DRAMA
for Students

DRAMA
for Students

Presenting Analysis, Context and Criticism on
Commonly Studied Dramas

Volume 6

David Galens, Editor

GALE GROUP

Detroit
San Francisco
London
Boston
Woodbridge, CT

National Advisory Board

Drama for Students

Staff

Editorial: David M. Galens, *Editor*. Tim Akers, *Contributing Editor*. James Draper, *Managing Editor*. David Galens and Lynn Koch, *"For Students" Line Coordinators*. Jeffery Chapman, *Programmer/Analyst*.

Research: Victoria B. Cariappa, *Research Manager*. Andrew Guy Malonis, Barbara McNeil, Gary J. Oudersluys, Maureen Richards, and Cheryl L. Warnock, *Research Specialists*. Patricia Tsune Ballard, Wendy K. Festerling, Tamara C. Nott, Tracie A. Richardson, Corrine A. Stocker, and, Robert Whaley, *Research Associates*. Phyllis J. Blackman, Tim Lehnerer, and Patricia L. Love, *Research Assistants*.

Permissions: Maria Franklin, *Permissions Manager*. Kimberly F. Smilay, *Permissions Specialist*. Kelly A. Quin, *Permissions Associate*. Sandra K. Gore, *Permissions Assistant*.

Graphic Services: Randy Bassett, *Image Database Supervisor*. Robert Duncan and Michael Logusz, *Imaging Specialists*. Pamela A. Reed, *Imaging Coordinator*. Gary Leach, *Macintosh Artist*.

Product Design: Cynthia Baldwin, *Product Design Manager*. Cover Design: Michelle DiMercurio, *Art Director*. Page Design: Pamela A. E. Galbreath, *Senior Art Director*.

Copyright Notice

Table of Contents

The Study of Drama

We study drama in order to learn what meaning others have made of life, to comprehend what it takes to produce a work of art, and to glean some understanding of ourselves. Drama produces in a separate, aesthetic world, a moment of being for the audience to experience, while maintaining the detachment of a reflective observer.

Drama is a representational art, a visible and audible narrative presenting virtual, fictional characters within a virtual, fictional universe. Dramatic realizations may pretend to approximate reality or else stubbornly defy, distort, and deform reality into an artistic statement. From this separate universe that is obviously not ''real life'' we expect a valid reflection upon reality, yet drama never is mistaken for reality—the methods of theater are integral to its form and meaning. Theater is art, and art's appeal lies in its ability both to approximate life and to depart from it. By presenting its distorted version of life to our consciousness, art gives us a new perspective and appreciation of reality. Although, to some extent, all aesthetic experiences perform this service, theater does it most effectively by creating a separate, cohesive universe that freely acknowledges its status as an art form.

And what is the purpose of the aesthetic universe of drama? The potential answers to such a question are nearly as many and varied as there are plays written, performed, and enjoyed. Dramatic texts can be problems posed, answers asserted, or moments portrayed. Dramas (tragedies as well as comedies) may serve strictly ''to ease the anguish of a torturing hour'' (as stated in William Shakespeare's *A Midsummer Night's Dream*)—to divert and entertain—or aspire to move the viewer to action with social issues. Whether to entertain or to instruct, affirm or influence, pacify or shock, dramatic art wraps us in the spell of its imaginary world for the length of the work and then dispenses us back to the real world, entertained, purged, as Aristotle said, of pity and fear, and edified—or at least weary enough to sleep peacefully.

It is commonly thought that theater, being an art of performance, must be experienced—that is, seen—in order to be appreciated fully. However, to view a production of a dramatic text is to be limited to a single interpretation of that text—all other interpretations are for the moment closed off, inaccessible. In the process of producing a play, the director, stage designer, and performers interpret and transform the script into a work of art that always departs in some measure from the author's original conception. Novelist and critic Umberto Eco, in his *The Role of the Reader: Explorations in the Semiotics of Texts,* explained, ''In short, we can say that every performance offers us a complete and satisfying version of the work, but at the same time makes it incomplete for us, because it cannot simultaneously give all the other artistic solutions which the work may admit.''

Thus Laurence Olivier's coldly formal and neurotic film presentation of Shakespeare's *Hamlet* (in which he played the title character as well as directed) shows marked differences from subsequent adaptations. While Olivier's Hamlet is clearly entangled in a Freudian relationship with his mother, Gertrude, he would be incapable of shushing her with the impassioned kiss that Mel Gibson's mercurial Hamlet (in director Franco Zeffirelli's 1990 film) does. Although each of the performances rings true to Shakespeare's text, each is also a mutually exclusive work of art. Also important to consider are the time periods in which each of these films were produced: Olivier made his film in 1948, a time in which overt references to sexuality (especially incest) were frowned upon. Gibson and Zeffirelli made their film in a culture more relaxed and comfortable with these issues. Just as actors and directors can influence the presentation of drama, so too can the time period of the production affect what the audience will see.

A play script is an open text from which an infinity of specific realizations may be derived. Dramatic scripts that are more open to interpretive creativity (such as those of Ntozake Shange and Tomson Highway) actually require the creative improvisation of the production troupe in order to complete the text. Even the most prescriptive scripts (those of Neil Simon, Lillian Hellman, and Robert Bolt, for example), can never fully control the actualization of live performance, and circumstantial events, including the attitude and receptivity of the audience, make every performance a unique event. Thus, while it is important to view a production of a dramatic piece, if one wants to understand a drama fully it is equally important to read the original dramatic text.

The reader of a dramatic text or script is not limited by either the specific interpretation of a given production or by the unstoppable action of a moving spectacle. The reader of a dramatic text may discover the nuances of the play's language, structure, and events at their own pace. Yet studied alone, the author's blueprint for artistic production does not tell the whole story of a play's life and significance. One also needs to assess the play's critical reviews to discover how it resonated to cultural themes at the time of its debut and how the shifting tides of cultural interest have revised its interpretation and impact on audiences. And to do this, one needs to know a little about the culture of the times which produced the play as well as the author who penned it.

Drama for Students supplies this material in a useful compendium for the student of dramatic theater. Covering a range of dramatic works that span from the fifth century B.C. to the 1990s, this book focuses on significant theatrical works whose themes and form transcend the uncertainty of dramatic fads. These are plays that have proven to be both memorable and teachable. *Drama for Students* seeks to enhance appreciation of these dramatic texts by providing scholarly materials written with the secondary and college/university student in mind. It provides for each play a concise summary of the plot and characters as well as a detailed explanation of its themes and techniques. In addition, background material on the historical context of the play, its critical reception, and the author's life help the student to understand the work's position in the chronicle of dramatic history. For each play entry a new work of scholarly criticism is also included, as well as segments of other significant critical works for handy reference. A thorough bibliography provides a starting point for further research.

These inaugural two volumes offer comprehensive educational resources for students of drama. *Drama for Students* is a vital book for dramatic interpretation and a valuable addition to any reference library.

Source: Eco, Umberto, *The Role of the Reader: Explorations in the Semiotics of Texts,* Indiana University Press, 1979.

Carole L. Hamilton
Author and Instructor of English
Cary Academy
Cary, North Carolina

Introduction

Purpose of Drama for Students

The purpose of *Drama for Students* (*DfS*) is to provide readers with a guide to understanding, enjoying, and studying dramas by giving them easy access to information about the work. Part of Gale's ''For Students'' literature line, *DfS* is specifically designed to meet the curricular needs of high school and undergraduate college students and their teachers, as well as the interests of general readers and researchers considering specific plays. While each volume contains entries on ''classic'' dramas frequently studied in classrooms, there are also entries containing hard-to-find information on contemporary plays, including works by multicultural, international, and women playwrights.

The information covered in each entry includes an introduction to the play and the work's author; a plot summary, to help readers unravel and understand the events in a drama; descriptions of important characters, including explanation of a given character's role in the drama as well as discussion about that character's relationship to other characters in the play; analysis of important themes in the drama; and an explanation of important literary techniques and movements as they are demonstrated in the play.

In addition to this material, which helps the readers analyze the play itself, students are also provided with important information on the literary and historical background informing each work.

This includes a historical context essay, a box comparing the time or place the drama was written to modern Western culture, a critical overview essay, and excerpts from critical essays on the play. A unique feature of *DfS* is a specially commissioned overview essay on each drama by an academic expert, targeted toward the student reader.

To further aid the student in studying and enjoying each play, information on media adaptations is provided, as well as reading suggestions for works of fiction and nonfiction on similar themes and topics. Classroom aids include ideas for research papers and lists of critical sources that provide additional material on each drama.

Selection Criteria

The titles for each volume of *DfS* were selected by surveying numerous sources on teaching literature and analyzing course curricula for various school districts. Some of the sources surveyed included: literature anthologies; *Reading Lists for College-Bound Students: The Books Most Recommended by America's Top Colleges;* textbooks on teaching dramas; a College Board survey of plays commonly studied in high schools; a National Council of Teachers of English (NCTE) survey of plays commonly studied in high schools; St. James Press's *International Dictionary of Theatre;* and Arthur Applebee's 1993 study *Literature in the Secondary School: Studies of Curriculum and Instruction in the United States.*

Input was also solicited from our expert advisory board (both experienced educators specializing in English), as well as educators from various areas. From these discussions, it was determined that each volume should have a mix of ''classic'' dramas (those works commonly taught in literature classes) and contemporary dramas for which information is often hard to find. Because of the interest in expanding the canon of literature, an emphasis was also placed on including works by international, multicultural, and women playwrights. Our advisory board members—current high school teachers—helped pare down the list for each volume. If a work was not selected for the present volume, it was often noted as a possibility for a future volume. As always, the editor welcomes suggestions for titles to be included in future volumes.

How Each Entry Is Organized

Each entry, or chapter, in *DfS* focuses on one play. Each entry heading lists the full name of the play, the author's name, and the date of the play's first production or publication. The following elements are contained in each entry:

- **Introduction:** a brief overview of the drama which provides information about its first appearance, its literary standing, any controversies surrounding the work, and major conflicts or themes within the work.

- **Author Biography:** this section includes basic facts about the author's life, and focuses on events and times in the author's life that inspired the drama in question.

- **Plot Summary:** a description of the major events in the play, with interpretation of how these events help articulate the play's themes. Subheads demarcate the plays' various acts or scenes.

- **Characters:** an alphabetical listing of major characters in the play. Each character name is followed by a brief to an extensive description of the character's role in the plays, as well as discussion of the character's actions, relationships, and possible motivation.

  Characters are listed alphabetically by last name. If a character is unnamed—for instance, the Stage Manager in *Our Town*—the character is listed as ''The Stage Manager'' and alphabetized as ''Stage Manager.'' If a character's first name is the only one given, the name will appear alphabetically by the name.

Variant names are also included for each character. Thus, the nickname ''Babe'' would head the listing for a character in *Crimes of the Heart,* but below that listing would be her less-mentioned married name ''Rebecca Botrelle.''

- **Themes:** a thorough overview of how the major topics, themes, and issues are addressed within the play. Each theme discussed appears in a separate subhead, and is easily accessed through the boldface entries in the Subject/Theme Index.

- **Style:** this section addresses important style elements of the drama, such as setting, point of view, and narration; important literary devices used, such as imagery, foreshadowing, symbolism; and, if applicable, genres to which the work might have belonged, such as Gothicism or Romanticism. Literary terms are explained within the entry, but can also be found in the Glossary.

- **Historical and Cultural Context:** This section outlines the social, political, and cultural climate *in which the author lived and the play was created.* This section may include descriptions of related historical events, pertinent aspects of daily life in the culture, and the artistic and literary sensibilities of the time in which the work was written. If the play is a historical work, information regarding the time in which the play is set is also included. Each section is broken down with helpful subheads.

- **Critical Overview:** this section provides background on the critical reputation of the play, including bannings or any other public controversies surrounding the work. For older plays, this section includes a history of how the drama was first received and how perceptions of it may have changed over the years; for more recent plays, direct quotes from early reviews may also be included.

- **For Further Study:** an alphabetical list of other critical sources which may prove useful for the student. Includes full bibliographical information and a brief annotation.

- **Sources:** an alphabetical list of critical material quoted in the entry, with full bibliographical information.

- **Criticism:** an essay commissioned by *DfS* which specifically deals with the play and is written specifically for the student audience, as well as excerpts from previously published criticism on the work.

In addition, each entry contains the following highlighted sections, set separate from the main text:

- **Media Adaptations:** a list of important film and television adaptations of the play, including source information. The list may also include such variations on the work as audio recordings, musical adaptations, and other stage interpretations.

- **Compare and Contrast Box:** an ''at-a-glance'' comparison of the cultural and historical differences between the author's time and culture and late twentieth-century Western culture. This box includes pertinent parallels between the major scientific, political, and cultural movements of the time or place the drama was written, the time or place the play was set (if a historical work), and modern Western culture. Works written after the mid-1970s may not have this box.

- **What Do I Read Next?:** a list of works that might complement the featured play or serve as a contrast to it. This includes works by the same author and others, works of fiction and nonfiction, and works from various genres, cultures, and eras.

- **Study Questions:** a list of potential study questions or research topics dealing with the play. This section includes questions related to other disciplines the student may be studying, such as American history, world history, science, math, government, business, geography, economics, psychology, etc.

Other Features

DfS includes ''The Study of Drama,'' a foreword by Carole Hamilton, an educator and author who specializes in dramatic works. This essay examines the basis for drama in societies and what drives people to study such work. Hamilton also discusses how *Drama for Students* can help teachers show students how to enrich their own reading/viewing experiences.

A Cumulative Author/Title Index lists the authors and titles covered in each volume of the *DfS* series.

A Cumulative Nationality/Ethnicity Index breaks down the authors and titles covered in each volume of the *DfS* series by nationality and ethnicity.

A Subject/Theme Index, specific to each volume, provides easy reference for users who may be studying a particular subject or theme rather than a single work. Significant subjects from events to broad themes are included, and the entries pointing to the specific theme discussions in each entry are indicated in **boldface.**

Each entry has several illustrations, including photos of the author, stills from stage productions, and stills from film adaptations.

Citing Drama for Students

When writing papers, students who quote directly from any volume of *Drama for Students* may use the following general forms. These examples are based on MLA style; teachers may request that students adhere to a different style, so the following examples may be adapted as needed.

When citing text from *DfS* that is not attributed to a particular author (i.e., the Themes, Style, Historical Context sections, etc.), the following format should be used in the bibliography section:

> ''Our Town,'' *Drama for Students*. Ed. David Galens and Lynn Spampinato. Vol. 1. Farmington Hills: Gale, 1997. 8–9.

When quoting the specially commissioned essay from *DfS* (usually the first piece under the ''Criticism'' subhead), the following format should be used:

> Fiero, John. Essay on ''Twilight: Los Angeles, 1992.'' *Drama for Students*. Ed. David Galens and Lynn Spampinato. Vol. 1. Farmington Hills: Gale, 1997. 8–9.

When quoting a journal or newspaper essay that is reprinted in a volume of *DfS,* the following form may be used:

> Rich, Frank. ''Theatre: A Mamet Play, 'Glengarry Glen Ross'.'' *New York Theatre Critics' Review* Vol. 45, No. 4 (March 5, 1984), 5–7; excerpted and reprinted in *Drama for Students,* Vol. 1, ed. David Galens and Lynn Spampinato (Farmington Hills: Gale, 1997), pp. 61–64.

When quoting material reprinted from a book that appears in a volume of *DfS,* the following form may be used:

> Kerr, Walter. ''The Miracle Worker,'' in *The Theatre in Spite of Itself* (Simon & Schuster, 1963, 255–57; excerpted and reprinted in *Drama for Students,* Vol. 1, ed. Dave Galens and Lynn Spampinato (Farmington Hills: Gale, 1997), pp. 59–61.

We Welcome Your Suggestions

The editor of *Drama for Students* welcomes your comments and ideas. Readers who wish to suggest dramas to appear in future volumes, or who have other suggestions, are cordially invited to contact the editor. You may contact the editor via

E-mail at: **david.galens@gale.com.** Or write to the editor at:

David Galens, *Drama for Students*
The Gale Group
27500 Drake Rd.
Farmington Hills, MI 48331-3535

Literary Chronology

484 B.C.: Euripides born on the island of Salamis.

406 B.C.: Following Athen's defeat in the Peloponnesian War and his subsequent flight, Euripides dies in exile in Macedonia.

405 B.C.: Produced posthumously by his executors, Euripides's *The Bacchae* debuts.

1818: Ivan Turgenev is born on October 28 (some sources cite November 9), 1818, in Orel, Russia.

1828: Henrik Ibsen is born in Skien, Norway, on March 20.

1850: Ivan Turgenev's *A Month in the Country* is completed; the work is met with harsh treatment from Russian censors, who object to certain social aspects of the play. It is finally produced in 1872 in Moscow.

1856: George Bernard Shaw is born on July 26 in Dublin, Ireland.

1883: Ivan Turgenev succumbs to cancer in Paris, France, dying on September 3; he is buried in Volkovo cemetery in St. Petersburg, Russia.

1888: Eugene O'Neill is born on October 16, 1888, in the Barrett House family hotel on Broadway in New York City.

1890: *Hedda Gabler* by Henrik Ibsen is first published; the play is first performed in Munich, Germany, on January 31, 1891, with subsequent productions in Berlin, Stockholm, Copenhagen, and Christiania (Oslo). The play debuts in English in London, on April 20, 1891.

1891: Zora Neale Hurston is born January 7 in Eatonville, Florida.

1899: Noel Coward is born on December 16, 1899, in Teddington-on-Thames, Middlesex, England.

1902: Langston Hughes is born James Langston Hughes in Joplin, Missouri, on February 1.

1903: *Man and Superman* by George Bernard Shaw is first published; the play debuts in London, England, at the Royal Court Theatre on May 21, 1905.

1906: Henrik Ibsen dies after a series of strokes on May 23 in Oslo, Norway.

1920: *The Emperor Jones* by Eugene O'Neill is first produced in New York City by the Provincetown Players at the Provincetown Playhouse on November 1; the play is so successful in its Off-Broadway setting that it moves to a larger Broadway theatre in 1921.

1925: *Hay Fever* by Noel Coward debuts in London, England, at the Ambassador's Theatre; the play is produced in New York at Maxine Elliot's Theatre later in the year.

1927: Neil Simon is born on July 4, 1927, in the Bronx, New York.

1930: *Mule Bone* by Zora Neale Hurston and Langston Hughes is completed; following a dispute between the authors, production is delayed until the 1990s.

1931: Peter Barnes is born on January 10 in the East side of London, England.

1932: Athol Fugard is born in Middleburg, Cape Province, South Africa, on June 11.

1933: Joe Orton is born John Kingsley Orton on January 1 in Leicester, England.

1943: Sam Shepard is born Samuel Shepard Rogers in Fort Sheridan, Illinois, on November 5.

1947: David Mamet is born on November 30 in Chicago, Illinois.

1950: George Bernard Shaw dies on November 2, 1950, following an injury sustained in a fall, in Ayot Saint Lawrence, Hertfordshire, England.

1953: Eugene O'Neill dies in a rented hotel room in Boston, Massachusetts, on November 27, of pneumonia; he is buried in Boston's Forest Hills cemetery on December 2.

1954: Harvey Fierstein is born on June 6 in Brooklyn, New York.

1960: Zora Neale Hurston dies at the Saint Lucie County, Florida, Welfare Home on January 28; she is buried in an unmarked grave in the Fort Pierce segregated cemetery.

1967: Langston Hughes dies on May 22 of congestive heart failure in New York City.

1967: Joe Orton is bludgeoned to death by his lover, Kenneth Halliwell, on August 9 in London, England.

1968: *The Ruling Class* by Peter Barnes is first produced in Nottingham, England.

1969: *What the Butler Saw* by Joe Orton is posthumously produced in London's West End; the play is produced in New York City at the McAlpin Rooftop Theatre in 1970.

1969: *Boesman & Lena* by Athol Fugard is first produced in a private setting at the Rhodes University Little Theatre in Grahamstown, South Africa, on July 10; the play is subsequently produced Off-Broadway in 1970.

1973: Noel Coward dies on March 26, of a heart attack in Blue Harbor, Jamaica.

1978: *Buried Child* by Sam Shepard premieres at New York City's Theater for the New City on October 19; the playwright later revised and augmented his play for a revival at the Steppenwolf Theatre in Chicago, Illinois, before transferring to Broadway in April, 1996.

1981: *Torch Song Trilogy* by Harvey Fierstein is first produced Off-Off-Broadway at the Richard Allen Center in October; the play is produced on Broadway at the Little Theater, June, 1982.

1982: *Brighton Beach Memoirs* by Neil Simon is first produced in Los Angeles, California, at the Ahmanson Theatre in December; the play is produced on Broadway at the Alvin Theatre, March 27, 1983.

1988: *Speed-the-Plow* by David Mamet debuts on Broadway at the Royale Theater on May 3.

Acknowledgments

The editors wish to thank the copyright holders of the excerpted criticism included in this volume and the permissions managers of many book and magazine publishing companies for assisting us in securing reproduction rights. We are also grateful to the staffs of the Detroit Public Library, the Library of Congress, the University of Detroit Mercy Library, Wayne State University Purdy/Kresge Library Complex, and the University of Michigan Libraries for making their resources available to us. Following is a list of the copyright holders who have granted us permission to reproduce material in this volume of **DFS.** Every effort has been made to trace copyright, but if omissions have been made, please let us know.

COPYRIGHTED EXCERPTS IN *DfS,* VOLUME 6, WERE REPRODUCED FROM THE FOLLOWING PERIODICALS:

Commonweal, v. CXV, June 17, 1988; v. CXVIII, June 1, 1991. Copyright © 1988, 1991 Commonweal Publishing Co., Inc. Both reproduced by permission of Commonweal Foundation.—*The Explicator,* v. 46, Fall, 1987. Copyright © 1987 by Helen Dwight Reid Educational Foundation. Reproduced with permission of the Helen Dwight Reid Educational Foundation, published by Heldref Publications, 1319 18th Street, NW, Washington, DC 20036-1802.—*Maclean's,* v. 102, February 20, 1989. © 1989 by *Maclean's* Magazine. Reproduced by permission.—*The Nation,* New York, v. 211, No-vember 30, 1970; v. 246, June 18, 1988; v. 254, March 2, 1992. Copyright 1970, 1988, 1992 *The Nation* magazine/The Nation Company, Inc. All reproduced by permission.—*The New Leader,* v. LXXIV, February 11-25, 1991. © 1991 by The American Labor Conference on International Affairs, Inc. Reproduced by permission.—*The New Republic,* v. 215, July 15-22, 1996; v. 218, April 27, 1998. © 1996, 1998 The New Republic, Inc. Both reproduced by permission of *The New Republic.*— *New York,* Magazine, v. 14, December 14, 1981; v. 16, April 11, 1983; v. 24, February 25, 1991; v. 25, February 10, 1992; v. 29, May 13, 1996. Copyright © 1981, 1983, 1991, 1992, 1996 K-III Magazine Corporation. All rights reserved. All reproduced with the permission of *New York,* Magazine.—*The New Yorker,* v. LIX, April 11, 1983 for "Portrait of the Artist as a Young Saint" by Brendan Gill; v. LXI, December 23, 1985 for "Country Pleasures" by Brendan Gill; v. LXIII, January 25, 1988 for "Don Bernardo in Hell" by Mimi Kramer; v. LXVII, February 10, 1992 for "Stopover" by Edith Oliver. © by the authors 1983, 1985, 1998. All rights reserved. All reproduced by permission.—*The New Yorker,* v. LXX, February 21, 1994 for "Laughing It Off" by John Lahr. © 1994 by The New Yorker Magazine, Inc. All rights reserved. Reproduced by permission of Georges Borchardt, Inc. on behalf of the author.

COPYRIGHTED EXCERPTS IN *DfS,* VOLUME 6, WERE REPRODUCED FROM THE FOLLOWING BOOKS:

Nash, Jay Robert and Stanley Ralph Ross. From a review of *The Ruling Class* in *The Motion Picture Guide:* N-R, 1927-1983. Edited by Jay Robert Nash and Stanley Ralph Ross. Cinebooks, Inc., 1986. Copyright © 1986 by Cinebooks, Inc. All rights reserved. Reproduced by permission.

PHOTOGRAPHS AND ILLUSTRATIONS APPEARING IN *DfS*, VOLUME 6, WERE RECEIVED FROM THE FOLLOWING SOURCES:

Coward, Sir Noel, photograph. AP/Wide World Photos. Reproduced by permission.—Euripides, photograph of a bust. Archive Photos, Inc. Reproduced by permission.—Fierstein, Harvey, photograph by Angel Franco. AP/Wide World Photos. Reproduced by permission.—From a movie still of *Brighton Beach Memoirs* by Neil Simon, Directed by Gene Saks, with Jonathan Silverman as Eugene, 1986, Universal, Eugene is under the kitchen table looking up the women's skirts, photograph. Universal. Courtesy of The Kobal Collection. Reproduced by permission.—From a movie still of *Brighton Beach Memoirs* by Neil Simon, Directed by Gene Saks, with Jonathan Silverman as Eugene and Bob Dishy as Jack, 1986, Universal, Eugene helps his father carry a package home from work, photograph. Universal. Courtesy of The Kobal Collection. Reproduced by permission.—From a movie still of *The Ruling Class* by Peter Barnes, Directed by Peter Medak, with Peter O'Toole as Jack Arnold Alexander Tancred Gurney, 14th Earl of Gurney and Arthur Lowe as Tucker, 1972, An Avco Embassy Film, photograph. United Artists. Courtesy of The Kobal Collection. Reproduced by permission.—From a movie still of *Torch Song Trilogy* by Harvey Fierstein, Directed by Paul Bogart, with Harvey Fierstein as Arnold, 1988, New Line Cinema, impersonator Arnold Beckoff, aka nightclub entertainer ''Virginia Hamm'' is on stage with another female impersonator and two muscle men, photograph. New Line Cinema. Courtesy of The Kobal Collection. Reproduced by permission.—From a movie still of *Torch Song Trilogy* by Harvey Fierstein, Directed by Paul Bogart, with Matthew Broderick as Alan and Harvey Fierstein as Arnold, 1988, New Line Cinema, Alan and Arnold are laying on a bed while Alan is writing, photograph. New Line Cinema. Courtesy of The Kobal Collection. Reproduced by permission.—From a theatre production of *Buried Child* by Sam Shepard, Directed by Marcus Stern, with Jack Willis as Tilden at the American Repertory Theatre and Institute for Advanced Theatre Training, 1995-96 season, Tilden standing in a field of corn holding a child, photograph by Richard Feldman. AMERICAN REPERTORY THEATRE. Reproduced by permission of the photographer.—From a theatre production of Eugene O'Neill's *The Emperor Jones* with Paul Robeson as Emperor Jones, circa 1933, a smiling Emperor Jones sits on his throne, photograph. Corbis-Bettmann. Reproduced by permission.—From a theatre production of George Bernard Shaw's *Man and Superman* with Peter O'Toole at the Haymarket Theatre, London, August, 1983, photograph by Richard Olivier. Richard Olivier/Corbis. Reproduced by permission.—From a theatre production of Henrik Ibsen's *Hedda Gabler* with Catherine Wilkin at the Downstage Theatre Company, Edinburgh International Festival, Edinburgh, Scotland, 1990, Hedda is holding a gun to her right temple, photograph by Robbie Jack. CORBIS/Robbie Jack. Reproduced by permission.—From a theatre production of Joe Orton's *What the Butler Saw* with Richard Wilson and Debra Gillet at the National Theatre, London, March, 1995, Gillet is standing in her underwear while Wilson holds a gun to her, photograph by Robbie Jack. Robbie Jack/Corbis. Reproduced by permission.—From a theatre production of Noel Coward's *Hay Fever* with Constance Collier at Shaftesbury Theatre, London, 1932, photograph by Sasha. Hulton-Deutsch Collection/Corbis. Reproduced by permission.—From a theatre production of *Speed the Plow* by David Mamet, Directed by Gregory Mosher, Produced by Lincoln Center Theater, with Joe Mantegna, Madonna and Ron Silver at the Royal Theatre, May, 1988, photograph. AP/Wide World Photos. Reproduced by permission.—From a theatre production of *The Bacchae* by Euripides, with Roger Frost as Teiresias and Wilbert Johnson as Cadmus, Shared Experience/Lyric Theatre, Hammersmith, London, 1988, photograph. © Donald Cooper/Photostage. Reproduced by permission.—Fugard, Athol, photograph. AP/Wide World Photos. Reproduced by permission.—Hughes, Langston, photograph. AP/Wide World Photos. Reproduced by permission.—Hurston, Zora Neale, photograph. AP/Wide World Photos. Reproduced by permission.—Ibsen, Henrik, photograph. AP/Wide World Photos. Reproduced by permission.—Mamet, David, photograph by Brigitte Lacombe. Grove/ Atlantic, Inc. Reproduced by permission.—O'Neill, Eugene G., photograph. The Library of Congress.—Orton, Joe, photograph. Archive Photos, Inc. Reproduced by permission.—Shaw, George Bernard, photograph. The Library of Congress.—Shepard, Sam, photograph. Archive Photos, Inc. Reproduced by permission.—Simon, Neil, photograph. AP/Wide World Photos. Reproduced by permission.—The January, 1991 PLAYBILL for Langston Hughes and Zora Neale Hurston's *Mule Bone,* Directed by Michael Schultz by the Ethel Barrymore Theatre, at Lincoln Center Theater, some men and one woman are sitting on a porch listening to a man playing a guitar, photograph. PLAYBILL (r) is a registered trademark of Playbill Incorporated, N.Y.C. All rights reserved. Reproduced by permission.—The July, 1970 PLAY FARE, Playbill for Athol Fugard's *Boesman and Lena,* Directed by John Berry, with James Earl Jones as Boesman, Ruby Dee as Lena and Zakes Mokae as Old African, at the Circle in the Square Theater, NY, silhouettes of a man and a woman, photograph. PLAYBILL (r) is a registered trademark of Playbill Incorporated, N.Y.C. All rights reserved. Reproduced by permission.—The July, 1970, Playbill for Athol Fugard's *Boesman and Lena,* Directed by John Berry, with James Earl Jones as Boesman, Ruby Dee as Lena and Zakes Mokae as Old African, at the Circle in the Square Theater, NY, Credit page, photograph. PLAYBILL (r) is a registered trademark of Playbill Incorporated, N.Y.C. All rights reserved. Reproduced by permission.—Turgenev, Ivan, photograph. The Library of Congress.

Contributors

Clare Cross: Doctoral candidate, University of Michigan, Ann Arbor. Entry on *What the Butler Saw.*

John Fiero: Professor Emeritus of Drama and Playwriting, University of Southwestern Louisiana. Entry on *Hedda Gabler.*

Lane A. Glenn: Author, educator, director, and actor, Lansing, Michigan. Entries on *The Bacchae* and *Buried Child.*

Carole Hamilton: Freelance writer and instructor at Cary Academy, Cary, North Carolina. Entries on *Man and Superman* and *The Ruling Class.*

Dustie Kellett: Freelance writer. Entry on *A Month in the Country.*

Erika Kreger: Doctoral candidate, University of California, Davis. Entry on *Hay Fever.*

Sheri Metzger: Freelance writer and Ph.D., Albuquerque, NM. Entries on *Mule Bone* and *Torch Song Trilogy.*

Terry Nienhuis: Associate Professor of English, Western Carolina University. Entry on *The Emperor Jones.*

Annette Petrusso: Freelance author and screenwriter, Austin, TX. Entries on *Boesman & Lena, Brighton Beach Memoirs,* and *Speed-the-Plow.*

The Bacchae

EURIPIDES

405 B.C.

Euripides was more than seventy years old and living in self-imposed exile in King Archelaus's court in Macedonia when he created *The Bacchae,* just before his death in 406 B.C. The play was produced the following year at the City Dionysia in Athens, where it was awarded the prize for best tragedy. Ever since, *The Bacchae* has occupied a special place among Greek dramas and particularly among the eighteen surviving plays of Euripides. It was a favorite of the Romans in the centuries following the decline of the Greek Empire. It persisted through the "dark ages" of Medieval Europe and was among the first classical plays translated into vernacular languages during the Renaissance. Alongside *Medea* and Sophocles's *Oedipus the King* (also known as *Oedipus Rex*) it is one of the most produced ancient plays of the twentieth century.

The simple plot of *The Bacchae* mixes history with myth to recount the story of the god Dionysus's tumultuous arrival in Greece. As a relatively new god to the pantheon of Olympian deities, Dionysus, who represented the liberating spirit of wine and revelry and became the patron god of the theatre, was not immediately welcomed into the cities, homes, and temples of the Greeks. His early rites, originating in Thrace or Asia, included wild music and dancing, drunken orgies, and bloody sacrifice. Many sober, conservative Greeks, particularly the rulers of the many Greek city-states, feared and opposed the new religion.

Pentheus, the king of Thebes, stands as a symbol in the play for all those who opposed the cult of Dionysus and denied the erratic, emotional, uninhibited longings within all human beings. He confronts the god, faces him in a battle of wills, and is sent to his bloody death at the hands of his own mother and a frenzied band of maenads, female worshipers of the god.

In half a century of playwriting, Euripides tackled many difficult and controversial topics and often took unconventional stands, criticizing politicians, Greek society, and even the gods. *The Bacchae,* however, has proven frustratingly ambiguous in its treatment of gods and men. Writing the play in exile, while watching the glory of Athens disintegrate near the end of the Peloponnesian War, Euripides explores the disintegration of old systems of belief and the creation of new ones. He questions the boundaries between intellect and emotion, reality and imagination, reason and madness. At the end of it all, however, it is not quite clear whether the tragic events were meant to glorify the gods and reinforce their power and worship among the Greeks, or condemn the immortals for their fiendishness, their petty jealousies, and the myriad sufferings they inflict on humankind.

AUTHOR BIOGRAPHY

The life of Euripides, one of the great tragic playwrights of Classical Greece, spans the ''Golden Age'' of 5th century B.C. Athens. This single stretch of a hundred years saw the reign of Pericles, the great Athenian statesman and builder of the Parthenon; the final defeat of the Persians at the Battle of Salamis; the philosophical teachings of Anaxagoras, Protagoras, and Socrates; the construction of the Theatre of Dionysus; the playwriting careers of Aeschylus, Sophocles, and Aristophanes; and, ultimately, the decline of the Greek Empire following the devastating Peloponnesian War.

Although accounts of Euripides's life differ, some elements seem relatively certain. He was born on the island of Salamis in 484 B.C. but spent most of his life on the Greek mainland, in Athens. Based on the education he received, and the personal library he reportedly owned, his family was likely at least middle-class. His father, upon hearing a prophecy that his son would one day wear many ''crowns of victory,'' led him to begin training as an ath-

lete. Later, he studied painting and philosophy before finally turning to the stage and producing his first trilogy of plays in 455 B.C., just after Aeschylus's death.

Third in the line of great Greek tragedians, behind Aeschylus and Sophocles, Euripides's plays were quite different from his traditional-minded predecessors and stirred much controversy when they were presented at the annual theatre festivals (called the Dionysia) in Athens. To begin with, Euripides shared a healthy intellectual skepticism with the philosophers of his day, so his plays challenged traditional beliefs about the roles of women and men in society, the rights and duties of rulers, and even the ways and the existence of the gods. He had been influenced by the Sophists, a group of philosophers who believed that truth and morality are matters of opinion and by the teachings of Sophocles, who sought truth through questioning and logic. His own doubts, about government, religion, and all manner of relationships, are the central focus of his plays.

Additionally, Euripides did not adhere to accepted forms of playwriting. He greatly diminished the role of the chorus in his plays, relegating them to occasional comments on his themes and little or no participation in the action onstage. Furthermore, he was criticized for writing disjointed plots that didn't rise in a continuous action and for composing awkward prologues that prematurely reveal the outcome of plays. When seeking a resolution for the conflicts in his work, he often turned to the *deus ex machina,* or ''god from the machine,'' and hastily ended a play by allowing an actor, costumed as a god, to be flown onto the stage by a crane to settle a dispute, rather than allowing the natural events of the story to run their course.

Perhaps most importantly, Euripides provided characters for his plays that seemed nearer to actual human beings than those of any of his contemporaries. Figures like Medea, Phaedra, and Electra have conflicts rooted in strong desires and psychological realism, unlike the powerful, but predictable, characters in earlier tragedies. It has been said that Aeschylus wrote plays about the gods, Sophocles wrote plays about heroes, and Euripides wrote plays about ordinary humans.

During his fifty year career as a dramatist, Euripides wrote as many as ninety-two plays, yet won only five prizes for best tragedy in competitions. In contrast, Sophocles wrote more than 120 plays and won twenty-four contests. During his lifetime, Euripides was not always appreciated by his audiences or his critics—he, in fact, found himself the object of ridicule among writers of comedies like Aristophanes, who lampooned the tragedian and his techniques in his satire *The Frogs*. Time, however, has proven Euripides's merits. While Aeschylus and Sophocles are each represented by only seven surviving plays, eighteen of Euripides's tragedies still exist, along with a fragment of one of his satyr plays. They have been preserved over the centuries as admirable models of classical tragedy and helpful examples of spoken Greek. Due largely to his progressive ideas and realistic characters, the same qualities that once earned him scorn, he is now one of the most popular and widely-produced writers of antiquity.

PLOT SUMMARY

The setting of *The Bacchae* is the royal palace of Thebes, where Pentheus has succeeded his grandfather, Cadmus, as king. The play begins with a prologue spoken by Dionysus, the great god of wine and revelry himself. He announces that he has successfully spread his cult throughout Asia and returns now to the land of his mother, Semele, in order to teach the Greeks how to worship him through dancing, feasting, and sacrifices.

Some of the women of the city, including his own mother's sisters, have denied his status as a god, claiming he is simply a mortal and that the great Zeus killed his mother for lying about her lover. In threatening tones he describes how he has already driven the women of Thebes mad and sent them to the hills around the city, where they wear the animal skins of bacchants, priestesses of Dionysus, carry the ivy-entwined thyrsus (a symbol of his worship), and dance and sing hymns of praise to the new god. Now he is ready to turn his attention to King Pentheus, who opposes his worship and denies his existence.

To accomplish his task, he has come to Thebes disguised as a mortal and brought with him a chorus of his Asian followers. Together, he claims, they will try to persuade the Thebans to accept him into their rites of worship, even fight them if necessary. Then he will leave Thebes and spread his cult throughout Greece.

Dionysus leaves to join the bacchants on Mount Cithaeron as his Chorus enters to sing and dance for

A bust of Euripides

the people of Thebes. The Chorus' song explains the origins of the god and describes how the Greeks can become worshipers themselves. They sing about Dionysus's mother, Semele, who conceived the god with Zeus, ruler of all the immortals on Mt. Olympus; and how she was tricked into asking Zeus to reveal himself to her in all his godlike glory. Zeus complied, appearing to Semele as a lighting bolt and killing her instantly in his flame. Zeus himself plucked the unborn Dionysus from the fire and sealed him up in his thigh, later giving birth to his half-human, half-divine son.

To worship Dionysus, the Chorus sings, followers need only to crown themselves with ivy, wear deer skins lined with goat hair, carry the branches of oak and fir trees, delight in the bounty of the vine, and make ritual animal sacrifices. If they do, the land will overflow with natural beauty and riches—fawns and goats, wine and honey.

The women worshipers of Dionysus are interrupted in their revels by the arrival of Tiresias, the famous blind prophet. Tiresias has come to collect Cadmus; the two elders have rediscovered their youth in the worship of Dionysus, and they are headed to the hills around Thebes to dance and sing the god's praises. Before they can leave, however, King Pentheus returns to the city from a trip abroad.

He heard about the flight of women from his city and hurried back to contain the madness. He proclaims the worship of Dionysus false and immoral, reveals he has already caught and jailed many of the mad women, and soon will have them all captured and safely imprisoned.

Although both Tiresias and Cadmus try to convince Pentheus not to spurn the new god, on peril of his life, the king is unconvinced. He has heard about the arrival of a mysterious stranger in Thebes, a sorcerer with golden curls who is always surrounded by women. Not knowing the man he seeks is actually the god Dionysus himself, he orders the stranger caught and brought back to the palace in chains, to face death by stoning. As a further insult, he orders Tiresias's home—where he divines his prophecies—destroyed and even threatens his grandfather, Cadmus, before rushing off in search of Dionysus.

After a brief interlude by the Chorus, which chants a warning about human pride and men who will not give in to the pleasures of life, Pentheus returns and is met by a Servant, leading the disguised Dionysus in chains. The Servant reports that the stranger turned himself in willingly, but that all the women Pentheus had captured have escaped from their jails by some miracle of the gods. In a brief exchange, Pentheus accuses the Stranger of worshiping a false god and undermining the morals of women and orders him imprisoned, to await his death. The Stranger (Dionysus) warns Pentheus that he will free himself and that the god's wrath will fall heavily on the king and his city, but Pentheus, filled with arrogance, doesn't listen and leads the god away to his punishment.

The Chorus provides another interlude, this time worrying about the fate of Dionysus. They wonder if the god has forsaken them in Thebes. Suddenly, in the midst of their chanting, the Chorus is startled by a roar of thunder and the brilliant flash of lightning that engulfs the palace and the nearby tomb of Semele. When the blaze dies, the Stranger appears again and tells the bacchants how he escaped by tricking Pentheus into shackling a bull, tearing down the prison, and fighting phantom images.

Worn down by his struggles, Pentheus reappears in pursuit of the Stranger. They are met by a Herdsman from Mount Cithaeron, who describes a terrible battle he has just witnessed between Dionysus's frenzied female worshipers, the maenads, and the villagers on the mountain. Stumbling upon the

bacchants in the forest, the villagers hid and saw the women perform strange miracles. They seemed to communicate with the wild animals and draw water from rocks and wine from the earth itself. Among the crazed women was Agave, Pentheus's mother, and they decided to help their king by capturing her and bringing her home again. When the women saw the villagers, however, they attacked them ferociously. Weapons could not harm the bacchants, but with simple branches or their bare hands Dionysus's priestesses wounded their attackers, then turned on their cattle, ripping the cows and bulls to pieces and feeding on the raw flesh.

Though the Herdsman and the Chorus implore Pentheus to accept the fearsome new god, the king is more resolute than ever. He orders his soldiers called to arms in preparation for an attack on the bacchants in the hills. Dionysus, still in the guise of the Stranger, again warns Pentheus not to tempt fate by taking arms against a god, but it is too late to change his mind: Pentheus, like all tragic figures, is blind to his errors, and stumbling inexorably toward his doom.

Seeing no way to deter the king, Dionysus instead begins to prepare Pentheus for his punishment. He offers to lead the hapless man to the forest to spy on the women in their revels. To prevent him from being discovered, Dionysus convinces Pentheus to dress himself as a woman. Thus, attired in women's robes and deerskins, and carrying the Thyrsus of Dionysus, Pentheus is led, in a hypnotic trance, through the streets of Thebes and into the hills where the bacchants dance. The Chorus, knowing the fate that awaits him, sings a song of celebration, cheering the impending death of the foolish king and exalting the name of Bacchus—Dionysus—the god of wine and revelry.

Soon afterward, a Messenger arrives to relay the news of Pentheus's grisly destruction: When the king and his soldiers arrived near the grassy glade occupied by the maenads, the Messenger tells the Chorus, Pentheus complained he could not see the women through the trees. The Stranger reached up and pulled down the top of a tall fir tree, set Pentheus in its branches, then gently straightened the trunk again, sending the king upward to the top of the forest. As soon as he was aloft, the Stranger disappeared and the voice of Dionysus boomed across the hillside, calling the women to attack the non-believer perched helplessly atop the tree.

The Messenger watched while the women pulled the tree from the ground, roots and all, sending

Pentheus plummeting to earth. They descended upon him like animals with Agave, his own mother, in the lead. Pentheus tore off his disguise and pleaded with his mother to recognize him and spare him, but in her madness she thought he was a mountain lion and helped tear him apart, limb from limb, taking his head as a trophy of the hunt.

Finishing his tale, the Messenger hurries away as Agave approaches, bearing Pentheus's head on her thyrsus. Still in a Dionysian frenzy, Agave boasts that she was the first of the maenads in the hunt to reach the lion, whose head she claimed as a prize. Cadmus enters with servants, carrying some of Pentheus's remains on a bier. Sorrowfully, the founder of Thebes forces his daughter, Agave, to shake off her trance and recognize her own son's bloody head in her hands. He laments that it was her own blindness, and that of Pentheus and the women of Thebes, that led to this disaster. Because they mocked the god and dishonored his name, Dionysus has punished them all.

Dionysus himself returns and pronounces their final punishment: Cadmus will be driven into exile, later to be turned into a serpent with his wife Harmonia. Agave, too, will be banished from Thebes and forced to wander as an outcast for the remainder of her days. As father and daughter bid each other a tearful goodbye, the Chorus delivers the play's final lesson—that the gods may appear in many forms and accomplish wondrous, unexpected things. Let mere mortals beware.

CHARACTERS

Agave

Agave is daughter to Cadmus, the founder and former king of Thebes, and mother to Pentheus, the city's current ruler. As revealed by Dionysus in the play's prologue, Agave insulted the god by saying he was not the son of Zeus; that Semele, Dionysus's mother and Agave's own sister, lied about her lover, who was actually some mortal. For her heresy, Dionysus has driven Agave, and all the women of Thebes, mad and sent them into the hills where they have been wearing animal skins, dancing, and singing hymns of praise to the god of wine and revelry. Near the end of the play, Agave, still in a mad frenzy, leads the women in a bloody attack on

Pentheus, her own son, who she mistakes for a mountain lion. She returns to Thebes triumphant, carrying her son's head as a trophy. Cadmus finally breaks the spell she has been under, bringing her back to sanity and the painful realization of what she has done. She and her father are both condemned to exile by the angry Dionysus.

Cadmus

In Greek mythology, Cadmus was the ancient founder of Thebes. He populated the city by sowing the teeth of a dragon he and his brothers had slain. The planted teeth grew into soldiers called Spartoi, who became the Theban nobility and helped Cadmus build the city's citadel. Interestingly, because one of Cadmus's daughters, Semele, was Dionysus's mother, Cadmus is actually the god's uncle. In *The Bacchae,* Cadmus appears in his old age, after he has resigned the throne to his grandson, Pentheus. Cadmus and his friend, the blind prophet, Tiresias, have discovered the joys of the worship of Dionysus and thereby discovered a second youthful spirit. Try as he will, however, he cannot convince the headstrong Pentheus to accept Dionysus into the pantheon of gods in Thebes. At the end of the play, he is banished by Dionysus and told he and his wife, Harmonia, will become serpents before perishing in another land.

Chorus

The Chorus is a group of Asian ''Bacchae,'' women followers of Dionysus who wear deer skins and crowns of ivy, carry the thyrsus wand and fennel stalk, drink, dance, and sing hymns—or ''dithyrambs''—in honor of the god of wine and revelry. They watch all the action of the play, never becoming direct participants but providing, through their songs, important background information about the life and worship of Dionysus. As with most choruses in Greek tragedies, they often address the audience directly, moralizing about the actions of the play's characters, as when these Bacchae warn the onlookers that the gods punish mortals who do not honor them properly. Their pure spirit and beneficent actions contrast with the view Pentheus has of Dionysus and his cult.

Dionysus

The Greek god of wine and revelry, Dionysus was also known as Bacchus to the Romans. In Greek myth, he is said to have been the son of the

MEDIA ADAPTATIONS

- *The Bacchae* has inspired a handful of operas, including at least three that are available on CD: Szymanowski's *King Roger* (1926) and Hans Werner Henze's *The Bassarids* (1966), each available from the Koch Schwann label; and Harry Partch's *Revelation in the Courthouse Park* (1961), available on the Tomato label. Other operatic versions include Egon Wellesz's *Die Bakchantinnen* (1931); Daniel Bortz's *Backanterna* (1991); and John Buller's *Bakxai* (1992).

- Italian director and writer Giorgio Ferroni produced a filmed adaptation of Euripides's play in 1961 called *Le Baccanti*. The film stars Taina Elg as Dirce (a character Ferroni introduced to his version of the story), Pierre Brice as Dionysus, and Elberto Lupo as Pentheus. An English version, called *Bacchantes* is available on video.

- In 1968 the avant-garde American theatre producer Richard Schechner formed his own company called the Performance Group. Their first production, staged in a converted garage, was *Dionysus in 69,* a reworking of *The Bacchae* that explored sexuality, freedom, and societal repression through a series of ritual vignettes.

---

immortal king of the gods, Zeus, and Semele, the mortal daughter of Cadmus, founder of Thebes. When jealous Hera, Zeus's Olympian wife, tricked Semele into asking Zeus to show her his real identity, the hapless woman caught only a glimpse of the god in his glory before she perished in his divine fire. Zeus plucked the unborn baby Dionysus from her womb and concealed him in his thigh, until his proper birth.

As a young god, Dionysus did not receive the recognition he deserved in Greece, so he left for Asia, where he gathered his power and his followers before returning to conquer his homeland and spread the worship of the vine. It is at this point in the god's life where the play begins. He has returned to Thebes, the home of his mother, Semele, leading a chorus of "Bacchae," his female followers. He wants the Thebans to be the first among the Greeks to learn the songs, dances, and rites of the Dionysian cult. He has encountered difficulty, however: While the old founder and ruler of Thebes, Cadmus, and the wise seer Tiresias have chosen to honor him, the people of Thebes, and especially their new king, Pentheus, deny his name and refuse his worship.

A jealous but patient god, Dionysus has driven the women of Thebes mad and sent them into the hills where they have been dancing and singing his praises. Disguising himself as a mortal, a priest of his own cult, he tries to convince King Pentheus to accept the new god into Thebes. Pentheus, however, doubts Dionysus's existence and finds the drinking and dancing associated with his worship immoral, especially among women. He orders the Stranger (Dionysus) placed in chains and led off to prison to await his death. Dionysus escapes, wreaking havoc on the king and his court. Unable to reason with Pentheus, he finally devises a gruesome punishment for the prideful mortal: He places Pentheus in a trance, then convinces him to dress as a woman and spy on the Bacchae dancing Dionysus's rites in the hills. When the women discover him, they tear Pentheus limb from limb, and his own mother carries his head back into the city. In the end, Dionysus banishes what is left of the royal family of Thebes and declares his cult newly established in Greece.

First Messenger

Messengers in Greek drama are typically minor characters whose principal function is to relay important information about plot developments offstage, so the action of the play can continue unabated. The First Messenger in *The Bacchae* is a herdsman from Mount Cithaeron, who appears halfway through the play to describe a terrible battle he witnessed between the "maenads" (another name for Dionysus's female followers) and the villagers of the mountain. During the battle, he claims, the women were impervious to the villagers' weapons but were themselves able to wreak terrible havoc with simple branches and reeds. Furthermore, they tore cattle apart with their bare hands and caused wine to flow from the earth. Like others before him, the First Messenger encourages King Pentheus to accept Dionysus and his cult before it is too late.

Pentheus

Pentheus is the son of Agave and grandson of Cadmus, making him cousin to the god, Dionysus. He has inherited the throne of Thebes from Cadmus, and early in the play he is abroad on business of his realm. He returns quickly, however, after hearing that the women of his city have been driven mad and are cavorting in the hills around Thebes, dressed in the manner of Dionysian priestesses. Though Cadmus and Tiresias each try to convince him to accept the new god and his rituals, Pentheus is, in the manner of all Greek tragic protagonists, too filled with pride and blind to his errors to see the folly of his ways.

Even when he is confronted with the god himself, disguised as a priest of his cult, Pentheus calls Dionysus a false divinity, sends him off to prison, and orders soldiers to attack his Bacchae in the hills. As punishments for his crime, Pentheus is entranced by Dionysus, who convinces him to don women's clothes and suffer humiliation walking through the streets of his city out to the forest, to spy on the women worshiping the god. He is placed atop a tall tree to see the women dancing and singing but once there they see him and, in their frenzy, pull the tree up from the roots, tumbling the ill-fated king to the ground. The women fall on him, led by his own mother, Agave. They tear him limb from limb, and Agave, thinking he is a mountain lion, claims his head as a prize.

Second Messenger

For the most part, scenes of death and destruction in Greek tragedy occur offstage. It is usually left to messengers to report the bloody deeds to the other characters and the audience, using words that often describe the scene as vividly as if it were taking place before their eyes. The Second Messenger in *The Bacchae* is given the task of reporting the

grisly death of Pentheus. He was part of Pentheus's retinue of soldiers who followed the king to the forest and witnessed him being torn to pieces by the maenads. Near the end of the play, he arrives back in Thebes just ahead of Agave and tells the Chorus about the tragic events on Mount Cithaeron.

Servant

Playing only a small part in the play, the Servant is one of King Pentheus's men. He leads the group that captures the Stranger (actually Dionysus in disguise), and he reports the escape of the captured Bacchae from their jail cells.

Tiresias

In Greek mythology, Tiresias was the famous blind prophet of Thebes, and he appears in many stories, including Homer's *Odyssey,* Sophocles's *Oedipus* cycle, and another play by Euripides, *The Phoenician Women.* He was a descendant of the Spartoi sown by Cadmus, and he was given the gifts of prophecy and long life by Zeus, after being struck blind by the goddess Hera.

In *The Bacchae,* Tiresias appears briefly at the beginning of the play, as the voice of wisdom and experience. Along with Cadmus, he tries to persuade the headstrong Pentheus to accept Dionysus and his worship, telling him he is wrong to rationalize about the gods, whose ways cannot be known by mere mortals such as himself.

THEMES

Rational vs. Instinctual

The Greeks of the 5th century B.C. prized balance and order in their lives. Their art and architecture, laws, politics, and social structure suggest a culture that sought equilibrium in all things, including human behavior. Even their gods aligned themselves with opposing aspects of human essence. Apollo was the Greeks' god of prophecy, music, and knowledge. He represented the rational, intellectual capacity of the human mind and its ability to create order out of chaos. As the god of wine and revelry, Dionysus represented the opposite but equally important feature of human instinct: the emotional, creative, uninhibited side of people

TOPICS FOR FURTHER STUDY

- Research the agriculture and economy of Greece in the 5th century B.C. What products did the Greeks export? Which did they import? How was trade within the country, and outside the country, managed? How was the worship of Dionysus conducted to coincide with important phases of agriculture throughout the year?

- When writing his plays, Euripides seems to have concentrated his efforts mainly on characters and themes and often appears to have ignored important elements of plot. Sophocles, on the other hand, has been called the greatest constructor of plots in the ancient world, and Aristotle called his *Oedipus the King* the finest example of Greek drama. Research *Oedipus the King* and compare it to *The Bacchae*. Consider the similarities and differences between each play's plots, characters, and themes.

- By the end of the 5th century B.C., Greek theatres had developed a distinct shape and very particular elements of scenery, costuming, and special effects that affected the way plays such as

The Bacchae were produced. Research the physical properties of Greek theatres in the age of Euripides, then choose a scene from *The Bacchae* and describe how it might have been staged. As a group project, you may wish to actually recreate the scene you have chosen.

- In his time, Euripides was widely known as skeptic, someone who questioned authority and doubted traditional beliefs. His ideas were influenced by, among others, the *Sophist* philosophers, who believed that truth and morality were relative to the individual and largely matters of opinion. Who were some of the Sophists? What were their beliefs? How did they influence Western culture?

- In his *Poetics,* Aristotle suggests that the ideal tragic protagonist is someone who is highly renowned and prosperous, basically good, and suffers a downfall not through vice or depravity but by some error or frailty—a "tragic flaw" as it has often been called. Does this description suit Pentheus? Why/why not?

---

that balances their daily rational, structured, law-abiding behavior. The main conflict in *The Bacchae* is between these two conflicting behavioral patterns, the rational and the instinctual, disciplines often referred to as the Apollonian and the Dionysian.

The fruits of Dionysus's worship are extolled by Cadmus, the former king of Thebes; Tiresias, the elderly blind prophet of the city; and by the Chorus of Bacchae, the god's followers. Never too old to learn a new lesson, Tiresias and Cadmus have discovered the joys of the Dionysian rites and in them a new youth. "I shall never weary, night or day, beating the earth with the thyrsus," Cadmus boasts, "In my happiness I have forgotten how old I am."

The Chorus, who explain the history of the god and describe how to worship him, also warn about

his dual nature, and the peril of crossing him. "The deity, Zeus's son, rejoices in festivals," they sing. "He loves goddess Peace, who brings prosperity and cherishes youth. To rich and poor he gives in equal measure the blessed joy of wine. But he hates the man who has no taste for such things—to live a life of happy days and sweet and happy nights, in wisdom to keep his mind and heart aloof from over-busy men."

Pentheus's error in the play is his distaste for the simple pleasures Dionysus offers. He is totally dedicated to reason, and he refuses to acknowledge the need of his citizens, or himself, to occasionally release inhibitions—to dance, to sing, to eat, drink, and be merry. Ever the conservative moralizer, he warns Tiresias, "When the sparkle of wine finds a place at women's feasts, there is something rotten about such celebrations, I tell you." His sin is excessive pride, or *hubris* to the Greeks. He doesn't believe in Dionysus, a god of wine and celebration, and his fanatical obsession with order proves his downfall, in spite of the warnings he is given.

Individual vs. God

The struggle between individuals and their gods, whether actual or metaphorical, has been depicted countless times in literature, from the biblical stories of Moses and Job to modern plays like Peter Shaffer's *Amadeus* (1985) and Tony Kushner's *Angels in America* (1993). Each of these stories recounts the difficult, delicate relationship between mortals and the higher powers that may have created them—and possibly provides them their life force, their sustenance, and their inspiration. In spite of the love/hate relationship they often share in these stories, however, humans rarely encounter their divine nemeses directly, the way Pentheus battles Dionysus in *The Bacchae.*

At stake in the struggle is Dionysus's right to exist and to expect homage from the mortals of Greece, whether they wish to honor him or not. "This city must learn, whether it likes it or not, that it still wants initiation into my Bacchic rites," the god explains in the prologue to the play. "The cause of my mother Semele I must defend by proving to mortals that I *am* a god, borne by her to Zeus." Dionysus's jealous behavior is similar to that of God in the Old Testament, who tests his human creations, ravages entire cities, and floods the earth to purify it for his worshipers.

Pentheus, Dionysus's mortal opposition, is a cynical realist, unwilling to believe in the god or his fantastic powers. He believes he can shackle Dionysus, contain his followers, and stop the spread of his worship through sheer physical force, even though everyone near him warns against his folly. Cadmus and Tiresias encourage Pentheus to allow Dionysus's worship into the city. The Chorus sings the god's praises. The Herdsman from Mount Cithaeron declares, "If *he* exists not, then neither does Cypris, nor any other joy for men at all." In spite of all the warnings, however, Pentheus stays his course, and only experiences the mystery of Dionysus's powers when the god himself hypnotizes the hapless king and sends him to his death.

The result of the struggle between individuals and gods is often the same, though with different lessons to be learned. After battling his creation for

centuries, the Biblical God is reformed in the New Testament, following the life and martyrdom of his son, Jesus. Free will is offered to humanity, along with the freedom to suffer or prosper at the hands of others. In *Amadeus,* Shaffer's Salieri is consumed by his hatred for God and destroys himself. The characters in Kushner's *Angels in America* fight divinity to a draw. Pentheus, of course, learns a valuable lesson much too late.

Sex Roles

Of all the Greek tragedians, Euripides provided the most leading roles to women (although, in keeping with the theatrical conventions of the time, the parts would have been played by men). His plays also often seem to sympathize with the plight of women in Greek society. Medea, scorned by Jason, becomes an almost sympathetic figure, in spite of the fact that she murders her own children. Hippolytus's stepmother, Phaedra, is driven by a passion she cannot control and, like Pentheus, Hippolytus is a fanatical extremist who may deserve his grisly fate. In *The Bacchae,* the playwright's analysis and criticism of the Greeks' treatment of women may not be immediately obvious, but it exists in the portrayal of the Dionysian rites, the sympathetic Chorus of Bacchae, and Agave's suffering at the end of the play.

During Euripides's lifetime, women were mainly prohibited from politics, the arts, and many religious ceremonies. Dionysus's cult offered women an outlet for worship, equal or greater to that afforded to men. In the spirit of the wine and revelry he represented, women could become priestesses of Dionysus, or "Bacchae," simply by drinking, dancing, singing, and releasing their inhibitions. Although Pentheus, the conservative voice of male-dominated Greek culture, objects to women drinking and participating in religious ritual, Tiresias notes that women's own nature, not a god, will determine whether they are moral or not. "Even in Bacchic revels the good woman, at least, will not be corrupted," he claims. The Chorus of Bacchae in the play prove Pentheus wrong. They have followed the god from Asia minor, where he first established his cult, and now exist only to worship him and share in his peaceful bounty. "The ground flows with milk, flows with wine, flows with the nectar of bees," they sing.

Agave's punishment at the end of the play proves that women are equal candidates for suffering as well as for pleasure. It was Agave who originally denied Dionysus's divinity, claiming her sister, Semele, lied about her amorous relationship with Zeus, the king of the gods. Agave's false claims brought the wrath of Dionysus down on the women of Thebes, driving them mad and sending them into the hills around the city. Because her son, King Pentheus, chose to compound her mistake by denying the worship of the god to the people of Thebes, they both suffered horribly: The mother was forced to kill her own son and carry his severed head among the stunned Thebans.

STYLE

Climactic Plot Construction

Classical Greek tragedians were the creators of climactic plot construction, a form of playwriting that condenses the action of the story into the final hours or moments of the protagonist's struggle and places the most emphasis on the play's climax. This is quite different from an episodic plot, such as those created by Shakespeare or those used by most modern films, in which the protagonist, or hero, of the story encounters many harrowing episodes in a story that may take place across many days, months, or even years. Aristotle recognized the appeal of climactic plots in his *Poetics* when he suggested that "beauty depends on magnitude and order." In the case of a climactic plot such as *The Bacchae,* magnitude and order emerge from the simple structure of the plot: One man struggles against one overwhelming force, a god, and is defeated in the course of a single day.

In a climactic plot, the "point of attack," or starting point, of the play is relatively late in the entire story, requiring a great deal of exposition up front. In other words, a number of things have already occurred to propel the action to the point it is at when the play begins and all that is left is for the protagonist to make the fatal error that plunges him into tragedy. In *The Bacchae,* for example, Dionysus presents a prologue at the beginning of the play that sums up what has already taken place: He has been to Asia and successfully started his cult of worship there and now has returned to Greece to offer his homeland the rewards of his divinity. He has learned, however, that his own mother's sisters have denied his origins, and King Pentheus refuses to worship him. In retaliation, he has already driven the women mad and sent them into the hills. Almost immediately, Pentheus returns from abroad to confront the new menace, and the play's struggle begins in earnest. A few hours later, the battle has ended and, through his pride, Pentheus has suffered a grisly death.

Dialogue

One interesting convention of the Greek stage required playwrights to carefully structure their tragedies in short, distinct episodes and forced actors to be extremely versatile in approaching their parts. When Thespis, a dramatist and performer long credited with being the first "actor" (thus the term "thespian"), won the award for the best tragedy at the City Dionysia in 534 B.C., he alone played all the parts in his plays. For at least the next sixty years, tragedies were limited to a chorus and one actor. According to Aristotle, Aeschylus introduced the second actor, sometime around 470 B.C., and Sophocles is credited with adding a third. By the time Euripides began writing plays, dramatists were limited to no more than three principal actors to play all the parts.

To the dramatist, this means the plot of the play must be divided into distinct episodes in which the important characters of the story can confront one another in groups of two or three, with the chorus standing near, observing the action. Playwrights manufactured reasons for characters to leave the stage, so other characters (played by the same performers) could appear. To accommodate scene and costume changes, the chorus provided interludes consisting of song and dance that usually commented on the action of the play. A quick glance at the episodes in *The Bacchae* will reveal that three separate actors must play the parts of Pentheus, Cadmus, and Tiresias, since these characters all appear on stage at the same time; but the actor playing Tiresias might also portray Dionysus and the Stranger, while the actor playing Pentheus may double as his mother, Agave, since these combinations are never seen together on the stage.

Chorus

One of the most unique and recognizable features of the construction of classical Greek tragedies is the use of a chorus. Some historians have speculated that the very origins of Greek tragedy lie in the appearance of the chorus on stage. Before there was actual dialogue and characters in conflict in drama, performances consisted of large groups of men, perhaps as many as fifty, representing each of the various tribes in the hills around Athens, who would gather at festivals honoring Dionysus and dance and sing hymns (or dithyrambs), honoring the god of wine, revelry, and the theatre. After 534 B.C., the year of the first competition for tragedies at the City Dionysia festival in Athens, the role of the chorus began to diminish as the individual characters in the plays became increasingly important.

By the time Sophocles wrote *Oedipus the King* in the late 5th century B.C., the conventional size of the chorus had been fixed at fifteen. The chorus continued to sing, chant, and dance and occasionally interacted with the principal characters, but most often, as in *The Bacchae,* they stand outside the action and provide the audience with important background information, sometimes commenting on what they see happening or even warning characters that their choices may prove dangerous. Typically, the singing and dancing of the chorus occur during choral interludes that divide the episodes of the play. These interludes may help suggest the passing of time, as when the Chorus of Dionysus's followers in *The Bacchae* chant an appeal to the god for justice while Pentheus goes off to face his death. Practically speaking, they also may help delay the action in the play while scenery is replaced or actors change costumes to appear in other roles. Of the three Greek tragedians whose work has survived, Euripides used the chorus least, preferring instead to allow his individual characters more time to develop his themes.

HISTORICAL CONTEXT

Greece in the 5th century B.C. was a collection of many small, independent city-states, each called a "polis." While these tribal communities would occasionally band together in a common cause, as the Athenians and Spartans did to overthrow Persian control of Greek colonies early in the century, they remained, for the most part, separate, autonomous entities, constantly suspicious of each other and forever questing for greater wealth and control in the realm.

The 5th century B.C. has been called the "Golden Age" of Greece, and for most of the era, the polis of Athens was the centerpiece of a burgeoning culture that has left an indelible imprint on more than two thousand years of science, religion, philosophy, and the arts. Golden Age Athens produced the philosopher Socrates and his pupil, Plato. Phidias, the famous sculptor, lived in the same community

as the great dramatists Sophocles and Euripides. Pythagoras, Protagoras, and Herodotus, some of the greatest scientists and thinkers of all time, lived in the shadow of the famous Parthenon, perched atop the city's Acropolis.

Politically, Athens accomplished what has been called the world's first democracy nearly 2,500 years ago. Beginning with the "tyrannos," or popular leader Pisistratus, who fought against aristocratic power in the 6th century B.C., Athens was led by a series of governors who included its citizens in the creation and enforcement of its laws, even though those citizens did not include women, foreigners, or slaves, which the Athenians took from various wars and kept as household servants and tutors for their children. The democratic system established by the Athenians divided the society into ten tribes, each of which provided fifty men for the city's "boule," a legislative body that was on duty year round, night and day, with each tribe on duty for thirty-six days at a stretch, working three daily shifts. Additionally, all eligible Athenians were expected to participate in the "ekklesia," a meeting of at least 6,000 citizens held about every nine days, during which the entire city would debate issues raised by the boule.

Between them, the boule and the ekklesia created laws, empowered a police force, established a law court, the Helaia, and developed a trial by jury system. Interested as they were in fair, impartial decisions, the Athenians demanded a minimum jury size of 201 citizens, with larger juries of 501, or even 1001 or 2001 not uncommon.

As presented in *The Bacchae,* ancient Greek religion was "polytheistic." The Greeks believed in a "pantheon" of twelve main gods, along with a host of lesser deities, heroes, and local, household gods. Each of the gods represented a different facet of human knowledge and experience, though they were recognized as something superior, or at least different from, earthly mortals. Stories about the gods often depict them interfering in human affairs, though no god was ultimately viewed as entirely good or entirely bad. Each was capable of helping, or harming, humans.

Religious ritual was extremely important in the daily lives of the Greeks. Their cities were often set up around the various temples to Zeus, Hera, Poseidon, Demeter, Apollo, and the other immortals who were thought to live atop Mount Olympus; many days in the Greek calendar were set aside for the worship of these gods, which included prayer, sacrifice, and divination.

COMPARE & CONTRAST

- **5th Century B.C.:** The Athenian democracy which evolved during the 5th century B.C. is considered to be the first of its kind in the world. Matters of the state are decided by a vote of the citizen assembly, known as the *ekklesia.*

  Today: The United States is considered the world's leading democratic nation, though American democratic practices are quite different. Officials of the state are elected to one of three branches of the government: the executive, the legislative, or the judicial. Each branch is given different responsibilities and authorities to act on behalf of the citizens of the country, all of whom, men, women, and naturalized citizens included, may vote, or choose to run for office, during periodic public elections.

- **5th Century B.C.:** Education in Athenian society is reserved for boys, who learn reading, writing, arithmetic, and music. Once the boys reach age twelve, physical education becomes a priority, and they are taught gymnastics and sports such as wrestling, running, the discus and javelin toss, which will serve them well during their mandatory military service at age eighteen. Middle and upper class girls, expecting to marry well, may learn to read and write, and perhaps play the lyre, from a female tutor at home. They rarely, if ever, participate in physical education or sports.

  Today: Equal education for women, in both academic subjects and sports, is recognized as important in a majority of the world's industrialized nations. In the United States, some type of formal education is required of all children and public education is available for everyone from kindergarten through the twelfth grade. A limited amount of music and physical education may be required of students but intense training in these areas is largely elective. Military service is not mandatory for young men, though American boys must still register to be drafted when they turn eighteen.

- **5th Century B.C.:** Theatre in Greece is associated with religious worship and the cult of Dionysus, the Greek god of wine and revelry. Plays are produced each March during the Dionysia. Production of the plays is financed by rich and public-spirited citizens, known as *choregoi,* who are assigned a playwright and up to three actors and charged by the state with employing a chorus, hiring a trainer for the group, and providing costumes, scenery, and props.

  Today: Most theatre is no longer associated with religious worship, though "Passion Plays," commemorating the lives of Jesus and the saints, are common in American Christian churches. Plays are performed year-round, mainly for recreational and entertainment purposes. In the United States, professional play production is concentrated mainly in larger cities, such as New York, where individual financiers or groups of wealthy investors provide the funds necessary to pay large groups of performers and buy often extravagant sets, costumes, and lighting effects, which may cost millions of dollars.

- **5th Century B.C.:** Many of the most popular Greek tragedies impart a lesson that is central to Athenian society: the gods are all-knowing and all-powerful and human beings should not allow hubris to let them think they are equal or superior to the deities.

  Today: The European Renaissance of the fifteenth and sixteenth centuries encouraged exploration and experimentation in the fields of science, geography, philosophy, and the arts. As a result, in the twentieth century, a variety of mainly monotheistic religions offer the opportunity to worship at will, while individual human endeavors and accomplishments are regularly recognized for superior achievement, and pride in ability, within reason, is encouraged as an important feature of personal development.

Greek theatre emerged from the worship of one of the minor gods, Dionysus, who was thought to be the son of Zeus and Semele, a mortal, and was associated with wine, fertility, and celebration. Although Dionysus had been worshiped in Thrace and Asia Minor since at least 700 B.C., it wasn't until the 6th century B.C. that his cult reached into Athens. Worshiping Dionysus involved the sacrifice of animals and feasts, accompanied by wine drinking, dancing, and singing dithyrambs, ritual hymns honoring the god. Eventually, a contest for dancing and dithyramb singing evolved among the tribes of Athens and from this singing and dancing, it is believed, drama developed. The first contest for tragedies was held in Athens at the City Dionysia, an entire festival honoring Dionysus, in 534 B.C. During the next hundred years, through the playwriting careers of Aeschylus, Sophocles, and Euripides, the great stone amphitheatres of Greece, some seating as many as 17,000 people, were built and production practices involving costuming, masks, and machinery evolved.

Throughout its Golden Age, Athens's great rival was Sparta. While Athens assembled a confederacy of city-states in the North through peaceful agreements and trade negotiations, Sparta, known primarily for its military might, built a minor empire to the South out of smaller territories it conquered. While the two rivals found a common interest in defeating the Persians early in the 5th century B.C., old jealousies and new affronts stirred renewed animosity and led to the Peloponnesian War. This terrible series of battles between Spartan and Athenian forces lasted from 431 to 404 B.C., eventually destroying Athens and elevating Sparta to supremacy in mainland Greece. At the end of the war, to avoid having all their soldiers killed and their women and children sold into slavery, the Athenians agreed to Spartan terms of peace, which included government of Athens by thirty pro-Spartan aristocrats, who became known as the Thirty Tyrants. Athens's democracy was dead, and though it would struggle to its feet again in the fourth century, the glory of Greece belonged next to the Thebans, the Macedonians, and, finally, the Romans.

It was in the historical context of Athens's decline, just before its defeat at the hands of the Spartans, that Euripides chose to leave the city he had called home for so many years and journey into self-imposed exile to King Archelaus's court in Macedonia. There, he wrote *The Bacchae* and, according to popular account, was accidentally killed

by the king's hunting dogs while walking in the woods—just two years before the fall of Athens.

CRITICAL OVERVIEW

While the original productions of classical Greek tragedies were not reviewed for potential audiences the way theatrical performances are today, some measure of their critical success may be determined by the awards they received (or did not receive) during the festivals at which they were produced, and by the subsequent number of times the plays were revived over the years.

Euripides spent most of his playwriting career pursuing the elusive top prize at the City Dionysia, Athens's famous annual festival honoring Dionysus, the Greek god of wine and revelry. While Aeschylus, Sophocles, and dozens of other tragedians whose work has not even survived the ages received many honors and a great deal of popular acclaim, Euripides took only four first prizes during his lifetime and, as often as not, his plays came in last. Whether it was his own death in 406 B.C. or the radical departure in subject matter from his earlier plays, he achieved a new level of fame and appreciation by the time *The Bacchae* was produced in Athens in 405 B.C. The avant-garde playwright was posthumously awarded the top prize for that year's festival.

Scattered references to the play suggest that it was revived continuously on Athens's stages for the next hundred years and that it continued its popularity during the period of the Roman Empire, when it was translated into Latin and performed across Italy. There is evidence that the work was familiar to Horace, Virgil, and Ovid. During the Middle Ages, it is commonly known, Euripides received more attention than either Aeschylus or Sophocles as a first-rate tragedian and brilliant writer of spoken Greek. *The Bacchae* and other plays by Euripides were among the first to be translated into Latin prose and Italian during the Renaissance and seventeenth and eighteenth century writers from Milton to Goethe praised the play's singular purpose and intense depiction of man's conflict with his god.

In the modern era, criticism of *The Bacchae* has largely been divided between scholarly commentary on the text and history of the play and popular reviews of occasional performances. In *Dramatic Lectures,* a collection of his scholarly analyses of dramatists and their plays, the nineteenth century German critic August W. Schlegel wrote, ''In the composition of this piece, I cannot help admiring a harmony and unity, which we seldom meet with in Euripides, as well as abstinence from every foreign matter, so that all the motives and effects flow from one source, and concur towards a common end. After the *Hippolytus,* I should be inclined to assign to this play the first place among all the extant works of Euripides.''

In his autobiographical *Life of Macaulay,* the famous English historian G. M. Trevelyan praised Euripides, writing, ''*The Bacchae* is a glorious play. I doubt whether it be not superior to the *Medea,* it is often very obscure; and I am not sure that I fully understand its general scope. But, as a piece of language, it is hardly equaled in the world. And, whether it was intended to encourage or to discourage fanaticism, the picture of fanatical excitement which it exhibits has never been rivaled.''

Twentieth century productions of *The Bacchae* are not as common as stagings of Euripides's other masterpiece, *Medea,* and they tend to meet with mixed or unfavorable reaction. In his review of Michael Cacoyannis's adaptation of the play, which Cacoyannis himself directed for Broadway in 1980, *New York* magazine critic John Simon wrote, ''There is serious doubt in my mind about whether Greek drama can be performed today.'' Simon complained about the artificial, melodramatic qualities of classical tragedies, Cacoyannis's translation of the play, which he deemed embarrassing and accidentally comic, and the problems inherent in staging plays that were originally meant to be performed in enormous outdoor amphitheatres before crowds of several thousand.

In his review of the same production for *Newsweek* magazine, critic Jack Kroll observed that mounting modern productions of classical tragedies is a difficult feat, requiring immense creativity and, often, radical reinterpretation for contemporary audiences. ''Euripides's *The Bacchae* is a stupendous, searing play,'' Kroll noted, ''but like most productions of Greek tragedy, Michael Cacoyannis's staging at Broadway's Circle in the Square can't really break through the centuries-old crust to the white-hot life beneath. Directors have gone to great lengths to solve this problem. In America, Peter Arnott used marionettes instead of actors. In Italy, Luca Ronconi used one actress . . . to speak the entire play as the audience moved with her through a series of rooms

and spaces. In Germany, Klaus Michael Gruber used nudity, horses, glass walls and 100,000 watts of neon lights.''

In the *Nation,* reviewer Julius Novick echoed Kroll's comments, and asked, ''Am I alone in having difficulty with the elaborate passages of woe in which the Greek and Elizabethan tragic playwrights so frequently indulged themselves? If my sensibilities are typical at all, modern audiences are conditioned to be moved obliquely, by irony, or poignant understatement, rather than by lines like 'O Misery! O grief beyond all measure!'''

At least part of the reason *The Bacchae* has been applauded as a literary text and dismissed in performance during the twentieth century may lie in Greek tragedy's original purpose: religious ritual. Several critics have observed that, since modern audiences do not feel the same ritual impulses as the ancient Greeks, their plays do not have the same effect on us in performance. In 1969, the avant-garde theatre producer Richard Schechner assembled a group of performers and created a modern version of *The Bacchae* they called *Dionysus in 69.* In his collection of criticism called *God on the Gymnasium Floor,* Walter Kerr explained his objections to the production this way:

> Mr. Schechner has gone all the way back—as far as our literary history permits—in his search for a religious impulse capable of breeding a fresh form of drama. He really does wish us to act on the impulse he has attempted to borrow: to get up from our places on the floor and to enter, to *feel,* the interior Dionysiac pressure toward abandon that the Greeks felt and that exists as a record in Euripides's play. We do not in fact feel this specific religious impulse today, however; we do not bring it into the theatre with us as a deposit or guarantee. The specific religious impulse is dead. It has been dead for a very long time. Because it is dead, the gesture dependent upon it must, for the most part, be empty, effortful, artificial. We can try to let ourselves go, but there is nothing genuine pushing us.

CRITICISM

Lane A. Glenn

Glenn is a Ph.D. specializing in theatre history and literature. In this essay he examines Euripides's ambiguous treatment of Dionysus as a god to be either worshipped or abhorred in The Bacchae.

A contemporary interpretative staging of The Bacchae, *depicting Bacchants Tiresias (the blind prophet) and Cadmus, the former king*

For half a century, Euripides was known as a playwright unafraid to speak his mind. Very often what he had to say disturbed his audiences. In plays like *Medea, Hippolytus,* and *Alcestis,* he recalled stories and myths familiar to ancient Greek audiences. Yet, viewed from the perspective of their respective protagonists, they also function as harsh criticisms of the Athenian society they inhabited. These plays show the Greeks' utter disregard for women, bastards, and foreigners. In addition, they lampoon some of the culture's most cherished heroes and even call into question the wisdom of the gods. Euripides was not one to follow rules of literature, pander to audience tastes, or shy away from public controversy. Plot and character were usually subverted by the themes in his plays, and he was as likely to indict his audiences as his villainous characters for crimes against humanity.

Euripides's reputation as a hard-nosed, cynical critic of contemporary society makes the ambiguous thematic statements of *The Bacchae* all the more puzzling. Was he, true to earlier form, questioning the motives of the gods and condemning the damaging effects of religious excess? Or as an old man, well into his seventies when the play was written, did he finally choose to accept the Dionysi-

an rites that might make him youthful again? Was he making an appeal to the great god of wine, revelry, and the theatre? Critics have disagreed for centuries over this fundamental question raised by *The Bacchae,* and, confoundingly, the play itself offers evidence to support either view.

To begin with, Dionysus has the largest speaking role and controls the play from start to finish, suggesting his order is the order of the day, and perhaps the playwright meant to justify his ways and glorify his godhead. It is the god, rather than the Chorus or some secondary figure, who appears at the beginning of the play to deliver the prologue, describing how he has developed his worship abroad and only recently returned to his homeland, the land of his dead mother, Semele, to teach the Greeks the glory of the vine and provide for them his bounty. Very likely, he raises sympathy from the audience when he recalls the tragic circumstances of his birth. His mother was seduced by Zeus, impregnated, then tricked by Hera into asking to see Zeus's real identity. He obliged, and in an instant she was burned to ashes by the lightning flash of Zeus's divinity. "Close by the palace here I mark the monument of my mother, the thunderblasted," the orphaned Dionysus tells the audience, "The ruins

WHAT DO I READ NEXT?

- Eighteen of Euripides's plays have survived, each of which contains elements of the dramatist's non-traditional style that raised criticism from his contemporaries and earned him the respect and admiration of later generations of play readers and theatergoers. One of his most popular works is *Medea,* Euripides's 431 B.C. retelling of the myth of the sorceress who, faced with abandonment and exile in a strange land, murdered her own children and cursed her unfaithful husband. *Hippolytus* (428 B.C.) is the story of King Theseus's bride Phaedra, who falls in love with her stepson, Hippolytus, leading them both down a path toward destruction.

- Classical historian Michael Grant has written several books about the ancient Greeks and Romans, including *The Rise of the Greeks* (1987), which largely examines the political and military history of the Greek Empire; *The Classical Greeks* (1989), which provides a profile of Greek society through brief biographical essays about prominent Greek writers, philosophers, and leaders; and *A Social History of Greece and Rome* (1992), an exploration of the roles of women and men, slaves and citizens in Greek society.

- *The Mask of Apollo* is a novel of historical fiction by Mary Renault. Niko, the story's protagonist, is an actor in the 4th century B.C. who travels the Greek Empire, performing for kings and tyrants and befriending Plato, the famous philosopher, and Dion, a great soldier and statesman. The book draws on Renault's lifetime of classical research and presents an engaging glimpse into the life of the Greeks thousands of years ago.

- Much of what is known of classical Greek tragedy is recorded in Aristotle's *Poetics,* a 4th century B.C. treatise in which the philosopher attempts to describe dramatic poetry (tragedy). Aristotle suggests the six essential ingredients of good tragedies are plot, character, theme, diction, music, and spectacle; and he refers specifically to the plays of Aeschylus, Sophocles, and Euripides as examples. While several translations and editions of the *Poetics* exist, S. H. Butcher's version, which first appeared in 1902, is one that is often used in the classroom and appears frequently in literary anthologies.

- For nearly 150 years, students and teachers alike have relied on *Bulfinch's Mythology* as a dependable and entertaining way to learn about the great heroes, gods, and myths of the world. In this great collection of legends, originally published in 1855 but readily available in recent editions, Thomas Bulfinch has carefully researched and retold some of the greatest stories the world has ever known, including tales about the full pantheon of Greek gods and the mortals who dared to cross them.

- Peter Connolly's *The Ancient City: Life in Classical Athens & Rome* is an introduction to the history and culture of two of the world's greatest empires. Filled with original drawings, suggesting what ancient theatres, temples, and homes may have looked like, as well as photographs and helpful maps, Connolloy's carefully researched text is simple, straightforward, and entertaining.

---

of her home, I see, are smoldering still; the divine fire is still alive—Hera's undying insult to my mother.''

Dionysus has brought with him a Chorus of Bacchae, Asian women followers from the North, who recount his history and sing his praises at every

opportunity. In fact, while the choruses of most Greek tragedies sound a variety of themes between the episodes of their plays, from beautiful paeans honoring nature to moral judgments on the actions of characters, the *Bacchae* Chorus sings each of their five choral odes—four stasima and the parados—in honor of Dionysus. They know no other theme, and in Greek tragedy this may be an indication of the author's intent. As John Edwin Sandys noted in *The Bacchae of Euripides,* "The chorus in Greek tragedy is, again and again, the interpreter to the audience of the inner meaning of the action of the play; and the moral reflections which are to be found in the lyrical portions of *The Bacchae* seem in several instances to be all the more likely to be meant to express the poet's own opinions, when we observe that they are not entirely in keeping with the sentiments which might naturally have been expected from a band of Asiatic women."

Sandys may be right. Throughout the play, this Chorus provides sage bits of wit and wisdom that sound decidedly like a classically educated scholar—or playwright. "If man, in his brief moment, goes after things too great for him, he may lose the joys within his reach," the Bacchae lecture in their first choral ode. More important to the stature of the god within the play, however, is the passion and poetry the Bacchae display for Dionysus. In their opening song, the parados, they rejoice:

> My love is in the mountains. He sinks to the ground from the racing revel-band. He wears the holy habit of fawn-skin; he hunts the goat and kills it and delights in the raw flesh. He rushes to the mountains of Phrygia, of Lydia. He is Bromius, the leader of our dance. Evoe! The ground flows with milk, flows with wine, flows with the nectar of bees. Fragrant as Syrian frankincense is the fume of the pine-torch which our bacchic leader holds aloft.

The spirit of the Bacchae is contagious, and, while it has been unable to move Pentheus, the new king of Thebes, it has reached the wise in the upper echelons of Theban society. Cadmus, the city's original founder, and Tiresias, the famous blind prophet of Thebes, have both discovered the joys of Dionysus's worship. As the Chorus completes their ode, Tiresias appears at the city gate, calling for his friend and fellow cultist to "dress the thyrsus and put on skins of fawns and wreathe our heads with shoots of ivy." Unlike the women of Thebes, they do not need to be compelled, or driven mad, to find the spirit in their hearts to worship a god who makes them feel young again. In a voice that could be that of the aged (and reformed) Euripides himself, Tiresias lectures, "We do not rationalize about the gods. We have the traditions of our fathers, old as time itself. No argument can knock *them* down, however clever the sophistry, however keen the wit." If Tiresias's sentiment does indeed mirror Euripides's at the time he wrote the play, then the author had certainly come a long way from his earlier work, which

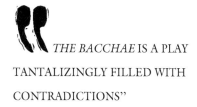

THE BACCHAE IS A PLAY TANTALIZINGLY FILLED WITH CONTRADICTIONS"

typically criticized, satirized, or simply ignored the gods.

Perhaps the most compelling evidence to suggest Dionysus was meant to be the hero, and not the villain, of *The Bacchae* is the personality of his nemesis, Pentheus. The new king of Thebes, though descended from the wise and noble Cadmus, is immature, headstrong, and puritanically conservative. The fault common to each of these flaws is the Greek concept of *hubris,* or excessive pride. He is convinced he is right, and he simply will not be told what to do. Encountering Tiresias and Cadmus on their way to the hills and the bacchic rites, Pentheus rails, "This is *your* instigation, Tiresias. This is another device of yours to make money out of your bird-gazing and burnt sacrifices—introducing a *new* god to men." He threatens the old, blind prophet with imprisonment and complains, "When the sparkle of wine finds a place at women's feasts, there is something rotten about such celebrations, I tell you."

Pentheus's position on the moral high ground makes him unsympathetic to audience members who have very likely experienced lapses in ethical behavior, as most humans have. Pentheus's *hubris* is that he claims to be something more than human, something perfect. Like Hippolytus, who wears his virginity like a badge of honor and refuses to worship Aphrodite, the goddess of love, Pentheus is heading for a fall from the moment he appears on the stage.

Taking only these elements into account—Dionysus's supremacy, the recommendations of the Bacchae, and the wise instincts of the Theban elders—it seems likely that Euripides intended *The Bacchae* as a moral lesson on the proper worship of the gods. As German scholar K. O. Muller suggested in his *History of the Literature of Ancient Greece,* "This tragedy furnishes us with remarkable conclusions in regard to the religious opinions of Euripides at the close of his life. In this play he appears, as it were, converted into a positive believer, or, in other words, convinced that religion should not be exposed to the subtleties of reasoning; that the understanding of man cannot subvert ancestral traditions which are as old as time, that the philosophy which attacks religion is but a poor philosophy, and so forth.''

With Cadmus and Tiresias, two of Thebes' most distinguished and respected elders, shuffling off the infirmities of age to toss their heads and beat the earth and Dionysus's chorus of devotees dancing and singing his praises between each episode of the play, it is difficult to find sympathy with Pentheus, the lone abstention from the merriment of the bacchic rites; he's the lone square at a hipster ball. Still, Dionysus has his devilish side, and there is enough in the play to also suggest that Euripides may have been less interested in appeasing the god in his old age and more determined to chastise the drunken deity for his reckless, damaging behavior. To establish his cult in Thebes, Dionysus has had to drive the women to madness, a state of artificial religious frenzy. In spite of the bounty he offers those who worship him, he can be jealous and petty, and even his most devoted followers may suffer terrible fates.

If Dionysus were held to the same standard of *hubris* as his mortal adversary, Pentheus, he would likely have to suffer a fate worse than the king's for his outrageous, unreasonable pride. After boasting of his success establishing his Asian cult, he threatens, ominously, ''This city must learn, whether it likes it or not, that it still wants initiation into my Bacchic rites.'' God or no, his tactless, overbearing rant detracts from the dignity his divinity should afford. While Pentheus is overreaching for the status of a god on earth, Dionysus is cutting himself down to the stature of a mere man through his bullying and hypersensitivity.

Then there is the matter of the justice the god dispenses at the end of the play. While it is true he gave Pentheus many opportunities to change his mind and accept the bacchic rites as part of the Theban rituals, does the errant king's punishment really fit his crime? For denying Dionysus's rightful place in the pantheon of gods and for imprisoning his servant (actually the god himself in disguise), Pentheus is hypnotized, fooled into donning women's clothes and walking through the town, and led to the forest to spy on the maenads. The crazed women, led by his own mother, Agave, shake him down from atop a tree and tear him limb from limb. Agave herself carries her unfortunate son's head back to the city as a trophy, thinking it is the head of a lion she has helped to kill.

Pentheus's destruction is gruesome enough, but how bad was Agave's crime that she must suffer this way—with the knowledge that she murdered her own son and carried his head aloft through town. Then, to make matters even worse, Dionysus decrees exile for Agave, her sisters, and their father, Cadmus. While Agave and her sisters insulted the god directly, by claiming he was not the son of Zeus, Cadmus's ''crime'' was far less malevolent. He is punished simply for allowing Pentheus, a nonbeliever, to ascend to the throne in Thebes, once he himself had finally become too old to rule.

The Bacchae is a play tantalizingly filled with contradictions. Whether Euripides intended his audiences to become more devout worshipers or hone their cynicism, however, may be beside the point. There is more to the play than whether or not Dionysus's claim to divinity is a legitimate cause for disrupting the life of a city. As G. M. A. Grube noted in *The Drama of Euripides,* ''The tragic beauty of *The Bacchae* does not arise from a purely external conflict between a ruthless god and a mortal who defies him; it arises from a conflict within the nature of the god himself.''

It is worth remembering that Dionysus is the god of wine and revelry. Wine sets free inhibition and releases passions that are locked inside every one of us. The Greeks adored balance and order and recognized the need for each thing, as well as its opposite. Laws, civility, and propriety govern the day-to-day world, but passion is the essence of life and fighting against passion destroys the soul, as surely as Pentheus was flung from his tree and torn limb from limb. Dionysus is also the god of *passion,* and, Grube continued, ''It is this god, and this worship, that Euripides has dramatized in all its aspects, its beauty and its joy, its ugliness and terror; he has even included the disgusting and the merely silly. Few will deny that it is from the very completeness of the picture that the play derives its power and its greatness.''

Source: Lane A. Glenn, for *Drama for Students,* Gale, 1999.

J. Michael Walton

In this essay, Walton delineates the plot of The Bacchae *and discusses its historical significance in relation to Euripides's other works and those of his ancient Greek contemporaries.*

The god Dionysus returns in disguise to Thebes where he was born. Rejected by his family, he is now set on punishing his cousin Pentheus, king of

Thebes, for denying his divinity. Pentheus has Dionysus imprisoned but he escapes and persuades the king to dress up as a woman so as to witness the Dionysiac rites. Pentheus's mother, Agave, and the other women tear Pentheus to pieces believing him to be a lion. Cadmus, the grandfather of both Pentheus and Dionysus, restores Agave to sanity while Dionysus looks on unrepentant.

Euripides went to live in Macedon for the final years of his life. *The Bacchae* was written there and performed posthumously in Athens in 405 B.C. The play revolves around the clash between a traditional culture in the person of Pentheus, and a foreign invasion in the figure of Dionysus, the god intent on introducing his religion to Thebes. Dionysus opens the play with a prologue, disguised as a man, in which he outlines his progress through Asia with his chorus of Bacchae before returning to his birthplace. The son of Zeus and Semele, he is both an individual and a representative of a religion of freedom and mystical powers. Introduced primarily as a religion for the women of Thebes, this religion has claimed Cadmus, founder of Thebes, and the prophet Teiresias among its converts. The young Pentheus sees his authority under threat when, under the influence of the god, the women of Thebes abandon the city and roam the mountains, apparently performing miracles.

Whether or not such miracles occur in the play is an open question. When Dionysus and Pentheus meet face to face, it soon becomes apparent that Dionysus's power is related to his ability to confuse and delude. This is how he escapes from imprisonment. It is never quite clear whether an earthquake, which the chorus "see" destroy the palace, really takes place. When Dionysus begins to exert his influence over Pentheus he persuades him to dress in women's clothes, believing these will serve as a disguise. He is torn apart by women who think he is a lion, his head returned on a Bacchic wand brandished by his mother. Cadmus, now freed from Dionysus's influence, has the task of bringing his daughter to see what she has done. At the end of the play Dionysus reveals himself as a god and Cadmus and Agave depart into exile.

A bloodthirsty enough story, the play is pervaded by a sense of theatrical power. For the Greeks, Dionysus was the god of ecstasy, as well as the god of wine. He was also the god of illusion and the god of the theatre. The play is full illusions: Dionysus is in disguise; Cadmus and Teiresias deck themselves out as Bacchants; Pentheus dresses up; a messenger

> THE PLAY CAN STAND A VARIETY OF TREATMENTS BUT FUNCTIONS BEST AS A WARNING AGAINST EXCESS OF ANY KIND, THUS LINKING IT TO EURIPIDES' EARLIER *HIPPOLYTUS.*"

reports remarkable events he claims to have witnessed—milk pouring from the earth, women unharmed by weapons that bounce off them, superhuman strength, snakes licking blood off human faces.

This world beyond reason is one with which Pentheus is ill-equipped to cope, but his clash with Dionysus is not a simple meeting of rational and irrational. Pentheus is no Apollo-figure for all his claims that he stands for order in a world that threatens to become chaotic. Dionysus destroys Pentheus by locating the Dionysiac elements in him: his conceit, his childishness, his prurience, turning him into a voyeur who contributes to his own destruction. Dionysus does so in the name of his religion which he claims as benign and beneficial except when opposed. Yet his motives are personal. Half-god, but from a mortal mother, he resents as a human being that he is excluded from his human family. As a god he has divine power to execute a revenge that is fearsome in its callousness. This ambiguity about where an audience's, or indeed the author's, sympathies may lie, has led to widely divergent interpretations and productions. For some, Dionysus is a destructive force whose cat-and-mouse cruelty disqualifies him from any claims to approval. At least one rationalist critic refused to believe him a god at all, but a sinister conman with skill as a hypnotist. His defenders regard Pentheus as a "fascist" dictator in opposition to the life-force. Popular in the 1960's, this view led to bizarre adaptations like the Performance Group's *Dionysus in '69.*

The play can stand a variety of treatments but functions best as a warning against excess of any kind, thus linking it to Euripides' earlier *Hippolytus.* The power that Dionysus represents, and of which the Chorus of Bacchae serve as a living manifesta-

> "THE PLAY HAS ITS PASSAGES OF WILD GRANDEUR THAT ARE ALMOST AESCHYLEAN, AND A SOLEMN, DREADFUL TREATMENT OF MADNESS INFLICTED BY DIVINE POWER, IN WHICH THE AUDIENCE IS SPARED NOTHING OF HORROR AND PITY."

tion, is both formidable and mysterious. It exists and, whether the story is seen primarily at a literal or at a figurative level, the implications are the same. There are aspects of the individual and of the collective which transcend reason and should be recognised. Pentheus, in trying to maintain order in Thebes, is suppressing not only the instinctive desire of the women to escape from the constant drudgery of their everyday lives, but also those aspects of himself which are part of the feminine side to his nature. Dionysus, who wins all the arguments and all the battles, does so at the expense of both humanity and compassion. To an audience of any age such a sacrifice is likely to seem too great.

Source: J. Michael Walton, '' *The Bacchae* '' in *The International Dictionary of Theatre,* Volume 1: *Plays,* edited by Mark Hawkins-Dady, St. James Press, 1992, pp. 39–41.

Anonymous

In this positive review, the critic praises a 1930 British production of Euripides's play, noting the strength of the chorus and the director's faithfulness to the original play text.

Cambridge has broken new ground in producing the *Bacchae.* Of Euripides the *Ion* was produced forty years ago and the *Iphigenia in Tauris* a little later, and now with admirable enterprise the finest, to many minds, and assuredly the most difficult of his plays to appraise and explain has been performed, for the first time, so far as we know, for many centuries. The executors of *Euripides* produced it just after his death, and it was acted in Athens and elsewhere for a time. Pagan and Christian writers have borrowed from it at all times since then. There is little here of ''Euripides the human'' or of ''the

touches of things common till they rose to touch the spheres,'' that Mrs. Browning found in other plays. The play has its passages of wild grandeur that are almost Aeschylean, and a solemn, dreadful treatment of madness inflicted by divine power, in which the audience is spared nothing of horror and pity. The more ghastly scene of Agave with her son's head is scarcely more weird than the ''fascination'' scene in which Dionysus gradually asserts his power over Pentheus until he has a crazy victim at his bidding.

Very wisely and mercifully the production last week attempted no indication of controversial interpretations. There were no laboured hints of matriarchal legends, of women's rights, or of Dr. Verrall's theories, whose delightful ingenuity would have puzzled Euripides. The play was not one of the Euripidean series written in Athens for competition at the Dionysia. It was the work of his old age at the Court of Archelaus, and seems to us to be the teaching of his disillusion over human intelligence, summed up in . . . the Second Chorus; ''the foolishness of God is wiser than men''. . . . The lesson of thankfulness for the good and pleasant things that Dionysus brought to man as against a stark puritanism is simpler and is rarer in tragedy. No tricks were played with the text, but the last scene, where the god pronounces the doom of Cadmus and Agave, was sensibly and substantially cut on account of the well-known mutilations and imperfections.

The scenery was novel and effective, with departures from antiquarian correctness. There was no pretence of reproducing the altar of Dionysus which was invariably the central object at Athens, but the play, none the less, kept that ultimate sense of worship which prevails in other plays in which Dionysus himself does not appear. The royal palace was placed to the right instead of in the centre of the stage, to give that honour to the shrine of Semele. The dresses of the Chorus were original rather than beautiful, but their merit appeared in the colour schemes of the dances, though they did not lend the grace of line which could be seen, for instance, in the robes of the Bacchantes on a beautiful little altar which was in Lansdowne House. The figure of Dionysus himself had the right effeminate charm of the dispenser of pleasure. Pentheus was the handsome blusterer that we expect until he is undone by the ''fascination.'' All the acting was good except at two points. To our mind the ''fascination'' was taken too abruptly and lost the gradual growth of horror. Secondly, the comic sporting of Cadmus and in a less degree of Tiresias (whose blindness the actor seemed to forget), when they set out for the revels, was out of place. They were following a divine instinct, not a ''lark,'' and the Cadmus of that scene could never have been the infinitely tender father of the last, when he brings Agave to her senses. The elocution was admirable. The two long narrative speeches were so delivered that every word could be followed and the two actors without any labouring spoke with great feeling. The music was a surprise to many. It was not, as is usual, composed for the play, but entirely adapted from operas of Handel that are known only to musical scholars. The ingenuity expended must have been great, but was not apparent. All the necessary dignity was there. . . .

These plays, carefully mounted and performed at Oxford, Cambridge, Bradfield or elsewhere in England, revived, too, abroad in ancient Sicilian or other theatres, are classics, and a classic work is one upon which time has no effect. The spirit survives through the ages. Even the Roman comedies, Greek at second hand, as played at Westminster, are alive to-day: and great passages can be spoken by Eton boys in knee-breeches and silk stockings without seeming absurd. Pedantry may have a hand in preparation: mere antiquarianism may prevail over art or intelligence on a small point here or there. But the works of Aeschylus, Sophocles, Euripides, and Aristophanes are immortal classics. Time after time the man who vaunts himself to be ''practical'' has come to mock and always he has remained to pray. He has thought that his emotions (if he had any) were proof against the purging by pity and fear as threatened by ''an old tag,'' until he has suffered the experience and felt a better man therefore. So, too, it seemed a joke to call a classical education ''fortifying.'' Yet the man who has learnt the lessons of the Bible (we do not speak here of its sacred side as well) and of the Greek tragedians, lessons of beauty, nobility and awe, is fortified for the struggles of life as other men are not All round us we hear complaints of the results of a narrow education that is no education, but a futile specializing aimed at securing quick material returns. The War opened the eyes of many to the effects of that materialism. Since the Peace we have heard of the gradually but steadily growing appreciation of a classical education It holds its own in the Universities and Public Schools and is spreading healthily into the schools provided from our rates and taxes, where scholars have until now had little chance of its blessings. This performance of the *Bacchæ* last week is not an action isolated from the movement, but it has been a vivid, stimulating and delightful event within that movement.

Source: Anonymous. Review of *The Bacchae* in the *Spectator,* Vol. 144, no. 5307, March 15, 1930, pp. 421–22.

SOURCES

Kerr, Walter. *God on the Gymnasium Floor,* Simon and Schuster, 1971, p. 42.

Kroll, Jack. Review of *The Bacchae* in *Newsweek,* October 13, 1980, p. 135.

Muller, K. O. *A History of the Literature of Ancient Greece: Volume I,* Parker, 1858, p. 499.

Novick, Julius. Review of *The Bacchae* in the *Nation,* October 25, 1980, pp. 417-18.

Sandys, John Edwin. *The Bacchae of Euripides,* Cambridge University Press, 1880.

Schlegel, Augustus Wilhelm. *A Course of Lectures on Dramatic Art and Literature,* translated by John Black, H. G. Bohn, 1861.

Simon, John. Review of *The Bacchae* in *New York,* October 20, 1980, p. 101-02.

FURTHER READING

Arnott, Peter. *The Ancient Greek and Roman Theatre,* Random House, 1971.
  An accessible, basic introduction to the drama and stagecraft of the classical Greeks and Romans that includes theories about the origins of tragedy, suggestions about the evolution of the Greek performance space, a handful of illustrations, and a helpful bibliography.

Bieber, Margarete. *The History of the Greek and Roman Theatre,* Princeton University Press, 1961.
  An in-depth, scholarly look at the evolution of the classical Greek and Roman theatres, including many photographs, illustrations, and conjectural drawings.

Foley, Helene P. ''The Bacchae'' in her *Ritual Irony: Poetry and Sacrifice in Euripides,* Cornell University Press, 1985.
  In this essay, Helene suggests one of the things Euripides accomplished with *The Bacchae* was an investigation of the relationship between ritual and theatre and between the spirit of festival and the society that creates it.

Grube, G. M. A. ''The Bacchants'' in his *The Drama of Euripides,* Barnes and Noble, 1961.

A careful episode-by-episode examination of the plot of *The Bacchae,* with running commentary by Grube explaining terminology and the possible historical and cultural significance of words and deeds in the play.

Hamilton, Edith. *The Greek Way,* W. W. Norton, 1993.

Hamilton's research and writing about the minds and culture of the ancient Greeks have been popular reading for decades. This relatively slim volume includes references to Euripides.

Segal, Charles. *Dionysiac Poetics and Euripides's* Bacchae, Princeton University Press, 1982.

In this exhaustive, scholarly tome, Segal examines many of the popular questions about *The Bacchae,* including whether or not Euripides approved of Dionysus's worship himself, the importance of the Dionysiac cult to Greek society, and sex roles in the plays of Euripides.

Stapleton, Michael. *The Illustrated Dictionary of Greek and Roman Mythology,* Peter Bedrick Books, New York, 1986.

A helpful collection of brief descriptions of some of the most famous Greek gods, heroes and myths, arranged alphabetically.

Winnington-Ingram, R. P. *Euripides and Dionysus: An Interpretation of the Bacchae,* Cambridge University Press, 1948.

A careful examination of *The Bacchae* that explores each action of the play, setting it in its literary and historical context, with special emphasis on Euripides's possibly negative opinion of Dionysus and the Greek gods.

Boesman & Lena

ATHOL FUGARD
1969

Athol Fugard's *Boesman & Lena* is one of the playwright's best-known and most widely respected dramatic works. It established Fugard's reputation as a major playwright. *Boesman & Lena* was first produced at the Rhodes University Little Theatre in Grahamstown, South Africa, on July 10, 1969. Fugard played Boesman in this production. The play was first produced in the United States in an Off-Broadway production at the Circle in the Square Theatre in 1970. This production won an Obie Award from the *Village Voice* for Most Distinguished Foreign Play of the season.

Like many of Fugard's plays, *Boesman & Lena* focuses on non-white characters and includes an element of social protest. Set in the mudflats outside of the playwright's native Port Elizabeth, South Africa, the title characters are an ill-matched ''colored'' (a South African term that describes people of mixed race) couple who have been beaten down by society. From its first productions, the play has been praised for its frank depiction of the affects of apartheid on people of color.

But critics also applaud Fugard because his play transcends time and place. *Boesman & Lena* can be seen as a metaphor for oppressed people of all nationalities, an exploration of the difficulty in relationships between men and women, and the need for human kindness, compassion, and hope. In a review of the original Off-Broadway production, the *New Republic*'s Stanley Kauffmann wrote: ''This

is not a protest play, though the pain of race hatred flames through it; it becomes, quickly and surely, a drama of all human beings in their differing captivities, suffering from and inflicting hate.''

AUTHOR BIOGRAPHY

Athol Fugard was born in Middleburg, Cape Province, South Africa, on June 11, 1932, the son of Harold David Fugard, of English descent, and his wife, Elizabeth Magdalena, who was an Afrikaner descended from the original Dutch settlers of South Africa. His parents ran a general store at the time of his birth, but when Fugard was three, they sold it and moved the family to Port Elizabeth. Port Elizabeth was home to every racial group and social strata found in South Africa. Growing up, Fugard was keenly aware of the racial divisions and their economic and social consequences. His family had two black male servants, one of whom, Sam, Fugard came to regard as a father figure. Fugard's own father was an alcoholic. As a child, Fugard spat in Sam's face in anger, an incident that Fugard felt tremendous guilt over for many years until he worked it out in his 1984 play ''*Master Harold*'' *and the Boys.*

Fugard attended the University of Cape Town on a scholarship and studied philosophy and social anthropology. In the middle of his senior year, in 1953, Fugard dropped out and became a sailor. He was the only white crewmember on the ship for two years. Fugard said the experience left him stripped of any racial prejudice. When he returned to South Africa, he met and married Sheila Meiring, an actress, in 1956. Fugard wanted to be a novelist and composed a manuscript, but watching his wife audition, Fugard became interested in, then involved with the theater. The couple eventually formed the Circle Players in Johannesburg.

In 1958, Fugard took a job as a clerk with a local court to support his family and art. There, Fugard saw racial injustice firsthand in the interworkings of the laws of apartheid (the South African political system that relegated the native blacks to second class status). The playwright was appalled at what he saw. As Fugard developed friendships with black people and saw their living conditions, their plight became even more evident to him. These experiences inspired his first play, *No-Good Friday,* which was performed privately for white audiences.

Fugard left the court position, and in 1959 he and his wife went to London to gain more theatrical experience. Within a year, a campaign against apartheid was being mounted, and Fugard and his wife returned to South Africa.

Upon his return, Fugard wrote the first of his ''Port Elizabeth'' plays, *The Blood Knot.* In 1962, five Xhosa tribesmen approached Fugard wanting to start a theater company. After some initial reluctance, Fugard formed the Serpent Company, which became the first successful non-white theater company in South Africa. Because of this success, several members were arrested. Fugard's passport was withdrawn by the South African government from 1967 until 1971. Still Fugard continued to write plays exploring racial and economic issues stemming from apartheid in South Africa.

During this time period, Fugard wrote his most successful and reputation-building play, 1969's *Boesman & Lena.* Performed both Off-Broadway and in London, the play garnered Fugard international praise. In the early-1970s, Fugard experimented with developing scripts in an improvisational theater format. The best known result is 1972's *Sizwe Bansi Is Dead.* In the early-1980s, Fugard became associated with the Yale School of Drama, which hosted the first production of ''*Master Harold*'' *and the Boys.* Widely acclaimed, this play is representative of Fugard's autobiographical period. In the 1990s, he split his time between the United States, where his actress daughter Lisa lives, and South Africa.

PLOT SUMMARY

Act I

Boesman & Lena opens with Boesman, a colored man, finding a spot to make camp in the Swartkops mudflats outside of Port Elizabeth, South Africa. He is heavily burdened, carrying all his possessions as well as a piece of iron with which to make a shelter. Tired, he drops his load. A few moments later, his woman Lena, who is also colored, enters. She carries all her possessions in a bundle on top of her head and a load of firewood in her arms. She walks past Boesman, realizes her mistake, and comes back. She asks him if they are going to stop here, and through his silence, she realizes that they are. She drops her baggage and looks around. Lena knows this place, and asks

Athol Fugard at the premiere of his play "Master Harold" and the Boys

Boesman why they have walked so fast to get here. She continues to address him, though his only response is stare at her with animosity. Through her dialogue, it is revealed that their previous home, a shanty, was destroyed by white people bulldozing the area, forcing them to leave.

Boesman finally speaks and threatens to leave her next time they walk. They argue, and Lena acknowledges that they are opposites: when she wants to cry, he wants to laugh. Boesman accuses her of looking back as they walked because she was trying to find a dog that had been following the couple. Lena says that Boesman did not know where he was going. When they rested earlier in the day, Lena says she counted her bruises, the result of Boesman beating her, as some white children watched her. She says she asked them if their mother needed a servant, but they didn't want her. Boesman says he did not want her either.

Lena tells Boesman that she wants him to talk to her, but he says that he does not have anything to say to her. He starts to unpack their belongings and build their shelter. Lena tries to figure out the last time they lived in this location, and Boesman does not help her. Lena then tries to figure out the many other places they have been, attempting to catalog the places in correct chronological order. When she

believes she has succeeded, she is happy. Boesman sees her happiness and is certain she has broken into their wine supply. He goes back to building the shelter, while trying to make Lena believe she has got the order wrong. Lena gets frustrated, and threatens Boesman, telling him that someday something will happen to him. Boesman counters by trying to make Lena doubt her own name.

Lena continues to try to reconstruct their past, while Boesman says the only thing that matters is today. Lena threatens to leave and takes a few steps away from the camp. She sees someone out walking on the mudflats, and Boesman comes to look. Lena waves the person over, much to Boesman's disgust. He does not want anyone to join them. The stranger is a "kaffer," an African man. When they try to figure out who he is, the man, who comes to be called "Outa," can only reply in Xhosa, a language neither Lena nor Boesman can understand. Lena makes the old man sit by the fire and tries to communicate with him. She grows frustrated because he can only speak Xhosa. Boesman threatens to hit her when she tries to go for a bottle of wine. Lena tells Outa that he is a witness to Boesman's abuse of her. She shows the old man the bruises on her arms that she received from Boesman when she dropped the sack of empty bottles that were to be returned for money. Boesman beat her, accusing her of breaking three of the bottles.

Boesman goes in search of more metal scraps and other materials for their shelter. Lena again grows frustrated with the old man's incomprehension, but finally gets him to understand that her name is Lena. With this breakthrough, Lena gives him water and tells him her about her life: her dog, the incident with the bottles, their walking, and their children (all but one born dead and that one only lived six months). He responds to her in his own language throughout, then tries to leave. Lena makes him stay, then Boesman returns. He is suspicious again, and watches them carefully as he continues to make the shelter.

Lena starts to make supper, asking Boesman if their bread can be cut into three pieces to share. Boesman says no, and Lena promises to share her portion with the old man. Lena seems happy, and Boesman insists the old man must go. Lena barters with Boesman foregoing her wine for the old man's presence. Lena wants the old man to sleep with them in the shelter, but Boesman refuses to allow it. Lena decides to sleep outside with the old man wrapped in a blanket. This upsets Boesman, and he shoves the old man when Lena goes in search of firewood. Lena returns and shares her bread and tea with the old man while Boesman does not eat or drink at all.

Act II

An hour later, Boesman is on the second bottle of wine while Lena and the Old Man are huddled under the blanket. Boesman is drunk and taunts Lena and the old man. He goes on to verbally torture Lena for trying to save things and crying while the bulldozers destroyed their home. He says that the experience liberated him, made him free, and he thought about going somewhere else. But his feelings of freedom were short-lived, when he says he realized that they were the whiteman's rubbish. Boesman does not understand why Lena traded a bottle of wine for the old man's company. Lena says it is because he sees where her life has lead: to this place at this time. As Boesman goes into the shelter for the night, he tells her that she cannot join him.

Lena starts talking to the old man again, telling him about dances they used to do. After she demonstrates some steps and sings bits of several songs, she huddles under the blanket again with him. Boesman watches them from the shelter and tells Lena that he is the one who dropped the empty bottles. Lena asks him why he hurt her and what she has done to deserve his bad treatment. Boesman strikes her several times, and Lena finally says that he should hit himself. When he says it does not hurt, she asks him if hitting her hurts him. Boesman says she is there and he hears her.

Lena shakes the old man to get him to stay awake, but he does not respond. Lena begs Boesman to say that he hit her for nothing, but he will not, nor will he hit her when she begs him to. Lena loses her composure and wonders what she has done aloud. Lena sits next to the old man and realizes that he has just died. Lena wants Boesman's help in putting him down, but Boesman refuses and decides to go to sleep instead. He goes into the shelter, then comes out and tells Lena to get rid of the dead man. Lena tells him to go back to sleep, but Boesman is agitated by the old man's continued presence. He worries that there will be trouble in the morning when people find out about the dead man.

Boesman gets so upset that he almost hits Lena, but she says that he has to be careful because there is already one body present. She taunts him further, suggesting the old man might not really be dead. Boesman checks the status of the old man by kicking him. Lena eggs him on, and Boesman kicks and beats the old man's body. Lena says she now knows what it looks like to be beaten and that the bruises he has caused will be suspicious. Boesman panics and starts packing up their things to leave. Lena refuses to help. She does not want to leave. Boesman smashes their shelter, and tries to carry everything on his body. She turns away from Boesman and goes to the old man's body to say goodbye. Lena returns to Boesman and takes up her share of their belongings. Boesman tells her the real order of the places they have been. She tells Boesman to walk slowly and that the next time he hits her, he should hit her hard enough to kill.

CHARACTERS

Boesman

Boesman is a middle-aged "colored" man (in South Africa, this means that he has the blood of both Europeans and Africans). He is downtrodden and poor, carrying all his possessions on his back. He has been with Lena for many years and is abusive towards her in many ways. He beats her regularly with his fists. He also abuses her verbally, taunting her and making her doubt herself. For example, he makes Lena believe that she broke three bottles they were going to sell at an exchange when in fact he broke them.

Boesman does not want Lena to invite the old man, Outa, to their camp. He cannot understand why Lena would give up her part of the wine for the company of the old man. There are a number of explanations for Boesman's behavior, most related to the oppressive atmosphere the white minority have created for the blacks in South Africa. The immediate source of stress is the recent bulldozing of Boesman and Lena's shanty. Unable to look toward the future, Boesman is only concerned with the present.

Lena

Lena is Boesman's woman. Like him, she is also "colored," middle-aged, and poor. She carries her possessions on her head and is gaunt. Lena is covered with bruises from the beatings that Boesman has given her. She says she wants to leave him—going so far as to ask some white children if their mother needed a maid while Boesman was selling the bottles—but she never does.

Lena tries to get a grasp on where she has been before and who she is, but her efforts are always undermined by Boesman. Unlike Boesman, Lena feels sympathy. She invites the old man over to the fire and talks to him in a way that Boesman does not approve of. She tells him that she and Boesman had many children born dead, except for one that lived for six months. While revealing herself to the old man, Lena uses Outa as her only weapon to fight Boesman's hold over her. She uses the old man to make Boesman doubt himself, and she nearly leaves him in the end.

Old Man
See Outa

Outa

Outa is a very old African man who only speaks the tribal Xhosa language. Lena sees him wandering on the mudflats and brings him to the campfire. Though he does not understand Lena's language, he is a sounding board, someone to whom she can talk. She likes Outa because his presence annoys Boesman. Lena is delighted when he learns her name. Outa gratefully takes the water she offers him.

When Outa tries to leave, however, Lena will not let him. He allows her to cover him with a

MEDIA ADAPTATIONS

- *Boesman & Lena* was adapted as a film in 1974. It was directed by Ross Devinish.

blanket and share her food with him. In Act II, Outa dies while holding Lena's hand. Following his death, Boesman takes out his rage on the old man's body, kicking and beating the body. Because Outa's death and bruises could be interpreted by the authorities as a crime, Boesman and Lena leave the mudflats.

THEMES

Violence and Cruelty

Acts of violence and cruelty underlie much of the action and character motivation in *Boesman & Lena*. Boesman acts out his frustrations, which are caused by his substandard place in South African society, by beating Lena. She is covered in bruises from such beatings. Boesman is also mentally cruel to Lena. He neglects and ignores her, refusing to talk to her at their campsite. He tells her several times that he wishes she would make good on her threats to leave him. When Lena tries to figure out where they have been, Boesman deliberately confuses her.

Lena cannot physically match Boesman, but she can return his mental cruelty. To cure her loneliness, she calls over Outa, an old African man wandering the flats. Lena uses the old man to make Boesman doubt his power over her. She gives up her ration of wine in exchange for the old man's presence in their camp, an act which Boesman cannot understand and which enrages him. After the Old Man dies, Boesman rails against Lena, but she turns the tables and makes Boesman doubt that the Old Man is really dead. To prove it to himself, Boesman kicks the body, then starts to beat on it. After

TOPICS FOR FURTHER STUDY

- Compare and contrast *Boesman & Lena* with Samuel Beckett's *Waiting for Godot.* Why do you feel the characters in *Boesman & Lena* change while those in *Waiting for Godot* do not?

- Research the psychological phenomenon of battered woman syndrome. Does this apply to Lena in *Boesman & Lena?*

- Compare and contrast *Boesman & Lena* with Fugard's play *Blood Knot,* which is also about familial opposites existing in a small space. Why does Boesman's violence explode while Zach's does not?

- Research the writings of Albert Camus, a French existentialist philosopher and playwright who influenced Fugard. How does Camus's philosophy play into the themes of *Boesman & Lena?*

Boesman is through, Lena points out that it now looks as though Boesman murdered the old man. These taunts play upon Boesman's fears and are as cutting as his fists. These words are Lena's only means of expressing her rage, of fighting against the oppression she suffers at his hands—and the white society at large.

Race and Racism

Boesman & Lena focuses on two ''colored'' people. In South Africa, this term refers specifically to people who have both African and white blood in them (a mix often referred to as mulatto in America). In this period (the 1960s) in South Africa, dark-skinned people were denied certain rights and forced to live in certain areas—predominantly ghettos and lower class projects. Boesman and Lena are essentially homeless, though they did live in a shanty town until bulldozers destroyed their home and forced them on the journey that led to the mudflats. The oppressiveness of racial separatism also fuels Boesman's anger, which he often takes out on Lena. At one point, Boesman refers to himself and Lena as trash discarded by white men.

Despite being the victim of such practices, Boesman also expresses racial prejudice. When Lena calls over the old man, Outa, Boesman does not want him to stay because he is black, an African. When Lena wants to give him water, just as other black people have previously done for the couple, Boesman does not want her to, in part because Outa is black and not brown. Lena does not share this racism and gives the old man water when Boesman's back is turned. Boesman treats the old man as white people have treated him. Despite her mistreatment at Boesman's hands, Lena identifies with humanity as a whole, separate from racial boundaries.

Search for Identity

Lena tries to understand her life and where she has come from in *Boesman & Lena.* She often looks to the past, especially in Act I, though Boesman repeatedly tells her she should be concerned with the present. One of Lena's first dilemmas is trying to figure out how she arrived in the mudflats. That is, she wants to know, in the correct order, where they have lived before now. Boesman tries to subvert these efforts when Lena comes up with a list by naming other possible areas, but by the end of the play, he relents and tells the exact order.

Lena also tries to quantify her existence by counting her bruises. Each has a story. Lena repeats one story several times. Boesman beat her that morning because he says she dropped three bottles they were trying to sell. Lena believes that this is the truth (because she has forgotten how to question the validity of what Boesman says) until the end of the play, when Boesman admits he broke the bottles, blaming her for his mistake.

Through Lena's ''conversations'' with the old man, she uses him as a sounding board to reconstruct her life. She recalls the stillborn children she has borne, the dog that she tried to keep, and the times when life with Boesman was not as hate filled. These recollections, which occur mostly in Act I, fuel Lena's actions in Act II, when she gains some power in her relationship with Boesman and nearly breaks away from him.

STYLE

Setting

Boesman & Lena is a drama set in contemporary South Africa. Specifically the action takes place in the Swartkops mudflats outside of the city of Port Elizabeth. Only owning possessions that they can carry with them, the characters are exposed to the elements. In order to survive in such a homeless state, Boesman builds a shelter out of scrap iron and other found materials. Yet once it is built, only he enters the shelter. Lena tends the fire and sits outside of it for the duration of the play. These desperate, temporary circumstances emphasize Boesman and Lena's precarious place in the world, but even they seem to have it better than the old man, Outa, who wanders in from the flats with nothing but the clothes he wears.

Language and Dialogue

In the standard English translation of *Boesman & Lena,* Afrikaan phrases pepper the text. (Afrikaan is South Africa's official language, a derivation of Dutch.) This emphasizes the setting of the play and the background of the characters. It also works as a contrast when Outa appears. He speaks Xhosa, a tribal language, when he says anything at all. The language difference underscores the fact that the old man is an outsider to even Boesman and Lena, themselves outcasts from mainstream (predominantly white) South African culture. It also allows Lena to use Outa as a sounding board; she can talk at him and interpret his responses to suit her own purposes.

Monologue

A monologue is defined as a long speech in a drama, spoken by one character. It can be used in the context of one person monopolizing a conversation or a character speaking more or less directly to the audience. Monologues can be used as a form of exposition to quickly relate dramatic events that the playwright may not wish to stage. A form of this is also called interior monologue—so named because it relates what a person is thinking by saying it aloud. William Shakespeare used such a device to great effect in his plays. Also known as a soliloquy, Shakespeare employed this technique to relate the emotions and inner thought processes of his characters; a famous Shakespearean soliloquy is the "To be or not to be" speech spoken by the title character in *Hamlet.*

Both of *Boesman & Lena*'s primary characters reveal their innermost thoughts and feelings via monologues. Lena has the majority of the monologues in the text. Most of her monologues occur in Act I and essentially relate what has transpired in the time leading up to the start of the play's action. Because Boesman will not talk with her, Lena talks

A Play Fare cover advertising a production of Fugard's play

at him—and to herself—while he is unpacking and building the shelter. Later, Lena talks at Outa, who does not speak her language. In both circumstances, Lena talks about herself: where she has been, what has happened to her in the past (her dead children, the dog that followed her), and the circumstances of her life (the reason why Boesman beats her). Lena's monologues serve to orient her and the audience in time and place.

In Act II, Boesman has several monologues. His monologues are more angry than Lena's and often derisively make fun of something she has said. He describes such things as the white man's bulldozer that destroyed their home, the so-called "freedom" the incident gave them, and how they are the white man's rubbish and no longer people. Boesman's monologues give insight into how he perceives the world, a stark contrast to Lena's world view.

Symbolism

Boesman and Lena, as well as their actions, can be interpreted as symbols. Boesman's violence towards Lena represents the violence white South Africans inflict on citizens of color. Lena represents hope and life: despite her setbacks and hardships, she marches forward, believing the future holds better times for her. She retains a sense of compassion, as her actions with the old man indicate. Boesman acts on his most bitter and jealous instincts, trying to destroy the hope and life inside of Lena. Also, Lena carries all her possessions on her head. Her baggage does not impair her ability to still see the world around her; it is also symbolic of the way she reflects on life with her mind. In contrast, Boesman carries everything on his back, hunched over and barely able to look up to the sky, symbolic of manner in which oppression has affected him.

HISTORICAL CONTEXT

In the late-1960s, as it had been for many years before, South Africa was controlled by its white citizens, Dutch settlers who colonized the country and displaced the indigenous black people. People of color were not allowed the same rights as these whites under the policies of apartheid. Apartheid stipulated that races be strictly segregated so that the white minority (only about 14% of the population) could maintain its hold on power. People of color did not have access to the same kinds of education and social services afforded the whites, and their movements within the country were strictly limited—while white children had to attend school from ages seven to sixteen, compulsory education for African children was *limited* to ages seven to eleven. Colored and black people were forced to live in specifically designated "homelands," "townships," and "national states" that were often overcrowded and without basic amenities. Jobs were also scarce, and many lived in poverty while the white minority grew more wealthy. People of color were also not represented in the South African Parliament.

Controlled by the all-white Nationalist Party, the South African government tried to insure the continued practice of apartheid in many ways. In 1969, the Bureau of State Security was formed. Among other things, this organization controlled the admission of evidence in courts. Thus there was no public control over their actions, and those in power consequently had a more restrictive grasp on society. White power in South Africa was also increased in 1969 when a new political party, the Reconstituted National Party of South Africa, was formed. This organization favored even more restrictive and repressive apartheid policies.

Not all whites in South Africa agreed with apartheid. When the government restricted membership in political parties to whites in 1968, the Liberal party disbanded rather than comply. The South African Council of Churches declared their nonsupport of apartheid in 1969. Despite protests from legal scholars and the world press, the South African government, led by B.J. Vorster, passed the General Law Amendment Act which prohibited cabinet members from giving evidence if it would be prejudicial to the interests of the public or state security. They also could not reveal, under punishment of law, any matter the Bureau of State Security was handling. These kinds of restrictions insured secrecy among those in power and a greater hold on the populace.

Despite such ominous security measures, there were forces moving against apartheid within South Africa. One such organization was the African National Congress (ANC), which was formed in 1912. With members of color, both radical and moderate, the ANC countered apartheid using both political and terrorist tactics. The South African government outlawed the ANC in 1960, and its leader, Nelson Mandela, was imprisoned in 1964. Still, these organizations had problems organizing resistance or protest against the repressive policies because interracial contact was so difficult under the law.

The policy of apartheid was routinely condemned by most countries in the world, including the United States. African-American leaders, their own battles for civil rights still fresh in their minds, were outspoken in their opposition to such policies.

CRITICAL OVERVIEW

From its first productions, critics praised *Boesman & Lena* for its powerful insights into the affects of apartheid as well as the human condition. Of the original Off-Broadway production, Harold Clurman in the *Nation* wrote, "Surely *Boesman & Lena* could not have been written by anyone who was not wholly immersed in the tortured realm of apartheid. Yet it is something more than a black play. It is about a man and woman, husband and wife, on a path of life beset by constant adversity." Stanley Kauffmann of the *New Republic* saw the deeper elements at work. "The play's epic quality derives from the wide and simple arch of its compass: shelter, food, fire, children, quarrels, dependence,

COMPARE
&
CONTRAST

- **1969:** The titular head of the African National Congress, Nelson Mandela, has been imprisoned by the South African government for five years.

  Today: Nelson Mandela has been the President of South Africa since 1994, when Dutch president F. W. de Clerk abolished apartheid, stepped down from his office, and helped to organize the popular elections that resulted in Mandela's rise to power.

- **1969:** Interracial marriage is banned in South Africa (the practice is not socially acceptable in many areas of the United States). Only .007% (310,000) of marriages in the United States are interracial.

  Today: The ban on interracial marriage was lifted in South Africa in 1978. In 1995, the percentage of interracial marriages in the United States was .025% (1,392,000).

- **1969:** The South African government segregates living areas, limiting people of color to certain areas. In the United States, President Nixon tries to delay efforts to desegregate schools.

  Today: In South Africa, laws are enacted to fairly redistribute land among its citizens of color. In the United States, there is a controversial movement to end busing students to aid in the desegregation of schools.

- **1969:** Under apartheid, education among people of color is only compulsory between ages seven and eleven and is not readily enforced.

  Today: Education for people of color is compulsory for students through age sixteen. Approximately 94% of school age children are enrolled in schools.

---

ego needs, death, endless pilgrimage. The rubbish that this pair gathers is the detritus of experience.''

Many critics saw deep meaning in Lena and Boesman, and how the play draws unexpected parallels between them and the rest of the world. Jack Kroll of *Newsweek* wrote, ''It is a powerful image—these two tattered, feral figures, like creatures neither human nor animal, hunched over with chronic fear and exhaustion, lurching and clattering through a wasteland that is neither nature nor civilization. The play in a sense is like a dramatic poem in which nothing much happens except the deepening of this basic image to a point of utmost terror and pathos.''

Kauffmann concurred with Kroll, arguing that ''Fugard makes very clear that, within the circumference of their lives, they represent the larger world. He is not saying that racial injustices do not signify; he is saying that those injustices are an extremity of the cruelty in all men. The reason that his play achieves towering height—as in the main it does—is because it *includes* the agony of *apartheid*

and shows that *apartheid* is not devil-inflicted but man-made, and that Boesman is a man, too.''

Several critics believed that one aspect of the play did not work: they found *Boesman & Lena* to be too literary. Kroll summarized these comments when he wrote, ''Fugard's plays are filled with understanding and compassion, and written with power and eloquence. But somehow, they bear that faint taint of 'literature' in which the eloquence and power seem to struggle unsuccessfully to break out of a self-regarding void and into that mysterious realm in which art has its radical effect and becomes primary rather than secondary experience. And this is true of . . . *Boesman & Lena.*'' Kroll added later in his review, ''For all its strength and authentic feeling, the play seems to beat its fists against its own eloquence.''

A few critics found *Boesman & Lena* to be unwatchable. Among them was T. E. Kalem of *Time,* who wrote, ''It may sound odd, but misery needs to be entertaining. Appalling calamities befall some people; yet they manage to make them sound drab and boring. Others possess the gift of making a minor mishap vividly compelling. Unfortunately, *Boesman & Lena* is one of those accounts of unlimited woe that try the playgoer's patience.'' Several critics agreed with this assessment; despite their praise for the play, they found its pace ''challenging.''

In 1992, Fugard directed a production of *Boesman & Lena* at the Manhattan Theater Club in New York City. Despite the twenty-three year gap since its debut, critics still found the play to be relevant, though the situation in South Africa had changed and apartheid polices had grown less oppressive. John Simon in *New York* wrote, ''This is an important play, no less so since conditions in South Africa have somewhat improved: The misery may now be as much existential as social. Outside oppressors add to it, but we carry oppression within us.''

Frank Rich, writing in the *New York Times,* agreed that in the two odd decades since its debut, the play's depths stood the test of time. ''Even at the time of its premiere *Boesman & Lena* was recognized as a universal work that might speak to audiences long after apartheid had collapsed.'' Later in the review, Rich added, ''Their [Boesman and Lena's] shared life, alternately a refuge and a brutal prison, is above all a marriage, observed by the author at a microscopic range Strindberg might have admired and as elemental and timeless a primitive campsite where the play's single evening of action takes place.''

CRITICISM

A. Petrusso,

In this essay, Petrusso discusses the evolution of Lena's character and why she decides to stay with her abusive mate, Boesman, at the end of Fugard's play.

In Athol Fugard's *Boesman & Lena,* the title characters, de facto husband and wife, seem to have an adversarial relationship. Though they are a couple, Boesman and Lena have no love lost between them. Boesman is impatient with Lena and often threatens her. He beats her regularly, and she has the bruises to prove it. Yet Lena stays with Boesman despite this mistreatment. During the play, however, Lena undergoes a transformation that shows she is more than an object for Boesman's fists. By

looking at Lena's nature and clues to her evolution, the reasons for her decision to stay with Boesman become much clearer.

When Lena and Boesman make their entrance in Act I, Fugard writes in the stage directions that ''She has been reduced to a dumb, animal-like submission.'' Lena trails behind Boesman, though she once, a long time ago, walked beside him. Boesman tries to ignore her as much as possible. When she starts complaining about their walk and the loss of their home that morning to bulldozers run by white men, he threatens to leave her behind next time. He says, ''It's useless to talk to you,'' though he never says much to her. She is there to share the burden that is life and provide a convenient whipping post for his anger and frustration. Boesman regularly tries to erase Lena's humanity. Early in Act I, he accuses her of faking her need to rest so she could look for a dog that she had been feeding.

But Lena wants more. What emerges in Act I is Lena's need for an individual, human identity. She needs to know who and where she is. She wants her humanity back. One way she achieves this goal is physical appearance. Her bruises, markers of Boesman's beatings, prove to her that she is flesh and blood. Each bruise also has a past. They are reminders of where she has been and what she has done. By counting them, as Lena does several times in the course of the play, she can recount something about her past.

Lena also affirms her existence by talking aloud, mostly to herself since Boesman refuses to communicate with her for most of Act I. This practice allows her to remember the past, something Boesman wants to forget. Unlike Lena, Boesman does not have to think about where he is. In Lena's early monologues, she tries to orient herself in place. She recounts the places they have lived and attempts to reconstruct their chronological order. When she thinks she has gotten a segment of it correct, Boesman makes her doubt herself, first feigning disinterest in her triumph, then making her mix-up the cities. Boesman goes on to say that someday Lena will not remember who she is, but Lena turns the tables when she asks him, ''Who are you?'' Self-examination throws Boesman off completely.

The incidents that fully forge Lena's identity and humanity in the play involve an old African man she invites to their camp. His presence highlights the contrast in Lena and Boesman's attitudes. After she threatens to leave Boesman, Lena sees this old man, whom she dubs ''Outa,'' wandering in the

WHAT DO I READ NEXT?

- *Hello and Goodbye,* a play by Athol Fugard written in 1965, is a drama that explores the lives and conflicts of a white brother and sister also living in Port Elizabeth, South Africa.

- *Writing South Africa: Literature, Apartheid, and Democracy, 1970-95* is a book published in 1998 and edited by Derek Attrige and Rosemary Jolly. Exploring how apartheid is portrayed in various forms of literature, the book includes original writings on the subject.

- *Lifetimes under Apartheid* is a book published in 1986 which contains both non-fiction and fiction writing as well as photographs by Nadine Gordimer and David Goldblatt. The book explores how people lived under the restrictions of apartheid.

- *The Smell of Apples,* a novel by Mark Behr published in 1995, explores life under apartheid in South Africa, highlighting events of 1961.

mudflats. Lena wants to help him, while Boesman says "We got no help." Later, after the old man has joined them, Lena wants to give the old man some of their precious water supply, as other black people have given them water in the past. Boesman will have none of it. He says, "He's not brown people, he's black people." Lena points out, "They got feelings too." By acknowledging another's humanness, her own identity grows stronger.

Even though the old man only speaks Xhosa, a language that Lena is unfamiliar with, she can talk *at* him. He manages to learn her name, which means she is a person with an individual identity. At the moment he learns her name, Lena decides the old man is truly her ally, her link to her humanity. She gives him water, and they talk at each other. The old man listens to Lena reconstruct her past, which acknowledges that she is alive. She tells him more of her story, and when she believes she has told him most everything, she says, "That all? *Ja.* Only a few words I know, but a long story if you lived it."

Lena's sense of self becomes nearly complete when she sacrifices everything she values to keep the old man in camp. Boesman will not let her cut their bread and tea into three parts, so she shares her food with the old man. Boesman throws his bread away and dumps his tea on the ground. Lena gives up her share of their wine in exchange for Boesman allowing the old man to stay with them. This is important because Boesman has previously called

Lena "a drunk." When Boesman will not let the old man sleep inside the shelter he has built, Lena stays outside, huddled under her blanket with the old man. By sacrificing for another, she has become human. She says, "I'm on this earth, not in it." Boesman cannot understand this at all.

But Lena is also violent towards the old man. When he arrives in their camp, she yells at him to sit in an angry tone. When she first tries to talk to him, he can only respond in Xhosa, which frustrates her. She shows him her bruises, and expects him to laugh at the story behind one of them just as some white men did earlier in the day. When the old man does not, she lets her exasperation show. When he tries to leave, she pushes him down and makes him stay. She needs, in some measure, to control Outa, the only sympathetic human contact she has received in a long time. She tells the old man at one point, "You can't just go, walk away like you didn't hear."

Lena's relationship with the old man confuses Boesman. He cannot leave them alone, especially once Lena has decided that she will give up her wine to keep the old man there. He tries to humiliate them at the beginning of Act II, making them say submissive words and mocking Lena, but it does no good. Lena's power has already grown beyond Boesman's comprehension. She questions his claims of freedom and is able to ask him questions like why he hurts her and why he hits her. Boesman tells her it is

> LENA'S SENSE OF SELF BECOMES NEARLY COMPLETE WHEN SHE SACRIFICES EVERYTHING SHE VALUES TO KEEP THE OLD MAN IN CAMP"

because "You cry." In other words, this is the only way he knows he is alive. All Boesman has is Lena.

Lena never lets the old man go. The old man's death makes Lena's human identity complete. She was holding his hand when he died and felt him slip away. Lena now knows the physical difference between life and death, self and nothingness. Lena is more than Boesman thinks she is. After the old man has died, Lena can finally trick Boesman. Lena makes Boesman doubt the moment he is living in. She convinces him the authorities could question the old man's death as suspicious and he could be implicated in it. As Boesman's anger grows, he comes close to attacking Lena, but she says "*Ja,* got to be careful now. There's one already." She goads him into beating up the body by pointing out that he could still be alive. Lena then makes Boesman believe that the bruises could further implicate him. She has reclaimed her life from Boesman and now has power over him.

During *Boesman & Lena,* Lena talks about leaving Boesman several times. While Boesman sold the bottles, Lena asked some white children if their mother needed a maid. She was rejected but swears she would have gone had a position been available. Lena was trying to leave Boesman again when she saw the old man wandering the flats. Finding him made Lena change her mind. But at the end of the play, Lena stays with Boesman. This happens only after he admits that he broke the bottles he accused her of breaking and after he tells her the order of places they have lived. These admissions acknowledge Lena's new identity, that of an equal to Boesman.

For Lena, it seems, the known is more scary than the unknown. She has found what she was looking for and to push her luck would not bring any discernable benefits. More importantly, Boesman is the only discernable link to her past. If she wants to

continue her journey of self-exploration, she needs Boesman. Also, Lena has held the hand of death and emerged alive. She is not afraid, but Boesman fears the old man's death and what it could say about him. She ends the play with more than she began. Her sense of self has grown while Boesman's has diminished. In her last speech of the play, Lena tells Boesman, "You still got a chance. Don't lose it." Lena took her chances and has more than survived.

Source: A. Petrusso, for *Drama for Students,* Gale, 1999.

Thomas M. Disch

Disch reviews a 1992 New York production of Boesman and Lena, *directed by Fugard himself. The critic lauds the playwright's work for its powerful depiction of "the horror of homelessness and vagrancy so tellingly."*

At the same time that the Manhattan Theatre Club is offering *Sight Unseen* in its Stage II space, the larger Stage I is offering a revival of *Boesman and Lena,* which is directed by its author, Athol Fugard. The two acts are presented without intermission, and for once this practice seems justified by the resulting tautness. Too often, eliminating intermission is simply a way to prevent the audience from escaping.

Boesman and Lena, which premiered in South Africa in 1969, presents one desolate night in the life of its title characters, who have just witnessed the destruction of the shantytown they'd lived in and have no other home than a featureless wasteland, represented in this production by a dead tree trunk. I know of no other play that depicts the horror of homelessness and vagrancy so tellingly, and surely the reason for this is that homelessness is not really Fugard's theme. The extremity of the situation in which Boesman and Lena find themselves is like Lear's heath or the desert with its single dead tree in *Waiting for Godot.* Boesman and Lena's straits are presented as emblematic of the human condition and hence not to be protested—only, if possible, endured.

Very little happens in Act I. Once they've set down their bundled possessions, Lena starts a fire and Boesman scavenges junk, from which he constructs a crude hut. In his absence Lena talks to herself, and in his presence she continues to talk to herself. The arrival of a derelict who speaks a language neither of them understands triggers a battle between them, as Lena resists Boesman's efforts to evict the intruder from "their" space. In the second act Fugard has two such effective *coups de théâtre* that it would be sinful for a reviewer to say what happens, even though this play has already acquired the status of a classic. Keith David as Boesman has the more difficult role, since he must somehow win our sympathy while glowering through most of Act I. He does, and when his glower finally explodes into speech he is tremendous. Come to think of it, it may be that the role of Lena is the more demanding, since she must keep the audience attentive to at least an hour's worth of nattering complaint before the tension mounts perceptibly. Lynne Thigpen turns these soliloquies into arias. Tsepo Mokone as the catalytic intruder should get this year's award for best performance in a foreign language. Score one more for the Manhattan Theatre Club.

Source: Thomas M. Disch, review of *Boesman and Lena* in the *Nation,* Vol. 254, no. 8, March 2, 1992, p. 283.

Edith Oliver

In this favorable review, Oliver praises the 1992 revival production of Fugard's play. She notes that it positively recalls the original production.

The revival of Athol Fugard's ''*Boesman & Lena,*'' at the Manhattan Theater Club, as directed by Mr. Fugard himself, is by far the most openly emotional of the three productions I've seen. This time, Keith David and Lynne Thigpen are the couple—the Cape Coloureds—who trudge the mud flats of the Swartkops River, in South Africa, escaping time after time from the white man's bulldozer, which destroys their shanties. When they enter, Miss Thigpen's face is filthy, her clothes are slovenly and ragged, and her bare feet are covered with mud. There are bruises on her face and arms from recent beatings. Boesman and Lena are carrying all their possessions on their backs, and silently, sullenly, they set up camp. Their work in this place is digging worms for fishermen. What is acted out on the stage is one evening and night of their life—an evening and night in which they come to realize that they are not human rubbish but a man and a woman of some identity. Lena has found and, over Boesman's protests, insists on sheltering at their fire (which she has built in a large metal container) a feeble old black man, a Bantu speaker, who is in very bad shape. The old man eventually dies, and, the rules of apartheid being what they were, Boesman and Lena are in such danger that they must now move on with all possible speed, one step ahead of the police. This time, however, both of them realize as they load up

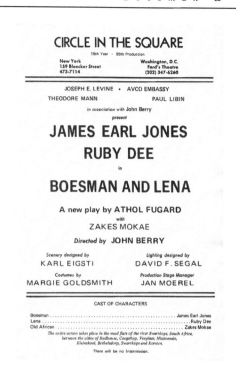

A marquee for a Circle in the Square production of Boesman & Lena

that something has changed forever: they have connected in a way that they never have before. They know who they are and what binds them together.

Miss Thigpen and Mr. David and their play are spellbinding for all its hundred and five unbroken minutes. For me, the performance was haunted—pleasantly so—by Ruby Dee, of the original New York production; by Frances Foster, of the first revival I saw; by James Earl Jones; and, above all, by the late Robert Christian, who was profound and indelible. Mr. David, much of the time silently on the boil, and Miss Thigpen, her hurt and defiance almost spilling over, are worthy of their predecessors, and so is Tsepo Mokone, as the black African. The dramatic setting—a backdrop strip of hot oranges and yellows—and the costumes were designed by Susan Hilferty, who was also the associate director. Lighting by Dennis Parichy.

Source: Edith Oliver, ''Stopover'' in the *New Yorker,* Vol. LXVII, no. 51, February 10, 1992 , p. 76.

John Simon

Calling Boesman and Lena *''Athol Fugard's profoundest play,'' Simon lauds the playwright for his probing examination of the injustices of Apart-*

> "THIS PLAY HAS ALREADY ACQUIRED THE STATUS OF A CLASSIC"

heid. Despite his respect for the text, however, the critic offers only mixed praise for the cast of this 1992 revival production.

Boesman and Lena, when it comes off, is Athol Fugard's profoundest play. Almost nothing happens—as in Beckett—yet all the injustices of the world are encapsulated in it. Two South African Coloureds—neither black nor white but in between—are wandering about the mud flats with their few belongings on their backs. They'll hunt for prawns in the riverbed in the morning, but tonight they'll pitch their makeshift tent, eat a little, drink, sleep, and maybe forget. Instead, they argue. Because Boesman relieves misery by beating his woman, and she, smarter and more verbal, relieves it with taunts. They fight, therefore they are.

Then a third person, even lower than they, is latched on to by Lena: Outa, a stray, decrepit Kaffir, who speaks Xhosa, not even Afrikaans, and with whom Lena can communicate only as with a child or dog. But she has someone now to witness her being and suffering, to corroborate the bruises Boesman and life have imprinted on her. She feeds Outa; Boesman bullies him. The old man dies, and Lena uses his death to scare Boesman. They flee. Prawnless and hopeless, the two trudge on into their daily drudgery. That is all, but it's enough. Enough for Fugard to convey that "both are . . . victims of a . . . shared predicament, and of each other. Which . . . makes it some sort of love story. They are each other's fate."

This is an important play, no less so since conditions in South Africa have somewhat improved: The misery may now be as much existential as social. Outside oppressors add to it, but we carry oppression within us. Unfortunately, no one in the cast is wholly right. Keith David, a black American, cannot, good actor though he is, quite convey a South African Coloured in looks and furtiveness. Ditto Lynne Thigpen, a fine actress, but one too robust and powerful. In the original American production (1970), the delicate yet resilient Ruby Dee

was a more moving Lena. And though Tsepo Mokone gets across the dazed marginality of Outa, he lacks the unearthly fragility that Zakes Mokae brought to the part. None of this, though, is a serious blemish on a production that the author has directed with his customary unblinking honesty.

Source: John Simon, "Benoit & Marcelle & Henri & Angelique" in *New York,* Vol. 25, no. 6, February 10, 1992, pp. 86–87.

SOURCES

Fugard, Athol. *Boesman & Lena* in *Boesman & Lena and Other Plays,* Oxford University Press, pp. 237-99.

Kalem, T. E. Review of *Boesman & Lena* in *Time,* July 13, 1970, p. 63.

Kauffmann, Stanley. Review of *Boesman & Lena* in the *New Republic,* July 25, 1970, pp. 16, 25.

Kroll, Jack. "On the Mud Flats" in *Newsweek,* July 6, 1970, p. 78.

Rich, Frank. "Fugard's Sad Wanderers, with Imitations of Now" in the *New York Times,* January 30, 1992, p. C15.

Simon, John. Review of *Boesman & Lena* in *New York,* February 10, 1992, pp. 86-87.

FURTHER READING

Davenport, T. R. H. *South Africa: A Modern History,* Cambridge University Press, 1977.
   This book covers South African history, focusing on the nineteen and twentieth centuries.

Fugard, Athol. *Cousins: A Memoir,* Theatre Communications Group, 1997.
   In this autobiography, the author discusses his life, focusing primarily on his childhood.

Fugard, Athol. *Notebooks, 1960-1977,* Knopf, 1983.
   This book contains the playwrights notes on many of his plays written in this time period, including *Boesman & Lena.*

Richards, Lloyd. "The Art of Theater VIII: Athol Fugard" in *Paris Review,* Summer, 1989, p. 128.
   This interview with Fugard includes information on his inspirations and the mechanics of writing his plays, including *Boesman & Lena.*

Vandenbroucke, Russell. *Truths the Hand Can Touch: The Theatre of Athol Fugard,* Donker, 1986.
   This book discusses Fugard's background and work in depth, including *Boesman & Lena.*

Brighton Beach Memoirs

NEIL SIMON

1983

Neil Simon's *Brighton Beach Memoirs* is one of his most widely respected plays. Simon earned kudos for what many critics consider the best example of his efforts to combine his trademark humor with a level of drama and character introspection. *Brighton Beach Memoirs* was first produced at the Ahmanson Theatre in Los Angeles on December 10, 1982. It debuted on Broadway on March 27, 1983, at the Alvin Theatre. Like many of Simon's successes, *Brighton Beach Memoirs* enjoyed a lengthy run and financial success. The play won Simon the New York Drama Critics Circle Prize for Best Play.

Critics attributed much of the success of *Brighton Beach Memoirs* to Simon's newfound sophistication. Before this play, Simon had a long career of successful plays that were either comic or serious. His previous attempts to combine the two rarely impressed critics or audiences. Critics praised *Brighton Beach* for its deft characterizations and meaningful humor. Some attribute this to the fact that Simon knew his material well. Though not strictly autobiographical, Simon based the play on his memories of growing up in New York City in the years just before World War II. Despite the play's success, some critics found *Brighton Beach Memoirs* superficial, comparing it to a soap opera, albeit one with good jokes.

The success of *Brighton Beach Memoirs* led to two more plays featuring protagonist Eugene Jerome and his family, 1985's *Biloxi Blues,* which

dealt with Eugene's armed service years, and 1986's *Broadway Bound.* Each of these plays received more positive reviews and contained more extensive autobiographical material than *Brighton Beach Memoirs.* With the success of this trilogy, Simon's reputation as a premiere American playwright was cemented.

AUTHOR BIOGRAPHY

Simon was born on July 4, 1927, in the Bronx, New York. His father, Irving, worked as a garment salesman. Irving Simon's job forced him to leave his family periodically during Simon's childhood. Simon's mother, Mamie, was forced to work during these periods in such places as Gimbel's department store to support Simon and his elder brother Danny. After his parents divorced, Simon lived for a time in Forest Hills, New York, with relatives. From an early age, Simon displayed comic and writing talents, and his elder brother encouraged his efforts.

After graduating from high school in 1944, Simon attended several colleges, served in the Army, and taught himself to write comedy from books and imitating successful comics. After being discharged from the military in 1946, Simon was hired to work in the mailroom at Warner Brothers studios. Danny Simon already worked in the publicity department there. The brothers Simon were given an opportunity to audition as comedy writers, and they were immediately hired by Goodman Ace on the basis of their sample. The brothers worked as a comedy writing team for the next decade in radio and television.

Danny Simon decided to pursue a career in television directing in 1956, while Simon continued to write television comedy for several shows. He won two Emmy Awards for his television writing. But Simon felt restricted by television and began working on a play around 1959. Titled *Come Blow Your Horn,* Simon rewrote the play for several years. It was finally produced on Broadway in 1961 and was a minor success. Simon immediately began work on his next play, a comedy called *Barefoot in the Park.* The play opened in 1962 and was an immediate smash hit.

The success of *Barefoot in the Park* established Simon's reputation as a playwright, and he began turning numerous plays. Almost all of them were moneymakers on Broadway. Many of his plays in the 1960s were straight comedies, including 1965's *The Odd Couple.* By the late-1960s, Simon attempted to combine comedy with serious issues. These efforts were not always successful or critically well-received, especially 1970's *The Gingerbread Lady.* After Simon's wife Joan died in 1973, leaving him with two young daughters, Ellen and Nancy, Simon's career temporarily floundered.

Simon remarried soon after his wife's death, to actress Marsha Mason, and moved to California in 1975. He wrote both successful comedies, such as *California Suite* in 1976, and more serious plays that dealt with his personal turmoils, such as 1978's *Chapter Two* (based on Joan's death and his subsequent remarriage). His comedies were usually bigger successes, both critically and at the box office. By 1983, however, Simon was able to combine the comic with the serious in his semi-autobiographical *Brighton Beach Memoirs,* the first play of a trilogy. The result was acclaim from the audience and critics alike.

Simon continued to use *Brighton Beach Memoirs*'s main character in two more plays, each more successful than the last. Though plays written after the trilogy were not always as successful, Simon's reputation as a gifted playwright was firmly solidified, and Simon continued to write Broadway plays well into the 1990s.

PLOT SUMMARY

Act I

Brighton Beach Memoirs opens in September, 1937, in the Jerome household. The Jeromes live in a lower middle class neighborhood in Brighton Beach, New York. It is about 6:30 in the evening and fourteen-year-old Eugene Morris Jerome is playing a semi-imaginary game of baseball outside. As his ball hits the house, Eugene's aunt, Blanche Morton, gets a headache. Eugene's mother Kate yells at her son to stop the game and come inside. Eugene reluctantly comes inside. He tells the audience that he wants to play professional baseball or be a writer. He is sent upstairs, and he begins writing in his journal.

Eugene tells the audience that his Aunt Blanche and his two cousins, Nora and Laurie, live with his family because Blanche's husband died of cancer six years ago. Eugene's father, Jack, has worked two jobs to support everyone for three and a half years. Eugene's writing is interrupted when Kate demands that he come down and set the table instead of Laurie. Laurie has a heart flutter, and Eugene complains that he has to do everything because of his cousin's illness.

As Eugene sets the table, sixteen-year-old Nora comes in and is very excited. She has been offered a chance to audition for a dancing role in a Broadway show. Nora says that the producer assured her that she would get the part if her mother gave her permission. Blanche hesitates because it would mean Nora would have to drop out of school, but Nora argues that she could support Blanche and Laurie if she took the job. Blanche can't make the decision, leaving it up to Jack when he returns.

Eugene's mother sends him to the store. Nora and Laurie talk in their room. They discuss their dead father and they resolve to spend no more money on anything so they can buy a house for their mother. When Eugene returns, his elder brother Stanley is waiting for him. Stanley tells Eugene that he was fired from his job for standing up for a coworker. To regain his position, he must apologize to his boss. Stanley wants to stand up for his principles, but the family desperately needs the money. Stanley decides to talk it over with his father.

A tired-looking Jack Jerome arrives home carrying several large boxes. They contain noise makers and party favors. Jack's second job was selling these items to hotels and nightclubs, but the business closed that day and he was left without employment. Jack worries about being able to support the large family. At the dinner table, everyone is tense. Jack suggests to Stan that he ask his boss for a raise. Laurie brings up Nora's offer, much to her chagrin. After dinner, Nora insists on talking about the audition with Jack, though her mother tries to prevent her. Jack offers his advice as they walk down to the beach.

Meanwhile, Stanley and Eugene talk in their room. Eugene describes an erotic dream he has had, and Stanley tells him it was a wet dream. Eugene presses him for information on puberty and girls, especially their cousin Nora, but Stanley's focus is on his employment problem. Kate and Blanche have a conversation downstairs. Kate tries to convince Blanche to come to a party that Jack's company is giving next week, but Blanche reveals that she

Neil Simon

has a date with Frank Murphy, a man who lives across the street with his mother. Nora and Jack return, and Nora presses her mother to make a decision. Blanche, like Jack, thinks Nora should finish high school. This angers Nora, and she storms upstairs.

Jack is growing more tired, and Kate wants him to come to bed. Stanley appears and asks to talk to his father. Stanley tells Jack what happened, and his father understands his dilemma. Stanley decides to write the letter and apologize. Stanley hires Eugene to write the letter in exchange for a detailed description of the time Stanley saw Nora naked in the shower.

Act II

This act takes place one week later. The household is in disarray because Jack has had a heart attack in the past week and is resting at home. Also, Blanche is getting ready for her date with Frank Murphy. Stanley sneaks into the house and talks to Eugene in their room. Stanley has lost his entire week's salary playing poker and is desperate about what to do.

Jack decides to get up and go downstairs to meet Blanche's date. Kate is appalled at her husband's disregard for his health, and they argue. Nora comes downstairs and leaves for her date, not wanting to see her mother. Blanche makes an appearance, and everyone present thinks she looks like a movie star. Jack sends Eugene and Laurie to get ice cream. Kate goes upstairs to ask Stanley for his pay so she can give emergency money to Blanche. Stanley tells her that he lost it in a poker game. Kate tries to remain calm and decides not to tell anyone about the matter until later.

Kate comes back into the kitchen in a very agitated state. Blanche is still worrying about Nora. Kate gets angry at Blanche for only focusing on her own problems. The sisters get into a fight which is interrupted by Laurie's return. On her way to get ice cream, Frank Murphy's mother gave the girl a note. Frank had a car accident and will not be able to keep their date because he is in the hospital. This leads to another argument between Kate and Blanche. Kate expresses her resentment at Blanche for things that go back to their childhood. Blanche decides that she will move out and live with a friend while she looks for a job. When she has a job, she tells Kate, she will take her daughters and move into her own home.

Eugene is sent upstairs to get Stanley and Laurie for dinner. Stanley demands money from Eugene in case he has to sleep out that night. Stanley has decided to join the Army because he might be able to make more money that way. Eugene becomes very upset, but Stanley still leaves. Eugene cannot tell his family about where Stanley has gone during dinner. After the meal, he tells Laurie.

Several hours later, Blanche waits outside for Nora to return. Blanche tells Nora about her decision. Nora tells her that she feels that Blanche does not care for her as much as she does Laurie. They make an awkward peace. Kate comes downstairs because of the noise, and Kate asks Blanche not to leave. Kate convinces Blanche to stay while she looks for work.

The next day, Stanley comes back just in time for dinner. Stanley says he passed the physical, but he could not join up knowing how much the family needed him at home. Stanley and Jack talk. Stanley made some money at a bowling alley, which he gives to his mother. He promises to make up the rest. Jack tells him that war is coming.

Upstairs, Stanley gives Eugene a present: a postcard with a naked woman on it. Eugene is overwhelmed. Jack gets a letter saying that his cousin and family have escaped Poland and are coming to New York City. He begins making plans for fitting the extra family members into the house.

CHARACTERS

Eugene Morris Jerome

Eugene is the fourteen-year-old narrator of *Bright Beach Memoirs*. He wants to be a baseball player, but if that does not work out, he'll settle for being a writer. He keeps a detailed journal of his family's eccentricities. Eugene is concerned for his family, especially his overworked father, but complains about their demands on him. He feels like a slave to his mother, who is constantly sending him to the store on one errand or another. He also feels that he is blamed for everything that goes wrong. Eugene has a love-hate relationship with his elder brother, Stanley. For the most part, though, Eugene worships his brother because he has integrity and tells Eugene about girls and masturbation. Eugene is at the beginning of puberty and just beginning to notice the opposite sex, especially his pretty cousin Nora. Eugene writes a letter of apology for Stanley in exchange for details about the time Stanley saw Nora naked.

Jack Jerome

Jack is the patriarch of the family. He works two jobs to support everyone in the household and looks older than his forty years. He is constantly tired, but makes time to guide both Nora and Stanley through their tough decisions. Between the action depicted in the acts, Jack has a heart attack and is confined to his bed. Though he finds someone to cover for him at work for several weeks, Jack still worries about taking care of everyone. This becomes especially important when relatives who have escaped from Poland write of their imminent arrival in America.

Jacob Jerome

See Jack Jerome

Kate Jerome

Kate is Eugene's mother and nearly forty-years-old. She is also Blanche's elder sister. Kate takes most of the responsibility in keeping the household running smoothly, acting as mother to everyone. She ensures everyone eats and is properly taken care of according to their needs. She also manages the money, scrimping to feed everyone. While Kate might inject her opinion on situations, she refuses to make decisions for other people. Eugene believes that she is illogical about some of the things she yells at him about, and that she has some sort of second sight. Kate feels especially protective of her sister, Blanche. She does not like the Murphy family living across the street, especially when Frank Murphy shows an interest in her sister. In the second act, Kate reveals that she has also resented Blanche at times.

Stanley Jerome

Stanley is Eugene's elder brother, nearly nineteen-years-old. He works in a hat store to help support his family. Stanley has a moral dilemma in the first act of the play. At work, his boss treated a black employee unfairly and Stanley stood up to him. Stanley must apologize for his actions or he will lose his job. After discussing the matter with his father, Stanley decides to apologize, but only because his family needs the money. In the second act, Stanley gambles away his weekly paycheck that the family desperately needs. Stanley leaves to join the army, but he does not enlist. He ultimately returns to the family and his job. Stanley is usually kind to his brother, Eugene, teaching him about the opposite sex and other worldly lessons, such as masturbation.

Blanche Morton

Blanche is Kate's younger sister. She has been a widow for six years because her husband David died of cancer. Since then, she and her daughters have lived with the Jeromes because her husband left her penniless. Blanche has asthma. Blanche takes in some sewing to contribute to the household, but it does not amount to much money. Blanche feels guilty about her lack of earnings. She lets her sister dominate her. Though Blanche has not shown much interest in getting remarried, much to her sister's chagrin, she agrees to go on a date with a neighbor, Frank Murphy. He is in a car accident and it does not happen. After she and Kate fight following the aborted date, Blanche decides that she will move out and get a job. Kate convinces her to stay until she finds employment.

Laurie Morton

Laurie is Blanche's younger daughter. She has a heart flutter and is rarely required to do any household labor. Laurie spends much of her time studying and reading.

Nora Morton

Nora is Blanche's elder daughter. She is sixteen-years-old and very pretty. Nora takes dancing lessons and has a chance to audition for a Broadway producer. She is very angry throughout the play because she is not allowed to audition. Everyone insists that she graduate from high school instead. In the second act, Nora reveals that she is angry with her mother for favoring her younger sister because of her illness. She and Blanche reconcile after this revelation.

MEDIA ADAPTATIONS

- *Brighton Beach Memoirs* was adapted as a film in 1986. Simon adapted the script from his own play. Directed by Gene Saks, the movie features Jonathon Silverman as Eugene, Blythe Danner as Kate, Bob Dishy as Jack, and Judith Ivey as Blanche.

THEMES

Coming of Age

Eugene Jerome, the main character of *Brighton Beach Memoirs,* is nearly fifteen-years-old and in the grip of adolescence. He is both a child and an adult. Eugene feels that he is a slave to his mother because he has to go to the store for her several times a day. Yet he does not have to work to support his family, and he still attends school. Eugene still has choices to make in his life: He wants to be a baseball player or a writer. His family wants him to attend college. Eugene is noticing girls for the first time and constantly asks his older brother for information about the opposite sex. Stanley tells his

TOPICS FOR FURTHER STUDY

- Compare and contrast *Brighton Beach Memoirs* with Paul Osborn's 1939 play *Morning's at Seven,* a comedic play about familial relations. How do the different settings (urban versus rural, respectively) affect the manner in which the families are perceived?

- Research the history of the Depression in the United States, focusing on the effect it had on families. How do the Jeromes compare with the average American family during the Depression?

- Explore the psychology of puberty. Discuss how puberty affects the actions and decisions of Eugene Jerome. Is Eugene a typical pubescent male?

- Research the history of Europe in 1937, focusing on the hostile actions of Nazi Germany towards other countries and Jewish populations. How do these political policies affect the relatives of the Jeromes in Europe as well as their American counterparts?

---

brother about masturbation and buys him a postcard with a naked woman on it. Eugene lusts after his beautiful sixteen-year-old cousin Nora. Eugene's adolescent concerns sometimes seem petty when compared to the rest of the family's problems. But Eugene realizes this by the end of the play, and this realization marks the beginning of his maturity.

Family

Everyone in *Brighton Beach Memoirs* is related and the importance of family is emphasized throughout the text. After Blanche's husband Dave died six years ago, the Jeromes took her and her daughters in. Jack and Stanley work to support Blanche's family as well as their own. Blanche tries to contribute to the household by taking in sewing. At the end of the play, it is revealed that a number of Jack's relatives have escaped the invading German Nazis in Poland and are making their way to New York City. The family decides how to make room for the new arrivals.

Despite the cramped quarters and occasional lack of privacy, everyone takes care of everyone else in the Jerome/Morton family. Jack does not complain about having to work two jobs to support seven people. Stanley feels guilty about losing his paycheck in a poker game because he knows how much the family needs the money. Though Eugene sometimes resents his mother's constant nagging and his frequent trips to the grocery store, he does his part to keep things running smoothly. There are numerous arguments between family members, especially between Blanche and her daughter Nora as well as Blanche and Kate, but their familial bonds endure.

Duty and Responsibility

Most every member of the Jerome household accepts their duties and responsibilities in life. Jack Jerome works two jobs to support his family and suffers a heart attack in the process. He does everything he can to make sure the bills are paid and everyone has food and clothing. Stanley Jerome also works to support the family. His sense of duty goes beyond money, though. Stanley stands up to his boss when he thinks the man has wronged another employee over an accident. No one else stood up for the man, and Stanley's sense of responsibility for his fellow man nearly costs him his job. Stanley is still young (eighteen), however, and still makes mistakes. He irresponsibly loses a whole week's pay in a poker game the same week his father is out of work because of his heart attack. Stanley decides to join the Army, ostensibly to make more money for the family and avoid their wrath over the lost wages. His sense of duty kicks in, however, and he realizes that his family needs him nearby.

The younger kids also feel a sense of duty and responsibility, though they sometimes manipulate it for their own benefit. When Nora is offered a chance to dance on Broadway, she tries to convince her mother to let her go by arguing that she will be able to support their family. Blanche wants Nora to finish high school instead and argues that is will be better for the girl in the long term. Nora resents the decision, but her desire to help out her family is sincere. Similarly, Eugene is often forced to run errands and perform household chores that he resents. But his sense of duty to his mother and his family forces him to set the table and go to the store, even if the request made of him seems stupid or unreasonable. This sense of duty and responsibility to each other keeps the family together.

A scene from the film adaptation of Simon's play; Jonathan Silverman as Eugene retrieves his napkin and takes the opportunity to look up his cousin Nora's dress

STYLE

Setting

Brighton Beach Memoirs is set in Brighton Beach, New York, in September, 1937, near the end of the Great Depression and just before the start of World War II. The Jerome household is located in a lower middle class section of the area near the beach, where most of the inhabitants are Jewish, German, and Irish. All of the action takes place in and around the Jerome house, a frame house with a small porch. Inside the house, the audience can see the dining room and living room on the first floor as well as the steps leading to the second floor. On the second floor the audience can see a hallway and three small bedrooms: Nora and Laurie's; Stanley and Eugene's; and Kate and Jack's. This setting emphasizes the familial themes of the play and the close-knit nature of their relationships.

Narrator

Eugene Jerome is the narrator of *Brighton Beach Memoirs*. He directly addresses the audience, commenting on the action and relaying information. Much of what Eugene says is humorous in nature and acts as a release for the play's dramatic ten-

sions. By talking directly to the audience, Eugene establishes a link between them and the heart of the play. The device also allows the audience to better understand Eugene and his feelings. For example, from these musings the audience knows that he hates his name and how he really feels about his family. Sometimes his actions contradict his words, but his true feelings come through.

In his narration, Eugene also reveals information about his family that the audience might not otherwise receive. One example is the details surrounding Aunt Blanche and why she and her daughters live with the Jeromes.

Metaphor

One way to interpret the Jerome and Morton family household is as a metaphor or microcosm of America in the late-1930s. *Brighton Beach Memoirs* takes place in 1937 during the Depression and the beginning of the Nazi horrors in Europe. Many members of the household remember a better life, before the economic and political turmoil. Nora, for example, remembers life before her father's death. The tensions in the household increase with each new problem, mirroring the increasing tensions in Europe as the Nazi aggressions increase. Because the Jerome and Morton families are Jewish, this metaphor works on another level as well. The family's endeavor to survive and maintain their dignity under extreme circumstances echoes the problems Jewish people faced with the onslaught of the virulently anti-Semitic Nazis.

HISTORICAL CONTEXT

In 1983, the United States was a country that looked to its past for inspiration. Nostalgia was a strong cultural force. Older ideas were reworked and recombined into new philosophies and styles. Little was truly original. This was evident in several ways. For example, 1930s-style Art Dèco was influential in fashion. Rap music, a burgeoning music form in the 1980s, was often built on samples (recorded snippets) of other artists' music. Some of the decades most popular films, *Star Wars* and *Raiders of the Lost Ark,* for example, were essentially reworked B-movie serials straight out of the 1930s. Adding to the country's fascination with the entertainment of the past, America's president was a former film star, Ronald Reagan. His populist rhetoric and simplistic, common sense approach to the office hearkened back to the heroic film cowboy attitudes that germinated in the films of the 1930s.

Reagan was also the oldest man ever to be elected president, and by 1983, he was seventy-two-years-old. The American population was "graying," with the percentage of senior citizens quickly growing; improved health care was extending the average life span. This senior segment of the population joined together to assert its power. The AARP (American Association of Retired Persons) grew significantly in membership and became a powerful lobbying force in Congress. There was talk of a generation gap, as the demands of senior citizens often collided with those of younger generations. This came to a head in the controversy over funding for Social Security.

Reagan was a Republican who operated from a conservative platform. The country as a whole seemed to embrace such right-leaning philosophies as an antidote to the liberal 1970s. Many voted Reagan into office hoping he would solve the country's economic problems, but in 1983, unemployment was still at record levels. Inflation had fallen to 3.2 percent, however. While conservatives touted the family-oriented, traditional life as the "new" ideal, these concepts did not mesh with the reality of rising divorces, single-parent homes, and the threat of the AIDS virus. Such contradictions showed the shallow nature of the time period, where superficial concerns held sway over substantive issues. In reality, the minority rich increased their wealth as the middle class shrunk and more and more people faced economic hardship.

To pump up the economy (and divert attention from their meager domestic policies), Reagan and the Republicans spent a record amount of money on defense, justifying their expenditures with anti-Communist rhetoric (the United States was still in the midst of the Cold War with the Soviet Union). In 1983, an incident occurred which allegedly proved the "evil" intent of the Soviet Union. A Korean airliner accidentally strayed into Soviet airspace and was shot down. Everyone aboard the aircraft was killed.

The Reagan administration seized the incident as proof that the Soviet threat was real, as was the threat of nuclear war. There was a controversy over whether a nuclear war could be won. One of the most highly watched television movies of 1983 was ABC's *The Day After,* which speculated what might happen in the aftermath of a nuclear war. Despite such precarious events, the United States and the Soviet Union were in negotiation for arms reduction treaties for much of the decade. But the American policy of massive spending on defense significantly increased the federal budget deficit, leading to an uncertain economic future.

CRITICAL OVERVIEW

While Simon has enjoyed a great deal of financial success on Broadway for many years, critics have generally been disdainful of his work. *Brighton Beach Memoirs* is regarded as the play which changed that. Many critics believed the play was the first time Simon successfully combined comedy with serious themes, and many expressed hope that Simon would finally be taken seriously by scholars. Not all critics agreed on the work's merit, but Simon did receive some of the best reviews of his career for *Brighton Beach Memoirs.*

T. E. Kalem of *Time* wrote: "Without slighting his potent comic talents, Simon looks back, not in anger, remorse or undue guilt but with fondly nour-

COMPARE & CONTRAST

- **1937:** The United States is in the middle of the Great Depression. The unemployment rate is very high, with approximately one quarter of the workforce unable to find work.

  1983: The United States is in a recession and the unemployment rate is at record levels.

  Today: The United States' economy is relatively stable. The national unemployment rate is extremely low and the stock market is experiencing record highs. In early-1999, the market hits the 10,000 mark for the first time.

- **1937:** War seems imminent in Europe because of German leader Adolf Hitler's aggressive foreign policy. Within two years, war will engulf all of Europe.

  1983: The Cold War, a political standoff between the United States and Russia that has lasted for decades, is near its end. When Mikhail Gorbachev is elected to the Russian presidency a few years later, the Cold War will end.

  Today: There are pockets of political instability in the world, especially the Middle East and the Balkan states, but almost of Europe is stable.

- **1937:** Social Security, a New Deal policy that ensures an income for people of retirement age, was introduced in 1935 and is in full force by 1937.

  1983: The graying of America (between twenty-six and thirty million people are sixty-five or older) puts unprecedented demands on the Social Security system. President Reagan signs a bill to ensure funding of Social Security for the next seventy-five years.

  Today: There are lingering worries that Social Security will go bankrupt as the Baby Boom generation ages. There is debate over alternative means of supporting social security, including the U.S. government making investments in the stock market.

ished compassion at himself as an adolescent in 1937 and at the almost asphyxiatingly close-knit family around him.'' Frank Rich of the *New York Times* concurred, stating ''Mr. Simon makes real progress towards an elusive longtime goal: he mixes comedy and drama without, for the most part, either force-feeding the jokes or milking the tears. It's happy news that one of our theater's slickest playwrights is growing beyond his well-worn formulas of the past.'' But Rich went on to argue that the play is not as good as it could be. He called it superficial, and criticized its skirting of deeper issues. Rich also felt that the character/narrator Eugene was too glib. Rich's colleague at the *New York Times,* Walter Kerr, disagreed, writing: ''The shrewdest of Mr. Simon's ploys, and very probably the best, is not simply to have made the boy hilarious in his likes and dislikes, his comings and goings, his sexual gropings. Mr. Simon lets us watch the comic mind growing up.'' Kerr, though, felt the second act

faltered in part because ''we tend to lose Eugene'' in favor of the rest of the family.

Critics who disliked the play often focused on the weakness of Eugene. Jack Kroll, writing in *Newsweek,* said that Simon's ''young hero, Eugene, wants to be a writer but Simon gives him so much dialogue about masturbation and naked girls that it gets unfunny and embarrassing.'' But the reviewer conceded, like many other critics, that ''There are moments of tenderness and insight.'' Catharine Hughes in *America* agreed. She wrote: ''His youthful narrator almost always steps in to diffuse seriousness with a facile, albeit usually funny, remark. After a time, this becomes too predictable as a device.''

Other critics found *Brighton Beach Memoirs* as a whole to be problematic. The *Nation*'s Richard Gilman stated, ''The first act contains the usual complement of more or less amusing episodes and funny lines. But the second act turns serious. That is to say, Simon wants to be a *dramatist* and so devises some hokey stuff about family life in the Depression, the growing menace of fascism, intergenerational conflict, and youth's awakening to sex. It's all obvious, derivative and flaccid.''

Many critics who criticized the play often focused on Simon and his background. While Simon says that he based *Brighton Beach Memoirs* on his adolescence, he did not intend it to be wholly autobiographical. None of the play's dramatic incidents actually occurred in his own youth, though he experienced many family difficulties. Critics suggested that Simon could have written a better play if it had been more autobiographical. Kroll wrote, ''In an interview Simon talks about his 'extremely painful' childhood, how he lived with a pillow over his head to block out the bitter fights of his parents, how his father would leave for long periods, how he was abused as the only Jewish kid in school. Why isn't this in the play? He didn't go all the way with his own truth.'' John Simon, in *New York,* brought up a similar issue, claiming ''The first problem with *Memoirs* is that it has no intention of being truthful,'' before relating details of Simon's childhood.

Similarly, critics were divided over Simon's use of Jewish characters. Kalem in *Time* said that ''Simon is openly comfortable with his Jewish characters '' Rich in the *New York Times* took a mixed point of view, writing, ''Though some of the Jewish mother gags are overdone, others are dead-on.'' John Simon took the most negative view, stating that ''as a final dishonesty, his Jewish family talks and looks as un-Jewish as possible (through the writing, casting, and directing).'' The only thing that critics could agree upon was Simon's draw at the box-office and the wide appeal of his brand of humor.

CRITICISM

A. Petrusso

In this essay, Petrusso discusses how the concept of dignity drives each of the characters in Simon's play.

In Neil Simon's play *Brighton Beach Memoirs,* there is an underlying theme overlooked by many critics. Each major character in the play is driven by or looks for some measure of dignity in his or her life. This measure of self-worth is an important part

of why the Jerome-Morton household survives despite the cramped quarters and the economic duress of the Great Depression. The quest for human dignity does not take the same form for each character, but the variety of experiences makes the tapestry of *Brighton Beach Memoirs* a rich composite of the problems people face to this day.

For Stanley Jerome, the eighteen-and-a-half-year-old brother of narrator Eugene Jerome, the quest takes on several forms. This is fitting for a young man on the verge of adulthood. In Act I, Stanley nearly loses his job when he stands up for a co-worker, defending the man's honor in the face of what Stanley perceives as an injustice. This dilemma makes Stanley heartsick, but because his family needs the money so desperately, he ultimately swallows his pride and writes (or has Eugene write) the letter of apology.

While Stanley's sweeping dirt on Mr. Stroheim's shoes is immature, the rest of his actions show that he is a young man willing to speak up when he perceives that an injustice has occurred. Jobs were hard to come by during the Depression, but Stanley's instincts put dignity before commerce. If it were not for the Depression and the scarcity of jobs, it is implied that Stanley would not have apologized. In Act II, Stanley's dignity-related dilemma takes on a much different form. It is a week later, and Stanley has lost his entire week's salary at a poker game. To save face with his family, Stanley decides that he will join the Army, rationalizing that he will earn more money as a soldier, especially when he makes sergeant. He promises Eugene that he will send all his salary home. Though his parents are angry when they learn about the lost salary, they are relieved when Stanley returns having not enlisted. Though Stanley thought he could find dignity in escaping, he decides that his family will benefit more from having funds now rather than later. Simon implicitly argues that to be dignified is to face up to one's responsibilities, even when mistakes are made and great shame is the result.

One of the reasons Stanley's salary is so important in Act II lies in the fact that his father, Jack Jerome, has had a heart attack and cannot work for several weeks. Like Stanley, much of Jack's quest for dignity lies in his ability to support his family. Jack must do everything he can, no matter what the cost to his health, to pay the bills for the seven members of his household and ensure some quality of life. The weight of the family's dignity lies on his shoulders. In Act I, Jack loses his night

WHAT DO I READ NEXT?

- *Biloxi Blues,* a play by Neil Simon first produced in 1984, is the second in the trilogy begun by *Brighton Beach Memoirs.* This play focuses on Eugene Jerome's experiences as a recruit in the Army during World War II.

- *Broadway Bound,* a play by Neil Simon first produced in 1986, is the third in the trilogy. This play focuses on Eugene Jerome's quest to become a professional writer.

- *A Portrait of the Artist as a Young Man,* a novel published by James Joyce in 1916, concerns the coming of age of writer Stephen Dedalus.

- *Our Town,* a play by Thorton Wilder first produced in 1938, is a nostalgic look at families living together in Grover's Corner, New Hampshire.

- *New York Jews and the Great Depression,* a nonfiction book published by Beth S. Wenger in 1996, discusses ethnic relations, economic conditions and life in the city.

---

job when the owner goes bankrupt. Jack worked as a party favor salesman to nightclubs and hotels. To compensate for this loss, Jack does several things. First, he takes as many noisemakers and party favors as he can carry to try to compensate for loss of income. Second, Jack finds another job, driving a taxi cab. This employment situation compounded by constant worry leads to his heart attack.

Though almost all of Jack's time and energy is sapped by his constant work, he does not neglect his duties as father and head of the household. He works hard to maintain the dignity of his family economically, but he does not forget their personal quests for dignity. Everyone looks to Jack for guidance. Stanley consults him on his work dilemma mentioned earlier. He also gives Nora counsel on her hard decision, and shows his support for both Kate and Blanche during their times of trouble. Because Nora's father is dead, and her mother will not make a decision about her audition, Jack steps in, though physically exhausted, and takes a walk with Nora to offer his advice. Though Jack is supposed to be restricted to bed rest because of his heart attack, he insists on getting up to be there for Blanche when she goes on her first date in many years.

When Frank Murphy does not come, and Kate and Blanche get into an argument, Jack does his best to be intercede and get them both to understand each other. He tells them to ''get it out of their systems''

and then make up. Individual dignity must be maintained in such a small space or the household would be an intolerable place to live.

The dignity-related dilemmas on the homefront are economically related on the surface. Nora is sixteen-years-old and has been taking dancing lessons, with considerable promise, for many years. In her class, she is offered an audition for a Broadway musical called *Abracadabra* along with a few other girls. The producer pulled her aside and said she basically had the job if she wanted it. Though she would have to drop out of school to take the role, Nora argues that she could help support her family and begin to pay back the Jeromes. Implicit in Nora's desire for the job, though, is a need for freedom, to be an adult.

When she and Jack return from their walk, Nora tells her mother, ''I don't want this just for myself, Momma, but for you and for Laurie. In a few years we could have a house of our own, instead of all being cooped up here like animals. I'm asking for a way out, Momma. Don't shut me in. Don't shut me in for the rest of my life.'' Nora wants dignity in two ways, but the adults decide that she should stay in school until she gets her diploma. Nora resents the decision, but eventually she and Blanche reach a mutual understanding.

Blanche's quest for dignity is not unlike Nora's by the end of *Brighton Beach Memoirs.* Blanche is

> "WHETHER WANTING TO EARN AN INCOME OR SIMPLY TO DEFINE ONE'S SELF AND ONE'S PLACE IN THE WORLD, IN *BRIGHTON BEACH MEMOIRS* THE QUEST FOR DIGNITY BEGINS AND ENDS AT HOME"

thirty-eight-years-old and has been a widow for six years. Because her husband left her nothing, she has had to rely on the kindness of her sister's family to survive. She does not work outside the home but takes in sewing work to contribute something to the household finances. During Act I, Blanche is content to let everyone around her make the decisions. When Nora presses her to decide if she can audition for the musical, Blanche defers to Jack's judgment. When Blanche feels tired from sewing, she lets Kate tell her when to stop. She does stand up for herself, though, when she decides to go on a date with Frank Murphy, an Irishman who lives across the street. Kate disapproves, but Blanche wins her over. After Murphy gets in an accident and the date is canceled, Blanche and Kate get into an argument. This argument leads to Blanche's realization that she has been too dependent on everyone for everything. She decides that she will get a job and move out of the house. She tells Jack, "I love you both very much. No matter what Kate says to me, I will never stop loving her. But I have to get out. If I don't do it now, I will lose whatever self-respect I have left. For people like us, sometimes the only thing we really own is our dignity." Though Kate convinces her to stay with them while she looks for work, Blanche is changed by the realization that dignity is a key to life.

Kate and Eugene have very slightly different concepts of dignity than the rest of the characters in *Brighton Beach*. Because they are the only two characters not concerned with supporting themselves directly, they are focused more on the home and family. Kate works to ensure a dignified household is maintained despite the limited space. She makes sure everyone eats and rests, according to their needs, and she manages the money. Though she can be insensitive, Kate wants her family to hold its collective head up. During her argument with Blanche, it is revealed that Kate sometimes resents

having to be the "workhorse," but she does what she can to keep her family together.

Though fourteen-year-old Eugene is the narrator and main character of *Brighton Beach Memoirs,* his pursuit of dignity is the simplest and one common to every teenager. He wants a little respect from his family. He does not want to be blamed for everything that goes wrong. He does not want to be the center of attention when something bad happens. He does not want to feel like the family slave, though he has to go to the store constantly for his mother. He wants to survive puberty in the Depression with his dignity intact, despite circumstances which seem to work against him. Because his concerns are universal, he is an ideal portal into the family depicted in *Brighton Beach Memoirs.* Though Eugene's quest for dignity might seem to be the least desperate and the most superficial of all the characters in the play, it emphasizes that dignity is irrevocably linked to family. Whether wanting to earn an income or simply to define one's self and one's place in the world, in *Brighton Beach Memoirs* the quest for dignity begins and ends at home.

Source: A. Petrusso, for *Drama for Students,* Gale, 1999.

John Simon

Simon is one of the best-known theatre critics in America. In this review of Brighton Beach Memoirs, *he praises Simon's facility with humorous dialogue, though he has reservations about the playwright's status as a master dramatist.*

Brighton Beach Memoirs is Neil Simon's *Long Day's Journey Into Night.* Simon is the world's richest playwright and he even owns the Eugene O'Neill Theater, but though you can buy the name, you cannot buy the genius. Actually, rather than into one night, the play takes us into two consecutive Wednesday evenings in 1937 (when Simon was ten rather than, as in the play, fifteen), but the pseudo-autobiographical hero is actually called Eugene, and there is an ostensible scraping off of layers of patina to get at the alleged truth; if no one takes dope, there are plenty of dopes around, not least the author, who, like all those comedians wanting to play Hamlet, imagines that he can write a serious play.

The first problem with *Memoirs* is that it has no intention of being truthful. In a *Times* interview with Leslie Bennetts, Simon tells of a father who would disappear for months, years, finally forever, and who'd have terrible fights with his wife. In the

Jack Jerome (Bob Dishy) is accompanied home by his son Eugene, returning from one of his many errands

play, Jack Jerome is the most responsible, wise, and generous man alive, and his wife, Kate, heroically coping with the deprivations of the Depression, is not a jot behind him in magnanimity. Her one true fight is with her widowed sister, Blanche, who, with her daughters Nora and Laurie, has been living with the Jeromes for years, working herself blind to earn her keep, but a drain nevertheless. Otherwise, the fights are harmless ones between various parents and children—a sort of *Life With Father* Jewish, but not too Jewish, style—and even the children's missteps are footling if not laudable: Nora's wanting to accept a role in a Broadway musical and quit school, elder brother Stanley's near loss of his job when he sticks up for a black handyman abused by the boss. Oh, hoping to make extra money for the family, Stanley does once gamble away a week's salary and run off intending to join the army; but he soon returns, makes back most of the money, and gets closer to Dad than ever.

Then why, you ask, the comparison to O'Neill's play? Because Eugene is a budding playwright with problems (not TB, to be sure, only puberty and lust for his cousin), there is a serious money shortage, there is near tragedy in the house across the street, there is the Depression and the threat of Hitler to

Jewish relatives in Europe, there is Father's losing one of his jobs and getting a minor heart attack, there is everyone's hurting everyone else's feelings and apologizing profusely and making up. What there isn't, though, is honesty. The first act is typical Simon farce cum sentimentality, and the better for it; the second, in which ostensibly grave themes and conflicts are hauled out, is fraught with earnest speechifying, ponderous and platitudinous moralizing, and heartwarming uplift oozing all over the place, with everybody's soul putting on Adler Elevator shoes and ending up closer to heaven. The dramaturgy itself becomes woefully schematic: Every character gets his tête-à-tête with every other character who has taken umbrage, and all ends in sunshine—even for the endangered relatives in Europe.

If all this were presented as farce, it might work. If it were honestly and painfully told, it might work. But Simon, who has also filled the play with those odious clean dirty jokes, wants to have his pain and let everybody eat cake, too. So everyone is funny and noble and ends happily, and Neil—Eugene—who is also a good student and obedient son—is funniest and noblest of all, even if given to somewhat excessive masturbation. Actually, the

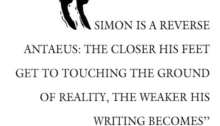

"SIMON IS A REVERSE
ANTAEUS: THE CLOSER HIS FEET
GET TO TOUCHING THE GROUND
OF REALITY, THE WEAKER HIS
WRITING BECOMES"

masturbation is more joked about than real—except, of course, in the playwriting. Simon is a reverse Antaeus: The closer his feet get to touching the ground of reality, the weaker his writing becomes. And, as a final dishonesty, his Jewish family talks and looks as un-Jewish as possible (through the writing, casting, and directing), so that Wasps should not feel excluded, let alone offended. In fact, the Irish family across the way—though drowning in drink and filth—are, we are sanctimoniously informed, very nice people indeed.

Gene Saks has directed adroitly and vivaciously; Patricia Zipprodt's costumes and Tharon Musser's lighting can nowise be faulted, and even a second-best set from David Mitchell is quite good enough. The cast is uneven: Zeljko Ivanek (Stanley) is marvelous; Matthew Broderick (Eugene) fine, but too young to begin doing shtick; Mandy Ingber (Laurie) a perfect stage brat, which, however, is not the same as a real kid; Elizabeth Franz (Kate) commanding but out of character; Peter Michael Goetz (Jack) given to breaking up his speeches nonsensically, and dull to boot; Joyce Van Patten (Blanche) nondescript to the point of vanishing; and Jodi Thelen (Nora) simperingly tremulous to the point of being sickening. Still, the man behind me was convulsed with laughter; if you like commercial theater at its most mercenary, you should love this one.

Source: John Simon, "Journeys into Night" in *New York,* Vol. 16, no. 15, April 11, 1983 , p. 55.

Brendan Gill

While calling the play's humor "surefire," Gill's ultimate appraisal of Brighton Beach Memoirs *finds the play stumbling into "shallowness" when Simon awkwardly strives for profound sentiments.*

Neil Simon's "*Brighton Beach Memoirs,*" at the Alvin, is a sentimental comedy decorated with surefire one-liners and inadvertently revealing its shallowness by means of an occasional awkward lunge in the direction of what the author evidently believes to be profundity. (In the midst of all his jokes about adolescent sex and domineering Jewish mothers in the nineteen-thirties, Simon manages to introduce the fate of European Jewry under Hitler, borrowing from that historic tragedy a weight of emotion that his ramshackle little comedy has done nothing to deserve.) Simon has acknowledged to the press that "*Memoirs*" has a greater autobiographical content than his other plays, and he finds, as autobiographers are wont to do, a seriousness it the heart of the play which members of the audience may perceive not as seriousness but as an exceptionally unabashed manifestation of self-approval. For the play is a posy presented to the author with love from the author, who appears unaware that he is telling the same story that hundreds upon hundreds of writers before him have written and that hundreds upon hundreds of writers after him are sure to write—the story of the gifted child who grows up to become the maker of the very work of art by which we are being entertained. Dickens, Joyce, O'Neill, Lowell, and scores of other novelists, playwrights, and poets have achieved masterpieces in this genre, but more commonly the product is narcissistic claptrap.

"*Memoirs*" has to do with seven members of a middle-class Jewish family in Brooklyn, whom we observe struggling to survive the dark days of the Great Depression. Remarkably, all seven of them have hearts of gold, and so do a couple of characters of some importance who remain offstage. Life is harsh, but everyone is doing his best to cope. Eugene, a.k.a. Neil, is a brilliant student and a successful wise-cracker; at fifteen, he is undergoing the despairs and delights of an inexplicably delayed sexual awakening. Eugene's curiosity about girls' bodies is feverish and unassuageable, though he learns what he can from his older brother, Stanley. The object of Eugene's unspoken passion is Nora, the elder of two cousins of his; unfortunately, Nora and Eugene share nothing but the unwelcome intimacy of the only bathroom in the house. Blanche, mother of Nora and Laurie (the snooty, pampered younger cousin), is a sister of Eugene's mother, Kate. Blanche is a widow and is well aware that, the house being too small for all of them and the burden of its upkeep too heavy for Eugene's sorely overworked father, she must find a new husband as quickly as possible; by ill luck, the likeliest candidate is an Irish Catholic alcoholic, living across the street with his aged mother. To Kate, everyone who is not a Jew is a cossack (at this point in the play we come close to echoing ''Abie's Irish Rose,'' a hit of half a century ago); the alcoholic gets into trouble and misses his first—and only—date with Blanche, and other vexations beset the family, but their essential saintliness remains undiminished. The last words of the play are a cry of joy from Eugene on having at last outdistanced the ignominious pangs of puberty.

''*Memoirs*'' provides the occasion for a virtuoso acting performance by Matthew Broderick, as Eugene. Without him, much of the pleasing humaneness of the play would degenerate into slapstick. Elizabeth Franz is a conventional Jewish scold of a mother, Joyce Van Patten is the woebegone Blanche, and Peter Michael Goetz is often touching as the exhausted paterfamilias. Zeljko Ivanek, Jodi Thelen, and Mandy Ingber play Stanley, Nora, and Laurie, respectively. The slick direction is by Gene Saks, and the setting, costumes, and lighting—all of the highest quality—are by David Mitchells, Patricia Zipprodt, and Tharon Musser.

Source: Brendan Gill, ''Portrait of the Artist As a Young Saint'' in the *New Yorker,* Vol. LIX, no. 8, April 11, 1983, p. 109.

THE PLAY IS A POSY PRESENTED TO THE AUTHOR WITH LOVE FROM THE AUTHOR, WHO APPEARS UNAWARE THAT HE IS TELLING THE SAME STORY THAT HUNDREDS UPON HUNDREDS OF WRITERS BEFORE HIM HAVE WRITTEN AND THAT HUNDREDS UPON HUNDREDS OF WRITERS AFTER HIM ARE SURE TO WRITE— THE STORY OF THE GIFTED CHILD WHO GROWS UP TO BECOME THE MAKER OF THE VERY WORK OF ART BY WHICH WE ARE BEING ENTERTAINED''

FURTHER READING

Bennetts, Leslie. ''Neil Simon Delves into His Past'' in the *New York Times,* March 27, 1983, Sec. 2, pp. 1, 6.
 Bennetts interviews Simon, discussing, among other topics, the inspiration for *Brighton Beach Memoirs.*

Johnson, Robert K. *Neil Simon,* Twayne, 1983.
 McGovern offers biography, criticism, and interpretation of Simon's works through the early-1980s.

McGovern, Edythe M. *Neil Simon: A Critical Study,* Ungar, 1978.
 McGovern offers criticism and interpretation of Simon's works through the late-1970s.

McGovern, Edythe M. *Not-So-Simple Neil Simon: A Critical Study,* Perivale Press, 1978.
 McGovern offers criticism and interpretation of each of Simon's plays, from *Come Blow Your Horn* to *Chapter Two.*

Simon, Neil. *Rewrites: A Memoir,* Simon & Schuster, 1997.
 Simon's autobiography covers both his career and his personal life through 1973.

SOURCES

Gilman, Frank. Review of *Brighton Beach Memoirs* in the *Nation,* May 21, 1983, p. 650.

Hughes, Catharine. ''Broadway Blooms'' in *America,* June 4, 1983, p. 441.

Kalem, T. E. ''Speak Memory'' in *Time,* April 11, 1983, p. 100.

Kerr, Walter. ''Seeing a Comic Mind Emerge'' in the *New York Times,* April 3, 1983, pp. H3, H13.

Kroll, Jack. ''Simon Says Laugh'' in *Newsweek,* April 11, 1983, pp. 66-67.

Rich, Frank. ''Stage: Neil Simon's 'Brighton Beach'' in the *New York Times,*March 28, 1983, p. C9.

Simon, John. Review of *Brighton Beach Memoirs* in *New York,* April 11, 1983, p. 55.

Simon, Neil. *Brighton Beach Memoirs,* Random House, 1984.

Buried Child

SAM SHEPARD

1978

After more than a decade as Off-Broadway's most successful counter-culture playwright, Sam Shepard achieved national fame and attention with his 1979 Pulitzer Prize-winning family drama, *Buried Child*. The play is a macabre look at an American Midwestern family with a dark, terrible secret: Years ago, Tilden, the eldest of three sons belonging to Dodge and Halie, committed an act of incest with his mother. She bore his child, a baby boy, which Dodge drowned and buried in the field behind their farmhouse.

The act destroyed the family. Dodge stopped planting crops in his fields and took to smoking, drinking, and watching television from a lumpy old sofa. Halie, apparently seeking salvation, turned to religion with fervor. She spouts Chritian platitudes and cavorts with the hypocritical Father Dewis. Tilden went insane with guilt and grief, spent time in jail in New Mexico, and has only recently returned to the farmstead, perhaps to set everything right. The secret is drawn out into the light of day, and the family curse apparently lifted, with the arrival of Vince, Tilden's estranged son, and his girlfriend, Shelly.

With its lower-class, sometimes humorous, recognizable characters and dialogue, *Buried Child* resembles the mid-century American realism and grotesquerie of Arthur Miller (*Death of a Salesman*) or Tennessee Williams (*A Streetcar Named Desire*). However, its roots in ritual and its approach to

monumental, timeless themes of human suffering—incest, murder, deceit, and rebirth—resemble the destruction wreaked by the heroes of Greek tragedy. The play contains many of Shepard's favorite motifs: a quirky, often frightening, family of antagonists contained in a claustrophobic farmhouse somewhere in the great American Midwest.

Reviews of the play's New York premiere at the Theater for the New City on October 19, 1978, were mainly complimentary and congratulatory. Critics who had followed his ten-year career Off-Broadway were happy for Shepard's mainstream success, while mainstream critics who were unfamiliar with the playwright were pleased with the new discovery. Even critics who weren't quite sure what it was they had found in *Buried Child* assured their readers that they liked the play. In the *Nation,* Harold Clurman wrote, ''What strikes the ear and eye is comic, occasionally hilarious behavior and speech at which one laughs while remaining slightly puzzled and dismayed (if not resentful), and perhaps indefinably saddened. Yet there is a swing to it all, a vagrant freedom, a tattered song. Something is coming to an end, yet on the other side of disaster there is hope. From the bottom there is nowhere to go but up.''

Shepard may have felt the same way. Whether he sought it or not, *Buried Child* marked a turning point in his career. With its success, he found his plays in demand in New York and across the country, and during the next ten years he created commercial successes like *True West, Fool for Love,* and *A Lie of the Mind* that found their way to Broadway and film. In 1995, Shepard rewrote *Buried Child* (the original director made changes to the play that went against the playwright's intentions). The new, author-approved version premiered at the Steppenwolf Theatre in Chicago before transferring to Broadway in April, 1996. In both cities, the play was hailed as a comical and insightful presentation of the disintegrating American dream.

AUTHOR BIOGRAPHY

Like the plays he writes, Sam Shepard's life and career have been unpredictable, wide-ranging, well-traveled, and, ultimately, quintessentially American. Shepard was born Samuel Shepard Rogers in Fort Sheridan, Illinois, on November 5, 1943. His father was in the Army Air Corps, and the family moved around from base to base before settling on an avocado ranch in Duarte, California. There, the future playwright found a love for horses and the outdoors that has remained with him ever since. He also picked up his father's drums and discovered a love for music that found its way into many of his plays.

In his semi-retirement, Shepard's father became an abusive alcoholic. After a series of violent confrontations, young Sam joined a touring repertory theatre group called the Bishop's Company, left home, and eventually found his way to the opposite coast: New York City. His arrival in New York in the early-1960s couldn't have been better timed. Although he was only nineteen years old, with a few months of acting experience and a single, unproduced play to his credit, the Off-Broadway theatre scene was just gaining momentum. It was there, in the tiny experimental studios and renovated churches of the underground theatre movement, that Shepard found his niche as a playwright.

His first professional production was a pair of one-acts, *Cowboys* and *The Rock Garden,* produced by Theatre Genesis at Saint Mark Church-in-the-Bowery in 1964. Although the popular press dubbed the new writer's work a pale imitation of Absurdist author Samuel Beckett (*Waiting for Godot*), the *Village Voice* and other counterculture publications gave him rave reviews and encouraged him to write more. Over the next several years, Shepard produced a series of experimental, poetic, musical one-acts and full-length plays that earned him a string of Obie Awards (Off-Broadway's equivalent of the Tony Award) and a cult following in New York and London, where he temporarily relocated in the early-1970s.

The Tooth of Crime (1972) and *Curse of the Starving Class* (1977) earned Shepard wider recognition, and larger audiences, but it wasn't until *Buried Child* (1978) that he gained mainstream acceptance. The play earned Shepard his tenth Obie Award (no other American playwright has won more than two) as well as the Pulitzer Prize for drama. With typical, Midwestern-style humility, Shepard declared, ''If I was gonna write a play that would win the Pulitzer Prize, I think it would have been that play, you know. It's sort of a typical

Sam Shepard

Pulitzer Prize-winning play. It wasn't written for that purpose; it was a kind of test. I wanted to write a play about a family.''

All of Shepard's plays are characterized by an obvious love of language and a flair for visual imagery. Often, the imagery he conjures is of the American West. His characters are obsessed with American myths and metaphors—cowboys and Indians, ranches, deserts, and other wide open spaces—and often the plots of his plays parallel familiar folk tales or religious parables. Thematically, he is often concerned with the American Dream and its effects on families, though the fathers, mothers, and sons that inhabit his work tend to be much darker, even more frightening aspects of those that appear in the plays, movies, and television of popular culture.

Since the success of *Buried Child,* Shepard has produced other popular plays, two of which, *True West* (1980) and *Fool for Love* (1983) have been turned into films. In the 1970s, Shepard himself turned to film, finding his way back to acting. He has appeared on screen in such films as *Days of Heaven, Frances, The Right Stuff,* and *Steel Magnolias,* as well as Robert Altman's film version of his play *Fool for Love* (1985).

PLOT SUMMARY

Act I

Buried Child occurs in a single setting: the large downstairs living room of a dilapidated Midwestern farmhouse. The creaky old estate is occupied by an odd, eccentric, and often frightening family who are removed from any traces of civilization outside. At the beginning of the play, Dodge, the clan's leader, is lying on a dingy old sofa, half-asleep, watching a television with no sound. As he listens to the rainfall outside, he begins to cough, tries to stifle his hacking with a slug of whiskey from a hidden bottle, and manages to stifle his choking only when his wife, Halie, calls to him from upstairs.

The opening dialogue between Dodge and the unseen Halie, though relatively short, provides a great deal of important exposition in a play that requires careful attention to clues and minor details. The plot of *Buried Child,* like most of Shepard's plays, is not often simple and direct but unfolds in a series of strange encounters and unsettling symbols.

Halie and Dodge, though married for quite a few years, seem estranged. She remains upstairs, except when she leaves the house. He seems to dwell downstairs, on the sofa, and he never goes out. He drinks, smokes, wears filthy clothes, and watches television almost constantly. She seems to have a preachy, religious streak in her, advocates propriety, and nags her lumpish husband incessantly.

Still, Halie, like almost all the characters in the play at one time or another, recalls the past, a time when things seemed more exciting, more normal. Remembering a day she once spent at the horse races, Halie says, ''Everything was dancing with life! Colors. There were all kinds of people from everywhere. Everyone was dressed to the nines. Not like today. Not like they dress today. People had a sense of style.'' It is obvious from the very beginning of the play that something happened to this family—something mysterious, secret, and tragic—that has forever altered their lives.

While Halie continues ranting from upstairs, and Dodge lapses into one of his coughing fits, their eldest son, Tilden, appears with an armload of corn which, he claims, he just picked from the field out back.

In spite of Dodge's protests that he never planted any corn, and that the produce was probably stolen from a neighbor's farm, Tilden pulls up a stool, puts down a milk pail, and begins husking the vegetables. While he works, Dodge questions him about his plans for the future. Apparently, Tilden has been away from home for more than twenty years, off in New Mexico by himself, and has only recently reappeared. Dodge seems eager to send him on his way again—an anxiety that begins to make sense later in the play, when Tilden's earlier illicit relationship with his mother surfaces.

Meanwhile, from upstairs, Halie continues her oration. She calls down to warn Dodge that they must care for Tilden, since he can no longer care for himself. Halie remembers the glory days of Tilden's youth, when he was an All-American football player and the family had such high hopes for his future. His younger brother, Bradley, they felt, was destined to fail, and all their dreams would come alive in Tilden. When Tilden turned out to be troublesome, Halie continues, they staked their hopes on Ansel, the youngest of the boys who, Halie claims, may not have been as handsome, but was by far the smartest. She rambles on about Ansel's accomplishments as a basketball player and a soldier, mourns his tragic death in a motel room on the night of his honeymoon, and suggests Father Dewis, their pastor, might help them erect a statue of their fallen son in the town square.

Halie finally descends the stairs. She is dressed completely in black, as though mourning, and on her way to a lunch appointment with Father Dewis. She argues with the two men about the rain outside, the corn on the floor, and Bradley, causing Dodge to complain, ''He's not my flesh and blood! My flesh and blood's out there in the backyard!'' A hush falls over the room. Dodge has spoken the apparently unspeakable in this household. While his comment goes unheeded and unexplained for the time being, it haunts the rest of the play, as the family's terrible secret is slowly revealed.

Halie finally leaves for her rendezvous with the pastor. Dodge curls up on the sofa and falls asleep. Tilden steals his whiskey and leaves. Then, in the silence that falls over the house, Bradley stomps in through the front door, the hinges of his wooden leg creaking as he walks. He removes Dodge's baseball cap, plugs in a pair of electric clippers, and begins cutting his father's hair while he sleeps. The lights fade on the first act.

Act II

Later the same night. Vince, Tilden's son, appears with his girlfriend, Shelly. They are travel-ing across the country from New Jersey to see Vince's father, who they think is still in New Mexico, and have stopped by unannounced to visit Dodge and Halie. They are expecting a joyful family reunion. Instead, they are greeted by the grumpy, drunken Dodge and the distant, half-crazed Tilden, neither of whom seem to recognize Vince.

Dodge hollers for more whiskey and rails about the haircut he was given while he was asleep, which has left him with patchy bald spots and cuts on his scalp. Tilden brings in an armload of freshly picked carrots, which he proceeds to cut and scrape in preparation for dinner. Shelly is initially terrified by the gloomy house and its strange inhabitants. She urges Vince to leave and at least spend the night in a hotel and return the next day. Vince, however, is adamant about staying. He tries to prove he is part of the family by making funny faces and noises he used to make as a child at the dinner table, but his father and grandfather ignore him.

While Vince becomes more and more exasperated, Shelly, oddly enough, is drawn into the fold. She sits down with Tilden and helps him clean the carrots. To clear his head and perhaps restore some sense of normalcy to the scene, Vince agrees to run to the store to fetch more whiskey for Dodge. He pleads with Tilden and Dodge to try to remember who he is while he is gone and assures Shelly that she will be safe in his absence.

Once Vince leaves, Tilden opens up to Shelly. He describes how he, too, used to drive across the country, through the snow and the deserts, admiring the trees and the animals. He, too, once had a sense of adventure. According to Tilden, his life changed with the arrival of a baby in the house—a baby that was quite small and simply disappeared. ''We had no service. No hymn. Nobody came,'' Tilden laments. Only Dodge knows where the corpse is, he insists.

Shelly, terrified once again, has little time to react to this macabre story of murder and deceit before Bradley comes stomping into the room from outside and immediately bullies Dodge and Tilden into submission. He insults and humiliates his older brother until Tilden scampers offstage. Dodge lies quivering and coughing on the floor while Bradley, to assert his control in the house, orders Shelly to stand still and open her mouth. He places his fingers in her mouth, then drops her coat over Dodge's head as the scene ends.

Act III

It is the next morning, and a change has come over the household. The rain has stopped, the sun is shining outside, and birds are singing. Bradley has fallen asleep on the sofa, his artificial leg lying nearby, while Dodge leans against the television, using Shelly's coat as a blanket. Shelly, meanwhile, has suddenly become a nurturing, motherly figure to the ailing Dodge. She emerges from the kitchen, bright and happy, with a bowl of warm soup broth for the man she now calls her "grandpa." Some things still haven't changed, however. Dodge is as irascible as ever. He refuses to eat the soup and complains loudly that Vince didn't return the previous night and probably stole the money he was given to buy Dodge's whiskey.

While Shelly attempts to calm and care for Dodge, Halie, who was also gone all night, returns home with Father Dewis. She is now wearing a bright yellow dress, with no sign of her black mourning clothes, and carrying an armful of roses. Both Halie and the Father are a little drunk and have obviously been out for a night on the town. Halie attempts to assume her usual position in the house, nagging Dodge, scolding Bradley, and completely ignoring Shelly.

The balance of power shifts again, and Shelly takes a stand. She grabs Bradley's artificial leg, wielding it like a weapon and leaving the once tyrannical bully helpless and whimpering on the sofa. As the shocked family and pastor listen in amazement, Shelly's frustrations pour out. She describes what she and Vince had hoped to find—the perfect American family he remembered from his past. She confronts them with what they really are: strangers in their own house who commit murder and bury the bodies in their backyard.

Shelly's outrage draws a confession from Dodge. Against the wishes of his wife and son, the old man breaks down and explains the family's gruesome, tragic secret: Years ago, after all the boys were already grown and the family and farm were quite prosperous, Halie unexpectedly became pregnant. She and Dodge hadn't been sleeping in the same bed for six years, so he knew the child wasn't his. The baby, it seemed, belonged to Tilden, who would carry the infant through the fields at night, singing to it and telling it stories. Unable to stand the insult or allow a child who wasn't his own to grow up in his household, Dodge drowned the baby and buried it in the yard.

Halie is mortified that Dodge has allowed the truth to surface and frantically cries for her lost Ansel. "What's happened to the men in this family!" she screams, "Where are the men!" As if on cue, Vince comes crashing through the screen door, drunk and hurling empty liquor bottles. The prodigal son has returned. As the youngest and strongest of the surviving male children, and the only member of the family who is free of guilt and complicity in the clan's awful crimes, Dodge immediately declares Vince the heir to the estate. While Dodge screams out his last will and testament, leaving almost everything to his grandson, Vince sets about restoring order to what is now his home.

Shelly finally reaches her breaking point and leaves. "I can't hang around for this," she complains to Vince, "I'm not even related." Vince tosses Bradley's artificial leg outside, and his now-pathetic uncle crawls out after it. Father Dewis excuses himself from the terrible scene, leaving Halie upstairs crying. Dodge, meanwhile, has quietly died. Vince covers the dead patriarch with a blanket and places Halie's roses on his chest. Then he takes Dodge's cap, puts it on, and lies down on the couch, staring at the ceiling. The play has come full circle, with the new man of the house once again stretched out on the sofa.

To complete this final tableau, Halie begins calling to Dodge from upstairs, just as she did at the beginning of the play. She tells him about the fields outside, filled with corn, carrots, and potatoes, miraculously produced by the recent rain and the day's bright sunshine. While she describes this impossible farmer's paradise, Tilden enters from outside and slowly walks upstairs, carrying the muddy, rotten corpse of a small baby he has just unearthed from the yard: the buried child.

CHARACTERS

Bradley

Bradley is Dodge and Halie's middle son and, accordingly, seems to have received the least attention and respect from his parents. As a child, he was never expected to amount to much. After he accidentally cut off one of his legs with a chain saw, they gave up all hope for him, praying that Tilden would be able to care for his younger sibling.

As an adult, he occupies a strange, not quite clear place in the household. Although he no longer lives with his parents, he visits often. Bradley has become a mean, sometimes violent, bully. For some reason, he cuts his father's hair while he sleeps, leaving him with bald patches and cuts on his scalp. When Tilden leaves corn husks scattered around the living room, Halie worries that Bradley will be upset. "He doesn't like the house in disarray," she warns. "He can't stand it when one thing is out of place. The slightest thing. You know how he gets." Initially, Bradley is even able to intimidate the strong-willed Shelly. Bursting in on the interloper when she is alone with Tilden and Dodge, he takes her coat away from his simpleton brother, runs him off, then forces her to stand still while he puts his fingers in her mouth.

Once separated from his artificial leg, however, Bradley is a simpering coward. Near the end of the play, Shelly regains her dignity by grabbing the leg away and threatening the family with it. Finally, Vince tosses the limb out in the yard and Bradley makes his final exit on his belly, crawling out the door after the prosthetic limb that he believes will make him whole.

Father Dewis

Father Dewis is the smallest part in the play, but he acts as an important foil to Halie. Claiming to be an upright Christian who abhors the sins of her family around her, Halie apparently spends a great deal of time in the company of the good reverend. She has been bargaining with him to help her convince the City Council to erect a statue honoring her dead son, Ansel. Early in the play she disappears for a lunch meeting with Father Dewis.

The two of them return the next morning, obviously drunk after a night on the town. Father Dewis does not acknowledge his indiscretion or the paradox of the family's religious advisor consorting with the mother of the household. When the scene becomes threatening, Father Dewis backs away, claiming, "This is out of my domain." In the end, faced with the strong will of Vince, the new patriarch of the house, Father Dewis leaves Halie upstairs crying and makes a tactical retreat.

Dodge

Dodge is one of the most important figures in the play. Once the strong, energetic, successful leader of the family and its farm, he is now in his seventies and has degenerated into a slovenly, drunk-

MEDIA ADAPTATIONS

- While *Buried Child* has not yet been turned into a film, other Shepard plays are available on video, including *Fool for Love,* directed in 1985 by Robert Altman and starring Kim Basinger and Shepard himself; and *True West* (1986), directed by Allan Goldstein and starring John Malkovich and Gary Sinise.

en, curmudgeonly old man who spends all his time smoking and drinking, curled up on the sofa watching television. The change in Dodge's lifestyle and personality is understandable, given his family's past: After raising three children and helping build a prosperous farm, his wife, Halie, conceived a fourth child with their eldest son, Tilden. Unable to live with the shame, and perhaps threatened by the presence of a male child in the house that wasn't his own, Dodge murdered the baby and buried it in the backyard.

For years since these terrible events the family has kept the buried child a secret. Each member of the household has found his or her own way of dealing with the guilt. Dodge's comfort, such as it is, has been in forcing the memory as far back in his mind as possible, through denial and slowly drinking himself to death. Although his general demeanor is grumpy and acerbic, his wry comments and sarcasm occasionally make him unintentionally funny.

In the end, it is Dodge who confesses the family's secret. Unable to live with the guilt any longer, he admits all the sordid details of incest and murder. Then, just before he quietly dies, he leaves the farm to Vince, his grandson who, it is assumed, will try to rebuild the family's shattered legacy.

Halie

Halie is the hypocritical, promiscuous mother and grandmother to the strange Midwestern clan of *Buried Child.* At the beginning of the play, she seems like an elderly wife who has been ignored and perhaps abused by her drunken, lazy husband. While Dodge lays in front of the television all day, drinking whiskey and smoking cigarettes, Halie stays upstairs, occasionally calling down to check on him and encourage him to take his pills. She seems devoutly religious and complains about modern ways that she finds anti-Christian. When she finally appears, she is dressed all in black, seemingly mourning the death of her favorite son years earlier. She is on her way to meet Father Dewis, the family's religious advisor, who, she hopes, will help her get a statue of her son erected in the town square.

In spite of her claims to propriety and family values, however, Halie is not a sympathetic character. She nags her husband incessantly, complains about the worthlessness of her sons who have survived, and ends up spending all night drinking with her reverend friend, returning home with him the next day, dressed gaily and carrying an armful of roses. Her actions are all the more reprehensible in light of the family's tragic secret: She committed incest with her eldest son, Tilden, sending a ripple of destruction through the entire family.

Shelly

Along with Father Dewis, Shelly is an outsider in the play. She is Vince's girlfriend from New Jersey and has been brought along on his odyssey into the past expecting to meet his father and grandparents, who, she has been told, are a typical, happy, friendly American family. Instead, she is met by a frightening band of eccentrics who insult and degrade her and don't seem to recognize her boyfriend as their blood relation.

Although she is initially intimidated and scared of the clan, Shelly is strong-willed by nature. First she tries to fit in by helping Tilden with the vegetables he keeps bringing in from outside. "I'll cook the carrots," she tells Vince. "And I'll do whatever I have to do to survive. Just to make it through this thing." Left alone with Dodge, Tilden, and Bradley for the night, Shelly appears the next morning renewed, energized, and ready to take on the responsibility of caring for the crazy crew. She tries to nurture Dodge, bringing him soup broth and calling him "grandpa." Her efforts go unrewarded, however. Dodge shuns her, Halie ignores her, and even Vince pushes her aside as he assumes control of the household. Finally, exasperated, she storms out, telling Vince, "I can't hang around for this. I'm not even related."

Tilden

Tilden is Dodge and Halie's eldest son and father to Vince. As a child, his parents expected great things from him. He was an All-American football player, and they hoped he would care for his less responsible younger brother, Bradley, after he accidentally lost his leg to a chainsaw. But somewhere along the way Tilden went astray. Although the details aren't described clearly, he disappeared for several years, apparently got into some trouble in New Mexico, spent some time in jail, and was eventually driven out of the state. Now he has returned home, penniless, withdrawn, and mentally unstable. Strangely, Tilden keeps bringing in armloads of vegetables he claims to have harvested from the fields outside, even though, Dodge insists, the fields haven't been planted in years.

Tilden's ability to pull crops from fallow fields is symbolic, and directly related to the secret of the "buried child" in the play's title. Years ago Tilden committed incest with his mother, Halie, and they produced a baby boy, which Dodge murdered and buried in the yard. His mother, like the fields on the farm, was past middle age and hadn't been with her husband or "fertilized," in a long time. Tilden's virility proved the family's undoing, and his ability to pluck corn and carrots from thin air shows his unfortunate talent still exists. At the end of the play, after Dodge confesses the grisly truth to Shelly, Tilden walks out into field, exhumes the corpse of his murdered son/brother, and carries it upstairs to his mother so they can finally be together—a ghastly little "family."

Vince

Vince is twenty-two, adventurous, and a sort of prodigal son figure in the play. After at least six years away, he has decided to take his girlfriend, Shelly, on a cross-country trip from New Jersey to New Mexico for a reunion with his father, Tilden. They stop along the way to visit his grandparents, Dodge and Halie, expecting a warm, friendly, familial welcome, with a turkey dinner on the table and excited conversation about the good old days. Instead, they encounter the surly, drunken Dodge and, unexpectedly, Vince's half-crazed father, Tilden, neither of whom recognize their estranged relative. A little panicked, but ever resourceful, Vince leaves Shelly behind while he goes to buy some whiskey for Dodge, in the hopes that the liquor will calm him and help him remember.

Vince is gone for the entire night, and while he is away a lot changes. His Uncle Bradley appears and terrorizes Shelly. His grandmother, Halie, returns home after a night of carousing with Father Dewis. Shelly confronts the quirky clan, and in the ensuing family feud, Dodge admits the truth about the "buried child" in the field outside. Just in time to pull all the loose ends together, Vince comes crashing through the door, drunk and hurling liquor bottles. Recognizing in Vince some hope for his family's future, Dodge promptly recites his last will and testament, leaving the farm and the house to Vince. He then promptly expires on the floor.

Vince takes on a new attitude with his unexpected windfall, and decides to stick around. "I've gotta carry on the line," he tells Shelly. "It's in the blood. I've gotta see to it that things keep rolling." Dismissing his confused girlfriend, he sets about putting his house in order by chasing out Bradley and Father Dewis. Then he reclines on the equivalent of the family throne—the living room sofa—to ponder his next move as the new man of the house.

THEMES

American Dream

In literature, as in life, the *American Dream* contains elements of adventure on the open road, the exploration of far frontiers, and family and financial success. These ideas permeate nearly all of Shepard's plays and are used effectively as a criticism of contemporary American society in *Buried Child*. In this dark vision of the American Midwest, Shepard presents the disintegration of the American family and suggests that, as a culture, Americans have an embarrassment of riches and a paucity of spirituality and morality. For most of the play, his view of America in the late-twentieth century is one of selfish, brutal, and hypocritical tyrant wannabees who care little for one another and are mainly interested in physical pleasures and power over others.

Dodge, the father and grandfather of the household, talks about things that American patriarchs are supposed to talk about—family, the farm, even baseball. But he is not the loving, nurturing father who knows best. "You think just because people propagate they have to love their offspring?" he growls. "You never seen a bitch eat her puppies?" His wife, Halie, is certainly no better. Though she feigns religious piety and pines for the days of traditional values, in her old age she is carrying on an affair with the family's pastor and in her younger days committed incest with her oldest son, an act

that resulted in a mid-life pregnancy. This American family is definitely not the happy, well-balanced stereotype portrayed in popular media.

Shepard's use of backwoods country twang in the voices of his characters, along with images of the land outside big cities and the uncharted vastness of open spaces in America suggest some of the country's earliest and most important myths—the frontiersman, westward expansion, and rugged individualism. Vince, initially one of the "outsiders" of the play, has a quintessentially American road experience late in the play that causes an epiphany that sends him back to the farm with a renewed sense of purpose. In a frenetic monologue, Vince describes how he drove all night through the rain with the windows open, "clear to the Iowa border." En route, he examined his reflection in the windshield and saw his face changing into the faces of generations of his past, "every last one. Straight into the corn belt and further. Straight back as far as they'd take me." Vince's experience is a reminder of the interconnectedness of individuals, families, and whole communities in America and lends the play's climax a faint glimmer of hope. As Vince assumes control of the household, and Tilden carries the corpse of the exhumed "buried child" upstairs to its mother, there is the sense that, through the lessons learned by mistaken generations, this family, and America as a whole, may revitalize itself, stir from the ashes of moral destruction, and rise, Phoenix-like, to soar again.

Family

Acknowledging his thematic interest in the concept of *family,* Shepard once observed, "What doesn't have to do with family? There isn't anything. Even a love story has to do with family. Crime has to do with family. We all come out of each other—everyone is born out of a mother and father. It's an endless cycle." Still, in spite of everyone's common evolution from a father and mother, the family ties in *Buried Child* become more twisted and significant than most people ever experience.

The play begins realistically enough, with the offstage voice of an elderly wife, Halie, nagging her semi-drunken, oafish husband (appropriately named Dodge) who lies on a lumpy sofa all day watching television. Very quickly, however, this stereotypical image of a marriage in its twilight years turns into a nightmarish vision of adultery, incest, and murder. The couple's eldest son, Tilden, has returned home after a twenty-year absence. He has been in some

TOPICS FOR FURTHER STUDY

- Shepard incorporates many symbols into *Buried Child* in order to communicate deeper levels of meaning to his audiences. Consider the importance of Bradley's artificial leg, Dodge's baseball cap, and the blanket from the living sofa as symbols in the play. What might each one represent? How are they used by different characters? How do they affect your understanding of the play's plot?

- Read another contemporary American family drama, such as Arthur Miller's *Death of a Salesman,* Edward Albee's *Who's Afraid of Virginia Woolf,* or August Wilson's *Fences,* and discuss the contrasting views of *family* each playwright presents in his work. Consider such things as: the responsibilities of parents; animosities among family members; sibling rivalries; and the effects of domestic violence.

- Sam Shepard has been called a *postmodern* writer. Research postmodernism as a style in late-twentieth-century drama. What elements of postmodernism does Shepard incorporate in *Buried Child?* Which does he ignore?

- Several scholars and critics pointed to corn and its harvest as one of the central images and ritual influences in *Buried Child.* Using an encyclopedia or the Internet, research the history of this important crop and try to find two to three examples of rituals associated with its planting and harvest. Be prepared to examine cultures as widely different as the ancient Egyptians, Europeans of the Middle Ages, and the Native Americans of a few hundred years ago.

kind of trouble in another state and is obviously suffering from mental illness. Bradley, their second son, has lost a leg in a chainsaw accident and terrorizes his father and brother. A third son, Ansel, was, according to Halie's skewed recollection, murdered on the night of his honeymoon. His mother remembers him as the accomplished adult he never grew to be; she wants to have a statue of him erected in the town square.

Into the midst of this motley clan plunges Vince, son to Tilden and grandson to Dodge and Halie. He has returned home after a six-year absence, hoping to find the perfect, warm, and normal American family he remembers from his youth, complete with turkey dinner on the table and smiling, kindly grandparents. Oddly, though, no one seems to recognize him, though the other men of the house quickly take a liking to his girlfriend, Shelly, who has come along for the ride. The most horrific aspect of this house of horrors is the terrible secret they have kept for decades: Tilden is the father, with Halie, of the slain Ansel; Dodge, resentful and

threatened, murdered the infant and buried it in the yard.

Shepard's view of family life in the American Midwest recalls some of the best-known family tragedies of dramatic literature, from the Greek tragedy *Oedipus Rex* to Shakespeare's *King Lear* to Miller's *Death of a Salesman.* Each of these works calls upon primal urges and fears buried deep inside humanity—lust, jealousy, love, and greed—to reveal essential, if undesirable, truths about family relationships and humankind.

STYLE

Symbolism

In literature, a symbol is something that represents something else. Symbols are often used to communicate deeper levels of meaning. In Nathaniel Hawthorne's famous novel *The Scarlet Letter,* for example, the red letter ''A'' worn by Hester Prynne is a symbol not only of her supposed crime (adultery) but also of her neighbors' bigotry and her own courageous pride. *Buried Child,* like most of Shepard's plays, is suffused with symbolism, which he uses to communicate deeper, though sometimes ambiguous, levels of meaning to his audiences.

Some of the strongest symbols in *Buried Child* are related to nature and fertility and reinforce the play's central image: the dead, buried child in the field. The vegetables Tilden continuously carries into the house are one such symbol. Crops have not been raised on the family farm for many years. In all that time, the fields have gone unplanted and have grown over with weeds and scrub brush. Still, Tilden manages to harvest the fallow fields, just as he was capable of conceiving a child with his own middle-aged mother years before (it is suggested that Halie was past menopause, and therefore fallow herself, when her tryst with Tilden occurred). Realistically, his harvest is nonsensical, but as a symbol, it complements his dreadful act of incest and illustrates his obsession with his lost child, his need to pull life from the dead ground.

The rain and sunshine that fall on the farm near the beginning and end of the play are also essential ingredients to understanding the play's deeper, partially obscured meanings. Rain and water have always been symbols of cleansing and purification, thus their use in baptismal ceremonies of the Christian church. At the beginning of *Buried Child,* a soft rain falls on the family's farmhouse and all its visitors, washing away the dirt and the smell and, symbolically, the sins of their past. By the third act, which takes place the following morning, the sun is shining brightly, birds are singing, and a new day, literally and figuratively, has dawned. The sunshine brings crops back to the fields and a new leader to the recently purified house. Dodge dies, Bradley is ejected, and Vince assumes the mantle of family head.

While there are several other objects that may function as minor symbols in the play, such as Bradley's wooden leg, Dodge's baseball cap, and the blanket on the sofa, the most obvious and important one is the dead child itself, which oddly might offer some hope in this otherwise grim drama. Doris Auerbach, in *Sam Shepard, Arthur Kopit, and the Off Broadway Theatre,* noted, "The play ends like a miracle play with the symbol of the resurrection. The child is taken from the tomb, tended by its father and carried up, not to the patriarchal figure who lies dead on stage before us,

but to the mother who is waiting above. *Buried Child* leaves the audience with hope for a revitalized America, for one that nourishes its children and holds the promise of the American dream once again.''

Archetypes

An archetype is an original—the pattern for all that follows. Throughout his career, Shepard has dealt with mythic subjects and archetypal characters in his plays, lending his work a sense of mystery, ritual, and atavistic purpose. In *Buried Child,* nearly all the characters are archetypes of one kind or another. Dodge, the aged patriarch of the family, is the archetypal domineering father figure who threatens, rather than nurtures, his children and ultimately must be overthrown. His type of character has appeared in the stories humans tell since time out of mind, from Oedipus's father, Laius, to Shakespeare's King Lear.

Each of the men in *Buried Child* represent some type of tragic son figure. Tilden, like Oedipus, lusted after his mother, even conceiving a child with her. Bradley suffers the humiliation of the male fear of castration, bearing a wooden leg as a symbol of his anxiety and attempting to compensate for his terror by bullying everyone around him. The long dead Ansel has been made into the heroic figure he never was by his mother, much like Willie Loman idealizes Biff and Happy in *Death of a Salesman.* Vince returns home with the expectations of the long-lost prodigal son and emerges as a conquering hero figure. As strange and frightening as these characters' actions become in the play, they always seem at least a little familiar to the viewer because of the archetypes they represent.

HISTORICAL CONTEXT

In many ways, *Buried Child* exists outside of time and apart from history. The plot of the play is the ages-old, familiar story of youth overthrowing age, intertwined with murder and incest, death and resurrection—terrible human impulses that have shocked and fascinated audiences for thousands of years. The play's characters are mainly archetypal figures, recognizable from centuries of stories and myths scattered across cultures and around the globe. Still, Shepard's family drama is anchored in a particular place and a particular age—1970s America—and

The most potent symbol in Shepard's play: Tilden emerges from the cornfield with the buried child

this environment, if not directly obvious in the play, certainly influenced the playwright and his work.

Although practically any era can be called an age of turbulent politics for one reason or another, the 1970s were particularly difficult and painful for the United States. The decade saw the end of the painful Vietnam War, which altered a great many Americans' perception of war as an unsavory but noble effort. It was also during this era that the country developed a cynicism toward the democratic process and the people it elevates to its highest offices. This cast of doubt has plagued American

politics ever since. The problem evolved from a series of unsuccessful presidents, corruption in public offices, and disastrous domestic and foreign policies.

In 1974, Republican President Richard M. Nixon, once a widely popular leader with daring foreign policy ideas, was forced to resign from the executive office in the wake of the ''Watergate'' scandal. Watergate involved illegal break-ins, wire taps, and subversion of the constitution for the cause of furthering Nixon's political career while simultaneously discrediting his enemies (a noted paranoid

COMPARE
&
CONTRAST

- **1978:** On April 17, trading on the New York Stock Exchange reaches a record single-day volume of 63.5 million million shares. On November 1, the Dow Jones industrial average soars 35.34 points, a record-breaking advance for a single day of trading.

  Today: Trading on the New York Stock Exchange is often ten times the volume of two decades ago, with over 600 million shares changing hands on a single day. Single day rises and drops of hundreds of points at a time are becoming common. In March of 1999, the Dow average closes above 10,000 points for the first time in history.

- **1978:** In *Bakke vs. the Regents of the University of California,* the U.S. Supreme Court affirms a lower court decision requiring the University of California Medical School to admit Allan P. Bakke, a white male who claimed he was a victim of "reverse discrimination" as a result of the school's minority admissions plan.

  Today: The *Bakke* case is again making headlines across the country as American universities and state governments wrestle with Affirmative Action policies that many, including a handful of vocal minority leaders, say are outdated and unfair. Colleges in Texas and Michigan are named in lawsuits by disgruntled student applicants, and forced to abandon admissions and hiring practices that favor minority applicants.

- **1978:** Various religious "cults" are in the news. A murder-suicide ritual claims the lives of 917 members of the "Peoples Temple" in Guyana, including spiritual leader Jim Jones.

  Today: On April 4, 1993, followers of spiritual leader David Koresh's Branch Davidians, are killed in an FBI raid on their Waco, Texas,

compound, after a fifty-one-day standoff. Many vocal critics claim the FBI conducted themselves improperly. In March, 1997, near San Diego, California, thirty-nine members of the "Heaven's Gate" cult, believing they will leave the corporeal world and ascend to "the next level," don purple shrouds, drink a mixture of vodka and poison, and lie down to die with plastic bags over their heads. As the world moves toward the new millennium, such "death cults" are reported to be proliferating.

- **1978:** Broadway, in New York City, is the center of America's theatrical world. The average cost of mounting a play on Broadway is around $200,000, and a few dozen plays are produced in the 1978-79 season. Tickets are considered high-priced, with seats averaging $18. Off- and Off-Off-Broadway theatres, where plays cost only a few thousand dollars to produce and ticket prices average $3-5, are on the rise. The Off-Broadway scene becomes a haven for new and experimental playwrights.

  Today: A smash on Broadway is still considered the height of success in the American theatre, though smaller, Off-Broadway theatres are everywhere (more than two-hundred by a recent count) and regional theatres in places like Chicago, Minneapolis, and Houston are becoming more influential. It costs well over $1 million to mount a play on Broadway, though only a handful are produced. In the 1992-93 season, only eighteen plays were presented. Increasingly, Broadway has turned to musicals, revivals, and imports from abroad, mainly England. Large-scale, multi-million dollar spectacles such as Andrew Lloyd Weber's *Phantom of the Opera* are the norm.

figure, Nixon was known to keep an "enemies list" that kept track of those who had in some way aggrieved him).

Nixon was succeeded by his vice president, Gerald Ford. Ford's brief term of office is remembered primarily for the mistakes Americans felt he made. He pardoned Nixon for any criminal offenses he may have committed in relation to Watergate, and he granted limited amnesty to Vietnam War draft evaders and military deserters. While both acts were meant to help the country heal old wounds and recover momentum, Ford was seen as a weak president, and Americans felt he had betrayed them. In 1976, Ford campaigned for the office he had inherited from Nixon and was defeated by Georgia Democrat Jimmy Carter.

Although he has since become a popular and effective negotiator and ambassador for the United States, Carter's presidency was afflicted with errors of judgment and bad fortune. The country experienced a terrible energy crisis during the late-1970s, leading Carter to encourage conservation of electricity and heating oil and causing gasoline rationing across the country. In 1977, Carter signed away the Panama Canal. Although the deal had been planned since the canal's construction a hundred years before, it was news to most of the country, who blamed the loss on Carter.

Finally, in the midst of an economic crisis and mounting domestic discontent, Carter's administration suffered a terrible foreign policy debacle. Because the United States agreed to harbor the Shah of Iran during his political exile in 1979, Iranian militants, led by the Muslim extremist Ayatollah Khomeini, seized the U.S. Embassy in Tehran and took more than fifty hostages. Carter approved a rescue mission that failed, resulting in more bad press for the president. His shame was compounded when the captives weren't released until more than a year later, when Republican Ronald Reagan became president in 1981.

While *Buried Child* has nothing to do directly with macro-politics, the sense of abandonment, helplessness, and cynicism many Americans felt in the 1970s is apparent in the micro-cosmic world of the play. The past, for this dangerously disturbed Midwestern family, was infinitely better than the present, and no one seems quite willing to stake much on what the future might hold. Any hope Bradley might have presented for a normal, productive life was cut short, literally, when he lost his leg. Tilden, Halie reports, was once an All-American

halfback, destined for greatness. Now he is an ex-convict with a shattered psyche and a tremendous burden of guilt. The unseen Ansel was next on his mother's pedestal. He was "the smart one," prepared to succeed where his brothers had failed. But he, too, lost his struggle against the barbaric world outside, and was killed in a hotel room on the night of his honeymoon. (Yet each of the sons' falls from greatness, save Bradley, could merely be fiction, since it is known that Ansel never reached adulthood. It can be construed that Tilden's accomplishments exist only in his mother's mind as well.)

One at a time, each member of the family stumbles forward, only to be driven back by catastrophe. Dodge summarizes their experiences in this bleak American landscape when he chides Shelly, "You're all alike, you hopers. If it's not God then it's a man. If it's not a man then it's a woman. If it's not a woman then it's politics or bee pollen or the future of some kind. Some kind of future."

While Shepard's characters were facing grim prospects in the America of the 1970s, the playwright himself was thriving in the burgeoning world of Off-Broadway theatre. Developed in the late-1960s and early-1970s as an alternative to the high-priced, predictable, popular entertainment offered by the mainstream Broadway scene, Off-Broadway was a collection of smaller, less expensive, often experimental theatres where the work of new playwrights, like Shepard and Arthur Kopit (*Oh Dad, Poor Dad . . .*), could be given a chance at production and a live audience. In an interview with *Theatre Quarterly,* Shepard once described the exhilaration he felt as a developing artist in this era:

> On the lower East Side there *was* a special sort of culture developing. You were so close to the people who were going to the plays, there was really no difference between you and them—your own experience was their experience, so that you began to develop that consciousness of what was happening . . . I mean nobody knew what *was* happening, but there was a sense that something was going on. People were arriving from Texas and Arkansas in the middle of New York City, and a community was being established. It was a very exciting time.

CRITICAL OVERVIEW

By the time *Buried Child* opened in New York in 1978, Sam Shepard was well-established as a counterculture playwright. The play earned him his unprecedented tenth Obie Award—no other American playwright had garnered more than two of Off-Broadway's highest honor. But with *Buried Child* Shepard had also found his way into the mainstream theatre, complete with larger audiences, critical raves from the popular press, and the Pulitzer Prize for drama in 1979.

Although admitting Shepard was definitely not "commercial," the *Nation's* Harold Clurman, in his review of the *Buried Child* premiere at the Theatre for a New City on October 19, 1978, called him "quintessentially American," and asserted, "I am convinced that he is not only a genuinely gifted but a meaningful writer." To illustrate Shepard's importance to the theatre and New York at the time of the production, Clurman observed, "The production cost $2,000: the actors receive a pittance. Two utterly worthless musicals now on Broadway cost more than $1 million each."

What was it about *Buried Child* that elicited such excited response? For several critics, it was Shepard's ability to tap into America's self perception in intriguing new ways. "*Buried Child,* for all its enigma, is a powerful reflection, no matter how 'funny' the mirror, of the dilemma of present day America," wrote William A. Raidy in *Plays and Players.* Raidy called the play Shepard's most interesting to date and the most stimulating play of the Off-Broadway season. He further noted, "Shepard reaffirms his position as one of America's most adventurous and imaginative playwrights."

In his review for *Time,* T. E. Kalem suggested, "If plays were put in time capsules, future generations would get a sharp-toothed profile of life in the U.S. in the past decade and a half from the works of Sam Shepard. His theme is betrayal, not so much of the American dream as of the inner health of the nation. He focuses on that point at which the spacious skies turned ominous with clouds of dread, and the amber waves of grain withered in industrial blight and moral dry rot."

Shepard was also praised for his use of language and unique, strong character portrayals. In *New York* magazine, John Simon declared of *Buried Child,* "This is the best Shepard play I have seen in some time, which means that it is powerful, obsessive stuff, intensely theatrical, not always disciplined but always wildly poetic, full of stage images and utterances replete with insidious suggestiveness even if they don't yield unequivocal meanings." Critic Jack Kroll wrote in *Newsweek:* "Like Tennessee Williams, Shepard writes strong parts. Even

the 'minor' characters—a futile Catholic priest here—are fully magnetized to the play's core."

Because he was still relatively young (thirty-five at the time of *Buried Child's* premiere) and hadn't established himself yet as a major popular playwright, Shepard's work still drew comparisons to many other writers. In the *New York Times,* Mel Gussow noted, "The buried child of the title, though actual, reminds us of the imaginary child in *Who's Afraid of Virginia Woolf?* It is a dark secret, whose existence is never to be acknowledged in public. Although the play deals with a homecoming—one of several points in common with Harold Pinter—it is equally connected to Edward Albee." In *American Playwrights: A Critical Survey,* Bonnie Marranca added, "An odd play for Shepard, in the sense that his plays have always been identifiable by their striking originality. This one has the most echoes of plays of other writers: Ibsen's *Ghosts,* Pinter's *Homecoming,* and Albee's *The American Dream* come immediately to mind."

In deeper explorations of *Buried Child's* literary conventions, scholars have observed Shepard's unique, tricky blending of realism with symbolism, which achieves unexpected results for audience members. "Shepard's play carefully sustains a realistic veneer, adhering almost formulaically to the familiar Ibsen/Strindberg brand of realism in theme and structure," observed Lynda Hart in *Sam Shepard's Metaphorical Stages.* Hart pointed out that *Buried Child* contains all the essential elements of a well-made, realistic drama, including a naturalistic set, meant to represent a shabby, middle-class American living room; psychologically real, motivated characters; and a fatal secret, hidden in the past and revealed gradually by exposition and character discoveries, until a horrifying climax pulls many of the clues together. Still, she noted, some pieces of the puzzle don't fit. "Motives are left undiscovered," Hart pointed out. "The past is revealed but fails to illuminate the present; character becomes increasingly disorganized and action unpredictable. The two antithetical forms [realism and symbolism] jarringly combine to produce an uneasy, inexplicable action that taunts our ability to make our observations intelligible."

Shepard revised the text of *Buried Child* for a Steppenwolf Theatre production in Chicago in 1995. His changes made it more clear that Tilden was the father of the "buried child," and, according to most reviewers, introduced more humor into the play. The Chicago production was successful enough to earn a Broadway run of the revised play in 1996, which has since prompted several revivals in regional theatres across the country.

CRITICISM

Lane A. Glenn

Glenn is a Ph.D. specializing in theatre history and literature. In this essay he examines the importance of the harvest ritual to the plot and character construction of Buried Child.

Sam Shepard has often been called a mythic playwright, one whose work summons the contradictory images and archetypes of American life—killers and cowboys, Hollywood and farmsteads, rock n' roll and the open road. He is, as Wynn Handman, the artistic director of the American Place Theatre once remarked in an interview with *Newsweek,* "like a conduit that digs down into the American soil and what flows out of him is what we're all about."

What often flows out of Shepard are characters and stories that are at once exciting and recognizable as American allegories as well as shocking and repulsive for what they tell us about human instinct and behavior, regardless of cultural background. His is the gift of sight where many fear to look—a sort of witch doctor of modern America or, as Jack Gelber wrote in his introduction to Shepard's *Angel City, Curse of the Starving Class & Other Plays,* a shaman. "Anthropologists define the shaman as an expert in a primitive society who, in a trance state induced by drugs or music or other techniques, directly confronts the supernatural for the purposes of cures, clairvoyance, the finding of lost objects, and the foretelling of the future," Gelber explained. "Sam Shepard . . . is a shaman—a New World shaman. There are no witches on broomsticks within these pages. That's the Old World. Sam is as American as peyote, magic mushrooms, Rock and Roll, and medicine bundles."

Shepard's unique brand of American shamanism has led him to explore the thoughts in the mind of a murderer seated in the electric chair in *Killer's Head* (1975), and the hip, dexterous verbal wit of dueling rock musicians in *The Tooth of Crime* (1972). He has plumbed the depths of the film industry and pop culture in plays like *Angel City* (1976) and *True West* (1980), and wrestled with quirky relationships in *Cowboy Mouth* (1971) and *Fool for Love* (1983). One of the most interesting features of these plays is their portrayal of recognizable *rituals.* From the seemingly random rules of engagement Hoss and Crow observe in *The Tooth of Crime* to the Indian bones and totems used by Rabbit to jump start the creation of a stalled disaster movie in *Angel City,* rituals of one kind or another figure prominently throughout Shepard's work.

Perhaps nowhere, however, is ritual as important as in *Buried Child.* On its surface, the play seems like a fairly typical, if somewhat dark, family drama, but surprises lie in wait below. In an article for *Modern Drama,* Thomas Nash noted, "here, behind the seemingly trivial squabbles and musings of a typical Midwestern family, are the shadows of sacrificial rites and the shades of dying gods."

The "sacrificial rites" found in *Buried Child,* though perhaps not immediately obvious, parallel primitive agricultural rituals associated with planting, tending, harvesting, and celebrating crops, activities which were essential to non-industrialized agrarian societies. As Venetia Newall noted in an article for *Man, Myth, and Magic,* "It is difficult for us to realize nowadays, with tins and frozen foods available throughout the year, and imported tropical fruits on our tables even in the middle of winter, the anxiety which our ancestors felt as they waited for the annual harvest."

To help relieve their anxiety, and to rejoice as a community when their efforts met with success, early farming cultures developed a variety of rituals meant to bless the earth and the seeds that were sown, appeal to the various gods that represented elements necessary to crop growth, such as rain and sunshine, and preserve the spirits that inhabited the fields and their bounty from year to year. Such rituals have surrounded the planting and harvesting of wheat, corn, and rice—the principal crops of most of the earth's population—for thousands of years. The ancient Greeks, for example, worshiped Demeter, the goddess of grain, and developed rituals designed to please her, keep her spirit alive within their crops, and promote its renewal each spring. American Indians developed Corn Dances, while many European communities from the Middle Ages to the present day make dolls from the last sheaf harvested, or leave a few ears standing in the field until the next planting. Once the harvest left the field, it was time for rituals of gratitude, which typically involved fellowship in the community and great feasts. To this day, the Jewish community celebrates Sukkot—the Feast of the Booths—and

WHAT DO I READ NEXT?

- In a career spanning more than thirty years, Sam Shepard has produced dozens of one-acts, full-length dramas, and screenplays. Some of his more popular plays include *The Tooth of Crime* (1972), *Curse of the Starving Class* (1977), *True West* (1980), *Fool for Love* (1983), and *A Lie of the Mind* (1985). These are all available in collected anthologies of Shepard's work such as *Sam Shepard: Seven Plays* and *The Unseen Hand and Other Plays.*

- *Buried Child* echoes the plots, characters, and themes of some of the greatest plays in Western dramatic literature. Consider reading *Oedipus Rex* (c. 430-425 B.C.), Sophocles's tragedy about murder and incest in ancient Greece.

- *Death of a Salesman* (1949) is Arthur Miller's modern tragedy about mediocrity and struggling with the American dream. *Buried Child* echoes

many of its themes of disillusionment, delusion, and shattered hope.

- *Who's Afraid of Virginia Woolf* (1962) is Edward Albee's dark and twisted portrayal of a middle-aged couple's fights and fantasies over their imaginary son.

- *Buried Child,* like many of Shepard's plays, recalls elements of popular myths and legends from society's shared past. The play is filled with symbolism and characters who resemble figures from the bible, childhood stories, and the myths of cultures around the world. For a scholarly exploration of the value of myths in human society, try Joseph Campbell's *Hero with a Thousand Faces* (1949). Campbell examines tales from *Oedipus the King* to *Beauty and the Beast,* and explains the archetypal hero common to all human beings.

most Americans and Canadians observe Thanksgiving in the fall, during harvest time, just as the Pilgrims may have done in Plymouth Colony in 1621.

In *Buried Child,* Shepard draws upon the essential elements of these rituals—fertility and nourishment, growth and maturation, death and resurrection—and symbolically provides each a chilling dual meaning. One of the most important and recognizable sacrificial rites dramatized in *Buried Child* is the death of the old Corn King and the birth or, in this case, resurrection, of a new Corn King. Behind this ritual, shared in one form or another by many different cultures, is the notion that a spirit inhabits the corn plant, and the spirit must be kept alive from the time the plant is harvested until the following year, when a new field is planted, in order to ensure a bountiful new crop.

The plot construction and characters of *Buried Child* contain echoes of this ancient corn ritual. Outside the house lies a fallow field, which hasn't been planted in years. Inside, sickly and near death,

lies Dodge, the patriarch of the family and, in ritual terms, the symbolic "Corn King" whose spirit must be kept alive until a successor is found. Like the old man with a long beard, leaning on a scythe, who is the symbol of the Old Year, annually dying on December 31, Dodge is almost helpless, and entirely dependent on his wife and sons while waiting for the infant New Year or, in this case, a young, strong new Corn King, to replace him. The play reaches its climax when the old Corn King dies and a new one, the outsider, Vince, assumes the throne.

Early in the play, one of Dodge's sons, the emotionally disturbed Tilden, covers his sleeping father with the husks of the corn he has mysteriously brought in from the field. Although he will not inherit the role of new Corn King at the end of the play, Tilden is nevertheless a symbolic part of the ritual. He represents the youth and virility his father, now dying on the stalk, once had, making him a threat to the old Corn King. To amplify his role as his father's aggressor, and possible heir to his

"WHAT OFTEN FLOWS OUT OF SHEPARD ARE CHARACTERS AND STORIES THAT ARE AT ONCE EXCITING AND RECOGNIZABLE AS AMERICAN ALLEGORIES AS WELL AS SHOCKING AND REPULSIVE FOR WHAT THEY TELL US ABOUT HUMAN INSTINCT AND BEHAVIOR, REGARDLESS OF CULTURAL BACKGROUND"

throne, Tilden is able to reap more than just crops from an empty field. Years before, he managed to impregnate his own mother, long after she and Dodge had stopped "planting the field" as it were. "We weren't planning on havin' any more boys," Dodge admits to Shelly late in the play. "We had enough boys already. In fact, we hadn't been sleepin' in the same bed for about six years."

Dodge's middle son, Bradley, is another candidate for the title of new Corn King, though he is even less likely to wrest the office from the cantankerous patriarch than Tilden. When Bradley is first mentioned by Halie, Dodge expresses contempt for his offspring, who has the unusual habit of sneaking into the house and cutting his father's hair while he sleeps. "You tell Bradley that if he shows up here with those clippers, I'll separate him from his manhood!" Dodge warns. But Bradley has already been symbolically castrated. He lost a leg in a chainsaw accident and, though he bristles and blusters as loud as any playground bully, without his leg he is reduced to a whining, pre-pubescent schoolboy.

Still, just as Dodge feared, Bradley appears after the old man falls asleep. Standing over Dodge's rumpled, wheezing form stretched out on the sofa, Bradley mutters, "Harvest's over, Pops," and proceeds to savagely cut his father's hair, as if he were husking an ear of corn. With this act, the old Corn King falls even closer to his death.

Vince's appearance on the scene in Act II finally signals the arrival of a potential new Corn King. Young, strong, and untouched by the terrible family secret that has crippled the rest of the men in the household, Vince introduces a renewed spirit of hope into the grim ceremony. For a time, Vince is at once the buried child, the lost Ansel, and himself—all the missing sons of the family. Perhaps recognizing the seriousness of the threat Vince represents, Dodge, the old King, and Tilden, a contender for the throne, claim not to recognize the boy, though both are eager to win the favor of Shelly, the new female Vince has brought into the male-dominated homestead.

To formulate a plan of attack, and perhaps steel himself for the battle to come, Vince leaves the house on a mission for Dodge, his symbolic nemesis in the fight for the Corn King title. While he is away, each of the inhabitants of the house makes a play for power. Halie returns home with a man from the outside—Father Dewis, who turns out to be completely ineffectual and metaphorically impotent. Bradley's bullying turns to whimpering when Shelly takes his artificial leg and wields it like a weapon. Tilden, left with no other choice, leaves the scene to exhume the "buried child," the root of all their troubles.

When Vince finally returns home from his overnight driving odyssey through the symbolically purifying rain, he cuts his way through the porch's locked screen door and steps through, like a baby emerging from its mother's womb. Nash observed: "Clearly, Shepard has used this dramatic moment as a *symbolic rebirth,* calculated to correspond to the exact moment when Tilden, alone in the rain, must be pulling the decayed corpse of the buried child from the mud of the cornfields." In terms of the symbolic ritual he is reenacting, he has returned just in time for the new season's planting. With his dying words, the old Corn King (Dodge) wills the house and fields to the new Corn King (Vince). Outside, after the cleansing rain and nourishing sunshine, the crops miraculously begin to burst through the soil of the fields. Inside, after a long season of blight and decay, hope is renewed as the buried child is carried upstairs for a homecoming with its mother, and a new Corn King reigns from his living room throne.

Source: Lane A. Glenn, for *Drama for Students,* Gale, 1999.

Robert Brustein

Examining Shepard's dual career as a Hollywood actor and an experimental playwright, Brustein reviews the heralded 1996 revival of Buried Child, *for which Shepard both revised and wrote new material. Comparing the play with the author's autobiographical* Cruising Paradise, *the critic finds that while the play deals with difficult themes, it is ultimately deserving of its status as a modern classic.*

Challenging the camera over a period of thirty years, Sam Shepard's face appears in sepia and black-and-white on the jackets of three newly issued books. The chiseled bones, the two deep furrows in his forehead, the uncombed mane and dimpled chin are physical constants. What the camera also reveals is how the acid of years and circumstance have etched radical mutations in Shepard's appearance. Something more than passing time is responsible for his transformation from the youthful hipster depicted in Bruce Weber's unposed photo for *The Unseen Hand and Other Plays,* to the engaging, rather shy young man of Weber's cover shot for *Simpatico,* to the unshaven, haggard, vaguely anguished figure in Brigitte Lacombe's portrait for *Cruising Paradise,* to the harrowing, glowering desperado in Richard Avedon's recent celebrity mug shot for *The New Yorker.* Avedon's black-bordered photograph shows the face and neck of its now middle-aged subject weathered by outdoor and indoor experience, his brow threatening, his mouth drooping at the edges with surly contempt. You can almost sense him tapping his foot, an unwilling subject, impatient to return to his horses and the open air, who doesn't know what in hell he's doing in a New York studio.

Why, he might be asking, is a man who prided himself on being a private, even reclusive writer now willing to cooperate with this cosmopolitan world of hype and fashion? Once a mysterious presence behind a wealth of cryptic plays, today he finds himself a highly publicized celebrity, not through his theater work, which never managed to draw a mainstream public, but largely as a result of screen appearances, beginning with *The Right Stuff,* which brought him momentary fame as the new Gary Cooper. It is true that Shepard's movie roles have been occasional, even desultory lately, and that the once-prolific dramatist has only produced three plays in more than a decade. Yet, we are told, this will be Shepard's jubilee year. He has just enjoyed his first Broadway premiere—a revised version of the 1979 Pulitzer Prize-winning play *Buried Child* in the splendid Steppenwolf production (which will soon be closing). The Signature Theatre will stage a series of Shepard works next year off-Broadway, some old, some revised, some newly written. And Knopf and Vintage are issuing a

"BURIED CHILD REVERBERATES WITH ECHOES OF *THE WASTE LAND, TOBACCO ROAD, OF MICE AND MEN,* EVEN *LONG DAY'S JOURNEY INTO NIGHT,* BUT IT IS AT THE SAME TIME AN ENTIRELY ORIGINAL SHEPARD CONCOCTION"

series of Shepard volumes, the latest among them a collection of "tales" called *Cruising Paradise.*

Reading *Cruising Paradise* after seeing *Buried Child* (Brooks Atkinson Theatre) reinforces the impression that Shepard's writing is becoming increasingly autobiographical, if not self-absorbed. By common consent his masterpiece, *Buried Child* was the beginning of a relatively new phase in Shepard's work. Not long before he was discovered by Hollywood, he turned away from the rock-androlling hallucinogenics of *Tooth of Crime* and *The Unseen Hand* ("impulsive chronicles," as he now calls them, "representing a chaotic, subjective world") to compose domestic plays in a relatively realistic style. It was around the same time that this itinerant road warrior settled into domesticity with Jessica Lange and permitted the studios to replace his broken front tooth. What was jagged and chaotic and parentless in the Shepard persona was now turning familiar and familial.

Indeed, *Cruising Paradise* suggests that the characters depicted in *Buried Child* (and other plays of the period: *Curse of the Starving Class, A Lie of the Mind, Simpatico*) bear a family resemblance to Shepard's own ancestors. As a matter of fact, a few *Buried Child* character names—Dodge, Vinnie, Ansel—are mentioned (though in different guises) in these brief stories, along with the weird names of some recurrent Shepard locales (Azusa, Cucamonga).

The name of Dodge, a cantankerous drunkard in *Buried Child,* reappears in the stories as his great-great-great-grandfather, Lemuel Dodge, who lost an ear fighting for the North and an arm fighting for the South. (These amputated parts may have inspired Bradley's prosthetic leg in *Buried Child.*) But Dodge, the dramatic character, is probably much closer to Shepard's own father, whose bourbon-soaked presence dominates the first half of *Cruising Paradise*. In ''The Self-Made Man,'' Shepard remembers his father as a World War II fighter pilot in a silk scarf, who mournfully concluded that ''aloneness was a fact of nature.'' In ''The Real Gabby Hayes,'' he recalls him as man who loved the open desert and loaded guns, two passions inherited by his son. In ''A Small Circle of Friends,'' he describes the way his father gradually estranged all his close companions as a result of his drinking bouts and temper tantrums. At one point, he attacked a man he suspected of having an affair with his wife, smashing his face on his raised knee and splitting his nose. And in ''See You In My Dreams,'' Shepard recounts (in an episode recapitulated in *A Lie of the Mind*) how his father was run over by a car in Bernalillo after a three-day binge of fighting, fishing and drinking with a Mexican woman. His son buried his ashes in a plain pine box in Santa Fe's National Cemetery, feeling ''a terrible knotted grief that couldn't find expression.''

Most of these stories, like many of his plays, take place in motor courts—Shepard may be the most inveterate chronicler of motel culture since Nabokov made Humbert Humbert chase Lolita through the back lots of America. (Both writers recognize that nothing better suggests the bleak rootlessness of American life than a rented room.) In one of the stories—''Hail From Nowhere''—a man (the author?) is looking for his wife in a motel room, and discovers that she has abandoned him. He can't remember what they fought about, but in a companion piece, ''Just Space,'' the woman describes him to her mother as someone who ''carries guns'' and tried to shoot her. I was reminded of a time when Shepard, having driven to Boston with a brace of shotguns in his trunk, threatened to use them on a *Herald* photographer who was stalking him and Jessica Lange through the streets of Beacon Hill. Rage, alcohol and a profound respect and awe for trackless nature—these constitute the basic Shepard inheritances.

They also constitute the essence of *Buried Child*. Set in central Illinois in 1978, the play is about an alcoholic couch potato (Dodge), his hectoring unfaithful wife (Halie), two dysfunctional sons (the half-wit Tilden and the sadistic amputee Bradley), a grandson (Vince) and his girlfriend (Shelly). Some past nastiness is afflicting this family, a secret that is gradually exhumed (along with the child) in Ibsenite fashion: Halie has borne a baby out of wedlock by her own son, Tilden.

Shepard monitors this story through strong and violent metaphors. At the end of the first act, Bradley cuts his father's hair until his scalp bleeds, and, at the close of the second, thrusts his fingers into Shelly's mouth in a gesture equivalent to rape. When Vince returns to the family, no one recognizes him. He responds by drinking himself into a stupor with his grandfather's whiskey. By the end of the play, Dodge has quietly expired, Vince has inherited his house, and Tilden—who earlier carried corn and carrots to dump them into Dodge's lap in some vague vegetative rite—enters with the decaying remains of the child who was buried in the garden. It is a remarkable moment, contrasting fertility and drought, invoking the lost innocence and failed expectations not just of a family but of an entire nation. *Buried Child* reverberates with echoes of *The Waste Land, Tobacco Road, Of Mice and Men,* even *Long Day's Journey Into Night,* but it is at the same time an entirely original Shepard concoction.

And the production that director Gary Sinise has fashioned with his Chicago company is a corker—easily the finest staging of a Shepard work I have ever seen. Robert Brill's vast set is composed of an endless staircase ascending to nowhere and wooden slatted walls decorated with the head of a lopsided moose that seems to be as drunk as the owner. The accomplished cast fills this space entirely, investing this dark gothic concerto of a play with elaborate comic cadenzas. James Gammon, a quintessential Shepard actor, is especially powerful as Dodge, rasping his part as if he were swallowing razor blades. Leo Burmester as Bradley drags his leg along the floor like Walter Slezak stalking John Garfield in *The Fallen Sparrow*. Terry Kinney plays the lobotomized Tilden in filthy boots and trousers, as if he had just been plucked from the earth himself. And Lois Smith is an eerie, frenzied, nattering Halie.

While *Buried Child* uses the family as a commentary on an entire nation, *Cruising Paradise* is oddly insulated from anything but Shepard memories. In most of these stories, this is not a pressing problem. Whether told in first or third person, they are drenched in a powerful nostalgia. ''I found myself lost in the past more often than not,'' Shepard writes in ''The Devouring Lion,'' which may explain why he has chosen the reflectiveness of narrative rather than the immediacy of drama for evoking his family history: the short tale is the perfect medium for reminiscing about yourself and your ancestors.

It is not, however, an ideal medium for talking about your experiences as a movie star. And what weakens and finally enfeebles *Cruising Paradise* is the self-regarding, oddly conflicted nature of the final stories. Here, in a series of twelve impressionistic vignettes, mostly written on location in 1990 for a film he was shooting at the time, presumably Volker Schlondorff's *Voyager,* Shepard goes by train to California for an initial meeting with the German director, then by car to Mexico for the filming. "I'm an actor now," he writes. "I confess, I don't fly. I've been having some trouble landing jobs lately because of this not wanting to fly; plus, I refuse to live in L.A." He also doesn't own a fax machine or a word processor, and he won't do "press junkets."

During appointments with costume and make-up, he realizes that he is going to be thrown together with perfect strangers on a long shoot. This makes him want to "either run or puke." He gets in a hassle with an assistant to the director who, because of Shepard's fear of flying, is required to make arrangements for a special limo. These arrangements are complicated by Mexican border regulations and Shepard's taste in cars. "I don't need a limo. Just get me a Chevy," he remarks. The L.A. weather reminds him of murder, "the perfect weather to kill someone in." Passing some "very chic people" in the hotel, "sinking into paisley, overstuffed sofas, reaching for silver trays full of cashews and almonds," he again thinks of murder. He remembers what Céline said in his very last interview: "I just want to be left alone."

Since he won't fly, or use technology, or engage himself socially, Shepard manages to create as much trouble for the studio as the most demanding star. He harasses his Austrian driver because he insists on wearing a tux while driving through the desert. He feels alienated from the director when, sick with "*la turista,*" he cries over a lost love ("I barely know the man"). In short, he behaves like a royal pain in the ass.

He arrives in Mexico finally after a series of harrowing adventures. The limo is stopped and stripped by some narcs looking for drugs. Shepard can only get a work permit by lying to a female bureaucrat, telling her he's Spencer Tracy. "I'm not an actor. I'm a criminal," he muses. "Maybe there is some inherent crime attached to pretending." These last stories contain some finely observed paragraphs about the Mexican landscape, the local villages and the Indian extras, but the very act of

"*BURIED CHILD* IS SAM SHEPARD'S BEST PLAY"

writing them while acting in a movie suggests the effort to maintain a literary identity.

Shepard knows that there is something inherently contradictory about his twin careers. It is a little jarring to find a man noted for his reserve and taciturnity talking about "this scene I'm playing now," about having "no idea whatsoever how to play this character." He has elected to follow the career of a public personality without sacrificing his privacy as an artist. This is not an easy choice. The face in the Avedon portrait suggests it's a choice that is tearing him apart.

Source: Robert Brustein, "Shepard's Choice" in the *New Republic,* Vol. 215, no. 3 & 4, July 15 & 22, 1996, pp. 27–29.

John Simon

Calling Buried Child *"Shepard's best play," Simon reviews the 1996 revival. The critic offers a highly favorable appraisal of the work, calling it "as good of its kind as it gets."*

Buried Child is Sam Shepard's best play. It is what the French call *misérabiliste* theater, but as good of its kind as they come, as much of a classic as *Christina's World* or a George Price cartoon. The central concept of a rural American family going down the drain because of—literally—a skeleton in the closet may be a bit schematic and the symbolism-cum-absurdism a tad dragged in by the cat. Even so, the flamboyant blend of the comic and the horrific, the verbally teasing and visually terrifying—in short, the hair-and-hackle-raising humor—takes you to a Shepard country where, laughing and shuddering, you never know when you'll be rolling in the aisle or scared out of your wits.

It is useless to try to retell the plot, minimalist yet convoluted, but sense can be made of the seemingly preposterous: Shepard gives us his family's and his country's history as reflected in a fun-house mirror, the very distortions grinning their way to the core of an insidiously incisive truth. The couch-bound grandfather (James Gammon), cursing his family and world as he revels in his filth; the mild-mannered near-idiot son (Terry Kinney) who keeps bringing in things that grow or fester outside; the one-legged and violent elder son (Leo Burmester) who practices petty viciousness on other people; the grandmother (Lois Smith) who berates everyone and hangs out with an addled priest (Jim Mohr); the grandson (Jim True) who escaped to the city, returning years later with his saxophone and a girlfriend (Kellie Overbey) who wants out of this madhouse in which none of the family recognize her boyfriend—all of these compel us to join their metaphysical staggers between farce and melodrama.

Gary Sinise has directed this Steppenwolf production with the trademark Chicago athleticism whose physicality sometimes detracts from the deeper meaning; he also introduces non sequiturs such as Grandma's leaving white-haired and returning a flaming redhead. But he does keep the mayhem spinning, even if the finish is less devastating than it might be. In the remarkable cast, only Jim True strikes me as too dopey a beanpole for what is, after all, the nearest thing to an authorial alter ego.

The set by Robert Brill, costumes by Allison Reeds, and lighting by Kevin Rigdon are fittingly, frighteningly good. And to think that it took Shepard's masterpiece 18 years to reach Broadway! But at least it gets there in style.

Source: John Simon, ''The Good Shepard'' in *New York,* Vol. 29, no. 19, May 13, 1996 , p. 60.

SOURCES

Auerbach, Doris. ''*Buried Child*'' in her *Sam Shepard, Arthur Kopit, and the Off Broadway Theatre,* Twayne, 1982, pp. 53-61.

Clurman, Harold. Review of *Buried Child* in the *Nation,* December 2, 1978, pp. 621-22.

Gussow, Mel. Review of *Buried Child* in the *New York Times,* January 2, 1979, p. C7.

Hart, Lynda. ''Realism Revisited: *Buried Child*'' in her *Sam Shepard's Metaphorical Stages,* Greenwood Press, 1987, pp. 75-87.

Kalem, T. E. Review of *Buried Child* in *Time,* December 18, 1978.

Kroll, Jack, Constance Guthrie, and Janet Huck, ''Who's That Tall Dark Stranger'' in *Newsweek,* November 11, 1985, p. 71.

Kroll, Jack. Review of *Buried Child* in *Newsweek,* October 30, 1978.

Marranca, Bonnie. ''Sam Shepard'' in *American Playwrights: A Critical Survey,* p. 108.

Nash, Thomas. ''Sam Shepard's *Buried Child:* The Ironic Use of Folklore'' in *Modern Drama,* Vol. XXVI, no. 4, December, 1983, pp. 486-91.

Newall, Venetia. ''Harvest'' in *Man, Myth, and Magic: An Illustrated Encyclopedia of the Supernatural,* Marshall Cavendish, 1970, pp. 1214-18.

Raidy, William A. Review of *Buried Child* in *Plays and Players,* February, 1979, pp. 36-37.

Simon, John. Review of *Buried Child* in *New York,* November 27, 1978, p. 118.

FURTHER READING

Bottoms, Stephen J. *The Theatre of Sam Shepard: States of Crisis,* Cambridge University Press, 1998.
    One of the most recent studies of Shepard's work, Bottoms's analysis of Shepard's plays begins with his early, experimental one-acts, performed in churches and garages around New York in the 1960s; through his mainstream, full-length dramas and films of the 1970s and 1980s; and ending with *Simpatico,* produced in 1994.

Dugdale, John, compiler. *File on Shepard,* Methuen Drama, 1989.
    This useful reference book, part of a series covering leading modern dramatists, contains a chronology of Shepard's career; descriptions and reviews of all his plays, from 1964-1985; selected quotes from the playwright himself; and a helpful bibliography of books and articles about Shepard and his work.

Shepard, Sam. *Cruising Paradise,* Vintage Books, 1997.
    A collection of forty short stories that explore some of the same motifs and themes found in Shepard's plays: America, the open road, solitude and loss, family, and the absurdity of life in show business.

Shepard, Sam. *Motel Chronicles,* City Lights Books, 1983.
    A sort of journal, filled with short stories, observations, and poetry by the playwright, mixed with black and white photographs.

Wade, Leslie. *Sam Shepard and the American Theatre,* Greenwood Press, 1997.
    Wade's study of Shepard's career is part of a series of books called *Lives of the Theatre.* The volumes are designed to provide scholarly introductions to important figures and eras in world theatre, from ancient Greece to the present day. *Sam Shepard and the American Theatre* examines Shepard's evolving place in American dramatic literature from a leading Off- (and Off-Off-) Broadway experimentalist to a mainstream dramatist and filmmaker.

The Emperor Jones

EUGENE O'NEILL

1920

The Emperor Jones was part of an amazing first year for O'Neill as a Broadway playwright. His very first Broadway play, *Beyond the Horizon,* had appeared in February of 1920 and eventually won him the Pulitzer Prize for drama, but *The Emperor Jones* was so successful in its Off-Broadway production in November that it moved to Broadway by the end of the same year and became another high-profile success for the newly acclaimed playwright. By 1930, at the end of an astoundingly productive first decade, O'Neill was widely recognized as America's greatest dramatist.

The Emperor Jones was also the first of several experiments with Expressionism for O'Neill. O'Neill found inspiration for Expressionism in the work of Swedish playwright August Strindberg (1849-1912), whose *A Dream Play* (1902) and *The Ghost Sonata* (1907) explored and represented on stage complex states of mind, eschewing realistic style and imitating instead the fluid associative structure of human consciousness. After *The Emperor Jones,* O'Neill used expressionistic techniques most fully in *The Hairy Ape* (1922) and to some extent in *Strange Interlude* (1928), where his five-hour play focused on the interior monologue of its main character, Nina Leeds.

The Emperor Jones was also the first American play to offer an racially integrated cast to a Broadway audience and feature a black actor in its leading role. Prior to O'Neill's ground breaking drama,

black roles in integrated productions were played by Caucasians in black-face makeup. But O'Neill insisted that black actor Charles Gilpin play Brutus Jones in the Provincetown Playhouse premiere of *The Emperor Jones,* and a precedent was set that would eventually lead to this country's present level of racial equality in the arts.

AUTHOR BIOGRAPHY

Apparently destined for a life in the theatre, Eugene O'Neill was not only born the son of an extremely popular American stage actor, James O'Neill (1846-1920); he was also literally born on Broadway—October 16, 1888—in the since demolished Barrett House family hotel on Broadway and Forty-third Street (the area presently called Times Square), while James O'Neill was touring in his most famous role as the Count of Monte Cristo. O'Neill's childhood and adolescence were mostly unhappy because of his unstable family life, and many of his plays, especially his most famous play, *Long Day's Journey into Night* (1956), focused on disturbed, dysfunctional families.

O'Neill's formal schooling culminated in very brief stints at both Princeton and Harvard. His short stay at Princeton included a two-week suspension in 1907 for an act of drunken vandalism. After a short and unsuccessful first marriage, O'Neill's next few years included a mining expedition to Honduras, several stints as a seaman, an attempted suicide, and a bout with tuberculosis. O'Neill spent an academic year at Harvard (1914-15) studying playwrighting under the famous teacher, George Pierce Baker.

In the spring of 1916, the twenty-seven-year-old O'Neill became acquainted with a group of New York actors doing informal summer theatre in Provincetown, Massachusetts, and these "Provincetown Players" gave O'Neill's one-act plays their first productions. When the group officially organized and moved back to Greenwich Village for a winter season, they brought O'Neill's plays with them, and he soon became known as a promising new playwright.

O'Neill's first Broadway play, *Beyond the Horizon* (1920), earned him his first Pulitzer Prize for Drama (he would earn three more, one posthumously), and this initial Broadway success was almost immediately followed in the same year by *The Emperor Jones.* Initially produced by the Province-

town group in Greenwich Village, this startlingly new "expressionistic" play starring black actor Charles Gilpin was so successful Off-Broadway that it moved "uptown" to a Broadway theatre and has since become one of O'Neill's most famous plays.

During the 1920s, O'Neill was enormously successful, becoming the first American playwright to garner an international reputation. However, by the late-1930s, interest in O'Neill's work had cooled, and though he had earned America's first Nobel Prize for Literature in 1936, O'Neill's reputation did not return to its former high status during his lifetime. After years of failing health, O'Neill died, ironically, as he had been born—in a rented hotel room—on November 27, 1953, of pneumonia. However, O'Neill's literary reputation soon soared again, starting in 1956, when director Jose Quintero began mounting definitive productions of O'Neill's plays. The subsequent rejuvenation of interest in O'Neill has helped maintain *The Emperor Jones* as a crucial component in O'Neill's canon and in the history of American drama.

PLOT SUMMARY

Scene I

The Emperor Jones takes place on an island in the West Indies and opens in the elegant throne room of the island's ruler or "emperor," Brutus Jones. It is late afternoon and no one is present except for an old black peasant woman sneaking through the palace. A white trader named Smithers enters and interrogates the woman, asking her why the palace is deserted. Smithers learns that the natives of the island, led by a former native chief named Lem, have stolen all the horses and have headed to the nearby hills to plan a revolt against their oppressive emperor.

When the Emperor, Brutus Jones, enters, Smithers gradually reveals this news, but Jones remains calm. He arrived on the island two years earlier from the United States, where he had worked as a porter on a fancy Pullman train before going to prison for killing a man named Jeff over a craps game. Escaping prison, Jones had come to the island and found Smithers cheating the black natives with his trade goods. After briefly joining Smithers as an associate, Jones eclipsed Smithers and named himself Emperor. Convincing the natives that he had magical powers and could only be killed by a silver bullet, Jones felt secure. He continues to feel secure in the face of this native revolt because he has carefully planned a response to it. He has money stashed in a foreign bank account, an escape route through the woods mapped out in his mind, and food buried at the edge of the forest. Jones has even made for himself a good luck charm out of what he thinks is the only silver bullet on the island.

But as Jones outlines his escape plan to Smithers, a drum begins to beat in the distant hills, and Jones is initially startled by it. Smithers informs Jones that the natives have begun a war dance to work up their courage for killing their "emperor." Smithers tells Jones that the natives will send ghosts after him into the dark forest, but Jones asserts that he's not afraid of ghosts and that by nightfall he will have gotten such a head start on Lem's troops that they will never catch up to him. At 3:30 in the afternoon, Jones casually sets off on foot for his getaway through the dense forest.

Scene II

Night has fallen sometime after 6:30 pm, and Jones has reached the edge of the dense forest. Fatigued from his afternoon hike in the hot sun, Jones rests, listening to the steady beat of the drum, pulsating at a little more than 72 beats a minute, the rate of the normal heart beat. However, Jones can't find the food he so confidently hid near this spot. As he lights a match to see more clearly, the rate of the drum beat increases and "the Little Formless Fears"—hallucinations that represent Jones's rising doubts—slide silently out of the darkness like black, shapeless grubworms "about the size of a creeping child." When the Formless Fears laugh at Jones's consternation, Jones notices them, pulls his pistol, and fires. In a flash, the Formless Fears are gone, and the drums begin beating more rapidly. Jones reassures himself and hurries into the dark forest.

Scene III

It is 9:00 at night and the beams of the newly risen moon create an eerie glow on the dark forest floor as Jones enters a small triangular clearing. There, the figure of black Jeff, the man Jones killed in a crap game in the United States, seems to be mechanically throwing dice. Jones enters the clearing, his face scratched and his elegant clothes torn from forcing his way through the thick underbrush in the dark. He hears the increasingly rapid beat of the distant drums, sees Jeff, and fires another shot.

Eugene O'Neill

The hallucinated image of Jeff disappears with the pistol shot and Jones leaves the forest path to plunge wildly into the underbrush.

Scene IV

It is an hour before midnight and from the forest Jones stumbles onto a wide dirt road running diagonally across the stage. His uniform is now ragged and torn, and he begins to discard parts of it to ease himself from the stifling heat. Exhausted, he throws himself down to rest but soon begins to hallucinate again. A small gang of black convicts in striped suits are working with picks and shovels. The white prison guard, armed with rifle and whip, demands that Jones join the convict group, and for a moment the nearly hypnotized Jones does. But when the hallucinated guard beats him, Jones responds by trying to hit the guard with his imaginary shovel. Realizing his hands are actually empty, Jones fires another shot from his pistol and all the imagined figures disappear. Jones plunges again into the forest, the drum beats increasing in volume and rapidity.

Scene V

It is an hour after midnight and Jones enters a large circular clearing and sits on a dead stump. In his exhaustion and misery, Jones hallucinates again and sees the stump as an auction block from the 1850s where a crowd has gathered to watch slaves bought and sold. When Jones becomes the slave being auctioned off, he fires at the auctioneer and planter trying to buy him, once again causing the images to disappear. Again Jones plunges into the forest as the drum beats quicken and increase in volume.

Scene VI

It is 3:00 in the morning and in a cleared space no more than five feet high under dense tree limbs Jones settles for another rest. The moonlight is shut out by the canopy and only a ''vague, wan light filters through.'' Jones's silver bullet is all that remains in his gun. His clothes have all been torn away and what remains is no more than a breech cloth. Gradually, two rows of seated figures appear behind Jones in his next hallucination. The small space in the forest becomes a ship at sea and Jones a member of a slave group being carried to the new world. As this hallucination fades, the drum begins to beat even louder and quicker.

Scene VII

It is 5:00 in the morning and at the foot of a gigantic tree near a river Jones imagines an African witch-doctor dancing and chanting before him. As the drum beat reaches a frenzied pitch, Jones is hypnotized by the Witch Doctor's performance. He begins to sway with the shaman and joins in the chanting. At the culmination of the dance, the Witch Doctor indicates that Jones must be sacrificed to the sacred crocodile river god, but Jones rouses a final defiance and fires his remaining silver bullet into the crocodile apparition.

Scene VIII

It is dawn and the final scene takes place in the identical spot at the foot of the forest where Jones started his journey in Scene II. Lem enters with his small band of soldiers, followed by Smithers. They examine Jones's tracks, Smithers complaining that they have wasted their evening beating the drum and casting spells, Lem confident that they will still ''kotch him.'' The sound of snapping twigs in the forest alerts the soldiers and they shoot Jones, who has simply run in a circle all night. The sound of the drum abruptly ceases and Lem reveals that part of the evening's ceremonies involved making their own silver bullets from melted coins. The soldiers

show Jones's dead body and exit, leaving Smithers to sneer at ''the lot of 'em.''

CHARACTERS

Jeff

The black man Brutus Jones killed over a crap game in the United States before the action of the play began. Appearing in Scene III as one of Jones's hallucinations, Jeff is brown rather than black-skinned, thin, middle-aged, and dressed in a Pull-man porter's uniform. In Jones's hallucination, Jeff tosses the dice like a robot.

Brutus Jones

The main character in *The Emperor Jones,* Brutus Jones is a tall and powerfully built American negro man of middle age. Formerly a Pullman (train) car porter in the United States, Jones comes to the West Indian island where the play takes place and becomes ''emperor'' after convincing the natives that he has magical powers. Before coming to the island, Jones had escaped from an American prison, where he was being confined for killing a man over a crap game. Jones exudes a strength and confidence that commands fear and respect from all around him even while he reigns quite ruthlessly as Emperor. His eyes indicate extraordinary cunning, intelligence, and a careful shrewdness.

To make himself appear regal, Jones wears a light-blue uniform decorated with brass buttons and heavy gold chevrons and braids. His pants are bright red with a light-blue stripe down the side and he wears patent leather boots with brass spurs and a holster with a long-barreled, pearl-handled revolver. In the play he speaks with a strongly marked black dialect, as in, ''who dare whistle dat way in my palace?'' Jones is filled with contempt for the former exploiter of the islanders, the white man, Smithers.

Lem

A former chieftain on the island and the leader of the natives who finally rebel against Jones's dictatorial rule. The heavy-set Lem appears on stage only in the last scene, where he is dressed in a loin-cloth with a revolver and cartridge belt around his waist. Lem hates Jones and once hired another native to shoot him, but when the gun misfired in the

MEDIA ADAPTATIONS

- *The Emperor Jones* was adapted as a full-length feature film in 1933 and starred Paul Robeson as Brutus Jones and Dudley Digges as Smithers. The screenplay adaptation for this black and white, seventy-two-minute film was written by Du Bose Heyward and directed by Dudley Murphy for United Artists. In 1980 the film was released on videocassette by Hollywood Home Theatre. In 1993, Janus Films joined Voyager Press to issue the 1933 film coupled with a thirty-minute documentary of Paul Robeson's life taken from the Janus Film Collection and originally released in 1980. The documentary, in color, is narrated by actor Sidney Poitier.

- In 1933, an operatic version of the play had its World Premiere at the Metropolitan Opera House in New York City. The composer and librettist was Louis Gruenberg, the conductor Tullio Serafin. The set was designed by Jo Mielziner, and the role of Brutus Jones was sung by baritone Lawrence Tibbett. The opera followed O'Neill's script faithfully except for the omission of the final scene and the changing of Jones's death to suicide (using his last silver bullet on himself). O'Neill approved the changes. As a result of the orchestration, the drum-beat was less effective.

- In 1971, Everett and Edwards released a thirty-two-minute audiocassette lecture on the play as part of their Modern Drama Cassette Curriculum Series. The lecturer is Jordan Yale Miller. In 1976, Everett and Edwards released a thirty-six-minute audiocassette lecture on the play as part of their World Literature Cassette Curriculum Series. The lecturer is Howard F. Stein.

- In 1974, Jeffrey Norton Publishers released a fifty-five-minute audiocassette interview between Heywood Hale Broun and O'Neill biographer Louis Sheaffer as part of the Jeffrey Norton Publishers Avid Readers in the Arts tape library.

- In 1975, Educational Dimensions Corporation released an eighteen-minute audiovisual filmstrip that examines and analyzes O'Neill's play.

---

assassination attempt, Jones proclaimed that only a silver bullet could kill him. As the play opens, Lem has finally convinced the rest of the natives to forge their own silver bullet, and they spend the night working up the courage to attack Jones. Lem and his men finally kill Jones in the forest where Jones had desperately run in circles trying to escape.

Little Formless Fears

In the second scene of the play, these fanciful creatures represent Jones's first hallucinations in the forest and they stand for his general anxieties. These ''fears'' are ''black'' and ''shapeless,'' like ''a grubworm about the size of a creeping child,'' and ''only their glittering little eyes can be seen.'' These shapes ''move noiselessly, but with deliberate, painful effort, striving to raise themselves on end, failing and sinking again.'' When these fears mock Jones with their laughter, Jones shoots at them and they disappear.

Henry Smithers

Smithers is the tall, bald, stoop-shouldered Cockney Englishman, about forty-years-old, who was successfully exploiting the black natives before Brutus Jones arrived on the island. Smithers has a long neck with an enormous Adam's apple, which looks like an egg. Deeply tanned, Smithers's naturally pasty face has taken on a sickly yellow color, and his nose is red from extensive drinking of native rum. Smithers has small, sharp features, including a pointed nose and little, red-rimmed eyes that dart around like a ferret's. He is mean, cowardly, and dangerous—afraid of Jones but openly defiant, as far as he dares to be, and is clearly delighted with Jones's downfall.

Smithers carries a riding whip and is dressed in a dirty white suit with a white cork helmet and a cartridge belt and revolver around his waist. Smithers speaks in a (British) Cockney dialect, which O'Neill indicates with idioms and spelling like "I got me 'ooks [hooks or hands] on yer [you]."

Witch Doctor

Jones's last hallucination, in Scene VII, includes this dancing and chanting shaman or medicine man of primitive African society. The Witch Doctor is shriveled, old, and "naked except for the fur of some small animal tied about his waist, its bushy tail hanging down in front." His body is stained a bright red, he has antelope horns on his head, and he carries a bone rattle and a "charm stick" made of white cockatoo feathers. The Witch Doctor finally indicates that Jones must serve as the ritual sacrifice for a crocodile god that rises from the nearby river. However, Jones's last act is to defy the sacrifice and shoot his pistol and the remaining silver bullet into the crocodile apparition.

THEMES

Race and Racism

The Emperor Jones examines race and racism on a number of levels. Most simply, it calls attention to the racial oppression that actually existed in America in 1920. In Scene I, Smithers expresses skepticism over Jones's claim that he killed a white man before coming to the island: "from what I've 'eard, it ain't 'ealthy for a black to kill a white man in the States. They burn 'em in oil, don't they?" And though Smithers is an Englishman, he clearly represents racist attitudes that were present in O'Neill's contemporary society. At times Smithers reveals his racism somewhat subtly, as in the opening moments of the play when he assumes that the peasant woman sneaking through the throne room must have been "stealin' a bit." At other times, Smithers is much less subtle, as when he delivers the vicious curtain line at the end of the play, dismissing all dark-skinned people as "Stupid as 'ogs, the lot of 'em! Blarsted niggers!"

And as Jones re-enacts in the forest the horrors of the slave trade that brought Africans to America, O'Neill's implication is that Jones is also a victim of American racism. However, at this point O'Neill takes the racism theme to another level of complexity: he reveals that Jones himself has become a racist

on this distant isle. After he becomes "emperor," Jones thinks of himself as being separate from and superior to the natives of the island, whom he characterizes as "de low-flung bush niggers," "dese fool woods' niggers," and "black trash." He sees himself as civilized, and he is contemptuous of "dis raggedy country." In Scene IV, as he is recovering from his vision of Jeff, Jones says to himself, "Is yo' civilized, or is yo' like dese ign'rent black niggers, heah?" And Jones is also contemptuously racist toward Smithers: "Talk polite, white man! Talk polite, you heah me! I'm boss heah now, is you forgettin'?" The suggestion that O'Neill seems to be making is that anyone who succumbs to the temptations of power is susceptible to racism, even those who themselves have so poignantly suffered from it.

But the most extraordinary feature of this theme is that even as O'Neill is attempting to expose the horrors of racism he seems himself to be guilty of it to some extent. His representation of the black dialect throughout the play, though an attempt to capture a unique vocal quality, perpetuates linguistic stereotypes about black speakers. And in Scene IV, when Jones sees the gang of prison convicts, O'Neill says of Jones in his stage directions that "his eyes pop out," relying on a stereotypical image of fear that is seldom applied to white characters. O'Neill's characterization of Lem in the final scene is especially insensitive. He describes Lem as "a heavy-set, ape-faced old savage of the extreme African type, dressed only in a loin cloth." And Lem's naive belief in the magic of the silver bullet is expressed in words that make him sound like a caricatured Native American Indian: "lead bullet no kill him. He got um strong charm. I took um money, make um silver bullet, make um strong charm, too. . . . Yes. Him got strong charm. Lead no good." Charles Gilpin, the original actor playing Jones, was so sensitive to the implied racism of the play that as the production continued he changed many of the lines, refusing at times to use the frequently repeated word "nigger." When United Artists made its 1933 movie version of the play they even cut Smithers's last line, a clear concession to the play's excessively vivid racism.

Change and Transformation

In addition to its treatment of racism, *The Emperor Jones* focuses on the disintegration of Brutus Jones and his transformation from an apparently self-confident human being to a whimpering shadow of his former self.

TOPICS FOR FURTHER STUDY

- Research the history of Expressionism in both painting and theatre in the early-twentieth century and discuss how *The Emperor Jones* illustrates expressionistic subject matter and technique.

- Research the lives of Charles Gilpin (1878-1930) and Paul Robeson (1898-1976), the black actors who portrayed Brutus Jones in the original stage (1920) and film (1933) versions of *The Emperor Jones.* Discuss the ways in which their skin color had an effect on their personal and professional lives.

- Research the history of how African Americans were portrayed in drama and film during the first thirty years of the twentieth century. Compare these portrayals with the one O'Neill creates in *The Emperor Jones.*

- Research the physiology and psychology of hal-

lucinations. What is happening in the human brain when people ''see'' and experience phenomena that are not actually present? Compare this information with what you see happening to Brutus Jones in *The Emperor Jones.*

- Research several biographies of Eugene O'Neill to see how his father, James O'Neill, had his promising acting career ''ruined'' by his extraordinary success in the stageplay, *The Count of Monte Cristo.* Then research in biographies (and the autobiography) of twentieth-century actor, Basil Rathbone, who had a similar experience with his success in the Sherlock Holmes film series. Finally, read O'Neill's *Long Day's Journey into Night* and discuss how ''success'' is not always what it seems to be, a theme that can be applied as well to *The Emperor Jones.*

When Jones first appears in Scene I and reports on his past, it is clear that there has already been a great transformation for Jones: ''from stowaway to Emperor in two years!'' he says. He is proud of his transformation and appears to be confident in its durability. When Smithers challenges him, Jones menaces the white trader and says ''No use'n you rakin' up ole times. What I was den is one thing. What I is now's another.'' Jones defends himself against the charge that his transformation has been the result of luck, asserting instead that it has been the result of diligence, intelligence, quick thinking, and careful planning. He wants to be seen as a man in complete control, one whose transformation has put a former and inferior self far behind him. Expressing ''real admiration'' Smithers says, ''Blimey, but you're a cool bird, and no mistake.''

But the opening scene reveals at the same time that Jones's confidence in his transformation from oppressed black man to ''emperor'' of this small island is really quite shallow and fragile. Very subtle and early indications of Jones's tenuous hold

on his new status appear throughout Scene I in O'Neill's stage directions. When Jones shows Smithers his silver bullet, Jones holds it in his hand and looks at it, ''strangely fascinated,'' as if he can't quite believe in its power himself. And when Smithers dares him in the opening scene to ring his throne room bell and summon the natives, Jones is ''startled to alertness but [preserves] the same careless tone.'' He is ''alarmed for a second'' over Smithers's news that all of the horses have been taken away by Lem and his men, but Jones is soon ''shaking off his nervousness—with a confident laugh.'' When the tom-tom is first heard, Jones ''starts at the sound,'' and ''a strange look of apprehension creeps into his face for a moment as he listens.'' Then he asks, ''with an attempt to regain his most casual manner: What's dat drum beatin' fo'?'' He is ''a tiny bit awed and shaken in spite of himself;'' his carelessness is ''studied.''

So, when Jones disintegrates so thoroughly during his night in the forest, it does not come as a total surprise. In Scene II he is already a man

---

whistling past the graveyard. ''With a chuckle'' he says, ''cheah up, nigger, der worst is yet to come,'' and then ''his chuckle peters out abruptly.'' With the first serious reversal of fortunes, his inability to find his hidden food, Jones begins to crumble and his ''little formless fears'' appear. O'Neill is suggesting that confidence so manufactured and hollow often responds to reversals with a desperation that is deep and long-lasting.

At the end of the play Smithers says of Jones, ''''e'd lost 'imself,'' and Jones is indeed a man in conflict with his past and the self he created to hide from it. The exalted position he claims for himself in order to obliterate that past has no real roots, and his inner self can't match the postured self that he aspires to. In spite of his blustering behavior, it is clear in the opening scene that Jones's status as ''emperor'' is fraudulent, and when this fiction gets sufficiently tested, Jones's recently assumed status crumbles because he is not aware of the power of his own self-doubts. Only dimly aware of the conflict between his real self and his postured self, Jones is like the schoolyard bully who is unaware of his basic fears. When forced to his knees, there is no genuine strength to call forth in defense.

STYLE

Exposition

The Emperor Jones is a one-act play in eight scenes. The first and last scenes contain several characters and employ a realistic style while the six scenes in the middle are an expressionistic monologue chronicling Jones's nightmarish trip through the forest. This middle section is the main part of the play and focuses as much on light, sound, and setting as on Jones's spoken words. The first and last scenes of the play, then, serve as a framing device, first setting up and then resolving Jones's night in the forest. However, the first scene of the play is vastly different not only from the middle scenes but also from its companion, frame scene at the end of the play. For it is in this opening scene that O'Neill must provide all of the ''exposition'' for the play.

''Exposition'' is the term used for that part of a play that must give the audience the necessary background information for the main action. It is a very demanding aspect of the playwright's craft and can be performed expertly or inexpertly, depending on whether or not the information is woven subtly

into the dramatic flow of the initial action. *The Emperor Jones* focuses on the last twenty-four hours in the life of Brutus Jones, but in the first scene O'Neill must inform the audience of Jones's past—that he is a non-native black man from America, that he has only been on the island for two years, and that in his former life he was a train car worker who killed a friend in a craps game, went to prison, and then killed a white guard in order to escape. O'Neill must also indicate that Jones's quick rise to ''emperor'' included a period where he served Smithers as an associate and survived an assassin's bullet. All of this and more must be indicated quickly and efficiently in order to effectively set up the middle scenes and Jones's experience in the forest.

At times in this first scene, O'Neill is not very subtle or clever as he reveals Jones's background. For example, Smithers says, ''I wasn't afraid to hire yer like the rest was—'count of the story about your breakin' jail back in the States.'' At other times, however, O'Neill delivers this exposition very adroitly, as when he reveals much of Jones's background in a single speech. Jones is responding to Smithers's skepticism about his claim that he killed a white man in the United States when he says:

> Maybe I goes to jail dere for gettin' in an argument wid razors ovah a crap game. Maybe I gits twenty years when dat colored man die. Maybe I gits in 'nother argument wid de prison guard who was overseer ovah us when we're walkin' de roads. Maybe he hits me wid a whip an' I splits his head wid a shovel an' runs away an' files de chain off my leg an' gits away safe. Maybe I does all dat an' maybe I don't. It's a story I tells you so's you knows I'se de kind of man dat if you evah repeats one word of it, I ends yo' stealin' on dis yearth mighty damn quick!

With the simple addition of the single, repeated word, ''maybe,'' O'Neill conveys much of the necessary background while at the same time suggesting that the information might be false, thus creating an air of mystery about this ''emperor.''

Of special interest in regard to the exposition in *The Emperor Jones* is that the 1933 movie version of the play drastically expanded O'Neill's script by fully dramatizing this background information. The movie added scenes in America and on the island that showed the entire process whereby Jones proceeded to his fateful last day. Thus, over half of the movie is an elaboration of the exposition that O'Neill provided so briefly in the play's first scene.

Symbolism

Jones's night in the forest is a symbolic journey that represents not only his process of personal self-destruction but also a confrontation with his racial past. Once he gets to the island, Jones tries to deny what he has been in order to imitate the successful white men he once served on the train in America. Like his former white oppressors, Jones wants to dominate and be all-powerful, treating other people like inferior ''trash'' and exploiting them for personal gain. In overcompensating excess, however, Jones tries to set himself apart from all other human beings, only to discover during his nightmare journey that he cannot escape his connection with other people or even with his repressed inner life.

The first scenes in the forest show Jones confronting his personal past—his killing of Jeff, his time in prison, and his lethal attack on the prison guard. After reliving these personal experiences, Jones begins to confront the history of his race. He re-enacts the experience of his ancestors coming to America in slave ships and being sold at auction like property. Then he goes even deeper into his racial past and confronts the primitive witch doctor who claims him as a sacrifice for the crocodile god. Jones's trip through the forest, then, becomes a trip back through time, perhaps even an expiation for his attempted denial of self as a member of the black race.

And the symbolism culminates in the strange figure of the crocodile god, which is the most evocative and puzzling symbol in the play. As the climax of Jones's journey, the crocodile might be seen as a symbol of Jones's primitive self or as a symbol of evil—either the evil of Jones or of humanity in general; perhaps it represents the pagan, non-Christian response to the world; perhaps it is a symbol of Jones's inner being, which he can't accept. Any number of interpretations can be made of this figure whose presence brings Jones to his final destruction.

HISTORICAL CONTEXT

Expressionism

Expressionism is a term used for an artistic movement that initially appeared in painting, as a reaction to Impressionism, near the beginning of the twentieth century. Eventually the term came to be applied to literary forms, including drama, where it served as a reaction against Realism. Expressionism was strongest in drama in the early-1920s.

Basically, Expressionism is an attempt to objectify inner experience, to express the reality of the inner self rather than to copy external reality. Expressionism is most often concerned with representing states of human consciousness and exploring the psychology of complex feelings. Often, the emphasis is on intense and rapidly changing emotional states, since these are considered more interesting than states of serenity and calm. In the late-nineteenth and early-twentieth century, the famous Viennese psychoanalyst Sigmund Freud had revolutionized the conception of humanity by introducing the world to the complexities of the subconscious mind. In the twentieth century many artists felt compelled to explore and accurately describe these complexities.

In theatre, expressionism appeared very prominently in the work of Swedish dramatist August Strindberg, whose *A Dream Play* (1902) and *The Ghost Sonata* (1907) explored intense feelings of human pain and disappointment. Filled with free association and fantasy, these plays seriously challenged conventional stagecraft with their multitude of characters, shifting scenes, and bizarre settings. Expressionism was even more widely represented by German playwrights like Frank Wedekind, Ernst Toller, and Georg Kaiser, in plays like *Spring's Awakening* (1891), *Man As the Masses* (1921), and *From Morn to Midnight* (1916).

O'Neill's experimentations with Expressionism were mostly influenced by Strindberg, and in *The Emperor Jones* and *The Hairy Ape* (1922) O'Neill is trying to find dramatic means to express the working of the subconscious mind. Perhaps the easiest places to see this are in O'Neill's use of the drumbeat to indicate Jones's heartbeat and in his dramatization of Jones's ''little formless fears.'' O'Neill also objectifies Jones's obsessive memories in the visions of Jeff and the prison experience. But perhaps the most powerful of O'Neill's dramatizations comes when he shows Jones's mind coming to grips with racial memories. Deep in the recesses of Jones's mind he relives black history, the culmination of which leaves him defenseless in the dark forest. From dramatizing fear as a state of mind to capturing the tormented soul of a race, *The Emperor Jones* earns its title as one of the stage's successful experiments with expressionistic technique.

By the middle-1920s expressionism in the theatre was losing its immediate impact, but the long-lasting effects helped to liberate many generations of artists. Freed from the boundaries of realism, playwrights like Luigi Pirandello (*Six Characters in Search of an Author*), Bertolt Brecht (*Mother Cour-*

COMPARE
&
CONTRAST

- **1920:** The African American population in the United States is about 10.5 million, or nearly 10% of the American population. The average life expectancy for African American males is 45.5 years, compared to 54.4 for whites. For females the comparable figures are 45.2 and 55.6.

  Today: The African American population in the United States is about 32 million, or nearly 12% of the American population. The average life expectancy for African American males is 67.5 years, compared to about 73.4 for whites. For females the comparable figures are 75.8 and 79.6.

- **1920:** After race riots break out in twenty-six U.S. cities in 1919, the recently rejuvenated Ku Klux Klan experiences tremendous growth in 1920, expanding to 100,000 members in twenty-seven states. According to Frederick Lewis Allen in *Only Yesterday,* the Klan will mushroom to 4.5 million by 1924. There are sixty-one documented lynchings of African Americans in 1920.

  Today: Klanwatch is an organization founded in 1980 to monitor residual Klan terrorism. In 1986, they estimated that there were only six to seven thousand active Klan members in the United States. In 1998, police and hate-group watchers in South Carolina estimated they had only two state Klan groups with fewer than fifty members, diminished from four groups of several hundred in the early-1990s. However, over the years the Klan has been joined by a hundreds of other hate groups. One group, the Skinheads, numbered about 3,500 members in the early-1990s and were considered by many to be a greater racist threat than the Klan.

- **1920:** Though proposals are defeated for regular

cooperation between white and black labor leaders, the national convention of the American Federation of Labor (the AFL) officially opposes discrimination and votes in support of the unionization of blacks. The Brotherhood of Railroad Clerks is asked to change their ''whites only'' membership policy. The Brotherhood of Dining Car Employees is organized on a national basis.

Today: The AFL-CIO is the most powerful labor organization in the United States. The merger of the AFL with the CIO (the Congress of Industrial Organizations) in 1955 brought both skilled and unskilled or semi-skilled workers together. Under the leadership of its president, George Meany, the AFL-CIO became completely integrated and openly supported civil rights initiatives in the 1960s.

- **1920:** The National Association for the Advancement of Colored People (NAACP)—founded in 1909 by an interracial group—makes James Weldon Johnson the Secretary and the first African-American on the national board. The original organization, though headed by W. E. B. DuBois, was predominantly white.

  Today: The NAACP remains one of the pre-eminent organizations attempting to assure black Americans their constitutional rights. Considered a radical organization in 1920, the NAACP is now considered much less radical than other civil rights groups born in the 1960s and 70s. Focusing mainly on litigation, legislation, and education, the NAACP has won numerous victories for civil rights in the federal courts, including the landmark legislation ending school segregation in 1954.

---

age and Her Children), Thornton Wilder (*Our Town*), Samuel Beckett (*Waiting for Godot*), Eugene Ionesco (*The Chairs*), and Jean Genet (*The Balcony*) enjoyed a significantly broadened range

of dramatic subject matter and technique. Even a play as nominally realistic as Arthur Miller's *Death of a Salesman* shows the influence of Expressionism. Miller's play attempts to dramatize the internal workings of protagonist Willy Loman's mind (the original title of Miller's play was ''The Inside of His Head'').

Novelists as diverse as Virginia Woolf (*To the Lighthouse*), Franz Kafka (*The Trial*), James Joyce (*Ulysses*), William Faulkner (*The Sound and the Fury*), Kurt Vonnegut (*Slaughterhouse Five*), and Thomas Pynchon (*Gravity's Rainbow*) show the influence of Expressionism, as do poets like T.S. Eliot, Gerard Manley Hopkins, and Allen Ginsberg. Early films like Robert Wiene's *The Cabinet of Dr. Caligari* (1920), Friedrich Murnau's *Nosferatu* (1922), and Fritz Lang's *Metropolis* (1926) were clearly experiments in Expressionistic techniques, and echoes of the influence can be found in the work of later filmmakers like Ingmar Bergman (*The Seventh Seal*), Federico Fellini (*Satyricon*), and Michelangelo Antonioni (*Zabriskie Point*).

The Harlem Renaissance

The year 1920 represents the early stages of an important cultural movement in America called the Harlem Renaissance. During the 1920s, an extraordinary number of African American poets, essayists, and novelists suddenly appeared, and their work constituted both a literary and social movement, gaining recognition and respect for black writers while at the same time increasing racial pride among blacks and awareness of black culture among whites. Journals like *Crisis,* and *Opportunity* published many of these new works, and influential editors like W. E. B. Du Bois, Charles S. Johnson, and James Weldon Johnson demonstrated that black writers were making genuine contributions to American literary culture. Other black writers of the Harlem Renaissance, like Countee Cullen and Langston Hughes, have become highly visible figures in the history of twentieth-century American literature.

O'Neill's *The Emperor Jones* was related to the Harlem Renaissance because it helped to stimulate an increased interest in African-American life. Other white playwrights like Paul Green and DuBose and Dorothy Heyward wrote of African-American life, as in the Heyward's *Porgy* (1927), which eventually spawned the still popular folk opera, *Porgy and Bess* (1935). Ironically, the strength of the Harlem Renaissance destroyed a vital Harlem theatre movement in the 1920s because interest in black stories led to such an array of Broadway musicals dealing with black subjects in the first half of the decade that indigenous Harlem theatre lost much of its audience base.

Later generations of black writers, including Richard Wright, Zora Neale Hurston, Gwendolyn Brooks, Ralph Ellison, James Baldwin, and many others owed much of their success to the pioneers of the Harlem Renaissance.

CRITICAL OVERVIEW

On the night of November 1, 1920, *The Emperor Jones* opened Off-Broadway for a short run at the 200-seat Provincetown Players' Playwright's Theatre on Macdougal Street, and it was an immediate and huge success. The first-night audience refused to leave even after repeated curtain calls, and early the next morning long lines formed at the box office. Because one had to be a ''member'' to see the company's productions, the group's subscription list doubled within days and the projected two-week run was extended. In part the play was a great novelty as it presented an integrated cast and a captivating black actor in the lead role, but an unusually powerful script and startling scenic effects for such a small theatre contributed greatly to the play's success. First-line theatre critics had been busy earlier in the week at Broadway openings and didn't see the play for three days, but when they arrived they generally concurred with the audiences.

Writing for the *New York Times,* Alexander Woollcott called *The Emperor Jones* ''an extraordinarily striking and dramatic study of panic fear.'' Production values were not first-rate—there were clumsy and irritating transitions between scene changes that interrupted the drum beat and produced long, silent blackouts—but even with these flaws Woollcott found that the play ''weaves a most potent spell.'' Charles Gilpin was singled out for praise, and Woollcott concluded that the play ''reinforces the impression that for strength and originality [O'Neill] has no rival among the American writers for the stage.''

New York Tribune critic Heywood Broun agreed with Woollcott, calling *The Emperor Jones* ''just about the most interesting play which has yet come from the most promising playwright in America'' and reiterated the high praise for Gilpin's performance. Broun also complained about the scene changes: ''unfortunately, production in the tiny Provincetown Theatre is difficult and the waits between these scenes are often several minutes in length. Each wait is a vulture which preys upon the attention. With the beginning of each new scene, contact must again be established and all this unquestionably hurts.''

Other critics concured—like Kenneth Macgowan of the *New York Globe,* Maida Castellun of the *New York Call,* and Stephen Rathbun of the *New York Sun*—and by the end of December the play was on Broadway in a series of special matinees at the Selwyn Theatre. There, the critics generally repeated their praise. Woollcott proclaimed that in the larger and better equipped space the play was still ''exciting and terrifying'' and ''quite as astonishing,'' with Gilpin continuing to be ''amazing and unforgettable.'' The move ''uptown'' seemed to improve the production because better facilities eliminated the long waits between scenes. Later, the production shifted to the Princess Theatre, where it enjoyed an unusually long and successful run followed by a two-year national road tour featuring Gilpin and numerous international productions. Paris, Berlin, London, Vienna, Stockholm, Buenos Aires, and Tokyo were some of the foreign cities it visited, and on the basis of *The Emperor Jones,* Eugene O'Neill was now the first American playwright with an international reputation.

In 1924 the play was revived at the Provincetown Playhouse, but this time O'Neill chose newcomer Paul Robeson to play the role of Brutus Jones. During the original run, O'Neill had become impatient with Gilpin's drinking during performances and with Gilpin's habit of changing the play's dialogue. Gilpin played Brutus Jones in two more 1926 revivals of the play, but he never recovered his commanding ownership of the role. After the 1924 revival, Robeson went on to play the role in London and also in the 1933 film version. Robeson's portrayal was praised almost as much as Gilpin's, especially because of Robeson's physical stature and deep bass voice, but contemporary observers and even O'Neill himself finally admitted that Gilpin's portrayal of Jones was more authentic and powerful. Still, in part because of Robeson's appearance in the enduring film version, Robeson's portrayal has come to be the one most closely associated with the role.

Ironically, the tremendous success of *The Emperor Jones* was both the best and the worst thing to happen to the Provincetown Players. Overnight they went from an experimental theatre struggling on a small budget to a profitable venture that could pay all its actors a salary. But they divided over the issue of moving *The Emperor Jones* to Broadway. Originated in 1915 as an informal group dedicated

to art rather than commerce, some of the actors and managers wanted to exploit the commercial success initiated by O'Neill's play while others wanted to retreat from it in order to stay small, amateurish, experimental, and faithful to their original vision.

When the production finally moved uptown, the original cast and most of the group's working actors went with it, leaving a depleted crew to continue the season downtown. Rising expenses and personal jealousies eventually destroyed the small group. Their leader, George Cram (Jig) Cook, finally declared a year's moratorium on productions, left for Greece, and died in 1924 after bitterly severing ties with his theatre. A new organization was formed in 1923, led by O'Neill, but the idealistic and non-commercial spirit of the original Provincetown Players was gone forever.

Today, *The Emperor Jones* is still recognized as one of O'Neill's finest plays. In 1921 it was considered ''a splendid achievement, easily the author's finest work to date,'' as O'Neill's biographer Sheaffer put it. However, O'Neill's major triumphs with autobiographical materials near the end of his life led to powerful full-length plays like *The Iceman Cometh* (1946) and *Long Day's Journey into Night* (1956) that have put O'Neill's early one-act play in a subordinate position.

CRITICISM

Terry R. Nienhuis
Nienhuis is a Ph.D. specializing in modern and contemporary drama. In this essay he discusses the theatrical elements in O'Neill's The Emperor Jones.

The critical enthusiasm for O'Neill's drama has always been tempered by a recognition that he was limited as a writer. As his foremost biographer, Louis Sheaffer, put it in *O'Neill: Son and Playwright,* ''of all the major playwrights, O'Neill is, with little doubt, the most uneven. During the larger part of his career ... he kept producing, almost alternately, good plays and bad.'' And even O'Neill's good plays sometimes seem to display his major faults: he is often melodramatic, clumsy and heavy-handed with dialogue, unpoetic in his use of language, obsessed with regional and ethnic dialects, verbose, unsubtle, labored, and simplistic.

But there is one area where O'Neill's skills are seldom questioned—he had an uncommon ability to

A 1933 production featuring Paul Robeson as the Emperor Brutus Jones, the second notable actor—following Charles Gilpin—to essay the role

create compelling theatrical effects. He was, as Croswell Bowen described it in *The Curse of the Misbegotten,* "the most theatrical playwright of his time." And *The Emperor Jones* is perhaps the clearest example of O'Neill's unequivocal strength as a "theatrical" playwright.

It is often said that O'Neill's dramas "play" better than they "read," that what sometimes appears lifeless and labored on the page often becomes quite vibrant in a theatrical performance. At their best, O'Neill's plays create an effective blueprint for his theatrical collaborators: actors, directors, set,

sound, light, and costume designers take his script and help transform the page into a thrilling theatrical experience.

In his introduction to *O'Neill: A Collection of Critical Essays,* the venerable scholar John Gassner expressed this commonly held appraisal of O'Neill. He said that O'Neill is "disproportionately effective on the stage and disappointing in print." As Gassner said of O'Neill, however:

> He acquired a strong aptitude for dramatic writing and theatrical effect. He was able to compensate for his defects as a writer with the power of his stage action;

WHAT DO I READ NEXT?

- The German silent film *The Cabinet of Dr. Caligari* (1919) is one of the classic examples of expressionistic technique in film. Odd angles of vision, distorted sets, and hypnotic acting enhance the dream-like portrayal of insanity in this film.

- *The Hairy Ape* (1922) is O'Neill's most completely expressionistic play. Set initially on an ocean liner and focusing on the social snub felt by the brutish, below-deck worker, Yank, the play creates a nightmare atmosphere as Yank searches for a place where he can ''belong.''

- *All God's Chillun Got Wings* (1924) is another of O'Neill's plays dealing with the black experience. The play caused a tremendous controversy because of the interracial kissing of a hand and the portrayal of an interracial marriage.

- In the history of theatre, *A Raisin in the Sun* (1959) by Lorraine Hansberry is one of the most famous and commercially successful dramas focusing on black life. A poignant protest against racial injustice, the play features a black family and its attempt to rise into the middle class.

- *Funnyhouse of a Negro* (1962) by Adrienne Kennedy is a one-act play that portrays the disturbed mind of a mulatto woman named Sarah as she contemplates suicide. Surreal, poetic, and mythic in its presentation, the play shows Sarah hallucinating and shifting between various alter egos—black and white, male and female—as she resists her Negro identity.

- *The Sound and the Fury* (1929), a novel by William Faulkner, tells a story from the point of view of four different characters, revealing the mental process of each narrator along the way. One of the speakers is a mentally deficient young man named Benjamin.

- *Expressionism* (1970), by John Willett, is a thorough examination of Expressionism in many different areas, including painting, drama, poetry, and film.

---

had he elected to write novels and been forced to rely on description and narration rather than dramatization and visualization, he might have proved a second-rate author. . . . Dramatic action, pictorial composition, and sound-effects such as the beating of the tom-toms in *The Emperor Jones* concealed, or minimized his literary infelicities, and sustained his intense—often, indeed, over-intense—dramatic intentions.

Where, then, in *The Emperor Jones* do we see this aptitude for theatrical effect? Perhaps it is most obvious in the simple idea of indicating Jones's emotional state through the beating of the drum. As Doris Falk wrote in *Eugene O'Neill and the Tragic Tension,* ''Nowhere in O'Neill's work is his theatrical skill more evident than in Jones's flight through the jungle to the drumbeat which begins at normal pulse rhythm, growing faster and faster, louder and louder.'' In fact, the drumbeat was one of the first ideas that led O'Neill to write *The Emperor Jones.* In a 1924 interview with the *New York World*

O'Neill said, ''One day I was reading of the religious feasts in the Congo and the uses to which the drum is put there; how it starts at a normal pulse-beat and is slowly intensified until the heart-beat of every one present corresponds to the frenzied beat of the drum. There was an idea and an experiment. How would this sort of thing work on an audience in a theatre?''

In Scene I, the sound of the drumbeat begins just as Jones boasts to Smithers that he is not afraid. The initial sound is faint but steady, beating ''at a rate exactly corresponding to normal pulse-beat—72 to the minute.'' As the drumbeat continues ''at a gradually accelerating rate from this point uninterruptedly to the very end of the play,'' it represents Jones's state of mind. But the art of the drumbeat is even more complex. It begins literally as a war drum and always remains so, even after the sound comes

---

to represent Jones's increasing anxiety. But in Scene VI, the sound also becomes the cadence for the moaning black slaves being carried by ship to America. Ultimately, the sound becomes as well the heartbeat of the audience itself as they get caught up in the action. At the end of each scene in the written text, O'Neill reminds the reader that the drumbeat is intensifying. In a theatrical production no audience member would have to be reminded, but adept readers have to be more imaginative to hear the constant drum and follow its complex theatrical effects.

The next most powerful theatrical element is perhaps light, for the shifting of light during the play is not only varied and complex but highly indicative of Jones's changing frame of mind. The play begins in late-afternoon light, still bright but on the edge of sunset, communicating heat and languor. As the play progresses, varieties of light become more and more oppressive for Jones. A "wall of darkness" greets him at the forest's edge in Scene II, and a "barely perceptible, suffused eerie glow" of moonlight envelops him as he encounters Jeff in Scene III. A "veil of bluish mist" colors the river in the final scene with the witch doctor and crocodile. In every scene the light is changing, reflecting Jones's mental state and providing the theatre audience with an immediately perceptible visual experience that the reader of the play must try to imagine. But as challenging as O'Neill's script is to the reader, it is even more so for the lighting designer. In Scene IV, for example, O'Neill specifies that "the road glimmers ghastly and unreal" in the moonlight, "as if the forest had stood aside momentarily to let the road pass through and accomplish its veiled purpose. This done, the forest will fold in upon itself again and the road will be no more." This light cue and set design would be more appropriate for a film project than for a stage designer!

Working closely with the theatre's lighting designer, then, is the set designer, who must create throne room and forest environments that complement the nightmarish quality of the play's light. The throne room is spacious and speciously elegant with its high ceilings, white walls, white floor, and garishly red throne. With the distant hills in the background, the white and spacious throne room contrasts with the dark forest environment that will gradually enclose Jones in ever smaller spaces. When he crouches in Scene VI in a tiny space that becomes the galley of a slave ship, Jones has retreated to an almost womb-like environment, and

> **"THERE IS ONE AREA WHERE O'NEILL'S SKILLS ARE SELDOM QUESTIONED—HE HAD AN UNCOMMON ABILITY TO CREATE COMPELLING THEATRICAL EFFECTS"**

Scenes IV and V both end with the walls of the forest once again folding in on him.

Given the importance of the set in *The Emperor Jones,* it is ironic that the play was first produced in a tiny Off-Broadway theatre whose budget could not accommodate elaborate scene design. But George Cram (Jig) Cook, the leader of the Provincetown Players and the director of the original production, saw immediately that the staging would require something special to capture its atmospheric qualities. As Ronald Wainscott put it in *Staging O'Neill,* "Cook's problem was finding a way to present O'Neill's sweeping nightmare on a stage the size of an ordinary living room." Cook insisted that an elaborate "dome" or cyclorama be built on stage to give the effect of great distances. He had seen such domes in small European theatres, and working with plaster, concrete, and iron, he created a sky against which hanging cloth and canvas could represent the forest. When light was bounced off the dome's textured surface, it gave an illusion of infinity.

Arthur and Barbara Gelb reported in their biography, *O'Neill,* that "viewers seated three feet from the stage had the illusion of vast distance; an actor could stretch his hand to within inches of its plaster surface and still seem to be far away from it." But Cook had to construct the dome over the protests of the other members of the theatre group because in building it he had to spend the theatre's entire budget on its first play of the season. According to Helen Deutsch and Stella Hanau, authors of *The Provincetown: A Story of the Theatre,* "Cook left just $6.40 in the treasury, drained the last measure of strength from his workers, and sacrificed eight feet of very limited floor space of the stage to build the first dome in New York." However, the dome was spectacularly successful and the visual effect one of the sources of the play's tremendous success.

Last, but certainly not least, the effects of the play's costume design have an enormous impact on a theatre audience. When Jones first appears, he is dressed in an outlandish military uniform that reflects his tenuous standing as emperor. As he bolts through the forest, pieces of this uniform are gradually torn away and then discarded until he is left in the last scene in a loincloth, and the primitive witch doctor now has, ironically, all the sartorial accouterments of high status. Timo Tiusanen speculated in *O'Neill's Scenic Images* that O'Neill might have specified Jones's light blue uniform as a way of further indicating Jones's disorientation. The uniform, he says, would fit well with the scarlet and white throne room but clash and be "out of harmony" with the dark green forest. "It is possible that O'Neill knew the physical qualities of light well enough to choose light blue for Jones, a color that remains visible on a relatively dark stage where green trees are turned into a menacing darkness."

Other examples of "theatrical" elements abound in the play. In an adept production, the "Little Formless Fears" of Scene II are almost spooky in their unearthly quality, moving noiselessly "but with deliberate, painful effort, striving to raise themselves on end, failing and sinking prone again." Their mocking laughter "like a rustling of leaves" contrast sharply with the loud report of Jones's gunshot, and those gunshots echo against the castanet-like clicking of Jeff's dice in Scene III and the silence of the guard's whip and the convicts' picks and shovels in Scene IV. The disappearance of the various hallucinations is a difficult visual effect to achieve on stage, but it gives a dream-like quality to the play. The film technology in 1933 was obviously not sufficient to make the hallucinations and their disappearance even the slightest bit convincing or powerful, but the technology of contemporary stage and (especially) film could make the hallucinations appear and disappear effectively.

Taken together, these theatrical effects make *The Emperor Jones* "a striking series of scenic images," and O'Neill's "early masterpiece," according to Tiusanen. But it is the theatrical elements working all together that creates the impact on an audience in a theatre. As Tiusanen asserted, "It is not the tom-tom, striking as this repetitious sound effect is; it is not the presence of the visions as such. It is the fusion of the scenic means employed; it is the interaction of the scenic images . . . the abundance of imaginatively used scenic means of expression within the space of thirty-odd pages or about an hour and a half of acting time." Croswell

Bowen summed up *The Emperor Jones* in *The Curse of the Misbegotten* by saying, "Although not the best play that Eugene O'Neill ever wrote, it is in many ways the most theatrical—the most theatrical play by the most theatrical playwright of his time."

Source: Terry R. Nienhuis, for *Drama for Students,* Gale, 1999.

Robert Brustein

Brustein is one of the most respected theatre critics of the late-twentieth century. In this review of a 1998 revival production of The Emperor Jones, *the critic offers a mixed appraisal of the work, citing troubles with both O'Neill's original script and liberties this new production has taken with the casting of the title character, Brutus Jones.*

The other O'Neill, the writer pursuing transcendence rather than domesticity, is also being represented on the New York stage these days, in a production of *The Emperor Jones* by the Wooster Group. This enterprising experimental troupe has already flexed its O'Neill muscles earlier this season with a powerful version of *The Hairy Ape. The Emperor Jones* is a reworking of a production that it first presented in 1993.

This relatively early work, written in the same rush of inspiration that produced *The Hairy Ape* and *Anna Christie,* would seem to be virtually unplayable today, owing to its clumsy effort to render the black idiom. Look at this typical passage: "Think dese ign'rent bush niggers dat ain't even got brains enuff to know deir own names even can catch Brutus Jones? Huh, I s'pects not! Not on yo' life." Or even worse, when Jones is preparing to flee: "Feet do yo' duty!" Perhaps recognizing that O'Neill's tin ear made almost all of his language sound stereotypical (Smitty's Cockney dialect, even in the mouth of the superb actor Willem Dafoe, is equally clumsy), the Wooster Group meets this problem head on. Brutus Jones, a role once played by the majestic Paul Robeson, is performed not by a black actor but by a white person in black face, and a woman at that (Kate Valk). Rather than normalize Jones's speech, Valk chooses to exaggerate the already exaggerated dialect into minstrel-show patter.

This is inviting trouble; but then so is the very act of producing the play. The only notes in the Wooster Group program are some generous comments from W.E.B. DuBois, defending O'Neill against those "preordained and self-appointed" judges of how black people should be represented on stage, those who would "destroy art, religion and good common sense in an effort to make everything that is said or shown propaganda for their ideas.'' DuBois believed that O'Neill in *The Emperor Jones* was trying to break through the defensive shells that prevent black people from being represented truthfully in the theater. Today, when even such black artists as Kara Walker and Robert Colescott are being attacked for creating black stereotypes, O'Neill's early effort at opening the doors of perception looks all the more brave and prescient.

As written, *The Emperor Jones* is a trip into the heart of darkness by an American black man who has persuaded himself that his Western reason and intelligence are protections against the voodoo spells of his native antagonists. He proves to be wrong. This former Pullman car porter and ex-convict is conquered less by external enemies than by his own terrors. Having set himself up as Emperor of a West Indian island and looted all its treasure, Jones has invented the myth that he can only be killed by a silver bullet. He eventually comes to believe the myth, too. Both the emperor Caesar and the assassin Brutus inhabit the same breast. In Trilling's words, Jones ''goes backwards through social fears to very fear itself, the fear of the universe which lies in primitive religion.'' This is a great theme. O'Neill never lacked great themes. He lacked only the art with which to express them.

Once again the Wooster Group, under its visionary director Elizabeth LeCompte, supplies that art by distracting attention from the play and the dialogue to the theatrical medium itself. The stage is bare except for a white linoleum floor, decorated with three television screens and, for one blinding moment, three bright headlights. While the screens register ghost images, Valk and Dafoe engage each other, both displaying great vocal range and variety, sometimes as characters in O'Neill, sometimes as samurai warriors and dancers in a Kabuki drama. Two prop masters solemnly hand them their properties. Each actor carries a microphone, which also has a prop function (a walking stick for Jones, a bat for Smitty). Valk sits in a high chair on wheels, rolling her eyes and roaring her lines through a reddened mouth, a bit like Hamm in Beckett's *Endgame*. The mikes and the music (often raucous rock) are set at a high decibel level.

Those who emerge from the theater without a headache can testify to a penetrating, if painful, encounter with the play. The Wooster Group's deconstructing of classic American drama can some-

> THE EMPEROR JONES IS A TRIP INTO THE HEART OF DARKNESS BY AN AMERICAN BLACK MAN WHO HAS PERSUADED HIMSELF THAT HIS WESTERN REASON AND INTELLIGENCE ARE PROTECTIONS AGAINST THE VOODOO SPELLS OF HIS NATIVE ANTAGONISTS''

times come perilously close to desecrating it. But when successful, such approaches can also open up new avenues of understanding. ''O'Neill's techniques,'' wrote Trilling, ''like those of any sincere artist, are not fortuitous—they are the result of an attempt to say things which the accepted techniques cannot express.'' The same might be said for the Wooster Group.

Source: Robert Brustein, ''The Two O'Neills'' in the *New Republic,* Vol. 218, no. 17, April 27, 1998, p. 28.

John Shand

In this review of an early production starring Paul Robeson as Brutus Jones, Shand offers a positive appraisal of The Emperor Jones, *despite some reservations that O'Neill was over-ambitious in his themes.*

Eugene O'Neill, the American dramatist, comes to Europe with a great reputation. Genius, we hear, is not too high a term for him. So that on going to see a new play of his some of us expect to see something ''Diff'rent'' from the usual. *The Emperor Jones,* produced last week at the Ambassadors, at first seems unconventional in form; and though few would argue that constructional novelty is any criterion of future fame, praise must always be given to any fresh attempt to loosen the girths of modern drama. In my opinion, the modern technique is too tight. The acquisition by any less vigorous mind than an Ibsen's of the highly specialised technicalities necessary for the construction of a modern play, is apt to produce a clever juggler rather than an artist. But, remembering always the exception, it is also a general rule that the genius in any art does not invent new forms, but uses to their full extent the forms moulded by others. The fact, then (I quote Mr. C. E. Bechhofer's preface to *Emperor Jones*) that "for years dramatists have been attempting to find a new kind of play, something that would pass the limits of contemporary drama," and that "in *The Emperor Jones* O'Neill may be said to have solved this problem," is no evidence of genius in the author, even if it be true. But, to put aside the feeling that G. Bernard Shaw, not to mention the Expressionists, may also be said to have solved this problem, it may be well to examine whether O'Neill is quite so original as some would have us believe.

Readers may remember that a few years ago the Everyman Theatre gave us some of this author's one-act plays, and a full play, *Diff'rent.* Afterwards, at a West End theatre, *Anna Christie* was produced. I should like to point out that O'Neill has written about a dozen one-act plays. Now this is very significant if we take in conjunction the fact (which is obvious to all who have seen or read *Diff'rent*) that this play is really two one-act plays divided by an interval of thirty years; and that in *Anna Christie,* which is in four acts, there is a decided declension of interest after the first act. After saying this, and after seeing *The Emperor Jones,* I am prepared to suggest that O'Neill is strictly a one-act playwright, and probably has not enough creative impetus to carry him the length of a full play. Of course, there is nothing derogatory to O'Neill in saying this. We cannot all be major artists. We cannot all be Shakespeares and Ibsens. The perfect painter of miniatures is no less to be admired than he who fills a mighty canvas with his genius. The miniaturist we do not admire is only he who, despising the real talent he possesses, endeavours to use a larger brush. In all the arts the same rules apply, and the same results obtain when they are forgotten. The perfect short story writer is rarely the great novelist as well. Just so, the one-act playwright may attain perfection in his own medium even while he fails in each attempt to write a full-length play. And he fails, as all like him must fail, because he is fluttering at the bars of his own talent, attempting to win a freedom that he will never be able to use. How many artists have been spoilt because they have tried, or have been persuaded that they ought to try, to do "important" work? It will be a pity if O'Neill is spoilt in this way, for he has an undoubted talent for the short piece; and if he does not, perhaps cannot, make his characters very significant, he is certainly a master of emotional effect, even if the emotions he plays upon are the very crudest.

With the suggestion in mind that this author's proper medium is the one-act play, let us examine *The Emperor Jones.* The action takes place on an island in the West Indies. Brutus Jones, an unusually intelligent and self-reliant negro of tall and powerful build, has made himself "Emperor" over the "trash" niggers. For years he had been in the States. Owing to a quarrel in which he killed his negro opponent, Jones had been given a twenty years' sentence; but he had escaped, after killing his warder, and had fled to this island. His personality and intelligence have enabled him to dominate the other negroes. As "Emperor," he has ground them down with taxes and appropriated the money. But he realises that they will sometime rise against him, and he has made all arrangements for a hurried departure.

The scene opens in a spacious audience chamber, bare of all furniture except a bright scarlet wooden throne. Through archways can be seen an unclouded sky of intense blue. This setting is very simple and very good. After an unnecessary scene between a negress and a white-livered, shiftless, aitchless Cockney trader who acts as chorus to the play, Emperor Jones appears. There follows a well-written scene of great interest. As the huge negro talks to the comic and sickly representative of Europe, we hear the necessary antecedent facts at the same time as we learn to appreciate the vigour of the negro. He boasts and swaggers, but O'Neill makes us believe that he has something to boast about. The trader tells Jones that his game is up, that the rebellion has started. Jones, incredulous, clangs the attendance bell. No one comes. After a moment of anger he accepts the situation, and decides "to resign de job of Emperor right dis minute." It is late afternoon, and a tropical sun burns hotly. He will have to reach the edge of the great forest by running over the plain, before evening. After resting, and eating the food he has buried there in readiness, he is going to run all night through the forest to the coast. And as he boasts to the Cockney of his cunning foresight, there comes from the distant hills the low vibrant throb of the tom-tom. It is the "trash" niggers weaving spells to aid them in their attack. It brings a moment's breath of fear to the superstitious negro in Jones. But he waves the fear away, and starts his flight from the palace, grandiloquently, through "the front door."

The rest of the play consists of seven very short scenes, in which we see Jones in various parts of the forest. Physically exhausted by hunger, mentally harassed by fear of the ghostly visions which appear every time he rests, he loses his way. Each vision disappears when he shoots, but every time be shoots he remembers that he has only six bullets and that he is also indicating his position. Throughout these scenes sounds the gradually accelerating thump of the tom-tom, which also quickens at each ghostly appearance, giving us out loud, as it were, the negro's heart-beats quickened by fear. The last scene is at the edge of the forest. Some natives are there, one frantically beating the tom-tom, the others armed with rifles. The Cockney is also there. ''Ain't yer goin' in an' 'unt 'im in the woods?'' he asks. ''We cotch him,'' answers the chief. There is a sound of snapping twigs. The natives shoot. The dead body of Brutus Jones is dragged in. By losing his way he had run in a circle, and he comes out of the forest where he went in.

All this reads much better than it acts. Indeed, the scenes in the wood are scarcely dramatic, and being almost repetitions of each other certainly do not create a crescendo of interest. Besides, ghosts and supernatural visions are hardly ever successful in the theatre. Shakespeare is the only dramatist who has dared to bring on a ghost three times in one play. He managed, it is true, to make the third visitation more effective than the first, but there are few dramatists who could do likewise. The first act of *The Emperor Jones* is good, and could almost stand by itself. The rest of the play is a monologue in a series of anticlimaxes. The author has found a good theme; but the play will never be a famous one because there are so many plays with good ideas spoilt by wrong treatment. It is worth seeing, if only for the first act; but mainly you ought to see it because of Mr. Paul Robeson in the leading part. I have nothing but admiration for his performance. Where the author was good he was magnificent. He failed, I think, only in those pitfalls of the author's which only a personality of the greatest magnetism could have o'erleaped. Mr. Robeson's voice, intelligence, physique, and sense of the stage immediately made me want to see him in *Othello*.

Of those readers who see this play many, I hope, will agree that the theory that O'Neill is a one-act dramatist holds good in *Emperor Jones* as in *Diff'rent*. And that in any case a series of monologues on a theme of fear hardly passes beyond the limits of contemporary drama. What are most plays written round a ''star'' actor but monologues on that well-known theme, the capabilities of that particular ''star''? But it is unfortunate for the theory that O'Neill is a good one-act dramatist that the curtain-raiser should have been *The Long Voyage Home*.

> O'NEILL IS STRICTLY A ONE-ACT PLAYWRIGHT, AND PROBABLY HAS NOT ENOUGH CREATIVE IMPETUS TO CARRY HIM THE LENGTH OF A FULL PLAY''

For in this piece is exposed to view the simple and conventional mind of the author, who at first sight surprises us by the unusualness of his characters, and his literal transcription of their language, but who is soon found to be developing them so conventionally that we know exactly what they will do and say next. So that although he ''piles on the agony,'' letting us know that the quiet, simple sailor about to be drugged, robbed, and put on to an outgoing ship, has all the virtues, that he has been saving up for two years to buy a farm, and that his aged mother is waiting for him, we are not very interested in him, and watch him being drugged, robbed and carried off without emotion. As in other plays and books of this kind, to use Wilde's perfect phrase: it is the suspense of the author which becomes unbearable.

Source: John Shand, review of *The Emperor Jones* in the *New Statesman*, Vol. XXV, no. 647, September 19, 1925, pp. 628–29.

SOURCES

Bowen, Croswell. *The Curse of the Misbegotten*, McGraw-Hill, 1959, p. 132.

Broun, Heywood. Review of *The Emperor Jones* in the *New York Tribune*, November 4, 1920, reprinted in *O'Neill and His Plays: Four Decades of Criticism*, edited by Oscar Cargill, New York University Press, 1961, pp. 144-46.

Falk, Doris V. *Eugene O'Neill and the Tragic Tension*, Rutgers University Press, 1958, pp. 67-68.

Gassner, John. ''Introduction'' in *O'Neill: A Collection of Critical Essays*, edited by John Gassner, Prentice-Hall, 1964, pp. 2, 4.

Gelb, Arthur, and Barbara Gelb. *O'Neill*, Harper, 1960, p. 444.

O'Neill, Eugene. Interview with Charles P. Sweeney in the *New York World*, November 9, 1924, p. 5M, reprinted in

Conversations with Eugene O'Neill, edited by Mark W. Estrin, University Press of Mississippi, 1990, pp. 57-58.

Tiusanen, Timo. *O'Neill's Scenic Images,* Princeton, 1968, pp. 104, 106, 338.

Woollcott, Alexander. "The Emperor Jones" in the *New York Times,* December 28, 1920, sec. 9, p. 1.

Woollcott, Alexander. "The New O'Neill Play" in the *New York Times,* November 7, 1920, sec 1, p. 1.

FURTHER READING

Allen, Frederick Lewis. *Only Yesterday: An Informal History of the Nineteen-Twenties,* Blue Ribbon Books, 1931.
    One of the classic accounts of the "roaring twenties," this very readable book discusses everything from daily life to the great stock market crash in 1929.

Deutsch, Helen, and Hanau, Stella. *The Provincetown: A Story of the Theatre,* Farrar and Rinehart, 1931.
    A history of the Provincetown Players with a chapter focusing on the production of *The Emperor Jones.* Appendices include reproductions of the company's theatre programs from 1916 to 1929.

Huggins, Nathan. *Harlem Renaissance,* Oxford University Press, 1971.
    A basic treatment of this important movement in American literary history.

Miller, Jordan Y. *Eugene O'Neill and the American Critic: A Bibliographical Checklist,* Archon Books, 1973.
    A reference book that lists detailed publication and production data for all of O'Neill's plays along with an annotated list of contemporary reviews of these productions.

Pfister, Joel. *Staging Depth: Eugene O'Neill and the Politics of Psychological Discourse,* University of North Carolina Press, 1995.
    Despite its foreboding title, a very readable book with an unusually detailed multi-disciplinary slant on O'Neill and the times in which he wrote.

Ranald, Margaret Loftus. *The Eugene O'Neill Companion,* Greenwood Press, 1984.
    This encyclopedia dedicated to O'Neill has entries for plays, characters, and important individuals and organizations in O'Neill's life and much more. Contains several valuable appendices.

Sheaffer, Louis. *O'Neill: Son and Playwright,* Paragon House, 1968, and *O'Neill: Son and Artist,* Little, Brown, 1973.
    These two-volumes constitute the best of the many biographies of O'Neill.

Turnqvist, Egil. *A Drama of Souls: Studies in O'Neill's Super-naturalistic Technique,* Yale, 1969.
    A very close reading of the plays, giving special attention to theatrical effects.

Wainscott, Ronald H. *Staging O'Neill,* Yale, 1988.
    Includes an unusually detailed chapter focusing on the theatrical elements of *The Emperor Jones.*

Hay Fever

NOEL COWARD

1925

Noel Coward's plays epitomize the sophisticated wit of the era between the two world wars, and *Hay Fever,* a comedy of manners about a family whose theatrical excesses torment a group of unsuspecting visitors, epitomizes the Coward play. Inspired by a weekend he spent at the house of the actor Laurette Taylor, Coward wrote the play in just three days. Upon its 1925 London debut on August 6, it won praise from both audiences and critics. Considered by many to be cleverly constructed, wittily written, slightly cynical, and undeniably entertaining, the work contains all the elements that would help establish Coward's reputation as a playwright.

Hay Fever is set in the hall of the Bliss family home. The eccentric Blisses—Judith, a recently retired stage actress, David, a self-absorbed novelist, and their two equally unconventional children—live in a world where reality slides easily into fiction. Upon entering this world, the unfortunate weekend guests—a proper diplomat, a shy flapper, an athletic boxer, and a fashionable sophisticate—are repeatedly thrown into melodramatic scenes wherein their hosts profess emotions and react to situations that do not really exist. The resulting comedic chaos ends only when the tortured visitors tip-toe out the door.

Designed to showcase the larger-than-life personalities of celebrated actors (many of whom were close friends of the playwright), *Hay Fever,* as Coward himself observed in the introduction to the

first volume of *Play Parade,* has ''no plot at all and remarkably little action. Its general effectiveness therefore depends on expert technique from each and every member of the cast.'' The play's humor is provided by context. When the show was revived in 1964, Coward remarked upon how the biggest laughs ''occur on such lines as 'Go on,' 'No there isn't, is there?' and 'This haddock's disgusting.' . . . the sort of lines . . . [that] have to be impeccably delivered.'' Although Coward claimed that he intended only to amuse and cared little about posterity, he might have been pleased that the simple dialogue in *Hay Fever* would continue to be well-delivered and well-received half a century after it was written.

AUTHOR BIOGRAPHY

Noel Peirce Coward—the celebrated actor, composer, and playwright once described as the person who ''invented the '20s''—was born on December 16, 1899, in Teddington-on-Thames, Middlesex, England, to Arthur Sabin and Violet Agnes (Veitch) Coward. His father worked as both a clerk for a music publishing company and a piano salesman. Young Noel attended Chapel Royal School in Clapham but learned his most vocational lessons while studying acting with Sir Charles Hawtrey's drama company. Working with this theater group, he developed comic timing and his trademark casual demeanor. Encouraged by his mother, Coward made his first professional theatrical appearance when he was only twelve. He continued to act in London throughout his teens, while also making both his first attempts at playwriting and his film debut in director D. W. Griffith's 1917 feature *Hearts of the World.*

Coward's first play was produced in 1920; three more of his compositions went on the stage in 1922. *The Young Idea* (1922), although deemed a pale imitation of playwright George Bernard Shaw's style, showed signs of the unique humor found in Coward's later work. Already prolific, Coward produced four more plays before writing *Hay Fever* in the three days following his first trip to the United States in the fall of 1924. He wrote seventeen more plays in the next decade, often acting in, directing, producing, and composing music for them as well. During this period he wrote what is widely considered his best work, the comedy *Private Lives* (1930), in which he starred with actress Gertrude Lawrence.

Lawrence was only one of the theater luminaries—including Laurence Olivier, Vivien Leigh, John Gielgud, Claudette Colbert, Mary Martin, Tallulah Bankhead, and Michael Redgrave—with whom Coward formed close friendships. Like these celebrities, the playwright cultivated a debonair public persona. He embodied—both on stage and off—the image of the suave, cynical gentleman who appears in evening dress, a cigarette in hand, ready to offer witty cocktail party repartee.

Among his sophisticated theatrical companions it was an ''open secret'' that Coward was a homosexual, but he never came out publicly. During most of his lifetime the British censors did not allow works containing homosexual themes to appear on stage, and Coward's one play which depicted gay characters, *Semi-monde,* although written in 1926, did not get produced until 1977.

After 1935, Coward wrote twenty more plays, including the hit *Design for Living* (1933) and his biggest box office success *Blithe Spirit* (1941), a comedy of manners that ran for two thousand performances in London and won the New York Drama Critics Circle Award for Best Foreign Play in 1942. After World War II public tastes changed, and Coward's work received less critical attention. Yet, his reputation was well established, and he continued to express his talents in diverse ways: publishing fiction, acting in films, and continuing to write songs, movie scripts, and plays. In 1970, he was honored with a knighthood as well as a special Antionette (Tony) Perry Award. Three years later, on March 26, 1973, he died of a fatal heart attack in Blue Harbor, Jamaica.

PLOT SUMMARY

Act I

When the curtain rises, the two adult children of the Bliss household are relaxing in the hall (main living room) of the Bliss family country home. The siblings' conversation reveals that the daughter, Sorel, wishes their family were more normal. She expresses a desire to change, but her brother, Simon, says it is fine to be different. They both observe that their mother, who has recently retired from a successful acting career, has been very restless. They speculate that she might return to the theater. Sorel also announces that she has invited a diplomatist named Richard Greatham down for the weekend.

Their mother, Judith, enters from the garden and says she hopes the housekeeper Clara has prepared the Japanese Room for her guest. The ensuing dialogue reveals that each family member has invited someone for the weekend and they all expected their guests to sleep in that same room. Irritated, each criticizes the others' prospective visitors. David—the father and Judith's husband—enters the room in the midst of this argument. He has come down from his study where he has been writing his latest novel. He casually tells everyone that he invited a young woman for the weekend to observe her behavior, and then heads back upstairs before anyone can say anything.

After David exits, Judith, Sorel, and Simon continue complaining about how awful the weekend is going to be. Soon, however, Judith announces that she has decided to return to the stage and revive one of her most successful plays, *Love's Whirlwind*. Recollecting favorite passages from this drama, she prompts the children to join her in acting out a scene that begins with the cue ''Is this a game?'' Their reenactment is interrupted when the doorbell rings.

Clara opens the door and lets in Sandy Tyrell, the athletic amateur boxer invited by Judith. The children go upstairs and Sandy and Judith's brief conversation reveals his infatuation with her. The doorbell rings again. This time, Clara admits Simon's guest, Myra Arundel, who greets Judith familiarly before Judith takes Sandy away, leaving the latest arrival to her own devices. Myra strolls around looking very much at home until Simon rushes in. He tries to kiss Myra, but she pushes him away. She continues to rebuff his advances as he expresses his adoration for her.

The bell rings once more, and Clara opens the door for Richard Greatham and Jackie Coryton. Richard asks for Sorel, and Clara goes in search of her. Simon immediately drags Myra outside leaving Richard and Jackie alone to make awkward small-talk until Sorel appears. She sends Jackie up to find David, then sits down with Richard, who expresses his admiration for her unconventionality while she offers similar praise of his propriety.

Clara enters with tea. Simon, Myra, David, and Jackie rejoin Richard and Sorel. The visitors all

Noel Coward

attempt to begin some polite conversation, but they keep starting sentences at the same time and eventually give up. The scene ends in dead silence.

Act II

After dinner that night all eight main characters are in the hall talking at once, trying to choose a game to play. They decide on ''Adverbs,'' which involves one person leaving the room while the rest choose an adverb. Then the person re-enters and tries to guess the word based on watching the others perform actions in the manner of that adverb. The shouted half-explanations of this enterprise confuse Jackie, but the Blisses begin the game anyway. Sorel goes out. The rest of the group argues over word selection. Richard proposes ''winsomely,'' David ''drearily,'' Judith ''saucily,'' and Myra—under her breath—''rudely.'' Jackie, who still does not understand the game, suggests ''appendicitis.''

Judith agrees with Richard that ''winsomely'' is best and calls Sorel back into the room. Judith performs the first action, handing a flower to Richard in a manner she considers winsome. Myra then attempts to do the next action but is criticized by Judith. They move on to Richard, but Judith stops him midway through because she does not think he is performing well either—and it turns out he had been acting out the wrong adverb. Finally, it is Jackie's turn but she refuses to do anything. Her shy protestations are so sweet and innocent, however, that Sorel guesses the word just as everyone starts yelling at each other. The game breaks up. Simon grabs Jackie's hand and pulls her out in the garden; Sorel drags Sandy into the library; and David takes Myra outside.

Left alone with Richard, Judith begins flirting, inducing him to lean forward and kiss her. She jumps back instantly and dramatically announces that David must be told everything. Confused, Richard listens to Judith go on about how heartbroken poor David will be that she is leaving him to be with her new love (the unwitting Richard). The diplomat tries to protest, but she sends him out into the garden, never letting him finish a sentence.

Judith then opens the library door and stands looking shocked as Sorel and Sandy emerge guiltily, suggesting they have been caught kissing. Switching roles, Judith now loudly laments what a fool she has been. Sorel initially tries to say that "it was nothing" but quickly gives up on this approach and begins playing along, claiming she and Sandy love each other. This allows Judith to nobly "give" Sandy to her daughter before exiting. Once her mother is gone, Sorel clarifies the situation for the befuddled young man, explaining that she knows they do not love each other but she had just said so because "one always plays up to mother in this house; it's sort of an unwritten law."

Sandy and Sorel exit while Myra and David enter talking about the plot of David's latest novel. As their conversation progresses, Myra confesses that she accepted the weekend invitation in order to meet David because she admires his books. David says that he writes bad novels and wonders if Myra has an ulterior motive in complimenting his work. She then expresses her affection for him, and he respond by asking first whether they should elope and then whether she wants him to make love to her. Offended, she pulls away but is drawn back when he takes her hand and says they can still "have a nice little intrigue." He grabs and kisses her; she resists but then gives in. At this moment, Judith appears and sees them. She immediately launches into the role of wronged wife. David starts out saying Judith is speaking nonsense, but then he begins to play his expected part. Interrupting Myra's protests, he says

he and Myra love each other and commends his wife's bravery in the difficult situation.

Just as David and Judith shake hands, Simon rushes in announcing excitedly that he and Jackie are engaged. This news brings Sorel and Simon out of the library and prompts Judith to shift roles again, now acting the part of the bereaved mother anticipating an empty nest. As Jackie tries to deny the engagement, Myra breaks in with a denunciation of the whole family's theatricality. Everyone talks at once as Richard enters and unsuspectingly asks, "Is this a game?" Recognizing the cue, Judith launches into the scene she and the children enacted earlier. Simon and Sorel catch on immediately and speak the appropriate lines. David starts laughing. The four visitors stand watching in absolute bewilderment.

Act III

Act III opens the following morning. A breakfast table has been set up in the hall and Sandy enters, sits and begins eating. He jumps at every sound, however, and when he hears someone approaching he runs into the library. Jackie then enters, takes some food, sits down, and starts to cry. Sandy comes out and the two have a conversation about how uncomfortable they were the night before and how crazy the Blisses are. When they hear people approaching, they both go into the library. Myra and Richard now enter and help themselves to breakfast. Their conversation echoes that of Sandy and Jackie, who subsequently emerge from the library. The entire group decides they are going to return to London. Sandy agrees to drive them in his car. They all go upstairs to collect their things

Judith comes down next, asks Clara for the papers and begins reading aloud the descriptions of herself in the gossip columns. Sorel and Simon enter soon thereafter, followed by David who wants to read them the last chapter of his novel. He begins by describing how his main character drives down one street in Paris to get to a particular plaza. Judith immediately interrupts to say he has the streets wrong and that the one he names does not go where he says it does. This sparks another family argument with everyone talking at once about what streets go where in Paris. As they continue to debate, the four visitors tip-toe down the stairs and out the door. The Blisses only notice their fleeing guests when they hear the door slam. Then after a momentary pause to comment on the guests' rude mode of departure, the Blisses return to their conversation. Judith makes the final statement of the play, announcing she will indeed return to the stage.

CHARACTERS

Myra Arundel

Well-dressed, confident, and sophisticated, Myra is invited to the Bliss house by her admirer Simon but coolly rebuffs his advances; her real motive in accepting the weekend invitation is to meet his novelist father, David. Before Myra even appears on stage, Simon's mother, Judith, describes her as a "self-conscious vampire" who "goes about using Sex as a shrimping net." So the audience is not surprised when Myra later begins a flirtatious conversation with David. Myra herself, however, is taken quite off-guard when David asks her directly, "Would you like me to make love to you?" and then refuses to believe that she is offended by the question, saying simply "You've been trying to make me—all the evening."

Although David will not play the game of subtle seduction in the typical manner that Myra expects, he does readily join in the game his wife instigates, pretending that they are ready to break up their marriage so he can be with Myra. Used to being the one who manipulates such situations, Myra is utterly frustrated by the way the entire family's odd behavior takes events out of her control. Towards the end of the play, she angrily denounces the Blisses in a statement which accurately sums up their way of life: "You haven't got one sincere or genuine feeling among the lot of you—you're artificial to the point of lunacy."

David Bliss

David, Judith's husband and Simon and Sorel's father, is an absent-minded writer, wrapped up in his latest book. Although his works—which have titles like *The Sinful Woman* and *Broken Reeds*—are popular, he admits that they are actually "very bad novels." Less melodramatic than his flamboyant wife, David nevertheless is equally self-involved and self-obsessed. He forgets he invited Jackie and, as she reports, rudely greets her by saying "Who the hell are you?" He behaves in a similarly unconventional way with Myra. At first bluntly calling her attempts to seduce him exactly what they are, he ruins the mood with his directness. Then, changing his attitude and willingly participating in the romantic "intrigue," he explains that he loves "to see things as they are first, and then pretend they're what they're not." He again demonstrates this inclination when he calls Judith's wronged wife routine "nonsense" initially, but then—after calling things "as they are"—goes on to "pretend

they're what they're not" by joining in the scene and acting as if he does love Myra. At the end of the play, his self-absorption is emphasized once more as he reads the last section of his new novel to the family and debates with them over the streets described in a certain passage, not noticing the departing guests.

Judith Bliss

Judith is David's wife and Simon and Sorel's mother. A well-known stage actress who has temporarily retired, she made her name in melodramatic plays with names like *Love's Whirlwind* and *The Bold Deceiver,* which she admits were not that good even though the public loved them. Bored with everyday life, she amuses herself by acting out exaggerated roles and theatrically misinterpreting ordinary situations. During the course of the play, she takes on the demeanor of the rural lady of the manor, the long-suffering mother, the glamorous star, the flirtatious coquette, the betrayed lover, and the wronged wife, among others. Vibrant and eccentric, she is unable to keep from slipping into dramatic personae constantly, and her family has learned to adapt to and play along with this tendency. She is also in the habit of bolstering her ego by inviting young male fans to the house and refuses to apologize for it, telling her daughter not to think that the younger woman has "the complete monopoly of any amorous adventure there may be about."

Judith's whims and inclinations dictate the action in many of the play's scenes, her dominant personality overshadowing those that are more quiet and conventional. Her every action supports her self-descriptive statement, "I won't stagnate as long as there's breath left in my body." Early on she tells her children, "I long for excitement and glamour," and the rest of the play shows her ability to create her own excitement when the world does not provide enough for her.

Simon Bliss

Simon is Judith and David's adult son. He first appears on stage looking disheveled and unwashed, and, like the rest of his family, he seems to care little about other people's opinions. In contrast to his sister, he has no desire to reform the Blisses' unconventional and often inconsiderate ways, remarking, "we see things differently, I suppose, and if people don't like it they must lump it." In typical Bliss fashion, Simon is given to extremes: expressing energetically his adoration for the worldly Myra one minute, then seducing the innocent Jackie the next.

MEDIA ADAPTATIONS

- A videorecording titled *Hay Fever: A High British Comedy* was produced by the George Washington University (Washington, DC) Department of Theatre and Dance in 1995. It is available on two VHS videocassettes running 110 minutes. This college production was directed by Nathan Garner and features the actors Carole Stover, John F. Degen, Maura Miller, Brian Coleman, Kristiana Knight, Alan Goy, Kerry Washington, Michael Laurino, and Rachel Flehinger.

- Another videorecorded production of *Hay Fever* is included on tape number seven of the Theater Department Productions 1989 VHS video series from Seton Hill College in Greensburg, Pennsylvania.

- A sound recording of a radio play adaption of *Hay Fever* featuring actors Peggy Ashcroft, Tony Britten, Millicent Martin, Julia Foster, and Maurice Denham is included in the 1988 British Broadcasting Corporation Enterprises audio collection entitled *A Noel Coward Double Bill.* These two analog cassettes run 180 minutes and

also contain a sound recording of *Private Lives.* The tapes were distributed in the United States by the Novato, California-based Mind's Eye Co.

- The Radio Yesteryear company of Sandy Hook, Connecticut, released a sound recording of *Hay Fever* featuring actors Everett Sloan and Ann Burr. First broadcast as a radio play on June 3, 1947, this audio version was released in 1986 as volume forty-six of the Radiobook series.

- Although *Hay Fever* has yet to be adapted into a feature film, at least seventeen of Coward's other plays and screenplays were made into movies between 1927 and 1987, including a 1946 British production of *Blithe Spirit* directed by David Lean, and a 1931 Hollywood version of *Private Lives* directed by Sidney Franklin and starring Norma Shearer and Robert Montgomery. Additionally, Coward acted in at least twelve films, including director Richard Quine's *Paris—When it Sizzles,* a 1931 feature starring Audrey Hepburn. A complete Coward filmography is available in the Internet Movie Database at http://us.imdb.com.

He shocks poor Jackie when he kisses her in the garden and then rushes into the house to announce their engagement, even though she has never agreed to marry him. He also willingly participates in his mother's theatrical scenes—both scripted and improvisational—just as his father and sister do. His own artistic inclinations tend toward drawing, and in the final act he brings a new sketch down to show the others.

Sorel Bliss

Sorel is Judith and David's adult daughter. She is the only member of the Bliss family who expresses any concern about their unorthodox behavior. At the start of the play she laments to her brother that they are all "so awfully bad-mannered" and "never attempt to look after people" and are essentially "abnormal," observations that will be clearly prov-

en true in the scenes to follow. Sorel, however, is "trying to be better," and so invites a man for the weekend whose perfectly proper behavior is the antithesis of the Blisses' wildly inappropriate actions.

Sorel's attempts at reform are only party successful, however, as the audience sees when she still regularly takes part in her mother's impromptu dramas. Although she does not truly have deep feelings for Sandy, she pretends she does so her mother can act the part of a betrayed lover who nobly gives away the man she loves. Sandy gets swept up in the moment and confesses his love for Sorel, but she clarifies the situation, telling him, "I was only playing up—one always plays up to mother in this house; it's sort of an unwritten law." This confession shows a change in Sorel's habits; as she tells Sandy further, "A month ago, I should have let you go on believing that, but now I can't—I'm bent on improving myself.'' Despite her attempts at self-improvement, Sorel remains very much a Bliss: eccentric and unconventional. At the end of the play she and her family are absorbed in their argument about the trivial details of David's novel, oblivious to the departure of the tormented weekend guests.

Clara

Described in the stage directions as ''a hot, round, untidy little woman,'' Clara is a long-suffering Bliss family employee. Originally Judith's dresser at the theater, she is now the over-taxed family housekeeper. Clara must deal with the imposition of four unexpected weekend guests all by herself because the maid is home sick with a toothache.

Jackie Coryton

Jackie is the ''perfectly sweet flapper'' David has invited for the weekend because ''she's an abject fool but a useful type'' and he wants ''to study her a little in domestic surroundings.'' Described in the stage directions as ''small and shingled, with an ingenuous manner,'' she is shy and ill at ease from the start. She feels awkward making small-talk with Richard when the two are left alone early in the play. Later she is completely confused and embarrassed by the word game but in her embarrassment acts out ''winsomely''—i.e. sweetly and innocently— so well that Sorel still guesses the adverb. She has no idea what to do when Simon suddenly announces their engagement. By the next morning she is so distraught that she bursts into tears when sitting alone at the breakfast table. Completely distressed, she concludes at the end of Act III that the Blisses are ''all mad,'' and is as eager as her fellow visitors to escape from the house.

Richard Greatham

Richard is the ''frightfully well-known diplomatist'' Sorel has invited for the weekend. Described in the stage directions as ''iron-gray and tall,'' his instinct for politeness is revealed in his first moments on stage when he manages to keep up some sort of conversation with the shy Jackie while they wait in the hall. Although Sorel admires him precisely because of his conventional manners, he is drawn to her and her family because they are ''so alive and vital and different from other people.'' He admires Judith's vitality and says he feels ''dead'' by comparison, but he hardly knows how to respond when after one brief kiss she leaps up and begins announcing plans to leave her husband. Later, when

he comes in from the garden to encounter a chaotic scene he unwittingly speaks the line, ''Is this a game?'' that is the cue for Judith and the kids to launch into the scene from *Love's Whirlwind.*

Sandy Tyrell

Sandy is the amateur boxer Judith has invited for the weekend. In her words, he is ''a perfect darling, and madly in love with me.'' But as Sorel says to her, he is just another one of the ''silly, callow young men who are infatuated by your name.'' Described in the stage directions as ''fresh-looking'' with an unspoiled, youthful sense of honor and rather big hands, owing to a ''misplaced enthusiasm for boxing,'' Sandy has an athletic form that contrasts with Simon's less-developed physique. Having fallen in love with Judith when he saw her on stage, Sandy at first can't believe his good fortune in being her houseguest. He is soon disillusioned, however, by the discovery that she has a husband. Later when he kisses Sorel in the library and is discovered by her mother, he gets swept up in Judith's interpretation of events—that Sorel has stolen him away from Judith—until Sorel admits that it was all just another act. Such strange encounters with the Blisses leave him so unnerved that the next morning he hides in the library when he thinks one of them might be about to enter the room.

THEMES

Absurdity

Much of the humor in *Hay Fever* derives from the way Coward's characters, despite being placed in ordinary situations, behave in odd and unexpected ways. These eccentricities make typical interactions seem ridiculous to the viewer. The Bliss family leaps to melodramatic and emotional extremes at the slightest provocation, leaving their guests at a loss for how to respond and highlighting the absurdity of social and romantic conventions that might otherwise be accepted as normal. While Coward's exploration of this theme was primarily in the service of entertainment, there are also elements of social criticism in his mocking of conformity.

Culture Clash

Although the characters in *Hay Fever* (save Clara) belong to the British upper class, they can still be divided into two separate groups, each

TOPICS FOR FURTHER STUDY

- Several critics have commented upon the strong connections between *Hay Fever* and Edward Albee's 1962 play *Who's Afraid of Virginia Woolf?* Compare and contrast these two works, considering how each playwright takes a similar situation and setting and develops it to very different effect.

- Both Coward as an individual and the plays he wrote are often associated with 1920s "Bohemi-an" culture. Research the meaning and evolution of the term "Bohemian" in early twentieth-century western culture. Once you have a good sense of what the term means, consider whether it accurately describes the worldview of Coward and his characters.

- In addition to being a playwright, Coward was a talented composer and lyricist. Locate and listen to some recordings of Coward's songs. Then consider how the lyrics and melodies of the music relate to the theme and tone of *Hay Fever.*

- More so than some artists, Coward is considered to have revealed facets of his personality in his plays. Research Coward's biography—including both his public persona and his private exist-ence as a closeted homosexual—and then con-sider the question of how his comedies, including *Hay Fever,* might be seen to reflect his character and/or life experience.

---

reflecting a different worldview or "culture." The four members of the Bliss family follow their own unique rules for personal interaction, rules that allow them to slip into fictional roles and act out melodramatic plots whenever the mood strikes them. The four weekend visitors, contrastingly, follow the conventional rules that instruct people to act accord-ing to their "real" social roles, behaving in a polite and predictable manner even if this means denying their genuine inclinations or feelings. These two cultures clash over the course of the weekend visit, resulting in the abundance of silly situations that amuse the audience.

Family

In this play, the members of the Bliss family have problematic relationships with outsiders, yet they are able to interact contentedly—if oddly—among themselves. In a reversal of the typical family drama plot, none of the potential romantic connections with their weekend visitors are able to rival or disrupt familial bonds; a fact that is clearly illustrated in the final scene when the four Blisses sit around the breakfast table absorbed in their own idiosyncratic conversation while their guests slip out unnoticed.

Illusion vs. Reality

The line between illusion and reality is con-stantly crossed in the Bliss household. Elements of theater and fiction are freely integrated into every-day life as family conversations slide into dialogue from a play or family members begin to act out melodramatic emotions they do not genuinely feel. But Coward also reveals—through the small decep-tions of the "normal" visiting characters—that the "real" world is just as full of play-acting as the Bliss world—only people accept these everyday illusions in the name of good manners and social convention.

Individualism

The unusual beliefs and behavior of the Bliss family, which confound their guests and amuse the audience, also reflect an individualistic ideology that celebrates people who rebel against the re-straining conventions of society at large. Each Bliss is a unique individual and follows his or her inclina-tions without considering the opinion of others. Being a homosexual, Coward was particularly sen-sitive to the narrow definitions of "normal" that society placed on people. His celebration of the

Blisses' individuality can be read as a veiled criticism of such prescriptive social mores.

STYLE

Dialogue

Coward was one of the first playwrights of his generation to use naturalistic dialogue, that is, to have his characters speak in the same ordinary phrases that people use in everyday conversation. Earlier dramatists had employed an epigrammatic style, wherein the actors on stage spoke in quotable "epigrams," complex and witty phrases that sound poetic or literary. By contrast, Coward's plays rely on the interaction between charismatic performers to grab attention and the context of a given line to generate laughs. Viewers might not leave the theater quoting a single clever phrase, however, chances are they laughed their way through the actual performance because of the amusing situations depicted on stage.

Comedy of Manners

In a comedy of manners, humor and interest derive from social interaction and conversation rather than from elaborate or suspenseful plots. Jane Austen's novels and Oscar Wilde's plays, for example, can both be categorized as comedies of manners. *Hay Fever,* with its focus on a series of amusing situations that all take place in one upper class home, is a sophisticated and irreverent adaptation of this comedic form.

Farce

Hay Fever employs many elements of farce, a comic theatrical form in which exaggerated characters find themselves in improbable situations and engage in wordplay and physical humor intended to provoke simple hearty laughter from the audience. Although Coward's play carries a bit more social weight than a traditional farce, it does make use of farcical word games and broadly drawn characters.

Irony

Many of the humorous comments made by the members of the Bliss family are good examples of dramatic irony. This type of irony comes from situations where the impact of a line or action depends upon the audience being aware of something the character is not. So for example, it is ironic, and therefore funny, when David—who both accepts unusual behavior from his family and behaves quite unconventionally himself—reacts to his guests' surreptitious departure by saying "People really do behave in the most extraordinary manner these days." Although the audience is aware of how David's comment actually describes his own behavior, David himself does not see this and so makes his observation free of self-reflection.

Juxtaposition

Throughout the play, Coward juxtaposes the carefree unconventional Blisses with their anxious, convention-bound guests. Each new pairing of characters provides an amusing contrast between one of the self-absorbed impulsive family members and an uneasy, confused visitor. These oppositions—both of personality types and personal expectations—produce much of the work's humor.

Pace

The success of a Coward comedy depends upon the live production maintaining a fast pace. The humor and impact of a play like *Hay Fever* comes partly from the rapid staccato dialogue, the type of syncopated speedy delivery of lines that would later become the hallmark of late-twentieth-century plays by writers like David Mamet (*Glengarry Glen Ross*).

Romantic Comedy

Coward generates a good deal of humor by disrupting the audience's expectations regarding the traditional plot of the romantic comedy, which is usually a story of a love affair between two people who must overcome obstacles before they can marry—or at least end the play in a happy conclusion. As *Hay Fever* opens, the viewer might expect a plot in which a series of mismatched couples swap partners in order to find happier pairings—in other words the typical romantic comedy plot multiplied by four. Yet Coward thwarts such expectations, making fun of the familiar storylines about illicit love and adulterous spouses during the course of the play and in the end leaving all the members of the Bliss family just as they were when the play started.

Satire

Satire is a type of humorous critique used in both fiction and drama to ridicule political or social philosophies. *Hay Fever,* with its depiction of self-absorbed bohemian artists and their misguided conventional admirers, can be seen as a gentle satire of the excesses both of pretentious creative people and of the adoring public who indulge such egotistical behavior because these people are famous. This has come to be known as the "cult of personality" or "cult of celebrity," in which famous people are so revered that they are above social reproach.

HISTORICAL CONTEXT

In the 1920s, Great Britain experienced political upheaval resulting from the first global war, as well as social transformations resulting from industrialization. Technological innovations also significantly altered the era's cultural landscape. Both the optimism and the anxieties induced by such extreme changes were reflected in the period's art and literature.

Before World War I (1914-1918) there was great optimism in Europe about the future of parliamentary government. After the war, political attitudes were very different. After witnessing both the war's terrible death toll and the perpetual chaos in Post-war continental legislatures, Europeans were more likely to question government action and demand social justice. For Britain in particular, events early in the century underscored the government's vulnerability. The Easter Rising in Dublin (1916), the granting of Irish Independence (1921), and the shootings in India that started Mahatma Ghandi's peace movement (1919), all indicated that the British Empire was no longer invincible.

Meanwhile, unrest on the European continent set in motion events that would culminate in a second world war. The Bolshevik Revolution took place in Russia in 1917. Benito Mussolini assumed dictatorial power in Italy in 1922. Germany, struggling under the burden of World War I reparation payments, experienced rapid inflation of its currency in 1923-24, resulting in worthless money and a demoralized populace. Finding support from a dissatisfied German citizenry, Adolf Hitler reorganized the New Socialist or "Nazi" party and published the first volume of his manifesto, *Mein Kampf,* in 1925; his rise to power in the next decade would set the stage for World War II.

The first World War also altered the international economic order. In 1914, most of Europe's economies depended on Great Britain and Germany. By the time the fighting stopped in 1918, the United States had become the main economic power. In the period between the wars, England would have to adapt to industrialized modes of production—factories that used assembly lines and electric power—and the resulting loss of jobs. The country suffered severe unemployment, with as many as two million people out of work in 1921-1922 and still a million unemployed in 1925. A lot of these people had lost coal mining jobs, and the miners would go on to lead a massive protest, known as the General Strike in 1926. These events augured the world economic crisis of 1929-1932 (a global event that manifested itself as the Great Depression in America).

Despite its economic difficulties, the British government had to meet the Postwar expectations of its people, who demanded more social services and greater civil rights. In the early-twentieth century, English legislative acts reflected changing perceptions of the rights of workers and the role of women. The 1911 National Insurance Act established some medical coverage and unemployment benefits for workers, while the 1925 Pensions Act set aside retirement funds for them. World War I brought many women into the national workforce, making them less dependent on male wage-earners and more willing to assert their property rights. Although the Divorce Bill (1902) and Female Enfranchisement Bill (1907) had taken some steps to empower women, significant changes only came after the war. It was not until 1918 that British women who met age and property requirements got the vote.

During the following decade women continued to agitate for full suffrage, which was finally won in 1928. Many of those involved in the suffrage debate were dubbed "New Women," women associated—both positively and negatively—with personal independence, unconventional attitudes, and less-restrictive fashions. The image of the high-spirited "flapper" wearing loose-waisted dresses with skirts above the knee was often equated with this newly liberated female role.

The daily life and attitudes of all British people changed a great deal in the first decades of the twentieth century. Rapid urbanization took the majority of citizens away from the country. By 1911,

COMPARE & CONTRAST

- **1925:** It is the height of the modernist period in literature, numerous books later considered classics are published. These works include Theodore Dreiser's *An American Tragedy,* Willa Cather's *The Professor's House,* T. S. Eliot's *The Hollow Men,* F. Scott Fitzgerald's *The Great Gatsby,* Ernest Hemingway's *In Our Time,* Gertrude Stein's *The Making of Americans,* and Virginia Woolf's *Mrs. Dalloway.* The 1925 Pulitzer Prize for fiction goes to Edna Ferber for her novel *So Big.*

  Today: Recent British and American books that have earned praise include Alice McDermott's novel about ill-fated romance and family deception, *Charming Billy,* which won the National Book Award; Ian McEwan's exploration of personal intrigue and public humiliation, *Amsterdam,* winner of the Booker Prize; Phillip Roth's examination of a father-daughter relationship in the turbulent 1960s, *American Pastoral,* honored with the Pulitzer Prize for fiction; and Rafi Zabor's uniquely humorous story about a talking saxophone-playing animal, *The Bear Comes Home,* which received the PEN/Faulkner Award for fiction.

- **1925:** The Charleston—a jittery, kinetic dance performed with a partner to music with a staccato, syncopated 4/4 rhythm gains great popularity. Although originating in Charleston, South Carolina, the dance soon became an international trend and, along with flappers, became emblematic of the "Jazz Age" of the mid-1920s.

  Today: After two decades in which rock and rap music dominated popular music, a revival of swing music and dancing is taking place in many parts of America and Europe. Partner dancing—including the lindy-hop, a variation on the Charleston developed in the 1930s—has made a comeback with American youth, and remakes of big band swing tunes are appearing on the top-ten record charts.

- **1925:** American writer Anita Loos publishes *Gentlemen Prefer Blondes,* which was made into a film in 1928. This popular novel's main character, Lorelei Lee, provides the prototype for the caricature of the "dumb blonde" that would resurface in many books, shows, and movies throughout the second half of the century; beginning in the late-1950s, film star Marilyn Monroe would come to epitomize the dumb blonde.

  Today: In the latest variation on this theme, writer/director Tom DiCillo's 1998 independent film *The Real Blonde,* starring Matthew Modine, Daryl Hannah, and Catherine Keener, offers a witty critique of the cultural ideal of feminine beauty and the "dumb blonde" stereotype. Modern culture has mostly abandoned the dumb blonde stereotype, though it does occasionally reappear.

- **1925:** Nellie Taylor Ross is elected governor of Wyoming, the first woman to be elected to such a post in the United States. Margaret Thatcher, who later became Britain's first woman Prime Minister (in 1975), is born this same year.

  Today: Although the number of female politicians still does not begin to adequately represent the number of female voters in either America or Europe, women continue to be elected and appointed to high office. In 1993, for example, Janet Reno was appointed the first female Attorney General of the United States, and in 1998 she became the first person in the modern era to hold the post for more than five years; serving in the same Clinton presidential cabinet, Madeleine Allbright becomes the first female secretary of state in 1997.

80% of the population of England and Wales lived in urban areas. Despite periods of crisis, there was a general rise in the standard of living. This increase in national income allowed people to spend more on luxuries; the demand for non-essential goods went up accordingly. There was also a great increase in literacy as school attendance became mandatory across Europe.

Thanks to innovations in communications media, even those no longer in school had greater access to all kinds of information. Radio and cinema became significant political and cultural influences. Right before the war the British silent film industry was thriving; there were six hundred cinemas in Greater London in 1913. After 1918, Hollywood—left largely unaffected by the fighting—dominated film production. Although Europeans like Sergei Eisenstein made great artistic innovations in the field, the United States industry had the money to produce costly extravaganzas like *Ben Hur* (1926) and establish world-wide stars such as Charlie Chaplin, who was, ironically, British.

The first American radio broadcast took place in 1920, the first British in 1922, inaugurating an era of mass persuasion. In the years between the two world wars, cinema, radio, and microphones became powerful communication tools manipulated by monolithic fascist and communist parties to incite public responses. Dictators used propaganda films and large public meetings to inspire the same kind of hero-worship elicited by movie stars.

All these developments created great hopes as well as great fears, both of which were articulated by the period's artists. The modern writers of the 1920s—including Americans F. Scott Fitzgerald (*The Great Gatsby*) and Ernest Hemingway (*For Whom the Bell Tolls*) and Britons James Joyce (*Ulysses*) and Virginia Woolf (*To the Lighthouse*)—broke with traditional novel form, emphasizing individual thought and expressing the alienation felt by the Postwar generation. Visual artists—such as the European painters Wassily Kandinsky, Paul Klee, Henri Matisse, and Pablo Picasso—also experimented with new techniques, developing the non-representational forms of abstraction and cubism.

At the same time aesthetic movements like Art Deco, a popular style in 1920s furniture, clothing and architecture, optimistically embraced modern materials and designs. A similarly positive tone carried through the music of composers such as Aaron Copland and George Gershwin. Although the era Fitzgerald dubbed the "Jazz Age" and W. H. Auden called the "Age of Anxiety" was marked by a loss of faith in society, the incredible creative output of the time shows a continuing faith in the power of art.

CRITICAL OVERVIEW

Throughout his career, Coward was generally praised as a skillful dramatist capable of constructing well-balanced comedies filled with natural-sounding dialogue and broadly humorous situations. Even those who criticized his work as being too trivial and lacking in deep meaning have usually acknowledged his plays as entertaining, which is precisely what Coward intended them to be. Today the playwright's critical reputation rests largely on his comedies of manners written between the two World Wars, works—including *Hay Fever*—that capture the sophisticated, irreverent and high-spirited mood of 1920s elite society.

When *Hay Fever* premiered in 1925, some critics like James Agate, the reviewer for London's *Sunday Times,* complained that the play offered neither a useful moral nor admirable personalities. As Agate wrote, "There is neither health nor cleanness about any of Mr. Coward's characters, who are still the same vicious babies sprawling upon the floor of their unwholesome creche." Yet even this critic had to acknowledge that "it would be foolish to insist upon attacking this play on the score of truth or morality. . . . As a piece of brilliant, impudent, and sustained fooling the play is very pleasant entertainment." The 1925 critical consensus supported this final observation, that *Hay Fever,* though certainly not educational, was undeniably entertaining.

Many of Coward's contemporaries underestimated the extent to which the play would continue to appeal to later generations of theatergoers. Some thought the casual dialogue would rapidly become dated. While others, like Agate, anticipated that the play would only be favored by a "purely Metropolitan audience." Yet such predictions have proved false. *Hay Fever* is still frequently performed for late-twentieth century audiences. In professional revivals, as well as community and college theater productions, its jokes remain fresh, garnering laughs from a wide range of viewers. Audiences today seem to agree with the assessment expressed by Coward's fellow writer W. Somerset Maugham in his introduction to the 1929 collection *Bitter Sweet and Other Plays,* that *Hay Fever* is a ''masterpiece in miniature.''

In the past three decades, productions of the play have consistently earned critical praise. In 1965, Penelope Gilliatt complimented a version of *Hay Fever* ''immaculately revived by the author'' himself. Writing for *Harper's* in 1982, John Lahr expressed his view that *Hay Fever* is ''Coward's finest light comedy.'' A 1985 production elicited similarly positive reviews. Clive Barnes, in the *New York Post,* noted that this brilliant revival of Coward's play reclaimed the playwright's ''reputation as a major twentieth-century playwright'' and gave the work the ''patina of a classic.'' Although Frank Rich may have complained in his 1985 *New York Times* review that *Hay Fever* has ''skin-deep characters, little plot, no emotional weight or redeeming social value and very few lines that sound funny out of context,'' like many critics before him he acknowledged that it was ''unlikely'' that the audience would ''stop laughing and start thinking'' long enough to notice. By contrast, Jack Kroll argued in *Newsweek* that this ''timeless comedy of ill manners'' actually ''isn't superficial,'' but rather ''it's *about* superficiality.''

Literary historians now rank *Hay Fever* among Coward's most enduring works. In 1964, A. C. Ward in his *Twentieth-Century English Literature, 1901-1960* identified it as a ''first-rate comedy.'' While in 1996, Jean Cothia in her *English Drama of the Early Modern Period, 1890-1940* expressed the generally agreed upon scholarly view that ''where Coward makes his continuing claim to attention is in his wonderfully symmetrical comedies of egoism, desire and bad manners: *Hay Fever* (1925), *Private Lives* (1931), and *Blithe Spirit* (1941).''

Starting in the 1970s, some critics also began to place Coward's works in the context of the homosexual literary tradition. When Coward died in 1973 near the time when a famous gay producer, Hugh Beaumont, also passed away, one columnist in the *Spectator* wrote that although the two men's deaths did not mean ''the whole edifice of homosexual domination of the British theatre will come tumbling down,'' the ''loss of these two pillars'' does make the ''structure . . . look a little less secure.''

Actress Constance Collier depicted in a scene from a 1932 production of Coward's play at the Shaftebury Theatre

But in the succeeding decades, gay issues and identity—in the theater as in the rest of society—were more freely acknowledged.

In the increasingly less restrictive academic world of the 1980s and 1990s, critics have begun to explore possible homosexual themes and perspectives in Coward's comedies, observing how plays like *Hay Fever* mock heterosexual romance, allow characters to form unorthodox connections, and generally flaunt conventions of all kinds. Lahr, in his 1982 book *Coward the Playwright,* even went so far as to argue that Coward has an ''essentially homosexual vision.''

The main reason Coward's reputation remains secure at the end of the twentieth century, however, seems to be that the sophisticated humor of well-crafted plays like *Hay Fever* still provide the sort of light entertainment that pleases audiences. As Cothia observed, when ''performed with panache by a team of actors . . . skilled in delivery of the well-bred insults and discourteous frankness that characterize the staccato dialogue,'' Coward's comedies ''are works that perceive the absurdities of sexual relationship and social organization,'' allowing us to gently laugh at ourselves.

CRITICISM

Erika M. Kreger

Kreger is a doctoral candidate at the University of California, Davis, and has served as a guest lecturer at the Johannes Gutenberg University in Mainz, Germany. In this essay she discusses how Coward's comedic touch in Hay Fever *reveals the artifice of both social and theatrical conventions, putting a uniquely humorous spin on the anxiety over loss of meaning expressed so seriously by many of his modernist contemporaries.*

"None of us ever mean anything." So the character Sorel Bliss describes her family in the second act of Noel Coward's 1925 comedy of manners *Hay Fever*. In context, her words explain the Blisses' endless play-acting, the cause of the work's humorously chaotic situations. Yet her statement also echoes the cultural anxiety expressed in many other forums during the post-World War I era, a time when many artists articulated concerns about the increasing hollowness and meaninglessness of the modern world. Disillusioned by the awful realities of total war, influenced by new psychological and scientific theories, and dissatisfied with traditional aesthetic forms, modernist writers such as James Joyce and Virginia Woolf experimented with stream of consciousness narratives and contemplated the frightening possibility of an unstable world where all reality was relative, constructed by the subjective view of an individual. Such deep and dreary thoughts might seem unrelated to Coward's light and sophisticated comedy, yet the very same idea that was a source of anxiety for such artists serves as the main source of humor in *Hay Fever*.

Coward's perfectly balanced play places the four unrestrained and idiosyncratic members of the Bliss family opposite the four unimaginative and conventional people they have invited for the weekend. During the course of the resulting comedic action, the playwright pokes fun at artistic pretensions as well as ordinary habits, revealing the artifice inherent in both. In the midst of all the good fun, we find a subtle critique of not only excessive individualism but also hypocritical propriety. The unsuspecting visitors arrive at the country house expecting to be entertained by their vibrant and celebrated hosts but instead end up feeling tricked and tortured as the Blisses repeatedly profess false emotions and create imaginary relationships.

This unexpected behavior confuses the guests, who are unsure how to respond in the face of such irrational behavior. It is not—as some critics suggest—that they find themselves unable to distinguish between truth and illusion. Rather, they recognize fairly quickly that they are witnessing "acts" of different kinds, but they resist changing the accepted social rules about when and where it is appropriate to "act." So it is not that the visitors fail to see that the Blisses are speaking untruths and constructing false situations; it is more that the guests have trouble figuring out why this is happening all of a sudden in the living room. In a theater, they would know what such actions meant. Removed from the traditional dramatic arena, however, they do not know what anything means. Coward skillfully turns this loss of meaning into a joke. He plays with the audience's definition of what is "real" and what is "illusion," ironically revealing that perhaps there is more honesty in the Blisses' unapologetic theatricality than in their guests' repressed normalcy.

The comedy's situational humor comes from the juxtaposition of these two contrasting modes of behavior; yet each is equally open to ridicule. *Hay Fever* depicts a world devoid of true meaning or genuine feeling, taking modernist fears to a ludicrous extreme and cleverly making us laugh at the futility and falseness of it all.

Judith and David Bliss are celebrities, she having won fame as a stage actress, he as a romance novelist. Each understands, just as Coward himself did, what the public expects and how to live up to these expectations. Long before theorists began writing about the idea of personality as a fictional construct, Coward was well aware of the artificiality of public identity, having taken great pains to construct his own. As Christopher Innes commented in *Modern British Drama, 1890-1990,* many commentators have considered "Coward's public image—the appearance of upper class elegance, inscrutable poise, cocktail party wit elevated to epigram—to be the most brilliant of his artistic creations. Like Oscar Wilde, Coward is judged to have put his genius into his life" as well as to have "notoriously put his personality into his plays—writing major roles for himself to act—and the characters he played were a pose that disguised the reality of his life."

In the early-twentieth century, with the increasing variety and availability of all kinds of communication media, performance was no longer restricted

WHAT
DO I READ
NEXT?

- *The Collected Short Stories,* a 1962 collection that brings together all of Coward's short fiction. Like his better plays, the author's short stories showcase his skill with wordplay and considerable wit.

- Poems by Dorothy Parker, an American contemporary of Coward's. Her work also captures much of the same irreverent wit and high energy that defined the 1920s artistic world in which they both circulated. Two notable collections are *Enough Rope* and *Death and Taxes.*

- *Private Lives,* Coward's 1929 comedy about a divorced couple who meet again when both are honeymooning with new spouses. As in *Hay Fever,* the main characters' behavior befuddles and confuses their new spouses. Some consider this to be Coward's best play.

- *Pygmalion,* a play by influential British play-

wright George Bernard Shaw. The story deals with the transformation of a lower-class woman to fit upper-class ideals; it was later adapted into the popular stage musical and film *My Fair Lady.*

- *Quicksand,* Nella Larsen's 1928 novel depicts the "Roaring '20s" from another perspective, that of a black woman trying to negotiate her racial identity as she travels between Europe and America.

- *Who's Afraid of Virginia Woolf?,* a 1962 award-winning play by Edward Albee that is much indebted to *Hay Fever* for its dramatic situation of a married couple tormenting guests who do not understand the familial tensions and deceptions that are being played out in front of the them. Unlike Coward's play, however, Albee's work also deals with a deeper theme of marital discord.

---

to the stage. Whether in a radio interview, a fan magazine photo, or a newspaper gossip column, celebrity images were widely distributed. The public had a sense of what a given star was like; they expected the star—in person or in performance—to live up to that image. In *Hay Fever,* Judith acknowledges this dynamic. As she says, "it isn't me really, it's my Celebrated Actress glamor" that her young infatuated visitor loves, but this does not trouble her a bit. To her, theatrical glamor is as good as the real thing. It is of no matter if she is not truly beautiful because, as she tells her children, "I made thousands think I was." If a good act earns the same rewards as the genuine article, what is the difference? The public is ready to accept false images, so long as they are pleasing. Celebrity itself has an attraction that for some reason goes beyond talent or substance.

Although Judith admits the plays that made her famous were often terrible, and David states plainly that he writes "bad novels," each still garners

wealth and admiration. Sandy has fallen in love with Judith's on-stage persona; and Myra has been longing to meet David because she likes his books. Coward underscores that the Blisses are not true artists, but merely spoiled and egoistic celebrities. The play emphasizes how misguided their young admirers are to be fooled by unsubstantial public images.

Coward takes pains to show that the Blisses are not creative individuals who deserve to have their eccentricities indulged for the sake of their great art. He stresses that they produce nothing of value, are utterly self-absorbed, and possess no personal philosophy beyond enjoying themselves. Unlike the admirable individualists of the American literary tradition who cause no harm and serve as potential role models for others, the Blisses do cause harm and could care less. They exploit their privilege to amuse themselves and torment others, avoiding responsibility through affecting absent-mindedness and blindness.

> WHEN WE PLACE A PLAY SUCH AS *HAY FEVER* IN HISTORICAL CONTEXT, IT IS POSSIBLE TO ACKNOWLEDGE NOT ONLY COWARD'S SKILLS IN CONSTRUCTING SITUATIONAL COMEDY BUT ALSO HIS CLEVER RESPONSE TO THE LITERARY AND PHILOSOPHICAL DEBATES OF HIS ERA"

Judith claims that "if dabbling gives me pleasure, I don't see why I shouldn't dabble." But the play reveals that others might be able to offer her many reasons why she should not dabble with people's lives. Judith may say that the arrival of a houseful of unexpected guests was inevitable since "everything that happens is fate," but the housekeeper Clara—who suffers the consequences of all the extra work—correctly adds that it is "more like arrant selfishness." Just like the unrepentant characters who sing the song "Regency Rakes" in Coward's 1934 play *Conversation Piece,* the Blisses could say of themselves, "each of us takes/A personal pride/In the thickness of hide/That prevents us from seeing/How vulgar we're being."

Sorel's attempts at self-reform throw into stark relief the absolute blindness—or thickness of hide—of the rest of the family. She knows she is "entirely lacking in restraint," thanks to being raised by parents who have "spent their lives cultivating their arts and not devoting any time to ordinary conventions and manners and things," but her efforts at improvement are only partly successful.

Although Sorel, in her desire to change, is charmed by her guest Richard's proper and conventional manners, neither he nor the other visitors are held up as a particularly appealing alternative to the Blisses. While the hosts bring spectacle and drama into ordinary life, the visitors engage in the everyday theater of "good manners," hiding their true feelings and motives behind polite behavior. Each has accepted the weekend invitation with some kind

of personal agenda, hoping to meet a celebrity or consummate a romance (or both). Sandy tells Judith, "I've been planning to know you for ages." Myra confesses she accepted Simon's invitation only to meet David. Such plans and schemes are comically thwarted by the Blisses' inconvenient spontaneity.

Coward contrasts the Blisses' lack of self-awareness with the outsiders' self-consciousness: Richard's careful propriety, Jackie's painful shyness, Sandy's awkward nervousness, Myra's worldly calculation. The visitors' false presentation of self is paired with their false perception of their hosts. Richard expresses the romanticized view that seems to have attracted them all to the house; he thinks the Blisses are "a very Bohemian family," "so alive and vital and different than other people." But perhaps the visitors are not so very different from their hosts after all. Complimenting Richard, Sorel unwittingly makes clear that his ways are no more transparently understandable than her mother's over-the-top theatricality. She tells him, "You always do the right thing, and no one knows a bit what you're really thinking." Later Judith comments on what she views as his excessive restraint, saying "do stop being noncommittal." Coward makes being habitually noncommittal seem as false as offering phony expressions of commitment. By the end of the play, the audience might acknowledge that Myra's angry description of her hosts could just as well apply to them all: "You're the most infuriating set of hypocrites I've ever seen. This house is a complete featherbed of false emotions—you're posing, self-centered egotists."

Yet the very self-centered, egocentric behavior that torments the on-stage guests, entertains the onlooking audience. Although outrageous and unpredictable acts cause problems in daily life, they remains the stuff of good theater. So although *Hay Fever* reflects what could be a frightening concept—the total absence of meaning in modern life—the play remains in comedic territory because its substanceless spectacle is safely contained in the sphere or performance. The audience gets a pleasurably voyeuristic glimpse of the leisure-class, while also getting to feel comfortably superior when noticing the foibles the characters do not recognize in themselves.

Although the viewers, too, might engage in daily deceptions and worship substanceless celebrities, the extreme scenarios on stage seem removed from their lives, keeping the parody from hitting too close to home. If, as Coward wrote in his lyrics to the 1923 song "London Calling," "Life is nothing but a game of make-believe," then the world would be as pointless and chaotic as the Bliss household. But having perfected the art of maintaining comic distance, the playwright is able to offer gentle critique in an entertaining, rather than alarming, package.

Coward himself—despite repeatedly stating he had no intention for his plays to do anything more than make people laugh—at times admitted that his work did address more substantial themes. In 1925 he wrote that he wanted his plays to deal with "the hard facts of existence," to "concentrate on psychological impulses" and to "enlighten." Later, in a 1956 diary entry, he noted "I am a better writer than I am given credit for being. It is fairly natural that my writing should be casually appreciated because my personality, performances, music, and legend get in the way. Some day . . . my works may be adequately assessed."

Today, when we place a play such as *Hay Fever* in historical context, it is possible to acknowledge not only Coward's skills in constructing situational comedy but also his clever response to the literary and philosophical debates of his era.

Source: Erika M. Kreger, for *Drama for Students,* Gale, 1999.

Thomas F. Connolly

In the following essay, Connolly provides an overview and brief history of Coward's play.

The Bliss family has invited four intimate friends down to their place in Cookham, meaning to seduce their guests. However the Blisses end up abandoning them. The Blisses live in their own world, a realm which has precious little to do with external reality and the visitors to it are so completely bewildered that they end up seriously pondering whether they actually will be served tea at "teatime". Driven to starvation by their hosts' indifference and to distraction by their antics the guests unceremoniously depart. "How very rude!" exclaims Mrs. Bliss on hearing that they have done so.

Nothing is supposed to happen over a weekend and in this play Coward takes this social dictum to absurdly comic levels. A retired actress, Judith Bliss, will have absolutely nothing to do with the care and feeding of her guests, the only things that seem to interest her are a word game of her own

> COWARD'S TENETS FOR COMIC PLAYWRITING ARE MOST COGENTLY ILLUSTRATED BY *HAY FEVER*"

creation called "Adverbs" and the replaying of scenes from her old stage vehicles over and over again. Coward's choice of a word game whose rules are incommunicable artfully telegraphs the point of his play: one cannot learn the rules of life; one must simply have them. The Bliss menage creates its own milieu through a family code whose idiom is basically theatrical. Even though her children appear to loathe their mother's self-indulgent theatrics, they effortlessly feed her her "lines", practically on cue.

In its way the comedy is a sort of social reportage. Coward has identified the source of *Hay Fever* as being the evenings he spent at the Riverside Drive apartment of the actress Laurette Taylor in New York City, during which Miss Taylor subjected her guests to frenzied parlor games.

Thus on one level, *Hay Fever* presents us with an ancient and even severe situation: the observance of the laws of hospitality. Granted that in the beaumonde context of the play the laws of hospitality have degenerated into mere social graces, but rarely has the gracious living of high society been shown to be as graceless as it is in *Hay Fever*. For what we see and hear in this play is the merest lip service courtesy, indeed the laws of hospitality are flagrantly flouted, decorum is ignored, etiquette non-existent. No one is adequately or even inadequately introduced; no provisions are made for the feeding of guests; people wander in and out indiscriminately; conversations are interrupted and there is hardly a trace of civility. The Blisses do not even go through the motions of wanting to be polite; they are so staggeringly self-obsessed as to be completely incapable of legitimate social exchange. They treat everyone else as supernumeraries in the theatrical extravaganza of their lives.

One of Coward's cleverer devices is the bedroom controversy that develops among the Bliss family when each member finally realizes that the other has invited someone down for the weekend.

Something called "The Japanese Room" is the coveted sleeping chamber and each member of the family desires it for his or her own particular guest. Each tries to palm off a place called "Little Hell" on the other's chosen companion. We become privy to this information during a dialogue between Sorel Bliss and her brother Simon—with their mother presiding—which elegantly limns the barbarous nature of their way of life. Coward sets up the discussion as a sort of apologia for indecency. We learn that the Blisses are quite proud of their ways and believe themselves to be a breed apart.

It is this "otherness" that reflects Coward's own feelings about the way of the world in the early 20th century. John Lahr has said that Coward's comedies focus on a "talentocracy" whose self-awareness stems from its feeling of difference from, and indifference to, the traditional aristocracy's modes. In *Hay Fever* Coward shows how this self-conscious differentiation becomes self-propelling. As Sorel says of her parents, they have: "spent their lives cultivating their arts and not devoting any time to ordinary conventions and manners and things"—note that "arts" is modified with a possessive.

The playwright himself was the first person to admit that *Hay Fever* is awfully short on plot development or even action. In his introduction to *Hay Fever* (*Play Parade, 1*) Coward goes so far as to call it "one of the most difficult plays to perform that I have encountered". He goes on to posit that the work is wholly dependent upon "the expert technique" of its performers. If the dialogue is delivered with any archness—for example should the actress playing Myra Aryundel indicate in the slightest that she *knows* beforehand that her "haddock is disgusting"—the play will become insufferable. The characters must never revel in their "upper-class ellipticalness" (to use Robert Kiernan's phrase). They must simply take it for granted.

Coward's tenets for comic playwriting are most cogently illustrated by *Hay Fever*. It does not achieve its effects via epigrammatic flourishes, but rather by simple phrases being delivered in very complicated situations. Taken out of context the "laugh lines" are vacuous, but within the dramatic situation of the play they are hilarious.

In 1964 the National Theatre chose this play to be the first work that it presented by a living English dramatist. Coward directed the revival himself and its success started a tremendous renewal of interest in his works.

Source: Thomas F. Connolly, "*Hay Fever*" in *The International Dictionary of Theatre,* Volume 1: *Plays,* edited by Mark Hawkins-Dady, St. James Press, 1992 pp. 318–19.

Brendan Gill

In this excerpt, Gill provides a brief history of Coward's inspiration for writing Hay Fever *in addition to offering a positive appraisal of a 1985 revival of the play at the Music Box theatre.*

Noël Coward's "*Hay Fever*" has found a perfect home for itself at that exquisite toy of a theatre the Music Box (designed in 1921 for Irving Berlin and his partner, Sam H. Harris, by the celebrated theatre architect C. Howard Crane). Moreover, in Michael H. Yeargan the play has found the perfect designer for the setting that Coward called for—a country house in Berkshire, not far from London and with a view, in fair weather, of the pleasing green valley of the Thames. Mr. Yeargan has provided an interior straight out of Voysey, with leaded-glass French doors opening onto a garden, an arts-and-crafts oak staircase, plenty of chintz-covered overstuffed furniture, and a pantry door that is constantly swinging open and shut at the prompting of perky Clara, a much put-upon maid-of-all-work (played with appropriately vulgar brio by Barbara Bryne). The felicity with which the architecture onstage marries the architecture of the theatre itself is a symbol of the felicity of the occasion as a whole; this is an ideal production of "*Hay Fever,*" and I wish it the longest possible run.

Coward wrote "*Hay Fever*" in 1924, when he was not yet twenty-five (the next year, he would have five shows running simultaneously in London, including "*Hay Fever*"). His inspiration for the comedy sprang, so he reported years later, from weekends he had spent at the summer place on Long Island of the playwright Hartley Manners and his wife, the actress Laurette Taylor. The Mannerses' hospitality was notably errant and intermittent, though well intended, and Coward in the charming, self-delighting, and mischievously flirtatious Judith Bliss sketches a benignly exaggerated portrait of Miss Taylor. To play an outrageous person who is also an actress is for any actress a delectable opportunity, and Rosemary Harris as Judith Bliss makes the most of it. In the course of a sensationally amusing performance, there is scarcely a theatrical trick she doesn't stoop to, but then Judith Bliss/Laurette Taylor was evidently someone who stopped at nothing in the way of stoops. Enslaved by her wiles are Judith's self-important husband (Roy Dotrice), her burgeoning daughter (Mia Dillon), and her rather giddy son (Robert Joy).

The structure of the play consists, as so often in Coward, of a social symmetry placed in jeopardy and then more or less successfully patted back into temporary balance, if not restored. Unbeknownst to the others, each of the Blisses has invited a guest from London for the weekend: an innocent young man (Campbell Scott) who has fallen in love with Mrs. Bliss, or thinks he has; a somewhat older man, a diplomat (Charles Kimbrough), who is perhaps ready to fall in love with the daughter; a fey flapper (Deborah Rush) whom the father has summoned to his side and then forgotten; and a slinky woman of the world (Carolyn Seymour) with whom the son is infatuated. The guests are understandably dismayed by the reception they are subjected to; little by little, they begin to establish new relationships with their assorted hosts and one another. The play ends with the Bliss family locked in combat at the breakfast table while the guests make good their escape. That is the scanty sum of *Hay Fever,* and yet it suffices; Coward's high spirits (and evident delight in his talent) turn what appears at first to be a mere sparkling and sputtering pin-wheel into a quite substantial work of art. The witty period costumes are by Jennifer yon Mayrhauser, the lighting is by Arden Fingerhut, and the superlative direction is by Brian Murray.

Source: Brendan Gill, ''Country Pleasures'' in the *New Yorker,* Vol. LXI, no. 44, December 23, 1985, p. 44.

Harold Clurman

Clurman is a highly respected literary critic and theatrical director. In this review, he offers the opinion that Coward's play is a distinctly British work that holds little appeal for American audiences.

It was Shaw, I believe, who said that America and England were two countries separated by the same language. I thought of the remark at the performance of Noel Coward's 1925 play *Hay Fever* at the Helen Hayes Theatre. I am not a theatrical chauvinist, but it has struck me on several occasions that certain English plays had best be left to the English. Coward's plays are among them.

The trouble with the present revival of *Hay Fever* is not confined to its lack of English actors, but that is part of it. The proper way to speak Coward's lines is to appear unaware of and superior to them, to pretend that they have not been spoken at all.

> THE STRUCTURE OF THE PLAY CONSISTS, AS SO OFTEN IN COWARD, OF A SOCIAL SYMMETRY PLACED IN JEOPARDY AND THEN MORE OR LESS SUCCESSFULLY PATTED BACK INTO TEMPORARY BALANCE, IF NOT RESTORED"

The American, no matter how hard he tries to be casual or inexpressive in speaking Coward's witticisms, can't help seeming to mean them. And they shouldn't be meant: they should, ever so lightly, be ''assumed.'' An American who tries to take on the Coward guise becomes false and hoity-toity. But Coward's artifice is a reality, a habit of mind and spirit so fixed that it becomes not second but very nearly ''first'' nature.

If any Americans are able to approximate the manner successfully, none of them is in the cast of *Hay Fever.* Shirley Booth is a natural comedian and often a touching character actress, but she is not a *poseuse,* an actressy actress. Her forte is the middle middle class, and she is out of her element in this play. Worse still, everyone and everything else—including the set and clothes—are misplaced. Carole Shelley, who is English and capable of authentic cockney speech, replaces her person by a characterization which seems to precede her entrance on the stage.

Still, the play retains some of its inherent attributes and arouses occasional laughter. I was shocked some years ago to read in Ronald Bryden's column of theatre criticism in the London *Observer* that he thought Coward England's finest living playwright. In a sense it is so: if the term means to indicate the deftest of stage craftsmen with a marked persona typical of certain aspects of English society and something of a mocking commentary on it. Coward's trick is to mask his own approval and enjoyment of what he is doing in an attitude of indifference. One is never sure how much of this is calculated and how much the real thing.

Source: Harold Clurman, review of *Hay Fever* in the *Nation,* Vol. 211, no. 18, November 30, 1970, p. 572.

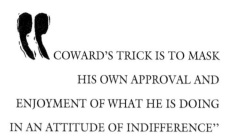

COWARD'S TRICK IS TO MASK
HIS OWN APPROVAL AND
ENJOYMENT OF WHAT HE IS DOING
IN AN ATTITUDE OF INDIFFERENCE"

SOURCES

Agate, James. Review of *Hay Fever* reprinted in *Red Letter Nights,* Jonathan Cape, 1944, pp. 240-42.

Barnes, Clive. "For Rosemary Harris—Love & Gesundheit!" in the *New York Post,* December 13, 1985.

Cothia, Jean. "Noel Coward" in her *English Drama of the Early Modern Period, 1890-1940,* Longman, 1996, pp. 101-02.

Coward, Noel. Introduction to *Three Plays,* Benn, 1925, pp. viii-ix.

Coward, Noel. Introduction to *Play Parade,* Vol. I, Doubleday, Doran, 1933.

Gilliatt, Penelope. "Coward Revived" in her *Unholy Fools: Wits, Comics, Disturbers of the Peace: Film and Theater,* Viking, 1973, pp. 242-43.

Innes, Christopher. "Noel Coward (1899-1973): Comedy as Social Image" in his *Modern British Drama, 1890-1990,* Cambridge University Press, 1992, pp. 238-60.

Kroll, Jack. "Serving up the Guests" in *Newsweek,* Vol. 106, no.26, December 23, 1985, p. 77.

Lahr, John. *Coward the Playwright,* Methuen, 1982, pp. 66-68.

Lahr, John. "The Politics of Charm" in *Harper's,* Vol. 265, no. 1589, October, 1982, pp. 64-68.

Maugham, W. Somerset. Introduction to *Bitter Sweet and Other Plays,* Doubleday, 1928, pp. v-xiii.

Rich, Frank. "'Hay Fever,' Noel Coward Comedy" in the *New York Times,* December 13, 1985, p. C3.

Ward, A. C. *Twentieth-Century English Literature 1901-1960,* Methuen University Paperbacks, 1964, pp. 131-32.

Waspe, Will. "A World Suddenly Less Gay" in the *Spectator,* March 31, 1973, pp. 399-400.

FURTHER READING

Coward, Noel. *Present Indicative,* Doubleday, 1937.
This first volume of Coward's autobiography covers his youth and early career up to 1931.

Hoare, Philip. *Noel Coward: A Biography,* University of Chicago Press, 1998.
This well-researched biography of Coward offers a good balance of insight into his private life and discussion of his literary works.

Payne, Graham, with Barry Day. *My Life with Noel Coward,* Applause Theater Books, 1997.
This memoir by Coward's longtime companion provides both a detailed personal portrait of the playwright and excerpts from his previously unpublished writings.

Payne, Graham, and Sheidan Morley, editors. *The Noel Coward Diaries,* Little, Brown, 1982.
Although clearly written with publication in mind, these diaries give the reader further examples of Coward's sophisticated wit and unconventional opinions.

Hedda Gabler

HENRIK IBSEN

1890

Hedda Gabler, published in 1890, was first performed in Munich, Germany, on January 31, 1891, and over the next several weeks was staged in a variety of European cities, including Berlin, Stockholm, Copenhagen, and Christiania (Oslo). Its premier performance in English occurred in London, on April 20 of the same year, in a translation by Edmund Gosse and William Archer (a translation that has continued to be employed throughout the twentieth century).

Many scholars link the play with what Ibsen described as the happiest event in his life, his brief liaison with Emilie Bardach, an eighteen-year-old Viennese girl whom he met in the small Alpine town of Gossensass in September of 1889. It is an ironic association, for in the months after the sixty-two-year old playwright stopped corresponding with Emilie, he wrote *Hedda Gabler,* which Herman Weigand termed the "coldest, most impersonal of Ibsen's plays" in *The Modern Ibsen: A Reconsideration.* It is almost as though the normally reserved and distant Ibsen had to exorcize his emotional attachment to Emilie by struggling to become yet more detached and objective in his art.

In its printed version, even before production, *Hedda Gabler* received the worst reviews of any of Ibsen's mature plays. Its earliest stagings fared little better. Conservative critics, predominately males, condemned the work as immoral, just as they had condemned many of Ibsen's earlier social-problem

plays. It survived the critical deluge, however, thanks in no small part to the efforts of the dramatist's ardent admirers, many of whom—including playwright George Bernard Shaw—belonged to the new intelligentsia shaped by the revolutionary thinking of such philosophers and scientists as Karl Marx and Charles Darwin.

Hedda Gabler's reputation steadily rose in the twentieth century, engaging the interest of many important actresses who found in Hedda one of the most intriguing and challenging female roles in modern drama. They helped earn the play the eminence it now enjoys as one of Ibsen's premier works and a landmark of realist drama.

AUTHOR BIOGRAPHY

At the time Henrik Ibsen wrote and published *Hedda Gabler* (1890) he was sixty-two and a well-established but highly controversial dramatist, but the road to that success had been paved with deprivation and hardship. Although he was born in a well-to-do family in Skien, Norway, on March 20, 1828, financial reversals led to poverty, making Henrik's youth a dismal one. At sixteen, he began a lonely and unhappy six-year apprenticeship to an apothecary (a pharmacist). He found his principal solace in the theater and writing, which he hoped would provide a means of escaping from his misery.

His first serious attempt at drama, *Cataline* (1850), earned him the support of friends who helped him escape from drudgery. He moved to Christiania (Oslo), where he undertook an apprenticeship as dramatist with the Bergen National Theatre. He also spent time in Copenhagen, studying at the Royal Theatre.

Ibsen's first plays borrowed freely from the French intrigue drama that he derided for its artificiality. Hoping to write something new, in 1857 he left the Bergen Theatre to become the director of the Norwegian Theatre in Christiania. The next year, despite his wretched financial state, he married and began a family. Nothing seemed to go right, however. His plays and poetry gained no influential following, and his theater went bankrupt within five years.

Lack of public support forced him into exile. In 1864, he moved to Rome. It was the first major turning point in his long career, for it was as an expatriate that he wrote most of the plays on which his great international reputation was built. Not only did he leave Scandinavia, he left behind a direct participation in theater. While in Italy, he wrote *Brand* (1866) and *Peer Gynt* (1867), two important poetic dramas. The former play was an immediate success and helped alleviate Ibsen's dire poverty.

In 1868, the French invasion of Italy obliged Ibsen to move to Germany, where he began writing the series of plays on which his fame largely rests. He turned from writing mythic-poetic drama to realistic, social-problem drama in prose, starting with *The League of Youth* in 1869, which, like so many of its successors, caused an uproar when first staged. Although his success was limited, by the time he returned to Rome in 1878, he had permanently freed himself from debt.

In the next year, 1879, he published *A Doll's House,* garnering international acclaim and putting him, critically, at center stage. Each succeeding social-thesis play brought increased recognition and notoriety, for each was, in some quarters, condemned. For example, *Ghosts* (1881) created such a furor that it could not be staged immediately. Others, like *An Enemy of the People* (1883) and *The Wild Duck* (1885), though less sensational, still caused critical controversy. Ibsen's fame and his notoriety spread quickly.

By 1890, when *Hedda Gabler* was published, he had even become a national hero in Norway. He returned home in 1891, where, before his death, he wrote *The Master Builder* (1892), *Little Eyolf* (1894), *John Gabriel Borkman* (1896), and *When We Dead Awaken* (1899), dramas that are more symbolic and introspective than any of his previous works. He died on May 23, 1906, widely regarded as the most important dramatist of the age.

PLOT SUMMARY

Act I
Hedda Gabler opens in the drawing room of the Tesmans' villa in the prestigious west-end district of Christiania, Norway. George Tesman and his new wife, Hedda, have just returned from a six-month honeymoon. Juliana Tesman, George's maiden aunt, and Berta, the Tesmans' servant, talk about George's invalid Aunt Rina, Hedda's father, General Gabler, and George's fortunate marriage and bright career prospects.

George enters, greets his aunt, and sends Berta off to store his valise while he helps Juliana remove her new bonnet. They discuss his good fortune in winning the much-admired Hedda, who, Juliana hopes, may already be pregnant. The journey and the villa and its furnishings, arranged by Judge Brack, have put both George and his aunts in debt, but Juliana assures her nephew that he is sure to get his anticipated academic appointment. Eilert Lovborg, George's chief competitor for the position, remains in disgrace, despite his popular new book.

When Hedda enters, she is both brusque and ill-mannered. After implying that Juliana's visit is too early, she complains about the room's stuffiness. She refuses to take any interest in George's favorite slippers, newly embroidered by his invalid aunt, and declares that Berta will have to be discharged for carelessly leaving her old bonnet on a chair. She also gets annoyed with George when he talks of her robust health, of how she seems to have "filled out" on their journey.

When George sees his aunt to the door, Hedda reveals her mounting frustration and rage by raising clenched fists over her head. He returns and they talk briefly about Aunt Juliana and Hedda's refusal to become closer to her. Berta then shows in Mrs. Elvsted, who explains that Eilert Lovborg is in town; she implores the Tesmans to befriend him. After Hedda sends George off to write Lovborg an amiable letter, she begins grilling Thea about her marriage to Sheriff Elvsted and her relationship to Lovborg. Accepting Hedda's apparent friendship, Thea confides that she has helped reform the dissolute Lovborg. She also confesses that she has left her husband, but that Lovborg has not encouraged her feelings for him because he remains emotionally bound to a former lover who had once driven him away at gunpoint.

George returns to find that they have another visitor, Judge Brack. After introductions, Hedda sees Thea out and returns to find the men talking about Lovborg, his book, and his moral reclamation. Brack then tells George that his academic appointment is not a certainty, that there is to be a competition for the post, pitting him against Lovborg—this news greatly upsets the financially-strapped Tesman. He voices his concerns to Hedda after Brack leaves, explaining that they will have to become much more frugal. She tells him that she will be bored but will amuse herself with her father's pistols.

Henrik Ibsen

Act II

It is late-afternoon on the same day. Judge Brack, approaching the Tesmans' villa from the rear, is dismayed when Hedda fires a pistol in his direction. After chiding her, Brack presses Hedda for a more intimate friendship. She reveals her disenchantment with marriage, complaining that the unexciting Tesman is simply too absorbed in his dull studies. She scoffs at the idea of love, admitting that she married George, not from affection, but because he is solid and respectable and has good prospects.

George enters laden with several books, one of which is Lovborg's new work. When he goes into the study, Hedda confesses her dislike for Tesman's aunts and even the married couple's villa. She admits she had only pretended to believe that Juliana's new bonnet belonged to Berta. She also tells Brack that she has hopes of interesting George in politics, but he offers no encouragement. His suggestion that she might find an alternative interest in raising a child makes her bristle.

When George re-enters, the talk turns to Lovborg and Judge Brack's bachelor's party. Shortly after, Eilert arrives, hoping to read part of his manuscript to George. He refuses an invitation to the party but defers to Hedda's insistence that he stay for dinner with her and Thea Elvsted. He also indicates that he will not stand in the way of Tesman's appointment, much to George's relief.

Lovborg stays alone with Hedda while the other men go into an adjoining room to drink punch. They speak of their former intimacy, of a time when Eilert confided in her. She confesses that she dreads the scandal that their love might have occasioned, a fear she still carries. He then allays her concern by revealing that he has never told Thea of their love, that Thea was too stupid to understand it.

When Mrs. Elvsted arrives, she tells Hedda of her happiness in being a catalyst in Lovborg's moral and professional reformation. Hedda suggests that Eilert is not really very secure, that both he and others, including Brack, suspect a possible relapse. She then betrays Thea's trust by revealing to Lovborg that Thea had come to her in a distracted state, herself fearful of what Eilert might do. To Thea's chagrin, Lovborg reacts bitterly, resolving to go off to the party with Tesman and Brack, with plans to read his manuscript there.

The men depart, leaving the worried Thea and exultant Hedda alone. Hedda is convinced that Eilert will return ''with vine-leaves in his hair.'' She admits that she desires the power to shape one person's destiny, and, reverting to a girlhood threat, says that she will yet have to burn the frightened Thea's hair off. At the curtain, she restates her conviction that Eilert will return in all his vine-leaf (drunken and disorderly) glory.

Act III

It is early the following day. Hedda and Thea have spent the night awaiting the return of Lovborg and Tesman. Hedda is asleep on the sofa, but Thea, restless, merely dozes in a chair. She wakes fully when Berta enters with a letter for George. Hedda also wakes, and after allaying Thea's concern, sends her off to rest in another room.

When Tesman returns, he tells Hedda that Lovborg had read part of his new manuscript to him and that is an extraordinary work. He also reveals that he has the manuscript with him, that he picked it up after Eilert carelessly dropped it, something only George knows. Hedda insists that he leave it with her. He is hesitant, but when he learns from the letter that his Aunt Rina is dying, he prepares to go to his aunt's bedside. Hedda stashes the manuscript out of sight, on the bookcase, just before Brack enters.

Brack describes Lovborg's behavior of the previous night, of how the scholar had gone to Mademoiselle Diana's room, charged everyone with stealing his papers, and, after striking a constable, been taken to jail. Eilert's fate comforts Brack, who had seen Lovborg as a threat to his plans to ensnare Hedda in an intimate relationship.

After Brack leaves, Hedda takes the packet of Lovborg's papers from the bookcase, but hearing voices in the hall, locks them in the drawer of a writing table. Lovborg barges in over the protests of Berta. Shortly after, Mrs. Elvsted also enters, and he tells her that she must leave him and go home again, that he is ruined. He lies to her, claiming to have torn his manuscript to pieces, scattering it on the fjord. She exits in despair, blaming Lovborg for destroying their work, their ''child.''

After Thea's exit, Eilert tells Hedda the truth, that he has lost the manuscript, and that he plans ''to make an end of all.'' Hedda then begs him to end it ''beautifully,'' and gives him one of General Gabler's pistols. After he leaves, she retrieves his manuscript and destroys it in the drawing room's stove.

Act IV

It is evening of the same day. Juliana talks of her sister's death with Hedda and George. She announces her desire to find another invalid to nurse, then adds the hope that Hedda will also have another to care for, a baby. After Juliana leaves, Hedda confesses that she had burned Eilert's manuscript to ashes. George is horrified, but when she claims that she did it for his sake, and lets on that she is with child, his regret turns to joy, and he agrees that they should keep her destruction of Eilert's papers a secret.

Mrs. Elvsted then joins them. She has heard rumors that Eilert was taken to the hospital. These are soon confirmed by Judge Brack, who enters shortly after. He claims that Eilert is in the hospital, dying from a self-inflicted gunshot wound in the chest, news that only slightly distresses Hedda, who had expected him to shoot himself ''beautifully,'' in the temple. When the talk shifts to Lovborg's destroyed manuscript, Thea suggests that from notes she has with her, she and Tesman might be able to recreate Eilert's work. George is at once enthusiastic, and the pair go into an adjoining room to begin what George now perceives as his life's work.

Alone with Hedda, Brack tells her the truth about Lovborg, that he is already dead, having bled to death from a wound to his bowels accidentally inflicted while Eilert was with Mademoiselle Diana in her boudoir. George then re-enters to say that he wants to work with Thea at the writing table. Hedda, after covering the remaining pistol with music sheets, moves apart, continuing her conversation with Brack *sotto voce* ("under the voice," in drama, a whispering technique that allows an audience to hear the dialogue). He reveals that he recognized the pistol that Lovborg used and warns her that a scandal could follow were he to disclose what he knows. She realizes what he is insinuating, that Eilert's death and her fear of scandal will put her completely in Brack's power.

As Thea and George work on Eilert's notes, Hedda goes into the adjoining room with music sheets and the pistol. She begins frenzied playing on the piano, prompting Tesman to protest the music's inappropriateness, given the death of Rina. George also tells Thea that they should work at Juliana's house in the evenings, leaving Brack to keep Hedda company. Brack is immediately agreeable, knowing that he can turn such occasions into sexual trysts. Hedda then fires the pistol, and when the men jump up and go into the room, they discover that Hedda has shot herself in the temple, something, according to the astonished Brack, that people just "don't do."

CHARACTERS

Berta

Berta is the Tesmans' middle-aged, maid. She is a loyal family retainer, formerly employed by George Tesman's maiden aunts but now in the service of George and Hedda at their newly purchased villa. Her closeness to Juliana Tesman makes her a minor threat to Hedda, who intensely dislikes George's aunt. Early on, Hedda threatens to discharge Berta, partly to discomfort George, but also because she clearly identifies Berta with George's family and its deeply affectionate binds that Hedda loathes. Although Berta appears often, she has no significant part in the play's action. She is very protective of George Tesman and his privacy.

Judge Brack

Judge Brack hides his desire for an intimate relationship with Hedda with an outward friendship for George Tesman and a cloak of respectability. He is, in truth, quite sinister and unprincipled, a sophisticated stalker who awaits an opportunity to seduce Hedda, to become the "one cock in the basket."

Brack is particularly dangerous because he is a fair judge of character, except, finally, in Hedda's case. He is genuinely shocked by her suicide, something he did not anticipate would result from his success in maneuvering her into a compromising position. He is otherwise a glib and masterful manipulator. At the outset, it is made clear that he has put George Tesman in his debt by arranging the loans for purchasing the villa. George, ingenuous to a fault, sees Brack only as an unselfish friend, one he trusts implicitly. Brack also challenges the hapless Lovborg, inviting him to his party, knowing full well that Eilert might slip again into his former dissolution. Hedda, on the other hand, penetrates Brack's mask of good will, identifying the leering innuendo in much of his seemingly harmless conversation with her.

It is Brack who forces Hedda into her last desperate act, her self-destruction. He knows that the pistol used by Eilert Lovborg was one of a pair of General Gabler's pistols in Hedda's possession. That he can expose her and subject her to scandal gives him the advantage he has sought, but Hedda, unwilling to become his "slave," elects to escape such a predicament through death.

Mrs. Elvsted

During the course of *Hedda Gabler,* Thea confesses that she has fled from her loveless and boorish husband, Sheriff Elvsted, and her stepchildren, destroying her reputation to follow Eilert Lovborg to Christiania. For the prior two years, she had both reformed the debauched Lovborg and inspired his new work. Despite her great influence on the brilliant Eilert, her hopes of securing his love are faint. A shadow sits on their relationship: Eilert's residual feelings for a former lover, who, unbeknownst to Thea, is Hedda Gabler.

Thea and Hedda, like Eilert and George Tesman, are sharply contrasting characters. Thea has courage and hope, selflessness and warmth. She is willing to risk all for love, even the kind of scandal that cowers Hedda, and though she knows her love for Eilert Lovborg is futile, her chief concern is for him, not herself. Hedda, on the other hand, is selfish and severe, incapable of the generosity of spirit necessary to love.

The two women even contrast physically. Thea seems made of softer stuff, rounded, not chiseled like the obdurate, stone-cast Hedda. Both have a kind of beauty, but Thea's greater beauty lies within. It is reflected in her outer femininity, in her rich

MEDIA ADAPTATIONS

- By the time film became commercially viable, Ibsen's reputation as one of the world's greatest dramatists was secure. In Europe and the United States, many early film directors tried their hand at adapting Ibsen's plays to the early cinema. *Hedda Gabler* was adapted to the silent screen at least three times: in the United States in 1917, by Frank Powell; in Italy in 1919, by Giovanni Pastrone; and in Germany in 1924, by Franz Eckstein.

- A 1963 British television version of *Hedda Gabler,* directed by Alex Segal, cast major film stars Ingrid Bergman as Hedda, Trevor Howard as Lovborg, Michael Redgrave as Tesman, and Ralph Richardson as Judge (Assesor) Brack.

- Another television version of the play was produced by the British Broadcasting Corporation (BBC-TV) in 1972. Directed by Waris Hussein, its cast includes Tom Bell, Ian McKellen, and Janet Suzman. A video version is available from Time-Life Multimedia in the United States.

- A film version of the Royal Shakespeare Company's stage production was released in the U. K. in 1975 under the title *Hedda.* Directed by Trevor Nunn, it features Glenda Jackson, Peter Eyre, Timothy West, Jennie Linden, and Patrick Stewart. It is generally available on video.

- In 1976, Films for the Humanities issued an educational film entitled *The Theatre of Social Problems: Ibsen, Hedda,* featuring an abridged version of the play, which, with commentary, runs 60 minutes. Produced by Harold Mantell, directed by Philip Hedley, and narrated by Irene Worth, its cast includes Darlene Johnson, Brian Protheroe, Rhys McConnochie, Sam Kelley, and Sara Stephenson. It is available in both video and 16 mm. formats from Films for the Humanities.

- Another British television version, directed by Deborah Warner, was first aired in 1993. The cast includes Fiona Shaw as Hedda, Nicholas Woodeson as Jorgen Tesman, Donal McCann as Judge Brack, Stephen Rea as Eilert Lovborg, Brid Brenan as Mrs. Elvsted, and Susan Colverd as Berte.

---

and luxuriant hair, particularly. Hedda's beauty is sharper, more masculine or androgynous.

Above all, Thea is devoted, her desertion of her oafish step-family not withstanding. Her loyalty to Lovborg inspires her to work with George Tesman to reconstruct Eilert's manuscript, their "child," which, she believes, Lovborg destroyed before his death. That Hedda is excluded from participating in their work contributes to Hedda's despair and suicide.

Hedda Gabler

Hedda is a complex character torn by opposing desires that make her both victim and victimizer. Her willfulness completely dominates the play, so much so that the other characters, even the more intriguing ones—Eilert Lovborg and Judge Brack

seem to exist primarily to help sculpt her character in high relief.

Hedda is selfish, proud, and cold, cruelly heedless of the pain she inflicts on others in her efforts to satisfy the inner desires that she is unwilling to deal with honestly or directly. Inhibited by her upbringing, she is unwilling to sacrifice her own comfort to satisfy those longings, even though she finds her respectable marriage wearisome and her doting husband contemptible. Instead of dealing openly with her dissatisfaction and her growing fear of drowning in boredom, she becomes desperate, even hysterical, as is revealed in her sometimes treacherous and destructive behavior.

First of all, she rejects George's efforts to bring her closer to his family. In fact, from the start, she seems bent on ruining George's ties to his past. She refuses to address his Aunt Juliana with the familiar form of the pronoun ''you'' and, instead, treats her rudely. She also threatens to dismiss Berta, the loyal family servant. But her calculated coldness towards the Tesmans is most pronounced in her total lack of concern for George's Aunt Rina, whose death seems to affect Hedda not at all.

Secondly, Hedda responds only negatively to her new role as wife. Most particularly, she refuses to accept her own pregnancy, something in which she is unable to take any joy at all. She seems to sense that a child will forever bind her to a life of suffocating boredom. At best, marriage seems only to offer her a sort of sanctuary from a far more exciting but dangerous world beyond, the world of Eilert Lovborg, a world that she perceives as romantic and beautiful but also terrifying. She does not love George, and she deeply resents having to rely on him for security, but she has almost a parasitical need for his respectability.

Thirdly, Hedda attempts to manipulate others, either from spite or to satisfy her needs vicariously. The doting George is an easy pawn in Hedda's cruel games. So is Thea Elvsted, a woman too trusting of Hedda's seeming good will. Hedda's jealousy of Thea, a feeling that extends back into their school days, makes her betray the woman's confidence, setting in motion the tragedy that at the last will destroy both Lovborg and Hedda. It particularly goads Hedda that Thea has played a major role in Eilert's reclamation, corralling his free spirit and directing his energies in a way she herself was unable or unwilling to do. Her dislike of Thea goes yet deeper, however. Thea, as her appearance suggests, is warm and engaging, even sensual, whereas Hedda, though attractive, is steely and distant. Thea's large, blue eyes are fixed with ''an inquiring expression,'' while Hedda's ''steel-grey eyes express a cold, unruffled repose.'' Most especially, Hedda is obsessed with Thea's luxuriant and abundant hair, which she treats like a hated thing to be destroyed, almost as if it were a reminder of the passion that, from fear, she represses in herself. Her own hair is described by Ibsen as ''not particularly abundant.''

As long as Hedda is able to manipulate others, she can deal with her dangerous passions, including her sexuality. She had once driven Eilert off, threatening him with her father's pistols, and she threatens Brack in the same way. However, her options run out when Brack gets her in a compromising position, one in which she can be manipulated,

something that she will not endure. Her only alternative is to take her own life.

While it is impossible to excuse Hedda's selfish and destructive character, at least some of the blame for her behavior rests with external influences, particularly her upbringing and the social dictates of her age. As the daughter of a general, she had learned to shoot and ride—hard, masculine activities that did not fit a respectable woman's role. That she is unable to make a mature adjustment to a feminine role, surrendering her freedom, is not entirely her fault.

Aunt Julia
See Miss Juliana Tesman

Eilert Lovborg
Eilert Lovborg is George Tesman's potential nemesis. Unlike Tesman, he is both a visionary and genius, but he is cursed with an inability to moderate his behavior. He carries disreputability on his back, luggage from a past in which he ruined his reputation by unspecified but dissolute conduct. However, when he first appears, he has renewed hopes. He has been inspired by Thea Elvsted, who has both prompted his reformation and been his able assistant in his scholarship and writing. He has also published a successful book and is close to finishing its more brilliant sequel.

Newly arrived in Christiania, Lovborg hopes to befriend George and interest him in his work, even though he is a threat to Tesman. He also attempts to refrain from any activity that might lead to a lapse into scandalous activity. However, his reformation proves both fragile and tragic when Hedda, his old love, reveals to him that Thea lacks sufficient faith in his self-control. He begins drinking, then goes off to Judge Brack's party. In the early morning, after heavy imbibing, he carelessly drops his manuscript on the street, where Tesman picks it up. It is later destroyed by Hedda, leading to Eilert's death and her own.

Lovborg offers a sharp contrast to Tesman. He is a disreputable and somewhat jaded genius, whereas George is a totally respectable and ingenuous plodder. Eilert has a creative, moody, and somewhat arrogant spirit; Tesman is unimaginative but steady and diligent. Hedda finds the latter boring but safe, and the former exciting but threatening.

Mrs. Rysing
See Mrs. Elvsted

George Tesman

George Tesman is a well-intentioned young man on his way to becoming a harmless drudge. He is a research scholar whose chief abilities, "collecting and arranging," are more clerical than insightful. He also seems more devoted to the minutia of history, the domestic industries of medieval Brabant, than he is to his wife, Hedda, around whom he usually seems doltish and imperceptive. He is unaware, for example, that she is pregnant, a fact that does not escape his Aunt Juliana. He also seems insensitive to Hedda's incivility and sarcasm, as well as her obvious discontent and bitterness.

On the other hand, George is devoted to his aunts, especially Juliana, who has been like a surrogate mother to him. He cares for her deeply, and he is upset that Hedda finds herself unable to develop a familiar relationship with her. To Hedda, Juliana is too much a busybody and too cloying in her affection.

Although professionally ambitious, Tesman is also essentially honest and fair. He recognizes in Lovborg the visionary genius that he utterly lacks, knowing, for example, that he could never make projections about the future the way Eilert has done in his manuscript sequel to his successful book. At the end of the play, he is willing to put aside his own work to collaborate with Mrs. Elvsted in an effort to reconstruct Lovborg's destroyed manuscript.

Tesman both bores and annoys Hedda. He treats life like his work, unimaginatively. At times he acts like a nincompoop, especially in his habit of responding to the most serious turn of events with the same inane enthusiasm accorded matters of no consequence. His tag expression, "fancy that," registers his apparently equal astonishment at the fact that his aunt has bought a new bonnet as, at the end, the fact that Hedda has shot and killed herself.

Hedda Tesman

See Hedda Gabler

Miss Juliana Tesman

Juliana Tesman, George Tesman's maiden aunt, has a deep affection for her nephew, who regards her with equal fondness. She is, in fact, a parental figure for Tesman, who calls her "father and mother in one" to him.

Juliana, who is sixty-five, is also devoted to her sister, George's Aunt Rina, who is an invalid. Juliana selflessly cares for her, and when she dies, Juliana immediately starts thinking about taking in an invalid boarder whom she might nurse. Her life, in short, is given over to ministering to the needs of others. She is the quintessential nurse, willing to sacrifice herself for others. Only in that does she find much meaning in life. In this respect, and in most others, she is a stark contrast to Hedda, who detests her.

Thea

See Mrs. Elvsted

THEMES

Betrayal

At a critical point near the end of Act II of *Hedda Gabler,* the titular character betrays the trust of Mrs. Elvsted by revealing Thea's fears regarding Lovborg. Hedda does this out of pure malice. She is jealous of Thea's influence over Eilert, a man with whom Hedda had once been involved but, afraid of her own passions, had driven off (at gunpoint). Hedda's betrayal is the last manifestation of a hatred that extends all the way back to her school years, when she had bullied Thea. She despised the younger woman from a deep-rooted jealousy of Thea's comfortable and natural femininity. The betrayal starts a chain of tragic events in motion, ultimately leading to Lovborg's death and Hedda's suicide.

Courage and Cowardice

One admission that Hedda openly makes to Lovborg is her fear of scandal, which prompts him to charge that she is a "coward at heart," which she confirms. It was her fear of scandal that compelled Hedda to drive Eilert away, a fear that overwhelmed her love for him. Lovborg, as a free spirit, had represented too much of a risk, for he had already been tainted by his scandalous, immoderate behavior.

Although she, unlike Thea Elvsted, is unwilling to be drawn into Eilert's life again, to sacrifice her respectability, she is willing to sacrifice him. She provides him with a pistol, expecting him to exit life with a grand and triumphant display of scorn for the tedium and convention of human existence. From his death, Hedda hopes to confirm that there is still beauty in the world and partake of it vicariously. She is, however, deluded by her romantic fantasies, even less capable of guiding Eilert's behavior than Thea Elvsted had been. He destroys Hedda's triumphant vision by accidentally shooting himself in the

TOPICS FOR FURTHER STUDY

- Investigate the influence of Ibsen's drama on the women's rights and emancipation movements of his day.

- Investigate "Ibsenism" in England in the last two decades of the nineteenth century, especially the dramatist's influence on Eleanor Marx (Karl Marx's youngest daughter), William Archer, and George Bernard Shaw.

- Research realism and naturalism as literary movements of the late-nineteenth century, relating their tenets to Ibsen's dramatic technique and themes in *Hedda Gabler*. You may want to

consider reading Emile Zola's celebrated essay "Naturalism in the Theatre" (1880) in your investigation.

- Much modern drama reflects the strong influence of Henrik Ibsen, Anton Chekhov, and August Strindberg. Investigate and compare their particular contributions to the development of twentieth-century theater.

- Research the official morality of Ibsen's day that led to his notoriety and the condemnation and censorship of his plays, especially *Ghosts* and *Hedda Gabler*.

---

abdomen. In the play's final irony, it is Hedda who shoots herself in the temple, not in a grand escape from life but from a cowardly fear of scandal and an unwillingness to become Judge Brack's sexual pawn.

Deception

Hedda, from selfish motives, uses deception as a tool in her efforts to manipulate others, particularly her husband and Mrs. Elvsted. Because they are both forthright and somewhat ingenuous, they are susceptible to Hedda's machinations. Hedda feigns a friendship with Thea, one that she does not and never has felt. She is, in fact, jealous of the younger woman and despises her. In her relationship with George, Hedda never has been honest. She finds him and their marriage boring, but she is unwilling to confront him with such truths for fear of losing the secure respectability that he provides. He is, as she says, "correctness itself." He is also a man with good if dull prospects.

Hedda is more open with Judge Brack, possibly because she recognizes in him a kindred spirit, a fellow deceiver, one who is too sly to fool. She knows that Brack's friendship with George is at least part sham. He also hopes to manipulate Tesman, ingratiating himself in order to enter a triangular relationship with the Tesmans, which, through innuendo, Brack suggests will involve more than a

Platonic friendship with Hedda. She is able to play a verbal cat and mouse game with Brack until he gains the upper hand; it is the prospect of submitting to his will that compels her to destroy herself.

Duty and Responsibility

Hedda Gabler is a study in contrasts. Both Juliana Tesman and Thea Elvsted are foils to Hedda, for in their distinct ways they reveal that duty and responsibility must arise from a loyalty prompted by love, not fear. Unlike Hedda, Juliana is a selfless person, willing to sacrifice her life for those she loves: her sister, Rina, and her nephew, George. She profoundly annoys Hedda, who cannot understand how such devotion can give Juliana a sufficient purpose in life.

Thea Elvsted has a similar selflessness, but her circumstances are very different. She is willing to sacrifice her reputation in her love for Lovborg, leaving behind a loveless, joyless marriage. Society might condemn her for betraying her duty and responsibility, but Ibsen makes it obvious that society would be wrong. She had been exploited, turned into a mere household servant in her marriage to the Sheriff. In following Lovborg to Christiania, Thea is heedless of imminent scandal, showing the moral courage that Hedda lacks. The difference is that Thea allows love to guide her, an emotion that Hedda represses in allowing her fears to rule her.

Good and Evil

"Evil" is too strong an adjective to apply to Hedda in any absolute sense. She does exhibit self-centered traits, as do most intriguing, dramatic villains, but these tendencies are muted by the playwright's dedication to realism. Hedda's wretched behavior cannot be forgiven, but at least it can be partially understood. It comes not from the deep recesses of a corrupt soul but from emotional needs that have been warped by environmental influences—her upbringing by a military father and her context within a morally strict social climate.

Despite this background, Hedda is proud and wanton in her cruelty. She cares little that she inflicts pain on others. She burns Lovborg's manuscript, not from love for her husband, which she leads George to believe, but from utter spite and jealousy. She views the work as Eilert and Thea's surrogate child, something to be destroyed because it was created from a love that she deeply resents and cannot understand. No less vicious is her effort to shape Eilert's final destiny, the "beautiful" and "triumphant" death she envisions for him. Her misdirected passion only destroys, for in Eilert's death there is no beauty at all, only a terrible waste of genius.

The shame is that to be good in Hedda's terms means living with unrelieved boredom, married to a "proper" but dull, plodding, and predictable scholar whose only virtue is his "correctness" in all things. Without real love or devotion, her duties and responsibilities become major irritants. She reacts with precipitous and thoughtless behavior, running the gamut between the petty and the tragic.

Sex Roles

Much of the conflict in *Hedda Gabler* arises from Hedda's resistance to the role of wife and mother, a role defined by the straight-laced, paternalistic society of the time and place. Women were expected to behave in accordance with traditional values that placed them in subservient and dependant relationships with men, from whose labors and leisure activities, both by custom and law, they were largely excluded. One hope they might have is that they could have a positive influence on men, such as Thea Elvsted has on Eilert Lovborg. Hedda even imagines that she might have a similar impact on George. She hopes to persuade him to enter politics, where, because of her ability to manipulate him, she might yield some clandestine but substantial power. However, when she confides her hopes in Judge Brack, he dampens her enthusiasm with observations about George's unsuitability for and disinterest in politics.

Hedda clearly feels both trapped and bored by her role. Her unwanted pregnancy only serves to remind her of just how much more confining her existence is to become, but she is paralyzed by her deep-rooted fear of scandal. She is simply unwilling to sacrifice respectability to be her honest self. The conflict between desire and fear finally perverts her character, turning her increasingly frantic and destructive. Her only respite is to cling to her father's pistols, symbols of a male freedom that she has lost as an adult and can never regain.

By contrast, Juliana Tesman and Thea Elvsted are comfortable and untroubled in their roles. Juliana, as nurse and caretaker for her sister, is selfless. Her respectable role is personally rewarding. Thea, who has sacrificed her reputation by abandoning her husband, is untroubled by such things. She sees that her path lies outside of respectability, and she is not afraid to follow it. Hedda scorns both women, masking her envy with contempt. It galls her that they are both at peace with themselves, something she can never be.

Victim and Victimization

Paradoxically, Hedda is both victim and victimizer. In her desperate boredom, she attempts to use others, even for petty amusement. As she confesses to Judge Brack, she had known that the bonnet about which she complains in Act I was not old and did not belong to Berta, but she could not resist her cruel whimsy. At first, there is little harm done. Besides, Hedda's discontent enlists some sympathy, for her husband is something of a ninny, who, for all his doting behavior, is all but oblivious of her needs.

Hedda must bear the responsibility for the marriage, however. As she acknowledges, she had been the one to fashion it, not from love, but from her need for comfort and respectability. That she cannot abide either her husband or her marriage is her own fault, and in that sense she is her own victim. She responds with anger and resentment, taking her desperation out on others, those she envies because they have found a contentment that completely eludes her.

At the same time, Hedda is very vulnerable. The fears that had led her to reject Eilert Lovborg and enter a loveless marriage with George Tesman finally ensnare her in Brack's power, something that she can not tolerate. The alternative is scandal, which Hedda elects to evade by suicide, her final destructive act.

STYLE

Setting

While it is important, the physical setting of *Hedda Gabler*—the Tesmans' newly purchased villa in Christiania, Norway—is of less importance than the social environment of the time and place. The comfortably furnished house reflects both the class status of the Tesmans and their future expectations. In the first act, Hedda makes it clear that they plan to move beyond mere comfort to new levels of luxury. Her old piano, unsuited for the drawing room decor, must be moved into another room, to be replaced by a second, more elegant piano— at best a frivolous and impractical expense. Hedda wants both the security of respectability and the extravagant lifestyle of the wealthy, something threatened by Lovborg's arrival.

There is a price to be paid, though, a price that makes the villa a kind of prison. Against her innermost desires, Hedda must act like a proper wife, deferring to her husband's authority. She attempts to feign that role, but she finds it extremely boring. She grows desperate, especially when George warns that his appointment is no certainty. Fearing the loss of comfort as much as the loss of respectability, Hedda destroys Eilert's manuscript and bamboozles George into believing that she did it out of love for him. Hedda will not live in such a cage unless it is extremely well-appointed and all her material needs are met. She is simply that selfish and abusive of others.

Structure

Hedda Gabler, a four-act play, has what at the time was probably the most common formal pattern of dividing full-length plays into discrete segments. Works from earlier eras are usually divided into five acts, while more modern plays are generally divided into either three acts or, as is the case with many contemporary plays, into two acts. As is also traditional, the acts of *Hedda Gabler* mark divisions in time, segments in which significant action occurs

over the course of two days. The plot is linear in its progression, strictly adhering to a straight-forward, chronological order.

Equally important, each act reaches a climactic moment when something decisive or irreversible is said or done. These are memorable moments, when, for example, at the end of the second act, Hedda burns Eilert's manuscript or, at the end of the play, kills herself with one of her father's pistols. Each act has the classic dramatic structure characterizing the play as a whole, and the warp and woof of each is a rising action that takes the whole to a new plateau of tension. In short, *Hedda Gabler,* provides an excellent example of what constitutes "a well-made play."

Realism

Like the other social-problem or thesis plays of Ibsen, *Hedda Gabler* follows the tenets of realism prevalent in late nineteenth-century Europe. Principal among these was the idea that the writer should render life both objectively and faithfully, concentrating on fairly ordinary people who face problems that can only be resolved in a manner that is true to life. In his realistic works, Ibsen sought to capture a sense of reality by using the characteristics of ordinary conversation, unencumbered with ornate diction and insistent poetic effects. In their cadences and diction his characters speak like real people, if, from dramatic necessity, somewhat more effortlessly and pointedly, and, in Norwegian at least, somewhat more sonorously.

Generally, too, characters in such works have discernible and valid motives for their behavior, even if they are complex, as they are in Hedda's case. If they are not clear, they must at least have verisimilitude, that quality that allows the viewer to conclude that even very puzzling characters are true to life and have validity. Ibsen allows his audience glimpses into Hedda's deeper motives, those things which do not wholly surface in the play's verbal matrix but are suggested, for example, both in persistent symbols and in her actions.

It is in *Hedda Gabler* that Ibsen takes his realism in drama to his limits. It has been described as the dramatist's most objective work, almost clinical in its coldness and distance. His plot driver, Hedda, is a vicious, petty, and extremely selfish woman, for whom, in Ibsen's time, few could find an iota of sympathy. Perhaps to underscore her brusque incivility and abrupt mood changes, Ibsen experimented with a new technique, eliminating long speeches altogether. He also used insistent words and phrases to reveal and even encapsulate his characters, a prime example being the ''fancy that'' of George Tesman.

Foil

An important device used by Ibsen in *Hedda Gabler* is the character foil. Contrasting figures help define their counterparts, providing a heightened sense of each character's personality. Hedda has two principal foils: Thea Elvsted and Juliana Tesman. Both women are very unselfish and at peace with life, willing to sacrifice themselves for others, even though, in Thea's case, it will destroy her reputation. Hedda's paralyzing fear of losing respectability stands in sharp contrast.

George Tesman and Eilert Lovborg are also foils. Tesman is ''correctness'' itself, a dull but steady plodder with a very limited imagination. His principal interest as scholar lies in rooting through the relics of the past, taking and organizing notes about the domestic industries of medieval Brabant. Lovborg, in contrast, is an erratic genius, prone to excess and easily drawn to hedonistic pleasures. As a visionary scholar, he is much more interested in the past for what it may reveal about the future, the unknown. He is, however, arrogant, self-destructive, and, at the last, somewhat pathetic.

Symbol

Ibsen makes it impossible to ignore some important symbols in *Hedda Gabler*. Primary are the pistols, Thea Elvsted's hair, and Eilert's manuscript. Because of the association made by both Hedda and Thea, the most obvious of these is Lovborg's manuscript. In the minds of both, the work is Eilert and Thea's ''child,'' born of their love and affection for each other. It is partly from her intense jealousy that Hedda destroys it and sets out to break the bond between Thea and Lovborg.

Less open in symbolic significance is Thea's luxurious and abundant hair, especially as it contrasts with Hedda's own. Thea's hair is a point of fixation for Hedda, something that she despised in Thea when the two were schoolgirls; it continues to annoy her during the course of the play. Thea's hair seems to embody those qualities in Thea's character that Hedda lacks, including an engaging femininity that Hedda envies, perhaps even a sensuality that Hedda hates because she represses it in herself.

The pistols, on the other hand, suggest masculinity, and have long been identified as phallic symbols. It is noteworthy that both George Tesman

and Judge Brack are appalled by the fact that Hedda plays with them. As extensions of Hedda's character, the guns suggest a masculinity, a hardening that has resulted from her repressed femininity. They represent the freedom that Hedda longs for but must sacrifice to respectability.

HISTORICAL CONTEXT

When Ibsen returned to his native Norway in 1891, he journeyed to a land that to a great degree was isolated from the revolutionary movements affecting both society and culture in the more cosmopolitan centers of Europe. That isolation was partly the result of inaccessibility. Modern communication and transportation were still in their infancy, awaiting the second major stage of the industrial revolution. The post and telegraph were the only real means of exchanging information over long distances, for the telephone was not yet in general use and wireless or radio communications were still the yet-to-be-realized dreams of Guglielmo Marconi and other inventors and engineers.

But Norway was also isolated in other ways. The dominate religion, Evangelical Lutheranism, was a conservative force in the social thinking of the country and one that, through his creative life, had not treated Ibsen well. The dramatist's frank treatment of taboo subjects and rigorous scrutiny of traditional mores offended many of his straightlaced countrymen. As a result, Ibsen was forced into a long artistic exile from his homeland.

A continent away, in the United States, as the historian Frederick Jackson Turner noted, the frontier was finally closing. In 1890, the last great Indian uprising was savagely crushed at the Battle of Wounded Knee, South Dakota, the final brutal ''taming'' of the West. The United States would soon look across the seas for new challenges and new opportunities.

Meanwhile, the British Empire was still in a major stage of development, making inroads in the near and far East by dint of its superior naval power. Indeed, it ruled the seas, though in Africa and other undeveloped areas of the world it had major competitors, including Germany and France, which, like Great Britain, looked for raw materials and markets to exploit.

The seeds of more revolutionary changes were also sown in the 1890s. By the middle of the decade,

COMPARE & CONTRAST

- **1890s:** The world stands on the threshold of the second major phase of the industrial revolution, revolutionary changes in communications and transportation, the advent of the automobile, airplane, radio, phonograph, and film. These innovations will bring isolated communities into virtual proximity with the cultural and political centers of the world.

  Today: In the advanced nations of the world, the industrial revolution has ended. It is the time of technological revolution, leading the world into the space and information ages. Satellite communications and the computer make it possible for even the most isolated people to communicate with anyone in the world.

- **1890s:** Puritanical codes of acceptable behavior govern the social mores of Ibsen's day. Throughout Europe, social sanctions against such things as pre-marital sex, divorce, and family abandonment are strong, forcing many people to live miserable lives. The so-called ''Victorian underground'' teems with prostitutes and thieves, many of whom are ''fallen women'' who had to resort to such a life or face abject poverty. Officially, however, moral sanctions in society were strict and penalties for infractions severe.

  Today: Life in most post-industrial societies is permissive. In the United States, many marriages end in divorce. In many urban areas, single-parent families are prevalent, with pregnancy among unmarried teenage girls reaching epidemic proportions, despite the availability of birth-control drugs and devices. Homosexuality has not only been decriminalized, it has reached considerably wide acceptance, at least in some quarters. The overall nature of this ''non-taboo'' society has led many conservatives to call for a return to ''family values'' and the respectable morality of Ibsen's day.

- **1890s:** Official and unofficial protectors of the strict community moral standards put theatrical performances under close scrutiny, and many have the authority either to shut down productions or lead boycotts or protests, some of which result in riots. Plays can even be censored before they are performed.

  Today: Both on stage and in media, especially film, there is virtually no official censorship. In the United States, for example, whatever moral codes relate to the substance of produced and broadcast works are self-imposed by the industries themselves. Frank treatment of what were once considered indelicate subjects is common, as are nudity, sex, and violence. Only the boycott remains as a possible avenue of protest, and it is rarely effective.

- **1890s:** In Ibsen's day, men and women live separate lives. Although there are various women's organizations dedicated to change, women remain ''unliberated,'' except, perhaps, in groups on the fringes of respectable society. They are educated in their own finishing schools and are excluded from most professions. Much of their leisure time is spent in the company of other women, segregated from men. They lack political power because, even in the democracies, they lack the vote. Their possibilities in life outside of marriage are limited, unless, like Mme. Diana in Ibsen's play, they are willing to sacrifice their reputations.

  Today: Although many feminists still argue that women have yet to complete their liberation, enfranchisement and greater freedom have resulted from the revolutionary changes that have occurred in this century. Women who sacrifice marriage and family for a career still earn reproach from more reactionary corners, but they are hardly censured or demonized by society at large. There remain few male-only bastions, and these are all under siege, at least in the United States. Women take the same jobs as men, go to the same schools, study the same subjects, and mix freely with men at all functions, from corporate board meetings to sporting events. The feminist complaints of today are not so much about exclusion now as they are about equal treatment and compensation.

Sigmund Freud had begun developing his psycho-analytical method, Louis and Auguste Lumière had introduced moving pictures, William Roentgen had discovered X-rays, and Joseph Thomson had isolated the electron. The world was still reeling from the influence of two important thinkers, Karl Marx and Charles Darwin, whose impact was being felt in everything from religion and politics to arts and letters. Marx's theories of group ownership and a government run by the people were the first seeds of the communist movement that would later sweep across Eastern Europe and Asia. Darwin's theories of evolution challenged the religious notions of immaculate conception and divine spark. Great changes were underway, and they were coming at a rate never before experienced.

In the last decade of the nineteenth century, *fin de siecle* ("end of the century") artists were self-consciously abandoning traditional and convention-al forms and techniques in favor of more experi-mental ones. It was a complex period of transition, having as one of its maxims "art for art's sake." It also reflected the new philosophies that called so much into doubt. The naturalistic school, for exam-ple, viewed humanity on the lower end of the socio-economic ladder, trapped there by environmental forces beyond its control.

Two *fin de siecle* British writers of importance were Oscar Wilde (*The Importance of Being Ear-nest*) and George Bernard Shaw (*Man and Super-man*), both of whom wrote plays. Shaw was Ibsen's bulldog in England, his great apologist and advo-cate. In the course of his own long life, he would become the greatest British dramatist of his age, and, next to Shakespeare, the second greatest in the history of British theater.

CRITICAL OVERVIEW

Hedda Gabler was published in December of 1890, a few weeks before it was first performed. Norwe-gian, English, German, French, Russian, and Dutch versions were printed almost simultaneously, with the result that the consternation many readers felt quickly spread throughout Europe. The play gar-nered the worst press reviews of any of Ibsen's mature plays, even *Rosmersholm,* which had been critically mauled four years earlier. The newer work offended many and puzzled more critics, who, as Hans Heiberg noted in *Ibsen: A Portrait of the Artist,* found the main character too monstrous, a "revolting female creature" who "received neither sympathy nor compassion." Just as damning, the work seemed to lack a message, a corrective pur-pose, the sort of social critique for which Ibsen had become so famous.

Hedda's character was the principal target of much of the negative criticism. Quoted in *Ibsen: A Biography,* Alfred Sinding-Larsen called her "a horrid miscarriage of the imagination, a monster in female form to whom no parallel can be found in real life," suggesting that the great realist had completely missed the mark in creating her and that he was only "pandering to contemporary European fashion." Similar complaints came from even the most ardent admirers of Ibsen, including Bredo Morgenstierne. Reprinted in *Ibsen,* the critic opined: "we do not understand Hedda Gabler, nor believe in her. She is not related to anyone we know." Also quoted in *Ibsen,* Gerhard Gran observed that while the play aroused his curiosity, it did not and never could satisfy it. For Gran, a figure as complex as Hedda was not suited to drama and could only be satisfactorily treated in the novel; the play, he argued, only "leaves us with a sense of emptiness and betrayal."

Much of the criticism was lodged on moral grounds, renewed objections that Ibsen had faced with earlier plays like *A Doll's House* (1879) and *Ghosts* (1881). Some Scandinavian critics suggest-ed that the printed play "should not be found on the table of any decent family." Others dismissed the work as either too puzzling or too decadent. Harald Hansen, reviewing stage productions of 1891, dis-missed it in as single sentence as "an ungrateful play which hardly any of the participants will re-member with real satisfaction" (*Ibsen*).

Ibsen and his play had their champions, includ-ing Henrik Jæger in Norway and Herman Bang in Denmark. Jæger, who had once gone on tour lectur-ing against *A Doll's House,* had become a pro-Ibsen convert. He saw Hedda as a very realistic, earth-born female, "a tragic character who is destroyed by the unharmonious and irreconcilable contrasts in her own character" (*Ibsen*). He suggested that the poor reception of *Hedda Gabler* stemmed from the general unpopularity of tragedy, not from faults in the play. Meanwhile, Bang, in some of the play's most perceptive early criticism, argued that Hedda was the female counterpart of a familiar Ibsen character, the egotistical male. Without the socially-sanctioned outlets afforded men, she is driven "into isolation and self-adoration." "Hedda," Bang observed, "has no source of richness in herself and must constantly seek it in others, so that her life becomes a pursuit of sensation and experiment; and her hatred of bearing a child is the ultimate expression of her egotism, the sickness that brings death" (*Ibsen*).

Most criticism, both of the printed play and first staged productions, was hostile, which, in retrospect, suggests a remarkable short-sightedness on the part of Ibsen's contemporaries. Now, over a century later, *Hedda Gabler* is considered one of the principal stars in the dramatist's artistic crown, and it has been for some time. In his 1971 biography *Ibsen,* Michael Meyer said that the work was then "perhaps the most universally admired of Ibsen's plays," and noted that it was Ibsen's most frequently performed work in England. Today, its chief competitor in Ibsen revivals is *A Doll's House,* in part because of its protagonist Nora Helmer's appeal to the women's liberation movement. Unlike Hedda, there is nothing vicious about Nora, who is mostly pure victim in a society under male control.

Interestingly enough, it is because Hedda so completely dominates her play that her role soon became very attractive to actresses, and because it proved a great vehicle for the most talented and highly regarded among them, it evolved from its maligned beginning into a stage favorite. Among those who undertook the role were leading international stars, including Eleonora Duse, Eve Le Gallienne, Nazimova, Mrs. Patrick Campbell, Claire Bloom, Joan Greenwood, Ingrid Bergman, and Glenda Jackson. That is the final irony, for it was the "monstrous" Hedda who, in the minds of the early critics, condemned the play, whereas it is now her character that makes it one of Ibsen's most durable works. The attraction of the part remains, despite the fact that the society that the play depicts is virtually extinct.

The climax of Hedda Gabler: *unable to face her lot in life, Hedda kills herself (scene from a Downstage Theatre Company production at the Edinburgh International Festival)*

CRITICISM

John W. Fiero

Fiero is a Ph. D., now retired, who formerly taught drama and play writing at the University of Southwestern Louisiana. In this essay he investigates the significance of the secondary female characters in Hedda Gabler, *with a focus on their function both as foils to Hedda and as women who* *themselves fail to meet the woman's primary role as wife-mother in the conventional thinking of the time.*

Because the titular character so completely dominates Henrik Ibsen's *Hedda Gabler,* discussions of the play from a gender perspective seem to almost exclusively focus on Hedda. It is easy to understand why. She is clearly the central figure, the one whose grating dissatisfaction arises from a

WHAT DO I READ NEXT?

- *Madame Bovary* (1857), by Gustave Flaubert, is one of the important early works of French realism. The novel offers a brilliant and fairly sympathetic portrait of a shrewd and ambitious woman who attempts to better her circumstances by marrying and manipulating a country physician.

- *The Awakening* (1899), Kate Chopin's long neglected novel of feminine self-consciousness offers a portrait of a woman defying conventional morality, including marital fidelity and taboos against miscegenation.

- *Sister Carrie* (1900), Theodore Dreiser's first novel, depicts an immoral, self-serving woman with an unusual degree of sympathy.

- *Margaret Fleming* (1890), by James A. Herne, is the first genuinely realistic play in America.

Although now considered sentimental, it depicts a woman who defies convention in undertaking to care for the illegitimate child of her husband.

- *The Quintessence of Ibsenism* (1913) may be more about George Bernard Shaw, its author, than it is about Ibsen, but it gives considerable insight into how Shaw and the British intelligentsia were attempting to transform theater into a vehicle for social improvement. The work grew out of a lecture Shaw gave in 1890, the same year that Ibsen published *Hedda Gabler.*

- *Women in Modern Drama: Freud, Feminism, and European Theater at the Turn of the Century* (1989), by Gail Finney, offers an excellent survey of the depiction of women in European drama towards the end of Ibsen's career.

---

conflict pitting her needs against conventional notions of propriety and female fulfillment as an adoring, dutiful, submissive wife and nurturing, loving mother. She is, moreover, the play's prime mover, the plot driver, the one who has the most at stake, and the one whose name answers the most important question: whose play is it? It is, of course, her play, pure and simple.

Hedda struggles violently against the conventional wife-mother role, a role she does not want but is mortally afraid to reject. She suffers most from what Gail Finney called in *The Cambridge Companion to Ibsen* ''victimization by motherhood''; she is unable to face or to escape the suffocating reality of marriage and motherhood. That surely is as big a factor in her self-destruction as is her fear of being held sexual hostage to the sinister Judge Brack, who threatens to expose her to scandal, of which she is at least equally terrified.

More is learned about Hedda than any of the other female characters. She alone is prone to self-analysis, to confessing her fears and dissatisfactions, which, ironically, she reveals to the two men

besides her husband who have pursued her: Judge Brack and Eilert Lovborg. Hedda has no real female friends, no confidantes with whom she is either close or honest. In fact, she perceives each of the other women as an antagonist. The fact that they seem at peace with themselves profoundly annoys her and contributes to her mounting hysteria. Towards Thea Elvsted, she feigns a friendship, and she quickly betrays what trust Thea places in her. She is also meanspirited towards her husband's well-intentioned aunt, Juliana, whom she views as an insufferable busybody, an unwelcome intruder, and a possible threat to Hedda's control of George. She is also determined to rid her house of Berta, the household servant whose loyalty to the Tesman family daunts Hedda as well.

Also, just as there is much more divulged about Hedda's past, there is also much more implied about Hedda than any other female character in the play. As Finney claimed, ''the influence of her motherless, father-dominated upbringing is everywhere evident.'' Her inheritance reveals itself in her masculine traits, her fondness for horses and pistols, for example, or her excitement over the impending contest between Eilert Lovborg and her husband George, or her interest in manipulating George into the male arena of politics, where she might exercise some real power. In some ways, she seems more masculine than George, the fussy foster-child of two maiden aunts who is uninterested in politics and is afraid of Hedda's handling of her father's pistols.

George also seems prone to what from a male point of view seems to be a typical female trait: excited chatter about trivial matters. His ubiquitous ''fancy that'' seems more appropriate to the tea table than the smoking room, saloon, or other haunt that in Ibsen's time were visited exclusively by men, unless, as in some saloons, disreputable females women like the unseen ''singing woman,'' Mademoiselle Diana, were allowed. To Hedda, the masculine ideal is represented by her father General Gabler. His portrait, a constant reminder of his influence, hangs in a prominent place in her inner sanctum, her room adjoining the drawing room. There are hints of an Electra complex, a deeply-rooted but repressed incestuous and terrorizing desire that is an important strain in Hedda's enigmatic character. Under her father's tutelage, she had become a fit masculine companion for him, but not one suited for her husband, who merely bores her. As for the woman's world, the society of the tea table, she is clearly a pariah, though certainly by willful choice.

The other women in *Hedda Gabler,* even those unseen, have one thing in common with Hedda. They are women who have either failed to meet the male ideal of woman as wife-mother or have rejected it, as Hedda, the least suited to the task, desires to do. They also differ from Hedda in a vitally significant way: they have made peace with themselves. And therein they represent some of the limited alternatives to what society at large viewed as a woman's primary goal—marriage and motherhood. George Tesman's two aunts are maiden aunts, Thea Elvsted has fled a brutal and loveless marriage, and Berta, having given her life over to service, remains, presumably, unattached outside the Tesman family. Their relative contentment speaks volumes about Hedda's discontent, but they are, of course, very different kinds of women, interesting in their own right and not just because as foils they set off Hedda's more complex character.

Like so many secondary characters in drama, the other women of *Hedda Gabler* run much closer to stereotypes than the play's enigmatic protagonist.

> THE OTHER WOMEN IN
> *HEDDA GABLER,* EVEN THOSE
> UNSEEN, HAVE ONE THING IN
> COMMON WITH HEDDA. THEY ARE
> WOMEN WHO HAVE EITHER FAILED
> TO MEET THE MALE IDEAL OF
> WOMAN AS WIFE-MOTHER OR HAVE
> REJECTED IT''

Two of them, Aunt Rina and Mademoiselle Diana, are superb examples of offstage characters whose presence is felt but never seen. The one is George Tesman's dying aunt; the other, ''a mighty huntress of men,'' is a lady of pleasure for those who can afford her.

The unseen Diana is, in fact, one of those notorious fallen women. Talk about her is strained through polite euphemisms which only thinly veil that she is a prostitute, though not of the crass sidewalk variety. She and her friends entertain gentlemen, both in salons and boudoirs, with the implication, too, that they are under some protection from the authorities, thanks to a double standard that permitted respectable men a sexual license denied to respectable women. Judge Brack tells Hedda that Eilert Lovborg had formerly been one of Diana's ''most enthusiastic protectors,'' even before his dissolution and disgrace. The implication is that during his wooing of Hedda, frustrated by her repression of sexual passion, Eilert had found easy solace in the ready arms of Mademoiselle Diana. Lovborg's renewed association with Diana helps ignite Hedda's perverse desire to see Eilert redeem himself through a triumphant and majestic suicide, a kind of ersatz expression of the sexual freedom Hedda had repressed in herself, if only because, unlike Mademoiselle Diana, she could never thumb her nose at respectability.

A sickly invalid, Rina is most important because she is her sister's main burden. Since Juliana is a selfless and loving person, she bears the burden with affection, dignity, and grace, all to Hedda's annoyance. To her, Rina's death only means that Juliana may become a more frequent and troublesome visitor, even though Juliana confides to both Hedda and George that she plans to devote herself to caring for some other sickly person. She tells them that ''it's such an absolute necessity for me to have one to live for.'' Juliana, a dedicated nurse, is simply beyond the selfish Hedda's comprehension. Juliana lives only for others, but Hedda lives only for herself. From Hedda's perspective, Juliana is both a fool and a threat.

Juliana is more than a nurse, however. For good or ill, she has also been a surrogate mother and father to George, as he cheerfully admits in the opening of the play. She and her sister helped shape her nephew's adult character, explaining why George utterly lacks the strong-willed and arrogant hardness of his wife. Unwittingly, they turned George into someone safe for Hedda. She can easily manipulate him, verbally beating down whatever objections the docile and compliant fellow raises. As regards Hedda, George is ''correctness itself'' not only because he is a respectable man with good prospects but because he lacks the intestinal fortitude to challenge her. She has none of the fear of George that Lovborg and Brack inspire in her.

Berta is another selfless woman who finds meaning and satisfaction in her service to others. In Act One, it is disclosed that she has been a loyal retainer in the Tesman family for years, and that with George's marriage to Hedda, she has come to the newlyweds' villa as servant and caretaker. Nothing is disclosed of her private life, but she speaks of ''all the blessed years'' that she spent with the Tesmans, suggesting that she has found fulfillment only in their employ and that she has had neither husband nor children. George and Juliana both treat her with affection and respect. Also, as if she were a member of the family, they confide in her, something that Hedda cannot do. That and her overly-protective behavior towards George irk Hedda, who wants to rid the house of Berta and threatens to do so with a petty complaint about her carelessness. Like Juliana, Berta represents a threat to Hedda's control over George, something that she will not tolerate *noblesse oblige* (''nobility obligates,'' a notion that those of high social standing were required to behave in an honorable manner) and familial gratitude be damned.

Hedda's most troubling female adversary is, of course, Mrs. Elvsted. She does not stand in Hedda's way of controlling George; she stands in Hedda's way of a greater challenge, controlling Eilert Lovborg. Hedda's frightful dislike of Thea is mixed with intense jealousy. It goads her that someone who seems like such a simpleton has been able to redeem Lovborg from his recklessness and inspire his work. Thea, for all her experience, acts like an innocent compared to Hedda. She is gullible and vulnerable, easily duped by Hedda into believing that Hedda is her friend, believing that Hedda's girlhood antagonism had been entirely vitiated over the years. She does not sense Hedda's spite and is both surprised and hurt when Hedda betrays her confidence.

Thea is, however, both a wholly sympathetic character and unlike Hedda—a survivor. She has devoted herself to redeeming the dissolute Lovborg with a love that he cannot fully return, even though she has sacrificed her reputation in the process by fleeing from her loveless and enslaving marriage to Sheriff Elvsted. It is her admirable courage and devotion that make Lovborg seem like an arrogant ingrate, someone at least partly deserving of his inept death. In fact, apart from his genius, nothing about his character is quite so memorable as his insufferable dismissal of Thea as being ''too stupid'' to understand the kind of love that he believes he has shared with Hedda.

Thea's eagerness to immerse herself with George Tesman in an effort to reconstruct Lovborg's manuscript has the aura of a magnificent obsession about it and argues that it is Thea who sees the truth about Eilert that the man's ideas are both more admirable and important than his life. Ironically, too, it is she who triumphs over her rival, Hedda, winning not Eilert but George, making him her co-conspirator in their efforts to breathe new life into Thea and Eilert's destroyed child, Lovborg's brilliant work. As much as Hedda's own unborn child and Brack's endgame sexual advantage, Thea's triumph drives Hedda to despair and suicide, proving that even in Ibsen's stark realism there is adequate room for at least a modicum of poetic justice.

Source: John W. Fiero, for *Drama for Students,* Gale, 1999.

Bert Cardullo

In this excerpt, Cardullo compares and contrasts elements of legacy in Ibsen's Hedda Gabler *and* Ghosts.

In Ibsen's *Hedda Gabler,* Hedda's ideal (to live beautifully, free from the constraints of her socialization) dies with her, but Løvborg's ideal (a book on the future of civilization, in which he frees himself, and potentially others, from the poisonous constraints of society by writing a prescription for that society's health or liberation) lives—it is reconstructed from notes by Tesman and Thea. Hedda kills herself *with child:* Løvborg and Thea speak of the manuscript as *their* "child." Hedda dies to achieve the ideal she could not achieve in life; Løvborg kills himself (or is killed in a mistaken attempt to retrieve his manuscript from "Mademoiselle Diana's boudoir") because he felt he had achieved, or helped to make possible, the ideal through his book and then senselessly lost the manuscript.

In the same way as Osvald's paralysis of mind could be said to be growing throughout *Ghosts,* to turn him at the end into a symbol of the paralysis of mind in Norwegian society, so too could the notes for Løvborg's book that Thea produces in *Hedda Gabler* be said to have been "growing throughout the play, to be given birth at the end as a symbol of hope for the future of civilization. Thea and Løvborg had spoken of the manuscript as their "child," as I mention above, and thus it is no accident that Thea "nurtures" these notes in the pocket of her dress throughout the play, (she says at one point, "Yes. I took them with me when I left home—they're here in my pocket—"), to produce them at the right moment for reassembly by herself and Tesman.

In the same way that Ibsen leads us to believe that in Osvald an artist of great promise is destroyed, ultimately, by the paralysis of mind of his society, so too does the playwright lead us to believe that in Hedda, a person of potential creativity, is destroyed by her upbringing as the daughter of the aristocratic General Gabler. Martin Esslin writes that

[Hedda's] sense of social superiority prevents her from realizing her genuine superiority as a potential creative personality. If the standards prescribed by the laws of noblesse oblige had not prevented her from breaking out into the freedom of moral and social emancipation, she might have been able to turn her passionate desire for beauty (which is the hallmark of real, spiritual, as distinct from social, aristocracy) to the creation of beauty, living beauty rather than merely a beautiful death. It is the creative energy, frustrated and damned up, that is finally converted into the malice and envy, the destructive rage, the intellectual dishonesty that lead to Hedda Gabler's downfall. (*Reflections: Essays on Modern Theatre,* Doubleday, 1969.)

Like Osvald, Hedda is a potential artist. Like Mrs. Alving, she has no true moment of recognition or perception: Ibsen is interested at the end more in whether Løvborg's ideal will be promulgated, to the benefit of future Heddas.

IN THE SAME WAY THAT IBSEN LEADS US TO BELIEVE THAT IN OSVALD AN ARTIST OF GREAT PROMISE IS DESTROYED . . . SO TOO DOES THE PLAYWRIGHT LEAD US TO BELIEVE THAT IN HEDDA, A PERSON OF POTENTIAL CREATIVITY, IS DESTROYED BY HER UPBRINGING AS THE DAUGHTER OF THE ARISTOCRATIC GENERAL GABLER"

Source: Bert Cardullo, "Ibsen's *Hedda Gabler* and *Ghosts*" in the *Explicator,* Vol. 46, no. 1, Fall, 1987, pp 23–24.

Max Beerbohm

Beerbohm is noted as one of the prominent voices of early twentieth-century drama criticism. In this review, which was originally published on October 10, 1903, he examines the expectations of typical theatregoers and the manner in which Ibsen's Hedda Gabler *goes against such preconceptions— and yet still manages to be a work of popular theatre.*

Eecosstoetchiayoomahnioeevahrachellopestibahntamahntafahnta . . . shall I go on? No? You do not catch my meaning, when I write thus? I am to express myself, please, in plain English? If I wrote the whole of my article as I have written the beginning of it, you would, actually, refuse to read it? I am astonished. The chances are that you do not speak Italian, do not understand Italian when it is spoken. The chances are that Italian spoken from the stage of a theatre produces for you no more than the empty, though rather pretty, effect which it produces for me, and which I have tried to suggest phonetically in print. And yet the chances are also that you were in the large British audience which I saw, last Wednesday afternoon, in the Adelphi Theatre—that large, patient, respectful audience, which sat out the performance of *"Hedda Gabler."* Surely, you are a trifle inconsistent? You will not tolerate two columns or so of gibberish from me, and yet you will profess to have passed very enjoyably a whole afternoon in listening to similar gibberish from Signora Duse. Suppose that not only my article, but the whole of this week's Review were written in the fashion which you reject, and suppose that the price of the Review were raised from sixpence to ninepence (proportionately to the increased price for seats at the Adelphi when Signora Duse comes there). To be really consistent, you would have to pay, without a murmur, that ninepence, and to read, from cover to cover, that Review, and to enjoy, immensely, that perusal. An impossible feat? Well, just so would it be an impossible feat not to be bored by the Italian version of *"Hedda Gabler."* Why not confess your boredom? Better still, why go to be bored?

All this sounds rather brutal. But it is a brutal thing to object to humbug, and only by brutal means can humbug be combated, and there seems to me no form of humbug sillier and more annoying than the habit of attending plays that are acted in a language whereof one cannot make head or tail. Of course, I do not resent the mere fact that Signora Duse comes to London. Let that distinguished lady be made most welcome. Only, let the welcome be offered by appropriate people. There are many of them. There is the personnel of the embassy in Grosvenor Square. There are the organ-grinders, too, and the ice-cream men. And there are some other, some English, residents in London who have honourably mastered the charming Italian tongue. Let all this blest minority flock to the Adelphi every time, and fill as much of it as they can. But, for the most part, the people who, instead of staying comfortably at home, insist on flocking and filling are they to whom, as to me, Italian is gibberish, and who have not, as have I, even the excuse of a mistaken sense of duty. Perhaps they have some such excuse. Perhaps they really do feel that they are taking a means of edification. "We needs must praise the highest when we see it"; Duse is (we are assured) the highest; therefore we needs must see her, for our own edification, and go into rhapsodies. Such, perhaps, is the unsound syllogism which these good folk mutter. I suggest, of what spiritual use is it to see the highest if you cannot understand it? Go round to the booksellers and buy Italian grammars, Italian conversation-books, the "Inferno," and every other possible means to a nodding acquaintance with Italian. Stick to your task; and then, doubtless, when next Signora Duse comes among us, you will derive not merely that edification which is now your secret objective, but also that gratification which you are so loudly professing. I know your rejoinder to that. "Oh, Duse's personality is so wonderful.

Her temperament is so marvellous. And then her art! It doesn't matter whether we know Italian or not. We only have to watch the movements of her hands" (rhapsodies omitted) "and the changes of her face" (r. o.) "and the inflections of her voice" (r. o.) "to understand everything, positively *everything*." Are you so sure? I take it that you understand more from the performance of an Italian play which you have read in an English translation than from the performance of an Italian play which never has been translated. There are, so to say, degrees in your omniscience. You understand more if you have read the translation lately than if a long period has elapsed since your reading of it. Are you sure that you would not understand still more if the play were acted in English? Of course you are. Nay, and equally of course, you are miserably conscious of all the innumerable things that escape you, that flit faintly past you. You read your English version, feverishly, like a timid candidate for an examination, up to the very last moment before your trial. Perhaps you even smuggle it in with you, for furtive cribbing. But this is a viva voce examination: you have no time for cribbing: you must rely on Signora Duse's voice, hands, face and your own crammed memory. And up to what point has your memory been crammed? You remember the motive of the play, the characters, the sequence of the scenes. Them you recognise on the stage. But do you recognise the masquerading words? Not you. They all flash past you, whirl round you, mocking, not to be caught, not to be challenged and unmasked. You stand sheepishly in their midst, like a solitary stranger strayed into a masked ball. Or, to reverse the simile, you lurch this way and that, clutching futile air, like the central figure in blindman's buff. Occasionally you do catch a word or two. These are only the proper names, but they are very welcome. It puts you in pathetic conceit with yourself, for the moment, when from the welter of unmeaning vowels and consonants "Eilert Lövborg" or *"Hedda Gabler"* suddenly detaches itself, like a silver trout "rising" from a muddy stream. These are your only moments of comfort. For the rest, your irritation at not grasping the details prevents you from taking pleasure in your power to grasp the general effect.

I doubt even whether, in the circumstances, you can have that synthetic power fully and truly. It may be that what I am going to say about Signora Duse as Hedda Gabler is vitiated by incapacity to understand exactly her rendering of the part as a whole. She may be more plausibly like Hedda Gabler than she seems to me. Mark, I do not say that she may have conceived the part more intelligently, more rightly, with greater insight into Ibsen's meaning. And perhaps I should express myself more accurately if I said that Hedda Gabler may be more like Signora Duse than she seems to me. For this actress never stoops to impersonation. I have seen her in many parts, but I have never (you must take my evidence for what it is worth) detected any difference in her. To have seen her once is to have seen her always. She is artistically right or wrong according as whether the part enacted by her can or cannot be merged and fused into her own personality. Can Hedda Gabler be so merged and fused? She is self-centred. Her eyes are turned inward to her own soul. She does not try to fit herself into the general scheme of things. She broods disdainfully aloof. So far so good; for Signora Duse, as we know her, is just such another. (This can be said without offence. The personality of an artist, as shown through his or her art, is not necessarily a reflection, and is often a flat contradiction—a complement—to his or her personality in life.) But Hedda is also a minx, and a ridiculous minx, and not a nice minx. Her revolt from the circumstances of her life is untinged with nobility. She imagines herself to be striving for finer things, but her taste is in fact not good enough for what she gets. One can see that Ibsen hates her, and means us to laugh at her. For that reason she ''wears'' much better than those sister-rebels whom Ibsen glorified. She remains as a lively satire on a phase that for serious purposes is out of date. She ought to be played with a sense of humour, with a comedic understanding between the player and the audience. Signora Duse is not the woman to create such an understanding. She cannot, moreover, convey a hint of minxishness: that quality is outside her rubric. Hedda is anything but listless. She is sick of a life which does not tickle her with little ready-made excitements. But she is ever alert to contrive these little excitements for herself. She is the very soul of restless mischief. Signora Duse suggested the weary calm of one who has climbed to a summit high above the gross world. She was as one who sighs, but can afford to smile, being at rest with herself. She was spiritual, statuesque, somnambulistic, what you will, always in direct opposition to eager, snappy, fascinating, nasty little Hedda Gabler. Resignedly she shot the pistol from the window. Resignedly she bent over the book of photographs with the lover who had returned. Resignedly she lured him to drunkenness. Resignedly she committed his MS. to the flames. Resignation, as always, was the keynote of her performance. And here, as often elsewhere, it rang false.

> HEDDA IS A MINX, AND A RIDICULOUS MINX, AND NOT A NICE MINX. HER REVOLT FROM THE CIRCUMSTANCES OF HER LIFE IS UNTINGED WITH NOBILITY"

However, it was not the only performance of Hedda Gabler. There was another, and, in some ways, a better. While Signora Duse walked through her part, the prompter threw himself into it with a will. A more raucous whisper I never heard than that which preceded the Signora's every sentence. It was like the continuous tearing of very thick silk. I think it worried every one in the theatre, except the Signora herself, who listened placidly to the prompter's every reading, and, as soon as he had finished, reproduced it in her own way. This process made the matinée a rather long one. By a very simple expedient the extra time might have been turned to good account. How much pleasure would have been gained, and how much hypocrisy saved, if there had been an interpreter on the O.P. side, to shout in English what the prompter was whispering in Italian!

Source: Max Beerbohm, ''An Hypocrisy in Playgoing'' in his *Around Theatres,* Simon & Schuster, 1954 , pp. 277–81.

SOURCES

Finney, Gail. ''Ibsen and Feminism'' in *The Cambridge Companion to Ibsen,* edited by James McFarlane, Cambridge University Press, pp. 99-100.

Heiberg, Hans. *Ibsen: A Portrait of the Artist,* University of Miami Press, 1967, p. 257.

Weigand, Herman J. *The Modern Ibsen: A Reconsideration,* Books for Libraries Press, 1970, p. 242.

FURTHER READING

Barranger, Milly S. *Barron's Simplified Approach to Henrik Ibsen,* Barron's Educational Series, 1969.
    This brief monograph offers uncomplicated readings of *Hedda Gabler* and two other major Ibsen plays:

The Wild Duck and *Ghosts.* It is a helpful guide to interpretation focusing on character, themes, and dramatic technique.

Durbach, Errol. *Ibsen the Romantic: Analogues of Paradise in the Later Plays,* University of George Press, 1982.
    Durbach discusses the romantic and counter-romantic currents in Ibsen that underlies his characters' search for meaning, their efforts to redeem themselves from an inhibiting and stultifying, uncreative life. It is a search that can be destructive, as in Hedda's case.

Lyons, Charles R. Hedda Gabler: *Gender, Role, and World,* Twayne, 1990.
    Lyons discusses both the cultural and historical milieu of *Hedda Gabler,* then discusses the play as a kind of mimetic snapshot of human behavior caught in that historical matrix and argues that reader responses should reflect that limitation.

McFarlane, James, editor. *The Cambridge Companion to Ibsen,* Cambridge University Press, 1994.
    A collection of articles by contemporary scholars, this anthology includes important pieces on such topics as Ibsen's realistic problem plays, his relationship to feminism, and his impact on modern drama. The work includes helpful aids, including a chronology and notes on the first publication and performance of each of Ibsen's works.

Meyer, Michael. *Ibsen: A Biography,* Doubleday, 1971.
    A well-documented critical biography, this study makes extensive use of Ibsen's correspondence and summarizes the critical reception of his works in his own day.

Northam, John. *Ibsen's Dramatic Method: A Study of the Prose Dramas,* Universitetsforlaget, 1971.
    A recommended starting place for the study of Ibsen's technique, this work approaches the plays by analyzing the playwright's language and its correlation with visual, on-stage images, as, for example, the opposing physical differences between Hedda and Thea Elvsted.

Young, Robert. *Time's Disinherited Children: Childhood, Regression, and Sacrifice in the Plays of Henrik Ibsen,* Norvik Press, 1989.
    Young's central thesis is that the motives and needs of many of Ibsen's major characters reveal the disinherited child in the adult.

Man and Superman

GEORGE BERNARD SHAW

1903

Subtitled "A Comedy and a Philosophy," George Bernard Shaw's *Man and Superman* is a comedy of ideas: its characters discuss ideas such as capitalism, social reform, male and female roles in courtship, and other existential topics in long speeches that resemble arias in an opera. The play's verbosity makes it unwieldy to produce full scale, so the Epistle in the beginning and the Revolutionist's Handbook at the end are usually not performed, and the scene in Hell, although containing the bulk of the play's philosophical musings, is often dropped.

What is left is basically a light-hearted parlor play demonstrating Shaw's idea of the Life Force, the force that drives women to pursue a mate in order to attempt to produce a Superman. This theory, along with a theory of eugenic breeding to accompany it, preoccupied Shaw for the rest of his life. The theories expounded in the play are full of contradictions, typical of Shaw's writing, and critics have devoted countless books and articles to sorting them out. Early critics called the play tedious and dramatically unsound, but today it is considered a landmark in the genre of the "idea play."

AUTHOR BIOGRAPHY

George Bernard Shaw was born in Dublin in 1856, the youngest child of George Carr and Lucinda Elizabeth Shaw. His mother was an opera singer

and voice trainer; his father was an unsuccessful businessman and alcoholic who could not pull his family out of poverty, in spite of belonging to the genteel class of Protestant Irish gentry. Shaw once described himself as a "downstart," one whose family had come down in the world. When Shaw was twenty, he moved to London with his mother. Lucinda earned the family's living with her music; Shaw wrote five unsuccessful novels and furthered his education through reading. Music was central to his world and would later come to be essential to his plays.

Shaw entered the theatrical world as a critic, writing music reviews for various papers until asked to write drama criticism for the *Saturday Review* in 1894. He also wrote pamphlets, tracts, and articles, spoke out for the labor movement, and established the Fabian Society, a socialist intellectual group, in 1884 with Beatrice and Sidney Webb. Shaw's interest in the theater soon led him to publish and then to produce what he called the "play of ideas," a shift in dramatic form that altered the course of dramatic structure irrevocably. *Man and Superman* was the first of these, published first in book form in 1903 and then produced on stage in 1905.

Shaw, a shy man despite his speaking ability, developed a public persona, G. B. S., who parried boldly with his critics in editorials and in irreverent comments within the plays themselves. G. B. S.— impudent and witty—contrasted greatly with the real Shaw, who was shy, prudish, and courteous. Shaw felt compelled to produce plays of social reform. The words spoken by Don Juan in *Man and Superman* might easily have been those of Shaw himself: "I tell you that as long as I can conceive something better than myself I cannot be easy unless I am striving to bring it into existence or clearing the way for it. This is the law of my life. That is the working within me of Life's incessant aspiration to higher organization, wider, deeper, intenser self-consciousness and clearer self-understanding." Admittedly a virtual "writing machine," Shaw worked relentlessly, writing plays, critical commentary, and letters of social reform, as well as maintaining a rigorous daily schedule of physical labor in his garden. Among his notable works are the plays *Pygmalion, Major Barbara,* and *Saint Joan.* At the age of 94 he fell from a tree he was pruning and broke a leg. The injury was soon followed by his demise; he died November 2, 1950, in Ayot Saint Lawrence, Hertfordshire, England, having become one of the most influential dramatists of all time.

PLOT SUMMARY

Epistle Dedicatory to Arthur Bingham Walkly

The printed play includes a dedication, in the form of a letter (epistle), addressed to Arthur Bingham Walkly, a drama critic and Shaw's friend of fifteen years, who, according to the letter, had once asked Shaw why he did not write a Don Juan play. The dedication defends the play's "preaching" tone, and sets out the premise of the play as "the natural attraction of the sexes," to be distinguished from a play about love or marriage. The rest of the rather long and digressive letter explains that Don Juan is a philosopher who follows his instincts, along with some of his theories. This is a play admittedly designed for "a pit of philosophers" as audience.

Act I

Respectable Roebuck Ramsden and brash John Tanner are shocked to discover they must share jointly the guardianship of Ann Whitefield, whose father has just died. Tanner's anarchistic book *The Revolutionist's Handbook and Pocket Companion* offends Ramsden, and Tanner finds Ramsden hopelessly obsolete. They both would like to marry her off to Octavius, who loves her, and be done with their obligation. They present their dilemma to Ann, but she charms them into accepting their partnership, for her sake, and retires upstairs to mourn her father. Octavius, or Tavy, or Ricky Ticky Tavy, as Ann calls him, is clearly smitten with her, somewhat to Tanner's disgust. Tanner compares her attention to Octavius as like that of a lion or tiger with its prey. Octavius says he would consider such treatment "fulfillment."

Ann returns downstairs, and Ramsden tells her that Octavius's sister, Violet, is pregnant by an unknown "scoundrel." Octavius and Ramsden want to find him and force a marriage, but Tanner's interest is in supporting Violet's need to raise her child, since the male contribution to her condition is essentially over. Octavius goes upstairs to comfort his sister, while Tanner and Ann reminisce about their childhood romance. Tanner accuses her of being a boa constrictor, encircling him in her flirtation. Now Miss Ramsden, Roebuck's maiden sister, comes downstairs, washing her hands of Violet because the young expectant mother does not show proper contrition. Violet shows her true mettle when she is outraged by Tanner's congratulations on her courage. She is offended because she *is* married, much to everyone's surprise, although she mysteriously withholds her husband's identity. She departs indignantly, leaving the others to contemplate their stupidity.

Act II

The scene opens in the drive of a country estate, where a competent chauffeur, Enry Straker, attends to a broken-down touring car while Tanner looks on helplessly. The chauffeur and Tanner banter nearly as equals about driving fast, which scares Tanner and exhilarates his employee. Tanner calls Straker the scion of the rising class of intelligent, successful but not wealthy, working men. Now Octavius comes out of the house, having arrived earlier with Ann Whitefield and her sister Rhoda, his own sister, Violet, and an American friend, Hector Malone. Ann has refused Octavius's marriage proposal, claiming to be too upset by her father's death to answer.

Tanner insincerely invites Ann to accompany him on a cross-country drive to Nice, Algiers, and Biskra, assuming she will refuse. Mr. Malone offers to take Violet along, in his car. Mrs. Whitefield and Ann discreetly go indoors, leaving Ramsden and Octavius to help explain Violet's embarrassing situation to the dense American. Alone, Hector and Violet kiss, for Hector is her secret husband. The secrecy evolves from the fact that Hector's father would cut off Hector's substantial inheritance if he learned that his son had failed to marry a girl whose station in life he can improve. Tanner has arranged for Ann to travel with Octavius, and it takes Straker to inform Tanner that Ann is really after him. Tanner escapes by leaving immediately for Biskra.

Act III

The stage directions to Act III consist of an ironic socialist mini sermon on the right of the working man to refuse demeaning labor, as represented by the band of vagabonds discussing "abstruse questions of politic economy" in an abandoned quarry in the Spanish Sierra Nevada. Their discussion parodies an intellectual club meeting, until Mendoza, the chief of the brigand, calls them back to earth. Their mode of redistributing the wealth of society lies in thievery: they are waiting to ambush the next automobile. They catch Straker and Tanner and hold the latter for ransom. To pass the time before morning, when the money can be procured, Mendoza offers to read his love poems, dedicated to one Louisa—who turns out to be Enry's sister, Louisa Straker. The poems are so bad that Tanner recommends he throw them in the fire. The bandits and their prisoners fall asleep in front of

George Bernard Shaw

the fire listening to, "Louisa I love thee; I love thee, Louisa; Louisa, Louisa."

The stage grows dark, and then a ghostly pallor, accompanied by violins playing a "Mozartian strain" reveals a man dressed as a fifteenth-century Spanish nobleman—it is Don Juan, but he looks remarkably like John Tanner. He is joined by an old woman, who turns out to be Dona Ana de Ulloa, Don Juan Tenorio's love, the one whose father Don Juan had killed in a duel over her honor. Dona Ana, a near twin for Ann Whitefield, has just arrived in Hell (for that is where they are) having lived to the age of seventy-seven. She is surprised to learn that her old lover and her father, Don Gonzalo, are now good friends who enjoy long philosophical discussions, along with the Devil, when the old commander visits from Heaven.

The commander is a statue resembling Roebuck Ramsden in all but his marble form and the style of his moustache. He is the statue that Dona Ana commissioned in her father's honor, after his death. They debate the relative merits of hell versus heaven, with the devil trying to convince Don Juan to go to heaven, since he "has no capacity for enjoyment" and thus doesn't like being in Hell. The good commander would rather be in Hell because heaven is "too angelically dull" for him. The three men discuss instinct, virtue, and love in lengthy speeches, while Ana expresses shock at their callousness toward women. She leaves in search of a father for the Superman she hopes to conceive.

The sleepers awake and hear a loud bang that turns out to be a flat tire on the car containing Ann Whitefield and the others. She has tracked John Tanner, driven by the Life Force.

Act IV

The scene shifts to a villa on a hillside that looks onto Alhambra, a Medieval Moslem castle. Here, the group learns that Violet's secret husband is the American, Hector Malone; the pair has kept their marriage a secret. Once the elder Malone meets the spirited Violet, however, he blesses the marriage and gives the couple a generous gift of money. Ann again rejects Octavius's marriage proposal. Octavius indicates that he will spend the rest of his life mourning this rejection. Ann then woos and wins Jack Tanner, despite his recognizing the wiles with which she ensnares him. They find compatibility in cynicism.

The Revolutionist's Handbook and Pocket Companion by John Tanner, M. I. R. C. (Member of the Idle Rich Class)

This section would frequently be printed in the playbill rather than presented on stage. It offers an argument for the breeding of the Superman and for eliminating marriage and describes an experimental commune in America, the Oneida Community. The tract then makes a call for a conference of people who seek the immortality such a program might bring. The handbook ends with "Maxims for Revolutionists" ranging in topic from royalty to the treatment of children and servants and ending with self-sacrifice.

CHARACTERS

The Chief
See Mendoza

The Devil

The Devil is the suave and sophisticated host of Hell and the alter ego of Mendoza. The devil debates with Don Juan, insisting that it is not the Life Force that governs the earth but Death and that humans are essentially destructive beings, not creative ones. The Devil points out that the country where he holds the largest following is England.

Duval

One of the bandits, a Frenchman, who helps Mendoza waylay travelers to hold them for ransom.

Jack
See John Tanner

Lucifer
See The Devil

Hector Malone

An American traveling in Europe who falls in love with and secretly marries Violet, since his father would disapprove of her social status. He is honorable but laughable because of his open-hearted good nature and because he does not know enough to be "ashamed of his nationality." He shows his mettle when he announces himself ready to support his new wife, without his father's financial assistance.

Mendoza

A Jewish Spaniard, a former waiter, and now leader of a band of vagabonds with an imposing "Mephistophelean affectation." Mendoza has thrown his life away over a lost love, Louisa Straker. He is transposed into the Devil in the Don Juan in Hell scene. Mendoza bores his hostages to sleep with the terrible poetry he wrote to Louisa. Mendoza knows most of the main characters because he waited on them at the Savoy Hotel. Tanner befriends him and provides a viable alibi rather than turning him in to the police when they arrive.

Miss Ramsden

Roebuck's maiden sister takes a high hand with Violet, assuming her unmarried, and succeeds in offending her completely.

Roebuck Ramsden

The quintessence of the well-to-do gentleman, Ramsden ("Granny" to Ann) fancies himself a freethinker but is in fact a conservative. He dresses and acts impeccably, professes to want to help Violet, yet blunders into offending her with his assumptions about her marital status and the presumptuous way that he starts making decisions for her. Underneath the limitations imposed by society's conventions, Roebuck is a kind person.

Ricky Ticky Tavy
See Octavius Robinson

Octavius Robinson
Octavius, a rather simple and idealistic soul, suffers for his love of Ann, who merely toys with him and then throws him over for Jack. Tavy will probably never marry but will enshrine his brief moment with Ann on the altar of his heart.

Violet Robinson
Violet, Octavius's sister, possesses a strong will and a firm step. Married and pregnant, she honors her new husband's strange request to keep his name a secret from her friends to delay his father finding out that he has foiled the elder Malone's plot to buy social advancement either for his son or his son's new wife through marriage. Even though marriage to Violet would not show ''a social profit'' for anyone, she so charms Mr. Malone that he instantly accepts the marriage and blesses it with his love, and his money.

Senor Commander
See Don Gonzalo Ulloa

The Statue
See Don Gonzalo Ulloa

Enry Straker
The modern Prometheus, Enry (or Henry without the dropped H), is a topnotch automobile mechanic with a penchant for fast cars. He has more competence, self-assurance, and wisdom than his employer Jack Tanner because Straker works for a living. It is Enry Straker who recognizes Ann's pursuit of Jack. He also pulls the wool from Jack's eyes about his own desire.

MEDIA ADAPTATIONS

- The classic version of the *Don Juan in Hell* segment of Act III was recorded in the 1950s by actors Charles Laughton, Sir Cedric Hardwicke, Charles Boyer, and Agnes Moorehead for Columbia; it is available on audio tape.

John Tanner
John, or Jack, would prefer to spend his days philosophizing about life rather than living it. He sees right through Ann's manipulations but falls for her anyway. He fancies himself a revolutionary, working for social reform, and to this end has published the *Revolutionist's Handbook,* the precepts of which are expounded to all who will listen by his alter ego and remote ancestor, Don Juan.

Tavy
See Octavius Robinson

Don Juan Tenorio
Don Juan is the old philosopher who once was a lover and repents not of his acts but of the foolishness of his dreams. In Hell, he expounds his theory of the Life Force, and he longs to live for eternity contemplating reality.

Ana de Ulloa
At the age of seventy-seven, Ana dies and finds herself in Hell with the unexpected option of going to Heaven if she wants. She is the alter ego of Ann Whitefield, though at her age she now lacks Ann's drive for the Life Force. She still remembers her young lover, Don Juan Tenorio, the brash man who wooed her and who killed her father in a duel over her honor.

Don Gonzalo Ulloa
A sincere and honorable man, the commander lived his life as a gentleman, doing what was

expected of someone of his class, including facing Don Juan, an expert fencer, in a duel. When he dies of wounds inflicted by the younger man, he goes straight to heaven, but he spends much time in Hell, chatting amiably with his new friend, Don Juan. Heaven and its saccharine occupants bore the Don. Influenced by his young friend, he is reconsidering the values that guided his life on earth.

Ann Whitefield

Ann is a huntress in the world of male and female relationships. Her instinct toward the Life Force drives her to seek a mate worthy of producing with her the new Superman. She is sophisticated, poised, and fully in command of the men who fall for her. When she breaks Octavius's heart, it causes her no remorse. Tanner is a good match for her because he sees through her hypocrisy. According to Shaw "Every woman is not Ann, but Ann is Everywoman."

Mrs. Whitefield

Ann's mother does not have to play the match-maker's role with a daughter who seeks her own mate, but she tries to lend a hand. Mrs. Whitefield tells Tanner that she doesn't care if Ann marries him, but when he asserts that he has no intentions along those lines, she slyly suggests that he'd be Ann's match. Mrs. Whitefield cannot help working for the Life Force.

THEMES

Sex

Man and Superman expounds Shaw's pointed view of humanity's sexual nature. In this play, Ann Whitefield woos her newly appointed guardian, John Tanner, and he, in spite of his anti-romantic persona, falls for her. He does not love her in the conventional sense, but falls prey to the "Life Force" that she exudes. It is more a matter of sexual attraction than it is of romanic love. Shaw's idea of this Life Force derives from French philosopher Henri Bergson's *Olan vital,* or spirit of life.

Bergson's concept proposed that intellect was an advanced form of instinct, and that intellect and

instinct together constituted the source of vitality shared between all creatures and God. Social niceties, such as the conventions of marriage and courting, merely mask the underlying drive toward life and procreation. The Life Force is the creative urge toward self-preservation and regeneration, the drive to evolve, adapt, and actualize. Bergson's philosophy parallels French naturalist Jean Baptiste Lamarck's biological concept of the organism's tendency to adapt to environment, to survive through self-transformation. Lamarck predated Darwin's theory of natural selection, which Shaw opposes by going back to the idea of Lamarckian determinism in the form of an unconscious will towards life.

Shaw draws on both philosophy and biological theory for his Life Force theory, which became a common theme in his work, especially in his prefaces. Nowhere else, however, is it so fully explored as in the Don Juan in Hell segment found in Act III, where Ann Whitefield transposes into Dona Ana de Ulloa and Tanner becomes Don Juan Tenario. They debate the relative merits of heaven and earth with the devil and "the statue," Ana's dead father. Don Juan insists that, "Life is a force which has made innumerable experiments in organizing itself . . . the mammoth and the man, the mouse and the megatherium, the files and the fleas and the Fathers of the Church . . . all more or less successful attempts to build up that raw force into higher and higher individuals, the ideal individual being omnipotent, omniscient, infallible, and withal completely, unilludedly self-conscious: in short, a god."

The purpose of the Life Force is to create a superior being, the Superman. In *Man and Superman,* Life Force flows through female intuition, whose sole purpose is to achieve union with a male of intellectual superiority. An exceptional woman, who has a strong and irresistible Life Force, scoffs at weaker intellects, such as Octavius, who, though not unintelligent, lacks charisma. She seeks instead someone like Tanner, whose intellect makes him surly and offensive to other men but irresistible to strong women like Ann.

Intellect may seem an odd property to combine with the Life Force, but Don Juan explains that "brains" are needed to avoid death, thus the woman seeks a mate whose offspring have a good chance of survival.

Ubermensch (Superman)

The German term *Ubermensch* first appeared in Goethe's *Faust* (1808) and later in Nietzsche's

Thus Spake Zarathustra (1892). Nietzsche meant the term to indicate the universal human goal that could only be achieved when man suppresses his natural passions and commits himself to intellectual creativity. This, according to Nietzsche, is the overarching goal of humanity, the one that transcends individual goals or those of a cultural group. The Superman would be morally and intellectually superior to the average man.

Nietzsche was influenced by Arthur Schopenhauer, a German philosopher who proposed that a single all-encompassing "Will" was the cosmic force that drives nature and individuals to act as they do. The Nietzschian concept of a Superman contributed to Hitler's drive for a superior Aryan race, and Shaw himself proposes that the Superman might be bred from humans of the highest intellectual and moral standards.

The Superman in *Man and Superman* has the potential to be forged through a union between Jack Tanner, due to his intellectual superiority, and Ann Whitefield, who embodies the Life Force. The Superman is explicitly mentioned in the play, when the devil calls Nietzsche's Superman "the latest in fashion among Life Force fanatics" in Act III. Shaw's Don Juan explains that the Life Force seeks to create a Superman, and that humanity's highest goal is to serve that purpose as well as to gain a philosophical mind in order to understand its purpose.

The intellect is needed because without it, man "blunders into death." The philosophic man "seeks in contemplation to discover the inner will of the world, in invention to discover the means of fulfilling that will, and in action that will by the so-discovered means." In other words, each human should seek its highest ability to comprehend its ultimate purpose and then bend willingly to the Life Force's urge to create the Superman.

Moral Corruption

The Don Juan story is an age-old tale of an obsessive lover and adventurer who is carried off by the devil after a lifetime of chasing women. It is probably best told by Mozart in his opera *Don Giovanni* (1787). In Mozart's version, Don Giovanni (Don Juan) woos Donna Anna, who rejects him and whose father, the Commander, he kills in a duel over her honor. Later Don Giovanni and his servant Leporello see a statue of the dead Commander in a

TOPICS FOR FURTHER STUDY

- In what ways are Shaw's heaven and hell different from conventional concepts of them? How do these differences inflect the meaning of the play as a whole?

- The character of Ann Whitefield has been criticized as being a calculating huntress of men, and Shaw has Tanner compare her unfavorably to several animals of prey (boa constrictor, lion, tiger). What does it mean that Ann pursues her man instead of waiting for him to pursue her? What does that say about her character?

- Jack Tanner is a member of the ruling class and the author of the *Revolutionist's Handbook,* in which he offers his theories of socialism and eugenics. Is Jack is the hero of this play? How is the idea of heroism refashioned to a new purpose in *Man and Superman?*

- How does Shaw's representation of the Life Force in *Man and Superman* compare with Darwin and Lamarck's ideas of instinct?

cemetery and Don Giovanni jokingly asks it to dinner. The statue nods its head and later appears at dinner, whereupon it chastises Don Giovanni for his reckless life. Then the Devil appears to carry him off, while the police arrive too late to arrest him for the murder of Donna Anna's father.

The origin of the Don Juan story is unknown, having first appeared in Spanish literature in 1630 as *Don Juan of Seville*. Moliere also wrote a version in the eighteenth century, and Lord Byron, in the early-nineteenth century, takes Don Juan from Spain to a Greek island, to Turkey and Russia, and then to England as a garrulous adventurer who intersperses his love affairs with philosophical musings on power, politics, and poets. Shaw's play is a kind of modernized and inverted comedic adaptation of Mozart's work, which Shaw knew intimately from his mother's participation in opera and which he learned to love.

In Shaw's Don Juan story, the woman, Ann Whitefield, plays the pursuer and the Don Juan figure of John Tanner is a reluctant lover. The commander/statue becomes Roebuck Ramsden, who threatens not with a sword but by throwing Tanner's book, *The Revolutionist's Handbook,* at him. Rather than fight over her virtue, they duel verbally over whether Ann should be allowed to read Tanner's book and how to share her joint guardianship. In a distinct role reversal, the theme of moral corruption in Don Juan is, in Shaw's work, cast aside in favor of a theme of moral passion (a term borrowed from Hegel)—a passion, on Tanner's part, to be moral in the face of Ann's seduction. Naturally, he loses, because Ann is without morals and because she is driven by the Life Force—as is Tanner—to procreate. In Shaw's Don Juan, moral corruption is portrayed as simply a side effect of the basic biological drive to preserve the species.

STYLE

The Idea Play

Typical of nineteenth-century drama was the "parlor comedy," which had its roots in the "comedy of manners" popularized during the Restoration period (late-seventeenth century). The dominant theme of the comedy of manners was society life, specifically as it related to courtship and marriage. In a comedy of manners, the plot both reflects and satirizes the moral behavior of the characters, who represent "types" of people rather than fully rounded individuals. The parlor comedy moved the action to the parlor, or sitting room, where the characters discussed their predicaments.

Shaw advanced the parlor comedy into the play of ideas. The play of ideas had evolved from Henrik Ibsen's serious parlor dramas, where characters discussed deep moral or social crises. There was more talk than action in Ibsen's work, and Shaw adapted the "talking" play into a dramatized dialogue between conflicting ideas instead of characters. Whereas Ibsen's plays put realistic characters into a parlor to discuss at some length their conflict with antagonists, Shaw loads the dialogue with philosophical ideas voiced by "types" who discuss ideas at great length. In an idea play, it is not the

action or the characters but the ideas that take center stage.

HISTORICAL CONTEXT

Women's Suffrage Movement

In 1889, Shaw considered running for public office as a Liberal candidate. His platform would include "suffrage for women in exactly the same terms as men." During Shaw's life, women discovered that they could earn an independent living. The next logical step was to demand the right to vote. Women in Britain had been fighting for the vote and the right to own property since 1875. Shaw's circle of friends included renowned suffragettes such as Emily Pankhurst and her daughter Christabel, who endured multiple imprisonments and force-feedings—tube-feedings to prevent them from dying (as a result of the hunger strikes they would pursue) and thus becoming martyrs—in their mission to liberate women.

Shaw supported the suffrage movement and spoke out against forcible feeding, which he considered torture. Although he frequently contributed witty editorials to the suffragettes' cause, however, he felt that women themselves were completely capable of fighting their own battles and that women should not need men's assistance to procure what was rightfully theirs. Furthermore, although he insisted that "the denial of any fundamental rights to the person of woman is practically the denial of the Life Everlasting," he so often couched his criticisms in flippant humor that women were not sure he was actually helping their cause. As it was, the cause dwindled by the turn of the century, after the press lost interest in it.

Finally, in 1918, women over the age of thirty were granted the right to vote and to hold positions in the House of Commons. At the same time, the property clause requiring male voters to own property (amounting to ten British pounds) was removed.

Fabian Society

George Bernard Shaw with his two friends Beatrice and Sidney Webb formed the core of the

COMPARE & CONTRAST

- **1903:** In Britain, women suffragettes take to the streets in protest marches. They also publish feminist newspapers in an effort to obtain the right to vote.

  Today: As of 1928, all British citizens over the age of twenty-one may vote and hold public office. Although inequalities still exist, women hold equal legal rights with men.

- **1903:** Socialism is a new political ideology fast

gaining support from intellectuals throughout Europe. Shaw's Fabian Society promotes it as the solution to Britain's social inequalities. In its infancy, socialism promotes a communistic economic model.

  Today: Socialists have strong organizations in Britain and Europe and still strive for worker rights and social equality. The economic model has shifted to contain elements of capitalism.

Fabian Society, named after the Roman general Fabius, who saved Rome from the invading Hannibal. Shaw's Fabian Society sought to obtain basic human rights through gradual reforms in society as a way to stave off what might otherwise lead inevitably to revolution. The society members took as their mission the simplification of their lifestyles, in order to expend their energy in bettering the lives of others.

The Fabian Society was an outgrowth of the Fellowship of the New Life, founded by Scottish philosopher Thomas Davidson in 1883 and centered on achieving ethical perfection in order to serve the larger society through promoting socialism. Cambridge fellow Edward Carpenter honed the group's belief to specifically endorse vegetarianism, hard physical labor, and handspun clothing, in a blatant rejection of the excesses of the Victorian upper classes. The Webbs and Shaw adopted this philosophy, taking the new Victorian work ethic to an extreme: they worked eighteen-hour days gardening, writing, and distributing pamphlets on socialist ideals. They abhorred any form of personal indulgence, from overeating and sex to the wearing of fine clothing. They abstained from eating meat and led celibate, spartan lives.

Besides their social and political mission, the Fabians also supported the arts, and it was under the auspices of the Fabian Society that Shaw presented

a series of lectures about the dramatic influence of Henrik Ibsen (*Hedda Gabler*), whose work he admired and promoted in Britain. Perhaps not coincidentally, all three founding Fabians lived productively until their eighties (nineties in Shaw's case), and they were still writing prolifically in their seventies. Their purpose in adopting their strict regime of personal hygiene was to subordinate their needs to greater cause of human equality.

Although others periodically joined the group, H. G. Wells (*The Time Machine*) the most notable among them, it was this trio that held the society together and made its greatest impact on British society. The Fabian Society was revived in 1960 and still serves as a liberal think tank for Britain's current Labour Party.

CRITICAL OVERVIEW

Man and Superman was first published in book form in 1903 before being produced on the stage. Shaw published this early play himself, supervising the work closely. He sold just over 2700 copies in Britain. Essayist and critic G. K. Chesterton, as quoted in *George Bernard Shaw: The Critical Heritage,* considered the book "fascinating and delightful'' but called his friend Shaw to task for showing little faith in humanity. Likewise, essayist and critic Max Beerbohm, writing in the *Saturday Review,* found Shaw's characters flat and priggish, so much so that ''The Life Force could find no use for them.''

By the time the play was produced, in May of 1905 at the Royal Court Theatre, many of the prominent drama critics had already read the printed version of the play. The leading critic of the day, E. A. Baughan, who wrote under the pseudonym ''Vaughan'' in the *Daily News,* called Shaw an ''anaemic idealist,'' who might become ''the comedy writer for men and women who have the modern disease of mental and physical anemia.'' A. B. Walkley, the critic to whom Shaw addresses his dedicatory epistle in the beginning of the printed play, wrote in the *Times Literary Supplement* that Shaw's ''idea-plot'' interferes with his ''action-plot,'' such that finds the former ''soon exhausts itself,'' while the latter is ''a mere parasite of the other.''

William Archer, a journalist who had helped Shaw get an early job writing art criticism, and who then wrote for the *World,* expressed distaste for the character of Ann Whitefield, calling her a ''man-devouring monster.'' Archer suggested that Shaw approached his subject with too broad a brush, painting male-female relationships in such general terms as to lose the realism demanded by theater. In spite of such criticism, the play ran for 176 performances and served as a turning point in Shaw's career, because the actor who played Jack Tanner, Granville Barker, was a producer who recognized Shaw's talent and helped him to stage several more plays at his theater over the next few years. The ''Don Juan in Hell'' scene was not included in this first production but was separately staged at the Royal Court Theatre in 1907. The tradition of producing this scene separately has continued.

Critics evaluating Shaw's career as a whole often point to his lack of feeling, complaining that his plays are ''as dry and flat as a biscuit'' according to V. S. Pritchett, quoted in *George Bernard Shaw: A Critical Survey.* These critics complained that his characters talk so much that the ideas in the idea play get lost in the verbiage. In his early years, however, Shaw had great influence over young minds, as drama critic Eric Bentley asserted in *Bernard Shaw,* because he questioned ''marriage, the family, education, science, religion, and—above

all—capitalism.'' His mode was to proselytize through discussion, presenting multiple sides of the debate through a dramatized dialectic. He stirred up the beehive and waited for his audience to reorganize their thinking according to higher principles.

That his audiences often simply enjoyed the show and failed to ''get'' his message was a source of tremendous disappointment for Shaw. He had the reputation of a gadfly or crank, not a profound social reformer. Misunderstood, Shaw created G. B. S. (George Bernard Shaw), an alter ego who would fight arrogantly with the public while Shaw the man shunned publicity. G. B. S. wrote scathing responses to the critics and was taken for a crank. ''Not taking me seriously,'' G. B. S. announced, ''is the Englishman's way of refusing to face facts.'' Even so, by the time he was seventy, Shaw was ''probably the most famous of living writers,'' according to a *New York Times* editorial.

As Bentley pointed out, ''Shaw's career is 'sounder' that any merely popular writer's, for his books have gone on selling indefinitely and his plays have returned to the stage again and again.'' Looking back, T. S. Eliot, quoted in *Discovering Authors,* said of him that ''It might have been predicted that what he said then would not seem so subversive or blasphemous now. The public has accepted Mr. Shaw not by recognizing the intelligence of what said then, but by forgetting it; we must not forget that at one time Mr. Shaw was a very unpopular man. He is no longer the gadfly of the commonwealth; but even if he has never been appreciated, it is something that he should be respected.''

CRITICISM

Carole Hamilton

Hamilton is a Humanities teacher at Cary Academy, an innovative private school in Cary, North Carolina. In this essay she discusses the ideological contradictions in Shaw's play and in his nature.

Shaw's *Man and Superman* holds a myriad of comic inversions, from the role reversal in which

Peter O'Toole in a scene from a Haymarket Theatre production of Shaw's play

the woman pursues the man, to the satiric switching of heaven and hell. His inversions confuse even the play's characters, whose conventional responses to unconventional situations make up the comedy of his play, while the underlying truths expressed by the inversions make up its philosophical content. For example, Ana, having recently arrived in Hell, finds it a delightful paradise, and she cannot wait to get into Heaven, since to her mind, "if Hell be so beautiful as this, how glorious must Heaven be!"

Don Juan, the Devil, and her deceased father, the Commander, protest: they too once shared her delusion, but they now know the truth. Don Juan is in Hell, where one would expect him to be after having killed the Commander. Having led a life of sin, Don Juan might well look forward to reveling in Hell, but in fact he cannot stand it. However, his reasons reveal an inversion in Shaw's structuring of heaven and hell. Don Juan's problem is not that heaven and hell are switched, but that what he expected from each is also switched. Hell is the Heaven of earthly imagination—but it is based on misguided imagination. Thus Shaw's inversions occur on multiple and intersecting planes.

Hell is a beautiful paradise (a commonplace inversion) that is hellish in its tedium (not an

WHAT
DO I READ
NEXT?

- *Man and Superman* has strong affinities to Mozart's *Don Giovanni,* the opera on which Shaw based his play. The opera is worth listening to as a way to understand Shaw's use of music and the musicality of the characters' language as well as to enjoy another version of the Don Juan story.

- The perennial favorite *Pygmalion* is a Shaw classic, being the story of a street girl whom, on a bet, a gentleman trains to "pass" in high society by teaching her how to act and speak like a lady.

- William Congreve's *The Way of the World* (1700) is an eighteenth-century comedy of manners centered on a courtship.

- Lord Byron's unfinished *Don Juan* is poem describing the adventures of the lover Don Juan, interspersed with philosophical musings similar to those of Shaw's Don Juan.

- Friedrich Nietzsche's *Thus Spake Zarathustra* presents his idea of the Superman, upon which Shaw based his idea of the Superman.

- Arthur Schopenhauer's essay "The World as Will and Idea" presents the philosophy of a community or cosmic Will that drives the actions of individuals as well as nature itself.

---

inversion) and the tedium consists of the continuation of earthly hopes and dreams (the key inversion). The latter inversion proves to be the most perverse and is one of the cornerstones of the philosophy Shaw explores in this play. In Shaw's Hell, the Devil is an earnest fellow, not an evil being. But his rather unexpected plea for sincerity and warmth make Don Juan ill. At the same time, the Commander, a good and kindly man, has gone to heaven as he might have expected. But because Heaven too is inverted, he finds it a place of boring contemplation, full of hypocrites. Don Juan wants to go to Heaven to contemplate reality, while the Commander wants to escape this "most angelically dull place in all creation."

Further inversions occur in the Devil's perception of humankind. The Devil abhors (rather than revels in) humanity's obsession with Death and deadly inventions, from the rack and gallows to patriotism and other "isms" that insidiously encourage destruction in their name.

With so many inversions competing for attention, Shaw is not able to avoid certain logical contradictions. For example, Hell is Hellish to someone like Don Juan partly because of the Devil's longing for "love, happiness, and beauty." Rather

than feeling inferior to God's creation, the Devil claims to have created Hell as a haven away from Heaven's hypocrisy. Such fatuousness nauseates Don Juan, who finds soul-searching hypocritical, although he himself wants to abide in Heaven where he can contemplate reality. He'll find only hypocrisy in Heaven, according to the Commander, who leaves Heaven "forever," having recently converted from hypocrisy himself.

According to the Commander, the truly blessed go to Hell. Meanwhile, the Devil finds offense in Dona Ana's preference for Heaven's brand of hypocrisy over his. In other words, both places harbor hypocrites as well as enlightened individuals who seek the reality they left behind on earth. Such contradictions led critics such as Bertrand Russell to declare Shaw "more bounder than genius" because the logic of his philosophy did not make sense.

Shaw's penchant for turning things upside down extended to real life as well as the closed fictional world of the stage and again inherent contradictions caused him difficulties. His almost perverse tendency towards opposing conventional thought rankled the suffragettes he tried to help when he suggested that the women's voting rights movement should, by definition, not need to enlist the support of men.

He told his sister Lucy that women were better off speaking for themselves than making use of men's entreaties. He wrote several essays in their support, but then, treating women as he did men, he ridiculed them for their voting follies once they were empowered. As he was quoted in *The Genius of Shaw:*

> Only the other day the admission of women to the electorate, for which women fought and died, was expected to raise politics to a nobler plane and purify public life. But at the election which followed, the women voted for hanging the Kaiser; rallied hysterically round the worst male candidates; threw out all the women candidates of tried ability, integrity, and devotion; and elected just one titled lady of great wealth and singular demagogic fascination, who, though she justified their choice subsequently, was then a beginner. In short, the notion that the female vote is more politically intelligent or gentler than the male voter proved as great a delusion as the earlier delusions that the business man was any wiser politically than the country gentleman, or the manual worker than the middle class man.

Shaw compares his disappointment in women voters with his disappointment in businessmen and manual workers. Even though common sense would predict that novice voters would necessarily lack political sophistication, Shaw derides women for it. He glosses over the fact that having never had the vote, they need time to get used to their new responsibility. It is as though, as a way of chiding others to live up to his ideals, Shaw stubbornly refuses to see things as they are but as they should be. At the same time, because he sets himself up as a critic and judge, he fails to attend to his own logical inconsistencies.

Shaw comes by his inversions naturally: born a Protestant in the Catholic city of Dublin, Ireland, he was never to enjoy either acceptance or shared values with his peers at school or at play. His religious and cultural otherness led him to experience painful isolation within a teeming city. He wrote of his year-long stint at a mostly Catholic school in a piece entitled "Shame and Wounded Snobbery," applying the phrase often applied to Hell and which he reiterates in *Man and Superman:* "All hope abandon, ye who enter here."

As a strategy for survival, Shaw eschewed relations with the lower class Catholic boys and instead "was a superior being, and in the play hour did not play, but walked up and down with the teachers in their promenade." Meanwhile, because of the "downstart" nature of his family's fortunes, he was also shunned by the more affluent Protestant middle-class boys of the neighborhood. If his outsider status trained his eye for social injustice, it also

> IN *MAN AND SUPERMAN,* SHAW APPLIES HIS INVERSIONS TO NO SMALLER A TARGET THAN HUMANKIND AND ITS MOST IMPORTANT DREAMS AND DELUSIONS: THE RELATIONS BETWEEN MAN AND WOMAN, THE PURPOSE OF LIFE, AND THE STRUCTURE OF THE HEREAFTER"

gave him the time and inclination to train his wit for imaginary reversals of fortune. Doubly shunned, he became doubly aloof, feeling philosophically and economically superior to his Catholic peers even though seen by them as socially inferior.

His memories of this period of his life so haunted him that he said "when ghosts rise up from that period I want to lay them again with a poker." He took his escape route into fantasy, creating an internal world where he righted the wrongs around him. What may have begun as playful imagining, became an ingrained habit of mind. In the preface to his long autobiographical essay *Immaturity,* he explains the creation of his G. B. S. persona as a derivative of his escape into fantasy:

> Whether I was born mad or a little too sane, my kingdom was not of this world: I was at home only in the realm of my imagination, and at my ease only with the mighty dead. Therefore I had to become an actor, and create for myself a fantastic personality fit and apt for dealing with men . . . I was outside society, outside politics, outside sports, outside the church. If the term had been invented then I should have been called the Complete Outsider.

Later within that preface Shaw notes that whenever he addressed "music, painting, literature, or science . . . the positions were reversed" and he became "the Insider." Being an Insider in Shaw's terms meant being perceived as capable of judging authoritatively, but ironically, this status implies being outside. In other words, essential inversion lies at the very core of Shaw's personality and in fact serves as a defining characteristic of all that is best in his nature and intellect. Just as he inverted his own self to become an "Insider," he went about constructing fictional worlds that he could breath into life on the stage. Worlds where his upside-down logic could flourish. An Outsider is at heart a critic who serves the world that rejects him by rejecting that which is offensive in the world.

In *Man and Superman,* Shaw applies his inversions to no smaller a target than Humankind and its most important dreams and delusions: the relations between man and woman, the purpose of life, and the structure of the hereafter. In so doing, he chides his fellow humans to reconsider the structures of the mind that delude them, and he builds a bridge, albeit shaky and tentative, between his world and theirs.

Source: Carole Hamilton, for *Drama for Students,* Gale, 1999.

Mimi Kramer

Calling Man and Superman *"Shaw's great treatise on sex, morality, and the war between men and women," Kramer offers a positive review of a 1988 revival of the play, though she expresses reservations about the lead actors essaying Jack and Ann.*

The heroine of "*Man and Superman,*" Ann Whitefield, is one of Shaw's strong-minded women. Like Candida, Barbara Undershaft, and Vivie Warren, she knows the world and what she wants out of life. But Ann isn't as immediately likable as Candida, Barbara, and Vivie; she lacks their forthrightness and their gift for argument. Where Barbara and Candida can hold their own with fathers, suitors, and husbands, Ann comments on speech instead of engaging in it, and she manages people—particularly men—instead of trying to reason with them. She's forever getting caught out in some manipulative lie—usually by Jack Tanner, the selfstyled radical who seems so anxious to escape her machinations. It's an undignified position for a young woman to put herself in, and one can easily see that Ann Whitefield might offend modern female sensibilities—especially since Jack's main attraction for Ann seems to lie in the regularity with which he insults and abuses her.

"*Man and Superman*" is Shaw's great treatise on sex, morality, and the war between men and women. Written between 1901 and 1903, it was both his answer to the conventional romantic comedy and a response to the joking suggestion, made some years earlier by the London *Times* critic Arthur Bingham Walkley, that he attempt a play about Don Juan. Shaw's modern "libertine" is a

man who runs from Woman instead of pursuing her and who outrages not her person or her honor but the tenets of conventional morality. Shaw referred to the long dream sequence in Act III, in which Tanner falls asleep and imagines a conversation, in Hell, between the Devil and the characters in Mozart's opera, as a "pleasantry" and "a totally extraneous act." But the play is full of lines that look yearningly forward—or hauntingly back—to the dream sequence: "Octavius, it's the common lot. We must all face it some day," "A lifetime of happiness! It would be hell on earth," "I'll call you after your famous ancestor Don Juan," "That's the devilish side of a woman's fascination," "There is a rascal in our midst, a libertine," "When you go to heaven, Ann . . ." And, finally, in Act IV, Tanner's "When did all this happen to me before? Are we two dreaming?" Whatever Shaw thought (or said he thought), "Don Juan in Hell" contains the key both to Tanner's essential character as an idealist and to the nature of his attraction for women.

The latest revival of "*Man and Superman,*" at the Roundabout Theatre, does not include "Don Juan in Hell." Instead, the production (which excises Act III entirely and renumbers Act IV as Act III) teases the audience with snippets of Mozart. (In Act II, Tanner's chauffeur, Henry Straker, keeps whistling the opening bars of "Là ci darem la mano," from "Don Giovanni.") The revival is standard Roundabout Theatre fare: it contains execrable performances by David Birney and Frances Conroy as Jack Tanner and Ann Whitefield and glorious performances in nearly all the secondary roles—Straker (Anthony Fusco), Taw (Michael Cumpsty), the American Hector Malone (Jonathan Walker), his father (John Carpenter). Kim Hunter proves a charming Mrs. Whitefield once she gets going, and of the supporting parts only Tavy's sister Violet is overplayed (by Harriet Harris).

It's typical of New York Shaw that secondary roles are played to perfection and leading roles to no purpose whatever. In recent seasons, what might have been first-rate productions of "*Arms and the Man,*" "*Mrs. Warren's Profession,*" and "*You Never Can Tell*" were marred by the performances of such leading ladies as Glenne Headly, Uta Hagen, and Amanda Plummer. (The Pearl Theatre Company's recent revival of "*Candida*" was an exception, held together, as it was, by Rose Stockton's performance in the title role.) What's unusual about the production at the Roundabout is the degree of difference between the levels of performance: Mr. Cumpsty and Mr. Fusco are *so* deft, Mr. Birney and

Miss Conroy *so* inept that the credit for good performances must clearly go to the actors rather than to their director, William Woodman. Mr. Birney's characterization is lodged entirely in the sort of mannerisms that Shaw worked so hard to abolish from the nineteenth-century stage: in putting his hands in his waistcoat pockets, scratching his nose, pulling his ear, brushing his forehead, and striking attractive poses against convenient pieces of furniture.

Miss Conroy's performance, meanwhile, seems motivated wholly by dislike for the character she is playing. She blinks a lot and speaks in a peculiar, repressed fashion (as though her jaws had been wired together) to show what a hypocrite Ann is, and emphasizes Ann's coquetry by reacting to everything onstage with an affected little moue. She fixes her hair when Tanner's back is turned. Her portrayal is openly hostile, as though she were anxious to divorce herself from the low, scheming creature that Jack divines Ann (and, by extension, all women) to be. I sympathize with Miss Conroy—I'm not wild about Ann Whitefield myself—but her performance seems dictated by an inability to take in the shape of the play. Even without the *"Don Juan in Hell"* sequence, *"Man and Superman"* takes us far beyond Jack Tanner's inadequate views of "the struggle between the artist man and the mother woman." It is Ann, after all, who proves to have the clearer vision, while Tanner, for all his intellectual chatter, is a fool.

Shaw was, in his way (as Eric Bentley has repeatedly observed), as subversive as Ibsen and, later, Strindberg when it came to recognizing women's sexuality. The whole point of *"Man and Superman "* is the role reversal in the courting game: here woman is the pursuer, not (as Jack thinks) because she is basically predatory but because there is something she *wants*. More subversive than any of Jack's verbal flying in the face of convention is the governing idea behind the play's dramatic situation: that the man a woman wants to marry is not the one who idealizes her but the one who knows how rotten she can be. What distinguishes Tanner from the crowd of other speechifying Shavian heroes is the pleasure—almost erotic in its intensity—with which we look forward to the moment when he will stop talking.

It's not impossible to play a character one doesn't have much sympathy with. Rose Stockton, in the circular issued by the Pearl Theatre Company, stated her basic discomfort with some views about

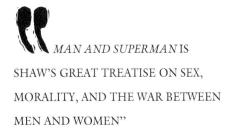

MAN AND SUPERMAN IS SHAW'S GREAT TREATISE ON SEX, MORALITY, AND THE WAR BETWEEN MEN AND WOMEN"

women that Shaw espoused, but that discomfort was not discernible in her portrayal of Candida Morell—though it very well might have been. Similarly, though Michael Cumpsty is clearly aware that Tavy is there to parody conventional idealism, that knowledge doesn't prevent him from making us care about Tavy. Perhaps in some future dream sequence there will be a meeting place imagined for the Rose Stocktons, the Michael Cumpstys, and the Anthony Fuscos of this world, where, without the distracting influence of commercially minded producers and casting directors, they can all come together and perform Shaw.

Source: Mimi Kramer, "Don Bernardo in Hell" in the *New Yorker,* Vol. LXIII, no. 49, January 25, 1988, pp. 85–87.

Max Beerbohm

In a review that was originally published on September 12, 1903, Beerbohm expounds on the nature of dramatists, using Shaw's play Man and Superman, *as an illustration. He also examines the play as a worthwhile theatrical experience.*

Aristotle, often as he sneered at Plato, never called Plato a dramatist, and did not drag the Platonic dialogues into his dramatic criticism. Nor did Plato himself profess to be a dramatist; and it would need a wide stretch of fancy to think of him dedicating one of his works to Aristotle as notable expert in dramatic criticism. On the other hand, here is Mr. Bernard Shaw dedicating his new book to "my dear Walkley," that pious custodian of the Aristotelian flame, and arguing, with Platonic subtlety, that this new book contains a play. Odd! For to drama Mr. Shaw and Plato stand in almost exactly the same relation. Plato, through anxiety that his work should be read, and his message accepted, so far mortified his strongly Puritan instincts as to give a setting of bright human colour to his abstract thought. He invented men of flesh and blood, to talk for him, and put them against realistic backgrounds. And thus he

MAN AND SUPERMAN, IS
SHAW'S MASTERPIECE, SO FAR.
TREASURE IT AS THE MOST
COMPLETE EXPRESSION OF THE
MOST DISTINCT PERSONALITY IN
CURRENT LITERATURE."

gained, and still retains, "a public." Only, his method was fraught with nemesis, and he is generally regarded as a poet—he, who couldn't abide poets. Essentially, he was no more a poet than he was a dramatist, or than Mr. Shaw is a dramatist. Like him, and unlike Aristotle, for whom the exercise of thought was an end in itself, and who, therefore, did not attempt to bedeck as a decoy the form of his expression, Mr. Shaw is an ardent humanitarian. He wants to save us. So he gilds the pill richly. He does not, indeed, invent men of flesh and blood, to talk for him. There, where Plato succeeded, he fails, I must confess. But he assumes various disguises, and he ventriloquises, and moves against realistic backgrounds. In one direction he goes further than Plato. He weaves more of a story round the interlocutors. Suppose that in the "Republic," for example, there were "Socrates (in love with Aspasia)," "Glaucon (in love with Xanthippe)," etcetera, and then you have in your mind a very fair equivalent for what Mr. Shaw writes and calls a play. This peculiar article is, of course, not a play at all. It is "as good as a play"—infinitely better, to my peculiar taste, than any play I have ever read or seen enacted. But a play it is not. What is a dramatist? Principally, a man who delights in watching, and can portray, the world as it is, and the various conflicts of men and women as they are. Such a man has, besides the joy of sheer contemplation, joy in the technique of his art—how to express everything most precisely and perfectly, most worthily of the splendid theme. He may have a message to deliver. Or he may have none. *C'est selon.* But the message is never a tyrannous preoccupation. When the creative and the critical faculty exist in one man, the lesser is perforce overshadowed by the greater. Mr. Shaw knows well—how could so keen a critic fail to detect?—that he is a critic, and not a creator at all. But, for the purpose which I have explained, he must needs pretend

through Mr. Walkley, who won't believe, to an innocent public which may believe, that his pen runs away with him. "Woman projecting herself dramatically by my hands (a process over which I have no control)." A touching fib! The only things which Mr. Shaw cannot consciously control in himself are his sense of humour and his sense of reason. "The man who listens to Reason is lost: Reason enslaves all whose minds are not strong enough to master her." That is one of many fine and profound aphorisms printed at the end of the book, and written (one suspects) joyously, as a private antidote to the dramatic tomfoolery to which Mr. Shaw had perforce condescended. Well! Mr. Shaw will never be manumitted by Reason. She is as inexorable an owner of him as is Humour, and a less kind owner, in that she does prevent him from seeing the world as it is, while Humour, not preventing him from being quite serious, merely prevents stupid people seeing how serious he is. Mr. Shaw is always trying to prove this or that thesis, and the result is that his characters (so soon as he differentiates them, ever so little, from himself) are the merest diagrams. Having no sense for life, he has, necessarily, no sense for art. It would be strange, indeed, if he could succeed in that on which he is always pouring a very sincere contempt. "For art's sake alone," he declares, "I would not face the toil of writing a single sentence." That is no fib. Take away his moral purpose and his lust for dialectic, and Mr. Shaw would put neither pen to paper nor mouth to meeting, and we should be by so much the duller. But had you taken away from Bunyan or Ibsen or any other of those great artists whom Mr. Shaw, because they had "something to say," is always throwing so violently at our heads, they would have yet created, from sheer joy in life as it was and in art as it could become through their handling of it. Mr. Shaw, using art merely as a means of making people listen to him, naturally lays hands on the kind that appeals most quickly to the greatest number of people. There is something splendid in the contempt with which he uses as the vehicle for his thesis a conventional love-chase, with motors and comic brigands thrown in. He is as eager to be a popular dramatist and as willing to demean himself in any way that may help him to the goal, as was (say) the late Mr. Pettitt. I hope he will reach the goal. It is only the theatrical managers who stand between him and the offchance of a real popular success. But if these managers cannot be shaken from their obstinate timidity, I hope that Mr. Shaw, realising that the general public is as loth to read plays as to read books of undiluted philosophy, will cease to dabble in an art which he abhors. Let him always, by all means, use the form of dialogue—that form through which, more conveniently than through any other, every side of a subject can be laid bare to our intelligence. It is, moreover, a form of which Mr. Shaw is a master. In swiftness, tenseness and lucidity of dialogue no living writer can touch the hem of Mr. Shaw's garment. In ''*Man and Superman*'' every phrase rings and flashes. Here, though Mr. Shaw will be angry with me, is perfect art. In Mr. Shaw as an essayist I cannot take so whole-hearted a delight. Both in construction and in style his essays seem to me more akin to the art of oral debating than of literary exposition. That is because he trained himself m speak before he trained himself to write. And it is, doubtless, by reason of that same priority that he excels in writing words to be spoken by the human voice or to be read as though they were so spoken.

The name of this play's hero is John Tanner, corrupted from Don Juan Tenorio, of whom its bearer is supposed to be the lineal descendant and modern equivalent. But here we have merely one of the devices whereby Mr. Shaw seeks to catch the ear that he desires to box. Did not the end justify the means, Mr. Shaw's natural honesty would have compelled him to christen his hero Joseph or Anthony. For he utterly flouts the possibility of a Don Juan. Gazing out on the world, he beholds a tremendous battle of sex raging. But it is the Sabine ladies who, more muscular than even Rubens made them, are snatching and shouldering away from out the newly-arisen walls the shrieking gentlemen of Rome. It is the fauns who scud coyly, on tremulous hoofs, through the woodland, not daring a backward-glance at rude and dogged nymphs who are gaining on them every moment. Of course, this sight is an hallucination. There are, it is true, women who take the initiative, and men who shrink from following them. There are, and always have been. Such beings are no new discovery, though their existence is stupidly ignored by the average modern dramatist. But they are notable exceptions to the rule of Nature. True, again, that in civilised society marriage is more important and desirable to a woman than to a man. ''All women,'' said one of Disraeli's characters, ''ought to be married, and no men.'' The epigram sums up John Tanner's attitude towards life even more wittily than anything that has been put into his mouth by Mr. Shaw. John Tanner, pursued and finally bound in matrimony by Miss Ann Whitefield, supplies an excellent motive for a comedy of manners. But to that kind of comedy Mr.

Shaw will not stoop—not wittingly, at least. From John Tanner he deduces a general law. For him, John Tanner is Man, and Ann Whitefield is Woman—nothing less. He has fallen into the error—a strange error for a man with his views—of confusing the natural sex-instinct with the desire for marriage. Because women desire marriage more strongly than men, therefore, in his opinion, the sex-instinct is communicated from woman to man. I need not labour the point that this conclusion is opposite to the obvious truth of all ages and all countries. Man is the dominant animal. It was unjust of Nature not to make the two sexes equal. Mr. Shaw hates injustice, and so, partly to redress the balance by robbing Man of conscious superiority, and partly to lull himself into peace of mind, he projects as real that visionary world of flitting fauns and brutal Sabines. Idealist, he insists that things are as they would be if he had his way. His characters come from out his own yearning heart. Only, we can find no corner for them in ours. We can no more be charmed by them than we can believe in them. Ann Whitefield is a minx. John Tanner is a prig. Prig versus Minx, with the gloves off, and Prig floored in every round—there you have Mr. Shaw's customary formula for drama; and he works it out duly in ''*Man and Superman.*'' The main difference between this play and the others is that the minx and the prig are conscious not merely of their intellects, but of ''the Life Force.'' Of this they regard themselves, with comparative modesty, as the automatic instruments. They are wrong. The Life Force could find no use for them. They are not human enough, not alive enough. That is the main drawback for a dramatist who does not love raw life: he cannot create living human characters.

And yet it is on such characters as John and Ann that Mr. Shaw founds his hopes for the future of humanity. If we are very good, we *may* be given the Superman. If we are very scientific, and keep a sharp look out on our instincts, and use them just as our intellects shall prescribe, we *may* produce a race worthy to walk this fair earth. That is the hope with which we are to buoy ourselves up. It is a forlorn one. Man may, in the course of æons, evolve into something better than now he is. But the process will be not less unconscious than long. Reason and instinct have an inveterate habit of cancelling each other. If the world were governed by reason, it would not long be inhabited. Life is a muddle. It seems a brilliant muddle, if you are an optimist; a dull one, if you aren't; but in neither case can you deny that it is the muddlers who keep it going. The thinkers cannot help it at all. They are detached from "the Life Force." If they could turn their fellow-creatures into thinkers like themselves, all would be up. Fortunately, or unfortunately, they have not that power. The course of history has often been turned by sentiment, but by thought never. The thinkers are but valuable ornaments. A safe place is assigned to them on the world's mantelpiece, while humanity basks and blinks stupidly on the hearth, warming itself in the glow of the Life Force.

On that mantelpiece Mr. Shaw deserves a place of honour. He is a very brilliant ornament. And never have his ornamental qualities shone more brightly than in this latest book. Never has he thought more clearly or more wrongly, and never has he displayed better his genius for dialectic, and never has his humour gushed forth in such sudden natural torrents. This is his masterpiece, so far. Treasure it as the most complete expression of the most distinct personality in current literature. Treasure it, too, as a work of specific art, in line with your Plato and Lucian and Landor.

Source: Max Beerbohm, "Mr. Shaw's New Dialogues" in his *Around Theatres,* Simon & Schuster, 1954 , pp. 268–72.

SOURCES

Evans, T. F. *George Bernard Shaw: The Critical Heritage,* Routledge, 1997.

Kronenberger, Louis. *George Bernard Shaw: A Critical Survey,* World Publishing, 1953.

FURTHER READING

Bentley, Eric. *Bernard Shaw,* Methuen, 1967.
   A leading drama critic looks at Shaw's drama from the perspective of his political and social ideas and the impact he has had on the theater.

Berst, Charles A. *Bernard Shaw and the Art of Drama,* University of Illinois Press, 1973.
   A close analysis of Shaw's major plays.

Brecht, Bertolt. "Ovation for Shaw" in *Modern Drama,* translated by Gerhard H. W. Zuther, Vol. 2, no. 2, 1959, pp. 184-87.
   Brecht, the author of such plays as *Mother Courage and Her Children* and a fellow innovative playwright and social reformer, praises Shaw's art.

Dukore, Bernard F. *Bernard Shaw, Playwright,* University of Missouri Press, 1973.
   Dukore praises Shaw as a watershed playwright of the twentieth century.

Hardwick, Michael, and Mollie Hardwick. *The Bernard Shaw Companion,* John Murray, 1997.
   Contains summaries of the plays and a brief biography of Shaw.

Hill, Eldon C. *George Bernard Shaw,* Twayne, 1978.
   A monograph on Shaw and his plays, part of the Twayne writers series.

Holroyd, Michael. *The Genius of Shaw,* Hodder and Stoughton, 1979.
   A biographical study of Shaw's life and times, including pictures of many of his associates and early productions.

Innes, Christopher. *The Cambridge Companion to George Bernard Shaw,* Cambridge University Press, 1998.
   Recent essays on Shaw and feminism, his dramatic structure, and his influence on the theater.

Kaye, Julian B. *Bernard Shaw and the Nineteenth-Century Tradition,* University of Oklahoma Press, 1955.
   Describes the legacy of eighteenth-century ideas of sociology and the socialist agenda of the nineteenth century and Shaw's place in this world of ideas.

MacCarthy, Desmond. *Shaw,* MacGibbon and Kee, 1951.
   In this biography, an esteemed drama critic evaluates Shaw's social agenda as it appears in his plays.

Meisel, Martin. *Shaw and the Nineteenth-Century Theater,* Princeton University Press, 1963.
   Shaw is assessed in relation to the conventions of nineteenth-century popular theater.

Weintraub, Stanley. "Bernard Shaw" in *Concise Dictionary of British Literary Biography,* Volume 6: *Modern Writers, 1914-1945,* Gale, 1992, pp. 348-68.
   Weintraub surveys Shaw's personal life and his work, focussing on his creation of the play of ideas.

Weintraub, Stanley. *The Unexpected Shaw: Biographical Approaches to G. B. S. and His Work,* Ungar, 1982.
   Weintraub makes connections between Shaw's personal life and his work, including a chapter on the influence of certain paintings on Shaw.

Whitman, Robert F. *Shaw and the Play of Ideas,* Cornell University Press, 1977.
   Examines Shaw as a proselytizer of philosophical, social, and religious ideas.

A Month in the Country

IVAN TURGENEV

1872

A Month in the Country was written during the
1840s and completed in 1850 when Turgenev was
thirty-two. Prior to this play, Turgenev had also
written poetry and short stories. His literary reputation was established in 1843 with the publication of
Parasha, a romantic story written in verse. Despite
Turgenev's past successes, *A Month in the Country*
was not permitted to be staged by the censor when it
was first published. As a result, the disheartened
Turgenev, who already did not think highly of his
plays, gave up writing for the theater. Instead, he
turned his talents toward novel writing, and by the
end of the 1850s, society and the government were
prepared to receive his next literary offerings.

Tsar Alexander II had come to power and in the
midst of a political climate still fraught with division, Turgenev's novels managed to appeal to people with diverse political perspectives. His works
became the most widely read and often the most
hotly debated. *A Month in the Country* was a gate-
way to this fame and is often attributed with developing Turgenev's craft as a writer. The play was
first staged in Moscow in 1872 and is often likened
to Honore de Balzac's *The Stepdaughter. A Month
in the Country*'s first showing was not received very
well; however, after a famous actress performed it
in 1879, the play became a success. It is still widely
performed today and because of its timeless themes
of youth, freedom, and love, it is likely to continue
attracting admirers well into the next century.

AUTHOR BIOGRAPHY

Ivan Turgenev was born to Sergey Nikolaevich Turgenev and Varvara Petrovna Lutovinova on October 20, 1818, in the town of Orel, located 200 miles South of Moscow. His father, who was from the minor gentry, was a colonel in the calvary, and his mother was a wealthy landowner with a reputation for being arbitrarily cruel, particularly to her approximately 5,000 serfs. Turgenev's childhood was spent with his two brothers, one of whom died in adolescence, on the family's country estate at Spasskoe. His family left the country for Moscow when Turgenev was nine, and in 1833, at the age of fifteen, he entered Moscow University to study what was then called the philological faculty— literature.

In 1834 Turgenev transferred to the University of St. Petersburg in order to share lodging accommodations with his father and eldest brother. During his collegiate years, Turgenev developed a strong affinity for western culture, and in 1838 he enrolled at the University of Berlin where he studied philosophy. Turgenev's stay in Germany fostered his growing distaste for serfdom and after his time there, he became a lifelong proponent of westernization. In 1841, he returned to Russia; however, through his remaining years, Turgenev spent a good portion of his time in the West. In 1842, he completed his Master's degree and had an illegitimate daughter with whom he was never close.

In the next year, Turgenev met the one woman with whom he would form an emotional bond— Pauline Viardot, a renowned opera singer. Until his death in 1883, Turgenev was a devoted friend and some say a besotted admirer of Pauline. Over the years that followed their meeting, Turgenev lived as near to Pauline and her husband Louis Viardot as possible. As he rose to prominence as a writer, Turgenev became acquainted with many notable artists and thinkers of the period, including Feodor Dostoevsky, Leo Tolstoy, Gustav Flaubert, Emile Zola, Alexander Pushkin, Guy de Mauppasant, George Sand, Henry James, and Nikolai Gogol. In fact, after writing Gogol's obituary, Turgenev was imprisoned for one month and placed under house arrest at Spasskoe for close to two years. Not popular with the government, but often celebrated by his public, Turgenev succumbed to cancer in Paris in 1883. Pauline was by his side. He is buried in St. Petersburg in the Volkovo cemetery.

PLOT SUMMARY

Act I

Rakitin and Natalya are reading a book while Anna, Liza, and Schaaf play a game of hearts at a nearby card table. Natalya and Rakitin do more talking than reading and the flirtatious tension between the two is obvious. Natalya is bored with Rakitin always agreeing with her, and she expresses her displeasure. Rakitin continues to act as her "obedient servant" despite her protestations. Natalya and Rakitin's bantering is intermittently interrupted by exclamations from the card players about Schaaf's skill at Hearts. Natalya and Rakitin's conversation turns a bit personal, and Natalya parallels their talks with making lace, which is done in stuffy rooms. Anna beats Schaaf at cards, and Kolya enters with Beliayev.

Kolya enthusiastically tells everyone how much he likes his new tutor. Natalya asks Rakitin what he thinks of the new tutor, and Rakitin notices that she is quite taken with him. Matvey enters to introduce Shpigelski, who greets everyone and goes on to tell a story about a woman who falls in love with two men. His story prompts Natalya to wonder out loud why someone can not love two people at the same time. She retracts her question by then stating that perhaps to love two people is really to love neither. As Natalya accompanies the exiting Anna and Liza to the door, Shpigelski and Rakitin confer about Natalya's curious mood. After Natalya's return, Shpigelski tells Natalya about his friend's interest in marrying Vera. Vera and Kolya enter and again exalt Beliayev.

Natalya and Rakitin continue talking and Beliayev and Islayev enter. Islayev and Beliayev discuss Islayev's dam project. Before exiting to accompany Islayev and Rakitin, Beliayev is summoned by Natalya to stay briefly. Natalya tells Beliayev of the life she hopes of for her son, and how she would like his life to differ from her own upbringing. Matvey announces dinner after Vera and Beliayev share a secret giggle with Natalya observing their playfulness.

Act II

Schaaf and Katya share a flirting exchange before they are interrupted by Natalya and Rakitin's entrance. Katya hides and Schaaf joins Natalya and Rakitin. Katya remains picking berries and is happened upon by Vera and Beliayev, who busy themselves fixing a kite. Vera and Beliayev discuss friends, poetry, and Natalya until she arrives with Rakitin and they exit. Natalya notices that they run off. After discussing Natalya's disposition, Bolshintsov, and youth, Natalya and Rakitin part. Rakitin reflects on his loyalty and devotion to Natalya and wonders why she is unhappy.

Beliayev enters and the two discuss Beliayev's laziness, his plan to make fireworks for Natalya's birthday, and his ability to translate French texts despite the fact that he does not speak the language. Rakitin lectures him about the importance of studying and tells him that Natalya finds him quite charming. Natalya reenters and is cheered by Beliayev, which Rakitin notices. Shpigelski returns with Bolshintsov. After being left alone, Shpigelski and an obviously nervous Bolshintsov discuss the possibility of a match between he and Vera. Shpigelski tries to comfort Bolshintsov with words of confidence and advice. The scene ends with everyone heading to the meadow to watch Kolya fly a kite.

Act III

Shpigelski admits to Rakitin that he has agreed to play matchmaker for Bolshintsov in return for a team of horses and urges Rakitin to find out if Bolshintsov can continue calling on Vera. In his next conversation with Natalya, which is mixed with much innuendo about her feelings for Beliayev, Rakitin tries to find out what she plans to do about Vera. She claims not to have made a decision, so Rakitin sends for Vera. While she talks with Vera about Bolshintsov, Natalya probes her about her feelings for Beliayev. Obviously shaken, Natalya concludes that Vera and Beliayev are in love and sends the girl away. Privately, Natalya questions her jealousy of Vera and decides that although she is in love with him, Beliayev must leave.

Rakitin reappears and confirms for Natalya that she is indeed in love with Beliayev and that it would be best if he and Beliayev both left. Natalya weeps on Rakitin's shoulder at the same time that Islayev and his mother enter. Natalya rushes out and following her, Rakitin tells Natalya's perplexed husband and mother-in-law that he will explain everything later. Together again, Natalya and Rakitin agree that Natalya must talk with Beliayev immediately. Beliayev enters and after Natalya questions him about Vera, whose love he is surprised to learn of, he decides that he must leave. His decision upsets Natalya and while he wavers on if he should leave or not, she decides that she should think about it before

Ivan Turgenev

a decision is made. Alone again, Natalya questions her motivations and intentions and finally concludes that the tutor must go.

Act IV

Liza and Shpigelski seek refuge from the rain in the same place where Katya is waiting to summon Beliayev for Vera. Katya hides and overhears the couple's conversation about Natalya's state of mind and their relationship. Shpigelski discusses some interesting merits for marrying, like the fact that he is aging and his "cooks always turn out to be thieves." He continues by proposing marriage and revealing a private persona that differs from his public facade. The two exit and as Beliayev walks by, Katya calls to him. While she summons Vera, Beliayev reflects on how unbelievable the whole situation has become. Embarrassed, Vera enters and tells Beliayev how sorry she is that he is leaving. She tells him that she never told Natalya that she was in love with him and that it is actually Natalya who is in love with him.

Natalya surprises the two as she enters, and Vera confronts her about being in love with Beliayev. Regretting her behavior, Vera flees, leaving Natalya and Beliayev alone. Natalya admits her love and in the midst of a seemingly mutual confession and their ensuing conversation about his staying or going, Rakitin enters. Natalya dismisses her previous conversation with Rakitin about Beliayev as childishness, and when the two run into Islayev, she takes his hand and exits followed by Rakitin and Shpigelski.

Act V

Islayev and his mother discuss the scene they happened upon between Natalya and Rakitin. Anna is suspicious and Islayev consoles her. Islayev calls for Rakitin, who, after admitting his love for Natalya, tells Islayev that he is leaving. After some discussion, Islayev says that maybe he should leave for just a few days. Rakitin runs into Beliayev and tells him why he is leaving. He continues to lecture Beliayev about the importance of a woman's honor and asks if Beliayev would do the same if he were Rakitin. Their conversation is interrupted by Natalya and Vera. Rakitin tells them his plan and seems jealous about Natalya's compliments to Beliayev.

After the men depart, Natalya apologizes to Vera, who receives the information quite bitterly and is obviously upset by the thought that Beliayev loves Natalya. Coming upon Vera alone, Shpigelski is happy to learn that Vera will marry Bolshintsov after all. After Shpigelski departs, Beliayev enters to tell Vera that he is leaving because he is unhappy with the problems he has caused. Vera confides her marriage plans and agrees to give Natalya his good-bye note. After giving Natalya the note, Vera tells her that she is leaving. They are interrupted by Islayev and then Rakitin. The men discuss Natalya's apparent illness and Islayev attributes it to her learning that Rakitin is leaving. Rakitin says his good-byes. Kolya, Anna, Liza, and Schaaf enter and ask what is wrong with Natalya. In the process of the inquiry, Islayev learns of Beliayev's departure and is perplexed by everyone's sudden departures. One by one, everyone exits the stage. In the end, only Anna and Liza remain. To her shock, Anna learns that Liza too has plans to leave.

CHARACTERS

Vera Alexandrovna

Vera is Natalya and Islayev's adopted daughter. As a seventeen-year-old, Vera is caught in the precarious situation of still being considered a naive child, when in fact she proves to be a perceptive and precocious young woman. Vera is smitten with Beliayev and when she comes to believe that he loves only Natalya, she agrees to marry Bolshintsov, who had been previously undesirable to her.

Alexei Nikolayich Beliayev

Beliayev is a twenty-one-year-old student hired by Natalya to tutor Kolya. In contrast to other characters in the play who profess their honorable nature, Beliayev's honor appears to be genuine when it comes to caring about others. He describes himself as lazy; however, his intelligence and ingenuity contrast with this quality. His translation of a book into French without knowing the language attests either to his facility with languages or his willingness to misrepresent himself and his capabilities.

Lizaveta Bogdanovna

Liza is a lady companion who plays cards with Anna and Schaaf, teaches Kolya piano, and becomes involved with Shpigelski. Liza accepts Shpigelski's marriage proposal, although the audience might wonder why she does this. During the proposal scene, she tells him that she is only thirty-years-old when in fact she is thirty-seven. She is apparently self-conscious of her age, and this is perhaps her motivation for accepting Shpigelski as a suitor and a husband.

Afanasy Ivanovich Bolshintsov

Bolshintsov is the forty-year-old single neighbor of Islayev and Natalya. He is not highly regarded by most of the characters and is quite nervous throughout the play about his courtship of Vera.

Anna Semyenovna Islayev

Anna is Islayev's fifty-eight-year-old mother. She spends her time leisurely and is suspicious of Natalya's behavior. She is concerned for her son and feels that Natalya's youth does not work in his favor.

Arkady Sergeyich Islayev

Arkady is a wealthy landowner in his mid-thirties, who spends much of his time working. His work keeps him away from his wife, who develops an interest in Rakitin, a family friend. He is not a jealous man, nor does he handle his wife's behavior with suspicion or malice once he learns of Rakitin's love for her.

Kolya Islayev

Kolya is Natalya and Islayev's ten-year-old son. He is an energetic youth who loves to play and is dazzled by his new tutor, Beliayev.

Katya

Katya is a twenty-year-old maidservant who acts as Vera's confidant. She entertains advances from Schaaf and seems to always be in the right place to overhear the conversations of the other characters in the play.

Matvey

Matvey is a forty-year-old servant who plays a small role introducing characters and announcing meals.

Natalya Petrovna

Natalya is the complicated main character of the play. She is a married twenty-nine-year-old who finds herself bored with much of the life and people around her. From childhood she has lived a structured and hence seemingly constrained life from which she would like to break free. Her domineering father kept her in line as a child, and it seems that her choice in marrying Islayev has continued her feeling of confinement. The claustrophobic feeling that she has is replicated in her relationship with Rakitin. When she hires a new tutor for her son; however, she sees a glimpse of a different life. Beliayev is a breath of fresh air for Natalya and through him, she hopes to give her son the fun, happiness, and freedom she never had. In the process, she develops a yearning to capture these things for herself as well. Ultimately she does not attain the freedom that she seeks, and she must accept her life as it is.

Mikhail Alexandrovich Rakitin

Rakitin is a thirty-year-old friend of Natalya and Islayev. While Islayev considers Rakitin a close friend to him, Rakitin most certainly has a stronger affinity for Natalya. After admitting his love for Natalya to Islayev, Rakitin departs the estate. In his lecture to Beliayev, Rakitin reveals his belief that a woman's honor is very important; however, his lecture can also be seen as self-serving. Rakitin

MEDIA ADAPTATIONS

- *A Month in the Country* was made into a film for Mastervision's arts series on drama. Produced in the 1980s, this ninety-minute version of the play stars Susannah York and Ian McShane. Derek Marlowe wrote the screenplay, Quentin Lawrence directed, and Peter Snell produced the film.

- In 1969, Melodiia in the U.S.S.R. published a recording called *Stseny iz spektaklei,* or *Scenes from Plays,* that included scenes from *A Month in the Country.* This recording is in Russian.

- *A Month in the Country* was performed as an opera and recorded in 1981 by the Boston and New England Conservatories. John Moriarty was the conductor and David Bartholomew directed the show.

- A 100-minute sound recording of the play was released in 1981 by A.B.C. in Sydney, Australia.

recognizes his devotion to Natalya and is perplexed by her coolness toward him. He sees only his passion for her and does not understand how such feelings are not mutual. On one level, he does the honorable thing by leaving Natalya; however, he also knows that he is welcome to return.

Adam Ivanich Schaaf

Schaaf is a forty-five-year-old German tutor who is playfully smitten with Katya. In the first scene, he demonstrates his skill at the card game Hearts as well as his willingness to attribute his loss to someone else.

Ignaty Ilyich Shpigelski

Shpigelski is the forty-year-old doctor who calls on the family and is interested in marrying Lizaveta. Though his public persona is one of an accommodating, thoughtful, and jovial country doctor, his private persona is quite different. He expresses disdain and dislike for the other characters in the play. He uses people for what they can provide for him and does not see himself as particularly kind, talented, or romantic. He has clear views about a wife's and a woman's place in society and prides himself on his honesty.

THEMES

Love and Marriage

The many pairings in this play make love a prominent theme—Schaaf and Katya, Liza and Shpigelski, Vera and Bolshintsov, Natalya and Rakitin, Natalya and Beliayev, and Natalya and Islayev. The play is not a glowing portrait of loving, stable marriages or relationships, however. Natalya's toying with Rakitin and Beliayev calls her fidelity into question, while Shpigelski's reasons for marrying hardly seem to be related to love (he mostly seems to desire a trustworthy housekeeper/cook). Marriage as such, becomes an institution or a commitment that either binds and inhibits people's freedom or serves a practical purpose.

In no instance is a loving relationship correlated with a passionate romantic relationship between two people. For example, the match between Shpigelski and Liza does not appear to be based on a mutual romantic affinity, nor does Natalya and Islayev's relationship appear to have the level of respect and commitment that one might characteristically associate with a good marriage. Natalya's feelings for Beliayev hint that a love full of passion and freedom is possible; however, by the end of the play, a happy, fulfilling love relationship seems ultimately unattainable for them.

Apathy and Passivity

The theme of apathy is largely introduced by Natalya's apparent boredom with most everyone and everything except Beliayev. She can't bother to listen to Rakitin when he tries to apologize to her, and she seems unconcerned that her husband will discover her true feelings about the young tutor. In concert with this apathy, much of Natalya's behavior is coupled with an extreme case of passivity. She rarely acts or makes decisions unless she is prodded by others. Even her relationship with Rakitin, though obviously charged, seems to be an unconsummated flirtation. Other characters seem to be haunted by this passivity as well, including Islayev, who, while

consoling his mother about Natalya's behavior, seems generally unaffected by what he encounters between his wife and Rakitin.

Greed

The theme of greed plays a large part in the development of Shpigelski's character. He is motivated by his greed and his desire to please only himself. It is ironic that he is a doctor; however, his profession serves as a good front for his otherwise undesirable personality. He agrees to help Bolshintsov in his pursuit of Vera, not because he hopes to make a perfect match between two people he cares about, but rather to advance his own concerns. He wants to replace his horse and for assisting with the matchmaking, he will gain not only one horse but a whole team. Shpigelski's self-absorption motivates much of his action, including his courtship of Liza. He finds that his cooks are often thieves and sees that having Liza as his wife would remedy that problem in his life.

Honor

Honor is a theme that swirls around many characters in the play including Natalya, Beliayev, Shpigelski, Rakitin, and Islayev. Natalya's honor is at stake because she is willing to engage in extramarital affairs. She questions her own honor in acting on behalf of these urges and consistently wavers on sending Beliayev away or not. Her behavior as Islayev's wife also calls his honor into question. His reputation is at stake and his judgment in choosing Natalya for a wife is up for review, particularly by his mother.

Rakitin's honor is likewise a bit questionable because although he claims to do the proper thing by leaving, he knows that he can return at any time. His honor is also in question because despite the fact that Islayev is his friend, he becomes involved with Natalya. Rakitin redeems himself a bit by being honest with Islayev. Honesty and honor are certainly not qualities that can be associated with Shpigelski, who, although he presents an honorable facade, is actually far from honorable when it comes to his personal relationships.

Coming of Age

Coming of age is a theme that is flushed out by the characters of Vera and Beliayev. Vera is perceived by Natalya as a child in the beginning of the play; however, as the situation develops with Beliayev, Natalya comes to see Vera as much less of a child. Vera's own thoughts on this subject confirm

TOPICS FOR FURTHER STUDY

- Climax is a literary term that refers to the turning point in a story during which the most important part of the action occurs. Identify the climax in *A Month in the Country* and discuss why you chose this point.

- Research Alexander II's reform policies in education, the judiciary, the military, and government. Discuss how you agree and disagree with his intentions. What was he trying to accomplish? Was he successful in your opinion?

- Research the Hohenzollern dynasty in Prussia and discuss the parallels between it and Nicholas I's rule of Russia during the first half of the nineteenth century.

- Research Philosophical Idealism, or slavophilism, movement of Russia's 1830s. Who were its major proponents and detractors? Given your vantage point in the twentieth century, discuss why you think the Philosophical Idealists' vision would or would not work in today's society.

- Discuss the similarities and differences between *A Month in the Country* and similar works, such as Balzac's *The Stepdaughter* and Ibsen's *Hedda Gabler*.

---

the fact that while Natalya thinks that Vera is a naive child who can be manipulated and tinkered with, she is in fact a mature perceptive woman who is quite aware of Natalya's motives.

In some ways, Beliayev also comes of age during the play, although he is perhaps less self-reflective about it than Vera. As the situation with Natalya unfolds, Beliayev is forced to confront adult love for the first time and as he does this, even Natalya notice the change in him. She says, "he is a man," not a boy any longer.

STYLE

Setting

A Month in the Country is set in Russia during the mid-1800s on the estate of a wealthy landowner. The entire play takes place within one week and the majority of the action takes place in the Islayev's drawing room. By setting the play during the 1840s, Turgenev adds a political dimension to the work. The expansion of the secret police and the increase in censorship during Tsar Nicholas I's reign limited the degree to which Russian citizens could express themselves freely. To the extent that Natalya wants to break free from the constraints imposed upon her by men and the institution of marriage, *A Month in the Country* can be symbolically read as a political commentary about Russian citizens wanting to assert their free wills and act in accordance with their desires and passions. Like Natalya, who seeks the freedom to do as she pleases without any fear of the consequences, Russia's citizens, including its artists, desired the same opportunity.

Realism

Realism is a literary term that describes the way that stories are told as well as a literary movement that was popular during Turgenev's lifetime. *A Month in the Country* is an example of a realist work because it depicts people and circumstances that could very well exist in everyday life. The characters and the plot are realistic as opposed to fanciful creations of the author's mind.

Biographical Elements

While *A Month in the Country* is not a biography of Turgenev's life, the play does include some elements that can be considered biographical. For example, his longtime love for Pauline Viardot can be paralleled to Rakitin's unwavering devotion to Natalya. Throughout his lifetime, Turgenev often moved so that he could be close to Pauline and her husband. Like Rakitin's relationship with Islayev,

Turgenev's relationship with Pauline's husband was a friendly one. In addition to hints of Turgenev being found in the character of Rakitin, the author can also be found in the character of Natalya. As an artist who faced the limitations of censorship, Turgenev shared Natalya's passion for freedom. Further, whereas Natalya was influenced by her fear of her domineering father, Turgenev was highly influenced by his fear of his mother, who was known for her unpredictable cruelty.

Foreshadowing

Foreshadowing is a technique used by authors to tip off readers/viewers about events that will come later in the story. Turgenev uses foreshadowing in the first act by having Anna, Schaaf, and Liza playing hearts. The card game is symbolic and its placement in the beginning of the play indicates that just as in the card game, there will be winners and losers in the game of love by the play's end.

Another use of foreshadowing involves Rakitin and Beliayev. Rakitin's decision to leave the estate suggests that, in the name of honor, Beliayev may make a similar decision and also decide to leave.

Symbolism

The card game, hearts, that Anna, Schaaf, and Liza play in the opening scene is one example of the symbolism used by Turgenev in this play. Although the card game is part of the action of the play, the name of the game has an added significance. Placing the game in the very first scene makes its symbolism even more weighty. It is as though from the start, Turgenev is signaling the reader that the play is about the heart or love. The game is symbolic because, as in love, not everyone who plays wins. In cards and in love, one runs the risk of losing, and indeed by the play's end, many have lost in love. Schaaf's disappointing loss mirrors the disappointment felt by other characters when their desires to succeed in love are not fulfilled.

Irony

Irony is defined as an outcome that is directly opposite an expected result. One of the central ironies in *A Month in the Country* is the fact that while love is one of the play's major themes, no one seems to sustain a romantic, loving relationship. While love is intended to be a passionate uplifting endeavor, none of the play's characters are happy in their romantic relationships. Further, the play does not suggest that any of the characters will likely be happy in their relationships. Vera agrees to marry Bolshintsov in order to leave the estate, Natalya remains with Islayev but wishes that she could be with someone else, and Anna joins with Shpigelski, with whom she is not in love.

HISTORICAL CONTEXT

The hope for reform and the tensions of revolution serve as the political backdrop against which much of Turgenev's work was created. From the 1820s and into the 1880s, Russia's government and its people were embroiled in the tenuous process of distinguishing an identity on the world stage. Nicholas I's reign, which spanned from 1825 to 1855, was characterized primarily by the idea that Russia should be independent from and uninvolved with the European West and its ideas. Nicholas I's highly nationalistic approach to government was coupled with his belief in having his government as centralized as possible. In his attempt to consolidate his power, Nicholas I expanded the role of the secret service and increased censorship.

During Nicholas I's rule, society was segmented by two growing forms of thought. While this segmentation was encouraged in academic circles where like-minded people met in discussion groups, mainstream thought was also divided along the same lines. The two primary groups were comprised of the Philosophical Idealists, or the Slavophiles, and the Westerners. According to Herbert J. Ellison in *History of Russia,* the Philosophical Idealists of the 1830s "conceived of Russia as a vigorous new civilization coming rapidly to maturity and leadership beside a declining Europe." While the Slavophiles favored a nationalistic approach to government, "they were opposed to the actual tyranny of the imperial regime," according to Sidney Harcave in *Russia: A History.*

On the other side of the spectrum, as Ellison noted, "The Westerners of the 1840s and 1850s . . . recommend[ed] the Western path of development for the future" and were not as nationalistic. In general, the Westerners saw a decided value in continuing to emulate the West. They supposed that Russia had not achieved the level of development that the West had and were critical of censorship and the great economic and social disparities between the serfs and the nobility.

Not surprisingly, the artists of this time were impacted by the political climate. While censorship

COMPARE
&
CONTRAST

- **Mid-1800s:** During Nicholas I's reign, there are many restrictions placed on education. In particular, there are restrictions on the use of western ideas and texts in the classroom. The government has a strong influence on curriculum. When Alexander II assumes power, he seeks educational reforms by relaxing censorship standards and increasing the autonomy of universities.

  Today: Along with the collapse of the Soviet system in the early-1990s came a marked increase in the number of private schools and institutions of higher education. In addition, the educational curriculum has been broadened to include previously banned works and reinterpretations of Russian and Soviet history.

- **Mid-1800s:** Land is primarily owned by the wealthy, who use serfs for labor. While there is growing agitation for freeing the serfs under Nicholas I, the official emancipation statues are not initiated until February 19, 1861. The statutes call for land ownership to pass from noble landowners to the serfs in three stages. Ultimately, serfs have to pay high prices in exchange for little land; however, despite the flaws in the reforms, they do substantially raise the social position of Russia's lowest class.

  Today: Since the dissolution of the Soviet Union, the agricultural industry has been slow to privatize. As late as the mid-1990s, 90% of agricultural land was in control of former collective and state farms. While these farms have been reorganized into cooperatives or joint stock companies, land ownership remains concentrated.

- **Mid-1800s:** Russia's most impressive industrial expansion takes place during the 1860s and 1870s; however, prior to this time, much had been done to pave the way. The completion of close to five thousand miles of roads and the Moscow-Petersburg railroad line contributed greatly to Russia's budding industrialization as did the growth of cities and cottage industries. During Alexander II's reign, wasteful excise tax collection is abolished, railroad construction continues, and the system of banks, joint stock companies, and credit institutions is expanded. Russia is primed for the industrial and commercial expansion it needs to strengthen its empire.

  Today: As the twentieth century comes to a close, Russia is finding itself, along with the rest of the world, in the midst of a new revolution—the technological revolution. Advances in the computer industry are transforming the global landscape and like the rest of the world, Russia is enjoying and eagerly anticipating the progress made possible by the new communication age.

- **Mid-1800s:** Russia is ruled by autocrats whose personal preferences and dispositions characterize and determine the goals of the government.

  Today: In the past two decades, Russia has been faced with the difficult task of transitioning from a single-party totalitarian style of government (communist) to a multiparty democratic style of government. The Communist Party of the Soviet Union (CPSU) has been replaced by hundreds of parties whose orientations range from monarchists to communists. In general, the political parties can be divided into three groups: 1) nationalist/communist, 2) pro-market/democratic, and 3) centrist/special interest.

---

certainly had a negative effect on the writing of many authors, Russia's cultural output during Nicholas I's reign did not suffer on the whole. According to Ellison, ''the reign of Nicholas I was in many ways a period of extraordinary growth and of great attainments ... particularly in literature.'' While this may be true, it is perhaps necessary to wonder what the cultural output would have been like, both in content and quantity, had censorship not been expanded during Nicholas I's reign.

Prior to the 1840s, Russia's literary canon had been largely dominated by poetry; however, with the advent of realism, prose fiction began to figure more prominently in the literary circles of the time. Realism, or naturalism as it was called in Russia, brought "everyday people who had hitherto been admitted neither to the homes nor to the writings of the fashionable" into the mainstream. Nikolai Gogol (*The Inspector General*) is perhaps one of the most well-known contributors to this body of Russian literature.

By the mid-1850s, the agitation for reform had become quite heated, and with Alexander II stepping in as ruler, the nation's policies began to change. As Ellison noted, Nicholas I had failed to stem "the tide of intellectual radicalism . . . to buttress the traditional social order . . . [and] to achieve a more enlightened and efficient government." This being the case, his successor set to work putting the wheels of change into motion. Alexander II relaxed censorship and began reforming all aspects of bureaucracy including the government administration, the judiciary, the educational system, the military, and the nation's economic policies.

Success can not be measured by intent alone, and as Ellison pointed out, Alexander II's "failures were of speed and scope, not of direction." Harcave concluded, "Although Alexander II, like Peter [the Great], failed to attain all the goals that he set for himself, his reforms helped to bring about such changes that his reign may be considered the second great watershed in Russian history."

CRITICAL OVERVIEW

Turgenev was and is a controversial author. As his brief stay in prison attests, his politics, which were often evident in his writing, placed him in a rather precarious position with a good portion of his contemporaries—particularly those in power. Turgenev supported the ideas of reform and westernization and detested serfdom. For these reasons, he fell into disfavor with many; however, for as much as he inspired dislike, Turgenev was equally liked by others. For those who agreed with his ideas, Turgenev was a master storyteller who had a unique facility for weaving realism with carefully developed characters and well-crafted prose.

As might be expected in the politically charged environment of nineteenth-century Russia, his champions and detractors were more often than not divided by their political leanings rather than their staunch literary convictions. Outside of Russia, readers and critics found Turgenev's works instructive and readily accessible, making him popular in the West as well. As A. V. Knowles noted in *Ivan Turgenev,* the playwright was "the first Russian novelist to achieve international recognition." During the mid-1800s, Turgenev reached his highest literary moments by locating the middle ground wherein his fans and previous skeptics could find cause to approve of him and his work.

The public's reception of *A Month in the Country* reflected the finicky tastes of his contemporary audiences. The play was finished in 1850, published in 1855, and performed for the first time in Moscow in 1872. Immediately after its release, the officialdom banned any performances of it, and after its debut in Moscow, it was not warmly embraced. Seven years later, however, when a young actress, Marya Savina, chose to star in the play, Russia's theater-going community changed its mind and the play began to be regularly performed—and enjoyed.

According to Knowles, "A production of 1909 at the Moscow Art Theatre with Stanislavsky directing and playing the part of Rakitin and Chekhov's widow Olga Knipper an Natalya Petrovna made it famous and established the interpretation it is usually given today. . . . Stanislavksy saw it as a psychological study and played down its social or political aspects." While Turgenev's political content, real or implied, caused some of his critics and the officialdom to reject his works on principle, his psychological explorations have come to be one of his signatures in more contemporary times. *A Month in the Country* originally suffered because of its implicit social commentary; however, it has now become more widely accepted and recognized for its literary merit rather than for its political overtones. As Knowles confirmed, "*A Month in the Country* is still successfully and regularly produced" today.

Turgenev's fame and notoriety have persisted into subsequent eras. His literary achievements and

A stage setting for A Month in the Country *at the Moscow Arts Theatre, where a revival of Turgenev's play was produced in 1909*

his portrayal of Russia's tumultuous nineteenth century have left him regarded both as one of Russia's finest literary figures and as one of its lesser achievers. He is most often praised for his keen character development, his knack for description as well as his realism; however, he has been criticized for his failure to measure up to some of Russia's other greats—Gogol, Tolstoy, Chekhov, and Dostoevsky. To Turgenev's credit, Knowles noted that "his best stories are models of construction, and his use of language superb. . . . Turgenev is at his best when he keeps things simple, when he describes rather than analyzes." Further, Knowles noted, "Turgenev once said that he was first and foremost a realist . . . [and perhaps] this provides a clue to the strengths of his methods of characterization and his writing style in general."

Though considered a skilled craftsman, Turgenev has been berated quite vehemently for falling short of his contemporaries' successes. Quoting from Charles A. Moser's *Ivan Turgenev,* Knowles noted that Turgenev "cannot boast the verbal exuberance and astounding inventiveness of a Gogol, the profound energy and conviction of a Dostoevsky wrestling with problems of a sort our age thinks very relevant, the epic sweep and inquiry to be found in

Tolstoy, the painstaking attention to detail and psychological analysis of a Goncharov." This statement reveals that Turgenev is both praised and criticized for the very same things.

His manipulation of the Russian language, his portrayal of his people and Russia's history, and his psychological characterizations all seem to be both his strengths and his weaknesses in the eyes of critics. The controversy over his work perhaps dates back to the highly dichotomized society in which his writings were first introduced; however, whatever the cause for such division, Turgenev and his works are sure to be a rich source for discussion for years to come.

CRITICISM

D. L. Kellett

Kellett has an M.A. in literature and works in corporate communications. In this essay she discusses Turgenev's use of dichotomies as a structural and character development device.

WHAT DO I READ NEXT?

- In his time, Nikolai Gogol was known for his unabashed criticism of Russia's bureaucracy. Today he is known as the Father of Russian realism. His short story ''The Overcoat'' was published in 1840 and reflects the author's skilled use of realism.

- *Hedda Gabler* is another play with a domineering aristocratic female heroine who is looking for happiness from within the confines of a dissatisfying marriage. This play was written by Norwegian Henrik Ibsen and was first published in 1890.

- Also a contemplation on what makes a life well lived, Leo Tolstoy's short story ''The Death of Ivan Ilych'' was first published in 1886. Tolstoy has long been considered one of Russia's finest prose writers and is best known for his novels *War and Peace* and *Anna Karenina.*

- The French author Gustave Flaubert was a contemporary of Turgenev's. In his novel, *Madame Bovary,* which was published in 1856, Flaubert explores the theme of disillusionment through a female protagonist who has an adulterous affair.

- The themes of love, youth, and happiness are all to be found in Anton Chekhov's *The Cherry Orchard,* which was written in 1903 and first performed at the Moscow Art Theater in 1904.

- *Fathers and Sons* is considered by some to be one of Turgenev's pinnacle works. Published in 1862, this novel favorably explores the rejection of all forms of tradition and authority through its male protagonist, Bazarov.

In the introduction that precedes Richard Newnham's English translation of *A Month in the Country,* Richard Schechner applauded Turgenev for what he called ''a masterful study of Natalya Petrovna,'' the play's main character. While Schechner discussed at some length the ways in which Natalya's fear of men is closely linked to her fear of her father, his analysis also culminated in an important conclusion: ''Natalya Petrovna is a failure in love, and that is the crux of her personality and the play. She cannot consummate love with her husband or Rakitin; Beliayev slips out of her grasp. She dissolves in a series of futile gestures and contradictions as the play draws to a close.''

It is certainly true that Natalya fails to achieve a fulfilling romantic relationship with any of her three leading men—Islayev, Rakitin, or Beliayev. Her attitude toward her husband seems at its best a benevolent tolerance, while her toying with Rakitin can be viewed as an ego-feeding, yet yawn-inspiring dalliance for her. As Schechner aptly noted,

there is only a chance for her with Beliayev, for ''he is young, athletic, virile,'' and because she perceives him to be naive, he is initially approachable. Ultimately, however, his departure from the estate also makes him inaccessible to her. Natalya is indeed a failure in love. Ironically, her eagerness to obtain the freedom and passion she desires is somehow too closely linked to her inability to attain the love that she believes will provide these things for her. She assigns value and ultimate happiness to the very things that she can not have, or does not attain, and thus, she dissolves into the ''futile gestures and contradictions'' of which Schechner spoke.

Schechner argued that it is Natalya's very fear of men that makes having any man impossible for her. She can only love that which is not a threat to her, yet all of her lovers either become threatening or boring, and as a result, love and the subsequent freedom and passion she seeks from it are unattainable for her. Her ultimate contradiction is perhaps a trite one—she wants what she can not have and does not want what is readily hers for the taking. As the play wraps up, all of Natalya's desires and realizations come to naught. Beliayev and Rakitin leave the estate, and she is left with her husband, who mistakenly believes that all happiness has been restored.

One way to understand the play's ending is offered by Schechner when he concluded that it is the "denouement of her [Natalya's] ineffectuality." Indeed, her ineffectuality is central to her character development. As she grapples with her own contradictions, she dissolves into a perpetual state of frustration with her unfulfilled wishes. The elements of contradiction and opposition manifest themselves very clearly in Natalya's inner conflicts—should she or should she not pursue Beliayev, does she like or dislike Rakitin, can she be free or will she always feel like a prisoner? Embedded in her questions are dichotomies like faithful/unfaithful, love/hate, freedom/entrapment, and honesty/dishonesty.

In addition to being defining characteristics of Natalya's character, such dichotomies are central elements in the work's overall structure. In fact, Turgenev's use of these elements permeates the play on almost every level. A quick glance at act one demonstrates the ways in which Turgenev incorporates these elements in his work from the very start.

When the curtains first rise, Schaaf, Liza, and Anna are playing hearts, a card game that is based not only on winning or losing but on a strategy that requires players to think in terms of all or nothing. To ensure a winning hand of hearts, one must hold all of the hearts in the deck and the queen of spades, or no hearts at all. Having any number of hearts in between these two extremes puts one at risk of losing the hand and eventually the game. Turgenev's placement of hearts in the opening scene signals to the reader that the play is about the heart, or the game of love, and at the same time it introduces one of the play's guiding organizational structures: dichotomies. Oppositions, contradictions, and contrast dominate *A Month in the Country*—all or nothing and winning or losing are just the beginning.

By interweaving the conversation about the card game with Natalya and Rakitin's interchange, Turgenev hints that the two lovers might also be considered in light of his structural web of contradiction and opposition. And indeed they can be. The two are very clearly at odds, and their romance is an

unconsummated one. At the same time that their love appears to be everything to Rakitin, it seems at times to mean nothing to Natalya. The tension surrounding the couple is obvious in the first scene when they quibble over Rakitin's reading of *Monte Cristo*.

As the act unfolds, it becomes apparent that Rakitin is caught up in a web of choices and consequences. He must either read or talk, obey Natalya or not, bore her or not, and as the audience later learns, he must decide to leave her or not. Their relationship is a balancing game. At some moments it appears that their affair is one-sided, and then in the next Natalya admits her love for him. Rakitin is aware of the precarious ground on which their relationship treads. He notes, "You know, Natalya Petrovna, the more I look at you today, the less I can recognize you." Contradictions abound even for Rakitin—that which should be most familiar to him becomes unfamiliar and almost unknowable.

When Shpigelski arrives, the oppositions and contradictions continue to grow. Of Verenitsm and his sister Shpigelski proclaims, "It's my opinion that they're either both mad or both normal, for there is nothing to choose between them." The choices offered by Shpigelski are extremes and as such they fall right in line with the other contradictory oppositions in the play. Natalya does not respond to Shpigelski's assessment; however,

THE OUTSTANDING SUCCESS
OF CHEKHOV'S PSYCHOLOGICAL
DRAMA IS ITSELF A VINDICATION OF
TURGENEV'S METHOD, WHICH WAS
SO UNPOPULAR IN ITS DAY"

her later comment about his story reveals that her reasoning parallels his. When responding to Shpigelski's story about the girl who loves two men, Natalya notes, ''I don't see anything surprising about that: Why shouldn't one love two people at once?'' As though this were not enough of a contradiction, she goes on to surmise, ''but no, I really don't know . . . perhaps it simply means that one isn't in love with either.''

The possibility of loving more than one man or no one at all goes hand in hand for Natalya, and in conclusion, she admits that she really just doesn't know what to think. Natalya is confused by what it means to love and almost immediately she adapts an all or nothing mentality. Rakitin echoes her sentiments about the perplexity of love when he ponders their relationship a bit later. He reflects, ''What does all this mean? Is it the beginning of the end, or the end itself? Or is it the beginning, perhaps?'' Rakitin's question is an appropriate one and it further epitomizes the dichotomies that populate Turgenev's play. The end and the beginning, though obviously opposite, are indistinguishable to Rakitin, who struggles to discover at which point he finds himself in his relationship with Natalya.

The presence of so many oppositions has a rather curious effect on the overall work. On the one hand, *A Month in the Country* is a highly charged play riddled with conflict. Natalya experiences a deep personal turmoil as she questions infidelity, to love someone so young, and if she should she act based on her own self-serving interests and marry Vera off to Bolshintsov. Interestingly, however, the contradictory nature of her options and the prevalence of so many other dichotomies in the play also add a feeling of balance to the work. Natalya is tortured and fragmented in terms of her personal loyalties, yet her struggle is set against a backdrop of opposites that create a certain sense of unity.

The idea of balance created by opposition is not a new concept. In fact, it traces back to the idea of yin and yang, the Chinese symbol for balance and harmony. This is not to suggest that the conflicted Natalya is in balance because she questions whether she should be unfaithful to her husband, yet it is to suggest that there is a certain sense of wholeness evoked by the presence of so many complementary oppositions in the play. In addition to presenting oppositions and contrasts in the development of the plot and the other characters, Turgenev includes such elements on a thematic level as well. Some of the more notable thematic contrasts he plays upon include young/old, public/private, work/play, truth/lies, upper class/lower class, and, of personal interest to the playwright, Russia/the West.

The world of opposites that populates *A Month in the Country* can also be said to swirl around its author. Attempting to draw parallels between Turgenev's fiction and his real life is merely speculative; however, it is intriguing that one of the elements that permeates *A Month in the Country* also dominated Turgenev's life. In *Turgenev: The Novelist's Novelist*, Richard Freeborn noted that Turgenev was ''a man of extraordinary, innate contradictions.'' Further he added, ''During his lifetime Turgenev acquired many reputations. He was a political figure whose views received approval and sympathy in some quarters, disdain and outright rejection in others, a man who regarded himself as European in Russia and a Russian in Europe . . . a man, finally, who never married but devoted the greater part of his adult life to a seemingly unrequited passion for a married lady.''

From his reception by his critics to his political views and his personal preferences, Turgenev was indeed a man haunted by contradiction. Some consider *A Month in the Country* to be at least somewhat autobiographical, and in that both the author and his work share such a dominant characteristic, one might assume that in an effort to achieve balance in his own life, Turgenev used his fiction as a forum for exploring his own conflicts. Whether *A Month in the Country* served personal purposes or not is difficult to say; however, from the distance of close to 150 years, one can certainly conclude that Turgenev's use of contradiction and opposition served his craft well. As a man and an artist, Turgenev grappled with the tenuous balance between life's greatest contrasts and while his success in walking this fine line was evident in much of his work, *A Month in the Country* serves as one of his best examples and as one of his greatest literary achievements.

Source: D. L. Kellett, for *Drama for Students,* Gale, 1999.

Anthony D. P. Briggs

In this essay, Briggs provides an overview of A Month in the Country *and discusses its significance within the canon of modern Russian drama, particularly the play's influence upon the pyschological dramas of Anton Chekhov.*

A Month in the Country is a five-act play in prose written by the Russian novelist Ivan Turgenev in the period 1848–50. After objections by the censors to some of its overt social criticism, the play was finally passed for publication in 1855. It was performed for the first time in Moscow (at the Maly Theatre) in 1872 and assured of continuing success in the 20th century by a famous Stanislavsky production at the Moscow Arts Theatre in 1909.

The story concerns a young tutor, Aleksey Belyaev, who is hired during the summer to teach the ten year old son of the Islaevs on their country estate. Despite his own mild manner the charming Belaev has a devastating impact on the household. Mme. Islaeva (Natalia Petrovna) vies with her own young ward, Vera, for his attention. Both women fall in love with him but Vera is no match for her protectress. Natalia maneuvers her into an arranged marriage with a ridiculous middle-aged neighbour. Belyaev departs, leaving all of the characters facing changes in their lives. In particular, Rakitin, a close friend of the family who has long been a secret admirer of Natalia, is forced to go away, suspected by her uncomprehending husband of having made advances towards her. Secondary interest, and not a little humour, arises from the down-to-earth love relationship between two middle-aged characters, Dr. Shpigelsky and Lizaveta Bogdanovna.

The play has had an unusual destiny. Its author was reluctant to believe in its quality because of the negative criticism which it received. He went so far as to admit that it was not really a play, but a novel in dramatic form. In fact, a good case could be made in the opposite direction: that Turgenev, with his skill in creating atmosphere, character, and dialogue far exceeding his narrative inventiveness, might be

regarded as a dramatist *manque.* This play has not only remained in the Russian repertory, it has travelled abroad with great success, proving particularly popular on the British stage.

Its major achievement is to have introduced into Russia, half a century too early for the author's own good, a wholly new theatrical genre, the pyschological drama. *A Month in the Country* is a play in which very little overt action occurs. There are arrivals and departures, one listens to conversations and gains a strong sense of hidden passions and tensions seething just below the surface of events. There are two or three moments of crisis, resolved with words rather than deeds, sufficient to raise an audience's involvement from interest to anxiety. But what is remarkable is the disparity between the radical nature of these developments and the lack of any external adventure or sensation. Ordinary people leading humdrum lives are subjected to turmoil and trauma; it is as if a whirlwind has passed through and blown away their comfortable routine, and no one saw anything happen.

Turgenev's characterization is remarkable. Not ony are the 13 characters extremely realistic, they actually develop and mature during the action of the play, without ever straining credulity. Particularly poignant are the two leading female roles. For all her understated depiction, Vera approaches tragic status and cannot fail to move the spectators as they watch her rapid transformation from girlishness to womanhood, followed by her painful resignation to a hopeless future. As for Natalia, she attracts some degree of sympathy because of her boring marriage and her forceful personality, but she is despicable in her ruthless treatment of the young girl whose interests she is supposed to be protecting. Her villainy is mitigated by a sense of her powerlessness before the forces which take control of her—physical love together with a sense of panic that her youth and beauty are rapidly coming towards their end. She is complex and fascinating. Alongside these leading characters there is much else to sustain the interest: the innocence of Belyaev, the sadly amusing remoteness of Natalia's husband, the bitterness of Rakitin who only now comes to full realization of how empty his life has been. There is a good deal of comic relief, particularly in the exchanges between Shpigelsky and Bogdanovna but also in the character of Shaaf, the German tutor, and the satirical picture of Bloshintsov, Vera's eventual husband-to-be. Productions which play upon the comedy and leave the more serious issues to speak for themselves in Turgenev's restrained manner bring out all the qualities of *A Month in the Country,* and, by keeping them nicely in balance, tend to be more successful than those which attempt to propel the complex drama explicitly in the direction of tragedy.

The question of Chekhov's debt to Turgenev has never been fully resolved. Chekhov himself denied it and claimed he had not even read *A Month in the Country* before writing his major plays. This can scarcely be true, as even a glance at the cast lists of this play and *Uncle Vanya* will reveal. Both plays (and also Balzac's *La Maratre* from which *A Month in the Country* derives) involve groupings of characters which are anything but conventional; all three are certainly interrelated. Critics tend either to take for granted a certain influence by Turgenev, or else to deny it almost entirely. The influence seems, however, beyond question, extending as it does to setting, characterization, atmosphere, dialogue, and even perhaps to thematic interest. The outstanding success of Chekhov's psychological drama is itself a vindication of Turgenev's method, which was so unpopular in its day. What is remarkable is the early date at which Turgenev attempted to introduce the Russians to a form of drama which would sweep to popularity half a century later; *A Month in the Country* was written ten years before Chekhov was even born.

Source: Anthony D. P. Briggs, '' *A Month in the Country* '' in *The International Dictionary of Theatre,* Volume 1: *Plays,* edited by Mark Hawkins-Dady, St. James Press, 1992 , pp. 531–32.

SOURCES

Harcave, Sidney. *Russia: A History,* J. B. Lippincott, 1968, pp. 248-74.

Schechner, Richard. Introduction to *A Month in the Country,* translated by Richard Newnham, Chandler, 1962, pp. vii-xviii.

FURTHER READING

Ellison, Herbert J. *History of Russia,* Holt, Rinehart, and Winston, 1964, pp. 134-218.
   This book chronicles Russia's history. The particular pages noted cover the years 1801 through 1881, roughly encompassing the period of Turgenev's life.

Freeborn, Richard. *Turgenev: The Novelist's Novelist: A Study,* Oxford University Press, 1960, pp. xi-36.
   While this book focuses upon Turgenev as a novelist, its beginning chapters provide an introduction to his guiding philosophies, political leanings, and development as a writer.

Garnett, Edward. *Turgenev,* Kennikat Press, 1966, pp. v-34.
   This work presents a discussion of Turgenev's childhood, family life, and his early works as well as a chapter about his critics.

Knowles, A. V. *Ivan Turgenev,* edited by Charles A. Moser, Twayne, 1988.
   This book offers an in-depth look at Turgenev with chapters devoted to his biography, literary career, reputation, six of his novels, and his final years. *A Month in the Country* is also discussed.

Schapiro, Leonard. *Turgenev: His Life and Times,* Oxford University Press, 1978.
   This book contextualizes Turgenev's life and works within the nineteenth century.

Yarmolinsky, Avraham. *Turgenev: The Man—His Art—His Age,* Hodder & Stroughton, 1926.
   Yarmolinsky's work offers a survey of Turgenev's life and his literary accomplishments.

Mule Bone

ZORA NEALE HURSTON

LANGSTON HUGHES

1930

Mule Bone was written in 1930. It was a joint collaboration between noted African-American authors Zora Neale Hurston and Langston Hughes, who joined forces to write a play based on a folktale, "The Bone of Contention," that Hurston had discovered in her anthropological studies. Both writers conceived the play as representative of authentic black comedy. Shortly after the play's creation, however, Hurston copyrighted the play in her name only. The two authors had a falling out and did not speak to one another again. A legal battle ensued and, because of those legal issues, the play could not be produced during either writer's lifetime.

Mule Bone remained locked away. Few people read the play and it was largely forgotten until critic and historian Henry Louis Gates discovered the play in the early-1980s. *Mule Bone* was not performed on stage until 1991.

In many ways, *Mule Bone* has the ability to evoke both discussion and controversy. Hurston and Hughes felt that by incorporating a black folktale and southern black vernacular English into their play, they could refute a racist tradition of black characters as ignorant. However, when the play was finally developed for the stage more than sixty years later, there were concerns that this comedy might, instead, recall stereotypes and bring back the very issues that the authors had hoped to refute. It was thought that the play, as viewed by a audience in the 1990s, might appear to cast blacks as backward or

ignorant. The director sought to mitigate that problem by including a section of Hurston's writings that explained her views on black vernacular English. Each writer brought separate talents to the writing of *Mule Bone*. Hughes was primarily a poet; Hurston was an essayist and novelist. Their quarrel ended what might have been a successful collaboration. As it stands today, *Mule Bone* is still considered a significant work of drama and is notable as an early work of African-American theatre.

AUTHOR BIOGRAPHY

Zora Neale Hurston was born January 7, 1891, in Eatonville Florida. She was forced to leave school at age thirteen so that she could care for her brother's children. She was later able to return to school and eventually studied Anthropology at Barnard College and Columbia University. During this time, Hurston began publishing short stories. In 1927, together with Langston Hughes and other artists, she founded a literary magazine, *Fire!,* which was devoted to African-American culture. The magazine quickly folded, and after graduation, Hurston returned to Florida to complete research for her anthropological studies.

The information she gathered on Negro folklore became the basis for much of her writing. Hurston published her first novel, *Jonah's Gourd Vine,* in 1934 and a collection of short stories, *Mules and Men,* in 1935. Her most famous work, *Their Eyes Were Watching God,* was published in 1937. By the 1940s, Hurston's career had begun to fail. Publishers, who thought that her recent work lacked the depth and insight of previous efforts, rejected her work. An autobiography, *Dust Tracks on a Road,* was published in 1942, and her last published novel, *Seraph on the Suwanee,* was published in 1948.

Hurston spent the last years of her life in Florida, where she worked variously as a cleaning woman, a librarian, a newspaper reporter, and a substitute teacher. She died penniless at the Saint Lucie County, Florida, Welfare Home January 28, 1960. Hurston was buried in an unmarked grave in the Fort Pierce segregated cemetery.

(James) Langston Hughes was born in Joplin, Missouri, on February 1, 1902. Hughes's parents separated shortly after his birth. His father eventually settled in Mexico, and his mother left him in the care of his maternal grandmother, who raised Hughes

until her death in 1910. For the next four years, Hughes lived with family friends and relatives until he joined his mother and new stepfather in Ohio in 1914.

Having encountered racism at Columbia University, Hughes dropped out of college after his freshman year and began working a series of odd jobs. While working as a bus boy in a hotel in Washington D. C., Hughes placed three poems on poet Vachel Lindsay's dinner plate. The resulting attention eventually led Hughes to a critic who helped him publish his first collection of poems, *The Weary Blues,* in 1926. Shortly after this publication, Hughes enrolled in Lincoln University in Pennsylvania, where he continued writing.

Hughes's first collection of short fiction, *The Ways of White Folks,* was published in 1934, and a series of sketches known as his "Simple Tales," which were about a black Everyman, were published in the *Chicago Defender.* The Simple Tales were very popular with black readers and were eventually published in a series of books. Hughes also began writing drama in the 1930s, but he always considered himself primarily a poet. Although his work sometimes received mixed reactions from blacks who were concerned that he emphasized lower-class life and presented an unfavorable image of his race, Hughes's work was a critical success and he received many honors and awards during his life, including a Guggenheim fellowship for creative work in 1935. Hughes died May 22, 1967, of congestive heart failure in New York City.

PLOT SUMMARY

Act I

Act I takes place in the area immediately in front of Joe Clarke's store. On this Saturday afternoon, a number of men are gathered on the porch talking, chewing sugar cane, whittling, or playing cards. There are children playing in the dirt in front of the store and women, who are shopping, are entering and leaving. The opening of this act introduces a number of minor characters who enter the stage for a few moments and then exit. Mrs. Roberts is the first to interrupt the group of men gossiping in front of the store. She is a huge woman whose role is to badger and whine her way into convincing Clarke to extend her more credit and more meat. After she leaves with her meat, the conversation turns to a mule bone that is brought into the store.

The audience learns that the bone is from a legendary mule. The mule is remembered as especially strong, stubborn, and even evil. Then the men began to speak of Daisy. This young woman is especially beautiful, but the discussion changes when two other young women enter the stage. Both of these women, Teets and Bootsie, used to date Jim and Dave. But both men are now enamored of Daisy instead.

In this manner, the audience learns that two young men, the best of friends since childhood, are now courting the same young woman. The audience also learns that Jim and Dave are not as close as they once were and that Daisy has come between them. Daisy enters briefly and is asked which man she prefers, but she declines to pick one. The men gathered on Clarke's porch continue gossiping, and a brief discussion about religion ensues. This establishes that there is some conflict in town between the Methodists and the Baptists. The audience also learns that there is no jail, and that the town marshal is really an errand boy for Clarke, who controls most elements of the town.

Eventually Jim and Dave enter. They have made some money playing and singing, and when Daisy appears and asks them to entertain, they do so. There is some jealous banter between the two men, but it is controlled until Jim notices Dave dancing in a corner with Daisy. Jim quits playing, and the two men begin to argue over the Daisy. Dave and Daisy enter the store to buy soda, and as they exit, Dave accidentally steps on Jim's foot. The two men begin to fight and Jim strikes Dave on the head with the mule bone, knocking him out. Clarke orders the marshal to arrest Jim and to lock him up in the barn.

Act II, scene 1

The action in this scene occurs on the street. Notice of the pending trial is being nailed to a tree. A number of women are gathered and begin talking. The audience learns from this conversation that Clarke is very antagonistic toward the Methodists, especially their minister, Elder Simms. The women state that this is because Simms is the only one who will stand up to Clarke, who has had control over the town since he bought land and built the basis of the town.

When Clarke enters, the women question him about trying Jim. Clarke defends his actions as

Zora Neale Hurston

maintaining order. The entry of other town women results in a confrontation that is largely accusations about religious differences. Even the town children enter into the fray and begin quarreling. At the end of the scene, both Methodists and Baptists exit the stage to begin preparing for the trial.

Act II, scene 2

The trial is set in the Baptist church. This scene opens with a great deal of arguing that threatens to become violent. Two of the women need to be restrained. Clarke attempts to maintain order but has only minimal success. When he asks that all testifying witnesses move to the front of the church, almost everyone present rises to do so. When questioned, their response is that although they were not present when the incident occurred, they have a biblical right to testify. An additional problem presents itself when Daisy's mother refuses to allow her daughter's name to be spoken in court.

Finally the testimony begins with Marshal Lum, who admits he did not see anything. In fact, no one who is called upon wishes to testify against Jim. Finally, Dave is forced to tell what happened. When it begins to look like Jim might be found guilty, Elder Simms, the Methodist minister, begins a defense that centers on the bible, which fails to

Langston Hughes

identify a mule bone as a weapon. Simms reasons that Jim cannot be guilty of assault, since he had no weapon (or at least none that is recognized in the Bible). Elder Childers, the Baptist minister, argues that an ass bone killed thousands according to the bible and that a mule is descended from an ass; therefore, since offspring are always more dangerous than their parents, the mule bone is a dangerous weapon. Clarke seizes on this latter argument, declaring Jim guilty and ordering that he be banished from town.

Act III

This act opens just outside town where Jim is preparing to leave. Daisy enters on her way into town to learn of the trial. She is clearly upset at the turn of events, since she claims to never have desired any animosity between Jim and Dave. Dave enters, and the two men begin bickering about Daisy. Daisy is asked to choose, and after Jim offers the most romantic pledge, she chooses him. But upon her insistence that he get a real job and quit playing his guitar, Jim hands her over to Dave. Daisy appears to accept this change easily enough, but then Dave insists that he—like Jim—does not want to work as a yardman or handyman, as Daisy wishes.

In the end, Dave would rather sing and dance than labor as Daisy's husband. Rejected, Daisy leaves the stage, Dave and Jim decide to continue their entertaining together, and both decide to return to town. Although Jim has been banished, it is clear that neither man fears Clarke or his authority.

CHARACTERS

Mrs. Dilcie Anderson

A Methodist housewife who, although she was not present at the fight, insists she can testify, since she heard all about it from her husband.

Daisy Blunt

Daisy has just moved back to town. Since her return from up North, she has emerged as the object of most men's attention. She is a flirt who enjoys seeing the men compete for her attentions. She is a domestic servant who must work and so does not come to the trial. After the trial ends, she meets up with both Jim and Dave just out of town. First she chooses Jim and suggests they live with her employers. But when Jim declines her invitation to work as a yard man, she chooses Dave. However, Dave would rather sing and dance. In the end, she has neither man.

Marshal Lum Boger

Boger is the town Marshal. His primary duty as the play opens is to chase after the small children who play in front of Clarke's store. He is subject to Clarke's orders and behaves more like a servant than an officer of the law. Most people make fun of Lum.

Dave Carter

Dave is a singer and dancer, who, with Jim, makes a living entertaining people. He is in love with Daisy. He and Jim have been friends all their lives, long before they began quarreling over Daisy. When Dave and Jim fight, Dave gets the first punches but is then hit in the head by Jim, wielding a mule bone. Dave recovers, and after Jim is found guilty and told to leave town, he searches out his friend. Although Daisy initially chooses Jim, she changes her mind and wants Dave, if he will get a job. Dave misses Jim and their entertaining. He rejects Daisy's offer and chooses to reunite with Jim instead.

Elder Childers

Childers is a long-time resident of the town. He is the Baptist minister and is calm and confident, willing to assume responsibility. Childers counters Simms argument at the trial and points out that a mule is kin to an ass and thus an ass bone is a weapon according to the bible.

The Mrs. Reverend Childers

Mrs. Childers is the minister's wife. She is focused on details.

Joe Clarke

Clarke is both the mayor of the town and a storekeeper. He bought the land on which the town was built and has been mayor since its inception. When Jim hits Dave, Clarke orders him arrested and decides to try the case in the Baptist church of which he is a member. Clarke sets himself up as judge and declares Jim guilty. Clarke is disliked by the Methodists, who say that he is dishonest.

Although Clarke is the mayor and founder of the town, there is no point in the play where he is clearly in charge. He orders his wife and Lum around because they are dependent on him, but even the town ladies know Clarke can be pushed and manipulated, and no one is afraid of his authority. As an authority figure, Clarke is just a subject of ridicule.

Mrs. Mattie Clarke

Mattie is the shopkeeper's wife. Joe sends her back in to work every time she emerges from the store. While her husband socializes on the front porch and struts his authority, Mattie is responsible for the actual running of the business.

Ada Lewis

Ada is the town tramp, whose reputation for promiscuity embarrasses her mother.

Della Lewis

Della is Ada's mother. She is a Baptist and considered to be a poor housekeeper.

Teets Miller

Teets is a local girl, who was dating Jim before Daisy returned to town.

Lige Mosely

Mosely is one of the town gossips.

Willie Nixon

Nixon is one of the Methodist men.

Bootsie Pitts

Bootsie is a flirtatious young woman and a friend of Teets. Before Daisy came to town, Bootsie was seeing Dave.

Elder Simms

Simms is the Methodist minister. He's only been in town three months and is in conflict with Clarke over how the town should be run. He is aggressive and ambitious. Simms argues in court that Jim's use of a mule bone to hit Dave does not make it an assault, since the bible says that a mule bone is not a weapon.

The Mrs. Reverend Simms

Mrs. Simms is a very large woman, the object of some jokes because of her size.

Daisy Taylor

See Daisy Blunt

Walter Thomas

Thomas is a village gossip who hangs out in front of Clarke's store.

Jim Weston

Jim plays guitar and with his friend Dave, the two make a living as entertainers. He is in love with Daisy and in competition with Dave for her attention. When a fight breaks out, Jim grabs a mule bone and strikes Dave with it, knocking him out. He is a Methodist, somewhat arrogant, and aggressive. Jim has more talent with words than Dave, and ultimately, he is able to sweet-talk Daisy into choosing him. However, after winning Daisy, Jim realizes he does not want a career as a yard cleanup man, as she suggests. He offers to give her back to Dave, but his friend also declines to work as a laborer. Like Dave, Jim realizes that there is greater value in his lifelong friendship with his partner than there is in romancing Daisy.

THEMES

God and Religion

The conflict between the Methodists and the Baptists has divided the town into factions, with

TOPICS FOR FURTHER STUDY

- Research the religious differences between Baptists and Methodists. Consider if the differences outweigh the similarities between these different branches of Protestantism.

- Discuss whether you think that *Mule Bone* is perpetuating stereotypes about southern blacks. Why or why not?

- Look at some early black sheet music. What do the lyrics tell the listeners about rural black life in the South in the first half of the twentieth century?

- A modern reader might wonder at the legitimacy of the trial Clarke holds for Jim. Research early town life in the rural South. Is Jim's trial representative of how small black communities might deal out justice?

- Joe Clarke thinks he has control in this town, and yet, at the play's conclusion a banished Jim can return to town in defiance of Clarke's orders. Who really maintains control? You might consider the role that church elders play or what women contribute to such action.

each side aligned with either Jim or Dave. That there is fundamentally little difference between sides is not apparent to either group. Both are Protestant and both believe in one God, and yet, each side is prepared to battle over which religion is superior. The argument and near-violent confrontation that opens Act II, scene 2, illustrates the ridiculous nature of the conflict.

Human Condition

Hurston and Hughes use black vernacular English to illustrate a type of black comedy. But the play's reliance on the common language of the people also reveals a great deal about the inhabitants of this small village. These people know one another intimately. They know each other's business and they feel free to comment upon their neighbor's private lives. Gossip is a big force in their lives.

There is poverty, and Clarke carries most of the people in the accounts of his general store. Extending credit is expected among neighbors in this small town, but even though the people owe him money, they still feel free to rebel against his claims of authority. Their language is populated with shortcuts and abbreviations that all the inhabitants know. This common language also helps to establish a sense of community. They are poor and they argue about religion, but they also argue as a close family does.

Justice

Clarke establishes himself as mayor and authority for this small town. He appoints the marshal and then he controls how the marshal enforces the law. When someone needs to be imprisoned, it is to Clarke's barn that he is taken. The trial is set in the Baptist church, of which Clarke is a member. Clarke presides over the trial and he pronounces sentence. Clarke finds it difficult to maintain order at the trial, and when Jim returns to town and ignores his banishment, it becomes clear that justice in this small village is more a matter for ridicule than it is a governing force.

Language and Meaning

Hurston and Hughes's decision to use black vernacular English illustrates the differences that exist in English. Most Americans define English according to the formal rules of grammar that are taught in primary and secondary education. But the language of this play is also the language of southern blacks. To the untrained ear, the villager's language may lack meaning or be difficult to understand. Such language may even be judged as ignorant or illiterate. In this way, people attach meaning to language. When it does not fit the accustomed model, listeners may seek to dismiss language as illegitimate. Hurston and Hughes sought to prove that, though unconventional, southern black vernacular English does have a role in defining a group of people within a particular location and time.

Race

Race is less a theme of the play than it is an issue for the audience. Because of the play's use of back vernacular English, there is a chance that the audience will make assumptions about the characters. The biggest fear is that members of the audience will embrace stereotypes of rural blacks as ignorant, silly, or as objects of ridicule. Blacks have worked hard to dispel old stereotypes and there exists a possibility that an uneducated audience might too quickly forget the reality of black life and fall victim to racial stereotypes.

Sex

In a play that focuses on romance, sexuality would be expected to be a motivating force for a character's actions and words. Teets and Bootsie are former girlfriends of Jim and Dave, and both young men are now intent on pursuing Daisy. These serial relationships, though intermingled, appear devoid of sexual tension. Teets and Bootsie have gone on to other young men. There is much gossip about which young man Daisy will ultimately choose, but there is no question about possible impropriety. Another man, Cody, has married and yet, in the months since his marriage, no one has seen his wife. The villagers gossip about this, but no one makes jokes about newlyweds. It is clear that people are intensely interested in personal gossip, but no one gossips about intimate matters. Sex is present in romance and marriage, but it is not a subject for idle talk.

Success and Failure

Jim and Dave are successful entertainers. That they make a satisfactory living can be based on their happiness with their work and because both appear to have access to available cash. They both consider what they do a success. But according to Daisy, neither one is really "working." She defines employment success as a job that involves physical labor and a salary, such as the position of yardman that she suggests Jim might assume. She will not marry a man who is not a success—according to her definition of success. This definition limits her prospects, since neither Jim nor Dave wants to meet her requirements. However, at the conclusion of the play, while both men seem slightly regretful as Daisy walks away, they are also clearly happy with their choices. Thus, their lives are a success by most definitions.

STYLE

Audience

Authors usually write with an audience in mind. Hughes and Hurston intended *Mule Bone* as a vehicle to bring southern black comedy to a larger audience. The two authors saw it as a way to keep alive black vernacular English and the rural folktales of southern blacks.

Character

The actions of each character are what constitute the story. Character can also include the idea of a particular individual's morality. Characters can range from simple stereotypical figures to more complex multi-faceted ones. Characters may also be defined by personality traits, such as the rogue or the damsel in distress. Characterization is the process of creating a life-like person from an author's imagination. To accomplish this the author provides the character with personality traits that help define who he will be and how he will behave in a given situation.

Drama

A drama is often defined as any work designed to be presented on the stage. It consists of a story, of actors portraying characters, and of action. But historically, drama can also consist of tragedy, comedy, religious pageant, and spectacle. In modern usage, drama explores serious topics and themes but does not achieve the same level as tragedy.

Genre

Genres are a way of categorizing literature. Genre is a French term that means "kind" or "type." Genre can refer to both the category of literature such as tragedy, comedy, epic, poetry, or pastoral. It can also include modern forms of literature such as drama, novels, or short stories. This term can also refer to types of literature such as mystery, science fiction, comedy, or romance. *Mule Bone* has elements of drama but is primarily considered a comedy.

Plot

This term refers to the pattern of events that take place in a play. Generally plots should have a beginning, a middle, and a conclusion, but they may also sometimes be a series of episodes that are thematically linked together—as in the epic plays of Bertolt Brecht (*Mother Courage and Her Children*). Basically, the plot provides the author with the means to explore primary themes. Students are often confused between the two terms; themes explore ideas, and plots simply relate what happens in a very obvious manner. Thus the plot of *Mule Bone* is the story of a fight and of the trial that ensues. But the themes are those of religious tolerance, friendship, and success.

Scene

Scenes are subdivisions of an act. A scene may change when all of the main characters either enter or exit the stage. But a change of scene may also indicate a change of time. In *Mule Bone,* Act II has two scenes. The scenes indicate two separate locations, a street and the interior of the Baptist church.

Setting

The time, place, and culture in which the action of the play takes place is called the setting. The elements of setting may include geographic location, physical or mental environments, prevailing cultural attitudes, or the historical time in which the action takes place. The locations for *Mule Bone* are all located in or near a small village. They include the front porch of Clarke's store, a street, the Baptist church, and the railroad tracks just outside town. The action occurs over a period of twenty-four hours.

HISTORICAL CONTEXT

In October of 1929, the American financial markets collapsed. By Christmas of 1929, the Great Depression had begun, and by the time *Mule Bone* was written two years later, the United States was solidly in the grip of a huge financial depression that affected almost everyone. The years after World War I had been prosperous for citizens of the United States. Employment was up, and the need for newly developed products had created a successful economy. For the first time, credit became an accepted way to buy durable goods. When people lacked enough money to buy something, they borrowed against future earnings. Demand for goods increased; jobs increased, and unemployment was down. When the market collapsed, jobs were cut, and there was no way to meet the demands of creditors. In a short time, the United States' economy collapsed. Banks closed and a lifetime of savings disappeared.

In the rural South, credit to buy automobiles or household goods never approached the levels it did in the larger cities to the North. Instead, credit was more often just as it appeared in *Mule Bone;* small country stores extended short lines of credit to steady customers. In a period when cash was often short, people's existence might be determined by the line of credit at a town grocery. This avenue for food was not available in many other American locations. Hunger was a serious problem. Many people lacked even the minimal food required to maintain nutrition. The United States' birthrate declined during the Depression because a lack of basic nourishment could not sustain life.

The hardships increased for blacks, many of whom had moved to northern cities from the rural South. Racism was never worse than it was during the Depression when jobs became scarce. Blacks were just more competition for already limited job opportunities. Blacks were not the only victims of discrimination in a shrinking job market, however. All racial minorities, such as Hispanics and Native Americans, found that jobs were reserved for white males. Even women, who had traditionally found work as domestics, discovered little opportunity for employment. To add to the already dismal picture, a severe drought in the southeastern United States created a dust bowl of once fertile farm land and added even more poverty and hunger to an already dismal picture.

Blacks had always been outsiders in the rural South, and little had really changed since the end of the Civil War. Although black men had joined the army and navy to fight overseas, they returned to the United States after World War I to find a life that was as segregated as it had been before the war. Blacks had been told that they were fighting for liberty and democracy, but they found little of either. Racist organizations like the Ku Klux Klan reached a level of new strength in the years after the war, and lynchings and violence against blacks increased.

How serious this racism was became evident in the Scottsboro case when nine black youths were convicted of raping two white women on a freight train in Alabama. In a case that involved questionable evidence, a lack of defense representation, jury problems, and which resulted in multiple trials and appeals, the defendants were finally all convicted and sent to jail, where they served a total of 130 years. Blacks not only had to combat the hunger and poverty of the Great Depression, they had to fight virulent racism just to survive.

CRITICAL OVERVIEW

Although written in 1931, *Mule Bone* was not performed on stage until 1991. In those intervening sixty years the world changed a great deal. Where Hurston and Hughes had envisioned a need for authentic black theatre in 1931, playwrights like

COMPARE
&
CONTRAST

- **1931:** U. S. unemployment tops 8 million.

  Today: Unemployment is very low, but while many employers claim they cannot fill jobs, many of the positions are for low paying menial jobs. As in the past, many of these jobs are filled with immigrants and minorities.

- **1931:** Detroit lays off another 100,000 workers, reducing employment at auto plants by 225,000 workers in two years.

  Today: Employment in automotive manufacturing has undergone many changes in the past seventy years. Production lines have become more mechanized and there have been periodic layoffs due to fluctuating demand, but the Ameri-can infatuation with the automobile has meant an increasing demand for cars and led to relatively steady jobs in the automotive sector.

- **1931:** The U. S. wheat crop breaks all records, driving down prices. Many farmers are forced off their land and banks foreclose on mortgages, thus adding to the poverty and food shortages of the Great Depression.

  Today: There are fewer farmers than at any time before. Large commercial farming operations have made it difficult for most small farmers to compete. Many have chosen to sell their farms and move to cities.

August Wilson (*The Piano Lesson*), Amiri Baraka (*Dutchman*), and Alice Childress (*The Wedding Band*) had stepped in to fill the void. Black theatre had moved from minstrel shows to dramas that reflect the black experience, and *Mule Bone,* which sixty years earlier might have been the start of black theatre, now seems more like a dated epilogue. This is the problem most often noted in the mixed reviews that greeted the play's debut at the Barrymore Theatre in February of 1991. In his review for the *New York Times,* Frank Rich found the play ''innocuous.'' Rich stated that the play was ''so watered down and bloated by various emendations that one can never be entirely sure if Lincoln Center Theatre is conscientiously trying to complete and resuscitate a lost, unfinished work or is merely picking its carcass to confer a classy literary pedigree on a broad, often bland quasi-musical seemingly pitched to a contemporary Broadway audience.''

While acknowledging that the play occasionally makes clear what Hurston and Hughes intended, Rich argued that the play appears dated. However, Rich did find that the trial scene in Act II and the final scene between Jim, Dave, and Daisy were especially good. As his review concluded, Rich summed up the problems with *Mule Bone:* ''the production design is mostly hokey, the performances often aspire to be cute, and even the fisticuffs are not played for keeps. While the authors intended *Mule Bone* to be funny, this production confuses corny affability with folk humor.''

The *Daily News*'s Howard Kissel found the play more likeable than Rich, but he also noted the ''aimless first act.'' In praising the play, Kissel pointed out that the work's strongest features are its ''earthy dialogue and the irresistible humor.'' Noting the especially large and strong cast, Kissel observed that there was ''an abounding affection for the material and for this irretrievable, innocent past.''

Another positive review was offered by Clive Barnes of the *New York Post.* Barnes stated that '''*Mule Bone*' positively sparkles with its rich dialect and vivid language, and it shines with the unaffected simplicity of a folk tale.'' Barnes also enjoyed the music (something many other reviews were divided on) and the dancing, which he felt added ''savor to the play.'' But the strongest elements of the play, said Barnes, are ''the sheer vigor of its life, the hyperbole of its language, the crosscut of its genial insults, the sharp-etched caricatures of its characters. And, of course, the acting.''

Offering a contrasting view, Linda Winer of the *New York Newsday* suggested that *Mule Bone* "missed its real time and now feels more like a vivid work of archeology than a universal work of theatre." She pointed out that the play had "no tension, not much shape, just a 30-member cast of experts dipping deep into their history to reclaim a tradition." Among the problems, stated Winer, are "the weak plot and a lack of dramatic momentum." An additional problem is that "much of the first act's nonstop chatter was hard to understand from the fifth row." Winer stated that the play's success may depend on the audience's patience "for caricature farce and one's willingness to hang around townfolk for a couple of hours and watch them amuse themselves."

John Beaufort, writing for the *Christian Science Monitor,* had few reservations about recommending *Mule Bone.* Citing the play's "exuberance," Beaufort singled out the "animated dialogue scenes" and the play's music for special note and referred to the play's debut as a "theatrical event." Proving that no two reviewers see or hear a play in quite the same way, Edwin Wilson's review in the *Wall Street Journal* referred to *Mule Bone* as "a pleasant but uneventful depiction of life in the small town of Eatonville, Fla., in the 1920s." Wilson stated that the "songs are mildly appealing but largely incongruous" but that the production lacks fire. Citing the last act as "sustained drama," Wilson stated that the play should have "gotten on track well before its final 15 minutes."

CRITICISM

Sheri E. Metzger

Metzger is a Ph.D. specializing in literature and drama at the University of New Mexico. In this essay she discusses some possible reasons why Mule Bone *has failed to find an audience.*

When *Mule Bone* finally opened on Broadway, it enjoyed only limited success, closing after sixty-seven performances and mixed reviews. Given the eager anticipation that greeted the play's opening and the audience's willingness to find a reason to accept and enjoy this long-awaited play, this brief run indicates that *Mule Bone* encountered some difficulties. Foremost is the fact that Hurston and Hughes left the play unfinished. The two wrote Acts I and III together, and Hurston wrote Act II later, but

the drama never received the kind of polishing and finishing that a play typically receives just before performance.

Although Hurston and Hughes quarreled over the play's completion and over authorship, *Mule Bone* was briefly scheduled to open in February 1931. When the two writers quarreled again, the play's production was canceled, and the play remained untouched for sixty years. Had the play opened as scheduled when both of its authors were still living, many of the problems might have been resolved. Instead, when *Mule Bone* finally opened in 1991, both playwrights were dead and any hope that some of the play's more confusing aspects might be cleared up died with them.

Even ignoring the play's unfinished state, however, significant problems with the large cast and with the play's use of black vernacular English make it difficult for the majority of audiences to make any connection with *Mule Bone.*

One significant reason for the play's lack of success is that there is no central protagonist with whom the audience can identify. While their music offers a few moments of entertainment on stage, the audience does not get to know either Dave or Jim well enough to cheer for one or both of them. It is important that an audience be able to identify with a play's protagonist. Quite simply, audiences need a focus. While both characters are funny, neither is endearing. Both men enter two thirds of the way through Act I. Their romance with Daisy has been discussed but only briefly. They fight, and Jim strikes Dave over the head with a mule bone. Both men appear briefly in Act II during the trial. But in this case, they are both more easily defined as onlookers and not participants.

The play's action seems to occur because of the duo's dispute, but the reality is that Jim and Dave serve more as a vehicle to center a plot around religious conflict. In the folktale upon which the play is based, the fight between the two men was about which one shot a turkey. It could have as easily been the same in the play, since it really does not matter why the men fight or even that they do. What is important is that the Baptists and the Methodists are permitted the opportunity to display their wit, to compare and contrast the benefits of each school of thought.

Unfortunately, this focus on the conflict between two competing religious factions means that the relationship between Jim and Dave has no focus or meaning for the audience until the third act, when both men appear on stage together. Although they are only alone on stage for a few moments before Daisy enters, these brief moments reveal what this play might have been.

Another reason why *Mule Bone* fails to capture our allegiance is found in the large cast of characters. John Lowe's analysis of this play suggests that the real voice of the play is a community. But even a community has to have a unifying force. This community of Eatonville, Florida, may have a purpose, but it is not readily identifiable to the audience. The cast, numbering nearly forty, is too large, too broad, and too unwieldy to keep track of. Who are these men, women, and children? They pop on and off stage, most with only a few lines of dialogue. There is no stage direction to provide context for their lines or their role. The audience receives neither background nor the nature of the relationships.

Consequently, too many characters remain anonymous as they speak their few brief lines. Except for a few characters, who play pivotal roles, the rest of the cast could have easily been filled by anyone. And that is the problem. Even characters listed as minor need to have appeal. To add confusion, in this case, actors listed in the play as major characters appear on stage with only one or two lines. Hurston and Hughes may have known these people's roles and their relationship to one another, but unless it is printed on the program, the audience does not. For example, Dave's aunt, Katie Carter, is listed as a major character, and yet, she has no dialogue. So how can the audience identify her as his aunt? Why make her a part of the cast?

Possibly, Hurston and Hughes intended to expand such roles, but since the play was never completed, they add more confusion. One effect of so many characters is that there is little left over for the leads. *Mule Bone* comes to life in Act III. Why? Because all the minor, ill-defined characters are off-stage. Only Jim, Dave, and Daisy remain. The focus is on their roles and on their relationship to one another.

In his discussion of the play in the *New York Times,* Henry Louis Gates noted that those lines reveal patterns of early black courtship. They reveal important cultural observations that are both humorous and revealing about black culture. According to Hurston's biographer, Robert E. Hemenway in *Zora Neale Hurston: A Literary Biography,* this is what Hurston and Hughes intended—to bring the

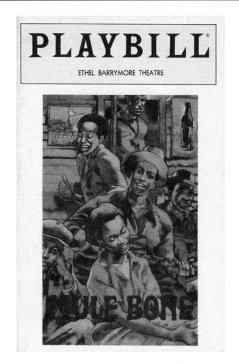

A playbill for Hughes and Hurston's play at the Ethel Barrymore Theatre

humor inherent in black folktales to an audience who would then find these new black comedies a more honest depiction of black life than the stereotypical minstrel shows that too often were identified with black life. Instead the large cast eclipses the small individual roles that are so central to a play's success.

Another problem with the play's large cast of undistinguishable characters is that, for the audience, the experience is akin to attending a huge reunion gathering—as the spouse of a member. Everyone is enjoying himself or herself, telling jokes, remembering stories, instantly understanding the kinship or relationship of all the other members. Everyone is laughing and exchanging in a kind of informal banter, everyone except the spouse, the outsider who feels left out. That is the experience that many viewers of *Mule Bone* have. The audience does not know these people and they do not know their stories.

The impression is of one arriving in the middle of a conversation. This can be effective in a limited arena, but in *Mule Bone* it is the entire long, first act of the play. During the first act, roughly thirty characters speak, most only a line of two. Many of

WHAT DO I READ NEXT?

- Zora Neale Hurston's *Dust Tracks on a Road,* is an autobiography published in 1942. In this work, Hurston offers her views on the role of black artists.

- *Their Eyes Were Watching God* (1937) is Hurston's best-known work. In this book, Hurston's main characters are white, rather than the black inhabitants of her previous work.

- *Fine Clothes to the Jew* (1927) is a collection of Langston Hughes's poetry. The central subject is Harlem's lower class. Hughes also includes several ballads.

- *The Ways of White Folks* (1934) is a collection of short stories that Hughes wrote after he noted similarities between his writing and that of D. H. Lawrence.

- Harriet Jacobs's *Incidents in the Life of a Slave Girl* (1861) is an autobiography that tells of the author's life as a slave in North Carolina and of her escape and struggle for freedom.

- In *Race, Writing, and Difference* (1985), Henry Louis Gates compiles a number of essays that discuss the role of race in literature.

---

the speakers are identified by name, although the name is essentially meaningless without some sort of context. Many of the speakers are simply referred to as Villager, Lounger, Voice, Man, Woman. All the audience can do is listen, smile politely, and hope that someone will explain the joke. It just is not fun to feel left out, and in *Mule Bone,* the audience feels excluded. John Lowe stated in the *Southern Quarterly* that the American theatre expects "individual central plots." Instead, this play delivers broad characterization, a large cast, and little plot to capture the audience's interest.

Even if an audience is willing to accommodate all the characters, there is another problem for the play which is even more difficult to overcome: the stereotyping of characters and of language is difficult to ignore. Even with an explanation of what Hurston and Hughes intended, the language appears condescending and racist. Even with an understanding of the authors' motives, this play seems a step backward to a period most African Americans do not want to revisit.

In her analysis of the play in the *Langston Hughes Review,* Lisa Boyd pointed out that when the play was first discussed in 1988, there was immediate concern about the language and depiction of characters. She stated that the play was

"revamped, toned down, and made more innocuous for the 1991 production." Use of the pejorative "nigger" was reduced to only one instance. But, in spite of this editing, many problems with language remained. The use of black vernacular English calls to mind an earlier period in American history. This in itself would be fine, except that this earlier period was fraught with racism and the odious practice of slavery.

For many blacks, the hope and need is to move beyond such a period, to build beyond it. *Mule Bone* is a little like moving backward, and even though it is only a perception, it is an illusion that no one desires. White audiences are made uncomfortable for much the same reason. Although most white members of the audience may have harbored no racist ideology, they feel a part of the community that created such a racist environment; they share a collective guilt. For both black and white, the language of *Mule Bone* creates an uncomfortable listening experience. Boyd maintained that *Mule Bone* makes critics so uncomfortable that they, instead, focus on the quarrel between Hurston and Hughes rather than the play's content. One exception is Gates, who championed the play and who acknowledged that this drama presents risks. Gates stated that the "precarious political and social condition within American society warrants a guarded attitude toward the way images of their culture are projected.'' While Gates's affection for *Mule Bone* is clear, his concern about language only serves to illustrate the gravity of the problems facing any production of *Mule Bone.*

Source: Sheri E. Metzger, for *Drama for Students,* Gale, 1999.

Gerald Weales

Weales reviews a 1991 production of Mule Bone, *the play's first in sixty years. The critic finds the play a ''slight tall tale'' that is ''buoyed by its tremendous sense of fun.''*

For years, the phrase ''Broadway play'' has been a favorite pejorative in critical circles—academic ones, particularly. It was familiar even when works like *Death of a Salesman* and *A Streetcar Named Desire* were Broadway hits, but no one ever knew precisely what it meant. Commercial? Predictable? Unlikely to disturb the patrons? Any or all of those, I suppose, but Broadway has never been quite the pigeonhole that play sorters have imagined it to be. There have always been producers who took chances on unusual works—not good ones necessarily—that outsiders, with the wisdom of the uncommitted, could recognize as sure losers. Even now, with fewer and fewer plays on Broadway, there have been some odd creatures turning up and, for the most part, disappearing before I could get a review into print. Come to think of it, most of the things I review are gone before my comments appear, but that is because much of the interesting work today is produced by nonprofit organizations for limited runs. The three plays I briefly consider here, however, were presumably hoping for old-fashioned Broadway success.

Mule Bone may be a special case since it was produced by the Lincoln Center Theater, heavily financed by foundation grants, but it was at the Ethel Barrymore because the Lincoln Center's own main stage was filled by the long-running *Six Degrees of Separation*—a Broadway play, if I ever saw one. *Mule Bone* was written in 1930 by Langston Hughes and Zora Neale Hurston, a collaboration that dissolved in disagreement, and it did not find its way to the stage or the page for more than half a century. For Hurston, presumably, it was still another of the works in which she wanted to present black life anecdotally in black vernacular; for Hughes, a poet who shared Hurston's concern with black language, it may have been an opportunity to turn to

''IT JUST IS NOT FUN TO FEEL LEFT OUT, AND IN *MULE BONE,* THE AUDIENCE FEELS EXCLUDED''

theater, a dream that would continue to draw him for the rest of his life.

This version of the play has been given a prologue and an epilogue by George Houston Bass, who according to a *Playbill* biography, is ''responsible for melding the 1920s sensibilities of Langston Hughes and Zora Neale Hurston with those of the audience in the 1990s.'' That means that he doctored the original script into stage life, greatly helped by the music of Taj Mahal. The play is a very slight tall tale—not unlike many of Hurston's stories—in which two friends, joined by the music one plays for the other to dance to, are split apart by a flirtatious young woman who likes the attentions of both. They finally fight over her, one knocking the other out with the titular mule bone, an event that leads to a trial which is mostly a confrontation between rival churches, an epic trading of insults which provides the main vitality of the piece. In the end both men reject the woman—who expects the man who gets her to take a real job—and stick with one another, their friendship, their music, and their freedom being more attractive than sparking which might turn into the trap of marriage. At the end, everyone forgets that the bone-wielder has been banished from the town, and the entire cast gets together for a musical finish which celebrates community that transcends any local quarrels. Those insults were never more than grand rhetoric, appreciated by insulter and insultee alike. *Mule Bone* ran for a few months, buoyed by its tremendous sense of fun and by a setting that drew black audiences who presumably had no desire to check out *La Bête* or *I Hate Hamlet.*

Source: Gerald Weales, ''To Hate or Not to Hate'' in *Commonweal,* Vol. CXVIII, no. 11, June 1, 1991, pp. 373–74.

John Simon

Simon is one of the best-known theatre critics in America. In this excerpt, he reviews the debut production of Hurston and Hughes's play, finding it

FOR HURSTON, MULE BONE WAS STILL ANOTHER OF THE WORKS IN WHICH SHE WANTED TO PRESENT BLACK LIFE ANECDOTALLY IN BLACK VERNACULAR; FOR HUGHES, A POET WHO SHARED HURSTON'S CONCERN WITH BLACK LANGUAGE, IT MAY HAVE BEEN AN OPPORTUNITY TO TURN TO THEATER, A DREAM THAT WOULD CONTINUE TO DRAW HIM FOR THE REST OF HIS LIFE"

worthwhile theatrical entertainment. While the critic calls the source material "skimpy," he nevertheless praises the presentation, stating "it was worth waiting 60 years for so accomplished a production to reach the stage."

Mule Bone was to have been the play (suggested at a 1930 party by Theresa Helburn to Langston Hughes) that would be neither heavy social drama nor minstrel show but a real comedy of black life that would extend the Harlem Renaissance to the stage. Hughes enlisted Zora Neale Hurston, and they started converting her brief folktale "The Bone of Contention" into the three-act *Mule Bone*. It was never quite finished because, under various inner and outer pressures, the co-authors quarreled, for reasons still not fully understood. The story of "The *Mule Bone* Controversy," now published together with the play, is longer and at least equally fascinating reading.

At the Barrymore, we get the play as edited by the late George Houston Bass, supplied with his prologue and epilogue and with music by Taj Mahal. In the story, two young hunters from an all-black Florida town each claim to have shot down the same wild turkey; in the ensuing fight, Jim knocks Dave unconscious with a handy mule bone. The mayor conducts a trial in the Baptist church, where the Baptists side with their boy, Dave, and the Baptist preacher defending him; the Methodists, occupying the other half of the church, back Jim and the Methodist minister defending *him.* The argument and counterargument are funny, as are the insults traded by Baptists and Methodists. And that is about the size of it.

This sweet but skimpy material had to be mightily stretched for the stage, and the stretch marks show. Instead of fighting over a dead turkey, Jim the singer-guitarist and Dave the dancer (best of friends who perform together) now fight over a live chick, Daisy, the prettiest girl in town, back from the North and working for whites whose stuck-up ways she's learned. This contest, too, has its entertaining aspects and a surprise ending, and is embedded in much racy talk, often heightened into perky song by Taj Mahal to both Hughes's and his own lyrics.

There is a nice blend of canniness and naïveté in the Lincoln Center production that Michael Schultz has staged into something as crisp as a white shirt fresh from the laundry. The 29 well-deployed actors acquit themselves, for the most part, pungently, with only Kenny Neal (Jim), Akosua Busia (Daisy), and Paul S. Eckstein (Marshal Lum Boger) not quite up to the rest. But Neal is handsome and a handy guitar-strummer, Miss Busia a remarkable beauty, and Eckstein miscast. There are catchy bits of dance staged by Dianne McIntyre, and scenery (Edward Burbridge), costumes (Lewis Brown), and lighting (Allen Lee Hughes) that are as frolicsome as they are functional.

I know that nothing is less thrilling than a list of names; but nothing would be more unjust than not mentioning at least a few personal favorites among so many nifty performers: Clebert Ford, Fanni Green, Donald Griffin, Leonard Jackson, Ebony Jo-Ann, Theresa Merritt, Reggie Montgomery, Eric Ware, Vanessa Williams, and Samuel E. Wright.

It was worth waiting 60 years for so accomplished a production to reach the stage. Far from patronizing blacks (as more whites than blacks seem to feel it does), *Mule Bone* is honestly alive and kicking; regrettable as their quarrel was, it is nice to know that what Hughes and Hurston fought over was not a turkey but a phoenix. And such salty dialogue as "Before you . . . went up North, I could kiss you every day . . . just as regular as pig tracks" is worth the slight effort our ears must make to adjust to an unaccustomed sound.

But what of the fear and indignation my companion and I observed among some white spectators, a couple of whom we overheard being politely and judiciously corrected by a black audience member? There are several things to bear in mind here. First, that this play (like the production) was created, from top to bottom, by black talent, and whatever ribbing there is is done tartly but affectionately. Next, we are dealing with a 1930 retelling of still-earlier folk material; would a white community, under the same conditions, emerge smelling any sweeter? Think of Erskine Caldwell or John Steinbeck, of George S. Kaufman and Morrie Ryskind (*Of Thee I Sing,* 1931).

Finally, and above all, the ultimate proof of maturity and sophistication in an individual, a group, a society is the gift of laughing at oneself. What is it that makes Gogol's *The Inspector General* the masterpiece it is if not laughter at Russia, all of Russia? Laughing self-criticism, even if the laughter is sharp and sardonic—perhaps especially then—is the greatest proof of coming of age that two black writers in 1930 could proffer: a sovereign demonstration of artistic (and therefore profoundly human) ripeness.

Source: John Simon, "The Learned Laddies or the Imagery Invalid" in *New York,* Vol. 24, no. 8, February 25, 1991, pp. 119–20.

Stefan Kanfer

While finding Hurston and Hughes's text to be somewhat outdated and "politically incorrect," Kanfer praises the production values of this 1991 presentation of Mule Bone, *concluding that the overall effect makes for significant theatre.*

Mule Bone, at the Ethel Barrymore Theater, is politically incorrect. Its protagonists refer to themselves as Negroes, say things like "Chile, if you listen at folkses talk, they'll have you in de graveyard or in Chatahooche," and when its village folk are depressed or excited they burst into song.

Nevertheless, it is the season's most rewarding exhumation. Although this "Comedy of Negro Life" was awarded a major grant from the Fund for New American Plays, the work is in fact 60 years old. Its authors, Langston Hughes and Zora Neale Hurston, had a falling out in 1930, and it has taken this long for scholars to pick up the pieces. Never mind. Scrupulous direction and an irrepressible cast have finally given *Mule Bone* the production it deserves.

Hughes and Hurston intended to "act out the folk tales, with the abrupt angularity and naïveté of

> *MULE BONE* WAS TO HAVE BEEN THE PLAY THAT WOULD BE NEITHER HEAVY SOCIAL DRAMA NOR MINSTREL SHOW BUT A REAL COMEDY OF BLACK LIFE THAT WOULD EXTEND THE HARLEM RENAISSANCE TO THE STAGE"

the primitive 'bama Nigger." Accordingly their play, based on Hurston's short story, is as elemental as a recipe for collard greens. A guitarist, Jim (Kenny Neal), and a dancer, Dave (Eric Ware), fight over a beautiful young woman (Akosua Busia). In the course of combat, Dave gets bopped upside the head with a mule bone. In Act Two Jim is put on trial before a gaggle of sunny Baptists and upright Methodists. The kangaroo court orders him out of town.

If narrative were all, *Mule Bone* would deserve to be exiled as well. The pleasures, though, are not in the text; they come from Taj Mahal's lilting score, and from a spirited and sensitive ensemble. Director Michael Schultz never allows a scintilla of condescension; the work seems to have been deliberately preserved in an ice floe so that it could be melted some fine night at the Barrymore. At a time of strangulated budgets, 29 actors are featured in this production, and every one of them embodies William Blake's dictum that energy is eternal delight. There are small parts but no undersized performances: Theresa Merritt was a powerful Ma Rainey years ago, and as a townswoman she becomes the lyrical, throaty Ma all over again; Sonny Jim Gaines, who has written better plays than this for the New Lafayette, here is content to animate the role of a local loudmouth; the hilarious "lawyers" for the prosecution and defense, Arthur French and Leonard Jackson, are abetted by some gifted veterans of the Negro Ensemble Company. If one 10,000-candlepower grin seems eerily familiar, but older than you remembered, look again. That face in the crowd is James Earl Jones' father, Robert.

Source: Stefan Kanfer, "Looking Backward" in the *New Leader,* Vol. LXXIV, no. 3, February 11–25, 1991, pp. 22–23.

MULE BONE, BASED ON HURSTON'S SHORT STORY, IS AS ELEMENTAL AS A RECIPE FOR COLLARD GREENS"

SOURCES

Barnes, Clive. Review of *Mule Bone* in the *New York Post,* February 15, 1991.

Beaufort, John. Review of *Mule Bone* in the *Christian Science Monitor,* February 26, 1991.

Boyd, Lisa. ''The Folk, the Blues, and the Problems of *Mule Bone* in the *Langston Hughes Review,* Vol. 13, no. 19, Fall, 1994, pp. 33-44.

Gates, Henry Louis Jr. Review of *Mule Bone* in the *New York Times,* February 10, 1991, pp. 5, 8.

Hemenway, Robert E. *Zora Neale Hurston: A Literary Biography,* University of Illinois Press, 1977, pp. 136-58.

Kissel, Howard. Review of *Mule Bone* in the *Daily News,* February 15, 1991.

Lowe, John. ''From *Mule Bones* to *Funny Bones:* The Plays of Zora Neale Hurston'' in *Southern Quarterly: A Journal of the Arts in the South,* Vol. 33, nos. 2-3, 1995, pp. 65-78.

Rich, Frank. Review of *Mule Bone* in the *New York Times,* February 15, 1991.

Short, Randall. Review of *Mule Bone* in *Mirabella,* March, 1991, p. 72.

Stearnes, David Patrick. Review of *Mule Bone* in *USA Today,* February 13, 1991.

Watt, Doug. Review of *Mule Bone* in the *Daily News,* February 22, 1991.

Wilson, Edwin. Review of *Mule Bone* in the *Wall Street Journal,* February 27, 1991.

Winer, Linda. Review of *Mule Bone* in *New York Newsday,* February 15, 1991.

FURTHER READING

Hughes, Langston, and Zora Neale Hurston. *Mule Bone: A Comedy of Negro Life,* edited by George Houston Bass and Henry Louis Gates, Harper, 1991.
  This book contains the full text of the play, and it also contains a selection of articles that deal with the controversy regarding its writing and the legal issues that resulted.

Kellner, Bruce, editor. *The Harlem Renaissance: A Historical Dictionary,* Greenwood, 1984.
  This text provides a brief literary biography of artists who wrote during the same period as Hurston and Hughes.

Pryse, Marjorie, and Hortense J. Spillers, editors. *Conjuring, Black Women, Fiction, and Literary Tradition,* Indiana University Press, 1985.
  This collection of essays attempts to place Hurston within a context of other American black women writers and demonstrates her influence on the women writers who followed.

Rampersad, Arnold. *The Life of Langston Hughes, 1902-1941,* Vol. 1, Oxford University Press, 1986.
  Rampersad relates Hughes's relationship with Hurston.

Watson, Carol McAlpine. *Prologue: The Novels of Black American Women, 1891-1965,* Greenwood, 1985.
  Watson compares Hurston to other writers and believes that she was unique among black women writers.

The Ruling Class

PETER BARNES

1968

Peter Barnes's *The Ruling Class* exploded onto the theatre scene when it was produced in Nottingham, England, in 1968. Its acerbic wit and tightly woven plot openly criticize England's social hierarchy, specifically targeting the foibles and greed of the upper—the *ruling*—class. Barnes's play peels back the veneer of respectability to reveal the ugly underneath, the rot that can exist at the very core of a life of privilege. The protagonist of the drama, Jack, the Fourteenth Earl of Gurney, is insane: he thinks he is Jesus Christ. His creed of Love proves completely unacceptable to the rest of the Gurney family, who try to get him committed so that they can take over the family estate.

Jack Gurney represents goodness, and it is for this breech of common sense that he does not fit into upper crust society. Ultimately a doctor of psychiatry succeeds in transforming Jack into a true Gurney—by the end of the play Jack believes he is God the Avenger, or Jack the Ripper, whose program of punishment and murderous intent is more consistent with the values of the ruling class. Thus the play ends unhappily but remains a comedy rather than a tragedy because of its quirky shifts in mood and its juxtapositions of music, dance, and playful dialogue; while it is a form of social criticism, it never appears to take its topic too seriously.

Relatively unknown until this play appeared, Barnes gained almost instant recognition as one of the moving forces in British theater after the pro-

duction moved to London. The play came at the height of the 1960s counterculture movement, when the youth of the western world began to openly question the establishment. Barnes's irreverent portrayal of upper class eccentricity, greed, and deviance fit in perfectly with the movement's ideals. Yet the playwright's ideas and facility with character have made *The Ruling Class* an enduring drama in subsequent decades as well.

AUTHOR BIOGRAPHY

Peter Barnes was born January 10, 1931, on London's East Side to parents of mixed religious backgrounds. His father was a British Protestant who willingly and rather superficially converted to Judaism to marry a Jewish woman. Although the family was not particularly religious, Barnes developed a fascination with the topic of religious belief and God, a fascination he explores in most of his major works. His other major theme is also believed to have originated from his family: an obsession with the ruling elite, its excesses and perversions—a contrast with his own working-class upbringing. Barnes did not finish secondary school and did not attend university but rather educated himself, believing that formal schooling corrupts the true artist.

Through his studies, Barnes developed a deep appreciation for Elizabethan playwright Ben Jonson (*The Alchemist*), considering his work superior to that of his contemporary William Shakespeare, whom Barnes found snobbish and pretentious in comparison to the more earthy Jonson. There are echoes of Jonson's straightforward plot lines and unaffected humor in all of the Barnes canon. Besides writing his own works, Barnes has adapted and translated plays that otherwise would not reach the English stage, including several Jonson plays and the Jacobean comedies of Thomas Middleton and John Marston. He has also produced and directed numerous works—including his own—for radio and television, especially for the BBC (British Broadcasting Company).

The BBC has supported Barnes's career by teaming him with some of the most accomplished actors in Great Britain for a radio series called *Barnes's People*. The original *Barnes's People* (seven monologues) and its sequels, *Barnes's People II* (eight duologues), *Barnes's People III* (seven plays for three voices), and *More Barnes's People* (more monologues) are "miniature" productions that fea-

ture stars such as Alan Bates, Claire Bloom, Sean Connery, John Gielgud, Ian McKellen, and Peter Ustinov. Barnes writes his plays in the Reading Room of the British Museum in London, where he can concentrate on his work, "cut off from disturbances," yet still be able to look up and "see other people, so you're not isolated."

Barnes's most notable work for the stage is 1968's *The Ruling Class*. The play received both the John Whiting Playwrights Award and the *Evening Standard* Annual Drama Award. Other plays of his that have gained critical and popular admiration include *The Bewitched* (1974), *Laughter!* (1978), and *Red Noses* (1985). Barnes has also written numerous works for film, including the screenplay adaptation of *The Ruling Class* in 1972. His other screenplays include a 1992 adaptation of Elizabeth von Armin's novel *Enchanted April*.

PLOT SUMMARY

Prologue
At the head of a long, formal banquet table, the Thirteenth Earl of Gurney presents a toast to England, "Ruled not by superior force or skill / But by sheer presence." As they drink, the scene shifts to his bedroom, where the Earl goes through his bedtime ritual: donning a ballet tutu and a three-cornered hat and swinging momentarily from a silk noose blithely prepared by his aged butler, Dan Tucker. Something goes wrong tonight, however, and the old Earl actually hangs himself.

Act I, scene i
The Earl's funeral is presided over by Bishop Lamptron, an asthmatic old man who appears magnificent in his stole and mitre.

Act I, scene ii
Back at the family castle, the family contends over who will inherit the estate. When the lawyer announces that it will be Jack, the Fourteenth Earl, Sir Charles, brother of the late Earl, and his wife Claire are aghast as is their dim-witted son, Dinsdale. Their protests are interrupted by Tucker, richer by the 20,000 pounds just bequeathed to him, who smashes a vase on the floor to get their attention. He announces Jack, the Fourteenth Earl, who enters, dressed like Jesus and spouting that he is God.

Act I, scene iii

Sir Charles brings in Jack's psychologist, Dr. Herder, to get Jack committed as a paranoid-schizophrenic.

Act I, scenes iv

Jack tells Claire that he knows he is God because when he talks to Him, he finds he is only talking to himself. Although there is logic to his madness, his ravings about love and equality are disturbingly "Bolshie" (communist) to his family.

Act I, scene v

Tucker tries to warn Jack that the family is plotting against him, but Jack repulses his "negativity."

Act I, scene vi

Jack reposes on a giant cross mounted to the wall while the others take tea. Two church ladies arrive to ask Jack to officiate at their Church party and are swept into a vaudeville chorus line with him. They want him to speak on a non-political topic, such as "Hanging, Immigration, the Stranglehold of the Unions." His talk of love—particularly as it pertains to sex—drives them away. Dinsdale suggests that if Jack would produce a legal heir, his relatives could control him. But Jack surprises them by announcing that he is already married—to the "Lady of the Camelias."

Act I, scene vii

Unsuccessful in convincing Jack he's married a myth, the family demands he produce a miracle. Jack tries to levitate a table but only the drunken Tucker sees it, just before passing out. Offstage there is singing; it is the Lady of the Camelias.

Act I, scene viii

Claire argues with Charles about his foisting Grace Shelley (who is playing the Lady of the Camelias at his bidding), his former mistress, onto Jack after first trying to foist her off onto his now-dead brother. But she demurs, realizing her husband's game might work.

Act I, scenes ix

Grace and Jack perform a love ritual, tweeting like courting birds. Dinsdale pops Jack's joyful bubble by disclosing Grace's true identity. Once again, Jack repulses this "negative insinuendo," which he defines as "insinuation towards innuendo,

brought on by increased negativism out of a negative reaction to your father's positivism." This confrontation with reality drives Jack to his wall-mounted cross for solace.

Act I, scene x

The Bishop and Sir Charles argue about Jack's marriage. Meanwhile, downstage, Dr. Herder seduces Claire after having learned that her husband sits on the board of foundation that may fund his research.

Act I, scene xi

Jack's time on the cross has purged him of doubts, and he blesses all and sundry, including the cockroaches, for it is his wedding day.

Act I, scenes xii through xv

The Earl plays the role of God in his own wedding. The marriage is consecrated with no one but the immediate family and Tucker to witness it.

The reception, too, is a lonely affair, with Bishop Bertie fretting about an actress daring to marry in white and Tucker "in his cups" (drunk). Sir Charles demands that they keep up the show, "The strength of the English people lies in their inhibitions. . . . Sacrifices must be made."

In their bedroom, Grace readies herself for her next "performance" and is panicked by the Earl's appearance on a tricycle. But he announces, "God loves you, God wants you, God needs you. Let's to bed." As the lights go out and the music swells, it becomes a successful wedding night.

Sir Charles and Claire interrogate Grace about her night, and she assures them that "His mind may be wonky but there's nothing wrong with the rest of his anatomy." Grace claims that she loves Jack. Dr. Herder admits that the "harsh dose of reality" of marriage might do Jack some good.

Act I, scene xvi

Dr. Herder stages a showdown designed to convince Jack he cannot be God. He has invited the insane McKyle, the "High Voltage Messiah," to "occupy the same space" as Jack. The encounter proves devastating to Jack, who convulses in agony with every shot of McKyle's imaginary volts. Claire herself convulses into labor, being nine months pregnant. When Jack comes to, he is reborn, calling

The mad Jack Gurney (Peter O'Toole) is offered his crown by his butler, Tucker, in the film version of Barnes's play

himself "Jack"—to Dr. Herder, a sign of sanity. Upstairs the newborn baby cries.

Act II, scene i

Act II opens in the drawing room, where the latest Gurney is being baptized. The room decor is now Victorian, and the cross is gone. Jack, dressed in a traditional suit and carrying a shotgun and now only "slightly out of 'synch'," goes out for a constitutional. A shot is heard outside. Charles hopes Jack has "done the decent thing at last."

Act II, scene ii

Jack has shot a game bird, barely missing Tucker. He has a moment of intimacy with Grace and realizes that he's "got to stop talking" since the Master of Lunacy is coming to assess Jack's sanity.

Act II, scene iii

The "Master," Truscott, denies that he does the actual committing of lunatics, his "main concern is property and its proper administration." Things look bad for Jack until he begins to sing an old Eton song and Truscott joins in. He pronounces Jack recovered.

Act II, scene iv

In a mad speech, Jack reveals that he has adopted the persona of Jack the Ripper.

Act II, scene v

Mrs. Piggot-Jones and Mrs. Treadwell visit again, and this time the Earl impresses them with the idea that fear is the answer to society's ills. Once again, they break into dance, then Grace takes them on a tour as Jack symbolically slits envelopes open at his desk.

Act II, scene vi

Claire has stayed behind to keep Jack company—and to attempt to seduce him. The lights dim and the set dissolves to Whitechapel, Jack the Ripper's haunt. He stabs Claire. When the lights come up, the family discovers the body. Tucker is elated.

Act II, scene vii

Two policemen investigating the murder settle on Tucker as the culprit—opting for the traditional "the butler did it" solution. During their questioning, silverware he'd been hoarding drops out of his pocket, sealing his fate. Jack is cleared of any suspicion as Tucker is taken away.

Act II, scene viii

When he realizes that Jack murdered Claire, Dr. Herder attacks the Earl. The stress turns the tables on the doctor, who himself goes insane.

Act II, scene ix

Jack dons his robes to take his seat in the House of Lords. Charles suddenly ages. Grace gently chides Jack that they were more intimate when he was "batty," but she voices her conviction that he'll get around to her.

Act II, scene x

Alone, Jack groans and screams, madly.

Act II, scene xi

Jack rouses the House of Lords—mostly a pack or dummies and nearly dead old men—with a speech about the merits of punishment and order. Sir Charles shouts "He's one of us at last!"

Epilogue

Grace pulls Jack close as the lights fade. Her scream reveals that Jack the Ripper has struck again.

CHARACTERS

Bertie

See Bishop Bertram Lampton

Detective Inspector Brockett

Called in after the murder of Claire, Detective Inspector Brockett discovers Lenin's books in Tucker's suitcase and therefore arrests him for the murder.

Detective Sergeant Fraser

Fraser is Brockett's assistant.

Sir Charles Gurney

Brother to the late Earl and uncle to Jack, the new Earl, Charles considers it is his family duty to get rid of Jack and take over the estate. He bickers with his wife Claire about how to eliminate his nephew and enlists the aid of his mistress to marry Jack and produce a legal heir he can control. He doesn't mind giving up his mistress, not being "the sensitive type," and is willing to sacrifice anything

MEDIA ADAPTATIONS

• The film version of *The Ruling Class* was produced by Keep Films, starring Peter O'Toole, in 1971. Barnes wrote the screenplay for the film, but because he did not like deferring to O'Toole's editing decisions, the playwright never viewed the completed film.

"for the family"—or rather for his own gain. He is blind to his wife's affair with Dr. Herder and his own son, Dinsdale, is a disappointment to him.

Lady Claire Gurney

Claire is married to Sir Charles, but that doesn't stop her from having an affair with Dr. Herder, which she undertakes to elicit his support in committing her nephew. She also attempts to seduce Jack when he begins to show signs of improvement. She displays a sophisticated, tough exterior when she blandly lets on that she knows of her husband's affairs. Claire is a caricature of the jaded granddame; she play-acts the role of a highborn lady while emptily pursuing the goal of saving the family name. She is a woman with no illusions.

Dinsdale Gurney

The dimwitted son of Claire and Charles who has the knack of upper class snobbishness but none of its class. Dinsdale reveals his father's plot to Jack, not out of honesty or distaste for the ruse but because he had been left out of the planning. Dinsdale's biggest concern is whether Jack's madness will affect his position in Parliament.

Jack Gurney, the Fourtheenth Earl of Gurney

Jack suffers from delusions of grandeur and, already a member of the peerage, the only step up for him is God. Therefore, he calls himself God, Yahweh, the Infinite Personal Being, and sleeps on a cross. He urges everyone to pray for "love and understanding." When confronted with another paranoid-schizophrenic who also thinks he is the sole divine being, he goes through a metamorphosis, or rebirth, and emerges as Jack. Although his family considers this a cure, he really has exchanged a divine and holy identity for an evil and profane one: Jack the Ripper. In his madness can be found a quirky logic that endears Jack to others.

Gurney, the Thirteenth Earl of Gurney

The prototypical British Lord, the Earl is very proper and dressed impeccably, complete with medals of honor on his chest, as he presides over the meeting of the Society of St. George. He is a judge, a "peer of the realm," and the owner of a huge estate. He is about to marry a common girl, Grace Shelly, in order to provide his estate with an heir. He is eccentric and mentally unstable. He dies accidentally while enacting a hanging ritual, dressed in underwear, a ballet tutu, and a three-cornered hat.

Dr. Paul Herder

A German psychiatric doctor who comes to the Gurney estate at Sir Charles's bidding to assess the possibility of committing Jack to an insane asylum. While at the estate, he seduces Claire so that she will aid him in obtaining funding for his experiments in rat schizophrenia, since Claire's husband sits on the grant board. Herder refuses to commit Jack, preferring instead to observe whether the "harsh dose of reality" of returning to his family will cure him. When that fails, Herder arranges a showdown between Jack and the High Voltage Messiah, another paranoid-schizophrenic. When Jack turns violent and murders Claire, Herder himself goes insane in a classic case of "transference."

Alexei Kronstadt, number 243

See Daniel Tucker

Bishop Bertram Lampton

The Bishop, Claire's brother, is an imposing figure at the funeral of the Thirteenth Earl, but without his robes, he is a wheezy, balding old man who collapses after the slightest exertion. He conveniently fails to understand the circumstances of the Earl's death.

Master of the Court of Protection

See Kelso Truscott, Q. C.

Master in Lunacy

See Kelso Truscott, Q. C.

McKyle, the High Voltage Messiah

The High Voltage Messiah, the Electric Christ, the AC/DC God, is clinically insane, a paranoid-schizophrenic who thinks he is the God of electricity. He's been told that Jack thinks he too is God. McKyle has "obliterated hundreds o' dupe-Messiahs" before; now he, being a Vengeful God, disabuses Jack of his megalomaniac pretensions as well.

Matthew Peake

The lawyer who reads out the Thirteenth Earl's will to the amazed family.

Mrs. Piggot-Jones

One of two church matrons who ask Jack to preside over the opening of their Church Fete. The ladies get swept up into a singing and dancing chorus line with Jack. They are affronted by the sexual innuendoes of his "God is love" litany.

Mr. Shape

Mr. McKyle's "assistant," who is really his warden.

Grace Shelley

Grace is Sir Charles's mistress, who willingly takes on the role of The Lady of the Camelias, or Marguerite Gautier, (both martyrs for love and important symbolically to Jack) as a way of advancing herself. Charles sets her up with Jack to provide the next Gurney heir. She starts out by using Jack, but his quirky innocence earns her genuine affection.

Toastmaster

Every proper British club has its toastmaster, who raps for attention and repeats the toast in a stentorian voice for all to hear. The toastmaster is a well-dressed servant.

Mrs. Treadwell

Another of the church matrons offended by Jack's irreverent behavior.

Kelso Truscott, Q. C.

Truscott prefers the title "Master of the Court of Protection" over "Master in Lunacy" since his "main concern is property and its proper administration," after all. Things do not go well for Jack's assessment until he breaks into an Eton school song and Truscott joins in. Being old school chums, they share certain values, such as the need for discipline against the barbarians and homosexuals. Truscott's verdict is that Jack is cured and sane.

Daniel Tucker

The Earl's personal manservant is aging but knows his place until he learns of the 20,000 pounds the Earl has left him in his will. Unfortunately, he lacks the imagination to leave, and so stays on as the family butler, though now he drinks to excess and makes rude remarks to the "Titled Turds." He has an alternate identity: Alexei Kronstadt, number 243, a dues-paying member of the Communist Party; but he admits, he doesn't *do* anything." He becomes an easy scapegoat for Claire's murder, since everyone tacitly agrees that "the butler did it."

THEMES

Greed

Greed is evident in all of Barnes's characters save the insane Jack. In the first half of the play, he represents the opposite of greed: Christian charity and "the unity of universal love." Alas, this unrealistic solution to life's challenges defines him as clinically insane. The so-called sane members of the Gurney family, who vie for control over Jack's ownership of the estate, are all driven by greed. Sir Charles hopes to commit his nephew so that he can manage the estate— and reap its power and riches— himself, Claire compromises her integrity by staying with Sir Charles even though they both have other lovers, and the Bishop seems more concerned about the late Earl's promise of "the Overseas Bishoprics Fund" than about guiding the family spiritually.

When Sir Charles hears the reading of the will, which transfers the Gurney estate to Jack, he complains that his brother has "let his personal feelings come before his duty to his family." Charles would never let love get in the way of money. By contrast, Jack seems singularly disinterested in the value of his inheritance, spending his time meditating on his personal cross and urging the others to pray to the God of Love. In his madness, Jack adheres to better values than do his sane family members. In Grace the greed that drove her to adopt the persona of the Lady of the Camelias contests with her growing love for a man who treats her unlike her other lovers have done. As Claire announces nastily, Grace has made her living "on her back," trading sexual favors for social advancement and money. But

TOPICS FOR FURTHER STUDY

- In what ways are Sir Charles and Claire representative of stereotypical upper class people? In what ways is Daniel Tucker representative of his class?

- Peter Barnes has said that "Laughter's too feeble a weapon against the barbarities of life"; however, his humor strikes deliberately at human pretensions, particularly those of the upper class. How does Barnes use humor in this play to sway the audience?

- Who is the hero of this play? How is the idea of heroism refashioned to Barnes's goals?

- Compare this play to a Jacobean play such as Ben Jonson's *Volpone*. What lessons has Barnes taken from his study of Jacobean comedy?

Jack's "insane" insistence on love, his refreshing perspective, and his ingenuous love begin to win her away from greed to true love. Eventually, Grace doesn't want Jack "cured" out of fear that he will simply become another Gurney.

On the other hand, Tucker, who revels in his inheritance of 20,000 pounds, wants "more, more, more." He is caught red-handed with stolen silverware; this petty theft libels his character enough to make it easy to pin Claire's murder on him. Here is where the classes divide in Barnes's world: Tucker's greed sends him to prison, while the Gurney family's greed lands them in Parliament.

Insanity

According to Dr. Herder, Jack's insanity consists of not believing "what other people believe"; he can't see reality but has his own reality designed to win him love. He is a paranoid-schizophrenic suffering from delusions of grandeur, and, since he is already at the top of British society, he can only satisfy his megalomania by being God himself. His insanity, however, rests on a logical basis. He finds that when he talks to God he is talking to himself.

He might have concluded, with the rest of modern western civilization, that God therefore does not exist, but he instead believes that he exists within himself.

As a peer of England with a vast estate, positions of honor, and a personal manservant, Jack is a kind of god. His God before his encounter with the High Voltage Messiah is the God of Love. He is peaceful and peace-loving, harming no one. But because he stands in the way of his family's greed, he either has to be cured or locked up, out of the way. When he transforms into Jack the Ripper, he declares that he has "finally been processed into right-thinking power." He is no longer "the God of Love but God Almighty. God the lawgiver, Chastiser and Judge." This new form of insanity is harder for the other characters to detect, for he acts like one of them. His reactionary speech at the House of Lords, a vitriolic plea to reinstate punishment as a way of controlling "the weak," leads Sir Charles to shout "He's one of us at last." In a sense, he is cured, as the Master of Lunacy has declared him. In fact, his newfound charisma proves irresistible to women—both Claire and Grace desire him and Mrs. Treadwell and Mrs. Piggot-Jones follow him slavishly.

Insanity is often defined in terms of legal responsibility. One who is insane cannot be held legally responsible. Jack as the God of Love was irresponsible and a social misfit. Jack as the God of Justice is eminently responsible, a leader in the highest social and legal circles of the land. The question of his sanity raises the question of the sanity of England's social system.

STYLE

Juvenalian Satire

Satire's goal is to effect social improvement—or at least chastisement for the follies of human nature. Although Barnes has stated that "nothing needs changing when it's all a joke," satire uses humor as constructive criticism. In *The Ruling Class* Barnes ridicules the pretensions of the upper class by exaggerating their pompous behavior to the point of absurdity. Thus the Thirteenth Earl carries the eccentric behavior of the stereotypical British lord to a ridiculous extreme—self-hanging as excessive masochism. Barnes's form of satire is known as Juvenalian satire, named for the Roman satirist Juvenal whose biting satires exposed the vices of the Roman elite. Horatian satire, named for Horace,

is gentler and more urbane. Juvenalian satire confronts its target viciously, with anger. In Barnes's version of this, no one is safe: from the bloated and sputtering Sir Charles and his dim-witted son, Dinsdale, to the grumbling butler Tucker and the two fatuous church ladies in grotesque hats—each is a butt of the playwright's pointed ridicule.

Jack is not simply mad, he is mad with the arrogance of a peer of England, who considers himself so high up on the social ladder that the only conceivable form of megalomania available is to be God. *The Ruling Class* uses indirect rather than direct satire, the characters make outrageous statements whose merit they never seem to question; they do not criticize human foibles directly. Dr. Herder says with perfect seriousness that the one commandment a doctor should never break is "Thou shalt not advertise." His statement constitutes a cynical assessment about a corrupt society, because he eschews the lesser vice of advertising while committing the greater vice of adultery in the service of advancing his career.

Satire has never gone out of style. Barnes admires the seventeenth century Jacobean comic dramatists—Ben Jonson, Thomas Middleton, and John Martson—some of whose works Barnes has adapted for the modern stage. He is also influenced by George Bernard Shaw (*Man and Superman*), a master of satiric barbs; Shaw, Barnes tellingly opines, "was at his most serious when least serious, most meaningful when most playful." Likewise, the most humorous moments of *The Ruling Class* convey Barnes's deepest disapprobation of England's class system and its impact on the moral worth of its members.

Burlesque

In *The Ruling Class,* Barnes not only satirizes human folly, he does so with elements of burlesque, in which the style of the work does not conform to the seriousness of the subject. Burlesque differs from satire in the form or style of the work. While satire pokes fun, burlesque puts the work's style in opposition to its matter, such that an important topic is trivialized by its treatment, or vice versa. Burlesque can include unexpected episodes of song or dance, as when Jack, Mrs. Treadwell, and Mrs. Piggott-Jones suddenly burst into a chorus line singing "The Varsity Drag." The song's lyrics outline the theme of adherence to social conventions: one must "learn how it goes" as the song says. Blind and instant conformance, as exhibited by the spontaneous dance and song, are burlesqued in both the action, instant conformity to ridiculous behavior, and the words of the song. When the church ladies meet Jack again, they join him in another vaudeville act, singing a bastardized version of the spiritual ''Dem Bones,'' which celebrates the necessary hierarchy of the skeleton that can be broken on the wheel; the ladies join in because they agree with Jack's social solution.

Barnes also burlesques phrases and high-sounding styles of speech, often pillaging literary works or pop culture and turning the phrases to his own use. When Jack intones biblically at the House of Lords, his message comprises the antithesis of Christianity, ''The strong MUST manipulate the weak. That's the first law of the universe—was and ever shall be world without end.'' Barnes parodies biblical style and turns its spiritual message inside out in a verbal burlesque. Moments later the mood of the musical comedy is burlesqued as Grace sings a ballad reminiscent of the love song from *The King and I,* and Jack responds by stabbing her to death. Thus burlesque itself is burlesqued into the grotesque, where serious matter is treated with gruesome frivolity. The result is devastatingly comic, as when Sir Charles responds to seeing his wife's corpse by saying, ''All right, who's the impudent clown responsible for this?''

HISTORICAL CONTEXT

The Liberal 1960s

The 1960s were a time of defiant liberation in society, from politics, art, and music to dress, hairstyles, and morals. The ''Liverpool poets'' reflected the mood of elation and questioning in its poetry of pop culture, while music throbbed to a new beat and students took to the streets to protest all forms of oppression. Alongside the monolithic publishing houses, small presses sprang into being and thrived, producing avant-garde works in a distributed network of artists.

Inroads were developing into every aspect of culture; power was being redistributed. In England, where the noble class had always enjoyed prestige, the attitude of the middle class toward gentility (and toward the whole concept of gentility) moved from muffled but tolerant resentment to active disrespect. While much of the rhetoric of the 1960s was rancorous, Barnes's *The Ruling Class* introduced

comedy to question the status quo. While the play does not urge social reform or raise an angry protest, it does prod the conscience—comedy being a gentle vehicle of liberation.

Theater

British theatre changed dramatically—if not swiftly—after Bertolt Brecht's Berliner Ensemble and his theatre of ''alienation'' or ''estrangement'' was introduced to London in 1956. In plays such as *Mother Courage and Her Children,* Brecht's ''alienation effects'' interrupt the dramatic flow of the plot through unexpected use of songs, music, cue cards, and asides to the audience by the players themselves. Although Brecht himself had died that year, his Marxist views and his interest in using theater to elicit social change were quickly embraced by the leftist playwrights working in London. Barnes admits the profound influence of Brecht on modern theater, and echoes Brecht's program of social reform when he says that his goal is ''changing conventions, changing ideas, changing attitudes.''

London theatre and Barnes were also affected by Samuel Beckett's ''Theatre of the Absurd,'' which further questioned dramatic conventions such as plot and character; Beckett's best-known example of this is his *Waiting for Godot.* Likewise, Antonin Artaud's Theatre of Cruelty introduced the notion of expressionistic drama, a huge departure from the genteel drawing-room theater London had known until the 1950s. Musicals such as *Hair* (1967) and *Oh, Calcutta* (1969) introduced nudity and profane language to the legitimate stage. At first these theatrical developments shocked audiences, but by 1968 stage censorship had been abolished in England and audience interaction, open staging, anachronistic costuming, and revolutionary content had become standard fare; audiences now expected to be challenged as part of their entertainment.

In comparison to the intensity of experimentation in the work of Harold Pinter (*The Birthday Party*) and others during the 1960s, Barnes's level of innovation seems rather tame. Rather than seeking to shock, his plays aim to ''disturb and entertain.'' Barnes picks and chooses among the fashions of the new theater, to create his own dramatic invention. The unexpected cuts to song and dance have a Brechtian flair, as does Jack's telling Dr. Herder that he will have to ''leave the stage'' if he cannot abide hearing about Claire's death. Like all of Barnes's work, *The Ruling Class* is highly self-conscious, aware of itself as a work of art, and forcing this awareness onto the audience as well.

COMPARE
&
CONTRAST

- **1969:** In England as in the United States, young people deepen the chasm between their generation and their parents' generation. In dress, hair styles, speech, music, and politics, young people express their opposition to the status quo.

  Today: There is still considerable difference between generations, though current forms of protest are less rooted in cultural significance (such as the Vietnam War that galvanized 1960s youth) and more in generic, youthful rebellion.

- **1969:** "Free love" and "love power" are mottoes of the hippie generation, who seek to cure the ills of society through acceptance and love. Sexual freedom, a natural outgrowth of their philosophy, is made viable through the introduction and wide availability of birth control.

  Today: Sexual conduct has swung to a more conservative status due to a shift in the moral majority and a greater threat of socially transmitted disease than existed in the 1960s. The practice of birth control and abortion is being questioned and vigorously debated.

- **1969:** Experimental theater is new and immensely popular. Audiences seek and expect to experience a "happening" at the theater, to be shocked and challenged as well as entertained.

  Today: As with other aspects of society, theater too has returned to a more conservative mode. Experimental theater continues but much of it has been absorbed and diluted by the mainstream.

The scene of Claire's murder has its roots in the Absurdist tradition, and Dan Tucker's card-carrying (but non-revolutionary) activities tip the hat toward the theatre of reform. *The Ruling Class* is an amalgamation of styles, with lines and references harvested from other works and humorously refashioned to Barnes's new purpose. The total effect has often been termed a kaleidoscope of dramatic action, fitting the fragmented experience of postmodern culture.

CRITICAL OVERVIEW

The Ruling Class opened in Nottingham, England on November 6, 1968, thanks to the foresight of two readers on the British Arts Council—drama critic Martin Eslin and director Stuart Burge—who read the script and pronounced Barnes "a bloody genius." Burge took the play to Nottingham and directed it himself. At opening night, London's *Sunday Times* drama reviewer Harold Hobson felt himself

"suddenly and unexpectedly faced with the explosive blaze of an entirely new talent of a very high order." Although he knew nothing of this playwright on that evening, he later wrote the introduction to the printed play, declaring that the performance he saw on its opening night was the perfect combination of "wit, pathos, exciting melodrama, brilliant satire, doubled-edged philosophy, horror, cynicism, and sentiment."

When it moved to London in February of 1969, Robert Bryden of the *Observer* pronounced *The Ruling Class* "one of those pivotal plays . . . in which you can feel the theatre changing direction, a new taste coming into being." Bryden's colleagues at the *Spectator* and the *Evening Standard* disagreed; Hilary Spurling of the former dismissed it as "too boring to go into" and the latter's Milton Shulman called the play "essentially shallow and glib." In spite of the mixed reviews, the *Evening Standard* honored Barnes as 1969's Most Promising Playwright and he earned the John Whiting Award for the Nottingham production.

The Ruling Class premiered in New York in 1971, directed by David William, who praised

Barnes for "the vision and the wit with which [he] has incarnated the life of the psyche: its tensions and paradox, hilarity and horror. For the play is both funny and frightening: a playful nightmare." Julius Novick of the *New York Times* also noted the play's psychological insights, stating that Barnes "has connected the perversions of privilege with the perversions of sexual feeling," which become "sources of both loathing and consequent power."

A year after the debut of *The Ruling Class* two other Barnes plays, *Leonardo's Last Supper* and *Noonday Demons,* opened as a double-bill. Irving Wardle of the London *Times* declared that now Barnes was confirmed as "one of the most original and biting comics working in Britain." The film version of *The Ruling Class,* released in 1972, earned Barnes more praise. Over the next ten years, Barnes cemented his status as one of the moving forces in modern British drama. He is considered an innovator whose critics do not always judge him by his standards but by the standards he is continually revising. Michael Billington of the *Guardian* praised him for having "broken the petty rules by which we judge plays."

Bernard Dukore, who has written two critical books on Barnes, *The Theatre of Peter Barnes* and *Barnestorm: The Plays of Peter Barnes,* placed the playwright alongside Harold Pinter and Alan Ayckbourn as "the playwriting giants of their generation in England." Although Dukore admitted that he remains in the minority in his choices.

CRITICISM

Carole Hamilton

Hamilton is a Humanities teacher at Cary Academy, an innovative private school in Cary, North Carolina. In this essay she discusses the ways in which the women's roles in The Ruling Class *reinforce its theme of social corruption.*

The liberated 1960s valued sexual freedom as a natural right, a legitimate form of expression for those who rejected the rigid morals of the previous generation and of the conservative "establishment." *The Ruling Class*'s protagonist, Jack, in his God-is-Love state expresses complete sexual freedom, courting his mate like a bird and successfully impregnat-

ing her. As Grace attests, "His mind may be wonky, but there's nothing wrong with the rest of his anatomy." His sexual freedom is of a part with his innocence and open-heartedness. But his naive attachment to an idealistic and impractical philosophy of "love and understanding" makes him unfit to "take his proper place in the world. "He is "living in a dream world" (but then, according to Tucker, so are all rich people).

Jack's family desperately explores legal avenues of removing him, while he further terrifies them with his entreaty that they pray together. He defines prayer as "to ask, to beg, to plead." Of course, pleading is distasteful to those who command, who "kick the natives in the back streets of Calcutta." Jack cannot take his place in the ruling class until he accepts its systematic and brutal oppression of other classes and leaves off pleading to God or anybody else. When, through a form of shock psychotherapy, he is transformed to a reactionary and oppressive upper class gentleman, Sir Charles declares Jack "one of us at last." He has changed socially, but this change has wrought the perversion of his sexual nature, too. As God the Avenger (or Jack the Ripper), Jack punishes prostitutes, including the one woman who met his ideal, Grace Shelley.

The transformation of his sexual feelings parallels the transformation of his social being as he embraces the most distasteful aspects of ruling class behavior: ruthlessness and sexual deviance. In *The Ruling Class,* playwright Peter Barnes has, according to *New York Times* writer Julius Novick, "connected the perversions of privilege with the perversions of sexual feeling ... [which] is an important source of both loathing and consequent power." For Barnes, social power and social deviance are inextricably linked.

The perversions of sexuality and its inflection on the perversions of power and privilege reveal themselves in Jack's relationships with the female characters, Mrs. Piggot-Jones and Mrs. Treadwell, Claire, and Grace Shelly. Although the first two are minor characters, they carry their weight in terms of symbolic significance in this carefully engineered play. It is not the fact that Jack is insane that shocks Mrs. Piggot-Jones and Mrs. Treadwell but that his insanity consists of rejecting values they hold dear: they become offended by his comment that England is "a country of cosmic unimportance," and they are miffed that he won't speak at their church fete on their preferred topics of "hanging, immigration,"

WHAT DO I READ NEXT?

- Barnes's play *Bewitched* (1974) sets his themes of greed, religious superficiality, and the corruption of the ruling elite in the context of seventeenth-century Spain, as King Carlos II tries to beget an heir. Once again, the self-indulgences of those in authority leads to chaos and futility.

- *The Ruling Class* may have been influenced by some of the ideas in Jean Renoir's *The Rules of the Game,* a 1939 film that exposes the moral bankruptcy of the French upper class.

- *Volpone,* Ben Jonson's satire about the lengths to which people will go to acquire an inheritance,

is arguably the finest comedy of the Jacobean era. The play also illustrates Jonson's influence on Barnes.

- Two plays by George Bernard Shaw, whose influence on Barnes is considerable, explore class inequalities and upper class hypocrisy: *Major Barbara,* about a Salvation Army officer disturbed by her father's morals, and the classic *Pygmalion,* a story of a street girl "passing" in high society after being trained how to act and speak like a lady.

---

or "the stranglehold of the Unions." They flee altogether when they realize that his ministry of love includes sexual love.

Mrs. Piggot-Jones and Mrs. Treadwell serve in the play as measures of upper class morality, which is uptight and repulsed by natural sexual expression. Their attitude toward sexual expression is conveyed by the wax fruit of Mrs. Treadwell's hat. Fruit traditionally symbolizes fertility, thus wax (fake) fruit symbolizes sterility. These are women who present a good front but do not "bear fruit."

Wax fruit first appears in the prologue, when the late Thirteenth Earl says that everything "tastes like wax fruit" after "the power of life and death" of being the hanging judge. The old Earl felt a sense of supreme power in his evening ritual of self-hanging; facing death made him feel fully alive. The Earl whets his appetite for dinner with his brush with death, in his zeal to avoid the wax fruit—or boring aspects of living. With the two church ladies, wax fruit is also equated with sexual frigidity or barrenness. Mrs. Piggot-Jones and Mrs. Treadwell mindlessly join with Jack in his song about toeing the line ("down on the heels, up on the toes") but cannot withstand his sermon of love that acknowledges their sexual natures. They have no sexual natures; they are wax fruit. When they return later in

the play, they find a Lord more along their lines, who, like them, disapproves of girls who "show their bosoms and say rude things about the queen." They accept the Earl when he accepts their value of suppressing sexuality.

Claire's sexual nature is suborned to her greed. An "ice-cold biddy" according the voluptuous Grace, Claire openly acknowledges that her husband seeks sexual gratification elsewhere—with Grace, in fact. At the same time, Sir Charles sanctions his wife's affair with Dr. Herder, essentially prostituting her as a means to wrest the estate away from his nephew. Claire plays this role dutifully and with feigned passion. She drops the affair without regret when the game changes, and Dr. Herder no longer needs to be kept quiet. Her passion is finally aroused when Jack trades his litany of love and understanding for a litany of vengeance and cruelty. Whereas she had found her nephew repulsive during his Jesus, God-is-love phase, he proves irresistible to her during his Jack the Ripper, God the Avenger phase.

Jack the Ripper exudes power; he can make Claire "feel *alive,*" and he is the acknowledged master of the estate. She can afford to love a man one step up on their social ladder. Her life of pretensions has deadened her, and now she wants

Jack to "wake" her, "with a kiss." Like the late Earl, however, she has an attraction to death. She tells Jack how a prowler outside her window made her shiver with excitement. But it is "impossible" for the ruling class "to feel," so she wants Jack to say he loves her "even if it isn't true." She blindly, and pathetically, plays a perverted duet with him, whispering "lover" in response to his filthy talk of "maggots," "gut-slime," and "gullet and rack." He calls her Mary, conflating her with Jack the Ripper's prostitute victims. Having scorned him in his loving phase, she becomes his first guilty victim in his avenging phase. Instead of feeling alive herself, Claire sacrifices her life so that Jack can shriek, "I'm alive, alive!" With dramatic irony, Sir Charles tells Jack that he has finally "behaved like a Gurney should"; that is, he has murdered a prostitute—Sir Charles's own wife—and blamed the crime on the butler.

Grace comes from the lower class but has "done it all, from Stanislavski to Strip . . . greasy make-up towels, cracked mirrors, rhinestones and beads." According to Claire, Grace made her living "on her back." However, although Grace freely indulges in sex, she is not sexually free: sex is her stock in trade. An actress-prostitute, she assists her lover Sir Charles by play-acting the role of the Lady of the Camelias, Jack's ideal lover. Dumas's Camille was a martyr to love, but Grace's Camille, as she points out to Claire, carries a wax flower, one that cannot wilt. In Grace's case, the wax flower takes on a new meaning, now symbolizing the resilience and artificiality of plastic. Like the wax camellia, Grace is here for show, but she is also required to blossom and bear fruit.

Grace plays the role of a twentieth-century Mary Magdalene, the whore-mother-lover, to Jack's Jesus. Unexpectedly, Grace falls in love with Jack, because of the very qualities that obstruct Jack's ascension to the ruling class. Perhaps because she is not of the upper class, she is more vulnerable and open to the truth contained within his madness. She has not been contaminated with upper class perversions, although she desperately wants to be called "Lady Grace Gurney."

Ironically, just when Grace begins genuinely to love Jack, having started the relationship as an empty charade, she becomes his victim. Like Claire, Grace finds the power of the Avenger God irresistible and wants his attentions, complaining that he was more loving when he was "batty." Of course, his new status as a proper gentleman precludes an

> " IRONICALLY, JUST WHEN GRACE BEGINS GENUINELY TO LOVE JACK, HAVING STARTED THE RELATIONSHIP AS AN EMPTY CHARADE, SHE BECOMES HIS VICTIM"

interest in healthy sex. Now Grace, like Claire, fulfils Jack the Ripper's appetite for vengeance against whores. It matters little when Jack says "She betrayed you," whether he refers to Grace's relations with his uncle or to her complicity in his "cure." Either way, she has prostituted herself, ruthlessly using her attractions to control him. When she voices genuine encouragement over his upcoming speech to the House of Lords, her words take on an ironic quality. "Don't worry, you'll kill 'em," she says, "and then you'll get around to me."

Once again, the threat of death is conflated with sex, since she means getting around to having sex with her, not killing her. Her murder is somewhat justified by her guilt, and Jack is deemed sane because "It's a sign of normalcy in our circle to slaughter anything that moves." She has become dispensable to the ruling class now that she has produced the wanted heir. The play becomes a tragedy with her death, since she and her love represented Jack's only hope for true redemption: salvation through love and the power to resist taking his place in the ruling class.

Source: Carole Hamilton, for *Drama for Students,* Gale, 1999.

Malcolm Page

In this essay, Page provides an overview of Barnes's play, delineating the action of the play and the manner in which the narrative satirizes the British class system.

The Ruling Class is a large-cast, epic, state-of-England play, resembling others of the 1960's and early 1970's, such as *The Workhouse Donkey,* by John Arden, and *Brassneck,* by Howard Brenton and David Hare. It is in 27 scenes, with prologue and epilogue, and opens with the 13th Earl of Gurney delivering a speech praising England, paro-

❝THIS LONG PLAY HAS A
JACOBEAN RICHNESS IN LANGUAGE,
INCIDENT, AND VARIETY"

dying Shakespeare's *Richard II:* "this teeming womb of privilege, this feudal state . . . this ancient land of ritual", followed by the National Anthem. An abrupt switch follows the first of many: the Earl returns home to Tucker, his faithful old butler, and speaks, with the rich language typical of Barnes' work, of passing the death sentence (for he is a judge, too): "If you've once put on the black cap, everything else tastes like wax fruit". Then the Earl disconcertingly puts on a cocked hat and ballet skirt, climbs a step-ladder, puts his head in a silk noose, swings and accidentally kicks over the steps and hangs himself. The Earl's funeral is conducted by a "magnificently dressed" Bishop, who then disrobes on stage and changes into "a small, bald-headed, asthmatic old man". The will is read and Tucker is left £20,000. He breaks into the Edwardian music hall song: "I'm Gilbert the Filbert the Knut with a 'K'"; Barnes continues using songs for contrast and surprise.

The heir, the 14th Earl, appears, dressed as a Franciscan monk. He believes he is God, explaining this with the brilliant line: "When I pray to Him I find I'm talking to myself", adding "What a beautiful day I've made". Shocked, his family decides to have him marry, and—as soon as he has fathered an heir—he is declared insane. He is convinced he is already married to the Lady of the Camelias, so Grace, his uncle's mistress, is dressed as Marguerite Gautier and makes a stunning entrance singing *La traviata.* The Earl arrives for his wedding night on a unicycle. In the continuing series of theatrical coups, a psychiatrist brings together the Earl and a Scotsman who also believes he is God, and the shock to the Earl is expressed by an eight-foot beast "dressed incongruously in high Victorian fashion", wrestling with him.

In the second half of the play the Earl changes to a stern, authoritarian, judgemental man, thinking he lives in the Victorian era. The Master of Lunacy, brought in to certify him, will not, for they are both Old Etonians. The Earl comes to believe that he is Jack the Ripper—an impression reinforced by the setting of "*a dark huddle of filthy houses . . . an*

impression of dark alleys". He murders his sister-in-law and lets Tucker be arrested for it, and Tucker reveals that secretly he is a Communist. The Earl, now seen as "normal" by his circle, goes to the House of Lords, represented very strikingly on stage, by "*tiers of mouldering dummies . . . covered with cobwebs*". Here he speaks as the Old Testament God, in favour of stern punishment, and finally he is seen stabbing the loving Grace.

Barnes wrote in a programme note, never reprinted:

> In a playhouse . . . we can use vivid colours, studied effects, slapstick, slang, songs, dances and blasphemies to conjure up men, monsters and ghosts. We can also raid mystery plays, puppet shows, Shakespeare (damn his eyes!) and demagogy to create a comic theatre of conflicting moods and opposites where everything is simultaneously tragic and ridiculous. This comedy is about the withdrawal of light from the world, the obstinacy of defeat, and asks again the question, is God a 10,000 foot tall, pink jelly bean?

The two acts of the play contrast the ideas of a loving God and a vengeful one and show that society is ruled by the latter concept. Along the way are satirical swipes at many aspects of British life: mockery of bishops, members of parliament, the House of Lords, the aristocracy, psychiatrists. Some of this is high-spirited, yet Barnes insists that this is a serious commentary on what was wrong with Britain: "I cared about the abuses and vices I was attacking. So much so that I was full of hate for them . . . I was taking the ruling classes as a symbol of what I was really attacking, which was something deeper than just blood sports".

This long play has a Jacobean richness (Barnes later adapted several of Ben Jonson's plays for stage and radio) in language, incident, and variety. It is also varied, surprising, and hugely theatrical. *The Ruling Class* anticipates aspects of the political debate of the 1980's: what were "Victorian values", and were they a good thing?

Source: Malcolm Page, "*The Ruling Class*" in *The International Dictionary of Theatre,* Volume 1: *Plays,* edited by Mark Hawkins-Dady, St. James Press, 1992, p. 694.

Anonymous

In this essay, the critic provides an overview of the 1972 film version of The Ruling Class, *which Barnes adapted from his stage text. In addition to a detailed plot synopsis, the review finds the film to be thought-provoking and highly entertaining.*

A controversial comedy with plenty of tragedy mixed in, this was adapted by the playwright for the screen and would have been better with a crueler set of fingers at the typewriter to remove some of the indulgences. It's too lengthy but has many wonderful moments and mixes satire with farce and pain to create a movie with many faults, though it remains unforgettable. Andrews is a member of the House of Lords. He comes back to the family manse after having delivered a scathing speech to Parliament, and his alcoholic butler, Lowe, helps him prepare for what is apparently his nightly ritual. He dons long underwear, a tutu, a Napoleonic hat, puts a silken noose around his neck, and will swing a few times before landing on the ladder top that gives him safety and his life. This night, he inadvertently kicks the ladder over and dies of strangulation, thus leaving his membership in the House of Lords and his estate to his insane son, O'Toole. The sum of 30,000 pounds has been bequeathed to Lowe, but the rest of the family, Mervyn (Andrews' brother), Browne (Merwyn's wife), and Villiers (their dotty son) are shocked upon hearing the will read by Sim, their local bishop. Lowe chooses to stay in service, but now that he is rich, his attitude changes. He begins spouting communist slogans, drinking in public, and telling everyone in the family exactly what he thinks of them. O'Toole has been in a mental hospital for the last several years and he returns dressed as Jesus, a role he insists he is playing for real. He admits that when he prays to God, he finds that he's talking to himself. O'Toole spends many of his hours on a huge cross in the large living room and prates about distributing the family's wealth to the meek and downtrodden, something that frightens the others in the family who would never stand for that. There is only one way to rectify matters: have O'Toole sire a child, then toss him back in the looney bin and the family can assume control of the money by becoming the unborn child's guardians. Mervyn has been keeping a woman on the side, Seymour, and his plan is to get O'Toole and her wed as soon as possible. O'Toole, however, keeps telling everyone that he's already married to The Lady of the Camellias. Seymour arrives, dressed as Camille, sings a snatch from "La Traviata," and O'Toole is convinced that she is who she says she is. They get married and Seymour falls in love with O'Toole and admits that this is all Mervyn's plan. O'Toole sighs, understands, and, in his Jesus fashion, forgives them as they know not what they do. He totally accepts Seymour, they sing a duet of "My Blue Heaven," and he rides her into the bedroom on his tricycle. She's instantly preg-

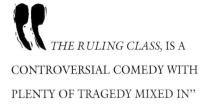

"*THE RULING CLASS,* IS A CONTROVERSIAL COMEDY WITH PLENTY OF TRAGEDY MIXED IN"

nant. O'Toole's doctor, Bryant, wants to help and works on the crazed peer through the months of the pregnancy. Seymour is about to deliver their child when Bryant shows O'Toole the folly of his ways by introducing him to Green, another nut-case who thinks that he, too, is Jesus. O'Toole is shattered by meeting Green and must admit that he isn't Jesus at all; he's Jack. Everyone in the family is thrilled that he's come to his senses and ceases preaching the gospel of love and truth. What they don't know is that the "Jack" he refers to is, in fact, "Jack the Ripper," which they learn the hard way when O'Toole kills his aunt, Browne, then tosses the blame for it on Lowe's drunken shoulders. O'Toole takes his seat in the House of Lords and makes a stinging speech that endorses bigotry and revenge and sets the sleeping peers on their feet, madly applauding the nonsense he's espoused. By this time, Mervyn, Bryant, and Sim have all gone bonkers themselves and so the castle is almost empty. O'Toole returns home and Seymour runs to put her arms around him. O'Toole responds by stabbing her. She screams her last and in the background, their child repeats, "I am Jack!" so there's no question that the genetic strain of madness has been passed through O'Toole's loins to his young son. There's hardly a segment of British society that comes out of this unscathed: the public school system, the Houses of Parliament, snobbism, the Church, Jesus, homosexuality, servants, the upper classes, and just about everything else it's fashionable to decry. It's caustic, funny, often goes too far and stays too long to make the points. O'Toole was oscar-nominated as the mad earl and bites off Barnes' speeches with Shavian diction. Lowe steals every scene he is in and the creators of the TV show "Benson" may have looked long and hard at Lowe's irascible butler before they turned him into a black man. There is more than just a passing similarity in the two. Sim's role as the aged bishop is one of his best in a long career. A lot of money was spent on this movie, making it one of the best produced British films of the year. Barnes' play was produced in England in 1969, then had a short run in Washington, D. C., in 1971, but it has yet to find anyone in the Broadway area to mount it. Joseph E. Levine, who made his fortune making sandals-and-swords Italian films was the presenter here, a far cry from his Steve Reeves epics. Interiors were done at Twickenham with locations shot in Buckinghamshire, Lincolnshire, Surrey, Hampshire and London.

Source: Anonymous. Review of *The Ruling Class* in *The Motion Picture Guide: N-R, 1927–1983,* edited by Jay Robert Nash and Stanley Ralph Ross, Cinebooks (Chicago), 1986, p. 2684.

SOURCES

Billington, Michael. Review of *The Ruling Class* in the *Guardian* January 25, 1978, p. 10.

Bryden, Ronald. "Tricks in Toryland" in the *Observer,* Vol. 2, March, 1969, p. 17.

Novick, Julius. Review of *The Ruling Class* in the *New York Times,* 1971.

Simon, John. Review of *The Ruling Class* in *New York Magazine,* September 10-October 2, 1972.

Shulman, Milton. "Huntin', Seducin', etc." in the *Evening Standard,* February 27, 1969, p. 17.

Spurling, Hilary. "Arts: Bond Honoured" in the *Spectator,* Vol. 222, March 7, 1969, p. 314.

Wardle, Irving. "Leonardo Clubbed" in the London *Times,* December 5, 1969, p. 7.

FURTHER READING

Bock, Hedwig, and Albert Wetheim, editors. *Essays on Contemporary British Drama,* Verlag, 1981.
    Essays on leading figures and issues in British theater today.

Dukore, Bernard F. *Barnestorm: The Plays of Peter Barnes,* Garland, 1995.
    Provides a detailed analysis of each of Barnes's plays and adaptations along with generalizations about his style.

Dukore, Bernard F. *The Theatre of Peter Barnes,* Heinemann, 1969.
    An earlier edition that discusses Barnes's work up to 1980.

Hobson, Harold. Introduction to *The Ruling Class,* Heinemann, 1981.
    An edition of the play that discusses Barnes's influence on British theatre.

Innes, Christopher. *Modern British Drama 1890-1990,* Cambridge University Press, 1992.
    Assesses Barnes as a major force in modern British comedy.

Speed-the-Plow

DAVID MAMET

1988

David Mamet's *Speed-the-Plow* is one of several successful plays he has written about the business world. Filled with Mamet's trademark, rapid-fire dialogue, *Speed-the-Plow* focuses on the ruthless nature of Hollywood and the movie industry. Mamet was familiar with this environment, having written several produced screenplays in the 1980s. The title *Speed-the-Plow* is derived from an old English farming phrase which was used to confer good luck and a swift and profitable ploughing. Critics and scholars have speculated that Mamet might be comparing Hollywood's fast pace and profit motivations to this past, for in the play cold business fact wins out over artistry and idealism.

Speed-the-Plow was first produced on Broadway in the Royale Theater, opening on May 3, 1988. The play was a box office success even before opening night, in part because pop star and cultural icon Madonna played the role of Karen, the temporary secretary. Advanced ticket sales exceeded $1 million. To many critics, Madonna's celebrity made an ironic comment on the play's action. Like many of Mamet's plays, *Speed-the-Plow* highlights men and their complicated relationships. Mamet has been routinely criticized for writing over-simple, objectified female characters over the course of his career, and this play received similar accusations regarding Karen.

Critics gave *Speed-the-Plow* generally good reviews during its Broadway production. Mamet

had won the Pulitzer Prize for drama several years earlier for his 1984 play *Glengarry Glenn Ross,* which also focuses on men in the business world. Many critics saw similarities between *Speed-the-Plow* and *Glengarry Glenn Ross* and found the latter superior. Still, most praised Mamet's use of dialogue and taunt plotting. Critics disagreed on the value of the play in the Mamet canon. Some saw it as a variation of Mamet's business dramas and therefore unoriginal, while others found deep meaning in the seemingly superficial depiction of two Hollywood producers looking for a big break.

AUTHOR BIOGRAPHY

David Mamet was born on November 30, 1947, in Chicago, Illinois, to Bernard Mamet, a labor lawyer, and his wife, Leonore. As a child, Mamet's parents had high expectations for their son and his younger sister, Lynn. Mamet's father especially emphasized the importance and potency of language. The family spent hours arguing for the sake of argument, and Mamet learned the subtleties inherent to well-spoken words. This experience had a direct bearing on Mamet's plays, for he is known as a master of dialogue.

Mamet's parents divorced when he was eleven, and he subsequently lived with his mother for four years before moving in with his father. At this time, Mamet got his first taste of theater, working backstage and doing bit parts at Chicago's Hull Theatre. At first Mamet wanted to be an actor, and to this end he studied the craft in New York City's famous Neighborhood Playhouse with Sanford Meisner. When it became evident that acting was not his true calling, Mamet returned to college (Goddard in Vermont) and began writing. His first full-length play, *Camel,* was his senior thesis and was performed as a student production.

Mamet continued to write following his graduation. He supported himself with small acting roles as well as working part-time teaching acting at Goddard and Marlboro, another college in Vermont. During this time, he began writing what would become his first hit: 1974's *Sexual Perversity in Chicago.* The play won the Joseph Jefferson Award for the best new Chicago play before it moved to Off-Off Broadway and Off-Broadway productions in New York City. Appraising the New York version of the show, *Time* named it among the ten best plays of 1976.

Mamet's next play, *American Buffalo,* was regarded as an ever bigger smash. As with its predecessor, the play debuted in Chicago. When the production moved to New York City in 1977, however, it went directly to Broadway. Several years later, in 1984, Mamet won the Pulitzer Prize for one of his most well-respected plays, *Glengarry Glenn Ross.* The story revolves around survival in a dog-eat-dog business environment: real estate. Similarly, Mamet's *Speed-the-Plow* (1988) revolves around another cutthroat business: Hollywood and the entertainment industry. Mamet wrote a number of screenplays, many of them adaptations of other's work, throughout the 1980s and 1990s and he became well-versed in the harsh business of film.

In 1992, Mamet produced one of his most controversial works, *Oleanna.* The play concerns the unfounded allegations of sexual harassment by a young, female student against a male college professor. Mamet directed the original Broadway production as he had previously done with several of his plays. The playwright also branched out into directing films. He has helmed (as well as written) such motion pictures as *House of Games* (1987), *Things Change* (1988), and *The Spanish Prisoner* (1997); he has also written the screenplays for *The Verdict* (1982), *The Untouchables* (1987), *The Edge* (1998), (with Hilary Henkin) *Wag the Dog* (1998), and *Lansky* (1999), among others. By the end of the 1990s, Mamet was regarded as one of the contemporary masters of the dramatic form, an emerging power in Hollywood, and a virtuoso of dialogue.

PLOT SUMMARY

Scene 1

Speed-the-Plow opens in Bobby Gould's new office in the morning. Gould, the newly promoted head of production at a movie studio is reading a book when Charlie Fox enters. Fox is very excited about something, but Gould continues to leaf through the book he is reading, making fun of its contents. Gould becomes suspicious when Fox asks if he can "greenlight" (approve) a movie deal, but his fears are quickly abated as Fox elaborates. Fox was visited earlier in the morning by a big movie star, Doug Brown, who is free to do a movie with him based on a prison script that Fox had sent him earlier; the star has given Fox until 10 am tomorrow to come up with a deal. Gould immediately calls his superior, Ross, and while he waits for him to call back, he and Fox discuss the Doug Brown story.

Ross calls back and says they will meet in ten minutes. In the meantime, Gould and Fox discuss the script, which is a prison movie/buddy picture, with "action, blood, and a social theme." Before Fox can ask, Gould assures him that he will get a co-producer credit. Gould thanks Fox for his loyalty because he could have taken the deal elsewhere. They discuss the strategy for the meeting. Gould will do the talking, summarizing the script in one line for Ross. Before they can finish, Ross calls telling Gould that he has to be out of town until tomorrow morning. Fox worries that his option will expire before they can talk to Ross, but Gould assures him they will talk to Ross in time. Fox realizes they are going to be rich, and Gould tells him that they will be very rich. Gould, though, says that money is not everything and people are more important in their business.

Gould calls for coffee, but the temp does not know where it is. While they wait for her to bring coffee in, Fox remains jumpy, finally picking up the novel Gould was reading earlier, titled *The Bridge; or, Radiation and the Half-Life of Society. A Study of Decay.* Fox suggests he make the book into a movie, then jokes that he should do it instead of the Doug Brown picture. Karen, the twentysomething temporary secretary, comes in with the coffee. While Karen is there, Fox and Gould talk about how they have been loyal friends for many years and how they are whores in their business. Gould says that most everything they make is garbage, and Karen asks why that is. The men try to answer, but can only come up with "That's the way it is."

Karen says that she does not know what she is supposed to do on her job. Gould says not to do anything but cancel all his appointments until the meeting with Ross, make lunch reservations for him and Fox, and then leave. She goes to the outer office to do these tasks, and Gould tells Fox to leave so he can get some work done. Fox says that he thinks Gould will make moves on Karen. Gould denies this, but after Fox speculates about Karen, Gould says that he thinks she would go out with him. They make a bet for $500 that Gould can get Karen to come to his house and have sex with him. Fox leaves.

After a moment, Karen comes back into Gould's office. She was unable to get the lunch reservation he wanted, but after Gould starts to point out her mistake, she realizes that she should have mentioned his name. Gould has her sit down and he

David Mamet

explains what happened in the office that morning. Gould offers her the opportunity to do the courtesy read on *The Bridge,* as long as she gives her report on it to him that night at his house. They also get into a discussion on purity and principles, and Gould admits he wishes he had them. He sends Karen back to make the proper reservations as well as call Fox and inform him that he owes Gould $500.

Scene 2

In Gould's apartment later that night, Karen is enthusiastically telling Gould about the novel. She explains that the author theorizes that all the radiation around us is sent by God and changes us constantly. Karen says that the novel has changed her. Gould thanks her, telling her that they have made a connection because she has shared this book with him. He offers to help her in the business, and she says that she wants to work on this film. She insists that this novel should be made into a movie, that it is a pearl. Gould does not think anyone will see the film. Karen says the script to Fox's prison film is not what people want. Gould talks about how everyone wants something from him. Karen tells him that she knows he wants to sleep with her, and she understands him. She tells him she knows that he is frightened. She says she is the answer to his prayers for purity, for the book has enlightened her.

Scene 3

In Gould's office the next morning, Fox comes in wanting assurance that they would be co-producers credited above the title. Gould informs him that he is not going to do the Doug Brown film. Fox sarcastically says that he should do the novel instead and ruin his career, then goes on a verbal rampage which ends with him asking Gould if he slept with Karen. Gould avoids the question, saying he will see Ross by himself and will not do the Doug Brown project. Fox points out that he promised him yesterday and that he could have taken the project elsewhere yesterday. When Fox asks, Gould says that he will be greenlighting the novel instead. Fox tells him he cannot make this book and he will lose his job if he does. Gould says that he was up all night thinking, and that he needs to do his job differently. Fox thinks he is totally crazy and says anything he can to convince Gould of this.

Fox finally asks if Karen played a role in his decision. When Gould admits that they talked, Fox is outraged and physically attacks Gould, cursing him. Gould insists that he has not changed his mind. Fox tries to convince him that Karen used her looks to get to him, speculating that she said she understands him. Fox says that she wants something from Gould. Gould tries to counteract his words, but he is not successful. Fox asks Gould to tell him about the novel, but Gould cannot. When Fox goes another verbal rampage, Gould asks him to leave.

Fox wants to ask Karen one question. Fox asks her what they talked about and if they became intimate. Karen is suspicious and answers in vague terms. Finally, Fox asks if she would have slept with Gould if he had not greenlighted her book. She admits that she would not have. Gould is confused as to what he should do until she reminds him that ''we have a meeting.'' At that point the executive decides to go the safe route and make the prison film with Fox. Gould changes his shirt and has Fox show Karen out. Fox berates her while Gould changes. The two men leave for the meeting. Gould assures Fox that above the title the names will read ''Fox and Gould.''

CHARACTERS

Charlie Fox

Fox is a movie producer who is about forty years of age. As his surname suggests, Fox is a sly, wily character who is above nothing if it means career advancement. He is a man looking for his big break; when he finds it in the form of a possible deal with film star Doug Brown, he fights viciously to keep it. Fox brings the deal to Bobby Gould, a long time friend and business associate. Charlie has a one-day option on the Brown picture and urges Gould to act upon it. When the executive agrees to take the project to his boss, Fox is pleased and believes his fortune is made when Gould assures him a co-producer credit.

As a competitive aside, Fox bets Gould that he cannot get his temporary secretary, Karen, to sleep with him. Fox is chagrined the next day, when Gould tells him that he has decided to produce an adaptation of a book that Karen liked instead of the Brown picture. To ensure his project gets made, Fox literally beats up Gould and verbally assaults him, arguing that Karen was using him. Gould realizes the folly of trying to do something different or artistic in Hollywood. In the end the executive agrees to the safer course of action, and the aggressive Fox gets his movie deal.

Bobby Gould

Bobby is a movie executive, around forty-years-old, and the most central character of the play. Before the action begins, he has just been given a promotion to head of production at a major movie studio. Gould seems to value loyalty. When Charlie Fox drops in and tells him that a big movie star, Doug Brown, has come to him wanting to do a movie deal, Gould immediately arranges a meeting with his boss to get approval on the deal. Fox and Gould also make a bet over whether or not Gould can get his new assistant, Karen, to sleep with him. To that end, the executive gives a her a book for ''courtesy read'' (essentially a review copy of a book sent to movie studios by the publishers in the hopes of having an adaptation made) and invites her over to his home to report. She finds something of value in it, and convinces him to pursue a film adaptation of the meaningful book instead of the movie with Doug Brown.

The next morning, when Fox arrives for the meeting, Gould has won the bet and tries to get rid of Fox. After Fox berates Gould, physically beating the executive and proving that Karen slept with him only because he decided to go with the book, Gould realizes that the Doug Brown picture is the better, safer choice. By the end of the play, Gould takes Fox to the meeting instead of Karen, for he is unwilling to take chances.

Karen

Karen is a young woman in her twenties. She is working as a temporary secretary in Gould's office. Because she is a temp, she does not know where the coffeemaker is nor the right way to make a lunch reservation for Gould. Karen believes in values and principles. She is also naive about the movie business, at least in the other characters' eyes, because she thinks films should be good. Still, when given an opportunity, she takes it. Gould lets her do a courtesy read on a book and give him a report at his home. Karen's enthusiasm for the book touches something in Gould, and she convinces him to pursue it as his next project over the Brown picture. Afterwards, Karen admits she slept with Gould only because he greenlighted (approved production of) the book, and the men are convinced that Karen was only using Gould to further her own ambitions.

In contrast to the cutthroat business tactics of Gould and Fox, Karen is the voice of art and reason in the play. While she may have had ulterior motives for sleeping with Gould, it is clear that she believes in high quality and artistry in motion pictures. While it is obvious that Gould and Fox do what they do to serve their own careers and make as much money as possible, Karen's motives are less clear. She may simply be a corporate climber, but there is also evidence to suggest that her motives are in the service of improving the films made by Hollywood.

THEMES

Friendship and Loyalty

The two main characters in *Speed-the-Plow*, Bobby Gould, the new head of production at a major motion picture studio, and Charlie Fox, a producer, have been friends for over twenty years. This friendship is at the center of the play, and their loyalty to each other makes it turn. Gould and Fox began their careers together in the mailroom at a studio and have remained loyal to each other over the years. When Fox unexpectedly gets the twenty-four-hour option to the next Doug Brown movie, Fox takes the project to his old friend Gould. Fox emphasizes that he could have taken the project "across the street," i.e. to another studio, but his loyalty and friendship compelled him to see Gould first. Gould seizes the opportunity, though his boss will be unavailable until the next morning.

TOPICS FOR FURTHER STUDY

- Research the history behind the phrase "speed the plow." How is the phrase's meaning related to the themes of Mamet's play?

- Compare and contrast *Speed-the-Plow* with Mamet's two other "business" plays, *American Buffalo* and *Glengarry Glen Ross*. What do these plays say about male relationships/friendships?

- Compare and contrast *Speed-the-Plow*'s Karen to Carol, the young female student in Mamet's *Oleanna*. Both claim to be naive young women, yet both are dishonest about themselves. Explore the psychological implications.

- Explore the idea of "the culture of success," a predominant cultural force in the United States in the 1980s, especially in Hollywood. How does this cultural concept affect the actions of each of the characters in the play?

The Gould-Fox friendship then undergoes a test of loyalty. Karen, the temporary secretary, is good-looking, and Fox bets Gould $500 that he cannot get her into bed. To accomplish this end, Gould has Karen do a reader's report on a novel and visit his home later to discuss her work. Karen does so, and convinces Gould that he would be doing "good" to make the novel into a movie rather than the Doug Brown project. The next morning, when Fox comes back for their meeting with the studio head, he is appalled to find that Gould has forsaken his loyalty and will go with Karen's project instead of the prison film.

Fox proceeds to do everything he can to make Gould act like a loyal friend and do his project instead. Fox only accomplishes his goal when he proves Karen is not what she seems, using her own words against her. Fox shows that Karen is using Gould to get ahead in Hollywood, while Fox's motivations are more pure. He has their best interests at heart, and wants to share success with his loyal friend. Fox argues, and Gould ends up agreeing, that they have more at stake with each other and that Karen is an outsider and a whore. *Speed-the-Plow* argues that Friendship between men is more important than a relationship—no matter what the motivation—with a woman like Karen.

Ethics, Honesty, and Idealism

Each of the characters in *Speed-the-Plow* has his or her own ethical standards. These ethics create conflicts between the characters. Charlie Fox is the simplest character ethically. He has no qualms about calling himself a ''whore.'' He wants to be successful at any cost and works only for the money, the power, and the prestige. He sees Bobby Gould as his ticket to that end. He is not idealistic about the movie industry in the least. He accepts that movies are a commodity and does not pretend otherwise.

Bobby Gould is much more conflicted and complex. Like Fox, he also admits to being a ''whore'' and knows that movies are a commodity. He sees the opportunity in the Doug Brown picture, no matter that the plot is a list of movie cliches. But Gould has some latent idealism. When he and Fox discuss how much money they will make off this project, it is Gould who points out that money is not everything. Much of Bobby's idealism is brought out by Karen. Gould tells her that he wants to do ''good'' films and that he wants to make a difference. To that end, Gould decides to greenlight the novel, which Karen believes is deeply meaningful, instead of the Doug Brown picture. Though Fox convinces him to do the Brown project by the end of the play, Gould has shown that he has deeper thoughts and motivations.

Karen, the temporary secretary, appears to be the least honest and ethical character. When she is introduced in Scene 1, she appears to be naive and idealistic. She thinks films should be ''good'' and be meaningful for their audience. Gould gives her an opportunity to do the courtesy read on a novel, and she finds deep meaning in it. She convinces him to do the novel instead of the Doug Brown project. But Fox, quick to spot his own kind, reveals Karen's true nature. Karen wants to be a part of the Hollywood dealmaking process. Karen admits she slept with Gould only because he agreed to do the novel. Karen also says that she read the script for the Doug Brown project and that is was not very good. This is suspect for a woman who claimed to know nothing about the movie-making world. At a key moment, Karen reminds Gould that ''Bob, we have a

meeeting.'' The ''we'' shows Gould that Karen has forced herself into the process and has been less than honest about her intentions. What Karen really believes, beyond her own self-service, is never made clear.

STYLE

Setting

Speed-the-Plow is a drama set in contemporary times. Though it is not explicitly stated, the play probably takes place in Los Angeles, the movie industry capital of the world, at a major studio. The action is focused in two settings. Scenes 1 and 3 take place in Bobby Gould's new office. Because he has just been promoted to the head of production, the office is sparsely furnished with ''boxes and painting materials all around,'' as the stage directions indicate. The brief Scene 2, where Gould and Karen meet to discuss her report on the novel, is set in Gould's home. It can be speculated that everything takes place in Gould's spaces because he is the man who ultimately makes the decisions. Charlie Fox and Karen are at his mercy, and they must try to influence him on his turf.

Karen nearly succeeds in getting her project off the ground because she is invited into Gould's private life. Fox uses the fact that this is a business deal—and the fact that Karen used sex to further her own ambitions—to his advantage in Scene 3. The office is where business is done, not at home. The spare sets also put Mamet's rapid-fire, though ultimately simple, dialogue at the forefront of *Speed-the-Plow*.

Foreshadowing

Several times in *Speed-the-Plow,* Mamet plays with lines that foreshadow future events in the play. However, the predicted events do not always work out exactly as intended. For example, Gould says that he ''don't fuck people'' in Scene 1, yet that is exactly what he does. Though it seems he will betray Fox and not get the Doug Brown picture made as he promised, Gould ends up backing out of his promise to greenlight Karen's novel. The novel itself is at the center of another example of foreshadowing. In Scene 1, Fox picks up the novel, *The Bridge,* and says in jest ''Why don't you do it? *Make* it.'' A few lines later he suggests ''Instead of our Doug, Doug Brown's *Buddy* film.'' Gould agrees with him, also in jest, saying ''Yeah. *I* could do that.''

By the end of Scene 2, however, Karen has actually convinced Gould to do this very thing. In the beginning of Scene 3, Fox repeats this idea, with a clause attached, not knowing what Gould has decided. Fox says, ''I were you, I'd do the film on Radiation. That's the project I would do; and then spend the rest of my life in a packing crate.'' Though Fox eventually convinces Gould not to do the novel, this kind of ironic foreshadowing adds texture to the play.

Dialogue

As a playwright, Mamet is often praised by critics for his realistic dialogue. Mamet writes dialogue in a way that reflects how people really talk to each other. Words overlap, people interrupt each other, and sentences are often short and complete with pauses. In *Speed-the-Plow,* Mamet's language choices reflect his subject matter. Charlie Fox and Bobby Gould use Hollywood cliches (the buddy picture, for example) and other lingo (greenlighting a picture), to set the tone. Sometimes characters hide behind these cliches. For example, when Karen serves coffee to Fox and Gould, they use more Hollywoodspeak to emphasize their positions of power within the business to the self-described naive woman.

HISTORICAL CONTEXT

Like much of the 1980s, American society in 1988 was consumed with the ideas of success and image, the bigger the better. By 1988, there were 1.3 million millionaires living in the United States. This number included 50 billionaires. (By comparison, when adjusting for inflation, there were only 180,000 millionaires in the United States in 1972.) Because of an economy that saw vast growth during the 1970s, at least on the upper end of the economic scale, many people wanted to display their new-found wealth with high-end status items. Both Bobby Gould and Charlie Fox in *Speed-the-Plow* discuss how much money they will make off their deal and what it will get them. During this discussion, Gould says, ''We're going to have to hire someone just to figure out the *things* we want to buy.'' Such

greed was typical of the media-enforced images of wealth and success in the 1980s. Television shows celebrated the wealthy lifestyle. One popular televison show, *Lifestyles of the Rich and Famous,* showed how celebrities and other rich people spent their money and lived their lives. Pop singer/actress/cultural icon Madonna, who played Karen in the original Broadway production of *Speed-the-Plow,* was a master at manipulating the media and toying with her image while making a big profit.

The attitude that bigger is better spilled over into the arts and mass media. On Broadway, large-scale musicals featured more elaborate sets and large casts. In the publishing world, there were many bidding wars for new novels. Neophyte authors received unheard-of advances on their work. Some of the most popular novels of the era were about the noveau riche and their hedonistic lifestyle. Authors like Jackie Collins, Judith Krantz, and Sidney Sheldon sold millions of books that celebrated the glitzy lifestyle.

Similarly, the film industry in the 1980s was concerned with big budgets and even bigger profits. The term ''blockbuster movie'' was defined by 1980s films like *The Empire Strikes Back* and *Batman.* Movies began being marketed and hyped by product tie-ins (such as action figures and soundtracks) released several months before the film itself hit the marketplace. But many of these movies put style and profit before substance. Gould chooses to greenlight the empty Doug Brown movie because it will profitable instead of the ''arty'' and unknown quantity contained in the novel. Still only a privileged few had enough power to get their movie projects made. Power was consolidated in a few hands, usually producers and studio heads. Mamet depicts Gould as being one of the powerful men in Hollywood whom Fox needs to get his Doug Brown project off the ground.

Hollywood, like many other aspects of society especially in the cultural milieu, was still very male-dominated. Though there were several prominent female film producers, such as Dawn Steel, and many prominent actresses with some clout, Meryl Streep for example, women had a hard time breaking into the industry. At the end of *Speed-the-Plow,* Fox throws Karen out of the studio. She has no place there in his eyes. The burgeoning feminist movement of the 1960s and 1970s lost its way in the 1980s. Though women made some progress in the workplace, their successes were seen as individual triumphs rather than collective steps forward.

CRITICAL OVERVIEW

When *Speed-the-Plow* was first produced on Broadway in 1988, the casting of Madonna in the role of Karen was debated in the press more than the merits of the play itself. Many critics found the play up to Mamet's high standards. William A. Henry III, reviewing the play in *Time,* wrote, "Of all American playwrights, Mamet, 40, remains the shrewdest observer of the evil that men do unto each other in the name of buddyhood." Not all critics were impressed, however. In *New York,* John Simon stated: "The plot is minimal, barely sufficient to poke fun at Hollywood and show some derision for human nature." Simon also added, "And when you reduce it to its essentials, it is really only variations on a basic bitter joke."

Mamet's use of language is often singled out for praise, and *Speed-the-Plow* is no exception. Robert Brustein in the *New Republic* argued, "His ear for language has never been more certain or more subtle, but what distinguishes him from other playwrights with a natural control of the American idiom (Paddy Chayefsky, for example) is the economical way he can advance his plot, develop his characters, and tell his jokes without departing from, or announcing, his strong social-moral purpose." *Newsweek*'s Jack Kroll added, "there's hardly a line in it that isn't somehow insanely funny or scarily insane."

Many critics compared *Speed-the-Plow* to other male-oriented business plays written by Mamet, including 1984's *Glengarry Glen Ross* and 1975's *American Buffalo. Speed-the-Plow* was often considered the inferior of the three. Brustein paid a back-handed compliment when he wrote, "*Speed-the-Plow* is the deftest and funniest of Mamet's works, and the airiest too, since the characters are playing for relatively low stakes. In *American Buffalo, Edmond,* and *Glengarry Glen Ross,* men are fighting for their very existence. In *Speed-the-Plow* they are skirmishing over movie deals and percentages of the gross." Moira Hudson in the *Nation* agreed, saying "*Speed-the-Plow* says nothing about Hollywood that hasn't already been said many times before, but Mamet manages through his language and timing to breathe life into old cliches. *Glengarry Glen Ross* a few seasons back was better."

Despite flaws, critics generally agree that Mamet writes challenging texts for actors. The *Nation*'s Hudson claimed, "Mamet is an actor's playwright, creating a language which is less simply overheard

and recorded whole-cloth then boiled down, crafted and reassembled to create an intense, hyperrealistic theatrical experience." Nearly every critic found the original Broadway production performances of Joe Mantegna as Bobby Gould and Ron Silver as Charlie Fox flawless. Simon in *New York* said that the actors "play off each other dizzingly and dazzlingly as they flesh out—or, rather, sound out—the potential of the script, which depends almost indecently on the skill of its interpreters."

More controversial was the role of Karen and the woman who played her in that original production, the popstar Madonna. Many critics debated if the character of Karen was well-written to begin with. Hudson stated in the *Nation* that "Madonna's line readings are less deft than Mantegna's (or Silver's). . . . Still, she isn't all bad—or if she is, it's hard to tell: The part she's been given is by far the least convincing of the three. . . . It is difficult to believe that someone as naive as Karen would actually be working in the movie business, and its just as difficult to believe someone like Bobby would be so easily swayed by her, despite her undeniable attractions."

Some critics thought Madonna's performance had merit. *Time*'s Henry wrote: "Madonna's awkward, indecisive characterization seems calculated to . . . sustain suspense by keeping the audience from reaching conclusions. Thus the question 'Can she act?' cannot be answered. The shrewdness in her performance is clear, but so, alas, is her thinking process: she lacks ease and naturalness." Kroll in *Newsweek* added, "She doesn't yet have the vocal horsepower, the sparks, and cylinders to drive Mamet's syncopated dialogue. But she has the seductive ambiguity that makes Karen the play's catalytic force. . . . Who better than Madonna—Virgin, Material Girl—to give embodiment to the conundrum at the heart of David Mamet's scathingly comic play?"

Other critics were much less kind. The *New Republic*'s Brustein acknowledged Madonna's importance as a pop star, but wrote, "Her performance is becomingly unshowy, but her modesty subdues her. . . . [She] gives a new dimension to the meaning of the word 'flat'." He concluded, "Her celebrity was bound to attract the wrong kind of attention to the play." John Simon in *New York* argued that "she is more of a temporary hindrance whenever she is on."

In September 1988, when the entire original cast left the production, several critics found the

A scene from the original Broadway production of Speed-the-Plow: *Joe Mantegna as Gould, Madonna as Karen, and Ron Silver as Fox; Madonna's presence in the production was controversial and often generated more publicity than the play itself*

new cast, which included a professional actress in the role of Karen, inferior in their interpretation of the play. Frank Rich in the *New York Times* wrote, "the deep, shudder-inducing chill of the original production is gone." Rich went on to comment on Felicity Huffman, who took over the role of Karen. He wrote, "Mrs. Huffman's skillful performance is in most details similar to Madonna's . . . yet less effective. . . . Madonna's awkwardness and, yes, star presence, added essential elements of mystery and eroticism to a character who doesn't reveal her true, shocking hand (and power over powerful men) until late in the play." Simon, who had earlier dismissed Madonna's performance, said, "though each of the trio is good, and Felicity Huffman surely better than Madonna, the work suffers."

CRITICISM

A. Petrusso

In this essay, Petrusso discusses the complicated role of Karen in Speed-the-Plow, *particularly the manner in which she exemplifies the problematic nature of female characters in Mamet's plays.*

Many critics have noted that David Mamet does not write strong female characters. Indeed, many of his best plays, including *American Buffalo* and the Pulitzer Prize-winning *Glengarry Glen Ross,* do not feature women at all. One critic, the *Nation*'s Moira Hudson, writing on the original New York production of *Speed-the-Plow,* observed: "Mamet's parts for women have never been the equal of his parts for men: Women in his plays always seem to function more as plot elements, as sources of complications than as rounded, living characters." Many reviewers of the play have agreed that the character of Karen works in this fashion but are divided over the merits of drawing her as such. Critics such as Hudson find Karen unbelievable while others believe that the assistant's enigmatic nature is very powerful. By looking at Karen and her role within the play, it becomes obvious that both arguments have merit. Ultimately, though, Karen is a weak caricature of a woman. Mamet condemns Karen for her ambitions, while the two male characters—who have far more suspicious values (though more pow-

WHAT DO I READ NEXT?

- *Glengarry Glen Ross,* a play that Mamet wrote in 1977, is a drama which also concerns men and their relationships in the business world. The play shows the lengths men will go to achieve success.

- *The Last Tycoon,* an unfinished novel by F. Scott Fitzgerald and first published in 1941, explores Hollywood and relationships formed within the industry.

- *The Last Mogul: Lew Wasserman,* a biography written by Dennis MacDougal, discusses the life of a Hollywood executive. The book includes insights into Hollywood business relationships.

- *Circus of Ambition: The Culture of Wealth and Power in the Eighties,* a nonfiction book by John Taylor published in 1998, is a collection of essays discussing the rich and the culture of success, including Hollywood.

- *Oleanna,* a play by David Mamet first produced in 1992, is a drama which concerns Carol, a young female university student who, like Karen in *Speed-the-Plow,* is also an enigma. The play focuses on a sexual harassment charge she brings against a male professor.

er)—are allowed to flourish in their rapacious environment.

Karen is by far the smallest role in *Speed-the-Plow;* this is brought into greater relief given the fact that the play is a three-character piece. Most of the text concerns the wheeling and dealing between Charlie Fox and Bobby Gould, the veteran Hollywood hustlers. Gould is the new head of production at a major movie studio; Fox is a producer with a twenty-four-hour option on a movie deal with a big, bankable star. Karen is merely the temporary secretary, filling in for Gould's usual assistant who is ill. Karen is not very competent in her position. Even before she is seen on stage in Scene 1, Gould is shown talking with her on the phone, helping her find the coffee machine.

The men also reduce Karen's character by commenting on her appearance. Fox says ''Cute broad, the new broad.'' They only consider her in the most superficial manner. When she does finally bring them coffee, the Fox and Gould talk about how they are ''old whores'' and their long-standing friendship. They also discuss how powerful they are and will be when the movie deal is made. In many ways the discussion is a verbal display of their importance in front of Karen. It both puts her in her

position as a lesser and works to impress her, like two male peacocks flouting their plumage during a mating ritual.

Gould and Fox continue to toy with Karen. Gould tells her she can go home after serving them coffee, canceling all his appointments, and making lunch reservations. After she leaves to do these tasks, Fox immediately begins to needle Gould about Karen. Gould decides to make a $500 bet with Fox ''That I can get her on a date, that I can get her to my house, that I can screw her.'' After Fox leaves, Karen's incompetence brings her back into Gould's office. Karen could not get reservations at the restaurant Gould wanted. Karen quickly realizes her mistake: she did not mention Gould's name when she was making the reservation. This reveals a problematic error in the persona Karen has chosen to present to Gould. First, how does one make a reservation without giving the name of the party who will using it? Second, it implies that Karen is somehow deeper because she might be hiding something. That is, she deliberately made the mistake so as to hide her true nature, that of a career-conscious, ambitious woman.

At this juncture, Karen begins to repeatedly call herself naive when talking to Gould, perhaps consciously reinforcing her status as a lesser to the man. This gives her some unexpected power, as Gould begin to believes that she is a green, helpless girl. There is no reason to believe otherwise. Karen services his ego by telling him that this job is allowing her to think in a business fashion. She politely listens to him describe some aspects of the business to her. While Gould is using this opportunity to win his bet, Karen is learning good deal about how business in Hollywood is accomplished. Gould looks at Karen only as an object when he offers her the opportunity to give a reader's report on a novel about radiation and the end of the world—even though the book has been deemed inappropriate for a film; he is using the "assignment" as an excuse to get her over to his house.

In the brief second scene (in Gould's apartment), Karen is the dominate force as she describes the book to Gould. Karen's appraisal of the novel does not make much sense, though she says it left her feeling "empowered" (a telling adjective regarding her rising status). She talks about how much the book touched her, but the dialogue as written by Mamet reveals little of who Karen really is. The scene illustrates her ambitions when Gould offers to help her get a job at the studio, and Karen says that she wants to work on the film adaptation of the novel. Karen continues to sound—in her own words—naive. She tells Gould "it would be so important to me, to *be* there. To help. If you could just help me with that. And, seriously, I'll get coffee, I don't care ." Gould is slightly taken aback, but Karen continues to press the issue. Like Fox, she sees her opportunity and aggressively pursues it.

A key revelation occurs in Scene 2 when Karen reveals that she has read the script that Fox wants to use for his Doug Brown project. Someone as unaware of Hollywood practices—as Karen claims to be—would have no idea how to get her hands on such a script. Fox did not bring the script into the office, so Karen obviously found out about the Fox project and procured the script through means of her own. Not only does this illustrate the depth of her wiles, it indicates that her work assignment to Gould was no random act. In having Karen disclose a knowledge of the script, Mamet hints at the considerable calculation that has gone into Karen's association with Gould: it becomes clear that she sought out the temporary assistant position with the express purpose of getting her foot in the door.

Karen also knows how to play the sex card. She tells Gould, "I knew what the deal was. I know you

> KAREN IS THE PLOT COMPLICATION IN *SPEED-THE-PLOW.* SHE IS THE SOURCE OF JEOPARDY IN TERMS OF THE 'RIGHT' SCRIPT BEING MADE, AND SHE FORCES THE OTHER CHARACTERS, PRIMARILY GOULD, TO QUESTION THEIR VALUES"

wanted to sleep with me. You're right, I came anyway; you're right." Karen proceeds to turn the tables on Gould, trying to reinforce their status as equals. She describes them both as people who need companionship and love. She says they have both been bad. She tells him that she is the answer to his prayers. And based on the discussions between Gould and Fox at the beginning of Scene 3, she appears to have succeeded.

The next morning, when Scene 3 takes place, Gould has decided to go with Karen's project instead of Fox's. Fox is appalled and immediately blames Karen, though he has no direct reason to believe it has anything to do with her. When Fox finds out it is because of her, he emphasizes their friendship and how Karen is an outsider. Fox asks at one point, "What is she, a witch?" Later, Fox says, "A beautiful and ambitious woman comes to town. Why? Why does *anyone* come here? Everyone wants power. How do we get it? Work. How do they get it? Sex. The End. She's different. Nobody's different. The broad wants power she trades on the one thing she's got, her *looks,* get into a position of authority—through you. She *lured* you in." Fox emphasizes Karen's difference, the fact that she is a woman and therefore cannot "work" to get success, to try to persuade Gould to change his mind.

Fox spends most of the scene cutting down Karen, her ambitions, and her project. He wants Gould to see her as a user rather than a savior. To salvage his project, Fox asks one question of Karen. Fox forces Karen to admit that she would not have become intimate with Gould if he had not agreed to make the radiation novel into a film. Gould cannot believe it. He says, "Oh, God, now I'm lost." Fox knows he has a leg up, and when Karen tries to save herself by saying "Bob. Bob, we have the opportunity," Fox goes in for the kill. The "we" is important here. It implies that Karen and Gould are linked, to the exclusion of Fox. Fox breaks that down when he says, "I know who *he* is, who are *you?* Some broad from the Temporary Pool. A Tight pussy wrapped around Ambition. That's who *you* are, Pal." Again, Fox focus on Karen's sex to bring her down. Gould is still uncertain, however, about his decision, and Karen and Fox say anything to get him to go their respective ways. But when Karen says, "Bob, we have a meeting," the issue is decided for him. Karen is only interested in getting her film made. The men regroup and go to the meeting together, effectively killing Karen's deal in favor of Fox's film. Fox tells Karen to leave the studio and never come back again.

Hudson's observation was correct: Karen is the plot complication in *Speed-the-Plow*. She is the source of jeopardy in terms of the "right" script being made, and she forces the other characters, primarily Gould, to question their values. Karen is not a fully drawn, realistic character but an excuse for the other characters to show off their maleness and power. Karen talks about values but in a superficial, manipulative fashion—despite hints that she may have altruistic intentions for her film. Any values she does have (idealism, for example) are condemned by Mamet. By having Karen sleep with Gould to get ahead, Mamet reinforces the idea that this is the only way for a woman to be successful in the business environment. The idea of her starting out in the mailroom, as Gould and Fox did, is never even considered—she wants to enter the business at the top. Thus, Karen is a series of contradictions that seem designed to make her enigmatic, but these contradictions serve the plot, not the character herself. Her potential to be anything more is never realized by Mamet.

Source: A. Petrusso, for *Drama for Students,* Gale, 1999.

Moira Hodgson

Proclaiming that "nobody in theater today has a better ear for the language of American business than David Mamet," Hodgson goes on to praise the realism, energy, and vitality of Speed-the-Plow.

Nobody in theater today has a better ear for the language of American business than David Mamet. Relentlessly on the make, his characters are not captains of industry but con men on the fringes of society, trying to batter down the doors of the bank with the only weapon at their disposal—their heads. Sometimes they succeed and fill their pockets, and sometimes they just give themselves colossal headaches. Without exception though, their language is vulgar and funny and charges the air with explosive energy.

In *Speed-the-Plow,* Mamet's latest play, directed by Gregory Mosher at the Royale Theatre, the subject is Hollywood. Bobby (Joe Mantegna) and Charlie (Ron Silver) have been friends for twenty years, ever since they started out together in a corporate mail room. Now Bobby is head of production at a major studio and Charlie is a producer who comes to him with a twenty-four-hour option on a "prison buddy" story starring (or directed by, it's not clear) the immensely bankable "Doug Brown." Bobby, snowed under a deskful of boring manuscripts — including one about radiation and the end of the world by an "Eastern sissy writer"— is delirious at the prospect. "Is there such a thing as a good film that loses money?" he asks rhetorically. "That's what we are in business to do—to make the thing that everyone saw last year!" The only problem is that Ross the Boss, whose approval Bobby needs to green-light a picture over $10 million, is flying to New York City on the company jet and won't be available until 10 o'clock the next morning. This is cutting Charlie's twenty-four-hour option a bit fine.

Mantegna and Silver, draped in off-white suits that look tailored by Bijan of Beverly Hills, are both excellent as two cynical hustlers about to hit the jackpot. (Mantegna's character, the one holding down a regular job, wears his suit with sneakers, no tie and no socks.) "It's lonely at the top," says Bobby ironically. "Yeah," agrees Charlie, "but it ain't crowded." Mamet captures the vernacular perfectly, littering the play with industry expressions and his signature repetitive phrases. It has often been observed that Mamet is a poor-man's Pinter, and it is true that the staccato exchanges are easy to mimic and at times threaten to turn cloying. But the two main actors' line readings are deft and point up the fact that Mamet is an actor's playwright, creating a language which is less simply overheard and recorded whole-cloth than boiled down, crafted and reassembled to create an intense, hyperrealistic theatrical experience. This, after all, is what art is all about.

That being said, the play is far from perfect. Its flaws center chiefly on its third character, Bobby's temporary secretary (played by Madonna). Karen is a semi-naïf who can't find the coffee machine and doesn't even know how to drop her boss's name when booking him a table at a fashionable restaurant. As the first act closes, Charlie says, "She's neither dumb enough or ambitious enough," and bets Bobby $500 she'll never go to bed with him. Accepting this challenge, Bobby shows Karen the sissy-writer's radiation novel; he asks her to give it a "courtesy read" and to file a report on it at his house later that evening.

The brief second scene takes place in Bobby's living room, sparsely furnished with pink curtains, a Turkish rug on the sofa and a Mexican chest which opens into a bar. Karen appeals to Bobby's vestigial noble instincts and convinces him that the movie he should pitch to Ross the Boss is not the exploitative prison buddy picture but the radiation picture. The fact that this scene drags terribly and that Madonna's line readings are less deft than Mantegna's (or Silver's) has something to do with her talent as a stage actress. Still, she isn't all that bad—or if she is, it's hard to tell: The part she's been given is by far the least convincing of the three. Mamet's parts for women have never been the equal of his parts for men: Women in his plays always seem to function more as plot elements, as sources of complication rather than as rounded, living characters. It is difficult to believe that someone as naïve as Karen would actually be working in the movie business, and it's just as difficult to believe that someone like Bobby would be so easily swayed by her, despite her undeniable attractions. (It is also difficult to watch Karen and not keep remembering it's actually Madonna.)

With the second act, and the return of Ron Silver, things go into high gear. When Charlie learns be is about to be screwed out of the chance of a lifetime, that his option on Doug Brown will expire through no fault of his own, his despair and desperation become palpable and even highly moving. All at once his beard grows unkempt and his natty suit seems to wrinkle up as if he's slept in it. Realizing he has only five or ten minutes to salvage his chances, he becomes a caged animal, lashing out with every argument at his disposal. When Bobby says he's going to green-light the radiation book because he believes in it, Charlie replies, "I believe in the Yellow Pages, Bob, but I don't want to film it." He asks Bobby to tell him what the novel is actually about, and when Bobby hesitates, he says, "If you can't put it to me in one sentence they can't

> *SPEED-THE-PLOW SAYS NOTHING ABOUT HOLLYWOOD THAT HASN'T ALREADY BEEN SAID MANY TIMES BEFORE, BUT MAMET MANAGES THROUGH HIS LANGUAGE AND TIMING TO BREATHE LIFE INTO OLD CLICHÉS"*

put it in *TV Guide.* " Our sympathies go out to him because he is totally vulnerable, a two-bit hustler who knows it and isn't afraid to face himself. The prison buddy film is garbage, but what matters above all is loyalty and friendship. Bobby has broken his word.

Speed-the-Plow says nothing about Hollywood that hasn't already been said many times before, but Mamet manages through his language and timing to breathe life into old clichés. *Glengarry Glen Ross* a few seasons back was better, but there is likely to be little else on Broadway this season with his new play's energy.

Source: Moira Hodgson, review of *Speed-the-Plow* in the *Nation,* Vol. 246, no. 24, June 18, 1988, pp. 874–75.

Gerald Weales

In this essay, Weales reviews Speed-the-Plow, *comparing it to Mamet's other works. While he found the play mean-spirited and often ugly, the critic admits his appreciation for the playwright's facility with dialogue.*

In Thomas Morton's *Speed the Plough* (1800), the most famous character is Mrs. Grundy, whose name became a synonym for British respectability, and she never appears at all. In David Mamet's *Speed-the-Plow,* the most pervasive character is also offstage: the American movie audience. As in Morton's play, where characters are constantly guessing what Mrs. Grundy would think, Mamet's Hollywood hacks, who have their commercial credibility rather than their reputations to lose, assume that they know what will bring the moviegoers to the boxoffice: what brought them there last week. Their

> MAYBE THE TARGET IS NOT HOLLYWOOD, NOT AMERICAN BUSINESS, BUT THE AUDIENCE ITSELF"

low estimate of the public is confirmed by the weekly listing of movie grosses; in the most recent *Friday the Thirteenth* topped *Beetlejuice.* Anyone for *Rambo III?*

Mamet's up-from-the-mailroom dealers are rough diamonds—zircons, at least—who know each other so well that they can overlap one another's speeches, communicate in reiterated platitudes decorated with sometimes elegant obscenity. Bobby Gould (Joe Mantegna) has just become head of production at what we are to accept as a major studio and Charlie Fox (Ron Silver), who comes to him on his first day in power, has snagged a bankable star for a buddy movie he is trying to peddle. They agree to join forces, go onward and upward with the sellable schlock, but the path of true greed never runs smooth. Enter the woman, for that is the way it is with buddy movies and has been at least since *Gunga Din. Speed-the-Plow* is a Mamet variation on the buddy movie. His best plays (*American Buffalo, Glengarry Glen Ross*) are set in male enclaves, and *Sexual Perversity in Chicago* follows the buddy formula in its story. So does *Speed-the-Plow.* After the requisite feminine interruption, the two men go off together to face the studio head— like Flagg and Quirt hurrying to the front in *What Price Glory?*—and the woman is tossed aside.

If there is a difficulty in *Speed-the-Plow,* it lies with the woman in the case. It is not, as some reviewers have insisted, because Madonna is playing Karen. Her performance is not as flashily free as those of Mategna and Silver, but she does a creditable job with a character who—unlike Bobby and Charlie—is never clearly defined. At first she seems to be the dumb secretary stereotype, too dense to find the coffee machine, but at this stage she may be only a reflection of Bobby's attitude toward women. He accepts Charlie's bet that the he cannot seduce her. In her big scene in Act II, having read and presumably been won over by the book on

nuclear destruction that Bobby asked her to give "a courtesy read," she persuades him to present it to the studio head rather than the buddy script. She does so not by arguments, but by sleeping with him. In the last act, she has a new authority, a taste of power that leads her to the plural pronoun ("we have a meeting"), but if she were just another ambitious broad, as Charlie insists, she would not answer his direct question as she does, admitting that she only went to bed with Bobby to get the film made. That revelation frees Bobby, of his flirtation with art and social conscience and sends him back to his true calling as a junk merchant.

It is possible that Mamet intends Karen as an innocent for whom the true heart of Hollywood is as elusive as the coffee machine—just the person to be taken in by the "Eastern wimp" author's pretentious book. It sounds like the kind of work which fondles the annihilation of the world while it whimpers its dessicated whisper of hope. There is a marvelous moment in which Karen tries to use the book to resnare Bobby after he allies himself again with Charlie. She reads a ponderous paragraph and then, faced with defeat, insists that that is not the passage she has in mind and keeps flipping the pages hopelessly. Mamet seems to be using the book and Karen's naive embrace of it as a matter for satire, but there is a problem there too. Reviewers tended to describe the book as an "anti-radiation" novel, but it is called *Radiation* and, from what we hear of the argument, the author is using *radiation* and Mamet uses *decay* and *decadence* in his essays in *Writing in Restaurants,* as a necessary destructive stage to revitalization. Mamet's theory of decadence seems to me fair game for the satirist, but I am not sure that he is Bernard Shaw enough to guy his own ideas for the sake of the play.

Whether Karen's projected movie is a joke or a serious option for Hollywood or a comic suggestion that serious options are possible, it is rejected. Greed and vulgarity triumph. Yet Mamet has more in mind than a ritual chiding of Hollywood venality. In a group interview in the *New York Times* (May 16), Madonna called the play a metaphor: "it's not just about Hollywood. It's about life." Silver modified her metaphor by suggesting that this was still another of Mamet's examinations of American business: "You show me one person in business who decides to do something that's good if the sacrifice is their quarterly statement." The Mamet point of view is clear enough, but the play's successful borrowing of the buddy plot muddies the social theme. Bobby and Charlie are a reprehensible pair (each would sacrifice the other for an edge up), but Mategna and Silver give them so much energy, so much *chutzpah,* so much tacky charm that we find ourselves roofing for Bobby's return to chicanery. Maybe that is the point. Maybe the target is not Hollywood, not American business, but the audience itself.

Source: Gerald Weales, ''Rough Diamonds'' in *Commonweal,* Vol. CXV, no. 12, June 17, 1988, p. 371.

SOURCES

Brustein, Robert. Review of *Speed-the-Plow* in the *New Republic,* June 6, 1988, p. 29.

Henry, William A. III. ''Madonna Comes to Broadway'' in *Time,* May 16, 1988, pp. 98-99.

Hodgson, Moira. Review of *Speed-the-Plow* in the *Nation,* June 18, 1988, pp. 874-75.

Kroll, Jack. ''The Terrors of Tinseltown'' in *Newsweek,* in May 16, 1988, pp. 82-83.

Mamet, David. *Speed-the-Plow,* Grove Press, 1987.

Rich, Frank. '''Plow' and 'Butterfly': New Leads, New Light'' in the *New York Times,* September 23, 1988, p. C3.

Simon, John. Review of *Speed-the-Plow* in *New York,* October 3, 1988, p. 79.

Simon, John. ''Word Power'' in *New York,* May 16, 1988, p. 106.

FURTHER READING

Dean, Anne. *David Mamet: Language as Dramatic Action,* Fairleigh Dickinson University Press, 1990.
    This book discusses the role of language in Mamet's plays.

Lahr, John. ''Profile: Fortress Mamet'' in the *New Yorker,* November 17, 1997, pp., 70-82.
    This biographical article gives a sweeping synopsis of Mamet's life and work.

London, Todd. ''Mamet vs. Mamet: He's Playwright, Director, Theorist—and His Own Worst Enemy'' in *American Theatre,* July-August, 1996, p. 18.
    This article discusses Mamet's extraordinary use of language in his plays and contrasts this aspect of his work with his persona as director of his own plays.

Mamet, David. *The Cabin: Reminiscence and Diversions,* Random House, 1992.
    This book contains a series of autobiographical essays.

Staples, Brent. ''Mamet's House of Word Games'' in the *New York Times,* May 29, 1988, pp. B1, B24.
    This article discusses Mamet's extraordinary ear for language and how it affects dialogue in his plays.

Torch Song Trilogy

HARVEY FIERSTEIN

1982

Torch Song Trilogy is a play that straddles genres, existing as both a comedy and a melodrama. Harvey Fierstein's play opened at New York's Richard Allen Center in October, 1981, and moved to the Off-Broadway Actors Playhouse in January of 1982. The play opened on Broadway in June, 1983, at the Little Theatre and continued for a long and successful run, having won several awards, including two Antoinette ''Tony'' Perry Awards.

The work is semi-autobiographical; Fierstein used his own experience as a homosexual to bring a sense of authenticity to the play. Critics have remarked that the language and situations ring true and not only to homosexual audience members. Fierstein states in a brief author's note to the play that he hopes members of the audience will recognize themselves in the exchanges between lovers and the relationship between mother and child. The play's popularity among a wide range of viewers indicates that the playwright's intentions succeeded.

Torch Song Trilogy began as *The International Stud,* a one-act play that was produced Off-Off-Broadway in 1978. This early work was combined with two other one-act plays, *Fugue in a Nursery* (1979) and *Widows and Children First* (1979), to create *Torch Song Trilogy.* Each element of the play focuses on an important passage in the life of its protagonist, Arnold. Although the play is about homosexuals, at its heart it is a play about family, love, and survival. Fierstein's play appeared just as

AIDS was recognized as a major medical problem. His reinforcement of the importance of love in all relationships, hetero and gay, served to counter the attacks against homosexuals as promiscuous pleasure seekers.

AUTHOR BIOGRAPHY

Harvey Fierstein was born June 6, 1954, in Brooklyn, New York. He received a fine arts degree from the Pratt Institute in 1973, but even before finishing school he had embarked on a career in theatre. After working as a female impersonator, and while still a teenager, Fierstein earned his first role as an actor in 1971. In Andy Warhol's *Pork,* Fierstein played an overweight, asthmatic lesbian maid. He began writing his own plays in 1976. *International Stud* was written as a form of therapy after the end of a two-year romance.

Fierstein later combined the semi-autobiographical *Stud* with two other one-act plays, *Fugue in a Nursery* and *Widows and Children First,* to form *Torch Song Trilogy,* which debuted Off-Broadway in 1981. *Torch Song Trilogy,* which Fierstein also starred in, is the play with which he is most closely identified; it is considered his defining work. The play won a number of awards, including an Obie, two Drama Desk awards, and two Antionette "Tony" Perry Awards for best actor and best play.

Fierstein also won awards for his stage adaptation of the popular French comedy film *La Cage aux folles,* including Tonys for best musical and best book of a musical. His other plays include, *Safe Sex* and *Forget Him.* In 1988, Fierstein wrote the screenplay adaptation for *Torch Song Trilogy* and reprised his role of Arnold in the film. Fierstein has also written a television drama based on his play *Tidy Endings,* as well as a second television drama, *Kaddish and Old Men.*

In addition to writing plays, Fierstein has also gained a considerable reputation as an actor. He has appeared in many theatrical productions, including *Xircus: The Private Life of Jesus Christ, The Trojan Woman,* his own *Safe Sex* trilogy, and *The Haunted Host.* Films in which Fierstein has appeared include *Garbo Talks, Mrs. Doubtfire, Bullets over Broadway,* and *Independence Day.* Fierstein has received a Rockefeller Foundation Grant in Playwrighting, a Ford Foundation Grant for new American Plays, and a special Obie Award for writing and acting.

Harvey Fierstein

When not writing or acting, he enjoys painting, gardening, and cooking. Fierstein is also a committed activist for AIDS research and gay rights.

PLOT SUMMARY

Act I: The International Stud, scene 1
The play opens with Arnold reciting a monologue to the audience. This speech sets the stage for the remainder of the play, since Arnold talks of his loneliness and of his need to love and be loved. He relates his disappointments in love and what he is looking for in a partner.

Act I: The International Stud, scenes 2-3
Ed Reiss is introduced, with the scene consisting of Ed's side of a conversation in which he meets Arnold. They are attracted to one another, and the two decide to leave together.

Scene 3 follows a brief exchange, heard over the sounds of a radio, in which Ed and Arnold both confess how scared they are. The scene is a telephone confrontation between Arnold and Ed. It has been some months since the action in scene 2.

Arnold, who has been waiting impatiently for Ed to call, finally calls Ed, and it becomes clear that Ed is seeing someone else. The someone else turns out to be a woman, Laurel. Ed is trying to deny his homosexuality and form a heterosexual relationship. Arnold is very hurt and the conversation ends when Arnold slams down the phone.

Act I: The International Stud, scene 4

The setting is a bar, where Arnold has gone out of loneliness. He is talked into going into the back room where men have anonymous sex. Arnold is not comfortable with this type of encounter, but he tries it, his nervous chatter revealing his anxiety. Arnold has sex with a stranger in the dark. The scene ends with him trying to be positive about the experience.

Act I: The International Stud, scene 5

Ed has gone to see Arnold five months after their break-up. It is not clear what his purpose is, since he tells Arnold he is happy with the woman he is seeing. But it is also obvious that Ed's relationship with Laurel is not ideal. Ed hints at wanting Arnold back, and he appears to want both Arnold and Laurel in his life. Ed reveals to Arnold that the depth of his feelings for Arnold scares him and that he sees Arnold as an impediment to the kind of straight life he—and his parents—wants. The scene ends with Arnold asking himself what he should do.

Act II: Fugue in a Nursery, "prologue"

The scene is one year after Ed and Arnold's meeting at the end of Act I. It is a telephone conversation between Arnold and Laurel. She has called to invite him to the country for the weekend. Arnold initially resists, but his new lover, Alan, wants to go, so Arnold agrees. All the scenes in this act occur in a large circular bed with all four characters (Arnold, Alan, Ed, and Laurel), but the lights focus on only the two who are speaking at the moment.

Act II: Fugue in a Nursery, "Nursery: a fugue"

This is a brief conversation between Ed and Laurel, in which the audience learns that Ed is unhappy that Alan has come to the country with Arnold. Ed was in favor of Arnold coming, but Ed is jealous of his former lover's new companion.

Act II: Fugue in a Nursery, "Subject"

This scene is a conversation between Alan and Arnold, in which it is revealed that Alan is very young and that he has been a hustler (a young gay man who prostitutes himself to other men). Intermingled is conversation between Ed and Laurel. Both sets of conversation include sexual banter. Ed again states his resentment and jealousy of Alan. When the conversation returns to Arnold and Alan, Alan questions Arnold about his relationship with Ed. Arnold insists that there can never be anything between him and Ed again.

Act II: Fugue in a Nursery, "Codetta"

This scene is a continuation of the previous, with the discussion now focused on young men and older women. Both sets of partners are reading from the newspaper and quizzing one another about their sexual desires and loves.

Act II: Fugue in a Nursery, "Stretto 1"

In this scene both couples are engaged in conversation about what happened during a three hour meeting between Arnold and Ed earlier that afternoon. Laurel and Alan want details, though both Ed and Arnold insist that nothing sexual happened. Alan tells Arnold that Laurel made a pass at him, another hint that Laurel is attracted to gay men. Laurel tells Alan how she met Ed and the details about their relationship, including that they have both been in therapy together. Coincidentally, Ed has told Arnold the same thing during their afternoon together. All partners insist that they have open and sexually free relationships.

Act II: Fugue in a Nursery, "Counter Subject"

Laurel has been trying to get Arnold and Alan to accompany Ed and her to church, but they have resisted. As the brief scene continues, Laurel confesses to Ed her apprehensions about the weekend and that she really just wanted Arnold to come up so that Ed could choose her rather than him.

Act II: Fugue in a Nursery, "Stretto 2"

It is just after lunch and Arnold decides to help Laurel with the dishes, allowing them time for a private conversation. At the same time Alan and Ed go off for some private time together. In the hour that follows, Laurel tells Arnold that she thinks he is trying to get Ed back. She knows about the telephone conversations they have been having, but she thinks Arnold is the one trying to rekindle the relationship. Arnold tells her that it is Ed who is calling him. At the same time, Alan is telling Ed about how he and Arnold met. The scene ends with Ed seducing the younger man.

Act II: Fugue in a Nursery, ''Coda''

It is after the weekend, and Ed calls Arnold to tell him that Laurel has left him following a fight they had. He asks Arnold to check on her, since she has come into the city. When Arnold talks to Laurel, he learns that she has left because of the sexual encounter between Ed and Alan. She does not realize that Arnold was unaware of Alan's betrayal. The scene ends with a confrontation between Alan and Arnold in which they both admit that they do not want an open relationship. Alan has not liked Arnold's trips to the back room of the bar for anonymous sex, and Arnold does not like Alan's hustling. Although Alan has been saying all along that he loves Arnold, Arnold has been afraid to commit to the relationship.

Act II: Fugue in a Nursery, ''Epilogue''

Laurel has come to visit Arnold. She brings a wedding present for Alan's dog, since Alan and Arnold have decided to be ''married.'' She also comes to tell Arnold that she and Ed are getting married and to ask him not to say anything to Ed that might cause him to renege on the marriage. At the end of the scene, Arnold sings a song about the end of a love affair.

Act III: Widows and Children First, scene 1

It is five years later, and Alan has died. Arnold has taken in a young fifteen-year old boy, David, that he and Alan were going to adopt. Ed has left Laurel and is staying with Arnold, temporarily. Laurel has called Ed, and only his side of the conversation is heard. It is clear that he is not planning on returning to the marriage. Arnold tells Ed that a social worker is coming to visit to determine Arnold's suitability as a parent for David. It turns out that Arnold's mother is also coming for a visit, and David is all dressed up to meet his prospective grandmother.

Ed approaches Arnold about the possibility of getting back together as a couple, but Arnold is resistant. Arnold's mother does not know about David as a prospective adopted son, she thinks he is Arnold's new roommate. David leaves to go to school and Ed leaves also. Arnold's mother enters. Arnold's mother quizzes him about Ed's presence in the apartment. She believes in the sanctity of marriage and thinks that Ed should go back to his wife. She also states her disapproval of Arnold's homosexuality. David enters and for a few moments Mrs. Beckoff thinks that her son has a child-lover. The scene ends with David revealing that his last name is Beckoff and that he is Arnold's son.

Act III: Widows and Children First, scene 2

Although Mrs. Beckoff and David spend the afternoon together, she is under the impression that the arrangement is temporary and that David will be going to another set of foster parents in a few weeks. When it becomes obvious that David's stay is permanent, there is a terrible fight between mother and son. She does not think Arnold's lifestyle is suitable for raising a child and the two explode, saying all the things they have been feeling and concealing for years. The audience also learns how Alan died. He was murdered by a group of gay-bashers with baseball bats. The scene ends with Arnold telling his mother to leave.

Act III: Widows and Children First, scene 3

At the beginning of this scene, David tells Ed how he met Arnold and about how lonely Arnold has been without a partner. But he also tells Ed that Arnold has been secluding himself from any possible relationship. When Arnold joins them, Ed leaves, and David tells Arnold that he needs to share his life with a partner.

Act III: Widows and Children First, scene 4

It is early morning and Ed and Arnold are talking. Ed again approaches Arnold with the idea that they get back together, but Arnold is still resistant. Ed is trying to tell Arnold that he loves him when David enters. David reassures Ed that Arnold will change his mind, that he always does. Indeed, within a few moments, Arnold indicates he may be willing to consider Ed's offer of love.

Mrs. Beckoff, who could not get a plane in the middle of the night, is still in the apartment. She enters the room, having thought about the argument from the previous evening. In a brief exchange with Arnold, she expresses a reserved approval, or at least acceptance, of her son's life-style. She also offers some ideas about how to grieve for the loss of a spouse. Since she had never accepted Alan as Arnold's spouse, it is a big step for her. The play ends with a reconciliation between mother and son.

CHARACTERS

Alan

Alan is a handsome young man, eighteen-years old, who models and aspires to be an actor. He enters into a relationship with Arnold following Arnold's break-up with Ed. He is considerably younger than Arnold, and he is accustomed to being wanted for his looks. Alan is a hustler, who has always been able to make money selling sex.

Arnold Beckoff

Arnold is the central character of the play. He first appears in *The International Stud* segment. It is Arnold who begins the play with a monologue in which he reveals his loneliness and his desire for a lover who will commit to him totally. Arnold finds Ed and the two begin a loving and passionate relationship, but Ed is tormented by guilt over being gay. After Ed leaves Arnold for a heterosexual relationship, he finds Alan, a much younger lover. They commit to a "marriage," but Alan is murdered in a street killing five years later.

Arnold continues with a plan he and Alan had to adopt a child, and David is placed with Arnold as a foster child. Finally, in *Widows and Children First,* Arnold confronts his mother and the two open up for the first time, but not before a terrible argument that nearly splits the family. In the end, Arnold is finally able to accept his mother and the possibility that Ed may once again have a place in his life.

Mrs. Beckoff

Mrs. Beckoff is Arnold's widowed mother. She disapproves of her son's homosexuality and continues to hope that he will find a nice girl to marry. She arrives to visit and finds David, who she did not know was to be Arnold's adopted son. Mrs. Beckoff and Arnold finally confront their differences and find a sense of resolution. At the play's end, she indicates a willingness to accept both Arnold's homosexuality and his adoption of a gay teenager.

Lady Blues

Lady Blues sings the songs that separate the scenes in *The International Stud.* She has no real role, but her songs help establish mood and in some ways act as a Greek chorus, enhancing the action and dialogue that occur on stage. Her songs are not intended to comment upon the action, but are left open to the interpretation of the audience.

David

David is a fifteen-year-old foster child that Arnold considers his son and who he wants to adopt. David is gay and has been abused by his parents. He has been in other foster homes and has been placed with Arnold so that he can have the example of an adult with a positive attitude toward homosexuality. David is bright and wise beyond his years. It is also clear that he loves and respects Arnold very much.

Laurel

Laurel is the woman Ed meets while he is still seeing Arnold and who later becomes Ed's lover. She is in her mid-thirties and has been involved in many relationships—though none of them have worked to her satisfaction; every man that she has been involved with was either bisexual or married. She seems to see Ed as a last chance for happiness, although it is also clear that she loves him. It is her idea to bring Arnold and Alan to the farm for a weekend getaway. She does this in an effort to prove to herself that Ed will choose her over Arnold.

Ed Reiss

Ed first appears in *The International Stud* as Arnold's love interest, and although he loves Arnold, he wants to belong to straight society, thus his heterosexual relationship with Laurel. By the end of *Fugue in a Nursery,* Ed and Laurel are engaged. Ed reappears at the beginning of *Widows and Children First.* He has separated from Laurel and the audience later learns that he has come back to Arnold looking for a reconciliation.

THEMES

Betrayal

Betrayal is a central theme in *Torch Song Trilogy,* since much of the play focuses on Ed's betrayal of Arnold's love. Ed loves Arnold but cannot accept his own homosexuality. In a very real sense, Ed betrays himself as well. He hurts the person he loves because he feels he must live as a heterosexual, fulfilling his parent's expectations. His betrayal of Laurel is also an issue, since he leaves her emotionally, long before he physically leaves their marriage.

Early in the play, Ed approaches Arnold, and although he wants to continue with Laurel, and in fact live with her, he also wants Arnold in his life. Ed wants the best of both worlds, Laurel and Arnold; he ends up betraying the two people who love him. Arnold is so wounded by Ed's treachery that he fears loving Alan, who certainly loves Arnold. It is only after a sexual betrayal that Arnold realizes that he and Alan need to have a more committed relationship. By the end of the play, Arnold is making his first tentative moves toward trusting Ed again.

Loneliness

The play opens with Arnold's monologue on loneliness. He wants a committed relationship with another person who will love him as much as he loves that person. Arnold is so lonely after Ed abandons him that he seeks out anonymous sex in the back room of a bar. Laurel has also been lonely; she meets Ed on a blind date and bonds with him. Having been abandoned by several previous lovers, Laurel views Ed as a means to end her loneliness. She agrees to a relationship in which Ed can still see other people—namely other men.

Loneliness is an important theme in *Torch Song Trilogy* because it illustrates how forlorn an existence can be when behavior does not fit certain defined social parameters. Because Arnold is gay, he feels isolated after Alan's death, since, as he points out, people do not think that queers can have feelings or grieve for a lover.

Love and Passion

That homosexuals can share love, passion, and a depth of feeling is an important theme in this play, since all too often the nature of homosexual love is misunderstood. Fierstein makes it clear to the audience that love offers the same joy and happiness and pain to gays as it does to heterosexual partners. Arnold's fight with Ed when he learns of Ed's betrayal sounds much like the argument that any other couple would have. Laurel's fears that Ed will love Arnold more echo the fears that any person might have when confronted with their partner's previous lover. And the nature of the love-hate relationship between mother and son is based on the same kinds of misunderstandings that any child and

MEDIA ADAPTATIONS

- *Torch Song Trilogy* was made into a film in 1988. The screenplay was written by Fierstein and directed by Paul Bogart. The film stars many of the same actors from the stage production. Fierstein reprises his role as Arnold and Matthew Broderick, who originally played David on stage, plays Alan. Anne Bancroft plays Mrs. Beckoff and Brian Kerwin plays Ed. What is notable about the adaptation is that many characters who are only discussed in the play actually appear in the film.

parent might experience. This play reveals to audience that love is the same whether it is between two men or between a man and a woman.

Prejudice and Tolerance

The violent death of Alan illustrates the danger of prejudice. He is beaten to death by a crowd of baseball bat-wielding bigots who fear what they cannot understand. The prejudice against gays is further illustrated by Arnold's mother who thinks that he cannot adopt a son because of his sexual orientation. She thinks that Arnold will teach David to be gay, and when she is told that David is gay, she responds with surprise that Arnold's conversion of the boy only took six months. Prejudice against gays is also the reason that Ed wants to have a girlfriend and later a wife. He thinks that a woman will provide him with a level of social acceptance and protection against prejudice. His sexuality is hidden in the closet because of his fear of prejudice.

Sex Roles

There is a lot of humor in the sex roles assumed in this play, especially in the last few scenes with David. David has several opportunities to joke about Arnold as his new mother, and he also jokes that with Arnold and Ed together, he would have a mother and father. Many of Arnold's dreams center on his desire to have a marriage as stable and happy

TOPICS FOR FURTHER STUDY

- Discuss the impact of AIDS on the gay population in the United States.

- Consider Arnold's pending adoption of David. Research the options for gay partners who wish to have children.

- Using both the relationship between Ed and Laurel and the relationship between Arnold and his mother, describe Fierstein's depiction of the tensions between homosexuals and heterosexuals.

- Although it is a comedy, there are many tragic elements present in *Torch Song Trilogy*. Explore this blending of humor and tragedy and discuss its effectiveness in relating Fierstein's themes.

- Investigate the legal problems that gay marriages face. What kind of limitations do the law, society, and custom present to gay couples?

as his parents. He wants a family and a home and that same kind of stability, but he states that his dream has only a few minor alterations. Arnold's dream substitutes male for female. He and a partner, whom he will love as much as his mother loved his father, will build the same kind of stable relationship that heterosexual partners enjoy.

Violence and Cruelty

Fierstein illustrates how dangerous the world can be for homosexuals when he tells the story about the death of his lover, Alan. Alan dies off-stage, between the second and third act, but his death casts a shadow over the last third of the play, since Arnold has now been left alone. That Alan was murdered on the street, in a violent attack provoked by the mere fact that he was a homosexual, illustrates the dangers for anyone who does not fit prejudiced people's idea of normal. Although the audience never sees the violence onstage, the effect becomes part of the story, and the telling of the details provides a horrifying moment in the last act of the play. Arnold uses the site of the attack as

a daily reminder of this violence when he rents an apartment overlooking the place where Alan was killed.

STYLE

Character

A character is a person in a dramatic work. The actions of each character are what constitute the story. Character can also include the idea of a particular individual's morality. Characters can range from simple stereotypical figures to more complex multi-faceted ones. Characters may also be defined by personality traits. "Characterization" is the process of creating a life-like person from an author's imagination. To accomplish this the author provides the character with personality traits that help define who he will be and how he will behave in a given situation. For instance, in the beginning of the play, Arnold tells the audience how important it is for him to find a partner who will love him freely and commit to a relationship. When he meets Ed and is later hurt by him, the audience is already aware of the depth of Arnold's pain, since it has already been stated how important love is to him.

Coda

A coda is a conclusion. It usually restates, summarizes, or integrates the themes of the literary work. In the case of *Torch Song Trilogy,* Fierstein uses a coda in the *Fugue in a Nursery* segment as a division in the act.

Drama

A drama is often defined as any work designed to be presented on the stage. It consists of a story, of actors portraying characters, and of action. Historically, drama can also consist of tragedy, comedy, religious pageant, and spectacle. In modern usage, the word drama is used as an adjective to describe a certain kind of play, typically one that explores serious topics and themes but does not achieve the same level as tragedy.

Fugue

A fugue is most often defined as a musical composition in which different parts successively repeat the theme. This is the case in Act II, when each set of partners repeat both the action and the

Playwright Fierstein as Arnold Beckoff in his alter ego, drag queen Virginia Hamm

dialogue in a type of round—almost like the repetition of a chorus in a song.

Plot

Plot refers to the pattern of events that occur within a play. Generally plots have a beginning, a middle, and a conclusion, but they may also be a series of episodes with a loose thematic connection, such as the epic plays of Bertolt Brecht (*Mother Courage and Her Children*). Basically, the plot provides the author with the means to explore primary themes. Students are often confused between the two terms; but themes explore ideas, and plots simply relate what happens in a very obvious manner. Thus the plot of *Torch Song Trilogy* is the story of how Arnold finally finds love. But the themes are those of loneliness, commitment, and love, what Arnold must experience and learn before arriving at the play's happy ending.

Scene

Scenes are subdivisions of an act. A scene may change when all of the main characters either enter or exit the stage. But a change of scene may also indicate a change in time or place. In *Torch Song Trilogy,* the third scene of Act I occurs several months later, and thus, indicates the passage of time in the play.

Setting

The time, place, and culture in which the action of the play takes place is called the setting. The elements of setting may include geographic location, physical or mental environments, prevailing cultural attitudes, or the historical period in which the action takes place. The locations for Fierstein's play are varied, but they include his apartment, a bar, and a country home. The action occurs over a period of several years.

Stretto

A stretto is a musical term for when the subject and the answer overlap. Fierstein uses a stretto in *Fugue in a Nursery* as a division in the act.

HISTORICAL CONTEXT

In 1981, when *Torch Song Trilogy* opened, the first cases of Acquired Immune Deficiency Syndrome (AIDS) were becoming important medical news. When AIDS was discovered, it was soon recog-

COMPARE
&
CONTRAST

- **1981:** The prime interest rate is at 21.5% and President Reagan ask for $13 billion in government spending cuts. The biggest victims of these cuts are social welfare programs.

  Today: The prime interest rate is 7.5% and the federal budget is as close to being balanced as it has been at any time in the last thirty years. Despite the relative prosperity, social programs are still in danger of being terminated. Many conservative politicians want to do away entirely with the funding of arts programs and many forms of social welfare.

- **1981:** AIDS cases are beginning to be reported. Doctors in New York and in San Francisco are seeing an increasing number of new cases of this especially deadly disease which attacks the immune system, rendering the victim unable to fight off even simple infections. Within the next few years, nearly 60% of all cases will end in death.

  Today: People with AIDS are living much longer, thanks to the discovery of new medications and a greater understanding of the body's immune system. Funding for research has made a critical difference in treating a disease that while still incurable is now treatable.

- **1981:** The world's population reaches 4.5 billion people. Female infanticide is on the increase in the People's Republic of China, where parents are limited in the number of children they can have and boys are more desirable than girls.

  Today: Female infanticide is still a problem in China, where male children are still greatly prized, but a greater effort is now being made to place infant Chinese girls for adoption in Western countries. The biggest benefit from this is that single, and often gay, parents can now adopt a child more easily.

---

nized as deadly and, at the time, untreatable. It was unknown exactly how the disease was spread. Public fear was probably similar to the panic that spread across Europe in the fourteenth century when the Black Plague claimed every third person as a victim.

Since the public had no real understanding about how the disease was transmitted, they focused on the early victims, who were largely homosexual men. Homosexuals were unfairly blamed for both the cause and spread of the virus and thus became the victims of even greater prejudice. Information that was disseminated by the press included data on the disease's growth pattern—including the assertion that gay bath-houses, where anonymous sex could be enjoyed, was responsible for much of the spread of the disease. In response, many people began to think that gays where preoccupied with promiscuity, anonymous sex with many different partners. The rumor spread that committed monogamous relationships were a rarity among gays.

One of the social points that Fierstein makes in *Torch Song Trilogy* is that gay men really desire the same committed relationships that heterosexuals enjoy. Through Arnold's speeches, the audience understands that love is the same regardless of the participants' genders. When Arnold tries to equate love with anonymous sex and fails, the play further reinforces the idea that love and sexuality are partnered with commitment.

Fear of AIDS also meant that homosexuals were even less likely to become accepted by mainstream America. In the 1980s, President Ronald Reagan squashed attempts by the government to fund additional research into the causes and cures of AIDS. He viewed the disease as solely a gay epidemic and saw no point in channeling large sums of money into research. It would be years before the government would start to fund research and only after it became clear that heterosexuals were also acquiring the disease.

The debate on the transmission of AIDS and funding of research—widely covered, sometimes to sensational effects, by the world media—fed into the public's paranoia that AIDS was a death sentence too easily caught. People became so afraid that violence against homosexuals increased. Another unfortunate side-effect of AIDS's proliferation was that the nation's blood supply had became contaminated by unwitting donors infected with the virus. As a result, the disease was spread to a number of new victims; where previous cases could be traced to either intravenous drug use or unprotected sex, these new victims became infected through routine blood transfusions. Especially at risk were hemophiliacs, people whose blood can not properly clot and who required frequent infusions. A young hemophiliac, Ryan White, became infected with AIDS by such a transfusion. His experience with prejudice regarding the disease—he was kicked out of his school solely because of his illness—made him a poster child for the movement to educate the public and humanize the disease.

White was not the only child to experience prejudice. When other children became victims of AIDS, they also became victims of the public fear. These infected children were banned from schools and from neighborhood businesses, and they were forbidden to enter other children's homes. Rational people became irrational and were afraid to touch anything that an infected individual have touched. Parents did not want their children to breath the same air as a child with AIDS, and they petitioned schools, sometimes violently, to have an infected child removed from school. Early in the epidemic, scientists made it clear that the only way to transmit the virus was through contact with infected blood, touching or breathing the air of an AIDS victim posed no threat. Despite this fact, irrationality and fear won out over common sense; people remained prejudiced and fearful of AIDS sufferers well into the 1990s.

The largest benefit of the public's acceptance of *Torch Song Trilogy* was that Fierstein was able to demonstrate to a large number of people the stupidity and hurt that comes from prejudice—and violence—against gays.

CRITICAL OVERVIEW

Reviews for *Torch Song Trilogy* were generally positive with most of the negative commentary focusing on the play's considerable length (four hours). In his review for the *New York Times,* Mel Gussow called Fierstein's play an "illuminating portrait of a man who laughs, and makes us laugh, to keep from collapsing." Fierstein's portrayal of Arnold (while other actors have assumed the role, the playwright is the actor most closely associated with Arnold) is often cited by reviewers as the centerpiece of the play. Gussow echoed this sentiment, equating Arnold and Fierstein as a single person. Gussow noted that he found himself "enjoying Arnold's wit—he has the pithy humor of a Fran Lebowitz—at the same time I was moved by his dilemma. He is a man of principle who compulsively plays the fool."

Gussow also observed that "the author is so accomplished at playing Arnold that he cannot resist an extra flourish or an easy wisecrack." Of the play, Gussow noted that the "sociological implications are complex and the author treats them with equanimity, demonstrating that the flamboyant Arnold is truly a reflection of his assertive mother, which is why they are destined to spend their lives at loggerheads." Arnold is, stated Gussow, in his own torch song, and "the role is inseparable from the actor-author. Gussow concluded that "Mr. Fierstein's self-incarnation is an act of compelling virtuosity."

In her review of *Torch Song Trilogy,* the *New York Post*'s Marilyn Stasio began by asking, "Who could resist Arnold Beckoff? He's more comforting than your mother, more understanding than your shrink, and funnier than your puppy." Stasio declared that Arnold's "lovable drag queen is a triumphant affirmation of the romantic soul in a cynical age." This assessment was seconded by Don Nelson of the *Daily News,* who noted that Fierstein's hoarse, gravelly voice is "the ideal vehicle for the character of Arnold." One of the strengths of the play, according to Nelson, is that the action "arises from contradictions that we also face as humans rather than as labels like homo or hetero."

The play's wide appeal is something that Jack Kroll mentioned in his review in *Newsweek.* Kroll argued that *Torch Song Trilogy* is a play for the whole family. He stated that Fierstein's play is "the most truly conservative play to come along in years . . . [with its commitment] to the classic values of fidelity, family, loving, parenting et al." Kroll added that the play is "very funny, poignant and unabashedly entertaining." Of special note, said Kroll, is "Fierstein's ability to combine almost nonstop humor with a complex texture of emotional levels.'' Kroll also commended the other members of the cast, stating that they do ''absolute justice to this play, which is both far out and central to the civilized values of loving and caring.''

Torch Song Trilogy's praises were also sung in Clive Barnes's review, which appeared in the *New York Post*. Barnes stated that ''Fierstein has written a devastatingly comic play with just the right resonances. It is a play about love and the merciless mayhem love wrecks.'' Noting that the play is just longer than four hours, Barnes nevertheless observed that ''it is a marathon very much worth running. It is—through Fierstein's fluent invention and buoyant humor—strangely untiring.''

Not all reviews were so positive, however. Gerald Clarke's mixed review in *Time* began by stating that the play ''is too long . . . it is often inconsistent; and for embarrassingly long periods it becomes as mawkish as an afternoon soap opera.'' But Clark also found that Fierstein ''has created characters so vivid and real that they linger in the mind, talking the night away, long after the lights have been turned out.'' Referring to Fierstein's Arnold, as ''arresting,'' Clarke declared that he ''seduces the audience.'' One major problem, said Clarke, is that there is ''enough material in act three to construct another separate three-act play, and consequently, there are too many rough edges.'' Despite his reservations, Clarke conceded, ''with all its flaws . . . *Torch Song Trilogy* is a remarkable achievement.''

CRITICISM

Sheri E. Metzger

Metzger is a Ph.D. specializing in literature and drama at the University of New Mexico. In this essay, she discusses the universal appeal of Harvey Fierstein's Torch Song Trilogy *and the nature of audience involvement in the play's success.*

When *Torch Song Trilogy* opened Off-Off-Broadway in the late fall of 1981, Harvey Fierstein's comedy became the first commercially successful play to openly feature homosexuality as both star and theme. Fierstein's play is a semi-autobiographical story. Thus homosexuality is central to the play,

since it is an essential part of the playwright's life; Fierstein takes special care in the opening lines to make clear his identity as a homosexual. But he does not announce he is gay; instead, Arnold/Fierstein offers a monologue that offers his position on any number of important issues: beauty, youth, love, dating, commitment. And while he never says, ''I am gay,'' the words are there, unspoken and just as visible as if he had held a sign up for the audience.

Indeed, Fierstein's stage mother's complaint in the final act is that Arnold's homosexuality is a part of every conversation. She tells him, ''You're obsessed by it. You're not happy unless everyone is talking about it.'' This is true of Fierstein's play, as well. The audience leaves the theatre equally obsessed with the topic and continues to talk about it. In his commentary on the play in *Maske und Kothurn: Internationale Beitrage zur Theatrewissenschaft*, Willliam Green attempted to determine the elements in Fierstein's play that made it ''Broadway's first successful play on the subject [homosexuality]'' Green offered the theory that it is Fierstein's positioning of homosexuality as normal and accepted that accounts for the play's popularity.

Instead of approaching his play as a means to make an abnormal behavior acceptable, Fierstein ''has not taken the negative view . . . but has built on the positive view of his own life,'' according to Green. Love, breakups, pain, loss, and death are all part of loving someone. Fierstein makes it clear that these events are the same for homosexuals as they are for heterosexuals. He uses comedy because it is an almost subversive form of theatre that can entice and seduce an audience before they are aware of it. Through the playwright's wit and his character's entertaining humor, the audience comes to appreciate and love Arnold and the characters in his life as human beings not stereotypes.

The viewer cannot help it; Fierstein insists upon it. Arnold's forthright manner and humor force the audience to realize that Arnold is no different from a heterosexual person; the basic truth that homosexuality is not abnormal is powerfully transmitted to the audience. His grief at Alan's death rings true for any person who has ever lost a loved one. He wins the audience's sympathy when he tries to explain to his mother that his ''widowing'' is much the same for him as her experience in losing her husband. Green declared that ''Fierstein uses it [homosexuality] to make a larger statement about the joys and the pain and the struggle which are the

WHAT
DO I READ
NEXT?

- Plato's *Phaedrus,* written c. 388 B.C., is a dialogue about love and passion. Although designed as an exploration of the subject of rhetoric, the examples used by Plato and Socrates are based on love. Plato's *Symposium,* written c. 370 B.C., explores the nature of beauty and examines the male response to male beauty.

- Fierstein's *Safe Sex* is a trilogy of plays that was first performed in 1987. These combined one-act plays deal with the problems that homosexuals face when AIDS becomes a factor in dating and intimacy.

- *M. Butterfly* (1988), by David Hwang is a play about a French diplomat who falls in love with an opera singer. The singer is a man disguised as a woman. Throughout the many years of their affair, the diplomat claimed not to recognize that his lover was male or that the singer was really a Chinese spy.

- Oscar Wilde's *Picture of Dorian Gray,* published in 1891, is an early gothic romance about homosexual love that scandalized the British public when it was published.

lot in life for most human beings—straight or gay.'' This is why audiences, whether homosexual or heterosexual, enjoyed *Torch Song Trilogy,* and it is why audiences found a way to identify with the central protagonist—a necessary act for any work to succeed. Quite simply, Arnold's loves and disappointments are the same as everyone else.

This is the same point that Madeleine Cahill made in *The Conception, Realization, and Reception of a Controversial Film,* a thesis on the film adaptation of Fierstein's play. Although she is discussing the film, the same points are applicable to the theatrical staging of *Torch Song Trilogy.* The audience, according to Cahill, cannot sit through a performance uninvolved. We cannot simply sit and watch; Fierstein will not allow that; he beckons us into his room, onto the stage, into his life. Cahill argued that ''we are being addressed directly, engaged in Arnold's life, forced to identify with him because of his frank expressions of human pain and longing.'' Although, Cahill was discussing only the opening scene in Fierstein's play where Arnold turns to the audience and tells us of his desires and dreams, this expression of sharing with the audience is present throughout the play. In performance, Fierstein often addressed the audience as if he were simply living his life up on the stage. But even beyond that, he is using a ''blend of pathos and

comedy,'' as Cahill noted, to keep the audience involved in his life. Before much of the play is completed, we are already involved. We already care about this character.

Fierstein uses our feelings toward Arnold to involve us as sympathetic participants in the gay issues that he is promoting. If the audience cares about Arnold, then we must also care about prejudice and anti-gay violence, and we also care about the conflicts between heterosexuals and homosexuals. In a review of *Torch Song Trilogy* for *Theatre,* Kim Powers drew an analogy between the mother-son conflict and the lines that separate gays from straights. Powers pointed out that when, in the last act, Arnold and Mrs. Beckoff argue, ''much of the anger from both combatants can be excused by the heat of battle, but a new and different truthfulness has been uncovered. The eternal bond (Mother/Son) has become less important than the sexual, societal conflict (homosexual/heterosexual).''

Instead of being simply a mother-son fight, their argument becomes an debate between homosexuality and heterosexuality. Initially, Mrs. Beckoff cannot find a way to compare her thirty-five year heterosexual marriage to Arnold and Alan's five year homosexual union. She cannot conceive of the loss being the same. She represents those people who would say, ''everybody knows that queers

"WHERE *TORCH SONG TRILOGY* DEALS WITH ACCEPTANCE BETWEEN HETEROSEXUALS AND HOMOSEXUALS, THE PLAYS THAT FOLLOWED IT DEAL WITH SURVIVAL"

don't matter! Queers don't love." The irony of these words, is that the audience knows just the opposite, the preceding portions of the play have proven it. When Mrs. Beckoff can finally admit to her son's pain and loss, the bridge between homosexuality and heterosexuality has been crossed—at least for a few moments. Fierstein forces the audience into accepting his homosexuality just as he forces his mother into some level of acceptance.

Powers stated that "The extremity of Fierstein's personality forces some sort of judgment [from the audience]. He is abrasive, shocking, flamboyant; the audience must resolve, or at least come to understand, any discomfort it may be feeling with an effeminate man. It must see beyond the bitchy gestures to the basic issues." Fierstein succeeds in opening the gay community to the heterosexual world. He puts the pain, the alienation and isolation, the loss, and the issues on stage, and he dares the audience to care. In the end, we do care. Arnold's love and fear and pain are very much the same for him as they are for anyone who has ever taken a chance on love. His portrayal of homosexuality as an emotional equal to heterosexuality helps to remove much of the fear that the uninformed may have about homosexual love.

In many ways, *Torch Song Trilogy* serves as a lonely sentinel to the past. The same year Feirstein's play was staged in New York, a new disease was being unmasked, starting in the gay communities of New York and San Francisco. Suddenly, doctors began noticing an unusually high number of men succumbing to diseases of the auto-immune system. The disease was named Acquired Immune Deficiency Syndrome (AIDS). It would forever change the homosexual community and it would change the way theatre and film approached gay issues. In a discussion of Fierstein's subsequent play *Safe Sex,*

Gregory Gross said in the *Journal of American Culture* that plays about gays have changed because of AIDS; there is a division in the theatre. Gross stated that "Gay writers know that both drama-time and real-time break down into pre-AIDS and post-AIDS."

Where *Torch Song Trilogy* deals with acceptance between heterosexuals and homosexuals, the plays that followed it deal with survival. How do gays confront a disease so insidious, so deadly? Gross stated that these new plays are "history plays that are performed in the midst of their own history." But that is true for *Torch Song Trilogy,* as well. The history of conflict between homosexuals and heterosexuals is more involved that a violent murder on a New York City street or in the argument between mother and son, but Fierstein uses these examples because the nature of their intimacy can involve the audience.

Gays have been the targets of violence in the past. They were victims of German leader Adolf Hitler and the Nazi death camps during the Holocaust of World War II. The Holocaust included the deaths of homosexuals, just as it included many other disenfranchised groups. But even before the Nazis made them a target, homosexuals were targeted by laws intended to punish or marginalize their behavior. British playwright and writer, Oscar Wilde (*The Importance of Being Earnest*), was imprisoned for "homosexual offenses" in 1895, thus proving that talent and notoriety offer no protection from persecution. But an audience for a play needs an emotional center with which to identify. They can sometimes be convinced of an issue's importance through emotional identification with the protagonist.

The history of Wilde's trial and imprisonment will no doubt appeal to a small, select audience, but Arnold's comedic travails will capture our hearts, as well as our intellects. Audiences need to belong to Fierstein if he is to make progress in his desires to promote gay issues, especially progress in the fight against AIDS. Gross argued that each new play about gays "laments the loss of a better time before the AIDS abyss." But, in truth, even pre-AIDS plays lament the lack of equality and acceptance that has been so long denied to homosexuals.

Source: Sheri E. Metzger, for *Drama for Students,* Gale, 1999.

Brian D. Johnson

In this review of the 1989 film adaptation of Torch Song Trilogy, *which Fierstein adapted from*

A scene from the film adaptation of Torch Song Trilogy, *with Fierstein as Arnold and Matthew Broderick as Alan (in the stage play, Broderick played Arnold's adopted son, David)*

his play text, Johnson praises the playwright for shedding light on "social terrain rarely explored in American movies."

It is a film about an eccentric Jewish drag queen struggling for some semblance of a normal life in New York City. It is also a funny, poignant and surprisingly wholesome tale of romantic love and old-fashioned family values. It could *almost* be a Hollywood movie—but it is not. Although *Torch Song Trilogy* as a stage drama captivated audiences on Broadway for two years—winning Tony awards for best play and best actor in 1983—Hollywood producers were nervous about bringing it to the screen. They proposed a sanitized version of the play with the sex cut out. They suggested Dustin Hoffman or Richard Dreyfuss for the lead role. And at least one studio executive said that *Torch Song Trilogy*'s 1970s-era "gay esthetic had been rendered obsolete by AIDS.

But Harvey Fierstein, the author and star of the play, persisted. He was encouraged by both Hoff-

"TORCH SONG PURGES
CYNICISM AND BURNS WITH A
CLEAR, HOT FLAME"

man and Dreyfuss: after seeing the play, the two actors individually told Fierstein that he himself was the best man for the part onscreen. Then, with the help of New Line Cinema, an independent U.S. producer, Fierstein wrote and starred in a movie made on his own terms. With a story that spans the years 1971 to 1980—before AIDS had begun to spread through the homosexual community—the film makes no mention of the virus. And Fierstein expresses outrage at suggestions by some critics that the omission of AIDS makes his story outdated. In Toronto last week to attend a benefit première of the movie for local AIDS groups, he told *Maclean's,* "Very well-meaning people have gone out of their way to mention AIDS in every review of the movie when it's not even an issue." Added Fierstein: "It's heinous to suggest that gay people have no issue other than AIDS."

One issue that the movie does deal with—aside from the right to be unapologetically gay—is the importance of being honest in matters of intimacy. Arnold (Fierstein), who performs in nightclubs as a female impersonator, is glibly pessimistic about his emotional future. He wants a loving relationship, and *Torch Song* encompasses his frustrating attempts to find one. The first is with Ed (Brian Kerwin), a confused bisexual who sleeps with men as a diversion from his romance with Laurel (Karen Young). The second is with Alan (Matthew Broderick), a pretty-boy prostitute who settles down with Arnold. Meanwhile, Arnold's most tempestuous relationship is with his caustic mother (Anne Bancroft).

Petulant, narcissistic and immature, Arnold is not an especially sympathetic character. And his liaisons with both Ed and Alan are unconvincing. As Alan, Broderick gives the movie its few faint sparks of erotic energy. In the original stage version, Broderick played David, the 15-year-old orphan adopted by Arnold, and that Broadway debut in 1982 led to starring roles in such movies as *Ferris Bueller's Day Off* (1986). Broderick fills the screen

with charm, but his character seems contrived, a fantasy figure all too eager to comply with Arnold's romantic game plan. In no uncertain terms, Arnold sets the agenda: "There are a couple of things we better get straight," he says. "A) I want children; B) If anyone asks, *I'm* the pretty one."

Fierstein's trenchant wit continually redeems the movie. But Arnold has a capacity for self-dramatization and self-mockery that tends to overwhelm everyone around him. Too often, the other characters seem like accessories in a would-be one-man show. The crucial exception is Arnold's mother. Although she represents all the prejudices that her son detests, she is also the only person with enough vitriol to penetrate his self-centred universe. In a cathartic series of verbal brawls between her and Arnold, *Torch Song* finally purges cynicism and burns with a clear, hot flame. Rising to the occasion, Bancroft breaks the tight Jewish-mother caricature that confines her in earlier scenes and delivers a heartrending performance. She fights guilt with guilt. "You cheated me outta your life," she tells Arnold, "then blamed me for not being there."

The script has the keenly whittled quality of stage drama. But the movie's naturalistic look and chronological structure depart radically from the play, which relied on flashbacks. In the opening shot, the camera sweeps from the skyline of Manhattan, down to the equally grey gravestones of a sprawling cemetery, and finally settles on the house in Brooklyn where Arnold grew up. Although such cinematic flourishes are rare, director Paul Bogart has at least succeeded in re-creating *Torch Song* as a movie in its own right rather than simply committing a play to film.

Since writing *Torch Song* in 1976, Fierstein has talked about it so much that, in an interview, an understandable fatigue darkens his voice, already a dry baritone. There are obvious parallels between Fierstein and his sardonic character in *Torch Song.* Explaining that his story is only semiautobiographical, Fierstein said, "I'm not as naïve as Arnold, not as moonstruck—Arnold is really a very specific personality, not a gay Everyman." *Torch Song* indeed has a deeply personal quality. Still, as Fierstein carries the torch from the stage to the screen, he illuminates social terrain rarely explored in American movies.

Source: Brian D. Johnson, "Drag Queen Romance" in *Maclean's,* Vol. 102, no. 8, February 20, 1989.

John Simon

Simon is one of the best-known and respected drama critics of the late-twentieth century. In this review he lauds Fierstein's play for successfully blending important social issues with comedy and moving human drama.

Kenneth Tynan created a stir some years ago by asserting that the two principal types of humor in the American theater were the Jewish and the homosexual. If this is so, and it well may be, the good news is that the two strains have been successfully crossbred in Harvey Fierstein's *Torch Song Trilogy,* which is a very amusing as well as moving affair for whose enjoyment, be it said right off, neither Jewishness nor homosexuality is a prerequisite.

This trilogy of shortish plays that lasts, all told (and is all ever told!), a little over four hours is about half the length of *Nicholas Nickleby,* but has at least twice as much to tell us about the way we live now. And when I say *we,* I mean people, any people, except perhaps those living in an offshore lighthouse or in the very buckle of the Bible Belt. Fierstein wrote, and performed the lead in, these three plays one at a time, but it is much better to see them as they are now: the long acts of one extended but not excessive work that gathers meaning as it progresses until, at last, all parts of it resonate in the mind in a bittersweet harmony made of dissonances, pain, resignation, and a little daredevil hope.

Arnold Beckoff, the protagonist, has all the earmarks of a stylized projection of the actor-author himself; yet even though one feels this potentially stifling closeness, one is not, or not for long, an embarrassed voyeur. Buttonholing immediacy is transmuted—by wit, irony, fair play to one and all—first into a bearable distance, then into a sense of wonder. For Beckoff-Fierstein emerges at the far end of identification in a state of liberated semidetachment that is not quite so good as serenity but that will—will have to—do.

In the first play, Arnold, a drag queen, is either backstage at the nightclub where he performs (a performance we do not see—an unfortunate evasion), or at a gay bar called the International Stud, which gives the play its name, or in his apartment, when not in that of his new lover, Ed, a bisexual who is also involved with a young woman called Laurel. The themes here are Arnold's drifting into the orgiastic back rooms of gay hotspots versus his yearning for a solid relationship, Ed's shuttling between two kinds of sexuality and styles of life,

> *TORCH SONG TRILOGY, WHICH IS A VERY AMUSING AS WELL AS MOVING AFFAIR FOR WHOSE ENJOYMENT, BE IT SAID RIGHT OFF, NEITHER JEWISHNESS NOR HOMOSEXUALITY IS A PREREQUISITE"*

and the difficulties with commitment to anything, even noncommitment. In dialogues, monologues, phone conversations with a homosexual friend, Arnold reveals himself and his world with a sweet campiness, an outrageousness whose bark is worse than its bite, an arrested development that does not preclude perceptions of devastating lucidity. "I always thought of myself as a kind person," says Arnold; "not small, but generous in a bitchy sort of way." Or: "To me a lap in bed is worth three in a [gay] bar, because deep down I know they don't marry sluts." Or: "That's really hitting below the belt: appealing to my Susan Hayward fantasies!"

Now, these lines may not be funny out of context, and they lose a lot on paper, without Fierstein's engagingly abrasive presence: the face of a weather vane whirling between corruption and innocence; the movements of an overgrown, precociously epicene baby; and the mind of a tirelessly impudent, lubricious wit that can instantly switch to self-mockery and comic *Weltschmerz* enunciated with a provocatively rasping voice that seems to be picking away at existential scabs on the self, on others, on the world. An upside-down world that one meets with tragicomic defiance: "I could make love to an 80-year-old woman. I could probably make love to an 80-year-old camel. I could make love to an 80-year-old anything as long as it kept its mouth shut."

In the second play, *Fugues in a Nursery,* it is a year later in the upstate farmhouse shared by Ed and Laurel, now living together and playing weekend hosts to Arnold and his new lover, Alan, a very young male model. Fierstein situates the entire action in an enormous symbolic bed in which the two couples talk, argue, copulate. and crisscross both emotionally and sexually. The writing is in the form of a fugue, which is clever, but also means something: The overlapping, intermingling dialogue, in which we are often not sure about who is talking to whom, conveys thought-provoking parallels between homo- and heterosexual relationships—though the captious might argue that Ed's bisexuality muddies the analogies. In any case, *Fugues* is an extremely droll and ingenious scrutiny of sexual politics whose humor, honorably, never hides the underlying cruelty or, still deeper down, the underlying pathos. With gallant gallows humor, Arnold wonders about this foursome: "If two wrongs don't make a right, maybe four *do*?"

It is the last play, *Widows and Children First!,* that rises to true heights and ties all the foregoing together. Ed is unhappily married to Laurel, has had a fight with her and is temporarily bunking *chez* Arnold, after whom he still hankers; Alan, who had been living with Arnold, has met a horrible, homosexual death; Arnold is trying to adopt legally a problem teenager, David, a tough, street-wise, homosexual kid, chock-full of precocious knowledge and sarcasm, but not without a touching residue of childishness. Into this *ménage,* on a visit from Florida, comes Mrs. Beckoff, Arnold's widowed mother. She knows about her son's homosexuality, but cannot really accept it, and keeps needling him. Mother and son try to love each other, but cannot quite make it; their defense, which is also an offense, is wit: her Jewish wit against his homosexual one. While they fumble for each other's affection out of one side of their mouths, they cleverly lacerate each other out of the other side. The combat, fought with bare tongues and occasional desperate gestures, is verbal Grand Guignol of matchless humor and horror.

It turns out that the two widowed creatures, mother and son, are, except for their different sexualities, deeply alike down to their very jokes. The Jewish ones, to be sure, suggest a sad, lonely stand-up comedian resorting to an almost metaphysical sardonicism; the homosexual ones suggest a sarcastic masquerader, flamboyantly theatricalizing everything. But they climax in a very similar, murderous and suicidal, bitchiness: envenomed chicken soup against poisoned paillettes. When mother accuses son of not knowing how to bring up David, Arnold answers: "What's there to know? Whenever there is a problem, I simply imagine how you would solve it. . . . *And then I do the opposite!*" But in fact—and here lies the play's subtlety—Arnold does the same, or nearly. And sometimes he realizes it. Reminiscing about Alan, he says: "It's easier to

love someone who's dead. They make so few mistakes. *Mother:* You have an unusual way of looking at things. *Arnold:* It runs in the family."

All values are inverted and subverted. *"Arnold:* What would you say if I went out and came home with a girl and told you I was straight? *Mother* (patronizingly): If you were happy, I'd be happy." There are ironies within ironies in this, a whole topsy-turvy world. And alongside the mother conflict are, cunningly and touchingly orchestrated, the David problem, the Ed problem, and even the Laurel problem. The author's ultimate achievement is the perfect blend of hard justice and warm empathy with which he embraces all characters, his own alter ego included. The performances by Joel Crothers, Diane Tarleton, Paul Joynt are very fine; more remarkable yet are Fierstein's Arnold, Matthew Broderick's wryly abstracted David aroused to sudden spurts of insistence, and Estelle Getty's quintessential Jewish mother.

There are flaws. Arnold's source of income grows unclear: Could a drag-queen single parent adopt even as unwanted a kid as David? Alan was presented as a fling in the second play; the third makes him out to have been a beloved spouse. No matter: Peter Pope's staging and the production values are good; the play is better. What are you waiting for

Source: John Simon, "The Gay Desperado" in *New York,* Vol. 14, no. 49, December 14, 1981.

SOURCES

Barnes, Clive. Review of *Torch Song Trilogy* in the *New York Post,* July 15, 1982.

Cahill, Madeleine A. Torch Song Trilogy: *The Conception, Realization, and Reception of a Controversial Film* (thesis), University of Massachusetts, 1992.

Clarke, Gerald. Review of *Torch Song Trilogy* in *Time,* February 22, 1982.

Green, William. *"Torch Song Trilogy:* A Gay Comedy with a Dying Fall" in *Maske und Kothurn: Internationale Beitrage zur Theatrewissenschaft,* Volume 30, nos. 1-2, 1984, pp. 217-24.

Gross, Gregory D. "Coming up for Air: Three AIDS Plays" in *Journal of American Culture,* Volume 15, no. 2, Summer, 1992, pp. 63-67.

Gussow, Mel. Review of *Torch Song Trilogy* in the *New York Times,* November 1, 1981.

Kroll, Jack. Review of *Torch Song Trilogy* in *Newsweek,* March 15, 1982.

Nelson, Don. Review of *Torch Song Trilogy* in the *Daily News,* November 11, 1981.

Powers, Kim. Review of *Torch Song Trilogy* in *Theatre,* Volume 14, no. 2, Spring, 1983, pp. 63-67.

Stasio, Marilyn. Review of *Torch Song Trilogy* in the *New York Post,* November 20, 1981.

FURTHER READING

Brozan, Nadine. ''When a Son or Daughter is a Homosexual'' in the *New York Times,* March 12, 1984, p. B11.
  In this article, Brozan discusses the reactions of parents who have discovered that their child is gay.

Dynes, Wayne and Stephen Donaldson, editors. *Homosexuality and Homosexuals in the Arts,* Garland, 1992.
  This book is the fourth volume in a series, ''Studies in Homosexuality.'' This volume contains a selection of essays that examines the role of homosexuality in film, stage, and fiction.

Helbing, Terry, editor. *Directory of Gay Plays,* JH Press, 1980.
  This book is a survey of the growth in the production of plays with homosexual themes.

Pastore, Judith L., editor. *Confronting AIDS through Literature: The Responsibilities of Representation,* University of Illinois Press, 1993.
  This is a collection of essays that examine the history of AIDS in literature.

Summers, Claude. *Gay Fictions: Wilde to Stonewall: Studies in a Male Homosexual Literary Tradition,* Continuum, 1990.
  This anthology of twentieth-century fiction includes works by Oscar Wilde, Willa Cather, Truman Capote, Tennessee Williams, James Baldwin, and several others.

Wilde, Oscar. *Novels and Fairy Tales,* Cosmopolitan, 1915.
  This book is a collection of Wilde's fiction, including *The Picture of Dorian Gray, The Canterville Ghost,* and *The Sphinx without a Secret.* All these works are considered seminal gay fiction.

What the Butler Saw

JOE ORTON

1969

Joe Orton's *What the Butler Saw* was first performed on March 5, 1969, a year and a half after its author's death. Like Orton's earlier plays, *What the Butler Saw* appalled and enraged audiences with its blatant sexuality and attacks on authority and conventional morality. The first audiences were so outraged that they disturbed the performance, yelling at the actors and destroying their programs. In the ensuing years, society's standards have become less restrictive, though there are many who would still be shocked and angered by Orton's work. Orton, however, has gained international respect and recognition as an important playwright. Most critics regard *What the Butler Saw* as his finest play.

The title of the play comes from an Edwardian peepshow, a type of entertainment in which people viewed pictures, often erotic, through a small lens. The implication behind the title is one of voyeurism. The audience is to be given a glimpse of private sexual conduct. Orton's title indicates the sexual nature of the play and implies that the audience will be put in the position of voyeurs, surreptitiously watching other people's lives. The content of the play is frankly carnal, and sexuality and sexual identity are explored at length. *What the Butler Saw* also looks at authority, particularly at the authority of psychiatrists and considers the question of madness, of who is sane and who is insane.

What the Butler Saw is a comedy, more specifically the comedic subgenre known as a farce. Orton's

themes, while serious, are intended to amuse. His witty dialogue is reminiscent of that of Victorian playwright Oscar Wilde (*The Importance of Being Earnest*). Like Wilde, Orton offers a criticism and exploration of society's standards. Entertaining as well as enlightening, *What the Butler Saw* is today considered a contemporary classic.

AUTHOR BIOGRAPHY

Joe Orton was born John Kingsley Orton on January 1, 1933, into a working class family in Leicester, England. Orton's father earned little as a gardener for the city, and his mother's extravagant taste ensured that the family was almost always in debt. Orton's parents fought continually, and there was little affection within the family; writing in his adolescent journal, Orton always put the word "family" in quotation marks.

As a teenager, Orton found escape from his family situation by acting in local theater productions. In 1951, at the age of eighteen, Orton left Leicester to study acting at the Royal Academy of Dramatic Arts in London. It was there that he met Kenneth Halliwell, an older and more sophisticated student who would become Orton's companion, collaborator, lover, and eventually his murderer. Halliwell encouraged Orton to begin writing, and the two co-authored several novels before Orton started writing on his own.

In 1959, the two began a bizarre act of literary vandalism. They would both steal library books, deface them in humorous ways, then return them to the library, where they would secretly watch the other patrons' reactions to their pranks. Orton often pasted over author pictures in the books, in one case replacing the photograph of the author of an etiquette book with a nude cut from a volume on art. Orton also typed his own mildly obscene blurbs onto book jackets. In 1962, Orton and Halliwell were arrested for these acts; each spent six months in jail.

In the meantime, Orton began writing plays and achieved his first success when the British Broadcasting Corporation (BBC) produced *The Ruffian on the Stair* (1964), which dealt comically with homosexuality and sexual ambiguity, themes which were to become Orton's hallmark. His next work, *Entertaining Mr. Sloan* (1964), in which the title

Joe Orton

character is blackmailed into granting sexual favors to the son and daughter of the man he murdered, brought Orton critical and financial success but also criticism for the supposed obscenity of the work. After the production of his next major play, *Loot,* Orton's writing was compared to that of such literary legends as Ben Jonson (*The Alchemist*), George Bernard Shaw (*Man and Superman*), and Lewis Carol (*Alice's Adventures in Wonderland*). *Loot* was named best play of 1966 by the *Evening Standard.* Orton also wrote a number of one-act plays and the screenplay *Up against It,* which was commissioned by the Beatles as the sequel to their film *A Hard Day's Night* but ultimately rejected for production (musician Todd Rundgren resurrected the text in the early-1990s, writing the music for a stage adaptation of Orton's unproduced work). *What the Butler Saw* (1969), Orton's last play, was not produced until after his death. It is generally regarded as his finest work.

Halliwell greatly envied Orton's success, and the relationship between the two became very strained as Orton began to draw away from Halliwell. Eventually, Halliwell sunk into a deep depression. On August 9, 1967, he murdered Orton, bludgeoning him with a hammer, then committed suicide. In the years since Orton's death, critical regard for his plays has grown, and he is now regarded as one of the finest playwrights of his era.

PLOT SUMMARY

Act I

Act I opens in a psychiatric clinic. Dr. Prentice, a psychiatrist, enters, followed by Geraldine Barclay, whom Prentice is interviewing for a secretarial position. Geraldine carries a small box, which she puts on the floor. Dr. Prentice begins to question her, and she reveals that she does not know who her father is and that she has not seen her mother, a chambermaid, in many years. Geraldine was raised by her stepmother, Mrs. Barclay, who recently died from a gas explosion that also destroyed a statue of Sir Winston Churchill. Parts of the statue were found embedded in Mrs. Barclay.

Under the pretense that he is conducting a medical examination required for the job, the psychiatrists asks the young woman to undress. Dr. Prentice attempts to seduce Geraldine, who seems to remain innocent of his intentions. Removing her dress, she lies on the couch, he pulls the curtains around her and puts her underwear on a chair. She is naked but hidden by the privacy curtains when Mrs. Prentice, Dr. Prentice's wife, arrives. Nick, a hotel page, also enters.

When Dr. Prentice leaves, Mrs. Prentice asks Nick to return her dress. The two have had a sexual liaison in a linen closet at the hotel, and Nick has taken photographs of Mrs. Prentice, which he threatens to sell unless she persuades her husband to give him the secretarial position. Dr. Prentice comes back on stage, Nick and Mrs. Prentice leave. Dr. Prentice tells Geraldine to get dressed, but before she is able, Mrs. Prentice comes back. Seeing Geraldine's dress but not Geraldine, Mrs. Prentice demands the dress and reveals that she is wearing only a slip beneath her coat.

Dr. Rance, a psychiatrist and government official, enters the room and asks about the clinic. Seeing the naked Geraldine, he assumes she is a patient and begins questioning her. Dr. Prentice gives Geraldine a hospital nightgown to wear, and Dr. Rance gives her an injection. Mrs. Prentice enters looking for Geraldine Barclay. When Geraldine identifies herself, Dr. Prentice attributes the girl's claim of identity to insanity. Dr. Rance insists that Geraldine was molested by her father, de-

spite her objections. He takes her from the room, and Mrs. Prentice comes in, again searching for "Miss Barclay."

Dr. Prentice leaves, supposedly to search for Geraldine, and when he is gone, Mrs. Prentice tells Dr. Rance that Dr. Prentice is behaving strangely and recounts what were in fact his attempts to keep her from learning of his attempt to seduce Geraldine. Dr. Prentice enters and is asked by Dr. Rance about the whereabouts of Geraldine; Dr. Prentice gives locations and Dr. Rance leaves to look for her. Mrs. Prentice leaves briefly, then returns, announcing that there is a policeman at the door. Nick enters with Mrs. Prentice's dress. Dr. Prentice is alone with Nick, whom he tells to undress. Looking for Nick, Mrs. Prentice finds only his clothes, which she takes with her. Dr. Prentice tells Nick to put on Mrs. Prentice's dress and wig and pretend to be Geraldine.

Fearing arrest for his recent molestation of a group of schoolgirls, Nick hides from Sergeant Match. Geraldine enters wearing Nick's clothes, however, and Sergeant Match reveals that he is looking not only for Nick but also for Geraldine, who is suspected of having a piece of the Churchill statue. Nick enters, wearing Mrs. Prentice's dress and claiming to be Geraldine, and Sergeant Match asks Nick for the missing piece of the statue. Mrs. Prentice takes Nick from the room to give him a physical examination. Dr. Rance returns and, thinking that Geraldine, whom he considers a mental patient, has escaped, pulls the siren bell. Sergeant Match discovers Geraldine, dressed as Nick, and says he needs to talk to him (her).

Act II

Act II begins in the same location one minute later. Geraldine complains to Sergeant Match, who believes her to be Nick, about Dr. Prentice's sexual misconduct. Dr. Prentice denies her account, and Sergeant Match says she must be given a physical examination. Rance says he will examine Geraldine, and Sergeant Match leaves the room. Attempting to avoid an examination, Geraldine says that she is, in fact, a girl. Mrs. Prentice enters, stating that Nick, still dressed in women's clothing, also refuses an examination. Prentice tells Rance that Nick has left and that Geraldine is Gerald Barclay. Rance says that Dr. Prentice is insane, and he relieves Dr. Prentice of his post.

Geraldine and Nick note that they are wearing each other's clothes, and the two confess their true genders. Nick announces that he wants to wear Sergeant Match's clothes so that he can claim he has arrested himself. When Sergeant Match enters, Dr. Prentice gives him a box of pills and orders him to undress for an examination. Sergeant Match takes off his clothes as Dr. Prentice secretly hands them to Nick. Both Dr. Prentice and Nick leave the room, and Mrs. Prentice enters with Dr. Rance. Dr. Rance attempts to explain the strange goings on to Mrs. Prentice, but his explanation is a skewed psychiatric narrative that "explains" everything but is actually professional sounding nonsense. Dr. Rance talks about publishing his "documentary type novelette" and is convinced he will make a fortune.

In the meantime, Sergeant Match enters the room, heavily drugged, and is taken out by Dr. Prentice. Dr. Rance and Mrs. Prentice notice the missing box of bills and first think Dr. Prentice has committed suicide, then speculate that he has murdered Geraldine. Dr. Rance asks for a straitjacket for Dr. Prentice, who now admits that he was trying to seduce Geraldine. When Mrs. Prentice suggests that he admit that he prefers young boys, Dr. Prentice orders her to remove her dress, then slaps her and tears the dress off of her. When Dr. Rance comes in, Mrs. Prentice gives him an exaggerated version of Dr. Prentice's attack.

Nick enters, wearing Sergeant Match's clothes, and says that he has arrested his brother, Nicholas Beckett, and put him in jail. Dr. Rance and Mrs. Prentice tell Nick that Dr. Prentice murdered his secretary, at which point Nick admits his true identity, stating that Dr. Prentice had asked him to pose as a woman. At Dr. Rance's request, Nick attempts to put Dr. Prentice in a straitjacket but is interrupted when Sergeant Match enters. Geraldine enters and Dr. Prentice tells her to remove Nick's uniform and put on a dress. A shot is heard, and Sergeant Match enters with blood pouring down his leg. Mrs. Prentice enters, holding a gun.

The next few moments are filled with confusion as the various actors enter and leave and Mrs. Prentice shoots at Nick several times. Geraldine enters, Rance announces that "the patient" has been found, and she is put into the straitjacket. Dr. Prentice enters saying that Mrs. Prentice has tried to shoot him because she believes he's mad. Nick attempts to put a straitjacket on Dr. Prentice. Dr. Rance puts a straitjacket on Mrs. Prentice, and Dr. Prentice gains control of the gun and threatens Dr. Rance, who pulls an alarm so that sirens wail and metal grilles come down over the doors. Dr. Rance

tells Dr. Prentice to put the gun down, but when he does, Dr. Rance grabs the weapon and points it at the psychiatrist.

Dr. Prentice then tells Dr. Rance the truth about Nick and Geraldine's identities. Dr. Rance then instructs Dr. Prentice to release Mrs. Prentice and Geraldine, who complains of the loss of her lucky elephant charm.

When Dr. Rance produces the charm, Nick says that he has one that's identical, and Mrs. Prentice, seeing both pieces of jewelry, shows that they fit together to form a brooch. She announces that she was given the brooch as "payment" when a young man raped her in a linen closet during a power outage while she was working as a chambermaid. The rape resulted in pregnancy, and when she subsequently gave birth to twins, she broke the brooch, pinned one piece to each of the children, then abandoned them in separate parts of town. She, therefore, is the mother of Geraldine and Nick.

Then Dr. Prentice says he has not seen the brooch since he gave it to a chambermaid he raped. He learns that the chambermaid is in fact his wife and that he is therefore Nick and Geraldine's father. Dr. Rance is delighted, for now he can say that Geraldine really is the victim of an incestuous assault, as is Mrs. Prentice.

As the "family" embraces, the skylight opens and a ladder descends. Sergeant Match is lowered from the skylight wearing Mrs. Prentice's leopard-print dress; he demands the missing piece of Churchill. Geraldine says that the undertaker gave her a box which she has not opened and which she brought with her to her interview. Sergeant Match opens the box and holds aloft the missing section of the statue—an oversized penis (an item that adds to the play's ribaldry when it is recalled that the statue pieces were imbedded in Mrs. Barclay; in the first production, a cigar was used to lessen the sexual outrage). The play ends as all gather their clothes and climb the ladder into the light.

CHARACTERS

Geraldine Barclay

Geraldine is the daughter of Dr. and Mrs. Prentice and the sister of Nick. At the beginning of the play, she does not know who her father is and believes her mother was a chambermaid. She was raised by a Mrs. Barclay, who was recently killed in a gas main explosion. Geraldine applies for a position as secretary to Dr. Prentice, but she can only take dictation at the speed of twenty words per minute and does not know how to type at all. She is a satire of an innocent, accepting Dr. Prentice's explanation of why she needs to undress for her job interview, and when Dr. Prentice asks her to help him test his new contraceptive device, she says she will be "delighted to help."

Of all of the characters in the play, Geraldine seems least able to take control of what happens to her. Attempting to hide his sexual misconduct, Dr. Prentice tells the others that Geraldine is a mental patient, and she is consequently dressed in a hospital gown, given a short haircut, and forcibly injected with drugs. At the end of the play, she is alternately described as "tearful," "weeping," and "unable to speak."

Nicholas Beckett

Nick is a hotel page, the son of Dr. and Mrs. Prentice, and the brother of Geraldine, though he only finds out about these relationships at the end of the play. He seems to have virtually no sexual ethics. When he first arrives on stage, through his discussion with Mrs. Prentice, the audience is told that Nick had sex with Mrs. Prentice and has taken photographs of their encounter. He has sold her dress and threatens to sell the photographs as well unless Mrs. Prentice persuades Dr. Prentice to hire him. Later in the play, he and Mrs. Prentice both claim that he attempted to rape her but did not succeed. The audience also discovers that after his encounter with Mrs. Prentice, he assaulted a group of schoolgirls and is trying to avoid arrest. In addition, Nick reveals that he prostitutes himself to strange men.

Nick

See Nicholas Beckett

Sergeant Match

Sergeant Match is a policeman who arrives at the clinic searching for Nick, because of Nick's assault on a group of schoolgirls, and Geraldine, because she possesses the missing piece of the statue of Winston Churchill. A figure of authority, Sergeant Match becomes an object of ridicule when he undresses on stage at Dr. Prentice's request and subsequently appears drugged and wearing a leopard-print dress.

Dr. Prentice

Dr. Prentice runs the psychiatric clinic in which the play takes place. He is married to Mrs. Prentice and is the father of Geraldine and Nick, although he does not know of his offspring until the end of the play. Dr. Prentice is a sexual predator who is completely lacking in ethics. He fathered Geraldine and Nick when he raped Mrs. Prentice, thinking that she was a chambermaid, shortly before their marriage. Because he raped her in a dark closet, he did not realize that she was his fiancee. In addition, he attempts to have sex with Geraldine, who is interviewing to be his secretary, by deceiving her into thinking that he must physically examine her before giving her the job.

The action of the play is set in motion by Dr. Prentice's efforts to hide this attempted rape/seduction from his wife. Dr. Prentice's relationship with Mrs. Prentice is primarily one of antagonism. He admits to having married her for her money, then attempting to beat her when he discovered she was not wealthy. He also physically attacks her during the course of the play.

Mrs. Prentice

Mrs. Prentice is married to Dr. Prentice and discovers at the end of the play that she is the mother of Geraldine and Nick, whom she abandoned at birth and, consequently, does not recognize. She is characterized as a nymphomaniac who pursues young men. When she first comes on stage, the audience discovers that she has recently had a sexual encounter with Nick, but the exact nature of that encounter is unclear. In her conversation with Nick, she indicates that she "gave herself" to him, implying that she willingly had sex with him. However, during the remainder of the play, she claims he attempted to rape her but did not succeed. She does not expect any sort of fidelity in marriage. She admits to numerous liaisons and seems to expect the same from her husband. For instance, when Dr. Rance leads her to believe that Dr. Prentice is attracted to young men, she volunteers to introduce him to some she knows (and with whom she has more than likely had sexual relations herself).

Dr. Rance

Dr. Rance is a government official in charge of psychiatric facilities. He is a figure of authority who boasts that he would "have sway over a rabbit hutch if the inmates were mentally disturbed." Dr. Rance sees everything that happens as a validation of his own preconceived notions. Upon being told by Dr. Prentice that Geraldine is a patient, Dr. Rance imposes his own ideas on whatever Geraldine says, concluding, for instance, that she is the victim of an incestuous attack by her father—an astute observation whose truth no one yet realizes. He even cites her denial of such an attack as proof that it occurred. Dr. Rance is quick to certify Geraldine as insane, again based on his own theories, not on actual symptoms that indicate such an illness.

Rance similarly imposes his own interpretations on the words and acts of all of the other characters, and those interpretations satirize the modern practice of psychiatry. For instance, believing Dr. Prentice to have murdered Geraldine based on the psychiatrist's statement: "I've given her the sack"—meaning that he fired her—Dr. Rance tells Mrs. Prentice: "He killed her and wrapped her body in a sack. The word association is very clear." From the events of the play, Dr. Rance creates a narrative which he intends to publish as a novelette, and he anticipates becoming rich and famous.

THEMES

Madness, Psychiatry, and Authority

Orton prefaces *What the Butler Saw* with a quotation from *The Revenger's Tragedy:* "Surely we're all mad people, and they/Whom we think are, are not." The perception of madness and, consequently, who is mad, is central to Orton's play. In the twentieth century, it is given to psychiatrists to answer this question. Although many may question psychiatric methods, it is nonetheless the case that psychiatrists have been given the legal authority to determine who is mad and, consequently, to commit those so diagnosed to psychiatric hospitals, to force them to take medications, and even to submit to electroshock therapy.

In recent years, safeguards against abuse of these powers have become strong; committing a patient to a psychiatric hospital requires clear evidence that he or she is a danger to themselves or others, and involuntary electroshock is used only in the most extreme cases. In Orton's time, however, the authority of the psychiatrist was more absolute. In *What the Butler Saw,* Orton calls the entire system into question, blurring the line between sanity and madness, questioning psychiatric methods, and subverting the authority of the psychiatrist.

TOPICS FOR FURTHER STUDY

- Orton has often been compared to Victorian writer Oscar Wilde. Compare *What the Butler Saw* with Wilde's play *The Importance of Being Earnest.* In what ways does Orton's play reflect Wilde's influence? How might the differences between the two plays reflect changes in society?

- Compare *What the Butler Saw* with Orton's earlier play *Loot.* In what ways do the two plays deal with the subjects of sexuality and authority?

- Orton has been accused of misogyny, hatred towards women. Discuss the female characters in *What the Butler Saw.* Does a reading of this play support this accusation?

- Research and discuss the elements of farce. In what ways does *What the Butler Saw* rely on these elements? Why might it sometimes be considered a parody of a farce? Use specific examples.

It would seem that in a psychiatric clinic, the line between who is mad and who is not would be most clear. Those in the clinic either are or are not patients. In *What the Butler Saw,* however, no one in the clinic is a patient and, to some extent, everyone is mad. There is madness in the way the characters speak; the dialogue is not rational. When Mrs. Prentice tells Dr. Rance that Nick attempted to rape her but did not succeed, Dr. Rance replies, "The service in these hotels is dreadful." When Mrs. Prentice suspects that Dr. Prentice wears women's clothing, her response is, "I'd no idea our marriage teetered on the edge of fashion." In addition, in performance, the appearance of the characters running on and off stage repeatedly, changing clothes and physically fighting each other, gives the audience a sense of chaos, of the abandonment of social constraints, of madness.

Psychiatrists are supposed to be able to treat madness, but that is not the case in this play; Orton satirizes psychiatry, particularly in the person of Dr.

Rance. Believing Geraldine to be a patient, Dr. Rance conducts a psychiatric examination that ridicules psychiatric methods. Dr. Rance is convinced that Geraldine was the victim of an incestuous attack by her father, and he uses even her denials as evidence. When Dr. Rance asks Geraldine if her father assaulted her, and Geraldine says, ''No,'' Dr. Rance remarks, ''She may mean 'Yes' when she says 'No.''' When he asks her again and she again says no ''with a scream of horror,'' Dr. Rance says, ''The vehemence of her denials is proof positive of guilt.''

There is nothing Geraldine can say that will change Rance's mind. No matter what the other characters say, Dr. Rance interprets their words to fit his preconceived theories. His psychiatric methods lead neither to truth nor understanding. He can make the words of others mean anything he chooses.

Orton aims not only at traditional psychiatry but also at new theories of madness that were becoming popular at the time he was writing. Some psychiatrists began to suggest that madness showed only a different way of dealing with reality and that the mad really had a kind of wisdom. Orton ridicules these theories as well. Mrs. Prentice says, ''The purpose of my husband's clinic isn't to cure, but to liberate and exploit madness.'' And Dr. Rance echoes the words of psychiatrist R. D. Laing, a major proponent of new interpretations of madness, when he says, ''You can't be a rationalist in an irrational world. It isn't rational.'' Orton's satirization of psychiatric theory is all inclusive.

Orton also focuses on the psychiatrist himself as authority figure. In much of his work, Orton attempts to subvert established authority, showing those with power as useless or corrupt. When ridiculing psychiatric methods, Orton is also ridiculing the authority society gives to psychiatrists. Dr. Rance and Dr. Prentice, for instance, exhibit what can easily be considered mad behavior. Dr. Rance even tries to certify Dr. Prentice as insane and have him put in a straitjacket. Showing the figures with power as madmen undercuts their authority, causing the audience to call that authority into question.

In addition, the psychiatrists in *What the Butler Saw* blatantly abuse their authority. Dr. Prentice uses his position as a doctor in his attempt to have sex with Geraldine. Dr. Rance is quick to certify the other characters as insane based on his ideas more than their words or actions. He also forces an injection on Geraldine, who is no more mad than he

is. It is unimaginable that he could ever be a help to the mentally ill.

In essence, Orton's use of these themes amounts to a criticism of societal conventions. Orton asks those in the audience to question their definitions of madness, their faith in psychiatry, their respect for authority. As funny as they may be, Orton's barbs and jests are aimed at serious issues.

Sex and Sexuality

Much of the action in *What the Butler Saw* revolves around sexual matters. The plot of the play is, in fact, driven by Dr. Prentice's attempted seduction/rape of Geraldine and his subsequent efforts to hide his sexual exploits from his wife. In addition to infidelity, Orton's play deals with rape, incest, and sexual identity. Orton's presentation of these sexual matters is comic, but there is a dark side as well.

Neither Dr. Prentice nor Mrs. Prentice is sexually faithful to the other. In the beginning of the play, the audience sees Dr. Prentice attempting a sexual tryst with Geraldine and Mrs. Prentice returning from a sexual encounter with Nick. The nature of the encounter with Nick is not clearly defined. When talking to Nick she says that she ''gave herself'' to him. However, later in the play, she claims he tried to rape her and he says this as well. What is clear is that Mrs. Prentice has affairs, and this is accepted within the reality of the play. When Dr. Prentice calls her a nymphomaniac, it seems he takes this condition as a fact of life. In fact, his simple acceptance of her nymphomania is what makes it funny.

Similarly, when Mrs. Prentice offers to find her husband young men, she acts as if his sexual infidelity is a matter of course. Again, that is what makes it funny. However, in the real world, infidelity is taken seriously. It destroys marriages and ruins lives. While the audience laughs at Orton's jokes, it is also aware of the serious nature of the matter. This adds a dark underside to Orton's play.

Similarly treated as humorous subjects, rape and incest also provide a dark background. Dr. Prentice's attempt to have sex with Geraldine would be construed by many as a type of rape. His deception takes no account of her will. He assumes, in fact, that she would not willingly have sex with him. In addition, Mrs. Prentice may have been raped by Nick, and she was raped by Dr. Prentice before the two were married. Again, these rapes are treated as the subject of humor.

In Orton's time, it would have been more socially acceptable to joke about rape, but recent changes in attitudes toward women have made such joking unacceptable. Even in Orton's time, however, rape was no laughing matter, especially to the victim. Incest, one of the most taboo of sexual activities, similarly, is no longer considered appropriate material for humor, if it ever was. Orton's play however, focuses on double incest, Dr. Prentice's attempt to have sex with his daughter and Nick's possible rape of his mother. Again, this provides a sort of dark humor.

In *What the Butler Saw,* Orton also deals with sexual identity, which he presents as fluid. Mrs. Prentice belongs to a lesbian club, despite the fact that she is married to Dr. Prentice, because the club counts him as a woman. Dr. Prentice's sexual identity can therefore change with other's perceptions of him. Later in the play, Dr. Rance and Mrs. Prentice come to believe that Dr. Prentice is gay. They then treat him as if he is gay, and the actual nature of his sexuality becomes less important than the way he is regarded.

Costume changes in the play also suggest the fluidity of sexual identity. When dressed as Nick, Geraldine is treated as a male, but she identifies herself as either male or female, depending on what is most convenient, saying in one case that she must be a boy because she likes girls. Nick appears on stage as a woman and as a man, but his sexual nature is not clear. He molests women but also has sexual relations with men for money. Thus the sexual natures of Dr. Prentice, Mrs. Prentice, Geraldine, and Nick are all in question. Orton suggests elements of homosexuality for each of these characters.

Orton, himself gay, did not see homosexuality as wrong, and in fact insisted, for other productions, that gay characters be played in the same way as other people, with no campiness. At the time he was writing, however, gays faced great discrimination (homosexuality was even outlawed in England for a time) and were considered by many to be ''sick.'' For the audience, therefore, changes in sexual identity could be perceived as dark, although that would be less likely to be the case today.

Critics have said that Orton uses sex as a weapon, that he wishes to shock and upset his audience. If this is the case, Orton certainly succeeded, in his own time, with *What the Butler Saw* and his other plays. Discomfort often results in laughter, and so Orton's blatant presentation of sexual matters also makes the play funny. In *What the Butler Saw,* the various reactions that an open look at sex causes—shock, disgust, laughter—all mix to create a play that shows sexual matters in all of their complexity.

STYLE

Farce

Farce is a type of comedy known for its humorous and extreme exaggeration. It is often characterized by a ridiculous plot, full of comic twists and turns and impossible coincidences, absurd dialogue, stereotyped characters, and physical comedy. Elements of farce exist in some plays of ancient Greece. The form first became popular in fifteenth century France, and it continues to this day. Examples of twentieth-century farce include movies by the Marx Brothers and Charlie Chaplin.

What the Butler Saw exhibits all of the attributes of farce, but many critics have said that the play is in fact a *parody* of a farce. This means that Orton is imitating the form of farce in order to ridicule it. It is difficult to distinguish a farce from a parody of a farce, but some elements of Orton's play move it outside of the traditional form.

The plot of *What the Butler Saw* can certainly be characterized as ridiculous. It begins with a job interview that quickly becomes absurd as Dr. Prentice attempts to seduce Geraldine. Immediately after Geraldine undresses, Mrs. Prentice enters the room. This initial coincidence sets the plot in motion as Dr. Prentice goes to more and more ridiculous lengths to keep the truth about Geraldine from his wife. As he grows more and more desperate, he causes Geraldine to be certified insane, forces Nick to dress in women's clothes, and has Sergeant Match take off his clothes before drugging him.

The madness of his actions convinces Dr. Rance and Mrs. Prentice that Dr. Prentice is himself insane, and so he almost ends up in a straitjacket. Unbelievable coincidences further the action of the plot as Mrs. Prentice finds Geraldine's nightgown and assumes she has been killed, and Sergeant Match arrives at the door looking for Nick and Geraldine. Of course, the most impossible coincidence occurs at the end of the play when Geraldine pulls out her elephant charm, Nick has a charm that matches it, Mrs. Prentice reveals that she is their mother, and Dr. Prentice realizes he is their father.

The absurd dialogue is also characteristic of farce. Throughout the play, the dialogue simply is not rational. Characters rarely say what one would expect them to say. Dr. Prentice remarks casually upon Mrs. Prentice's infidelities. Mrs. Prentice offers to introduce her husband to young men. Geraldine says she will be delighted to test Dr. Prentice's new contraceptive device. Nick says that the guardian of the schoolgirls he molested reported him because he did not molest her. Much of this dialogue concerns sexual matters. Orton pokes fun at societal conventions by having his characters act as if such mores do not exist. The characters' dialogue is not meant to be realistic.

Orton also uses stereotyped comic characters. Geraldine is the innocent girl, Dr. Prentice the sexual predator, Dr. Rance the mad psychiatrist, Mrs. Prentice the nymphomaniac wife. In farce, all of these characters are made to look ridiculous. They also look ridiculous because of the extreme physical comedy. Dr. Prentice desperately tries to hide Geraldine's clothes; Sergeant Match, drugged, falls down; Mrs. Prentice, wearing only a slip, crashes into a vase. Characters rush about the stage, dressing and undressing, and the play finishes with a free-for-all that involves screaming, fighting, and even gunplay.

Orton uses the expected elements of traditional farce, but he also upsets some of those elements, and that is what causes some critics to call this play a parody of a farce. In traditional farce, for instance, there may be onstage violence, but the violence is generally bloodless and nobody really gets hurt. In *What the Butler Saw,* Sergeant Match and Nick are shot and bleed and Mrs. Prentice's hands are covered with blood. Also, traditional farce is characterized by a return to the accepted social order after all of the madness of the play has passed.

Although *What the Butler Saw* ends with a scene of recognition that seems it will return the characters to a sort of normalcy, Orton's ending is dark. What is really discovered at the end is that Dr. Prentice raped his wife and attempted to seduce his child, and that Nick either attempted to rape his mother or had consensual sex with her. The play ends with the characters "weary, bleeding, drugged, and drunk," and although Dr. Rance's final words imply a new beginning, there is a strong sense of

corruption. Orton uses the basic forms of farce and many of its elements, but he twists those elements and so arrives at a play more complicated than the traditional form of farce.

deus ex machina

The Latin words *deus ex machina* literally mean "god from the machine." The term was first used in ancient Greek and Roman drama. In some of these plays, a complicated situation at the end of the play is resolved when a god appears and tells the characters what to do or creates an ending that does not always follow from the events of the play; the Greek playwright Euripides (*Medea*) was often accused of resorting to such quick fixes to end his plays. The god is "from a machine" because a sort of crane was used so that the god appeared in the sky, then was lowered down to earth.

Today the phrase is used to refer to an improbable event that creates a convenient ending for a dramatic work. For instance, in American western films, it is a well-known cliche to have the U.S. cavalry arrive at the last minute to save a hopeless situation. In modern times, the use of a *deus ex machina* ending, unless done for humorous effect, is generally considered a flaw in the writing.

In *What the Butler Saw,* Orton parodies the *deus ex machina* ending. The appearance of Geraldine's brooch creates an artificial ending for the play. Orton takes his parody further in the final scene, however. Sergeant Match appears descending from the skylight on a rope ladder as a god descended on a crane in ancient Greek theater. But Sergeant Match, instead of a glorified god, is a ridiculous figure wearing a leopard-print dress. Orton imitates the *deus ex machina* ending, but he does so for comic effect.

HISTORICAL CONTEXT

With the death of Sir Winston Churchill on January 25, 1965, Great Britain lost a major figure of political and moral authority. As Prime Minister through most of World War II, Churchill had become a national hero. During the war years, the British people suffered greatly, enduring daily deprivation as well as the terror and destruction of Nazi Germany's intense bombing of London, known as

COMPARE & CONTRAST

- **1969:** Society experiences a growing movement toward sexual freedom. Sex outside of marriage is gaining acceptance, at least in part because of the development of the birth control pill. Homosexuality has only recently become legal, and gays continue to suffer society's rejection and hatred.

  Today: The sexual freedom fought for in the 1960s has gained widespread acceptance, but concerns about the AIDS virus have caused more people to consider abstinence and monogamy. Gays have made great strides socially and legally but continue to be the victims of discrimination and hate crimes.

- **1969:** Psychiatrist R. D. Laing hypothesizes that madness is a sane reaction to an insane world, and some psychiatrists join him in opposition to traditional treatments for schizophrenia and related disorders.

  Today: Scientific research has shown that many mental illnesses are largely caused by biological factors. New and more effective medications revolutionize psychiatry. Success with medication results in the closing of mental hospitals, but many of the mentally ill will not take their medications on their own and are not capable of successfully living without assistance. Many of the mentally ill become homeless.

- **1969:** Young people protest, sometimes violently, against the restrictions imposed by the authority of the government. Opposition to American involvement in Vietnam gains worldwide support among young people.

  Today: Some opposition to the authority of the state continues, but formal protests are less common and less vehement. Many young people become more conservative.

---

the "blitz." Churchill's inspired leadership and his stirring radio speeches, still widely quoted today, sustained British morale during those dark years. He was a symbol of British unity and strength and, when he died, the nation and the world mourned.

It is difficult for contemporary Americans to understand the depth of British feeling for Churchill that existed when Joe Orton symbolically castrated the great man in *What the Butler Saw*. Audiences were outraged by Orton's disrespect for Churchill's memory and that is most likely the reaction Orton desired. Orton's *What the Butler Saw*, however, did not exist in a vacuum. The 1960s in Britain saw an unprecedented increase in personal freedom and a rejection of the symbols of authority.

Of particular importance in understanding Orton's work are the changes in attitude regarding sexual freedom. While there had been movements promoting what was called free love in earlier decades, it was not until the 1960s that such movements gained significant public support. There were,

as there are today, many who opposed sex without marriage and same sex relationships. Nonetheless, the predominant movement was towards sexual permissiveness, and the support for this movement is well illustrated by the changes in British laws which, before the 1960s, assumed a governmental interest in what are now widely regarded as private matters.

For most of Orton's life, the homosexual relationships with which he was involved were criminal offenses. It was not until 1967 that homosexual acts between consenting adult males became legally permissible. That same year, the Family Planning Act made it possible for local authorities to provide contraceptives, and the Abortion Act allowed for abortions to be performed under the National Health Service—though only if two doctors considered the procedure necessary for medical or psychological reasons. In 1969, the Divorce Reform Act permitted either party in a marriage to obtain a divorce, but only after five years of separation. Some of these laws may seem restrictive by today's standards, but at the time, their enactment was a significant step in the movement away from governmental authority over private lives.

Psychiatry was also undergoing a revolution during Orton's time. Then as now, psychiatrists had the power to deem an individual insane and forcibly place him or her in a locked mental hospital. Psychiatrists also have the authority to force medication or electroshock therapy on such committed patients. Since the 1960s, legal restrictions have made it much more difficult for a psychiatrist to restrict personal freedom unless such restriction is deemed absolutely necessary. During Orton's time, however, some psychiatrists were seeing their patients in a new way. Psychiatrist R. D. Laing popularized the idea that schizophrenia and other disorders were a logical reaction to living in a mad society (a theory which spawned the classic line from the *Star Trek* television series: "In an insane society, the sane man must appear insane").

The psychotic, according to Laing, emerged from the state of psychosis with a deeper understanding of the world. It was the so-called "normal" individual, in his or her blind acceptance of society's rules, who was truly insane. Laing's belief in a sort of wisdom in madness is also reflected in the widespread use of psychedelic drugs during this period. Those who used such drugs often believed that the experience opened their minds, made them more aware of their surroundings, and gave them a clearer understanding of the true nature of reality. Harvard Professor Timothy Leary, himself a user of LSD, urged young people to take psychedelic drugs, to reject authority, to "tune in, turn on, drop out." Leary's message shocked and angered many who still valued the orderly society represented by men such as Churchill, but rebellion against authority was the hallmark of the 1960s and of the work of Orton.

CRITICAL OVERVIEW

The first performance of *What the Butler Saw,* on March 5, 1969, was a critical and commercial disaster. Members of the audience shouted at the actors, disrupting the performance. In his Orton biography *Prick up Your Ears,* critic John Lahr noted that "Shouts of 'Filth!', 'Rubbish!', 'Find another play!' bombarded the actors as they struggled bravely through the lines." Lahr also quoted actor Stanley Baxter, who played Dr. Prentice, on his experience with the audience on opening night:

> At first I thought it was a drunk or someone mentally deranged. Then it became clear that it was militant hate that had been organized. . . . It was a battle royal. . . . The gallery wanted to jump on the stage and kill us all. The occasion had the exhilaration of a fight.

Barton also recalled "old ladies in the audience not merely tearing up their programmes, but jumping up and down on them out of sheer hatred."

The audience could not have really heard the play itself with all of the shouting going on, but they objected to what they saw as Orton's immorality. This reaction to Orton was not limited to members of the audience. Lahr noted that critic Harold Hobson "ignored the play in his initial review, using the space instead to portray Orton as the Devil's theatrical henchman." In a later essay in the *Christian Science Monitor,* Hobson still focused more on Orton than on the play. Lahr quoted, "Orton's terrible obsession with perversion, which is regarded as having brought his life to an end and choked his very high talent, poisons the play. And what should have been a piece of gaily irresponsible nonsense become impregnated with evil."

According to Lahr, the only review that recognized the play's importance was written by Frank Marcus, who predicted that "*What the Butler Saw* will live to be accepted as a comedy classic of English literature." Marcus's words proved prophetic. The 1975 revival received much more positive reviews, and the play is today widely considered Orton's finest work.

Although there are certainly many people today who would consider *What the Butler Saw* immoral, and even disgusting, in general attitudes toward sexuality have changed greatly since 1969. Most people would still find the characters' actions reprehensible, but sex is not the taboo subject it once was, and today's audiences are much less likely to be shocked. More recent criticism is less likely to focus on whether the play is immoral, but to look instead at what Orton is trying to say and whether the play is successful on its own terms. Nonetheless, Orton's presentation of amoral characters is still an important topic of discussion.

In *Joe Orton,* critic C. W. E. Bigsby suggested that Orton uses his plays to attack. Bigsby wrote that Orton's "primary weapons became parody, sexual affront, visual and verbal humour and macabre juxtaposition." The sexual affront of *What the*

Butler Saw is, in fact, what made the earlier audiences so angry. Bigsby called Orton's work "an act of aggression." Orton, according to Bigsby, believed he lived in "a very sick society" and attempted to "undermine [that society] at first with absurdist comedy and then with farce."

In *What the Butler Saw,* Orton's use of sexuality can be seen as an attack on the audience, whom Bigsby noted are granted, in all theater, "a privileged position" and "believe themselves to be in possession of a perceivable truth." But Orton destroys the complacency of the audience "at the end when they are made to see that what they took to be frivolous sexual games were in fact incestuous trysts in which a mother is raped by her son and a father attempts to strip and rape his daughter." According to Bigsby, the amorality of the characters serves to disturb the audience, to force them to see beyond convention, to attack their acceptance of society's rules.

In his book *Because We're Queers,* Simon Shepherd suggested that Orton's anger is directed not so much at the audience but at the status quo. Shepherd wrote that "Orton's most extended anger was ... reserved for a male figurehead who had explicit association with nationalism." Referring to the destruction of the statue of Winston Churchill and the symbolic castration of Churchill himself, Shepherd wrote, "To appreciate Orton's daring we have to recall the extent of national mythology surrounding the man."

Orton also shocked his audience with the final display of the statue's penis. "In dominant non-homosexual culture," Shepherd wrote, "it is taboo to make sexual advances to a man and it is taboo . . . to represent the erect penis. Both taboos preserve the dignity of the penis, defining it as a symbol of order and power." Shepherd further noted that "Conventional masculinity is founded on the notion that biological possession of the penis gives a person cultural or social power."

By exposing the statue's penis as an object of laughter, Shepherd wrote, Orton "has us look with a mocking gay look at the combination of elements—family, gender roles, nationalism, masculinity, propriety—which make up English fascism." So shocking was the display of the penis at the play's end, that the first production substituted the organ with Churchill's cigar, which can also be seen as a phallic symbol—albeit a far less explicit one. Subsequent productions have restored the use of the penis, which is a powerful symbol in the play, in part because of its shock value.

Not all critics, however, see Orton's use of shock and immorality as beneficial to the play. Benedict Nightingale, writing in *Encounter,* found flaws in *What the Butler Saw.* Nightingale reported that he saw the play twice "and twice failed to laugh even remotely as much as the swaggering language and frenetic encounters [seem] to demand." For Nightingale, the amorality of the characters weakened the play but not for the simplistic reason that such amorality is somehow "wrong." Instead, Nightingale believed that the characters keep the play from succeeding on its own terms, as a farce. Nightingale asked, "How can we laugh at someone's flouting of convention, or desperate attempt to regain respectability, when no one on stage is particularly convention, respectable or shockable? Farce simply can't breathe in an atmosphere of amorality and permissiveness." For Nightingale, the extremity of the characters' amorality defeated Orton's purpose.

There is no doubt that Orton intended *What the Butler Saw* to shock its audience, and early reactions show he succeeded; audiences and critics were shocked, even disgusted, by Orton's final play. Shock in itself, however, is ultimately not enough. There is critical disagreement on whether the play does succeed on its own terms. In spite of such disagreements, however, most critics today recognize the importance of *What the Butler Saw* and consider it Orton's finest play.

CRITICISM

Clare Cross
Cross is a Ph.D. candidate specializing in drama. In this essay she discusses the use of costume in Orton's play.

Joe Orton's *What the Butler Saw* is notable for its use of costume. Throughout the play, characters dress and undress, discarding and exchanging clothing, and thus furthering Orton's theme of the fluidity of identity. Orton also uses clothing and the removal of clothing in the play to establish and subvert authority, to highlight the vulnerability as well as the threat of the human body, and to create a confusing and comic effect. Costume in the play

Richard Wilson and Debra Gillet enact part of the chaos that ensues in the play's closing moments

provides much more than decoration or even character illumination. In *What the Butler Saw,* Orton's use of clothing is central to the play.

From the beginning of *What the Butler Saw,* the characters' clothing is used to establish who has authority and power and who does not. From the moment he arrives onstage, wearing an expensive, tailored suit, Dr. Prentice is identified as a member of the establishment and a figure of authority. Almost immediately, Orton undercuts that authority with Dr. Prentice's nonsensical dialogue, and the dissonance between Dr. Prentice's words and his sophisticated clothing creates a comic effect. Nonetheless, in the world of the play, he retains his power, power that is highlighted by his appearance, most of the time.

Later in the play, when Dr. Rance decides the psychiatrist is insane and Dr. Prentice loses his power, that loss is highlighted by Dr. Rance's attempt to change Dr. Prentice's clothing—to put him in a straitjacket. In the beginning, however, it is Geraldine whose clothes establish her subservient position. Dr. Prentice soon exchanges his suit coat for the traditional doctor's white coat, clothing that emphasizes his power as a psychiatrist. Geraldine, on the other hand, first appears wearing a dress. As a

woman in Orton's time (the 1960s)—and an aspiring secretary—she lacks power.

Dr. Prentice orders Geraldine to undress and, in spite of her doubts, because he is a doctor, she obeys. First standing on the stage in panties and bra, then lying naked behind a curtain, Geraldine is put in an extremely vulnerable position. Her lack of clothing takes away what little power she has. No longer a person in her own right, she becomes the object of Dr. Prentice's desire. Also, from a practical viewpoint, without her clothing, she is trapped; she cannot leave. While she undresses, becoming more vulnerable, Dr. Prentice puts on his white coat, thus increasing his appearance of authority. In addition, in production, as a nearly naked woman standing on a stage, the actress who plays Geraldine becomes vulnerable to the gaze of the audience. This adds a more complicated layer to Geraldine's loss of power. Both actress and character are set up as objects of desire.

After Geraldine undresses, Mrs. Prentice arrives, wearing an expensive coat that marks her as a wealthy woman, with all the power that money provides. Nick comes in shortly afterwards, seemingly subservient to her in a hotel page's uniform. The audience soon discovers, however, that Nick

WHAT DO I READ NEXT?

- *Loot,* an Orton play first produced in 1966, is a farce focusing on twentieth-century taboos surrounding death. In this send-up of the modern detective story, Orton also pokes fun at authority, focusing, in this play, on the police.

- *The Birthday Party* is a 1958 play by Harold Pinter, a British dramatist who influenced Orton's work, particularly in matters of comedy, social satire, and dialogue.

- *The Importance of Being Earnest,* an 1895 play by Oscar Wilde, had a great deal of influence on Orton's work. *What the Butler Saw* relies on dialogue very similar to Wilde's, and the ending of Orton's play parodies Wilde's final scene.

- *One Flew over the Cuckoo's Nest,* a 1962 novel by Ken Kesey, also focuses on the madness of psychiatry, though in a much more serious way.

Made into a 1975 film starring Jack Nicholson, Kesey's novel helped to foster a suspicious attitude toward the authority of mental health professionals the patients they are supposed to help.

- *A Day at the Races,* a 1937 Marx Brothers film, is a good example of farce. The film features Groucho Marx as a veterinarian who impersonates a doctor at a sanatorium and performs bogus medical examinations.

- *The Politics of Experience,* a 1967 work by psychiatrist R. D. Laing, explores Laing's belief that mental illness is the logical reaction to the madness of society. Neurobiological research has since discredited some of Laing's beliefs, but the influence of this work on attitudes toward mental illness is significant.

---

has taken Mrs. Prentice's dress and wig and that he has sold the dress. He has possession of her clothing, and so the wealthy woman loses power to the hotel page. This creates a loss of dignity, which becomes even more extreme when she later opens her coat, revealing that she is wearing only a slip underneath.

In *Because We're Queers,* Simon Shepherd wrote about the effect of the undressed character on stage, focusing on the difference between the audience's view of unclothed males and unclothed females. "The man with his trousers down is funny," Shepherd wrote, "because he loses his traditional dignity as he becomes uncovered (whereas the *woman* who is undressed is supposedly sexy)." While Shepherd's assessment of the effect of the unclothed male is correct, his remarks on the unclothed female are too simplistic. While the young undressed Geraldine is certainly a sexual object, she is also a figure of vulnerability. Her innocence in believing Dr. Prentice's reasons for having her undress is funny. Mrs. Prentice's situation, however-

er, is different from Geraldine's. As a wealthy and older woman, she has a certain dignity and power. Her lack of clothing does establish her as a sexual object. Her loss of dignity, however, is also funny. In this respect, she becomes more like the undressed male.

While Mrs. Prentice is briefly out of the room, Dr. Prentice tells Geraldine to get dressed and attempts to return the girl's clothes. When Mrs. Prentice returns before he has done so, Geraldine's clothing becomes an object of humor as Dr. Prentice attempts to hide the garments from his wife. He succeeds in dropping Geraldine's underwear in a wastepaper basket and tries to do the same with the dress, but Mrs. Prentice sees it, asks if he is a transvestite, and demands the dress for herself. She puts it on and thus regains her dignity and authority.

Geraldine, however, is in an even more powerless position. Not only is she not wearing her clothes, they have become unavailable to her. When Dr. Rance enters, his authority and power established by his white coat, Geraldine is completely naked. Dr. Rance, assuming she is a patient, sees her nudity as a manifestation of her madness, and Dr. Prentice gives her a hospital gown. With that change in clothes, she becomes, in effect, a mental patient, and thus loses power altogether. She also loses her identity. When the other characters become concerned because ''Miss Barclay'' is missing and begin to search for her, Miss Barclay cannot be found because, in effect, she no longer exists. In her place is a mental patient with no name, no power, and no dignity.

Geraldine's clothing change begins a series of character disguises that continue throughout the play. Again, the effect is comic. Writing of farce, Susan Rusinko, in her book *Joe Orton,* remarked that ''The single most necessary convention . . . is disguise—one that Orton carries to dizzyingly confusing heights. The multiplicity of Orton's disguises results in the expected confusions of names and identities, teeter-totter plot complications caused by a fast-paced series of exits and entrances, the big scene, and the deus ex machina ending.''

Disguise in *What the Butler Saw* certainly serves to confuse the characters and does create a comic effect, but for the audience, it raises a bigger question about the nature of identity. To what extent does Geraldine become a mental patient while wearing a mental patient's clothing? The changes in costume have real effects in the play because they affect the actions of the other characters. Because Dr. Rance believes Geraldine is a mental patient, he treats her as a patient, restraining her and giving her sedatives against her will. In the world of the play, Geraldine's increased vulnerability is real.

In the outside world as well, people are treated differently depending on how they dress. Lawyers routinely advise defendants not to wear their prison clothes in court because those clothes will cause the jury to see them as criminals. Women and men wear suits to job interviews so that the potential employers will see them as capable and responsible. In a

sense, such changes of clothing are disguises as well. People are judged by what they wear.

Geraldine is vulnerable without her street clothes, but Dr. Prentice becomes vulnerable because of his possession of her dress, stockings, bra, panties, and shoes. His attempts to hide these articles from Mrs. Prentice are comic, but her discovery of them causes him to lose power as both Dr. Rance and Mrs. Prentice see his possession of women's clothes as a manifestation of mental illness. Their beliefs are reinforced when Nick arrives with Mrs. Prentice's dress and wig, and Dr. Prentice promptly takes possession of them. ''The man dressed as a woman,'' Shepherd wrote, ''is . . . comic because this is supposedly improper for a man (and usually involves a mocking imitation of 'feminine' behaviour).'' Although Nick (and later Sergeant Match) will actually dress as a woman, the idea of Dr. Prentice dressing as a woman is comic. Because women are traditionally considered inferior to men, a man dressed in women's clothing loses power and dignity.

Sergeant Match's arrival as a uniformed figure of authority results in further clothing changes. Nick, worried that he will be arrested for sexual misconduct, needs a disguise, and Dr. Prentice, increasingly under suspicion because of Geraldine's disappearance, needs a Miss Barclay. Nick, therefore, puts on Mrs. Prentice's dress and wig and becomes the traditionally comic man in drag (women's clothing). Geraldine, still wearing a hospital gown and seen only by Dr. Prentice, enters and asks him for the return of her clothes. Dr. Prentice gives her her panties and bra, and she puts these on. Left briefly alone in the room, she takes Nick's hotel page uniform. The effect of these quick costume changes is comic, but also furthers one of Orton's themes. Geraldine and Nick have taken on each other's clothes, and thus, each other's identities. Except for Dr. Prentice, the other characters see Nick as Geraldine and Geraldine as Nick. In essence, it seems that they are identified by their clothes, not by their bodies and minds. In addition, because Geraldine has changed out of her hospital gown, the unnamed mental patient has disappeared, adding comic confusion.

Sergeant Match's interview with Geraldine, whom he believes to be Nick, results in further exploration of the issue of sexual identity. When Geraldine asks to be taken to the police station for protection from Dr. Prentice, Dr. Prentice says, ''What this young woman claims is a tissue of lies.''

After Sergeant Match replies, "This is a boy, sir, not a girl," Dr. Prentice begins to refer to Geraldine as he, even though he knows she is a girl. Geraldine initially insists that she is not Nick but still maintains that she is a boy. For Geraldine, however, her identity becomes a matter of convenience. "I'm not Nicholas Beckett," she says, "I want to go to prison." Sergeant Match replies, "If you aren't Nicholas Beckett, you can't go to prison. You're not under arrest." Geraldine pauses, then responds, "I am Nicholas Beckett."

Still attempting to maintain her disguise as a boy, Geraldine tells Dr. Rance that she wouldn't enjoy sexual intercourse. "I might get pregnant," she says, then catches herself and continues, "or be the cause of pregnancy in others." When Geraldine is told that she must undergo a physical examination, that she can no longer continue her façade, she is finally forced to insist that she is female. Ultimately, gender can be defined clearly only in strictly biological terms. Physiologically, an individual can be male or female. Psychologically and culturally, however, the boundaries are not so clear.

When Mrs. Prentice sees Geraldine and Nick, she asks what happened to the other young man, the boy who assaulted her, Nicholas Beckett. Now Geraldine is re-identified as Gerald Barclay. Nick persuades Dr. Prentice to tell Sergeant Match to undress so that Nick can have his police uniform. Now Sergeant Match loses his authority and his dignity with his clothes. Shepherd wrote, "Orton saves the conventional farce joke for the policeman Match, the figure of law and order. He is the one caught with his trousers down when the woman enters." Wearing only underpants, the officer becomes a comic figure. Mrs. Prentice sees first Sergeant Match, then Nick, wearing only underwear, and the unclothed human body is revealed as a potential threat. "You must help me doctor," she says, "I keep seeing naked men." Later, she says, "Doctor, Doctor! The world is full of naked men running in all directions."

This theme is continued when Mrs. Prentice finds the unnamed mental patient's gown. Dr. Rance takes note of this and of the fact that Nicholas Beckett left without his uniform. "Two young people," he says, "one mad and one sexually insatiable—both naked—are roaming this house. At all costs, we must prevent a collision." The unclothed body is now shown to be dangerous. Without clothing, there is the threat of unbridled sexuality. Of course, this presumed nudity, like the near nudity of Sergeant Match, is comic; the sense of danger lies below the surface. In addition, the naked or nearly naked body is also funny because it creates discomfort in the audience. People laugh when they are uncomfortable. Orton thus acknowledges society's fear of the human body and of sex but simultaneously draws attention to the body and sex as comic material. Orton uses the lack of clothing to reveal the complications of society's attitudes toward sex.

The following portion of the play is a scene of mass confusion and comedy as all characters participate in a wild and violent scene in which clothing is continually added, removed, and exchanged. At various times, Geraldine, Dr. Prentice, and Mrs. Prentice are all put in straitjackets, which creates in them a loss of dignity and power. Geraldine, Nick, Mrs. Prentice, and Sergeant Match all appear wearing only their underwear. Again, power and dignity are lost. It should be pointed out here that, in the last scene, some of the removal of clothing seems rather contrived. There appears to be no dramatic reason for Dr. Prentice to forcefully remove Geraldine's trousers or tear off Mrs. Prentice's dress.

At the end of the play, Dr. Rance and Dr. Prentice retain their white coats and Mrs. Prentice, Geraldine, and Nick all appear in their underwear. In the final moments of the play, Sergeant Match is lowered on a rope ladder from the ceiling. He wears Mrs. Prentice's leopard-spotted dress. Only Dr. Rance does not change clothes throughout the play. For the audience, he is nonsensical or insane, but he retains his power within the world of the play.

It is Dr. Rance who speaks the play's final words, "Let us put on our clothes and face the world." The line suggests a new beginning as, according to Orton's stage directions, the characters "climb the rope ladder into the blazing light." The traditional ending of farce is a return to normalcy, to the previous order. The implication is that the return of the old clothes will bring about the old order, will end the madness of the play. But Orton has shown that, like clothing, power, dignity, and identity can easily be discarded and changed.

Source: Clare Cross, for *Drama for Students,* Gale, 1999.

John Lahr

In this review of a 1994 revival of What the Butler Saw, *noted Orton biographer Lahr offers a laudatory appraisal of both Orton's skill as a farceur and the merits of this new production. Lahr calls* What the Butler Saw *Orton's "farce masterpiece."*

In May, 1967, Joe Orton sat with friends at a café in Tangier. He had every reason to feel free and full of fun. He was thirty-four, rich, newly famous after the award-winning success of "*Loot*" (1966), which he had turned, by his account, from "a failed farce into a successful farce," and with his new farce masterpiece, "*What the Butler Saw*"—now at the American Repertory Theatre, in Cambridge—completed and in the manuscript drawer under his bed in the tiny North London flat he shared with his mentor and eventual murderer, Kenneth Halliwell. Orton had already made a mental note to hot up the new play. "Much more fucking," he wrote in his diary, "and they'll be screaming hysterics in next to no time."

Orton wanted laughter to set off a panic—a combination of terror and elation that would create "a sort of seismic disturbance." Laughter was an exercise in freedom and a furious defense against the stereotyping and the received bourgeois notions that so oppressed him. Although Orton liked to brag about his sexual prowess both to friends and to his diary, his showy brilliance and his sexual athletics were displays of mastery that belied a deep-seated sense of inferiority. On that afternoon in Tangier, as Orton wrote in his diary, a "stuffy American tourist and his disapproving wife" sat at the table next to Orton's. The threat of judgment sent Orton into a comic attack that displayed the same psychic jujitsu that he practiced on the theatre audience, using the thrust of the public's prejudice to throw it off balance:

> They listened to our conversation, and I, realizing this, began to exaggerate the content. "He took it up the arse," I said. "And afterwards he thanked me for giving him such a good fucking." The American and his wife hardly moved a muscle. "We've got a leopard skin rug in the flat and he wanted me to fuck him on that," I said in an undertone which was perfectly audible to the next table, "only I'm afraid of the spunk, you see, it might adversely affect the spots on the leopard."

"It isn't a joke," Orton told his friends after the Americans "frigidly" moved away. "There's no such thing as a joke." He never said a truer word about his craft. Jokes were a method of disenchanting the credulous and of laughing the suffocating stereotypes off the stage. "Marriage excuses no one the freak's roll-call," says the arresting officer in "*What the Butler Saw*," which begins like a conventional boulevard farce, with a psychiatrist trying to seduce a would-be secretary, and ends as a tale of nymphomania, incest, transvestism, and attempted murder. Orton's combative, epigrammatic style demands capitulation, not discussion. When the lecherous psychiatrist, Dr. Prentice, protests to the government inspector, "I'm a heterosexual," the inspector, Dr. Rance, counters, "I wish you wouldn't use those Chaucerian words." The strut of Orton's dialogue—which honored and updated the discoveries of both Oscar Wilde and Ronald Firbank—was an irresistible amalgam of the highfalutin and the low comic. "My uterine contractions have been bogus for some time," Dr. Prentice's nymphomaniac wife says to her sexually inadequate husband. All Orton's characters speak in the same idiom. Their syntax is a model of propriety; their lives are models of impropriety. The very act of speaking demonstrates the thin line between reason and rapacity, which is the mischievous paradox that all Orton's comedies explore.

The other great stylists of modern English comedy—G. B. Shaw, Noel Coward, Harold Pinter—lived long enough to cajole actors and directors into realizing their vision. Orton, who was murdered in August, 1967, has had to endure a period of trial and error before graduating into the modern canon. In England, this elevation has been achieved by Lindsay Anderson's 1975 Royal Court revival of "*What the Butler Saw*," and by Jonathan Lynn's groundbreaking 1984 production of "*Loot*" with Leonard Rossiter. These examples of comic mayhem showed a generation how to stage and to play Orton for keeps and not just for laughs. In America—despite John Tillinger's firstrate productions of "*Entertaining Mr. Sloane*" and "*Loot*"—Orton's finest play, "*What the Butler Saw*," has not fared so well, both because of its verbal requirements, which defeat the diction of most American actors, and because of the nature of farce itself, which usually confounds an audience that likes stories where the self is inflated, not disintegrated. So David Wheeler's mostly sold-out Cambridge production comes as both a surprise and an improbable delight.

The ungainly fifty-foot-long proscenium of the Loeb Drama Centre, which serves as the American Repertory Theatre's main stage, poses an almost insoluble problem for any farce. Its length means that a sense of boundaries —that illusion of trapped, claustrophobic life which fuels farce's sense of chaos and collapse—is almost impossible to create. "*What the Butler Saw*"—a reference to British peep-show pier entertainments—parodies French farce and at the same time reinvents the farce form for more lethal dramatic purposes. Wheeler makes life harder for himself by eliminating Orton's French windows as well as the skylight, which figures large in Orton's brilliant finale. Derek McLane's set is also full of anomalies, which the production somehow succeeds in overcoming: a pea-green-and-chrome interior that looks more like a public swimming pool than like a private consulting room; and seven doors, five arc lamps, a utility desk, and scaffolding. The set announces the unconventional nature of the evening, whereas Orton's intention is to lull an audience into expecting the ordinary and then to sock them with the extraordinary. In French farce, stage life returns to the status quo ante, but in Orton's kind of farce, life and comic stereotypes are not just turned upside down but changed. In "*Loot,,*" the thieves escape, and the innocent father is framed by his son and hauled off to prison. ("I'm innocent, I'm innocent," Mr. McLeavy bleats, in one of postwar comedy's greatest exit lines. "What a terrible thing to happen to a man who's been kissed by the Pope.") In "*What the Butler Saw,*" promiscuity leads to redemption when the put-upon secretary, Geraldine, and the blackmailing page boy, Nick, turn out to be the abandoned children of Mrs. Prentice, fathered by her husband's anonymous rape of her in a hotel linen cupboard—a revelation that heals the Prentices' sexual standoff.

Orton was a voluptuary of fiasco, and in acting him the challenge is to keep the argument and the action operating at full tilt. Fluidity and reality are hard to deliver for all but the most experienced of players. Here, Nick, played by the excellent Benjamin Evett, gets closest to the true note of earnestness and agitation in Orton's demented characters. He hits the stage at high energy—a page boy who just wants his blackmail money but ends up in a dress, bleeding from a gunshot wound, and with his sanity in serious doubt. "If the pain is real, I must be real," he says to Dr. Rance, who replies, "I'd rather not get involved in methaphysical speculation." Margaret Gibson may occasionally tip the wink to the audience, but she brings to Mrs. Prentice (a wife Prentice claims "they'll send . . . to the grave in a Y-shaped coffin") the crucial requirement of robust comic acting and the added feature of a great pair of legs. Ms. Gibson makes up in comic invention what she lacks in comic gravity. When the frazzled and furious Prentice (played by Thomas Derrah, who is also slow to kindle but finally burns) rips off his wife's dress, the violence turns her on. "Oh, my darling!" says Mrs. Prentice, writhing on the floor in sexual ecstasy while Prentice dives for her abandoned garment. "This is the way to sexual adjustment in marriage." The moment is Ms. Gibson's invention, and it's terrific.

"ORTON WAS A VOLUPTUARY OF FIASCO, AND IN ACTING HIM THE CHALLENGE IS TO KEEP THE ARGUMENT AND THE ACTION OPERATING AT FULL TILT"

At a certain momentum, all things disintegrate; and "*What the Butler Saw*" acts out the notion of gender-collapsing. The credulous Geraldine (well played by Elizabeth Marvel) is so dizzy from the plots complications that she gets confused about her sex. "I must be a boy," she says, wearing a page-boy outfit and trying to pass as Nick to the police. "I like boys." But not all the actors feed the crazy brilliance of Orton's farce logic. Alvin Epstein, sporting a homegrown white mustache, plays Dr. Rance at a stately pace—a wrong choice, which keeps this excellent actor from maximizing the full comic menace of Rance's ranting psychiatric explanations and from raising the comic stakes for the other characters. "As a transvestite, fetishist, bisexual murderer Dr. Prentice displays considerable deviation overlap," says Rance, in a frenzy of psychoanalytic labelling. "We may get necrophilia, too. As a sort of bonus." But on the night I saw the play Epstein, who lost his way in the speech, also seemed to have lost his bead on the character. William Young's Sergeant Match is serviceable, but his unfortunate accent leaves whole areas of Match's hilarious stupidity unexplored. Still, with the complications of Orton's plot kicking in, the audience hardly notices or cares.

If Wheeler's production can't deliver the antic, it at least serves up intelligence and clarity. Wheeler has pruned Orton's jokes effectively, and in the end even his alteration of Orton's deus ex machina seems to work. Sergeant Match enters to a fanfare and on an automated trestle to demand the return of the missing part of a statue of Winston Churchill. The part, which was blown off when a gas main exploded, turns out to be not the great man's cigar but his penis. "Weary, bleeding, drugged and drunk, [they] climb the rope ladder into the blazing light": Orton's final stage direction is a vision of bruised transcendence. In Cambridge, there is no glaring light, no rope ladder, no "Hallelujah Chorus." But

> *WHAT THE BUTLER SAW IS A MAGNIFICENTLY COMIC CELEBRATION OF EXCESS THAT FOR THE FIRST TIME PROPERLY, OR PERHAPS IMPROPERLY, UNITED ORTON'S INTEREST IN THE COMIC POTENTIAL OF LANGUAGE WITH HIS WONDERMENT AT THE ABSURDITIES OF THE PHYSICAL MANIFESTATIONS OF BEHAVIOUR"*

there is a comic victory. The actors' final tableau fades out with a pinwheeling of psychedelic light and with the sound of the Beatles, which is what passed for hope and for Heaven in those bumptious, buoyant times.

Source: John Lahr, "Laughing It Off" in the *New Yorker,* Vol. LXX, no. 1, February 21, 1994, pp. 106–07.

John Bull

In this overview of Orton's plays, Bull delineates the plot and provides background history on the playwright's work, including the comparisons that have been made between Orton and Oscar Wilde.

What the Butler Saw turned out to be Joe Orton's final play, a magnificently comic celebration of excess that for the first time properly, or perhaps improperly, united his interest in the comic potential of language with his wonderment at the absurdities of the physical manifestations of behaviour. It is not only quite easily his best play, it heralds the arrival of what would have been one of the major post-war playwrights.

The plot is not readily summarised, its many and intricate complications being themselves a major part of the play's concern with the way in which rationalising words are ultimately always betrayed by the stronger imperatives of the body. Suitably enough the play is set in an asylum presided over by a psychiatrist, Dr. Prentice, whose intended sexual adventures and his continual attempts to lie his way out of the frustrated consequences are themselves a

part of the tension between the desire for liberation and the protective retreat into repression which lies at the heart of the play.

At the outset Prentice is interviewing a candidate for a secretarial position, an interview which inevitably concludes with a demand that the girl, Geraldine, undress for a complete physical examination. Surprised by the unexpected arrival of Prentice's wife, the naked girl is first hidden and then easily persuaded to borrow the clothes of Nicholas, a porter from the Station Hotel who has arrived bearing Mrs. Prentice's luggage.

Add to this initial sexual confusion the potential for chaos afforded by the introduction of, first, Rance, a visiting psychiatrist intent on examining the suitability of Prentice and his clinic for the treatment of the insane, and then a Sergeant Match in pursuit of anything remotely illegal—which covers just about everything that subsequently occurs to the characters or is revealed about their pasts—and one has a fair idea of the kind of revelations to follow. Incest is added to adultery and tranvestisism when it transpires that Geraldine and Nicholas are, unknown to all parties concerned, the twin children of the Prentices, conceived in the Linen cupboard of the Station Hotel—Orton's equivalent of Oscar Wilde's abandoned handbag in *The Importance of Being Earnest.*

It is obvious that the further the plot proceeds, the less Orton is concerned with anything like a moral evaluation of the characters' actions or motivations. Farce here is more than a technique; it is a way of life. On his first entrance Dr. Rance asks, "Why are there so many doors? Was the house designed by a lunatic?" It is a question that not only emphasises the function of the psychiatric clinic—a madhouse with openings for all tastes—but also recalls the play's epigram, from Tourneur's *The Revenger's Tragedy:* "Surely we're all mad people, and they whom we think, are not". Orton's redefinition of farce allowed for a complete abandonment of the naturalistic trappings of plot and character in favour of a world in which the repressions and sublimations of life are allowed a fully-articulated play.

The world of *What the Butler Saw* is a true Freudian nightmare of unleashed sexual repression. It is civilisation without its clothes. Indeed it is Dr. Prentice's inability to admit to the only comparatively straightforward heterosexual act in the entire play that sets things in motion. The wife he would deceive has just returned from a meeting of a club "primarily for lesbians", during the proceedings of which she has availed herself of the body of the young porter Nick, who has actually arrived at the asylum intent on demanding money for the photographs taken during the event; and Nick himself spent a large part of the previous evening sexually harrassing an entire corridor of schoolgirls.

Normality is never the norm in this play; as in the brothel in Genet's *The Balcony,* the asylum converts dreamed fantasy into actable reality. "Marriage excuses no-one the freaks' roll-call", Sergeant Match assures Prentice when he attempts to protest his absolute innocence. What follows is a sort of sexual *Bartholemew Fair* in which clothing is first removed and then redistributed in a confusion of sexual roles—the whole business being observed and interpreted by the lunatic inspector Rance, who offers a succession of psychoanalytical explanations of the characters' behaviour, the unlikelihood of which is only surpassed by the truths of the various cases.

It is a flawed play. It needs, and would certainly have received, considerable rewriting—in particular, the tedious running gag about the lost penis from the statue of Winston Churchill, which is eventually used to bring proceedings to a close, is a part of an interest in the over-facile shooting of sacred cows that characterised his earliest work, and could easily be removed. However, what it promises is a redefinition of farce, a complete liberation of libido in a glorious celebration of chaos and *fin-de-civilisation.* "'It's the only way to smash the wretched civilisation', I said, making a mental note to hot-up *What the Butler Saw* when I came to rewrite. . . Yes. Sex is not the only way to initiate them. Much more fucking and they'll be screaming hysterics in no time", noted Orton.

But sex is both the subject of the play and the vehicle which suggests potentially more serious matters. The tradition of farce inherited by Orton was diluted and trivial, confirming rather than questioning the assumptions of its audience. His awareness of the proximity of farce and tragedy—as seen, for instance, in the scene of the mad King Lear and the blind Gloucester on the beach at Dover—both as theatrical modes and as mirrors of psychological reaction to chaos, points to what he was really attempting. While the plays of those such as Tourneur and Webster move easily from farce to tragedy, the presentation of chaos counterpointed by the articulation of a sense of a moral order, in this play there is no possibility of a transition to a tragic definition of

farce. The characters end the play bloodied but unbowed; the ending is, however, purely mechanical. As Orton argued, farce had become an escapist medium, on the run from precisely that which it had originally presented—the disturbing manifestation of the human consciousness which threatens the stability of the social order.

Orton has frequently been compared to Oscar Wilde, and in this play in particular it is a useful comparison. But here more than ever there is a key distinction. Where Wilde invites us to look beyond the brittle and studied brilliance of his characters' dialogue to the hollowness underneath, Orton presents all his cards directly to the audience. What we are being shown *is* the underneath. What Orton was moving towards was the presentation of a pre-civilised world in which the awakened subconscious, at large in a decadent society, makes everyone a "minority group". Had he lived, his redefinition of the boundaries of comedy would have been a major feature of the modern theatre.

Source: John Bull, *"What the Butler Saw"* in *The International Dictionary of Theatre,* Volume 1: *Plays,* edited by Mark Hawkins-Dady, St. James Press, 1992, pp. 892–93.

SOURCES

Bigsby, C. W. E. *Joe Orton,* Methuen, 1982. pp. 49-61.

Nightingale, Benedict. "The Detached Anarchist: On Joe Orton" in *Encounter,* Vol. LII, no. 3, March, 1979, 55-61.

FURTHER READING

Lahr, John. *Prick up Your Ears: The Biography of Joe Orton,* Knopf, 1978.
  This is the most complete biography of Orton, featuring information on his life as well as his work. Lahr's work on the relationship between Orton and Halliwell was adapted to make the 1987 film on Orton's life, *Prick up Your Ears.*

Levin, Bernard. *The Pendulum Years: Britain and the Sixties,* Jonathan Cape, 1970.
  This thorough book covers many aspects of life in Great Britain during the time in which Orton was writing.

Rusinko, Susan. *Joe Orton,* Twayne, 1995.
  Rusinko provides a brief biography as well as extensive analysis of Orton's plays.

Shepherd, Simon. *Because We're Queers: The Life and Crimes of Kenneth Halliwell and Joe Orton,* GMP, 1989.

    In this study of Orton's work, Shepherd maintains that ''the Orton industry,'' as he calls it, reflects society's prejudice against gays. Shepherd seeks to present a ''radical gay viewpoint'' on Orton and his work.

Glossary of Literary Terms

A

Abstract: Used as a noun, the term refers to a short summary or outline of a longer work. As an adjective applied to writing or literary works, abstract refers to words or phrases that name things not knowable through the five senses. Examples of abstracts include the *Cliffs Notes* summaries of major literary works. Examples of abstract terms or concepts include ''idea,'' ''guilt'' ''honesty,'' and ''loyalty.''

Absurd, Theater of the: See *Theater of the Absurd*

Absurdism: See *Theater of the Absurd*

Act: A major section of a play. Acts are divided into varying numbers of shorter scenes. From ancient times to the nineteenth century plays were generally constructed of five acts, but modern works typically consist of one, two, or three acts. Examples of five-act plays include the works of Sophocles and Shakespeare, while the plays of Arthur Miller commonly have a three-act structure.

Acto: A one-act Chicano theater piece developed out of collective improvisation. *Actos* were performed by members of Luis Valdez's Teatro Campesino in California during the mid-1960s.

Aestheticism: A literary and artistic movement of the nineteenth century. Followers of the movement believed that art should not be mixed with social, political, or moral teaching. The statement ''art for art's sake'' is a good summary of aestheticism. The movement had its roots in France, but it gained widespread importance in England in the last half of the nineteenth century, where it helped change the Victorian practice of including moral lessons in literature. Oscar Wilde is one of the best-known ''aesthetes'' of the late nineteenth century.

Age of Johnson: The period in English literature between 1750 and 1798, named after the most prominent literary figure of the age, Samuel Johnson. Works written during this time are noted for their emphasis on ''sensibility,'' or emotional quality. These works formed a transition between the rational works of the Age of Reason, or Neoclassical period, and the emphasis on individual feelings and responses of the Romantic period. Significant writers during the Age of Johnson included the novelists Ann Radcliffe and Henry Mackenzie, dramatists Richard Sheridan and Oliver Goldsmith, and poets William Collins and Thomas Gray. Also known as Age of Sensibility

Age of Reason: See *Neoclassicism*

Age of Sensibility: See *Age of Johnson*

Alexandrine Meter: See *Meter*

Allegory: A narrative technique in which characters representing things or abstract ideas are used to convey a message or teach a lesson. Allegory is typically used to teach moral, ethical, or religious lessons but is sometimes used for satiric or political purposes. Examples of allegorical works include Edmund Spenser's *The Faerie Queene* and John Bunyan's *The Pilgrim's Progress.*

Allusion: A reference to a familiar literary or historical person or event, used to make an idea more easily understood. For example, describing someone as a ''Romeo'' makes an allusion to William Shakespeare's famous young lover in *Romeo and Juliet.*

Amerind Literature: The writing and oral traditions of Native Americans. Native American literature was originally passed on by word of mouth, so it consisted largely of stories and events that were easily memorized. Amerind prose is often rhythmic like poetry because it was recited to the beat of a ceremonial drum. Examples of Amerind literature include the autobiographical *Black Elk Speaks,* the works of N. Scott Momaday, James Welch, and Craig Lee Strete, and the poetry of Luci Tapahonso.

Analogy: A comparison of two things made to explain something unfamiliar through its similarities to something familiar, or to prove one point based on the acceptedness of another. Similes and metaphors are types of analogies. Analogies often take the form of an extended simile, as in William Blake's aphorism: ''As the caterpillar chooses the fairest leaves to lay her eggs on, so the priest lays his curse on the fairest joys.''

Angry Young Men: A group of British writers of the 1950s whose work expressed bitterness and disillusionment with society. Common to their work is an anti-hero who rebels against a corrupt social order and strives for personal integrity. The term has been used to describe Kingsley Amis, John Osborne, Colin Wilson, John Wain, and others.

Antagonist: The major character in a narrative or drama who works against the hero or protagonist. An example of an evil antagonist is Richard Lovelace in Samuel Richardson's *Clarissa,* while a virtuous antagonist is Macduff in William Shakespeare's *Macbeth.*

Anthropomorphism: The presentation of animals or objects in human shape or with human characteristics. The term is derived from the Greek word for ''human form.'' The fables of Aesop, the animated films of Walt Disney, and Richard Adams's *Watership Down* feature anthropomorphic characters.

Anti-hero: A central character in a work of literature who lacks traditional heroic qualities such as courage, physical prowess, and fortitude. Anti-heros typically distrust conventional values and are unable to commit themselves to any ideals. They generally feel helpless in a world over which they have no control. Anti-heroes usually accept, and often celebrate, their positions as social outcasts. A well-known anti-hero is Yossarian in Joseph Heller's novel *Catch-22.*

Antimasque: See *Masque*

Antithesis: The antithesis of something is its direct opposite. In literature, the use of antithesis as a figure of speech results in two statements that show a contrast through the balancing of two opposite ideas. Technically, it is the second portion of the statement that is defined as the ''antithesis''; the first portion is the ''thesis.'' An example of antithesis is found in the following portion of Abraham Lincoln's ''Gettysburg Address''; notice the opposition between the verbs ''remember'' and ''forget'' and the phrases ''what we say'' and ''what they did'': ''The world will little note nor long remember what we say here, but it can never forget what they did here.''

Apocrypha: Writings tentatively attributed to an author but not proven or universally accepted to be their works. The term was originally applied to certain books of the Bible that were not considered inspired and so were not included in the ''sacred canon.'' Geoffrey Chaucer, William Shakespeare, Thomas Kyd, Thomas Middleton, and John Marston all have apocrypha. Apocryphal books of the Bible include the Old Testament's Book of Enoch and New Testament's Gospel of Peter.

Apollonian and Dionysian: The two impulses believed to guide authors of dramatic tragedy. The Apollonian impulse is named after Apollo, the Greek god of light and beauty and the symbol of intellectual order. The Dionysian impulse is named after Dionysus, the Greek god of wine and the symbol of the unrestrained forces of nature. The Apollonian impulse is to create a rational, harmonious world, while the Dionysian is to express the irrational forces of personality. Friedrich Nietzche uses these terms in *The Birth of Tragedy* to designate contrasting elements in Greek tragedy.

Apostrophe: A statement, question, or request addressed to an inanimate object or concept or to a nonexistent or absent person. Requests for inspiration from the muses in poetry are examples of apostrophe, as is Marc Antony's address to Caesar's corpse in William Shakespeare's *Julius Caesar:* ''O, pardon me, thou bleeding piece of earth, That I am meek and gentle with these butchers!. . . Woe to the hand that shed this costly blood!. . . ''

Archetype: The word archetype is commonly used to describe an original pattern or model from which all other things of the same kind are made. This term was introduced to literary criticism from the psychology of Carl Jung. It expresses Jung's theory that behind every person's "unconscious," or repressed memories of the past, lies the "collective unconscious" of the human race: memories of the countless typical experiences of our ancestors. These memories are said to prompt illogical associations that trigger powerful emotions in the reader. Often, the emotional process is primitive, even primordial. Archetypes are the literary images that grow out of the "collective unconscious." They appear in literature as incidents and plots that repeat basic patterns of life. They may also appear as stereotyped characters. Examples of literary archetypes include themes such as birth and death and characters such as the Earth Mother.

Argument: The argument of a work is the author's subject matter or principal idea. Examples of defined "argument" portions of works include John Milton's *Arguments* to each of the books of *Paradise Lost* and the "Argument" to Robert Herrick's *Hesperides.*

Aristotelian Criticism: Specifically, the method of evaluating and analyzing tragedy formulated by the Greek philosopher Aristotle in his *Poetics.* More generally, the term indicates any form of criticism that follows Aristotle's views. Aristotelian criticism focuses on the form and logical structure of a work, apart from its historical or social context, in contrast to "Platonic Criticism," which stresses the usefulness of art. Adherents of New Criticism including John Crowe Ransom and Cleanth Brooks utilize and value the basic ideas of Aristotelian criticism for textual analysis.

Art for Art's Sake: See *Aestheticism*

Aside: A comment made by a stage performer that is intended to be heard by the audience but supposedly not by other characters. Eugene O'Neill's *Strange Interlude* is an extended use of the aside in modern theater.

Audience: The people for whom a piece of literature is written. Authors usually write with a certain audience in mind, for example, children, members of a religious or ethnic group, or colleagues in a professional field. The term "audience" also applies to the people who gather to see or hear any performance, including plays, poetry readings, speeches, and concerts. Jane Austen's parody of the gothic novel, *Northanger Abbey,* was originally intended for (and also pokes fun at) an audience of young and avid female gothic novel readers.

Avant-garde: A French term meaning "vanguard." It is used in literary criticism to describe new writing that rejects traditional approaches to literature in favor of innovations in style or content. Twentieth-century examples of the literary *avant-garde* include the Black Mountain School of poets, the Bloomsbury Group, and the Beat Movement.

B

Ballad: A short poem that tells a simple story and has a repeated refrain. Ballads were originally intended to be sung. Early ballads, known as folk ballads, were passed down through generations, so their authors are often unknown. Later ballads composed by known authors are called literary ballads. An example of an anonymous folk ballad is "Edward," which dates from the Middle Ages. Samuel Taylor Coleridge's "The Rime of the Ancient Mariner" and John Keats's "La Belle Dame sans Merci" are examples of literary ballads.

Baroque: A term used in literary criticism to describe literature that is complex or ornate in style or diction. Baroque works typically express tension, anxiety, and violent emotion. The term "Baroque Age" designates a period in Western European literature beginning in the late sixteenth century and ending about one hundred years later. Works of this period often mirror the qualities of works more generally associated with the label "baroque" and sometimes feature elaborate conceits. Examples of Baroque works include John Lyly's *Euphues: The Anatomy of Wit,* Luis de Gongora's *Soledads,* and William Shakespeare's *As You Like It.*

Baroque Age: See *Baroque*

Baroque Period: See *Baroque*

Beat Generation: See *Beat Movement*

Beat Movement: A period featuring a group of American poets and novelists of the 1950s and 1960s—including Jack Kerouac, Allen Ginsberg, Gregory Corso, William S. Burroughs, and Lawrence Ferlinghetti—who rejected established social and literary values. Using such techniques as stream of consciousness writing and jazz-influenced free verse and focusing on unusual or abnormal states of mind—generated by religious ecstasy or the use of drugs—the Beat writers aimed to create works that were unconventional in both form and subject matter. Kerouac's *On the Road* is perhaps the best-known example of a Beat Generation novel, and Ginsberg's *Howl* is a famous collection of Beat poetry.

Black Aesthetic Movement: A period of artistic and literary development among African Americans in the 1960s and early 1970s. This was the first major African-American artistic movement since the Harlem Renaissance and was closely paralleled by the civil rights and black power movements. The black aesthetic writers attempted to produce works of art that would be meaningful to the black masses. Key figures in black aesthetics included one of its founders, poet and playwright Amiri Baraka, formerly known as LeRoi Jones; poet and essayist Haki R. Madhubuti, formerly Don L. Lee; poet and playwright Sonia Sanchez; and dramatist Ed Bullins. Works representative of the Black Aesthetic Movement include Amiri Baraka's play *Dutchman,* a 1964 Obie award-winner; *Black Fire: An Anthology of Afro-American Writing,* edited by Baraka and playwright Larry Neal and published in 1968; and Sonia Sanchez's poetry collection *We a BaddDDD People,* published in 1970. Also known as Black Arts Movement.

Black Arts Movement: See *Black Aesthetic Movement*

Black Comedy: See *Black Humor*

Black Humor: Writing that places grotesque elements side by side with humorous ones in an attempt to shock the reader, forcing him or her to laugh at the horrifying reality of a disordered world. Joseph Heller's novel *Catch-22* is considered a superb example of the use of black humor. Other well-known authors who use black humor include Kurt Vonnegut, Edward Albee, Eugene Ionesco, and Harold Pinter. Also known as Black Comedy.

Blank Verse: Loosely, any unrhymed poetry, but more generally, unrhymed iambic pentameter verse (composed of lines of five two-syllable feet with the first syllable accented, the second unaccented). Blank verse has been used by poets since the Renaissance for its flexibility and its graceful, dignified tone. John Milton's *Paradise Lost* is in blank verse, as are most of William Shakespeare's plays.

Bloomsbury Group: A group of English writers, artists, and intellectuals who held informal artistic and philosophical discussions in Bloomsbury, a district of London, from around 1907 to the early 1930s. The Bloomsbury Group held no uniform philosophical beliefs but did commonly express an aversion to moral prudery and a desire for greater social tolerance. At various times the circle included Virginia Woolf, E. M. Forster, Clive Bell, Lytton Strachey, and John Maynard Keynes.

Bon Mot: A French term meaning ''good word.'' A *bon mot* is a witty remark or clever observation. Charles Lamb and Oscar Wilde are celebrated for their witty *bon mots.* Two examples by Oscar Wilde stand out: (1) ''All women become their mothers. That is their tragedy. No man does. That's his.'' (2) ''A man cannot be too careful in the choice of his enemies.''

Breath Verse: See *Projective Verse*

Burlesque: Any literary work that uses exaggeration to make its subject appear ridiculous, either by treating a trivial subject with profound seriousness or by treating a dignified subject frivolously. The word ''burlesque'' may also be used as an adjective, as in ''burlesque show,'' to mean ''striptease act.'' Examples of literary burlesque include the comedies of Aristophanes, Miguel de Cervantes's *Don Quixote,*, Samuel Butler's poem ''Hudibras,'' and John Gay's play *The Beggar's Opera.*

C

Cadence: The natural rhythm of language caused by the alternation of accented and unaccented syllables. Much modern poetry—notably free verse—deliberately manipulates cadence to create complex rhythmic effects. James Macpherson's ''Ossian poems'' are richly cadenced, as is the poetry of the Symbolists, Walt Whitman, and Amy Lowell.

Caesura: A pause in a line of poetry, usually occurring near the middle. It typically corresponds to a break in the natural rhythm or sense of the line but is sometimes shifted to create special meanings or rhythmic effects. The opening line of Edgar Allan Poe's ''The Raven'' contains a caesura following ''dreary'': ''Once upon a midnight dreary, while I pondered weak and weary. . . .''

Canzone: A short Italian or Provencal lyric poem, commonly about love and often set to music. The *canzone* has no set form but typically contains five or six stanzas made up of seven to twenty lines of eleven syllables each. A shorter, five- to ten-line ''envoy,'' or concluding stanza, completes the poem. Masters of the *canzone* form include

Petrarch, Dante Alighieri, Torquato Tasso, and Guido Cavalcanti.

Carpe Diem: A Latin term meaning "seize the day." This is a traditional theme of poetry, especially lyrics. A *carpe diem* poem advises the reader or the person it addresses to live for today and enjoy the pleasures of the moment. Two celebrated *carpe diem* poems are Andrew Marvell's "To His Coy Mistress" and Robert Herrick's poem beginning "Gather ye rosebuds while ye may. . . ."

Catharsis: The release or purging of unwanted emotions— specifically fear and pity—brought about by exposure to art. The term was first used by the Greek philosopher Aristotle in his *Poetics* to refer to the desired effect of tragedy on spectators. A famous example of catharsis is realized in Sophocles' *Oedipus Rex,* when Oedipus discovers that his wife, Jacosta, is his own mother and that the stranger he killed on the road was his own father.

Celtic Renaissance: A period of Irish literary and cultural history at the end of the nineteenth century. Followers of the movement aimed to create a romantic vision of Celtic myth and legend. The most significant works of the Celtic Renaissance typically present a dreamy, unreal world, usually in reaction against the reality of contemporary problems. William Butler Yeats's *The Wanderings of Oisin* is among the most significant works of the Celtic Renaissance. Also known as Celtic Twilight.

Celtic Twilight: See *Celtic Renaissance*

Character: Broadly speaking, a person in a literary work. The actions of characters are what constitute the plot of a story, novel, or poem. There are numerous types of characters, ranging from simple, stereotypical figures to intricate, multifaceted ones. In the techniques of anthropomorphism and personification, animals—and even places or things— can assume aspects of character. "Characterization" is the process by which an author creates vivid, believable characters in a work of art. This may be done in a variety of ways, including (1) direct description of the character by the narrator; (2) the direct presentation of the speech, thoughts, or actions of the character; and (3) the responses of other characters to the character. The term "character" also refers to a form originated by the ancient Greek writer Theophrastus that later became popular in the seventeenth and eighteenth centuries. It is a short essay or sketch of a person who prominently displays a specific attribute or quality, such as miserliness or ambition. Notable characters in lit-

erature include Oedipus Rex, Don Quixote de la Mancha, Macbeth, Candide, Hester Prynne, Ebenezer Scrooge, Huckleberry Finn, Jay Gatsby, Scarlett O'Hara, James Bond, and Kunta Kinte.

Characterization: See *Character*

Chorus: In ancient Greek drama, a group of actors who commented on and interpreted the unfolding action on the stage. Initially the chorus was a major component of the presentation, but over time it became less significant, with its numbers reduced and its role eventually limited to commentary between acts. By the sixteenth century the chorus—if employed at all—was typically a single person who provided a prologue and an epilogue and occasionally appeared between acts to introduce or underscore an important event. The chorus in William Shakespeare's *Henry V* functions in this way. Modern dramas rarely feature a chorus, but T. S. Eliot's *Murder in the Cathedral* and Arthur Miller's *A View from the Bridge* are notable exceptions. The Stage Manager in Thornton Wilder's *Our Town* performs a role similar to that of the chorus.

Chronicle: A record of events presented in chronological order. Although the scope and level of detail provided varies greatly among the chronicles surviving from ancient times, some, such as the *Anglo-Saxon Chronicle,* feature vivid descriptions and a lively recounting of events. During the Elizabethan Age, many dramas— appropriately called "chronicle plays"—were based on material from chronicles. Many of William Shakespeare's dramas of English history as well as Christopher Marlowe's *Edward II* are based in part on Raphael Holinshead's *Chronicles of England, Scotland, and Ireland.*

Classical: In its strictest definition in literary criticism, classicism refers to works of ancient Greek or Roman literature. The term may also be used to describe a literary work of recognized importance (a "classic") from any time period or literature that exhibits the traits of classicism. Classical authors from ancient Greek and Roman times include Juvenal and Homer. Examples of later works and authors now described as classical include French literature of the seventeenth century, Western novels of the nineteenth century, and American fiction of the mid-nineteenth century such as that written by James Fenimore Cooper and Mark Twain.

Classicism: A term used in literary criticism to describe critical doctrines that have their roots in ancient Greek and Roman literature, philosophy, and art. Works associated with classicism typically exhibit restraint on the part of the author, unity of design and purpose, clarity, simplicity, logical organization, and respect for tradition. Examples of literary classicism include Cicero's prose, the dramas of Pierre Corneille and Jean Racine, the poetry of John Dryden and Alexander Pope, and the writings of J. W. von Goethe, G. E. Lessing, and T. S. Eliot.

Climax: The turning point in a narrative, the moment when the conflict is at its most intense. Typically, the structure of stories, novels, and plays is one of rising action, in which tension builds to the climax, followed by falling action, in which tension lessens as the story moves to its conclusion. The climax in James Fenimore Cooper's *The Last of the Mohicans* occurs when Magua and his captive Cora are pursued to the edge of a cliff by Uncas. Magua kills Uncas but is subsequently killed by Hawkeye.

Colloquialism: A word, phrase, or form of pronunciation that is acceptable in casual conversation but not in formal, written communication. It is considered more acceptable than slang. An example of colloquialism can be found in Rudyard Kipling's *Barrack-room Ballads:* When 'Omer smote 'is bloomin' lyre He'd 'eard men sing by land and sea; An' what he thought 'e might require 'E went an' took—the same as me!

Comedy: One of two major types of drama, the other being tragedy. Its aim is to amuse, and it typically ends happily. Comedy assumes many forms, such as farce and burlesque, and uses a variety of techniques, from parody to satire. In a restricted sense the term comedy refers only to dramatic presentations, but in general usage it is commonly applied to nondramatic works as well. Examples of comedies range from the plays of Aristophanes, Terrence, and Plautus, Dante Alighieri's *The Divine Comedy,* Francois Rabelais's *Pantagruel* and *Gargantua,* and some of Geoffrey Chaucer's tales and William Shakespeare's plays to Noel Coward's play *Private Lives* and James Thurber's short story "The Secret Life of Walter Mitty."

Comedy of Manners: A play about the manners and conventions of an aristocratic, highly sophisticated society. The characters are usually types rather than individualized personalities, and plot is less important than atmosphere. Such plays were an important aspect of late seventeenth-century English comedy. The comedy of manners was revived in the eighteenth century by Oliver Goldsmith and Richard Brinsley Sheridan, enjoyed a second revival in the late nineteenth century, and has endured into the twentieth century. Examples of comedies of manners include William Congreve's *The Way of the World* in the late seventeenth century, Oliver Goldsmith's *She Stoops to Conquer* and Richard Brinsley Sheridan's *The School for Scandal* in the eighteenth century, Oscar Wilde's *The Importance of Being Earnest* in the nineteenth century, and W. Somerset Maugham's *The Circle* in the twentieth century.

Comic Relief: The use of humor to lighten the mood of a serious or tragic story, especially in plays. The technique is very common in Elizabethan works, and can be an integral part of the plot or simply a brief event designed to break the tension of the scene. The Gravediggers' scene in William Shakespeare's *Hamlet* is a frequently cited example of comic relief.

Commedia dell'arte: An Italian term meaning "the comedy of guilds" or "the comedy of professional actors." This form of dramatic comedy was popular in Italy during the sixteenth century. Actors were assigned stock roles (such as Pulcinella, the stupid servant, or Pantalone, the old merchant) and given a basic plot to follow, but all dialogue was improvised. The roles were rigidly typed and the plots were formulaic, usually revolving around young lovers who thwarted their elders and attained wealth and happiness. A rigid convention of the *commedia dell'arte* is the periodic intrusion of Harlequin, who interrupts the play with low buffoonery. Peppino de Filippo's *Metamorphoses of a Wandering Minstrel* gave modern audiences an idea of what *commedia dell'arte* may have been like. Various scenarios for *commedia dell'arte* were compiled in Petraccone's *La commedia dell'arte, storia, technica, scenari,* published in 1927.

Complaint: A lyric poem, popular in the Renaissance, in which the speaker expresses sorrow about his or her condition. Typically, the speaker's sadness is caused by an unresponsive lover, but some complaints cite other sources of unhappiness, such as poverty or fate. A commonly cited example is "A Complaint by Night of the Lover Not Beloved" by Henry Howard, Earl of Surrey. Thomas Sackville's "Complaint of Henry, Duke of Buckingham" traces the duke's unhappiness to his ruthless ambition.

Conceit: A clever and fanciful metaphor, usually expressed through elaborate and extended comparison, that presents a striking parallel between two seemingly dissimilar things—for example, elaborately comparing a beautiful woman to an object like a garden or the sun. The conceit was a popular device throughout the Elizabethan Age and Baroque Age and was the principal technique of the seventeenth-century English metaphysical poets. This usage of the word conceit is unrelated to the best-known definition of conceit as an arrogant attitude or behavior. The conceit figures prominently in the works of John Donne, Emily Dickinson, and T. S. Eliot.

Concrete: Concrete is the opposite of abstract, and refers to a thing that actually exists or a description that allows the reader to experience an object or concept with the senses. Henry David Thoreau's *Walden* contains much concrete description of nature and wildlife.

Concrete Poetry: Poetry in which visual elements play a large part in the poetic effect. Punctuation marks, letters, or words are arranged on a page to form a visual design: a cross, for example, or a bumblebee. Max Bill and Eugene Gomringer were among the early practitioners of concrete poetry; Haroldo de Campos and Augusto de Campos are among contemporary authors of concrete poetry.

Confessional Poetry: A form of poetry in which the poet reveals very personal, intimate, sometimes shocking information about himself or herself. Anne Sexton, Sylvia Plath, Robert Lowell, and John Berryman wrote poetry in the confessional vein.

Conflict: The conflict in a work of fiction is the issue to be resolved in the story. It usually occurs between two characters, the protagonist and the antagonist, or between the protagonist and society or the protagonist and himself or herself. Conflict in Theodore Dreiser's novel *Sister Carrie* comes as a result of urban society, while Jack London's short story "To Build a Fire" concerns the protagonist's battle against the cold and himself.

Connotation: The impression that a word gives beyond its defined meaning. Connotations may be universally understood or may be significant only to a certain group. Both "horse" and "steed" denote the same animal, but "steed" has a different connotation, deriving from the chivalrous or romantic narratives in which the word was once often used.

Consonance: Consonance occurs in poetry when words appearing at the ends of two or more verses have similar final consonant sounds but have final vowel sounds that differ, as with "stuff" and "off." Consonance is found in "The curfew tolls the knells of parting day" from Thomas Grey's "An Elegy Written in a Country Church Yard." Also known as Half Rhyme or Slant Rhyme.

Convention: Any widely accepted literary device, style, or form. A soliloquy, in which a character reveals to the audience his or her private thoughts, is an example of a dramatic convention.

Corrido: A Mexican ballad. Examples of *corridos* include "Muerte del afamado Bilito," "La voz de mi conciencia," "Lucio Perez," "La juida," and "Los presos."

Couplet: Two lines of poetry with the same rhyme and meter, often expressing a complete and self-contained thought. The following couplet is from Alexander Pope's "Elegy to the Memory of an Unfortunate Lady": 'Tis Use alone that sanctifies Expense, And Splendour borrows all her rays from Sense.

Criticism: The systematic study and evaluation of literary works, usually based on a specific method or set of principles. An important part of literary studies since ancient times, the practice of criticism has given rise to numerous theories, methods, and "schools," sometimes producing conflicting, even contradictory, interpretations of literature in general as well as of individual works. Even such basic issues as what constitutes a poem or a novel have been the subject of much criticism over the centuries. Seminal texts of literary criticism include Plato's *Republic,* Aristotle's *Poetics,* Sir Philip Sidney's *The Defence of Poesie,* John Dryden's *Of Dramatic Poesie,* and William Wordsworth's "Preface" to the second edition of his *Lyrical Ballads.* Contemporary schools of criticism include deconstruction, feminist, psychoanalytic, poststructuralist, new historicist, postcolonialist, and reader- response.

D

Dactyl: See *Foot*

Dadaism: A protest movement in art and literature founded by Tristan Tzara in 1916. Followers of the movement expressed their outrage at the destruction brought about by World War I by revolting against numerous forms of social convention. The Dadaists presented works marked by calculated madness and flamboyant nonsense. They stressed total freedom of expression, commonly through primitive displays of emotion and illogical, often senseless, poetry. The movement ended shortly after the war, when it was replaced by surrealism. Proponents of Dadaism include Andre Breton, Louis Aragon, Philippe Soupault, and Paul Eluard.

Decadent: See *Decadents*

Decadents: The followers of a nineteenth-century literary movement that had its beginnings in French aestheticism. Decadent literature displays a fascination with perverse and morbid states; a search for novelty and sensation—the "new thrill"; a preoccupation with mysticism; and a belief in the senselessness of human existence. The movement is closely associated with the doctrine Art for Art's Sake. The term "decadence" is sometimes used to denote a decline in the quality of art or literature following a period of greatness. Major French decadents are Charles Baudelaire and Arthur Rimbaud. English decadents include Oscar Wilde, Ernest Dowson, and Frank Harris.

Deconstruction: A method of literary criticism developed by Jacques Derrida and characterized by multiple conflicting interpretations of a given work. Deconstructionists consider the impact of the language of a work and suggest that the true meaning of the work is not necessarily the meaning that the author intended. Jacques Derrida's *De la grammatologie* is the seminal text on deconstructive strategies; among American practitioners of this method of criticism are Paul de Man and J. Hillis Miller.

Deduction: The process of reaching a conclusion through reasoning from general premises to a specific premise. An example of deduction is present in the following syllogism: Premise: All mammals are animals. Premise: All whales are mammals. Conclusion: Therefore, all whales are animals.

Denotation: The definition of a word, apart from the impressions or feelings it creates in the reader. The word "apartheid" denotes a political and economic policy of segregation by race, but its connotations— oppression, slavery, inequality—are numerous.

Denouement: A French word meaning "the unknotting." In literary criticism, it denotes the resolution of conflict in fiction or drama. The *denouement* follows the climax and provides an outcome to the primary plot situation as well as an explanation of secondary plot complications. The *denouement* often involves a character's recognition of his or her state of mind or moral condition. A well-known example of *denouement* is the last scene of the play *As You Like It* by William Shakespeare, in which couples are married, an evildoer repents, the identities of two disguised characters are revealed, and a ruler is restored to power. Also known as Falling Action.

Description: Descriptive writing is intended to allow a reader to picture the scene or setting in which the action of a story takes place. The form this description takes often evokes an intended emotional response—a dark, spooky graveyard will evoke fear, and a peaceful, sunny meadow will evoke calmness. An example of a descriptive story is Edgar Allan Poe's *Landor's Cottage,* which offers a detailed depiction of a New York country estate.

Detective Story: A narrative about the solution of a mystery or the identification of a criminal. The conventions of the detective story include the detective's scrupulous use of logic in solving the mystery; incompetent or ineffectual police; a suspect who appears guilty at first but is later proved innocent; and the detective's friend or confidant— often the narrator—whose slowness in interpreting clues emphasizes by contrast the detective's brilliance. Edgar Allan Poe's "Murders in the Rue Morgue" is commonly regarded as the earliest example of this type of story. With this work, Poe established many of the conventions of the detective story genre, which are still in practice. Other practitioners of this vast and extremely popular genre include Arthur Conan Doyle, Dashiell Hammett, and Agatha Christie.

Deus ex machina: A Latin term meaning "god out of a machine." In Greek drama, a god was often lowered onto the stage by a mechanism of some kind to rescue the hero or untangle the plot. By extension, the term refers to any artificial device or coincidence used to bring about a convenient and simple solution to a plot. This is a common device in melodramas and includes such fortunate circumstances as the sudden receipt of a legacy to save the family farm or a last-minute stay of execution. The *deus ex machina* invariably rewards the virtuous and punishes evildoers. Examples of *deus ex machina* include King Louis XIV in Jean-Baptiste Moliere's *Tartuffe* and Queen Victoria in *The Pirates of Penzance* by William Gilbert and Arthur Sullivan. Bertolt Brecht parodies the abuse of such devices in the conclusion of his *Threepenny Opera.*

Dialogue: In its widest sense, dialogue is simply conversation between people in a literary work; in its most restricted sense, it refers specifically to the speech of characters in a drama. As a specific literary genre, a "dialogue" is a composition in which characters debate an issue or idea. The Greek philosopher Plato frequently expounded his theories in the form of dialogues.

Diction: The selection and arrangement of words in a literary work. Either or both may vary depending on the desired effect. There are four general types of diction: "formal," used in scholarly or lofty writing; "informal," used in relaxed but educated conversation; "colloquial," used in everyday speech; and "slang," containing newly coined words and other terms not accepted in formal usage.

Didactic: A term used to describe works of literature that aim to teach some moral, religious, political, or practical lesson. Although didactic elements are often found in artistically pleasing works, the term "didactic" usually refers to literature in which the message is more important than the form. The term may also be used to criticize a work that the critic finds "overly didactic," that is, heavy-handed in its delivery of a lesson. Examples of didactic literature include John Bunyan's *Pilgrim's Progress,* Alexander Pope's *Essay on Criticism,* Jean-Jacques Rousseau's *Emile,* and Elizabeth Inchbald's *Simple Story.*

Dimeter: See *Meter*

Dionysian: See *Apollonian and Dionysian*

Discordia concours: A Latin phrase meaning "discord in harmony." The term was coined by the eighteenth-century English writer Samuel Johnson to describe "a combination of dissimilar images or discovery of occult resemblances in things apparently unlike." Johnson created the expression by reversing a phrase by the Latin poet Horace. The metaphysical poetry of John Donne, Richard Crashaw, Abraham Cowley, George Herbert, and Edward Taylor among others, contains many examples of *discordia concours.* In Donne's "A Valediction: Forbidding Mourning," the poet compares the union of himself with his lover to a draftsman's compass: If they be two, they are two so, As stiff twin compasses are two: Thy soul, the fixed foot, makes no show To move, but doth, if the other do; And though it in the center sit, Yet when the other far doth roam, It leans, and hearkens after it, And grows erect, as that comes home.

Dissonance: A combination of harsh or jarring sounds, especially in poetry. Although such combinations may be accidental, poets sometimes intentionally make them to achieve particular effects. Dissonance is also sometimes used to refer to close but not identical rhymes. When this is the case, the word functions as a synonym for consonance. Robert Browning, Gerard Manley Hopkins, and many other poets have made deliberate use of dissonance.

Doppelganger: A literary technique by which a character is duplicated (usually in the form of an alter ego, though sometimes as a ghostly counterpart) or divided into two distinct, usually opposite personalities. The use of this character device is widespread in nineteenth- and twentieth- century literature, and indicates a growing awareness among authors that the "self" is really a composite of many "selves." A well-known story containing a *doppelganger* character is Robert Louis Stevenson's *Dr. Jekyll and Mr. Hyde,* which dramatizes an internal struggle between good and evil. Also known as The Double.

Double Entendre: A corruption of a French phrase meaning "double meaning." The term is used to indicate a word or phrase that is deliberately ambiguous, especially when one of the meanings is risque or improper. An example of a *double entendre* is the Elizabethan usage of the verb "die," which refers both to death and to orgasm.

Double, The: See *Doppelganger*

Draft: Any preliminary version of a written work. An author may write dozens of drafts which are revised to form the final work, or he or she may write only one, with few or no revisions. Dorothy Parker's observation that "I can't write five words but that I change seven" humorously indicates the purpose of the draft.

Drama: In its widest sense, a drama is any work designed to be presented by actors on a stage. Similarly, "drama" denotes a broad literary genre that includes a variety of forms, from pageant and spectacle to tragedy and comedy, as well as countless types and subtypes. More commonly in modern usage, however, a drama is a work that treats serious subjects and themes but does not aim at the grandeur of tragedy. This use of the term originated with the eighteenth-century French writer Denis Diderot, who used the word *drame* to designate his plays about middle- class life; thus "drama" typically features characters of a less exalted stature than those of tragedy. Examples of classical dramas include Menander's comedy *Dyscolus* and Sophocles' tragedy *Oedipus Rex.* Contemporary dramas include Eugene O'Neill's *The Iceman Cometh,* Lillian Hellman's *Little Foxes,* and August Wilson's *Ma Rainey's Black Bottom.*

Dramatic Irony: Occurs when the audience of a play or the reader of a work of literature knows something that a character in the work itself does not know. The irony is in the contrast between the intended meaning of the statements or actions of a character and the additional information understood by the audience. A celebrated example of dramatic irony is in Act V of William Shakespeare's *Romeo and Juliet,* where two young lovers meet their end as a result of a tragic misunderstanding. Here, the audience has full knowledge that Juliet's apparent ''death'' is merely temporary; she will regain her senses when the mysterious ''sleeping potion'' she has taken wears off. But Romeo, mistaking Juliet's drug-induced trance for true death, kills himself in grief. Upon awakening, Juliet discovers Romeo's corpse and, in despair, slays herself.

Dramatic Monologue: See *Monologue*

Dramatic Poetry: Any lyric work that employs elements of drama such as dialogue, conflict, or characterization, but excluding works that are intended for stage presentation. A monologue is a form of dramatic poetry.

Dramatis Personae: The characters in a work of literature, particularly a drama. The list of characters printed before the main text of a play or in the program is the *dramatis personae.*

Dream Allegory: See *Dream Vision*

Dream Vision: A literary convention, chiefly of the Middle Ages. In a dream vision a story is presented as a literal dream of the narrator. This device was commonly used to teach moral and religious lessons. Important works of this type are *The Divine Comedy* by Dante Alighieri, *Piers Plowman* by William Langland, and *The Pilgrim's Progress* by John Bunyan. Also known as Dream Allegory.

Dystopia: An imaginary place in a work of fiction where the characters lead dehumanized, fearful lives. Jack London's *The Iron Heel,* Yevgeny Zamyatin's *My,* Aldous Huxley's *Brave New World,* George Orwell's *Nineteen Eighty-four,* and Margaret Atwood's *Handmaid's Tale* portray versions of dystopia.

E

Eclogue: In classical literature, a poem featuring rural themes and structured as a dialogue among shepherds. Eclogues often took specific poetic forms, such as elegies or love poems. Some were written as the soliloquy of a shepherd. In later centuries, ''eclogue'' came to refer to any poem that was in the pastoral tradition or that had a dialogue or mono-

logue structure. A classical example of an eclogue is Virgil's *Eclogues,* also known as *Bucolics.* Giovanni Boccaccio, Edmund Spenser, Andrew Marvell, Jonathan Swift, and Louis MacNeice also wrote eclogues.

Edwardian: Describes cultural conventions identified with the period of the reign of Edward VII of England (1901-1910). Writers of the Edwardian Age typically displayed a strong reaction against the propriety and conservatism of the Victorian Age. Their work often exhibits distrust of authority in religion, politics, and art and expresses strong doubts about the soundness of conventional values. Writers of this era include George Bernard Shaw, H. G. Wells, and Joseph Conrad.

Edwardian Age: See *Edwardian*

Electra Complex: A daughter's amorous obsession with her father. The term Electra complex comes from the plays of Euripides and Sophocles entitled *Electra,* in which the character Electra drives her brother Orestes to kill their mother and her lover in revenge for the murder of their father.

Elegy: A lyric poem that laments the death of a person or the eventual death of all people. In a conventional elegy, set in a classical world, the poet and subject are spoken of as shepherds. In modern criticism, the word elegy is often used to refer to a poem that is melancholy or mournfully contemplative. John Milton's ''Lycidas'' and Percy Bysshe Shelley's ''Adonais'' are two examples of this form.

Elizabethan Age: A period of great economic growth, religious controversy, and nationalism closely associated with the reign of Elizabeth I of England (1558-1603). The Elizabethan Age is considered a part of the general renaissance—that is, the flowering of arts and literature—that took place in Europe during the fourteenth through sixteenth centuries. The era is considered the golden age of English literature. The most important dramas in English and a great deal of lyric poetry were produced during this period, and modern English criticism began around this time. The notable authors of the period—Philip Sidney, Edmund Spenser, Christopher Marlowe, William Shakespeare, Ben Jonson, Francis Bacon, and John Donne—are among the best in all of English literature.

Elizabethan Drama: English comic and tragic plays produced during the Renaissance, or more narrowly, those plays written during the last years of and few years after Queen Elizabeth's reign. William Shakespeare is considered an Elizabethan dramatist in the broader sense, although most of his work was produced during the reign of James I. Examples of Elizabethan comedies include John Lyly's *The Woman in the Moone*, Thomas Dekker's *The Roaring Girl, or, Moll Cut Purse,* and William Shakespeare's *Twelfth Night.* Examples of Elizabethan tragedies include William Shakespeare's *Antony and Cleopatra,* Thomas Kyd's *The Spanish Tragedy,* and John Webster's *The Tragedy of the Duchess of Malfi.*

Empathy: A sense of shared experience, including emotional and physical feelings, with someone or something other than oneself. Empathy is often used to describe the response of a reader to a literary character. An example of an empathic passage is William Shakespeare's description in his narrative poem *Venus and Adonis* of: the snail, whose tender horns being hit, Shrinks backward in his shelly cave with pain. Readers of Gerard Manley Hopkins's *The Windhover* may experience some of the physical sensations evoked in the description of the movement of the falcon.

English Sonnet: See *Sonnet*

Enjambment: The running over of the sense and structure of a line of verse or a couplet into the following verse or couplet. Andrew Marvell's "To His Coy Mistress" is structured as a series of enjambments, as in lines 11-12: "My vegetable love should grow/Vaster than empires and more slow."

Enlightenment, The: An eighteenth-century philosophical movement. It began in France but had a wide impact throughout Europe and America. Thinkers of the Enlightenment valued reason and believed that both the individual and society could achieve a state of perfection. Corresponding to this essentially humanist vision was a resistance to religious authority. Important figures of the Enlightenment were Denis Diderot and Voltaire in France, Edward Gibbon and David Hume in England, and Thomas Paine and Thomas Jefferson in the United States.

Epic: A long narrative poem about the adventures of a hero of great historic or legendary importance. The setting is vast and the action is often given cosmic significance through the intervention of supernatural forces such as gods, angels, or demons. Epics are typically written in a classical style of grand simplicity with elaborate metaphors and allusions that enhance the symbolic importance of a hero's adventures. Some well-known epics are Homer's *Iliad* and *Odyssey,* Virgil's *Aeneid,* and John Milton's *Paradise Lost.*

Epic Simile: See *Homeric Simile*

Epic Theater: A theory of theatrical presentation developed by twentieth-century German playwright Bertolt Brecht. Brecht created a type of drama that the audience could view with complete detachment. He used what he termed "alienation effects" to create an emotional distance between the audience and the action on stage. Among these effects are: short, self-contained scenes that keep the play from building to a cathartic climax; songs that comment on the action; and techniques of acting that prevent the actor from developing an emotional identity with his role. Besides the plays of Bertolt Brecht, other plays that utilize epic theater conventions include those of Georg Buchner, Frank Wedekind, Erwin Piscator, and Leopold Jessner.

Epigram: A saying that makes the speaker's point quickly and concisely. Samuel Taylor Coleridge wrote an epigram that neatly sums up the form: What is an Epigram? A Dwarfish whole, Its body brevity, and wit its soul.

Epilogue: A concluding statement or section of a literary work. In dramas, particularly those of the seventeenth and eighteenth centuries, the epilogue is a closing speech, often in verse, delivered by an actor at the end of a play and spoken directly to the audience. A famous epilogue is Puck's speech at the end of William Shakespeare's *A Midsummer Night's Dream.*

Epiphany: A sudden revelation of truth inspired by a seemingly trivial incident. The term was widely used by James Joyce in his critical writings, and the stories in Joyce's *Dubliners* are commonly called "epiphanies."

Episode: An incident that forms part of a story and is significantly related to it. Episodes may be either self-contained narratives or events that depend on a larger context for their sense and importance. Examples of episodes include the founding of Wilmington, Delaware in Charles Reade's *The Disinherited Heir* and the individual events comprising the picaresque novels and medieval romances.

Episodic Plot: See *Plot*

Epitaph: An inscription on a tomb or tombstone, or a verse written on the occasion of a person's death. Epitaphs may be serious or humorous. Dorothy Parker's epitaph reads, "I told you I was sick."

Epithalamion: A song or poem written to honor and commemorate a marriage ceremony. Famous examples include Edmund Spenser's

"Epithalamion" and e. e. cummings's "Epithalamion." Also spelled Epithalamium.

Epithalamium: See *Epithalamion*

Epithet: A word or phrase, often disparaging or abusive, that expresses a character trait of someone or something. "The Napoleon of crime" is an epithet applied to Professor Moriarty, arch-rival of Sherlock Holmes in Arthur Conan Doyle's series of detective stories.

Exempla: See *Exemplum*

Exemplum: A tale with a moral message. This form of literary sermonizing flourished during the Middle Ages, when *exempla* appeared in collections known as "example-books." The works of Geoffrey Chaucer are full of *exempla*.

Existentialism: A predominantly twentieth-century philosophy concerned with the nature and perception of human existence. There are two major strains of existentialist thought: atheistic and Christian. Followers of atheistic existentialism believe that the individual is alone in a godless universe and that the basic human condition is one of suffering and loneliness. Nevertheless, because there are no fixed values, individuals can create their own characters—indeed, they can shape themselves—through the exercise of free will. The atheistic strain culminates in and is popularly associated with the works of Jean-Paul Sartre. The Christian existentialists, on the other hand, believe that only in God may people find freedom from life's anguish. The two strains hold certain beliefs in common: that existence cannot be fully understood or described through empirical effort; that anguish is a universal element of life; that individuals must bear responsibility for their actions; and that there is no common standard of behavior or perception for religious and ethical matters. Existentialist thought figures prominently in the works of such authors as Eugene Ionesco, Franz Kafka, Fyodor Dostoyevsky, Simone de Beauvoir, Samuel Beckett, and Albert Camus.

Expatriates: See *Expatriatism*

Expatriatism: The practice of leaving one's country to live for an extended period in another country. Literary expatriates include English poets Percy Bysshe Shelley and John Keats in Italy, Polish novelist Joseph Conrad in England, American writers Richard Wright, James Baldwin, Gertrude Stein, and Ernest Hemingway in France, and Trinidadian author Neil Bissondath in Canada.

Exposition: Writing intended to explain the nature of an idea, thing, or theme. Expository writing is often combined with description, narration, or argument. In dramatic writing, the exposition is the introductory material which presents the characters, setting, and tone of the play. An example of dramatic exposition occurs in many nineteenth-century drawing-room comedies in which the butler and the maid open the play with relevant talk about their master and mistress; in composition, exposition relays factual information, as in encyclopedia entries.

Expressionism: An indistinct literary term, originally used to describe an early twentieth-century school of German painting. The term applies to almost any mode of unconventional, highly subjective writing that distorts reality in some way. Advocates of Expressionism include dramatists George Kaiser, Ernst Toller, Luigi Pirandello, Federico Garcia Lorca, Eugene O'Neill, and Elmer Rice; poets George Heym, Ernst Stadler, August Stramm, Gottfried Benn, and Georg Trakl; and novelists Franz Kafka and James Joyce.

Extended Monologue: See *Monologue*

F

Fable: A prose or verse narrative intended to convey a moral. Animals or inanimate objects with human characteristics often serve as characters in fables. A famous fable is Aesop's "The Tortoise and the Hare."

Fairy Tales: Short narratives featuring mythical beings such as fairies, elves, and sprites. These tales originally belonged to the folklore of a particular nation or region, such as those collected in Germany by Jacob and Wilhelm Grimm. Two other celebrated writers of fairy tales are Hans Christian Andersen and Rudyard Kipling.

Falling Action: See *Denouement*

Fantasy: A literary form related to mythology and folklore. Fantasy literature is typically set in nonexistent realms and features supernatural beings. Notable examples of fantasy literature are *The Lord of the Rings* by J. R. R. Tolkien and the Gormenghast trilogy by Mervyn Peake.

Farce: A type of comedy characterized by broad humor, outlandish incidents, and often vulgar subject matter. Much of the "comedy" in film and television could more accurately be described as farce.

Feet: See *Foot*

Feminine Rhyme: See *Rhyme*

Femme fatale: A French phrase with the literal translation "fatal woman." A *femme fatale* is a sensuous, alluring woman who often leads men into danger or trouble. A classic example of the *femme fatale* is the nameless character in Billy Wilder's *The Seven Year Itch,* portrayed by Marilyn Monroe in the film adaptation.

Fiction: Any story that is the product of imagination rather than a documentation of fact. characters and events in such narratives may be based in real life but their ultimate form and configuration is a creation of the author. Geoffrey Chaucer's *The Canterbury Tales,* Laurence Sterne's *Tristram Shandy,* and Margaret Mitchell's *Gone with the Wind* are examples of fiction.

Figurative Language: A technique in writing in which the author temporarily interrupts the order, construction, or meaning of the writing for a particular effect. This interruption takes the form of one or more figures of speech such as hyperbole, irony, or simile. Figurative language is the opposite of literal language, in which every word is truthful, accurate, and free of exaggeration or embellishment. Examples of figurative language are tropes such as metaphor and rhetorical figures such as apostrophe.

Figures of Speech: Writing that differs from customary conventions for construction, meaning, order, or significance for the purpose of a special meaning or effect. There are two major types of figures of speech: rhetorical figures, which do not make changes in the meaning of the words, and tropes, which do. Types of figures of speech include simile, hyperbole, alliteration, and pun, among many others.

Fin de siecle: A French term meaning "end of the century." The term is used to denote the last decade of the nineteenth century, a transition period when writers and other artists abandoned old conventions and looked for new techniques and objectives. Two writers commonly associated with the *fin de siecle* mindset are Oscar Wilde and George Bernard Shaw.

First Person: See *Point of View*

Flashback: A device used in literature to present action that occurred before the beginning of the story. Flashbacks are often introduced as the dreams or recollections of one or more characters. Flashback techniques are often used in films, where they are typically set off by a gradual changing of one picture to another.

Foil: A character in a work of literature whose physical or psychological qualities contrast strongly with, and therefore highlight, the corresponding qualities of another character. In his Sherlock Holmes stories, Arthur Conan Doyle portrayed Dr. Watson as a man of normal habits and intelligence, making him a foil for the eccentric and wonderfully perceptive Sherlock Holmes.

Folk Ballad: See *Ballad*

Folklore: Traditions and myths preserved in a culture or group of people. Typically, these are passed on by word of mouth in various forms—such as legends, songs, and proverbs— or preserved in customs and ceremonies. This term was first used by W. J. Thoms in 1846. Sir James Frazer's *The Golden Bough* is the record of English folklore; myths about the frontier and the Old South exemplify American folklore.

Folktale: A story originating in oral tradition. Folktales fall into a variety of categories, including legends, ghost stories, fairy tales, fables, and anecdotes based on historical figures and events. Examples of folktales include Giambattista Basile's *The Pentamerone,* which contains the tales of Puss in Boots, Rapunzel, Cinderella, and Beauty and the Beast, and Joel Chandler Harris's Uncle Remus stories, which represent transplanted African folktales and American tales about the characters Mike Fink, Johnny Appleseed, Paul Bunyan, and Pecos Bill.

Foot: The smallest unit of rhythm in a line of poetry. In English-language poetry, a foot is typically one accented syllable combined with one or two unaccented syllables. There are many different types of feet. When the accent is on the second syllable of a two syllable word (con- *tort*), the foot is an "iamb"; the reverse accentual pattern (*tor* -ture) is a "trochee." Other feet that commonly occur in poetry in English are "anapest", two unaccented syllables followed by an accented syllable as in in-ter-*cept*, and "dactyl", an accented syllable followed by two unaccented syllables as in *su*-i- cide.

Foreshadowing: A device used in literature to create expectation or to set up an explanation of later developments. In Charles Dickens's *Great Expectations,* the graveyard encounter at the beginning of the novel between Pip and the escaped convict Magwitch foreshadows the baleful atmosphere and events that comprise much of the narrative.

Form: The pattern or construction of a work which identifies its genre and distinguishes it from other genres. Examples of forms include the different genres, such as the lyric form or the short story form, and various patterns for poetry, such as the verse form or the stanza form.

Formalism: In literary criticism, the belief that literature should follow prescribed rules of construction, such as those that govern the sonnet form. Examples of formalism are found in the work of the New Critics and structuralists.

Fourteener Meter: See *Meter*

Free Verse: Poetry that lacks regular metrical and rhyme patterns but that tries to capture the cadences of everyday speech. The form allows a poet to exploit a variety of rhythmical effects within a single poem. Free-verse techniques have been widely used in the twentieth century by such writers as Ezra Pound, T. S. Eliot, Carl Sandburg, and William Carlos Williams. Also known as *Vers libre.*

Futurism: A flamboyant literary and artistic movement that developed in France, Italy, and Russia from 1908 through the 1920s. Futurist theater and poetry abandoned traditional literary forms. In their place, followers of the movement attempted to achieve total freedom of expression through bizarre imagery and deformed or newly invented words. The Futurists were self-consciously modern artists who attempted to incorporate the appearances and sounds of modern life into their work. Futurist writers include Filippo Tommaso Marinetti, Wyndham Lewis, Guillaume Apollinaire, Velimir Khlebnikov, and Vladimir Mayakovsky.

G

Genre: A category of literary work. In critical theory, genre may refer to both the content of a given work—tragedy, comedy, pastoral—and to its form, such as poetry, novel, or drama. This term also refers to types of popular literature, as in the genres of science fiction or the detective story.

Genteel Tradition: A term coined by critic George Santayana to describe the literary practice of certain late nineteenth- century American writers, especially New Englanders. Followers of the Genteel Tradition emphasized conventionality in social, religious, moral, and literary standards. Some of the best-known writers of the Genteel Tradition are R. H. Stoddard and Bayard Taylor.

Gilded Age: A period in American history during the 1870s characterized by political corruption and materialism. A number of important novels of social and political criticism were written during this time. Examples of Gilded Age literature include Henry Adams's *Democracy* and F. Marion Crawford's *An American Politician.*

Gothic: See *Gothicism*

Gothicism: In literary criticism, works characterized by a taste for the medieval or morbidly attractive. A gothic novel prominently features elements of horror, the supernatural, gloom, and violence: clanking chains, terror, charnel houses, ghosts, medieval castles, and mysteriously slamming doors. The term "gothic novel" is also applied to novels that lack elements of the traditional Gothic setting but that create a similar atmosphere of terror or dread. Mary Shelley's *Frankenstein* is perhaps the best-known English work of this kind.

Gothic Novel: See *Gothicism*

Great Chain of Being: The belief that all things and creatures in nature are organized in a hierarchy from inanimate objects at the bottom to God at the top. This system of belief was popular in the seventeenth and eighteenth centuries. A summary of the concept of the great chain of being can be found in the first epistle of Alexander Pope's *An Essay on Man,* and more recently in Arthur O. Lovejoy's *The Great Chain of Being: A Study of the History of an Idea.*

Grotesque: In literary criticism, the subject matter of a work or a style of expression characterized by exaggeration, deformity, freakishness, and disorder. The grotesque often includes an element of comic absurdity. Early examples of literary grotesque include Francois Rabelais's *Pantagruel* and *Gargantua* and Thomas Nashe's *The Unfortunate Traveller,* while more recent examples can be found in the works of Edgar Allan Poe, Evelyn Waugh, Eudora Welty, Flannery O'Connor, Eugene Ionesco, Gunter Grass, Thomas Mann, Mervyn Peake, and Joseph Heller, among many others.

H

Haiku: The shortest form of Japanese poetry, constructed in three lines of five, seven, and five syllables respectively. The message of a *haiku* poem usually centers on some aspect of spirituality and provokes an emotional response in the reader. Early masters of *haiku* include Basho, Buson,

Kobayashi Issa, and Masaoka Shiki. English writers of *haiku* include the Imagists, notably Ezra Pound, H. D., Amy Lowell, Carl Sandburg, and William Carlos Williams. Also known as *Hokku.*

Half Rhyme: See *Consonance*

Hamartia: In tragedy, the event or act that leads to the hero's or heroine's downfall. This term is often incorrectly used as a synonym for tragic flaw. In Richard Wright's *Native Son,* the act that seals Bigger Thomas's fate is his first impulsive murder.

Harlem Renaissance: The Harlem Renaissance of the 1920s is generally considered the first significant movement of black writers and artists in the United States. During this period, new and established black writers published more fiction and poetry than ever before, the first influential black literary journals were established, and black authors and artists received their first widespread recognition and serious critical appraisal. Among the major writers associated with this period are Claude McKay, Jean Toomer, Countee Cullen, Langston Hughes, Arna Bontemps, Nella Larsen, and Zora Neale Hurston. Works representative of the Harlem Renaissance include Arna Bontemps's poems "The Return" and "Golgotha Is a Mountain," Claude McKay's novel *Home to Harlem,* Nella Larsen's novel *Passing,* Langston Hughes's poem "The Negro Speaks of Rivers," and the journals *Crisis* and *Opportunity,* both founded during this period. Also known as Negro Renaissance and New Negro Movement.

Harlequin: A stock character of the *commedia dell'arte* who occasionally interrupted the action with silly antics. Harlequin first appeared on the English stage in John Day's *The Travailes of the Three English Brothers.* The San Francisco Mime Troupe is one of the few modern groups to adapt Harlequin to the needs of contemporary satire.

Hellenism: Imitation of ancient Greek thought or styles. Also, an approach to life that focuses on the growth and development of the intellect. "Hellenism" is sometimes used to refer to the belief that reason can be applied to examine all human experience. A cogent discussion of Hellenism can be found in Matthew Arnold's *Culture and Anarchy.*

Heptameter: See *Meter*

Hero/Heroine: The principal sympathetic character (male or female) in a literary work. Heroes and heroines typically exhibit admirable traits: ideal-

ism, courage, and integrity, for example. Famous heroes and heroines include Pip in Charles Dickens's *Great Expectations,* the anonymous narrator in Ralph Ellison's *Invisible Man,* and Sethe in Toni Morrison's *Beloved.*

Heroic Couplet: A rhyming couplet written in iambic pentameter (a verse with five iambic feet). The following lines by Alexander Pope are an example: "Truth guards the Poet, sanctifies the line,/ And makes Immortal, Verse as mean as mine."

Heroic Line: The meter and length of a line of verse in epic or heroic poetry. This varies by language and time period. For example, in English poetry, the heroic line is iambic pentameter (a verse with five iambic feet); in French, the alexandrine (a verse with six iambic feet); in classical literature, dactylic hexameter (a verse with six dactylic feet).

Heroine: See *Hero/Heroine*

Hexameter: See *Meter*

Historical Criticism: The study of a work based on its impact on the world of the time period in which it was written. Examples of postmodern historical criticism can be found in the work of Michel Foucault, Hayden White, Stephen Greenblatt, and Jonathan Goldberg.

Hokku: See *Haiku*

Holocaust: See *Holocaust Literature*

Holocaust Literature: Literature influenced by or written about the Holocaust of World War II. Such literature includes true stories of survival in concentration camps, escape, and life after the war, as well as fictional works and poetry. Representative works of Holocaust literature include Saul Bellow's *Mr. Sammler's Planet,* Anne Frank's *The Diary of a Young Girl,* Jerzy Kosinski's *The Painted Bird,* Arthur Miller's *Incident at Vichy,* Czeslaw Milosz's *Collected Poems,* William Styron's *Sophie's Choice,* and Art Spiegelman's *Maus.*

Homeric Simile: An elaborate, detailed comparison written as a simile many lines in length. An example of an epic simile from John Milton's *Paradise Lost* follows: Angel Forms, who lay entranced Thick as autumnal leaves that strow the brooks In Vallombrosa, where the Etrurian shades High over-arched embower; or scattered sedge Afloat, when with fierce winds Orion armed Hath vexed the Red-Sea coast, whose waves o'erthrew Busiris and his Memphian chivalry, While with perfidious hatred they pursued The sojourners of

Goshen, who beheld From the safe shore their floating carcasses And broken chariot-wheels. Also known as Epic Simile.

Horatian Satire: See *Satire*

Humanism: A philosophy that places faith in the dignity of humankind and rejects the medieval perception of the individual as a weak, fallen creature. "Humanists" typically believe in the perfectibility of human nature and view reason and education as the means to that end. Humanist thought is represented in the works of Marsilio Ficino, Ludovico Castelvetro, Edmund Spenser, John Milton, Dean John Colet, Desiderius Erasmus, John Dryden, Alexander Pope, Matthew Arnold, and Irving Babbitt.

Humors: Mentions of the humors refer to the ancient Greek theory that a person's health and personality were determined by the balance of four basic fluids in the body: blood, phlegm, yellow bile, and black bile. A dominance of any fluid would cause extremes in behavior. An excess of blood created a sanguine person who was joyful, aggressive, and passionate; a phlegmatic person was shy, fearful, and sluggish; too much yellow bile led to a choleric temperament characterized by impatience, anger, bitterness, and stubbornness; and excessive black bile created melancholy, a state of laziness, gluttony, and lack of motivation. Literary treatment of the humors is exemplified by several characters in Ben Jonson's plays *Every Man in His Humour* and *Every Man out of His Humour.* Also spelled Humours.

Humours: See *Humors*

Hyperbole: In literary criticism, deliberate exaggeration used to achieve an effect. In William Shakespeare's *Macbeth,* Lady Macbeth hyperbolizes when she says, "All the perfumes of Arabia could not sweeten this little hand."

I

Iamb: See *Foot*

Idiom: A word construction or verbal expression closely associated with a given language. For example, in colloquial English the construction "how come" can be used instead of "why" to introduce a question. Similarly, "a piece of cake" is sometimes used to describe a task that is easily done.

Image: A concrete representation of an object or sensory experience. Typically, such a representation helps evoke the feelings associated with the object or experience itself. Images are either "literal" or "figurative." Literal images are especially concrete and involve little or no extension of the obvious meaning of the words used to express them. Figurative images do not follow the literal meaning of the words exactly. Images in literature are usually visual, but the term "image" can also refer to the representation of any sensory experience. In his poem "The Shepherd's Hour," Paul Verlaine presents the following image: "The Moon is red through horizon's fog;/ In a dancing mist the hazy meadow sleeps." The first line is broadly literal, while the second line involves turns of meaning associated with dancing and sleeping.

Imagery: The array of images in a literary work. Also, figurative language. William Butler Yeats's "The Second Coming" offers a powerful image of encroaching anarchy: Turning and turning in the widening gyre The falcon cannot hear the falconer; Things fall apart. . . .

Imagism: An English and American poetry movement that flourished between 1908 and 1917. The Imagists used precise, clearly presented images in their works. They also used common, everyday speech and aimed for conciseness, concrete imagery, and the creation of new rhythms. Participants in the Imagist movement included Ezra Pound, H. D. (Hilda Doolittle), and Amy Lowell, among others.

In medias res: A Latin term meaning "in the middle of things." It refers to the technique of beginning a story at its midpoint and then using various flashback devices to reveal previous action. This technique originated in such epics as Virgil's *Aeneid.*

Induction: The process of reaching a conclusion by reasoning from specific premises to form a general premise. Also, an introductory portion of a work of literature, especially a play. Geoffrey Chaucer's "Prologue" to the *Canterbury Tales,* Thomas Sackville's "Induction" to *The Mirror of Magistrates,* and the opening scene in William Shakespeare's *The Taming of the Shrew* are examples of inductions to literary works.

Intentional Fallacy: The belief that judgments of a literary work based solely on an author's stated or implied intentions are false and misleading. Critics who believe in the concept of the intentional fallacy typically argue that the work itself is sufficient matter for interpretation, even though they may concede that an author's statement of purpose can be useful. Analysis of William Wordsworth's *Lyri-*

cal Ballads based on the observations about poetry he makes in his "Preface" to the second edition of that work is an example of the intentional fallacy.

Interior Monologue: A narrative technique in which characters' thoughts are revealed in a way that appears to be uncontrolled by the author. The interior monologue typically aims to reveal the inner self of a character. It portrays emotional experiences as they occur at both a conscious and unconscious level. images are often used to represent sensations or emotions. One of the best-known interior monologues in English is the Molly Bloom section at the close of James Joyce's *Ulysses.* The interior monologue is also common in the works of Virginia Woolf.

Internal Rhyme: Rhyme that occurs within a single line of verse. An example is in the opening line of Edgar Allan Poe's "The Raven": "Once upon a midnight dreary, while I pondered weak and weary." Here, "dreary" and "weary" make an internal rhyme.

Irish Literary Renaissance: A late nineteenth- and early twentieth-century movement in Irish literature. Members of the movement aimed to reduce the influence of British culture in Ireland and create an Irish national literature. William Butler Yeats, George Moore, and Sean O'Casey are three of the best-known figures of the movement.

Irony: In literary criticism, the effect of language in which the intended meaning is the opposite of what is stated. The title of Jonathan Swift's "A Modest Proposal" is ironic because what Swift proposes in this essay is cannibalism—hardly "modest."

Italian Sonnet: See *Sonnet*

J

Jacobean Age: The period of the reign of James I of England (1603-1625). The early literature of this period reflected the worldview of the Elizabethan Age, but a darker, more cynical attitude steadily grew in the art and literature of the Jacobean Age. This was an important time for English drama and poetry. Milestones include William Shakespeare's tragedies, tragi-comedies, and sonnets; Ben Jonson's various dramas; and John Donne's metaphysical poetry.

Jargon: Language that is used or understood only by a select group of people. Jargon may refer to terminology used in a certain profession, such as computer jargon, or it may refer to any nonsensical

language that is not understood by most people. Literary examples of jargon are Francois Villon's *Ballades en jargon,* which is composed in the secret language of the *coquillards,* and Anthony Burgess's *A Clockwork Orange,* narrated in the fictional characters' language of "Nadsat."

Juvenalian Satire: See *Satire*

K

Knickerbocker Group: A somewhat indistinct group of New York writers of the first half of the nineteenth century. Members of the group were linked only by location and a common theme: New York life. Two famous members of the Knickerbocker Group were Washington Irving and William Cullen Bryant. The group's name derives from Irving's *Knickerbocker's History of New York.*

L

Lais: See *Lay*

Lay: A song or simple narrative poem. The form originated in medieval France. Early French *lais* were often based on the Celtic legends and other tales sung by Breton minstrels—thus the name of the "Breton lay." In fourteenth-century England, the term "lay" was used to describe short narratives written in imitation of the Breton lays. The most notable of these is Geoffrey Chaucer's "The Minstrel's Tale."

Leitmotiv: See *Motif*

Literal Language: An author uses literal language when he or she writes without exaggerating or embellishing the subject matter and without any tools of figurative language. To say "He ran very quickly down the street" is to use literal language, whereas to say "He ran like a hare down the street" would be using figurative language.

Literary Ballad: See *Ballad*

Literature: Literature is broadly defined as any written or spoken material, but the term most often refers to creative works. Literature includes poetry, drama, fiction, and many kinds of nonfiction writing, as well as oral, dramatic, and broadcast compositions not necessarily preserved in a written format, such as films and television programs.

Lost Generation: A term first used by Gertrude Stein to describe the post-World War I generation of American writers: men and women haunted by a sense of betrayal and emptiness brought about by the destructiveness of the war. The term is commonly applied to Hart Crane, Ernest Hemingway, F. Scott Fitzgerald, and others.

Lyric Poetry: A poem expressing the subjective feelings and personal emotions of the poet. Such poetry is melodic, since it was originally accompanied by a lyre in recitals. Most Western poetry in the twentieth century may be classified as lyrical. Examples of lyric poetry include A. E. Housman's elegy "To an Athlete Dying Young," the odes of Pindar and Horace, Thomas Gray and William Collins, the sonnets of Sir Thomas Wyatt and Sir Philip Sidney, Elizabeth Barrett Browning and Rainer Maria Rilke, and a host of other forms in the poetry of William Blake and Christina Rossetti, among many others.

M

Mannerism: Exaggerated, artificial adherence to a literary manner or style. Also, a popular style of the visual arts of late sixteenth-century Europe that was marked by elongation of the human form and by intentional spatial distortion. Literary works that are self-consciously high-toned and artistic are often said to be "mannered." Authors of such works include Henry James and Gertrude Stein.

Masculine Rhyme: See *Rhyme*

Masque: A lavish and elaborate form of entertainment, often performed in royal courts, that emphasizes song, dance, and costumery. The Renaissance form of the masque grew out of the spectacles of masked figures common in medieval England and Europe. The masque reached its peak of popularity and development in seventeenth-century England, during the reigns of James I and, especially, of Charles I. Ben Jonson, the most significant masque writer, also created the "antimasque," which incorporates elements of humor and the grotesque into the traditional masque and achieved greater dramatic quality. Masque-like interludes appear in Edmund Spenser's *The Faerie Queene* and in William Shakespeare's *The Tempest.* One of the best-known English masques is John Milton's *Comus.*

Measure: The foot, verse, or time sequence used in a literary work, especially a poem. Measure is often used somewhat incorrectly as a synonym for meter.

Melodrama: A play in which the typical plot is a conflict between characters who personify extreme good and evil. Melodramas usually end happily and emphasize sensationalism. Other literary forms that use the same techniques are often labeled "melodramatic." The term was formerly used to describe a combination of drama and music; as such, it was synonymous with "opera." Augustin Daly's *Under the Gaslight* and Dion Boucicault's *The Octoroon, The Colleen Bawn,* and *The Poor of New York* are examples of melodramas. The most popular media for twentieth-century melodramas are motion pictures and television.

Metaphor: A figure of speech that expresses an idea through the image of another object. Metaphors suggest the essence of the first object by identifying it with certain qualities of the second object. An example is "But soft, what light through yonder window breaks?/ It is the east, and Juliet is the sun" in William Shakespeare's *Romeo and Juliet.* Here, Juliet, the first object, is identified with qualities of the second object, the sun.

Metaphysical Conceit: See *Conceit*

Metaphysical Poetry: The body of poetry produced by a group of seventeenth-century English writers called the "Metaphysical Poets." The group includes John Donne and Andrew Marvell. The Metaphysical Poets made use of everyday speech, intellectual analysis, and unique imagery. They aimed to portray the ordinary conflicts and contradictions of life. Their poems often took the form of an argument, and many of them emphasize physical and religious love as well as the fleeting nature of life. Elaborate conceits are typical in metaphysical poetry. Marvell's "To His Coy Mistress" is a well-known example of a metaphysical poem.

Metaphysical Poets: See *Metaphysical Poetry*

Meter: In literary criticism, the repetition of sound patterns that creates a rhythm in poetry. The patterns are based on the number of syllables and the presence and absence of accents. The unit of rhythm in a line is called a foot. Types of meter are classified according to the number of feet in a line. These are the standard English lines: Monometer, one foot; Dimeter, two feet; Trimeter, three feet; Tetrameter, four feet; Pentameter, five feet; Hexameter, six feet (also called the Alexandrine); Heptameter, seven feet (also called the "Fourteener" when the feet are iambic). The most common English meter is the iambic pentameter, in which each line contains ten syllables, or five iambic feet, which individually are composed of an unstressed syllable followed by an accented syllable. Both of the following lines from Alfred, Lord Tennyson's

"Ulysses" are written in iambic pentameter: Made weak by time and fate, but strong in will To strive, to seek, to find, and not to yield.

Mise en scene: The costumes, scenery, and other properties of a drama. Herbert Beerbohm Tree was renowned for the elaborate *mises en scene* of his lavish Shakespearean productions at His Majesty's Theatre between 1897 and 1915.

Modernism: Modern literary practices. Also, the principles of a literary school that lasted from roughly the beginning of the twentieth century until the end of World War II. Modernism is defined by its rejection of the literary conventions of the nineteenth century and by its opposition to conventional morality, taste, traditions, and economic values. Many writers are associated with the concepts of Modernism, including Albert Camus, Marcel Proust, D. H. Lawrence, W. H. Auden, Ernest Hemingway, William Faulkner, William Butler Yeats, Thomas Mann, Tennessee Williams, Eugene O'Neill, and James Joyce.

Monologue: A composition, written or oral, by a single individual. More specifically, a speech given by a single individual in a drama or other public entertainment. It has no set length, although it is usually several or more lines long. An example of an "extended monologue"—that is, a monologue of great length and seriousness—occurs in the one-act, one-character play *The Stronger* by August Strindberg.

Monometer: See *Meter*

Mood: The prevailing emotions of a work or of the author in his or her creation of the work. The mood of a work is not always what might be expected based on its subject matter. The poem "Dover Beach" by Matthew Arnold offers examples of two different moods originating from the same experience: watching the ocean at night. The mood of the first three lines— The sea is calm tonight The tide is full, the moon lies fair Upon the straights. . . . is in sharp contrast to the mood of the last three lines— And we are here as on a darkling plain Swept with confused alarms of struggle and flight, Where ignorant armies clash by night.

Motif: A theme, character type, image, metaphor, or other verbal element that recurs throughout a single work of literature or occurs in a number of different works over a period of time. For example, the various manifestations of the color white in Herman Melville's *Moby Dick* is a "specific" *motif,* while the trials of star-crossed lovers is a "conventional" *motif* from the literature of all periods. Also known as *Motiv* or *Leitmotiv.*

Motiv: See *Motif*

Muckrakers: An early twentieth-century group of American writers. Typically, their works exposed the wrongdoings of big business and government in the United States. Upton Sinclair's *The Jungle* exemplifies the muckraking novel.

Muses: Nine Greek mythological goddesses, the daughters of Zeus and Mnemosyne (Memory). Each muse patronized a specific area of the liberal arts and sciences. Calliope presided over epic poetry, Clio over history, Erato over love poetry, Euterpe over music or lyric poetry, Melpomene over tragedy, Polyhymnia over hymns to the gods, Terpsichore over dance, Thalia over comedy, and Urania over astronomy. Poets and writers traditionally made appeals to the Muses for inspiration in their work. John Milton invokes the aid of a muse at the beginning of the first book of his *Paradise Lost:* Of Man's First disobedience, and the Fruit of the Forbidden Tree, whose mortal taste Brought Death into the World, and all our woe, With loss of Eden, till one greater Man Restore us, and regain the blissful Seat, Sing Heav'nly Muse, that on the secret top of Oreb, or of Sinai, didst inspire That Shepherd, who first taught the chosen Seed, In the Beginning how the Heav'ns and Earth Rose out of Chaos. . . .

Mystery: See *Suspense*

Myth: An anonymous tale emerging from the traditional beliefs of a culture or social unit. Myths use supernatural explanations for natural phenomena. They may also explain cosmic issues like creation and death. Collections of myths, known as mythologies, are common to all cultures and nations, but the best-known myths belong to the Norse, Roman, and Greek mythologies. A famous myth is the story of Arachne, an arrogant young girl who challenged a goddess, Athena, to a weaving contest; when the girl won, Athena was enraged and turned Arachne into a spider, thus explaining the existence of spiders.

N

Narration: The telling of a series of events, real or invented. A narration may be either a simple narrative, in which the events are recounted chronologically, or a narrative with a plot, in which the account is given in a style reflecting the author's artistic concept of the story. Narration is sometimes used as a synonym for "storyline." The recounting of scary stories around a campfire is a form of narration.

Narrative: A verse or prose accounting of an event or sequence of events, real or invented. The term is also used as an adjective in the sense "method of narration." For example, in literary criticism, the expression "narrative technique" usually refers to the way the author structures and presents his or her story. Narratives range from the shortest accounts of events, as in Julius Caesar's remark, "I came, I saw, I conquered," to the longest historical or biographical works, as in Edward Gibbon's *The Decline and Fall of the Roman Empire,* as well as diaries, travelogues, novels, ballads, epics, short stories, and other fictional forms.

Narrative Poetry: A nondramatic poem in which the author tells a story. Such poems may be of any length or level of complexity. Epics such as *Beowulf* and ballads are forms of narrative poetry.

Narrator: The teller of a story. The narrator may be the author or a character in the story through whom the author speaks. Huckleberry Finn is the narrator of Mark Twain's *The Adventures of Huckleberry Finn.*

Naturalism: A literary movement of the late nineteenth and early twentieth centuries. The movement's major theorist, French novelist Emile Zola, envisioned a type of fiction that would examine human life with the objectivity of scientific inquiry. The Naturalists typically viewed human beings as either the products of "biological determinism," ruled by hereditary instincts and engaged in an endless struggle for survival, or as the products of "socioeconomic determinism," ruled by social and economic forces beyond their control. In their works, the Naturalists generally ignored the highest levels of society and focused on degradation: poverty, alcoholism, prostitution, insanity, and disease. Naturalism influenced authors throughout the world, including Henrik Ibsen and Thomas Hardy. In the United States, in particular, Naturalism had a profound impact. Among the authors who embraced its principles are Theodore Dreiser, Eugene O'Neill, Stephen Crane, Jack London, and Frank Norris.

Negritude: A literary movement based on the concept of a shared cultural bond on the part of black Africans, wherever they may be in the world. It traces its origins to the former French colonies of Africa and the Caribbean. Negritude poets, novelists, and essayists generally stress four points in their writings: One, black alienation from traditional African culture can lead to feelings of inferiority. Two, European colonialism and Western education should be resisted. Three, black Africans should seek to affirm and define their own identity. Four, African culture can and should be reclaimed. Many Negritude writers also claim that blacks can make unique contributions to the world, based on a heightened appreciation of nature, rhythm, and human emotions—aspects of life they say are not so highly valued in the materialistic and rationalistic West. Examples of Negritude literature include the poetry of both Senegalese Leopold Senghor in *Hosties noires* and Martiniquais Aime-Fernand Cesaire in *Return to My Native Land.*

Negro Renaissance: See *Harlem Renaissance*

Neoclassical Period: See *Neoclassicism*

Neoclassicism: In literary criticism, this term refers to the revival of the attitudes and styles of expression of classical literature. It is generally used to describe a period in European history beginning in the late seventeenth century and lasting until about 1800. In its purest form, Neoclassicism marked a return to order, proportion, restraint, logic, accuracy, and decorum. In England, where Neoclassicism perhaps was most popular, it reflected the influence of seventeenth- century French writers, especially dramatists. Neoclassical writers typically reacted against the intensity and enthusiasm of the Renaissance period. They wrote works that appealed to the intellect, using elevated language and classical literary forms such as satire and the ode. Neoclassical works were often governed by the classical goal of instruction. English neoclassicists included Alexander Pope, Jonathan Swift, Joseph Addison, Sir Richard Steele, John Gay, and Matthew Prior; French neoclassicists included Pierre Corneille and Jean-Baptiste Moliere. Also known as Age of Reason.

Neoclassicists: See *Neoclassicism*

New Criticism: A movement in literary criticism, dating from the late 1920s, that stressed close textual analysis in the interpretation of works of literature. The New Critics saw little merit in historical and biographical analysis. Rather, they aimed to examine the text alone, free from the question of how external events—biographical or otherwise—may have helped shape it. This predominantly American school was named "New Criticism" by one of its practitioners, John Crowe Ransom. Other important New Critics included Allen Tate, R. P. Blackmur, Robert Penn Warren, and Cleanth Brooks.

New Negro Movement: See *Harlem Renaissance*

Noble Savage: The idea that primitive man is noble and good but becomes evil and corrupted as he becomes civilized. The concept of the noble savage originated in the Renaissance period but is more closely identified with such later writers as Jean-Jacques Rousseau and Aphra Behn. First described in John Dryden's play *The Conquest of Granada,* the noble savage is portrayed by the various Native Americans in James Fenimore Cooper's "Leatherstocking Tales," by Queequeg, Daggoo, and Tashtego in Herman Melville's *Moby Dick,* and by John the Savage in Aldous Huxley's *Brave New World.*

O

Objective Correlative: An outward set of objects, a situation, or a chain of events corresponding to an inward experience and evoking this experience in the reader. The term frequently appears in modern criticism in discussions of authors' intended effects on the emotional responses of readers. This term was originally used by T. S. Eliot in his 1919 essay "Hamlet."

Objectivity: A quality in writing characterized by the absence of the author's opinion or feeling about the subject matter. Objectivity is an important factor in criticism. The novels of Henry James and, to a certain extent, the poems of John Larkin demonstrate objectivity, and it is central to John Keats's concept of "negative capability." Critical and journalistic writing usually are or attempt to be objective.

Occasional Verse: poetry written on the occasion of a significant historical or personal event. *Vers de societe* is sometimes called occasional verse although it is of a less serious nature. Famous examples of occasional verse include Andrew Marvell's "Horatian Ode upon Cromwell's Return from England," Walt Whitman's "When Lilacs Last in the Dooryard Bloom'd"— written upon the death of Abraham Lincoln—and Edmund Spenser's commemoration of his wedding, "Epithalamion."

Octave: A poem or stanza composed of eight lines. The term octave most often represents the first eight lines of a Petrarchan sonnet. An example of an octave is taken from a translation of a Petrarchan sonnet by Sir Thomas Wyatt: The pillar perisht is whereto I leant, The strongest stay of mine unquiet mind; The like of it no man again can find, From East to West Still seeking though he went. To mind unhap! for hap away hath rent Of all my joy the very

bark and rind; And I, alas, by chance am thus assigned Daily to mourn till death do it relent.

Ode: Name given to an extended lyric poem characterized by exalted emotion and dignified style. An ode usually concerns a single, serious theme. Most odes, but not all, are addressed to an object or individual. Odes are distinguished from other lyric poetic forms by their complex rhythmic and stanzaic patterns. An example of this form is John Keats's "Ode to a Nightingale."

Oedipus Complex: A son's amorous obsession with his mother. The phrase is derived from the story of the ancient Theban hero Oedipus, who unknowingly killed his father and married his mother. Literary occurrences of the Oedipus complex include Andre Gide's *Oedipe* and Jean Cocteau's *La Machine infernale,* as well as the most famous, Sophocles' *Oedipus Rex.*

Omniscience: See *Point of View*

Onomatopoeia: The use of words whose sounds express or suggest their meaning. In its simplest sense, onomatopoeia may be represented by words that mimic the sounds they denote such as "hiss" or "meow." At a more subtle level, the pattern and rhythm of sounds and rhymes of a line or poem may be onomatopoeic. A celebrated example of onomatopoeia is the repetition of the word "bells" in Edgar Allan Poe's poem "The Bells."

Opera: A type of stage performance, usually a drama, in which the dialogue is sung. Classic examples of opera include Giuseppi Verdi's *La traviata,* Giacomo Puccini's *La Boheme,* and Richard Wagner's *Tristan und Isolde.* Major twentieth- century contributors to the form include Richard Strauss and Alban Berg.

Operetta: A usually romantic comic opera. John Gay's *The Beggar's Opera,* Richard Sheridan's *The Duenna,* and numerous works by William Gilbert and Arthur Sullivan are examples of operettas.

Oral Tradition: See *Oral Transmission*

Oral Transmission: A process by which songs, ballads, folklore, and other material are transmitted by word of mouth. The tradition of oral transmission predates the written record systems of literate society. Oral transmission preserves material sometimes over generations, although often with variations. Memory plays a large part in the recitation and preservation of orally transmitted material. Breton lays, French *fabliaux,* national epics (including the Anglo- Saxon *Beowulf,* the Spanish *El Cid,* and the Finnish *Kalevala*), Native American myths and legends, and African folktales told by plantation slaves are examples of orally transmitted literature.

Oration: Formal speaking intended to motivate the listeners to some action or feeling. Such public speaking was much more common before the development of timely printed communication such as newspapers. Famous examples of oration include Abraham Lincoln's "Gettysburg Address" and Dr. Martin Luther King Jr.'s "I Have a Dream" speech.

Ottava Rima: An eight-line stanza of poetry composed in iambic pentameter (a five-foot line in which each foot consists of an unaccented syllable followed by an accented syllable), following the abababcc rhyme scheme. This form has been prominently used by such important English writers as Lord Byron, Henry Wadsworth Longfellow, and W. B. Yeats.

Oxymoron: A phrase combining two contradictory terms. Oxymorons may be intentional or unintentional. The following speech from William Shakespeare's *Romeo and Juliet* uses several oxymorons: Why, then, O brawling love! O loving hate! O anything, of nothing first create! O heavy lightness! serious vanity! Mis-shapen chaos of well-seeming forms! Feather of lead, bright smoke, cold fire, sick health! This love feel I, that feel no love in this.

P

Pantheism: The idea that all things are both a manifestation or revelation of God and a part of God at the same time. Pantheism was a common attitude in the early societies of Egypt, India, and Greece—the term derives from the Greek *pan* meaning "all" and *theos* meaning "deity." It later became a significant part of the Christian faith. William Wordsworth and Ralph Waldo Emerson are among the many writers who have expressed the pantheistic attitude in their works.

Parable: A story intended to teach a moral lesson or answer an ethical question. In the West, the best examples of parables are those of Jesus Christ in the New Testament, notably "The Prodigal Son," but parables also are used in Sufism, rabbinic literature, Hasidism, and Zen Buddhism.

Paradox: A statement that appears illogical or contradictory at first, but may actually point to an underlying truth. "Less is more" is an example of a paradox. Literary examples include Francis Ba-

con's statement, "The most corrected copies are commonly the least correct," and "All animals are equal, but some animals are more equal than others" from George Orwell's *Animal Farm*.

Parallelism: A method of comparison of two ideas in which each is developed in the same grammatical structure. Ralph Waldo Emerson's "Civilization" contains this example of parallelism: Raphael paints wisdom; Handel sings it, Phidias carves it, Shakespeare writes it, Wren builds it, Columbus sails it, Luther preaches it, Washington arms it, Watt mechanizes it.

Parnassianism: A mid nineteenth-century movement in French literature. Followers of the movement stressed adherence to well-defined artistic forms as a reaction against the often chaotic expression of the artist's ego that dominated the work of the Romantics. The Parnassians also rejected the moral, ethical, and social themes exhibited in the works of French Romantics such as Victor Hugo. The aesthetic doctrines of the Parnassians strongly influenced the later symbolist and decadent movements. Members of the Parnassian school include Leconte de Lisle, Sully Prudhomme, Albert Glatigny, Francois Coppee, and Theodore de Banville.

Parody: In literary criticism, this term refers to an imitation of a serious literary work or the signature style of a particular author in a ridiculous manner. A typical parody adopts the style of the original and applies it to an inappropriate subject for humorous effect. Parody is a form of satire and could be considered the literary equivalent of a caricature or cartoon. Henry Fielding's *Shamela* is a parody of Samuel Richardson's *Pamela*.

Pastoral: A term derived from the Latin word "pastor," meaning shepherd. A pastoral is a literary composition on a rural theme. The conventions of the pastoral were originated by the third-century Greek poet Theocritus, who wrote about the experiences, love affairs, and pastimes of Sicilian shepherds. In a pastoral, characters and language of a courtly nature are often placed in a simple setting. The term pastoral is also used to classify dramas, elegies, and lyrics that exhibit the use of country settings and shepherd characters. Percy Bysshe Shelley's "Adonais" and John Milton's "Lycidas" are two famous examples of pastorals.

Pastorela: The Spanish name for the shepherds play, a folk drama reenacted during the Christmas season. Examples of *pastorelas* include Gomez

Manrique's *Representacion del nacimiento* and the dramas of Lucas Fernandez and Juan del Encina.

Pathetic Fallacy: A term coined by English critic John Ruskin to identify writing that falsely endows nonhuman things with human intentions and feelings, such as "angry clouds" and "sad trees." The pathetic fallacy is a required convention in the classical poetic form of the pastoral elegy, and it is used in the modern poetry of T. S. Eliot, Ezra Pound, and the Imagists. Also known as Poetic Fallacy.

Pelado: Literally the "skinned one" or shirtless one, he was the stock underdog, sharp-witted picaresque character of Mexican vaudeville and tent shows. The *pelado* is found in such works as Don Catarino's *Los effectos de la crisis* and *Regreso a mi tierra.*

Pen Name: See *Pseudonym*

Pentameter: See *Meter*

Persona: A Latin term meaning "mask." *Personae* are the characters in a fictional work of literature. The *persona* generally functions as a mask through which the author tells a story in a voice other than his or her own. A *persona* is usually either a character in a story who acts as a narrator or an "implied author," a voice created by the author to act as the narrator for himself or herself. *Personae* include the narrator of Geoffrey Chaucer's *Canterbury Tales* and Marlow in Joseph Conrad's *Heart of Darkness.*

Personae: See *Persona*

Personal Point of View: See *Point of View*

Personification: A figure of speech that gives human qualities to abstract ideas, animals, and inanimate objects. William Shakespeare used personification in *Romeo and Juliet* in the lines "Arise, fair sun, and kill the envious moon,/ Who is already sick and pale with grief." Here, the moon is portrayed as being envious, sick, and pale with grief—all markedly human qualities. Also known as *Prosopopoeia.*

Petrarchan Sonnet: See *Sonnet*

Phenomenology: A method of literary criticism based on the belief that things have no existence outside of human consciousness or awareness. Proponents of this theory believe that art is a process that takes place in the mind of the observer as he or she contemplates an object rather than a quality of the object itself. Among phenomenological critics

are Edmund Husserl, George Poulet, Marcel Raymond, and Roman Ingarden.

Picaresque Novel: Episodic fiction depicting the adventures of a roguish central character ("picaro" is Spanish for "rogue"). The picaresque hero is commonly a low-born but clever individual who wanders into and out of various affairs of love, danger, and farcical intrigue. These involvements may take place at all social levels and typically present a humorous and wide-ranging satire of a given society. Prominent examples of the picaresque novel are *Don Quixote* by Miguel de Cervantes, *Tom Jones* by Henry Fielding, and *Moll Flanders* by Daniel Defoe.

Plagiarism: Claiming another person's written material as one's own. Plagiarism can take the form of direct, word-for- word copying or the theft of the substance or idea of the work. A student who copies an encyclopedia entry and turns it in as a report for school is guilty of plagiarism.

Platonic Criticism: A form of criticism that stresses an artistic work's usefulness as an agent of social engineering rather than any quality or value of the work itself. Platonic criticism takes as its starting point the ancient Greek philosopher Plato's comments on art in his *Republic.*

Platonism: The embracing of the doctrines of the philosopher Plato, popular among the poets of the Renaissance and the Romantic period. Platonism is more flexible than Aristotelian Criticism and places more emphasis on the supernatural and unknown aspects of life. Platonism is expressed in the love poetry of the Renaissance, the fourth book of Baldassare Castiglione's *The Book of the Courtier,* and the poetry of William Blake, William Wordsworth, Percy Bysshe Shelley, Friedrich Holderlin, William Butler Yeats, and Wallace Stevens.

Play: See *Drama*

Plot: In literary criticism, this term refers to the pattern of events in a narrative or drama. In its simplest sense, the plot guides the author in composing the work and helps the reader follow the work. Typically, plots exhibit causality and unity and have a beginning, a middle, and an end. Sometimes, however, a plot may consist of a series of disconnected events, in which case it is known as an "episodic plot." In his *Aspects of the Novel,* E. M. Forster distinguishes between a story, defined as a "narrative of events arranged in their time- sequence," and plot, which organizes the events to a "sense of causality." This definition closely mirrors Aristotle's discussion of plot in his *Poetics.*

Poem: In its broadest sense, a composition utilizing rhyme, meter, concrete detail, and expressive language to create a literary experience with emotional and aesthetic appeal. Typical poems include sonnets, odes, elegies, *haiku,* ballads, and free verse.

Poet: An author who writes poetry or verse. The term is also used to refer to an artist or writer who has an exceptional gift for expression, imagination, and energy in the making of art in any form. Well-known poets include Horace, Basho, Sir Philip Sidney, Sir Edmund Spenser, John Donne, Andrew Marvell, Alexander Pope, Jonathan Swift, George Gordon, Lord Byron, John Keats, Christina Rossetti, W. H. Auden, Stevie Smith, and Sylvia Plath.

Poetic Fallacy: See *Pathetic Fallacy*

Poetic Justice: An outcome in a literary work, not necessarily a poem, in which the good are rewarded and the evil are punished, especially in ways that particularly fit their virtues or crimes. For example, a murderer may himself be murdered, or a thief will find himself penniless.

Poetic License: Distortions of fact and literary convention made by a writer—not always a poet—for the sake of the effect gained. Poetic license is closely related to the concept of "artistic freedom." An author exercises poetic license by saying that a pile of money "reaches as high as a mountain" when the pile is actually only a foot or two high.

Poetics: This term has two closely related meanings. It denotes (1) an aesthetic theory in literary criticism about the essence of poetry or (2) rules prescribing the proper methods, content, style, or diction of poetry. The term poetics may also refer to theories about literature in general, not just poetry.

Poetry: In its broadest sense, writing that aims to present ideas and evoke an emotional experience in the reader through the use of meter, imagery, connotative and concrete words, and a carefully constructed structure based on rhythmic patterns. Poetry typically relies on words and expressions that have several layers of meaning. It also makes use of the effects of regular rhythm on the ear and may make a strong appeal to the senses through the use of imagery. Edgar Allan Poe's "Annabel Lee" and Walt Whitman's *Leaves of Grass* are famous examples of poetry.

Point of View: The narrative perspective from which a literary work is presented to the reader.

There are four traditional points of view. The "third person omniscient" gives the reader a "godlike" perspective, unrestricted by time or place, from which to see actions and look into the minds of characters. This allows the author to comment openly on characters and events in the work. The "third person" point of view presents the events of the story from outside of any single character's perception, much like the omniscient point of view, but the reader must understand the action as it takes place and without any special insight into characters' minds or motivations. The "first person" or "personal" point of view relates events as they are perceived by a single character. The main character "tells" the story and may offer opinions about the action and characters which differ from those of the author. Much less common than omniscient, third person, and first person is the "second person" point of view, wherein the author tells the story as if it is happening to the reader. James Thurber employs the omniscient point of view in his short story "The Secret Life of Walter Mitty." Ernest Hemingway's "A Clean, Well-Lighted Place" is a short story told from the third person point of view. Mark Twain's novel *Huck Finn* is presented from the first person viewpoint. Jay McInerney's *Bright Lights, Big City* is an example of a novel which uses the second person point of view.

Polemic: A work in which the author takes a stand on a controversial subject, such as abortion or religion. Such works are often extremely argumentative or provocative. Classic examples of polemics include John Milton's *Aeropagitica* and Thomas Paine's *The American Crisis.*

Pornography: Writing intended to provoke feelings of lust in the reader. Such works are often condemned by critics and teachers, but those which can be shown to have literary value are viewed less harshly. Literary works that have been described as pornographic include Ovid's *The Art of Love,* Margaret of Angouleme's *Heptameron,* John Cleland's *Memoirs of a Woman of Pleasure; or, the Life of Fanny Hill,* the anonymous *My Secret Life,* D. H. Lawrence's *Lady Chatterley's Lover,* and Vladimir Nabokov's *Lolita.*

Post-Aesthetic Movement: An artistic response made by African Americans to the black aesthetic movement of the 1960s and early '70s. Writers since that time have adopted a somewhat different tone in their work, with less emphasis placed on the disparity between black and white in the United States. In the words of post-aesthetic authors such as Toni Morrison, John Edgar Wideman, and Kristin Hunter, African Americans are portrayed as looking inward for answers to their own questions, rather than always looking to the outside world. Two well-known examples of works produced as part of the post-aesthetic movement are the Pulitzer Prize-winning novels *The Color Purple* by Alice Walker and *Beloved* by Toni Morrison.

Postmodernism: Writing from the 1960s forward characterized by experimentation and continuing to apply some of the fundamentals of modernism, which included existentialism and alienation. Postmodernists have gone a step further in the rejection of tradition begun with the modernists by also rejecting traditional forms, preferring the anti-novel over the novel and the anti-hero over the hero. Postmodern writers include Alain Robbe-Grillet, Thomas Pynchon, Margaret Drabble, John Fowles, Adolfo Bioy-Casares, and Gabriel Garcia Marquez.

Pre-Raphaelites: A circle of writers and artists in mid nineteenth-century England. Valuing the pre-Renaissance artistic qualities of religious symbolism, lavish pictorialism, and natural sensuousness, the Pre-Raphaelites cultivated a sense of mystery and melancholy that influenced later writers associated with the Symbolist and Decadent movements. The major members of the group include Dante Gabriel Rossetti, Christina Rossetti, Algernon Swinburne, and Walter Pater.

Primitivism: The belief that primitive peoples were nobler and less flawed than civilized peoples because they had not been subjected to the tainting influence of society. Examples of literature espousing primitivism include Aphra Behn's *Oroonoko: Or, The History of the Royal Slave,* Jean-Jacques Rousseau's *Julie ou la Nouvelle Heloise,* Oliver Goldsmith's *The Deserted Village,* the poems of Robert Burns, Herman Melville's stories *Typee, Omoo,* and *Mardi,* many poems of William Butler Yeats and Robert Frost, and William Golding's novel *Lord of the Flies.*

Projective Verse: A form of free verse in which the poet's breathing pattern determines the lines of the poem. Poets who advocate projective verse are against all formal structures in writing, including meter and form. Besides its creators, Robert Creeley, Robert Duncan, and Charles Olson, two other well-known projective verse poets are Denise Levertov and LeRoi Jones (Amiri Baraka). Also known as Breath Verse.

Prologue: An introductory section of a literary work. It often contains information establishing the situation of the characters or presents information about the setting, time period, or action. In drama, the prologue is spoken by a chorus or by one of the principal characters. In the ''General Prologue'' of *The Canterbury Tales,* Geoffrey Chaucer describes the main characters and establishes the setting and purpose of the work.

Prose: A literary medium that attempts to mirror the language of everyday speech. It is distinguished from poetry by its use of unmetered, unrhymed language consisting of logically related sentences. Prose is usually grouped into paragraphs that form a cohesive whole such as an essay or a novel. Recognized masters of English prose writing include Sir Thomas Malory, William Caxton, Raphael Holinshed, Joseph Addison, Mark Twain, and Ernest Hemingway.

Prosopopoeia: See *Personification*

Protagonist: The central character of a story who serves as a focus for its themes and incidents and as the principal rationale for its development. The protagonist is sometimes referred to in discussions of modern literature as the hero or anti-hero. Well-known protagonists are Hamlet in William Shakespeare's *Hamlet* and Jay Gatsby in F. Scott Fitzgerald's *The Great Gatsby.*

Protest Fiction: Protest fiction has as its primary purpose the protesting of some social injustice, such as racism or discrimination. One example of protest fiction is a series of five novels by Chester Himes, beginning in 1945 with *If He Hollers Let Him Go* and ending in 1955 with *The Primitive.* These works depict the destructive effects of race and gender stereotyping in the context of interracial relationships. Another African American author whose works often revolve around themes of social protest is John Oliver Killens. James Baldwin's essay ''Everybody's Protest Novel'' generated controversy by attacking the authors of protest fiction.

Proverb: A brief, sage saying that expresses a truth about life in a striking manner. ''They are not all cooks who carry long knives'' is an example of a proverb.

Pseudonym: A name assumed by a writer, most often intended to prevent his or her identification as the author of a work. Two or more authors may work together under one pseudonym, or an author may use a different name for each genre he or she publishes in. Some publishing companies maintain ''house pseudonyms,'' under which any number of authors may write installations in a series. Some authors also choose a pseudonym over their real names the way an actor may use a stage name. Examples of pseudonyms (with the author's real name in parentheses) include Voltaire (Francois-Marie Arouet), Novalis (Friedrich von Hardenberg), Currer Bell (Charlotte Bronte), Ellis Bell (Emily Bronte), George Eliot (Maryann Evans), Honorio Bustos Donmecq (Adolfo Bioy-Casares and Jorge Luis Borges), and Richard Bachman (Stephen King).

Pun: A play on words that have similar sounds but different meanings. A serious example of the pun is from John Donne's ''A Hymne to God the Father'': Sweare by thyself, that at my death thy some Shall shine as he shines now, and hereto fore; And, having done that, Thou haste done; I fear no more.

Pure Poetry: poetry written without instructional intent or moral purpose that aims only to please a reader by its imagery or musical flow. The term pure poetry is used as the antonym of the term ''didacticism.'' The poetry of Edgar Allan Poe, Stephane Mallarme, Paul Verlaine, Paul Valery, Juan Ramoz Jimenez, and Jorge Guillen offer examples of pure poetry.

Q

Quatrain: A four-line stanza of a poem or an entire poem consisting of four lines. The following quatrain is from Robert Herrick's ''To Live Merrily, and to Trust to Good Verses'': Round, round, the root do's run; And being ravisht thus, Come, I will drink a Tun To my *Propertius*.

R

Raisonneur: A character in a drama who functions as a spokesperson for the dramatist's views. The *raisonneur* typically observes the play without becoming central to its action. *Raisonneurs* were very common in plays of the nineteenth century.

Realism: A nineteenth-century European literary movement that sought to portray familiar characters, situations, and settings in a realistic manner. This was done primarily by using an objective narrative point of view and through the buildup of accurate detail. The standard for success of any realistic work depends on how faithfully it transfers common experience into fictional forms. The realistic method may be altered or extended, as in stream of consciousness writing, to record highly subjec-

tive experience. Seminal authors in the tradition of Realism include Honore de Balzac, Gustave Flaubert, and Henry James.

Refrain: A phrase repeated at intervals throughout a poem. A refrain may appear at the end of each stanza or at less regular intervals. It may be altered slightly at each appearance. Some refrains are nonsense expressions—as with ''Nevermore'' in Edgar Allan Poe's ''The Raven''—that seem to take on a different significance with each use.

Renaissance: The period in European history that marked the end of the Middle Ages. It began in Italy in the late fourteenth century. In broad terms, it is usually seen as spanning the fourteenth, fifteenth, and sixteenth centuries, although it did not reach Great Britain, for example, until the 1480s or so. The Renaissance saw an awakening in almost every sphere of human activity, especially science, philosophy, and the arts. The period is best defined by the emergence of a general philosophy that emphasized the importance of the intellect, the individual, and world affairs. It contrasts strongly with the medieval worldview, characterized by the dominant concerns of faith, the social collective, and spiritual salvation. Prominent writers during the Renaissance include Niccolo Machiavelli and Baldassare Castiglione in Italy, Miguel de Cervantes and Lope de Vega in Spain, Jean Froissart and Francois Rabelais in France, Sir Thomas More and Sir Philip Sidney in England, and Desiderius Erasmus in Holland.

Repartee: Conversation featuring snappy retorts and witticisms. Masters of *repartee* include Sydney Smith, Charles Lamb, and Oscar Wilde. An example is recorded in the meeting of ''Beau'' Nash and John Wesley: Nash said, ''I never make way for a fool,'' to which Wesley responded, ''Don't you? I always do,'' and stepped aside.

Resolution: The portion of a story following the climax, in which the conflict is resolved. The resolution of Jane Austen's *Northanger Abbey* is neatly summed up in the following sentence: ''Henry and Catherine were married, the bells rang and every body smiled.''

Restoration: See *Restoration Age*

Restoration Age: A period in English literature beginning with the crowning of Charles II in 1660 and running to about 1700. The era, which was characterized by a reaction against Puritanism, was the first great age of the comedy of manners. The finest literature of the era is typically witty and urbane, and often lewd. Prominent Restoration Age writers include William Congreve, Samuel Pepys, John Dryden, and John Milton.

Revenge Tragedy: A dramatic form popular during the Elizabethan Age, in which the protagonist, directed by the ghost of his murdered father or son, inflicts retaliation upon a powerful villain. Notable features of the revenge tragedy include violence, bizarre criminal acts, intrigue, insanity, a hesitant protagonist, and the use of soliloquy. Thomas Kyd's *Spanish Tragedy* is the first example of revenge tragedy in English, and William Shakespeare's *Hamlet* is perhaps the best. Extreme examples of revenge tragedy, such as John Webster's *The Duchess of Malfi,* are labeled "tragedies of blood." Also known as Tragedy of Blood.

Revista: The Spanish term for a vaudeville musical revue. Examples of *revistas* include Antonio Guzman Aguilera's *Mexico para los mexicanos,* Daniel Vanegas's *Maldito jazz,* and Don Catarino's *Whiskey, morfina y marihuana* and *El desterrado.*

Rhetoric: In literary criticism, this term denotes the art of ethical persuasion. In its strictest sense, rhetoric adheres to various principles developed since classical times for arranging facts and ideas in a clear, persuasive, appealing manner. The term is also used to refer to effective prose in general and theories of or methods for composing effective prose. Classical examples of rhetorics include *The Rhetoric of Aristotle,* Quintillian's *Institutio Oratoria,* and Cicero's *Ad Herennium.*

Rhetorical Question: A question intended to provoke thought, but not an expressed answer, in the reader. It is most commonly used in oratory and other persuasive genres. The following lines from Thomas Gray's "Elegy Written in a Country Churchyard" ask rhetorical questions: Can storied urn or animated bust Back to its mansion call the fleeting breath? Can Honour's voice provoke the silent dust, Or Flattery soothe the dull cold ear of Death?

Rhyme: When used as a noun in literary criticism, this term generally refers to a poem in which words sound identical or very similar and appear in parallel positions in two or more lines. Rhymes are classified into different types according to where they fall in a line or stanza or according to the degree of similarity they exhibit in their spellings and sounds. Some major types of rhyme are "masculine" rhyme, "feminine" rhyme, and "triple" rhyme. In a masculine rhyme, the rhyming sound falls in a single accented syllable, as with "heat"

and "eat." Feminine rhyme is a rhyme of two syllables, one stressed and one unstressed, as with "merry" and "tarry." Triple rhyme matches the sound of the accented syllable and the two unaccented syllables that follow: "narrative" and "declarative." Robert Browning alternates feminine and masculine rhymes in his "Soliloquy of the Spanish Cloister": Gr-r-r—there go, my heart's abhorrence! Water your damned flower-pots, do! If hate killed men, Brother Lawrence, God's blood, would not mine kill you! What? Your myrtle-bush wants trimming? Oh, that rose has prior claims— Needs its leaden vase filled brimming? Hell dry you up with flames! Triple rhymes can be found in Thomas Hood's "Bridge of Sighs," George Gordon Byron's satirical verse, and Ogden Nash's comic poems.

Rhyme Royal: A stanza of seven lines composed in iambic pentameter and rhymed *ababbcc.* The name is said to be a tribute to King James I of Scotland, who made much use of the form in his poetry. Examples of rhyme royal include Geoffrey Chaucer's *The Parlement of Foules,* William Shakespeare's *The Rape of Lucrece,* William Morris's *The Early Paradise,* and John Masefield's *The Widow in the Bye Street.*

Rhyme Scheme: See *Rhyme*

Rhythm: A regular pattern of sound, time intervals, or events occurring in writing, most often and most discernably in poetry. Regular, reliable rhythm is known to be soothing to humans, while interrupted, unpredictable, or rapidly changing rhythm is disturbing. These effects are known to authors, who use them to produce a desired reaction in the reader. An example of a form of irregular rhythm is sprung rhythm poetry; quantitative verse, on the other hand, is very regular in its rhythm.

Rising Action: The part of a drama where the plot becomes increasingly complicated. Rising action leads up to the climax, or turning point, of a drama. The final "chase scene" of an action film is generally the rising action which culminates in the film's climax.

Rococo: A style of European architecture that flourished in the eighteenth century, especially in France. The most notable features of *rococo* are its extensive use of ornamentation and its themes of lightness, gaiety, and intimacy. In literary criticism, the term is often used disparagingly to refer to a decadent or over-ornamental style. Alexander Pope's "The Rape of the Lock" is an example of literary *rococo.*

Roman a clef: A French phrase meaning "novel with a key." It refers to a narrative in which real persons are portrayed under fictitious names. Jack Kerouac, for example, portrayed various real-life beat generation figures under fictitious names in his *On the Road.*

Romance: A broad term, usually denoting a narrative with exotic, exaggerated, often idealized characters, scenes, and themes. Nathaniel Hawthorne called his *The House of the Seven Gables* and *The Marble Faun* romances in order to distinguish them from clearly realistic works.

Romantic Age: See *Romanticism*

Romanticism: This term has two widely accepted meanings. In historical criticism, it refers to a European intellectual and artistic movement of the late eighteenth and early nineteenth centuries that sought greater freedom of personal expression than that allowed by the strict rules of literary form and logic of the eighteenth-century neoclassicists. The Romantics preferred emotional and imaginative expression to rational analysis. They considered the individual to be at the center of all experience and so placed him or her at the center of their art. The Romantics believed that the creative imagination reveals nobler truths—unique feelings and attitudes—than those that could be discovered by logic or by scientific examination. Both the natural world and the state of childhood were important sources for revelations of "eternal truths." "Romanticism" is also used as a general term to refer to a type of sensibility found in all periods of literary history and usually considered to be in opposition to the principles of classicism. In this sense, Romanticism signifies any work or philosophy in which the exotic or dreamlike figure strongly, or that is devoted to individualistic expression, self-analysis, or a pursuit of a higher realm of knowledge than can be discovered by human reason. Prominent Romantics include Jean-Jacques Rousseau, William Wordsworth, John Keats, Lord Byron, and Johann Wolfgang von Goethe.

Romantics: See *Romanticism*

Russian Symbolism: A Russian poetic movement, derived from French symbolism, that flourished between 1894 and 1910. While some Russian Symbolists continued in the French tradition, stressing aestheticism and the importance of suggestion above didactic intent, others saw their craft as a form of mystical worship, and themselves as mediators between the supernatural and the mundane. Russian symbolists include Aleksandr Blok, Vyacheslav Ivanovich Ivanov, Fyodor Sologub, Andrey Bely, Nikolay Gumilyov, and Vladimir Sergeyevich Solovyov.

S

Satire: A work that uses ridicule, humor, and wit to criticize and provoke change in human nature and institutions. There are two major types of satire: "formal" or "direct" satire speaks directly to the reader or to a character in the work; "indirect" satire relies upon the ridiculous behavior of its characters to make its point. Formal satire is further divided into two manners: the "Horatian," which ridicules gently, and the "Juvenalian," which derides its subjects harshly and bitterly. Voltaire's novella *Candide* is an indirect satire. Jonathan Swift's essay "A Modest Proposal" is a Juvenalian satire.

Scansion: The analysis or "scanning" of a poem to determine its meter and often its rhyme scheme. The most common system of scansion uses accents (slanted lines drawn above syllables) to show stressed syllables, breves (curved lines drawn above syllables) to show unstressed syllables, and vertical lines to separate each foot. In the first line of John Keats's *Endymion,* "A thing of beauty is a joy forever:" the word "thing," the first syllable of "beauty," the word "joy," and the second syllable of "forever" are stressed, while the words "A" and "of," the second syllable of "beauty," the word "a," and the first and third syllables of "forever" are unstressed. In the second line: "Its loveliness increases; it will never" a pair of vertical lines separate the foot ending with "increases" and the one beginning with "it."

Scene: A subdivision of an act of a drama, consisting of continuous action taking place at a single time and in a single location. The beginnings and endings of scenes may be indicated by clearing the stage of actors and props or by the entrances and exits of important characters. The first act of William Shakespeare's *Winter's Tale* is comprised of two scenes.

Science Fiction: A type of narrative about or based upon real or imagined scientific theories and technology. Science fiction is often peopled with alien creatures and set on other planets or in different dimensions. Karel Capek's *R.U.R.* is a major work of science fiction.

Second Person: See *Point of View*

Semiotics: The study of how literary forms and conventions affect the meaning of language. Semioticians include Ferdinand de Saussure, Charles Sanders Pierce, Claude Levi-Strauss, Jacques Lacan, Michel Foucault, Jacques Derrida, Roland Barthes, and Julia Kristeva.

Sestet: Any six-line poem or stanza. Examples of the sestet include the last six lines of the Petrarchan sonnet form, the stanza form of Robert Burns's "A Poet's Welcome to his love-begotten Daughter," and the sestina form in W. H. Auden's "Paysage Moralise."

Setting: The time, place, and culture in which the action of a narrative takes place. The elements of setting may include geographic location, characters' physical and mental environments, prevailing cultural attitudes, or the historical time in which the action takes place. Examples of settings include the romanticized Scotland in Sir Walter Scott's "Waverley" novels, the French provincial setting in Gustave Flaubert's *Madame Bovary,* the fictional Wessex country of Thomas Hardy's novels, and the small towns of southern Ontario in Alice Munro's short stories.

Shakespearean Sonnet: See *Sonnet*

Signifying Monkey: A popular trickster figure in black folklore, with hundreds of tales about this character documented since the 19th century. Henry Louis Gates Jr. examines the history of the signifying monkey in *The Signifying Monkey: Towards a Theory of Afro-American Literary Criticism,* published in 1988.

Simile: A comparison, usually using "like" or "as", of two essentially dissimilar things, as in "coffee as cold as ice" or "He sounded like a broken record." The title of Ernest Hemingway's "Hills Like White Elephants" contains a simile.

Slang: A type of informal verbal communication that is generally unacceptable for formal writing. Slang words and phrases are often colorful exaggerations used to emphasize the speaker's point; they may also be shortened versions of an often-used word or phrase. Examples of American slang from the 1990s include "yuppie" (an acronym for Young Urban Professional), "awesome" (for "excellent"), wired (for "nervous" or "excited"), and "chill out" (for relax).

Slant Rhyme: See *Consonance*

Slave Narrative: Autobiographical accounts of American slave life as told by escaped slaves. These works first appeared during the abolition movement of the 1830s through the 1850s. Olaudah Equiano's *The Interesting Narrative of Olaudah Equiano, or Gustavus Vassa, The African* and Harriet Ann Jacobs's *Incidents in the Life of a Slave Girl* are examples of the slave narrative.

Social Realism: See *Socialist Realism*

Socialist Realism: The Socialist Realism school of literary theory was proposed by Maxim Gorky and established as a dogma by the first Soviet Congress of Writers. It demanded adherence to a communist worldview in works of literature. Its doctrines required an objective viewpoint comprehensible to the working classes and themes of social struggle featuring strong proletarian heroes. A successful work of socialist realism is Nikolay Ostrovsky's *Kak zakalyalas stal (How the Steel Was Tempered).* Also known as Social Realism.

Soliloquy: A monologue in a drama used to give the audience information and to develop the speaker's character. It is typically a projection of the speaker's innermost thoughts. Usually delivered while the speaker is alone on stage, a soliloquy is intended to present an illusion of unspoken reflection. A celebrated soliloquy is Hamlet's "To be or not to be" speech in William Shakespeare's *Hamlet.*

Sonnet: A fourteen-line poem, usually composed in iambic pentameter, employing one of several rhyme schemes. There are three major types of sonnets, upon which all other variations of the form are based: the "Petrarchan" or "Italian" sonnet, the "Shakespearean" or "English" sonnet, and the "Spenserian" sonnet. A Petrarchan sonnet consists of an octave rhymed *abbaabba* and a "sestet" rhymed either *cdecde, cdccdc,* or *cdedce.* The octave poses a question or problem, relates a narrative, or puts forth a proposition; the sestet presents a solution to the problem, comments upon the narrative, or applies the proposition put forth in the octave. The Shakespearean sonnet is divided into three quatrains and a couplet rhymed *abab cdcd efef gg.* The couplet provides an epigrammatic comment on the narrative or problem put forth in the quatrains. The Spenserian sonnet uses three quatrains and a couplet like the Shakespearean, but links their three rhyme schemes in this way: *abab bcbc cdcd ee.* The Spenserian sonnet develops its theme in two parts like the Petrarchan, its final six lines resolving a problem, analyzing a narrative, or applying a proposition put forth in its first eight lines. Examples of sonnets can be found in Petrarch's *Canzoniere,* Edmund Spenser's *Amoretti,* Elizabeth Barrett

Browning's *Sonnets from the Portuguese,* Rainer Maria Rilke's *Sonnets to Orpheus,* and Adrienne Rich's poem ''The Insusceptibles.''

Spenserian Sonnet: See *Sonnet*

Spenserian Stanza: A nine-line stanza having eight verses in iambic pentameter, its ninth verse in iambic hexameter, and the rhyme scheme ababbcbcc. This stanza form was first used by Edmund Spenser in his allegorical poem *The Faerie Queene.*

Spondee: In poetry meter, a foot consisting of two long or stressed syllables occurring together. This form is quite rare in English verse, and is usually composed of two monosyllabic words. The first foot in the following line from Robert Burns's ''Green Grow the Rashes'' is an example of a spondee: Green grow the rashes, O

Sprung Rhythm: Versification using a specific number of accented syllables per line but disregarding the number of unaccented syllables that fall in each line, producing an irregular rhythm in the poem. Gerard Manley Hopkins, who coined the term ''sprung rhythm,'' is the most notable practitioner of this technique.

Stanza: A subdivision of a poem consisting of lines grouped together, often in recurring patterns of rhyme, line length, and meter. Stanzas may also serve as units of thought in a poem much like paragraphs in prose. Examples of stanza forms include the quatrain, *terza rima, ottava rima,* Spenserian, and the so-called *In Memoriam* stanza from Alfred, Lord Tennyson's poem by that title. The following is an example of the latter form: Love is and was my lord and king, And in his presence I attend To hear the tidings of my friend, Which every hour his couriers bring.

Stereotype: A stereotype was originally the name for a duplication made during the printing process; this led to its modern definition as a person or thing that is (or is assumed to be) the same as all others of its type. Common stereotypical characters include the absent- minded professor, the nagging wife, the troublemaking teenager, and the kindhearted grandmother.

Stream of Consciousness: A narrative technique for rendering the inward experience of a character. This technique is designed to give the impression of an ever-changing series of thoughts, emotions, images, and memories in the spontaneous and seemingly illogical order that they occur in life. The

textbook example of stream of consciousness is the last section of James Joyce's *Ulysses.*

Structuralism: A twentieth-century movement in literary criticism that examines how literary texts arrive at their meanings, rather than the meanings themselves. There are two major types of structuralist analysis: one examines the way patterns of linguistic structures unify a specific text and emphasize certain elements of that text, and the other interprets the way literary forms and conventions affect the meaning of language itself. Prominent structuralists include Michel Foucault, Roman Jakobson, and Roland Barthes.

Structure: The form taken by a piece of literature. The structure may be made obvious for ease of understanding, as in nonfiction works, or may obscured for artistic purposes, as in some poetry or seemingly ''unstructured'' prose. Examples of common literary structures include the plot of a narrative, the acts and scenes of a drama, and such poetic forms as the Shakespearean sonnet and the Pindaric ode.

Sturm und Drang: A German term meaning ''storm and stress.'' It refers to a German literary movement of the 1770s and 1780s that reacted against the order and rationalism of the enlightenment, focusing instead on the intense experience of extraordinary individuals. Highly romantic, works of this movement, such as Johann Wolfgang von Goethe's *Gotz von Berlichingen,* are typified by realism, rebelliousness, and intense emotionalism.

Style: A writer's distinctive manner of arranging words to suit his or her ideas and purpose in writing. The unique imprint of the author's personality upon his or her writing, style is the product of an author's way of arranging ideas and his or her use of diction, different sentence structures, rhythm, figures of speech, rhetorical principles, and other elements of composition. Styles may be classified according to period (Metaphysical, Augustan, Georgian), individual authors (Chaucerian, Miltonic, Jamesian), level (grand, middle, low, plain), or language (scientific, expository, poetic, journalistic).

Subject: The person, event, or theme at the center of a work of literature. A work may have one or more subjects of each type, with shorter works tending to have fewer and longer works tending to have more. The subjects of James Baldwin's novel *Go Tell It on the Mountain* include the themes of father-son relationships, religious conversion, black life, and sexuality. The subjects of Anne Frank's

Diary of a Young Girl include Anne and her family members as well as World War II, the Holocaust, and the themes of war, isolation, injustice, and racism.

Subjectivity: Writing that expresses the author's personal feelings about his subject, and which may or may not include factual information about the subject. Subjectivity is demonstrated in James Joyce's *Portrait of the Artist as a Young Man,* Samuel Butler's *The Way of All Flesh,* and Thomas Wolfe's *Look Homeward, Angel.*

Subplot: A secondary story in a narrative. A subplot may serve as a motivating or complicating force for the main plot of the work, or it may provide emphasis for, or relief from, the main plot. The conflict between the Capulets and the Montagues in William Shakespeare's *Romeo and Juliet* is an example of a subplot.

Surrealism: A term introduced to criticism by Guillaume Apollinaire and later adopted by Andre Breton. It refers to a French literary and artistic movement founded in the 1920s. The Surrealists sought to express unconscious thoughts and feelings in their works. The best-known technique used for achieving this aim was automatic writing—transcriptions of spontaneous outpourings from the unconscious. The Surrealists proposed to unify the contrary levels of conscious and unconscious, dream and reality, objectivity and subjectivity into a new level of "super-realism." Surrealism can be found in the poetry of Paul Eluard, Pierre Reverdy, and Louis Aragon, among others.

Suspense: A literary device in which the author maintains the audience's attention through the build-up of events, the outcome of which will soon be revealed. Suspense in William Shakespeare's *Hamlet* is sustained throughout by the question of whether or not the Prince will achieve what he has been instructed to do and of what he intends to do.

Syllogism: A method of presenting a logical argument. In its most basic form, the syllogism consists of a major premise, a minor premise, and a conclusion. An example of a syllogism is: Major premise: When it snows, the streets get wet. Minor premise: It is snowing. Conclusion: The streets are wet.

Symbol: Something that suggests or stands for something else without losing its original identity. In literature, symbols combine their literal meaning with the suggestion of an abstract concept. Literary symbols are of two types: those that carry complex associations of meaning no matter what their con-

texts, and those that derive their suggestive meaning from their functions in specific literary works. Examples of symbols are sunshine suggesting happiness, rain suggesting sorrow, and storm clouds suggesting despair.

Symbolism: This term has two widely accepted meanings. In historical criticism, it denotes an early modernist literary movement initiated in France during the nineteenth century that reacted against the prevailing standards of realism. Writers in this movement aimed to evoke, indirectly and symbolically, an order of being beyond the material world of the five senses. Poetic expression of personal emotion figured strongly in the movement, typically by means of a private set of symbols uniquely identifiable with the individual poet. The principal aim of the Symbolists was to express in words the highly complex feelings that grew out of everyday contact with the world. In a broader sense, the term "symbolism" refers to the use of one object to represent another. Early members of the Symbolist movement included the French authors Charles Baudelaire and Arthur Rimbaud; William Butler Yeats, James Joyce, and T. S. Eliot were influenced as the movement moved to Ireland, England, and the United States. Examples of the concept of symbolism include a flag that stands for a nation or movement, or an empty cupboard used to suggest hopelessness, poverty, and despair.

Symbolist: See *Symbolism*

Symbolist Movement: See *Symbolism*

Sympathetic Fallacy: See *Affective Fallacy*

T

Tale: A story told by a narrator with a simple plot and little character development. Tales are usually relatively short and often carry a simple message. Examples of tales can be found in the work of Rudyard Kipling, Somerset Maugham, Saki, Anton Chekhov, Guy de Maupassant, and Armistead Maupin.

Tall Tale: A humorous tale told in a straightforward, credible tone but relating absolutely impossible events or feats of the characters. Such tales were commonly told of frontier adventures during the settlement of the west in the United States. Tall tales have been spun around such legendary heroes as Mike Fink, Paul Bunyan, Davy Crockett, Johnny Appleseed, and Captain Stormalong as well as the real-life William F. Cody and Annie Oakley. Literary use of tall tales can be found in Washington Irving's *History of New York,* Mark Twain's *Life on the Mississippi,* and in the German R. F. Raspe's *Baron Munchausen's Narratives of His Marvellous Travels and Campaigns in Russia.*

Tanka: A form of Japanese poetry similar to *haiku.* A *tanka* is five lines long, with the lines containing five, seven, five, seven, and seven syllables respectively. Skilled *tanka* authors include Ishikawa Takuboku, Masaoka Shiki, Amy Lowell, and Adelaide Crapsey.

Teatro Grottesco: See *Theater of the Grotesque*

Terza Rima: A three-line stanza form in poetry in which the rhymes are made on the last word of each line in the following manner: the first and third lines of the first stanza, then the second line of the first stanza and the first and third lines of the second stanza, and so on with the middle line of any stanza rhyming with the first and third lines of the following stanza. An example of *terza rima* is Percy Bysshe Shelley's ''The Triumph of Love'': As in that trance of wondrous thought I lay This was the tenour of my waking dream. Methought I sate beside a public way Thick strewn with summer dust, and a great stream Of people there was hurrying to and fro Numerous as gnats upon the evening gleam,. . .

Tetrameter: See *Meter*

Textual Criticism: A branch of literary criticism that seeks to establish the authoritative text of a literary work. Textual critics typically compare all known manuscripts or printings of a single work in order to assess the meanings of differences and revisions. This procedure allows them to arrive at a definitive version that (supposedly) corresponds to the author's original intention. Textual criticism was applied during the Renaissance to salvage the classical texts of Greece and Rome, and modern works have been studied, for instance, to undo deliberate correction or censorship, as in the case of novels by Stephen Crane and Theodore Dreiser.

Theater of Cruelty: Term used to denote a group of theatrical techniques designed to eliminate the psychological and emotional distance between actors and audience. This concept, introduced in the 1930s in France, was intended to inspire a more intense theatrical experience than conventional theater allowed. The ''cruelty'' of this dramatic theory signified not sadism but heightened actor/audience involvement in the dramatic event. The theater of cruelty was theorized by Antonin Artaud in his *Le Theatre et son double (The Theatre and Its Double),* and also appears in the work of Jerzy Grotowski, Jean Genet, Jean Vilar, and Arthur Adamov, among others.

Theater of the Absurd: A post-World War II dramatic trend characterized by radical theatrical innovations. In works influenced by the Theater of the absurd, nontraditional, sometimes grotesque characterizations, plots, and stage sets reveal a meaningless universe in which human values are irrelevant. Existentialist themes of estrangement, absurdity, and futility link many of the works of this movement. The principal writers of the Theater of the Absurd are Samuel Beckett, Eugene Ionesco, Jean Genet, and Harold Pinter.

Theater of the Grotesque: An Italian theatrical movement characterized by plays written around the ironic and macabre aspects of daily life in the World War I era. Theater of the Grotesque was named after the play *The Mask and the Face* by Luigi Chiarelli, which was described as ''a grotesque in three acts.'' The movement influenced the work of Italian dramatist Luigi Pirandello, author of *Right You Are, If You Think You Are.* Also known as *Teatro Grottesco.*

Theme: The main point of a work of literature. The term is used interchangeably with thesis. The theme of William Shakespeare's *Othello*—jealousy—is a common one.

Thesis: A thesis is both an essay and the point argued in the essay. Thesis novels and thesis plays share the quality of containing a thesis which is supported through the action of the story. A master's thesis and a doctoral dissertation are two theses required of graduate students.

Thesis Play: See *Thesis*

Three Unities: See *Unities*

Tone: The author's attitude toward his or her audience may be deduced from the tone of the work. A formal tone may create distance or convey politeness, while an informal tone may encourage a friendly, intimate, or intrusive feeling in the reader. The author's attitude toward his or her subject matter may also be deduced from the tone of the words he or she uses in discussing it. The tone of John F. Kennedy's speech which included the appeal to ''ask not what your country can do for you'' was intended to instill feelings of camaraderie and national pride in listeners.

Tragedy: A drama in prose or poetry about a noble, courageous hero of excellent character who, because of some tragic character flaw or *hamartia*, brings ruin upon him- or herself. Tragedy treats its subjects in a dignified and serious manner, using poetic language to help evoke pity and fear and bring about catharsis, a purging of these emotions. The tragic form was practiced extensively by the ancient Greeks. In the Middle Ages, when classical works were virtually unknown, tragedy came to denote any works about the fall of persons from exalted to low conditions due to any reason: fate, vice, weakness, etc. According to the classical definition of tragedy, such works present the ''pathetic''—that which evokes pity—rather than the tragic. The classical form of tragedy was revived in the sixteenth century; it flourished especially on the Elizabethan stage. In modern times, dramatists have attempted to adapt the form to the needs of modern society by drawing their heroes from the ranks of ordinary men and women and defining the nobility of these heroes in terms of spirit rather than exalted social standing. The greatest classical example of tragedy is Sophocles' *Oedipus Rex.* The ''pathetic'' derivation is exemplified in ''The Monk's Tale'' in Geoffrey Chaucer's *Canterbury Tales.* Notable works produced during the sixteenth century revival include William Shakespeare's *Hamlet, Othello,* and *King Lear.* Modern dramatists working in the tragic tradition include Henrik Ibsen, Arthur Miller, and Eugene O'Neill.

Tragedy of Blood: See *Revenge Tragedy*

Tragic Flaw: In a tragedy, the quality within the hero or heroine which leads to his or her downfall. Examples of the tragic flaw include Othello's jealousy and Hamlet's indecisiveness, although most great tragedies defy such simple interpretation.

Transcendentalism: An American philosophical and religious movement, based in New England from around 1835 until the Civil War. Transcendentalism was a form of American romanticism that had its roots abroad in the works of Thomas Carlyle, Samuel Coleridge, and Johann Wolfgang von Goethe. The Transcendentalists stressed the importance of intuition and subjective experience in communication with God. They rejected religious dogma and texts in favor of mysticism and scientific naturalism. They pursued truths that lie beyond the ''colorless'' realms perceived by reason and the senses and were active social reformers in public education,

women's rights, and the abolition of slavery. Prominent members of the group include Ralph Waldo Emerson and Henry David Thoreau.

Trickster: A character or figure common in Native American and African literature who uses his ingenuity to defeat enemies and escape difficult situations. Tricksters are most often animals, such as the spider, hare, or coyote, although they may take the form of humans as well. Examples of trickster tales include Thomas King's *A Coyote Columbus Story,* Ashley F. Bryan's *The Dancing Granny* and Ishmael Reed's *The Last Days of Louisiana Red.*

Trimeter: See *Meter*

Triple Rhyme: See *Rhyme*

Trochee: See *Foot*

U

Understatement: See *Irony*

Unities: Strict rules of dramatic structure, formulated by Italian and French critics of the Renaissance and based loosely on the principles of drama discussed by Aristotle in his *Poetics.* Foremost among these rules were the three unities of action, time, and place that compelled a dramatist to: (1) construct a single plot with a beginning, middle, and end that details the causal relationships of action and character; (2) restrict the action to the events of a single day; and (3) limit the scene to a single place or city. The unities were observed faithfully by continental European writers until the Romantic Age, but they were never regularly observed in English drama. Modern dramatists are typically more concerned with a unity of impression or emotional effect than with any of the classical unities. The unities are observed in Pierre Corneille's tragedy *Polyeuctes* and Jean-Baptiste Racine's *Phedre.* Also known as Three Unities.

Urban Realism: A branch of realist writing that attempts to accurately reflect the often harsh facts of modern urban existence. Some works by Stephen Crane, Theodore Dreiser, Charles Dickens, Fyodor Dostoyevsky, Emile Zola, Abraham Cahan, and Henry Fuller feature urban realism. Modern examples include Claude Brown's *Manchild in the Promised Land* and Ron Milner's *What the Wine Sellers Buy.*

Utopia: A fictional perfect place, such as ''paradise'' or ''heaven.'' Early literary utopias were included in Plato's *Republic* and Sir Thomas More's

Utopia, while more modern utopias can be found in Samuel Butler's *Erewhon,* Theodor Herzka's *A Visit to Freeland,* and H. G. Wells' *A Modern Utopia.*

Utopian: See *Utopia*

Utopianism: See *Utopia*

V

Verisimilitude: Literally, the appearance of truth. In literary criticism, the term refers to aspects of a work of literature that seem true to the reader. Verisimilitude is achieved in the work of Honore de Balzac, Gustave Flaubert, and Henry James, among other late nineteenth-century realist writers.

Vers de societe: See *Occasional Verse*

Vers libre: See *Free Verse*

Verse: A line of metered language, a line of a poem, or any work written in verse. The following line of verse is from the epic poem *Don Juan* by Lord Byron: "My way is to begin with the beginning."

Versification: The writing of verse. Versification may also refer to the meter, rhyme, and other mechanical components of a poem. Composition of a "Roses are red, violets are blue" poem to suit an occasion is a common form of versification practiced by students.

Victorian: Refers broadly to the reign of Queen Victoria of England (1837-1901) and to anything with qualities typical of that era. For example, the qualities of smug narrowmindedness, bourgeois materialism, faith in social progress, and priggish morality are often considered Victorian. This stereotype is contradicted by such dramatic intellectual developments as the theories of Charles Darwin, Karl Marx, and Sigmund Freud (which stirred strong debates in England) and the critical attitudes of serious Victorian writers like Charles Dickens and George Eliot. In literature, the Victorian Period was the great age of the English novel, and the latter part of the era saw the rise of movements such as decadence and symbolism. Works of Victorian literature include the poetry of Robert Browning and Alfred, Lord Tennyson, the criticism of Matthew Arnold and John Ruskin, and the novels of Emily Bronte, William Makepeace Thackeray, and Thomas Hardy. Also known as Victorian Age and Victorian Period.

Victorian Age: See *Victorian*

Victorian Period: See *Victorian*

W

Weltanschauung: A German term referring to a person's worldview or philosophy. Examples of *weltanschauung* include Thomas Hardy's view of the human being as the victim of fate, destiny, or impersonal forces and circumstances, and the disillusioned and laconic cynicism expressed by such poets of the 1930s as W. H. Auden, Sir Stephen Spender, and Sir William Empson.

Weltschmerz: A German term meaning "world pain." It describes a sense of anguish about the nature of existence, usually associated with a melancholy, pessimistic attitude. *Weltschmerz* was expressed in England by George Gordon, Lord Byron in his *Manfred* and *Childe Harold's Pilgrimage,* in France by Viscount de Chateaubriand, Alfred de Vigny, and Alfred de Musset, in Russia by Aleksandr Pushkin and Mikhail Lermontov, in Poland by Juliusz Slowacki, and in America by Nathaniel Hawthorne.

Z

Zarzuela: A type of Spanish operetta. Writers of *zarzuelas* include Lope de Vega and Pedro Calderon.

Zeitgeist: A German term meaning "spirit of the time." It refers to the moral and intellectual trends of a given era. Examples of *zeitgeist* include the preoccupation with the more morbid aspects of dying and death in some Jacobean literature, especially in the works of dramatists Cyril Tourneur and John Webster, and the decadence of the French Symbolists.

Cumulative Author/Title Index

Nationality/Ethnicity Index

Subject/Theme Index

Patience
  What the Butler Saw: 236-237,
    240, 244
Persecution
  Hedda Gabler: 122, 127
  The Ruling Class: 197
  Torch Song Trilogy: 224-225
  What the Butler Saw: 240-241
Personal Identity
  What the Butler Saw: 234, 236-
    237, 241, 245, 248-249
Personality Traits
  Mule Bone: 175
  Torch Song Trilogy: 222
Philosophical Ideas
  The Bacchae: 11-12
  Man and Superman: 136-137,
    141-143
Plot
  The Bacchae: 1, 10
  Hay Fever: 94, 96, 100-101
  Man and Superman: 142, 144
  Mule Bone: 175, 178
  The Ruling Class: 185, 193
  Speed-the-Plow: 206, 208-209
  Torch Song Trilogy: 223
  What the Butler Saw: 240-241
Politicians
  Buried Child: 62, 64
  Hay Fever: 103
Politics
  The Bacchae: 2, 7, 9, 11-13
  Boesman & Lena: 31
  Brighton Beach Memoirs: 43-46
  Buried Child: 63-64
  Hay Fever: 96, 101-104
  Hedda Gabler: 122-123, 126
  Man and Superman: 137, 141-
    144, 147
  A Month in the Country: 153,
    159-162
  The Ruling Class: 189, 191-194
  What the Butler Saw: 242-244
Prejudice and Tolerance
  Torch Song Trilogy: 221
Pride
  The Bacchae: 4, 9-10
Prostitution
  The Ruling Class: 195, 197
Psychology and the Human Mind
  Buried Child: 64-65
  The Ruling Class: 187, 191-192
  What the Butler Saw: 234, 236-
    237, 240, 242-244, 249
Punishment
  The Bacchae: 4-5

R

Race
  Mule Bone: 174
Race and Racism
  Boesman & Lena: 28

  The Emperor Jones: 78
Race
  Boesman & Lena: 23-24, 30-31
  The Emperor Jones: 75,
    78, 81-83
  Mule Bone: 174-177
Racism and Prejudice
  Boesman & Lena: 28, 30-31
  The Emperor Jones: 82
  Mule Bone: 169, 174-176
  Torch Song Trilogy: 222, 224-225
Rational vs. Instinctual
  The Bacchae: 7
Realism
  Buried Child: 52, 65
  Hedda Gabler: 122-123
  A Month in the Country: 162-163
Recreation
  The Bacchae: 12
Religion and Religious Thought
  The Bacchae: 1-2, 5, 7, 9-15, 18
  Buried Child: 52, 54, 59, 63
  Man and Superman: 140,
    144, 147
  Mule Bone: 171-176

S

Satire
  The Ruling Class: 192, 194
Sculpture
  What the Butler Saw: 236, 245
Search for Identity
  Boesman & Lena: 28
Search For Knowledge
  Brighton Beach Memoirs: 46-48
Self-confidence
  Brighton Beach Memoirs: 46-48
  The Emperor Jones: 76, 78-80
  What the Butler Saw: 248-249
Selfless
  Hedda Gabler: 121-122
Setting
  The Emperor Jones: 80-81
  Torch Song Trilogy: 223
Sex
  Man and Superman: 140
  Mule Bone: 175
Sex and Sexuality
  What the Butler Saw: 240
Sex and Sexuality
  The Ruling Class: 195-197
  Torch Song Trilogy: 218-219,
    222, 224-228
  What the Butler Saw: 236-237,
    241-245, 248-249
Sex Roles
  The Bacchae: 9
  Hedda Gabler: 122
  Torch Song Trilogy: 221
Sexual Abuse
  What the Butler Saw: 237,
    239-242

Sickness
  Torch Song Trilogy: 225
  What the Butler Saw: 241, 245
Sin
  Buried Child: 61-62
  Hedda Gabler: 113, 122, 127
  The Ruling Class: 192
  What the Butler Saw: 236, 240,
    242, 244-245
Slavery
  The Emperor Jones: 76, 78, 81
Social Order
  A Month in the Country: 162
Socialism
  Man and Superman: 137, 143
Spiritual Leaders
  Buried Child: 55-56, 63, 65
Sports and the Sporting Life
  The Bacchae: 5, 12-13
Storms and Weather Conditions
  Buried Child: 54-56, 61, 65
Structure
  The Bacchae: 7, 10
Success and Failure
  Mule Bone: 175
Success and Failure
  Mule Bone: 171, 175, 178

T

Time and Change
  The Bacchae: 1, 12-13
  The Emperor Jones: 79
Tragedy
  The Bacchae: 1, 10, 14
Trust
  Hedda Gabler: 116, 120, 123

U

Ubermensch (Superman)
  Man and Superman: 140
Ubermensch
  Man and Superman: 135, 138,
    140-141
Understanding
  What the Butler Saw: 240,
    243-244
Upper Class
  The Ruling Class: 195-197

V

Victim and Victimization
  Hedda Gabler: 122
Violence and Cruelty
  Boesman & Lena: 27
  Torch Song Trilogy: 222

W

War, the Military, and Soldier Life
  The Bacchae: 2, 4, 11-13